STUNG

by William Deverell

Purchase the print edition
and receive the eBook free.
For details, go to ecwpress.com/eBook.

Published by ECW Press
665 Gerrard Street East
Toronto, Ontario, Canada M4M 1Y2
416-694-3348 / info@ecwpress.com

Cover design: David A. Gee

LIBRARY AND ARCHIVES CANADA CATALOGUING IN PUBLICATION

Title: Stung : an Arthur Beauchamp novel / William Deverell.

Names: Deverell, William, 1937- author.

Identifiers: Canadiana (print) 20200382446
Canadiana (ebook) 20200382497

ISBN 978-1-77041-595-9 (HARDCOVER)
ISBN 978-1-77305-712-5 (PDF)
ISBN 978-177305-711-8 (ePUB)
ISBN 978-1-77305-713-2 (KINDLE)

Classification: LCC PS8557.E8775 S78 2021
DDC C813/.54—dc23

The publication of *Stung* has been generously supported by the Canada Council for the Arts and is funded in part by the Government of Canada. *Nous remercions le Conseil des arts du Canada de son soutien. Ce livre est financé en partie par le gouvernement du Canada.* We acknowledge the support of the Ontario Arts Council (OAC), an agency of the Government of Ontario, which last year funded 1,965 individual artists and 1,152 organizations in 197 communities across Ontario for a total of $51.9 million. We also acknowledge the the support of the Government of Ontario through Ontario Creates.

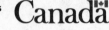

PRINTED AND BOUND IN CANADA

PRINTING: FRIESENS 5 4 3 2 1

MIX
Paper from
responsible sources
FSC® C016245
www.fsc.org

To Jan, in celebration of the love we share.
Always, truly, believe . . .

Chemicals sprayed on croplands or forests or gardens lie long in soil, entering into living organisms, passing from one to another in a chain of poisoning and death. Or they pass mysteriously by underground streams until they emerge and, through the alchemy of air and sunlight, combine into new forms that kill vegetation, sicken cattle, and work unknown harm on those who drink from once pure wells. As Albert Schweitzer has said, "Man can hardly even recognize the devils of his own creation."

— Rachel Carson, *Silent Spring*, 1962

PART ONE / HEAT OF SUMMER

CHAPTER 1 » RIVIE

1
Friday, August 10, 2018

So I'm in this gauche, fake-chichi pick-up bar on Queen West, all glass and glitter — it's called (get ready to barf) the Beaver's Tail. Five o'clock, and they're streaming in, the lonely and the desperate, fleeing the cubicles and workstations of their corporate prisons. It's a steamy mid-summer day, and the place already reeks of sweat and hastily applied deodorant.

Picture this, a kind of selfie: Our heroine commandeers two stools, one with my bag on it, the other propping up my fanny. I am nursing a vodka martini and am perched at an angle to the bar, arms bared to neck, and legs to mid-thigh, by sleeveless top and short skirt, strap-on heels, looking cool, in control, not too obviously hooky.

In a twenty-minute span I have sent off two applicants, slithering moves from snaky sales executives, calmly rebuffed with versions of I-am-waiting-for-a-friend.

Now enters a more interesting candidate for the ineffable charms of Rivie Levitsky — he's about six-three, manicured beard, longish brownish hair, square of jaw and shoulders, tucking in the tummy as he leads in two male shiny bums: sycophants, by their vibes, underlings to my tummy-tucking target. His suit jacket slung over a shoulder, shirt hanging loose. Distressingly attractive. Mid-forties, that frantic, omnivorous age on the cusp of dwindling powers.

His pals find an empty table on the mezzanine, and he does a slow scan, then — no surprise here — targets my reserved stool on the pretext of ordering from the bar.

"Oh, sorry," I say as I grab my bag. "I was saving it for a friend who didn't show."

And he goes, "He friend or she friend?" Giving me an up-and-down, all five feet, four inches.

"Former friend of the male persuasion."

"He's had rotten luck."

"Why?"

"If he reneged on a date with you he either had a serious accident or a psychotic breakdown. Mind if I take up his empty space?" Deep baritone, suffused with sincerity, like a voice-over in a TV commercial for a pain ointment. "Your martini looks decidedly empty. My pleasure."

"My mother told me never to accept drinks from strangers." Says the compulsive flirt. Comes with being aesthetically pleasing like my gorgeous mom, you do it because it's sort of expected, you learn to enjoy the power.

"Well, my mother taught me to respect the wishes of attractive young women who jump to the ridiculous conclusion I'm coming on to them."

I laugh, extend a hand. "Hi, I'm Becky."

"Howie. Howie Griffin. I come with a guarantee — I'm safe. I may be the safest guy in this room." Loopy grin, minty breath, no wedding ring. Long, strong fingers, like muscular tentacles enclosing my hand. He's really quite gorgeous, compared to the shots Doc took, mostly out of focus.

"And what makes you so safe, Howie?"

"I run security for a global. Canadian end of it, but they also send me on international troubleshoots."

He flips me a card: Howell J. Griffin, Director of Security Operations, Chemican-International, Canadian Division, corporate offices in a Bay Street tower. You can reach Howell by phone, fax, text, email, Skype, FaceTime, no mention of carrier pigeons. "For a sustainable planet," that's Chemican's hysterical motto.

I want this macher to think I'm in awe — wow, worldwide! — but I can't pull it off. I tell him I'm Becky McLean, and I'm a pharmacist's assistant. "It's not very glamorous." Nor is my real job, which doesn't exist. My degree is in comparative literature, so of course I'm basically unemployed, except for ESL classes for Syrians.

"Not very glamorous?" A glance down, thigh-ward, at the bicycle queen's legs of steel. "I don't know — glamour is mostly surface, isn't it? Hides natural beauty and good taste. I'll shut up."

I laugh. "Sure, I'll have another one. It hasn't been a good day."

"Hold that thought, Becky." He orders "the same for my friend," a Glenlivet and rocks for himself, and one each for his gawping friends up there. "I'll be back biggety bang."

Biggety bang. Howie may not be radically hip, but he's fairly smart and urbane. Unconsciously chill.

The Beaver's Tail is crowded now, standing room only, and Howie has to weave and squeeze, holding the two whiskies aloft as he makes his way to the mezzanine to look after his mates.

They're keen to exchange a few salacious sexisms about me, so his return is more biggety than bang. As he hoists himself up beside me, I can almost smell the testosterone. I hope he doesn't entertain any antediluvian notions about the meaning of consent.

A little musical ding as he touches his glass to mine. "Your imperfect day, Becky . . . Don't feel you have to talk about it."

"You don't want to hear."

"The friend who didn't show?" Looking into the fathomless depths of Agent Levitsky's darkly brown eyes.

"Yeah, he . . ." I shake my head, look sad, flick back a strand of auburn hair. "How was your day, Howie?"

"Oppressive. Desk was piled a mile high — I just got back from Peru. I have my Spanish, get along in Portuguese, so Kansas City — that's our head office — has me handling Latin America, putting out fires."

My eyes widen, a low-key wow reaction. Ghastly.

"So, given that your evening didn't work out . . . got any plans?"

"Not now."

"I'm not prying, but . . . let me speculate. Dinner date. He blew you off."

"You notched it — what am I, a crystal ball? Yeah, we were going to talk things out."

"I've been there, if it's any consolation. Got laid off in April by the significant other."

Stage One done. Smooth.

2

So I'm twenty-three, half Howie's age, but I've always had a thing about older men, maybe from my handsome hippie dad, but I got raped by a "mature" writer I used to admire, and . . . Let it go. Or it will eat you up. His next book bombed.

Then I had a bad rebound with a professor who'd taught me nineteenth-century French lit and who was unbearably in love with himself. I am currently without a male companion, and needy but not desperate . . . sorry, Howie.

He retains a gentlemanly aplomb through dinner: gracious, attentive, no flashes of masculine id. We're in this nouveau Italian place he likes, on Bathurst. He does lamb chops and I stick to my casually observed green diet, a nutty salad. I keep it down to two glasses of Pinot Gris, he goes through the rest of the bottle. And talks. About himself.

He's a cyberhead, has a master's in business computing. A jock-strap, handball, basketball, works out at Molloy's Gym on upper Yonge. Season passes to the Jays and the Chamber Music Society, which seems a weirdly unlikely combination. Keeps a sixty-horse launch at his cottage on Georgian Bay, near a town with a name that goes on forever: Penetanguishene.

His marriage bombed after fifteen years. A sports fan and a classical music enthusiast — sharing season tickets to the Jays and the Chamber Music Society wasn't the answer to saving their marriage. No kids, but his ex has two grown boys from a previous relationship. He goes on at some length about missing them, seems sincere.

You worry about loosened inhibitions, loosened hands, but the Pinot merely makes Howie a little soppy, carrying on about the ex, Maxine, his failed, brave fight to save their marriage — she left him for a concert violinist. Maxine is a cellist. Thus the chamber music tickets, I guess. Turns out he doesn't use them, he's more into jazz and seventies rock — tastes, he's pleased to learn, that I share.

I counter with my less intriguing ex-partner: a narcissistic doper who wrote cheesy pop songs.

He gives me his loopy, lopsided grin. Kind of cute.

Okay, that's Stage Two, and now we're off to his big apartment on Adelaide: uncoolly mannish, wood flooring that clacks under my heels, a honking big TV and stereo; CDs by Oscar Peterson, Django Reinhardt, Sarah Vaughan, and his 1970s rock, Stones, Pink Floyd, Santana, a lot of Dylan and some Cohen, whom I love.

A misty seascape dominates one wall, with breaching sperm whales — which is beyond hypocritical. A baseball in a glass case, signed by one of his heroes.

A big library dominates the opposite wall, adventure non-fiction but also spy novels, le Carré, Graham Greene, and, not shockingly I guess, Hemingway and Jack London, but also some high-end lit:

Pale Fire, Under the Volcano. I'm shocked. And there's Dostoevsky, Steinbeck, Rushdie, just for starters, and a whole section in Spanish: Marquez, Borges, Allende, many I don't know. These books actually look *read*. Does he stock up from used-book stores just to make an impression with the ladies he fetches here?

The kitchen is open to view, behind a bar at which he is pouring drinks. A viewette of Lake Ontario and the Islands from the balcony. A glassed-in office-in-home, tile floor, the door closed, likely locked, banks of computers in there, multiple screens, two filing cabinets.

"We're connected to every continent but one, and I'm working on Antarctica," he calls, and I laugh dutifully. "I have a duplicate system at HQ but they want me ready for calls in the middle of the night when it's noon in Cambodia or Belarus."

I hear myself going, "Awesome." This is a word I'd vowed would never pass my lips.

"We're always worried about sabotage from one of the rabid groups out there."

I've made note that Howie has an alarm system, a keypad mounted inside the front door, but I didn't catch the code he punched in to disable it. No way to tell if his inner office is also armed, no numeric pad, just a standard keyhole.

I wait until he goes off for a piss before dumping out most of a mondo martini in the kitchen sink. I now have to present as a little tipsier than I am, which has the unfortunate effect of encouraging him, an arm around my waist as he leads me toward a couch. He's pretty loaded, and I'm on alert — Danger! Assault Zone! — but I manage to detour him to the balcony, from where maybe neighbours could hear sounds of distress.

Another grope, those tentacles touring toward my left tit, and I pull away. I'm all about leaving but remember who I am. Rivke Levitsky, known to pals as Rivie, and she's tough, she's smart, she can control the situation. So I remind him of what my mother told me about strangers and drinks. The word mother is magic, he backs off, maybe thinking of his own mom, who raised him to be respectful.

"I'm not ready," I say. But hope must not be extinguished, and I add a modifier: "Yet."

That soothes the pain, and he takes his flippers off me. "Of course. I understand. I apologize, I went too far."

So we sit apart, still outside, on his all-weather chairs, and I ask about Peru, confess to being poorly travelled, and he flaunts his exotic locales. Chemican has plants in Europe, the Far East, but mostly in Latin America. Amazonia is opening up, you'd love it there, Becky, it's magical. Maybe someday if things work out I'd love to invite you down there.

I'd as soon walk into a burning building with dynamite strapped to my back. Baseball seems a safe topic, and I get him going on his eerie devotion to the Toronto Blue Jays, who are "rebuilding," and how he rarely misses a game when they're in town, which they are next week, and maybe I'd enjoy a trip to the Dome with him, great seats, right on top of third base.

I am a huge fan of this manly sport (I say with a straight face), catch the Jays on the tube when I can but can't afford tickets as I'm saving every cent to help my dad, who's on disability. He reels off a bunch of stats and averages, and did I catch that squeaker at Fenway, Smokey sending a walk-off boomer over the Green Monster, a parking lot shot. Fenway? Smokey? Green Monster?

This is a tune I can't sing, I don't know the lyrics, so I prod him for a short story of his unexceptional life. An only child, small-town Ontario, his dad retired from his hardware store, mom from a flower shop. Rotarians, churchy, Tory. Salt of the earth. Bedrock.

So with these embedded values, it doesn't shock me that he finds escape from the boring normality of it all with mood enhancers. After establishing that I don't have any attitudes against, he produces, maybe inevitably — something about him shouts coke-head — a packet of uncut blow, which he extols: "Never stepped on, unadulterated flake." I tell him, sorry, it's late, I have to work tomorrow. But I give him a teaser: "Maybe another time, Howie."

So with hope restored, but resigned to biding his time, playing the long game, he kind of staggers after me to the door, where I tell him by the way I have access at work to some dynamite behind-the-counter stuff. Howie is totally up for trying it. Maybe I'd like to go boating with him next weekend if the weather holds. Get high.

I remind him I'm not into anything serious. Yet.

He'll call me, text me, the Rangers are coming to town. How's Thursday? Yeah, I could really dig that, Howie. Take me out to the ball game.

The Dome seems a safe enough venue, grope-free. I give him the number of my Becky McLean phone — a throwaway I picked up last week.

He orders me a taxi on his corporate account. I thank him with a kiss, intended as a peck, but he returns it, a scratchy, failed effort. A pelvic thrust, a love message from his prodding dick. I peel away and go, "Let's keep it friendly." I don't want him to think I'm cheap.

3
Saturday, August 11

Our operations room is in the back of Ivor Antiques on St. Clair, near Keele, west of the Stockyards. It doesn't get much business, which is the way we like it. We usually enter by the alley, where no one goes except the occasional delivery truck, and always take our bikes inside.

It's a cluttered space, the big backroom, full of Ivor's unsalables, my favourite being a worn rolltop, my own personal workstation. Wicker and horsehair. Buffets, bureaus, vanities. Japanese, Oriental, Moorish. An oak dining table with its wings up is where we gather, on Louis Quatorze replicas, to wrangle endlessly about direct action.

Three comrades are doing just that as I stroll in, but turn silent, staring at me as, dripping sweat, I unbuckle my helmet and fluff out my hair, nonchalant, stringing out the tension.

Oklahoma Joe, who is this tall, shy, stringy thirty-year-old data dink with a wonky face like a cleaved rock, has a worried look, but that's basically his signature expression. Okie Joe, we call him, politically incorrectly. He's our in-house geek, did a stretch with Google in Silicon Valley. While coding for them, he fell under the benign sway of Bernie Sanders, fled to Canada as the Trumpian mafia began restyling America as a fascist state.

Lucy Wales is my best friend and is smart and wild and twenty-two and is currently an anarchist. She labels herself as post-left, believes in the propaganda of the deed — our escapade is right up her alley. She has her hands together in prayer, mocking the God she doesn't believe in. Magenta hair, nose rings but no tats, dark vampish makeup. Quite pretty underneath all that. She's my roomie — when she isn't sleeping over with her gorgeous boyfriend in the warehouse squat he's been camping in.

Helmut (Doc) Knutsen leans back with his feet on the table, pretending he's so fly and comfortable, which I know he's not. Two clowns and a monkey on a trampoline couldn't provoke a smile from this serious dude. Lucy and I have a thing for him nonetheless, another of my favourite older guys, sixty and sly as the Devil. Sort of sexy too despite the Einstein hair — he's never heard of a comb. He treats us like we're his grandchildren, though, doesn't get it that we'd both like to jump him. He's so old-fashioned he can't conceive of that, can't vault over the age difference.

He gets called Doc because he has a Ph.D. — it's in organic chemistry so that's why Operation Beekeeper is his baby. He wrote a widely ignored paper on neonicotinoids, bee-snuffing chemicals commonly known as neonics. He also authored a couple of angry op-ed pieces about how the planet could die without bees.

On top of which, he analyzed all of Chemican's research, found a pattern of deception even worse than Monsanto's, which made Chemican a more obvious target, more vulnerable.

Never married but he's had his lovers, though none of them stuck. He's too worried about germs to be a wild and passionate lover, I suspect. That's his only drawback: a slight hypochondria that seems to embarrass him.

And though Doc normally avoids crowded places for fear of infection he'd spent multiple evenings at the Beaver's Tail, watching Howie Griffin, charting his success rate in his relentless hunt for cunt: lucked out twice, struck out twice.

"I hate to ask" is how Doc had put it a few weeks ago. "If it gets weird, bail."

I pour a coffee. "Sweltering out there."

Lucy goes, "Come on, Rivie."

"I over-achieved."

"Elucidate," Lucy says.

"He was all over me."

Improbably, I am seeing a smile on Doc Knutsen's face, an actual smile, complete with never-before-witnessed crinkles. "You got in there? His apartment?"

"Seamlessly. Guy has a little powder habit, by the way."

Lucy again, master of subtlety: "Did you have to fuck him?"

"He wished. He has hand problems, but I didn't find him scary. He's not stupid, he actually reads *books*. I gave him a rain check and my Becky number. I expect a medal of honour for this."

"Think of the bees," Doc says.

4
Sunday, August 12

Howell J. Griffin waits all of a day and a half before calling the line registered to Becky McLean, who is a less brassy version of me, more wholesome but just as delectable. (And almost as vain.) Apologizes for having come on too strong. He doesn't do that sort of thing. That wasn't him. (Well, that wasn't me, either.) The thing is, he's been seriously lonely since his wife dumped him (not his phrasing) and doesn't want me thinking he's some kind of cocktail lounge hit man.

He'd like to repair the damage, give me a chance to know him better. We can start with that Rangers game on Thursday. Am I still up for it? Awesome, I say. Yay, Jays.

So I spend the next few days boning up on baseball so I can sound credible when I pretend I'm interested. Earbuds glued to some ghastly sports station, a couple of semi-literates rattling off stats and scores and standings. I record a couple of games, fast-forward through the beer-buddy and tough-truck ads: White Sox and Orioles, Jays and Rangers, memorizing players' names and accomplishments, the lingo. Some of it passeth understanding. What's a ribbie? A jam shot? An inherited runner?

Okie Joe, with his mid-America backwoods background, you'd think he'd know the game up the ass, but he's a full-time propellerhead.

Doc Knutsen doesn't do sports either, Major League Baseball being just another macho enterprise to keep the masses sedated. Prides himself on being a feminist. Wish he'd get off that. Why, when guys label themselves feminists, do I feel patronized?

5
Thursday, August 16

So we're in the eighth inning, and so far I'm throwing a no-hitter, tossing out phrases like picking corners, caught looking, getting doubled, impressing Howie that I actually give a shit. I'm the stats-master, rattling off numbers: Rangers chucker, ERA of 3.54 looking for his third straight, Grichuk hitless over four games, but Smoak has seventy RBIs (ribbies?) for the season, and he's working on more with runners on first and third.

A foul ball drifts toward us. I shy away, Howie jumps for it, but it sails overhead. Two strikes, no balls.

Howie shouts, "Drive one out of here, Smokey!" Pitcher shakes his head, nods, whips the ball to the plate. A ping, and the ball zips around the infield, biggety bang. Double play, inning over. The air goes out of the crowd, out of Howie.

He's been mostly hands off, except in the fifth, when the Jays finally got a run. That provoked a substantial bear hug, and I'm like a pressed flower, and I get this cowlike repentance as he unhands me. As usual, it's not him, he just got caught up in the moment. I'm totally hoping the good guys will lose, saving me from the full force of his jubilation and a possible cracked vertebra.

The first hitter up for Texas nails one, high and long, and I go, "Wow, that's a parking lot shot."

Howie chirps, "Parking lot?"

Right. This is an enclosed stadium. "Well, if there was a parking lot . . ."

I keep my mouth shut after that. The Jays give up two more, and their guys respectively whiff, fan, and are caught looking in the ninth.

We go to a bar after, and it's like a wake, the twin towers are collapsing again, planets are colliding, it's the death of civilization. I'm actually feeling sorry for Howie, I'm human, I can't help it, and I squeeze his hand. My touch is unexpected and apparently electric because he gives this jolt. I squeeze again, as an experiment, to test my powers, see if I can get him to jump even higher. Instead, he spills his beer on his Adidas.

He will hate me if I tell him it's only a game. I hear myself saying, "Sanchez gets a start Friday, he's due."

I get this astonished look. Kind of awed, wide-eyed, as if he just realized something unusual is going on, and I'm thinking, Holy

Fuckup, Batman, he's on to me. But it's not that, here comes the loopy grin, not like skeptical or ravenous, not at all.

"Becky, I am really quite wowed by you. You are sublimely, off-the-wall, delightfully unique."

6
Friday, August 17

"So things have gotten a little complicated." My understated summing-up of last night's date with Howell J. Griffin.

"You're sure he's not putting you on?" says Doc.

"I don't think he's capable of that. He's kind of guileless, your basic transparent middle-aged white male. His wife left him because he prefers Deep Purple to Debussy. He's infatuated with me, which is a little unnerving. Scary, in a way."

"Scary?" says Doc. "You're scared of him?"

"It's more like I'm scared *for* him."

The evening's balmy aftermath had us strolling along the water-front, hand in hand, enjoying the play of light on the lake, Howie rambling on all moose-eyed about how we clicked, our shared inter-ests, shared losses, both jilted, both free and on the rebound, and how his ex hated baseball, and made him turn the sound off while she rehearsed her Brahms and Beethoven.

He gets it that I'm maybe a little tentative and he doesn't want to push me, but what about a day on the water this weekend, maybe get a little buzz on, and he's got a lovely cottage, and we can overnight if I'd like but it would be my call . . .

I challenge Doc: "You said if things get weird, bail."

"He meant weird dangerous." Lucy interjecting.

She's to my right. A half-dozen of us, the nucleus of the Earth Survival Rebellion (not to be found on Facebook, Twitter, or Wikipedia) are gathered around the old oaken table, all except Okie Joe, who has more important things to do in his cluttered corner — he has hacked into a server for Canada's Pest Management Regulatory Agency, seeking evidence it bent to pressure from Big Agro to allow the use of neonics as seed treatment.

Ivor Antiques doesn't open till eleven, so Ivor Trebiloff is here, to my left, in shirt-sleeves but with his trademark ugly bow tie. To his other side is his wife, Amy Snider, a black activist from the Great State of Mississippi. Both in their late sixties (and children of the sixties), they met and bonded four decades ago when the cops shackled them to each other at a protest outside the church of a hate-spewing racist preacher.

Across from me: Selwyn Loo, our incredible lawyer. Sightless since fourteen when a virus struck his optic nerves. Turned down a Rhodes to work as a litigator with environmental groups in BC and Ontario. Reads a page of braille with a swipe of his hand. A chess master. Slim, greying, handsome. I have a crush on him too, even though he's halfway gay.

"Dangerous," I proclaim, "describes the jam I'm in when he learns I've been jiving him. Not *if* he finds out. Where am I going to hide? There'll be no cave dark enough."

"We've made arrangements, Rivie," Doc says. "If things go awry."

False ID, Stockholm, trusted comrades. Learning Swedish, eating raw herring. Maybe never seeing Toronto again, my home, my family. It seems an unbearable price to pay. But I think of the mass deaths of the planet's prime pollinator. And meanwhile, Selwyn's class-action suit against Chemican-International is faltering under a blitzkrieg of litigation, a SLAPP suit it's called: Strategic Litigation Against Public Participation.

Amy reaches over to take my hand: "We love you, Rivie. We are so proud of you."

"I'm okay with it, guys. Really." Rivie Levitsky is not a quitter. Rivie is a soldier. Tough, able to cast aside personal considerations. The end *does* justify the means. Exponentially.

Selwyn rises. "I have to run. Thank you, Rivke, for all you are doing. I am truly awed. Peace be on you."

Selwyn never stays for the planning. He knows the broad strokes of Operation Beekeeper but keeps his ears closed to the details. Can't counsel criminal behaviour. Pretty ethical for a lawyer.

His words embolden me. My tactics have been fucking brilliant. I will not be burdened with guilt over a schmuck with a broken heart.

7

Sunday, August 19

Two days later, Stage Four or maybe Five, it's cloudless and thirty-plus Celsius, and I'm on this fast, sleek twelve-metre cabin cruiser, high on cocaine, my hair flying all over the place, forested islets scudding by, terns to starboard, banking and diving, the Who blasting from a pair of speakers. I am refusing not to enjoy myself.

Howie, who has been totally hands off and agonizingly hon-ourable, throttles back as he aims for a pretty cove where we'll take lunch — we stopped at a deli on the way up. He has taken off his shirt, revealing lovely furry pecs and a belly flap that has defied the rigours of Molloy's Gym. Khaki shorts with pockets for everything. I'm in a bikini with shorts over. He can't stop goofing at me with that silly grin, his eyes weirdly filmy.

On the drive up, in his burly bourgeois BMW, he was mostly silent, as if struggling for words, until we pulled over for a snort, which gave him enough pluck to make the dreaded confession: "Becky, I'm afraid I may be falling in love with you."

Blurting out how he felt captivated with me, how he didn't know if his feelings were reciprocated in even a minor way but hoped so, a little anyway, and he wasn't going to push me, was going to earn my trust and maybe affection.

I told him I was flattered. Let's just take it day by day. Desperately trying not to show my discomfort. Part of my problem is lackanookie,

I really need to get laid, it's been four months. I worry that Howie picks that up, subliminally.

He asked if I brought any of my behind-the-counter dynamite. Next time, I told him. So he chopped a couple more lines of his unadulterated flake. It's excellent, though I'm no connoisseur. My thing is weed.

Howie drops anchor and begins slipping the knots from a powered inflatable at the stern. Beckoning is a mossy mesa above a thin crescent of sand. The water entices too, glassy and serene, a reprieve from the heat. Still on a cocaine high, feeling frisky, I slip off my shorts and dive in.

Halfway to shore, I turn, watch him gingerly step into the inflatable with the picnic hamper and towels. I holler at him not to forget my day pack with my lotion, and he scuttles back for it, like a good dog.

I have my hopes raised that I'll avoid having to sleep with this innocent mook. But how? *Sorry, Howie, I'm having another herpes outbreak.* I worry that I'll end up doing it, out of sheer need.

Okay, so now I am drying off naturally, on my stomach, my straps undone, not to tease, just to tan cleanly, but I know without looking that Howie is gawking, willing me to roll over. There's not much to see anyway, Howie, I don't want to disappoint.

I look up, and he's taking a photo of me with his iPhone. I tell him I don't like that, I'm a private person, it's intrusive.

He says he's sorry, and pockets the phone. He goes, "I can't get over how turned on I am by you. It's never happened before. Even with Maxine."

A minute later I open my eyes to his touch, he's applying sunblock to my back. "You're getting some extreme rays, don't want you to pay the price." He may think it's a cute gesture but I abhor the presumption. I try not to squirm.

He asks, "Your boyfriend ever call you back?"

Boyfriend? Oh, yeah, the writer of bad songs. "He sent flowers."

Let him know there's competition, that I'm still hurting, pining, so he'll back off.

Now he goes up my ankles and legs. I stiffen, totally mistrusting his vow of honour.

Ding-a-ling, a-ling goes his phone, just as I was contemplating a leg thrust to his groin. "Sorry, it's the hotline." As he scrambles through his pockets for his iPhone, I snap my top back on and wiggle my way to a protective squat position.

"Bryce?" A pause. "Yeah, well, I'm out of commission right now." Longer pause. "You and Farrell figure it out. They're trespassing. They're blocking traffic. Call the cops." He listens, frowns. "Then get the lawyers on it, for Christ's sake. Get an injunction, or whatever they call it down there. I'll call in two hours."

Brusque, forceful. I am dutifully impressed with his manliness. I go, "Gee, what's that all about?"

"Kansas City calling. Some punks blocking the entrance to one of our plants."

"In Kansas City? On Sunday?"

"Sao Paolo, Brazil. They work on Sunday."

"Why would they blockade the plant?"

"Apparently a lot of bees went missing down there. We've got a product that has practically doubled cereal crop output. You been following the news?"

"Um, not really. Everything is such bad news, I get depressed." Duh. Becky McLean, airhead.

"Let's not let it spoil the day." Don't let it bother your pretty little head. "I don't suppose you want me to do your front."

"I think I can handle that. Let's eat. I'm famished."

§

Two hours later, we are back on shore, and he's on the blower again, with his crisis in Sao Paolo. We're in his Ikea-inspired cottage, open space except for the one bedroom, its door yawning uninvitingly open. Bed, boudoir, a screen window offering a possible escape hatch. Bunk beds in the living room, for his ex's boys, I assume.

I have promised to see my father this evening. I made that point right at the start, when he picked me up at Finch Station.

The TV is on, the Jays hosting the Yankees. I'm totally absorbed in it, of course. Not listening to his bitching about Brazil's lazy cops and inefficient legal system. I pick up that a tanker truck has been blocked from leaving the Chemican distribution plant. A protester has somehow managed to chain herself to its front end.

"She's *what*? Breastfeeding? The hell! Hacksaw it!"

Bryce, on the other end, says something that Howie reacts to profanely. Stymied by a breastfeeding mom. I'm proud of that lady.

Howie clicks off. "Sorry, Becky, looks like I'm going to have to beat it back to town."

"No problem."

"How are the Jays doing?"

"Up by five. They cashed in two in the seventh."

"I'm going to make this up to you. Hugely."

He makes for the can, and it sounds like he's having a dump. Left his phone on a table, still on, so I grab it quick, go into his photo album, delete the pic he took of me, delete it from all devices.

8
Wednesday, August 22

Lucy Wales and I have been couching around a lot in Toronto, where rents are crushingly high, but we finally scored an ultra-urban loft with two cats, the owner on an eight-month sabbatical. It's in Roncesvalles, near High Park, where I charge my batteries, running and biking. Tension can soften the body, all that sitting and pacing and useless dicking around.

The flat is on the second floor of a groundscraper on Sorauren, a converted industrial building, and is high-ceilinged, open-space, upcycled furniture, full kitchen, but only one bedroom. We flipped, Lucy got it, and I sleep on a pullout in the living room.

The professor we're cat-sitting for is a leftie, his field is German literature. Two windowless walls are lined with books, mostly novels, an entire shelf reserved for his translations.

Howie's promised "big time" is on hold, praise Allah. He's in Brazil, putting the whip to the lawyers. Lawsuits are flying. Most of the protesters are out on bail. All have been named as defendants in yet another SLAPP suit. The claim is for thirty million, a number they snatched from the air. Supposed to scare off the protesters but they keep coming.

Selwyn Loo is there too, the chess master. He has cajoled some of Brazil's top counsel to appear pro bono, and they kicked ass on Chemican's motion to gag the defendants. The judge was offended by their gall. The protest is winning hearts and minds.

Howie phoned a couple of times, first from the Toronto airport and, yesterday, from Sao Paolo, where he's thinking about me "every waking minute" and "through every sleepless night." He'll be back by the weekend, so please, my princess, keep it free.

"How's it going?" I ventured, and he was like, "Storm in a teacup. Got these eco-fanatics on the run." Fuck yourself, gorgeous, because you ain't fucking me.

So it's now the rear end of Wednesday, and I'm just back from a five-K run in the park, and have turned on the Jays at Minnesota. We're up 1–0 in the third, bases loaded with one out. Wild pitch, two-zip. (I've become mildly addicted to the sport, and am hoping that will pass.)

During commercials I make a gesture at tidying up the indescribable mess in this funked-up joint. I love Lucy Wales, we've been pals and co-conspirators forever, but she's the roommate from the gutters of hell, and between her and Sinbad and Sleepy, the pampered cats, it's a chaotic situation, dirty dishes, flung underwear, smelly crap in the litter.

Lucy works half days at a Rexall in North York, behind the counter, so I'm well tutored for my cover. She's also a part-time chemical science student as well as full-time anarchist, portraits of her heroes on the wall, Sacco, Vanzetti, Kropotkin, L. Susan Brown. Property is theft, so just leave it lying all over.

Just as the Twins put three across in the fifth, she saunters in, back from work. She tosses her bag on the cat-chewed sofa, and grabs the remote.

"Hey, I'm watching that."

She studies me with her spooky, shadowed eyes. "Seriously? Get a life." She mutes the TV. "I got the goodies." Six hardshell capsules spill from a Ziploc. "Two of these little guys will knock him out for seven hours. But plan for five."

They make me nervous, these little yellow caps. "What's this stuff called?"

"Lucy's Mix."

Meaning she packed these caps herself. That doesn't give me comfort.

"Two are placebos, just flour and food colouring. Those are for you. I pinched one end of each just in case you mix them up, but you want to keep the dummies in a separate pocket or something."

The Mix, she explains with excessive confidence, combines Restoril, a high-end sleeping pill, and Rohypnol, which she scored on the black market, a drug favoured, ironically, by date rapists. "No hangover effect, he'll wake up as refreshed as Sleeping Beauty. More effective as a suppository, you want to stick it up his ass. Oh, yeah, I threw in something for the libido. Maximizes sexual heat."

"Whoa." She has to be joking, she's twisted.

"PT-141, it's a kind of testosterone. You're getting it on with this creep. You have to bring him off before he flakes out."

"I'm not fucking him."

"Well, you have to give him something. Head, at least. You don't make him come, he wakes up still horny, no sign of pecker tracks, he's going to wonder."

There's a dismaying logic in that. "What if he doesn't wake up?"

"Trust me."

"Have you tried it? Has anyone?"

"Hey, Ray is on his way with a pizza. He's up for anything short of junk."

Her boyfriend of three years, Ray Wozniak, Rockin' Ray, lead guitarist for Panic Disorder, four post-punk indie rockers who actually make enough loot playing bars and clubs to feed their drug habits. He's a Californian, a fellow traveller of the Action Network, but not a go-to-meetings kind of guy.

And as promised, here he is, at the door, his signal five-note rap, and Lucy lets him in, relieves him of the pizza. Guitar case slung over his shoulder. Blond, wild-haired, stringy, six-four, almost criminally handsome. Not exactly a candidate for Mensa.

Kisses Lucy, busses me, pot on his breath. Looks at the silent TV set, confused: Who around here gives a shit about baseball? Jays have closed the gap, a two-run homer.

Ray leans in for a close-up of the six capsules. "What's with the appetizers?"

Lucy gives him the full lowdown, then asks if she could interest him in doing a test run.

"Definotly," he says.

"For the cause. Yolo."

"Absonotly."

"Why?"

Ray ejects Sinbad from our one easy chair, sits, noodles on his guitar. "For one thing, I just woke up."

Lucy is pissed. "Then please delete yourself." Severe enough to perk up the ears of the cats.

I don't want a scene. "Hold on, I'll do the tester."

§

I emerge from the loo after a pee and a shower, in clean panties and a knee-length top, laying out my jeans by the pullout in case they have to take me to Emergency. Lucy announces she has set her bedroom alarm for four a.m., seven hours from now.

"I'll be up till then anyway," Ray assures me. He fingers a soft, sleepy melody. I take a deep breath, pop two caps with the tail end of a can of beer that I've been working on, for my nerves, and nibble at a slice, picking off the bacon, feeding the bits to Sinbad and his sister Sleepy.

We wait. Jays tie it up in the seventh. I go, "Yay." Lucy's Mix isn't taking.

I go back for another piss. Still not feeling sleepy after half an hour. There's an edginess, though, urgent little messages from my cunt. Maybe that aphrodisiac, the PT-141, cancels out the soporifics.

Lucy has made up my bed, and is sitting on it, thumbing her cell, waiting to tuck me in. Ray has laid his guitar aside and is lighting up a thin one. He looks delicious, sinewy, blond hair spilling over his shoulders.

A wild impulse propels me onto his lap, taking a hit from his joint. "Dress rehearsal," I say. "You be Howie."

I wrap my arms around him, give him a smooch. He doesn't seem to know what to do with his hands, so I place one on my left boob.

"Hey," Lucy yells. "That's not in the script."

"Script calls for an orgasm." She's an anarchist, right? All property is common.

Ray uses his tit-hold to kind of lever me away — gently, but I suddenly feel very foolish. And woozy. "Oh, God, I'm sorry. Wow, I'm going under."

I barely remember Lucy settling the covers over me.

9
Thursday morning, August 23

I awake to the sounds of voices. A woman: "She's been gone three weeks, Officer." His response: "I'm afraid I have bad news."

Sinbad jumps on me. I pry an eye open. Darkness. The TV on. Ray is watching something Netflixy, sprawled on the armchair, legs propped on a stool. The door to Lucy's bedroom closed. My phone tells me it's half past three. Six and a half hours.

There were vivid, uncomfortable dreams: fleeing from the cops on my bicycle down narrow lanes, into the protective cover of a cloud of bees, who lose their way as I arrive at a protest, fat men in red MAGA hats, their leader yelling, "Get her outta here!"

I nudge the cat off my feet and pull the covers off and sit up. Feeling okay except for that incessant carnal craving.

"Welcome back," Ray says, not rising, just turning his head. "You okay?"

"Almost."

I give him a hungry, lingering look.

"Absonotly," he says.

I go to the bathroom to engage in some lonesome love. Takes me two seconds to get off.

CHAPTER 2 » ARTHUR

1

Thursday afternoon, August 23

Arthur Beauchamp is in his underpants, seated, his right foot elevated, an inflated pink balloon, and it hurts like the wrath of God. Thirteen stab wounds for which a cold pack, calamine, and baking soda offer not a tittle of relief.

"They build nests in the ground," says Margaret Blake, his wife, who does not seem overcome with sympathy. "You should know that."

"I'm abundantly aware."

He had stepped on a wasps' nest in the north pasture and gone howling down the hill with them in hot pursuit. They got him in the shoulder and torso too, but the foot suffered the worst of it. He'd been sockless in scruffy tennis shoes. He should have known better, as Margaret insists on reminding him. He can't deny that. Senescence has finally begun to take its toll on the old fart.

Arthur is deep into his seventies, and though physically spry, unstooped, a tall, craggy man, he's become forgetful, error-prone, finds himself constantly making notes: little slips of paper haphazardly strewn on counters. Certainly, his days in court are over, though he still remains prominent on the letterhead as senior counsel for Tragger, Inglis, Bullingham in Vancouver: Arthur Ramsgate Beauchamp, QC, OC, LLD (hon.).

It's not pronounced Bo-Shaum, in the manner of the Norman conquerors of fair England, but Bee-ch'm, in the manner of the defeated Anglo-Saxons. But he answers to either, and has given up trying to correct those untutored in the nuances of Franglish phonics.

Arthur used to don his gown for occasional courtroom forays, always scuttling back to his sanctum sanctorum with great heaves of relief. That's history. Let his record of thirty-six straight wins be his legacy.

That legacy is enshrined in a book that sits on his shelf of biographies of notables far more famous than he. This warts-and-all history, wedged between Francis Bacon and Francis Beaumont, is titled *A Thirst for Justice — the Trials of Arthur Beauchamp*. The lawyer who authored it took great, chortling pleasure in laying bare Arthur's youthful alcoholic excesses and romantic failures.

Arthur tries meditation, to will away the pain in his foot, but again, as always, fails to find the peace it allegedly brings. The wasp attack was the second this month — yellow jackets have infested their waterfront island farm in these baking hot days of August. They infiltrate the house, though Margaret, insisting that all living things have their place in the biosphere, would shoo them out rather than put them to deserved death.

His wife — or life companion, as this over-liberated politician prefers — has a fortnight left of summer leave before her return to Ottawa, where she serves as the Member of Parliament for Cowichan and the Islands and as Canada's fiercely uncompromising Green Party leader.

She's a political animal, his wife, and is overburdened by her duties, but her many vows to retire have come to naught. So there'll be another few months of living apart, as the fall session of Parliament gets underway.

Arthur will at least have the company of his aging border collie, Homer, as well as one fat, farting horse, two lazy cats, four arrogant geese, ten frisky goats, thirty free-range chickens, and two clever young farmhands: Stefan Petterson from rural Oregon and Solara Lang from Houston, American refugees. Farm-bred Stefan is an animal behaviourist, with a degree in that esoteric art, and Solara is an African-American inner-city social worker learning the mysteries of rural life.

Solara has been here two months and Stefan only two weeks — socialists, escapees from Trumplandia — and they're out there now, as observed through the screen windows, engaged in the ticklish art of goat milking. Blunder Bay is a barely break-even farm since Arthur and Margaret stopped raising lambs — their annual slaughtering proved too painful. But the organic goat cheese and the roadside sale of eggs, apples, and veggies make enough to earn farm status, a tax break, and food on the table.

Margaret applies more calamine lotion to Arthur's tender foot, then leaves him to bear his pain like a man while she returns to the CBC news channel, a report on the protests in Brazil. Honeybee populations there have been decimated, the prime suspect a neonic, a crop-enhancing, insect-destroying, songbird-decimating, nicotine-based compound much touted by the chemical industry.

Vigor-Gro is the trademark, and now that the U.S. Department of Agriculture — under the Trump government — has rubber-stamped it, Vigor-Gro is being exported worldwide by Chemican-International. It's a U.S. corporation but one of its main production centres is a plant in Sarnia, Ontario, a border city serving the ravenous American market. Canadian regulators have blindly mimicked the Americans' endorsement of this pesticide.

In Sao Paolo, thirty protesters have been hauled into court for blocking traffic in and out of a Chemican distribution plant. Most are out on bail, all being sued — along with owners of several apiaries — in a form of litigation all too common in this age of corporate bullying, a SLAPP suit.

"Bastards," Margaret says. "We've got to do something, Arthur. A fundraiser at least."

Arthur agrees, of course, but his swollen foot has discouraged him from championing stinging insects in a country six thousand kilometres away. There are more immediate battles to be fought, right here on their island of Garibaldi, their little chunk of threatened paradise in British Columbia's Salish Sea.

A familiar face appears on the screen: Selwyn Loo, the brilliant, sightless environmental lawyer. He is running a class-action lawsuit against Chemican, on behalf of North American beekeepers. Now he is in Brazil, being interviewed about Chemican's motion to gag the defendants.

"Their SLAPP suit is intended not just to intimidate by suppressing the fundamental right of free speech, but to exhaust the defendants' legal resources with a host of frivolous and abusive court actions. The coalition will not bend."

Margaret is already on the phone, to her staff in Ottawa, instructing them to set up a website for donations and design a fundraising event.

Evening is nigh, time to put the chickens to bed. Arthur painfully pulls on his pants and hobbles to the door, grasping his walking stick to use as a crutch. The chickens are scattered around the yard, but here comes old Homer to help, arthritic but game, sucking it up, accepting pain as his lot, an inspiring example.

The fowl dutifully scurry toward the henhouse gate, Homer limping off to corral a straggler, which heads for home, flapping and squawking. Poor old Homer, he'd recently had a stroke, his rear legs barely working. Arthur can't bear the thought of putting his old pal down after fifteen years of loyal service.

He gives him a hug, limps back to the house to receive a call.

Margaret hands him the receiver. "Al says he feels your pain, but he couldn't help laughing."

Reverend Al, the acerbic Anglican minister, Arthur's best friend, cruelly finding humour in a wasp blitzkrieg.

"Quarry Park bylaw hearing tomorrow afternoon. You going to make it, old boy?"

"Even if I have to crawl." Garibaldi's two nutty Trustees are proposing to rezone twelve acres of parkland to industrial. Parkland!

2
Friday morning, August 24

Arthur spends much of the morning hobbling around with Stefan and Solara, repairing fences, bringing in hay, and reaping the rewards of garden and orchard. Twenty-year-old Solara has become a deft hand at tilling, weeding, and harvesting, and Stefan, who is twenty-five, not only has a deep understanding and love of animals, but is an innovative master of tools. Petite, mop-topped Solara is a chatterbox with a gentle Texas twang, and rangy, long-haired Stefan speaks rarely, though succinctly. Arthur will miss them when they go.

They are waiting for residency papers, hoping to find more lucrative employment than that offered by Blunder Bay — they are burdened with massive student loans, credit card debt, and, in Stefan's case, default of payment on his late-model mid-sized van. They found their way to Canada through the American Refugee Centre, seeking a bolthole from the depredations of their self-obsessed president and his supporting cast of wealthy misanthropes, crooks, and global warmers.

They reside in the house next door. Smaller and older than the main house, it was built in the 1890s by pioneer homesteader Jeremiah Blunder, who is famed equally for the potency of his homemade alcohol and for the ignominy of his death: a drunken slip down his stone well. Island old-timers claim they've seen his ghost occasionally roaming the island's byways with a jug of moonshine.

Arthur's feisty neighbour, the widow Margaret Blake, used to live in that old house with her late husband, a skilled tradesperson. Together, they painstakingly restored it, scoffing at island lore that it was haunted by Jeremiah's revenant, pouring new footings, adding a second bedroom, new shakes on walls and roof. Soon after, her husband died tragically in his prime.

After Margaret accepted a stumbling marriage proposal from the shy, besotted newcomer who'd bought next door — also a refugee, from the law — she moved to the more commodious main house. Their two farms were also married, into one forty-acre parcel of pasture and rolling hills on the banks of the Salish Sea.

Chores done, Arthur considers taking out his skiff to check the crab traps, but hesitates. Something is nagging at him. Yes, the bylaw hearing this afternoon about Quarry Park. He limps off to his ancient pickup, Homer dragging himself after him, like two wounded soldiers. The wasp swelling has abated, though it still feels like Arthur is walking on a dead, prickly stump.

He hoists Homer into the passenger seat, its window open so he can enjoy the rush of passing air. The engine coughs and sputters before igniting, then stalls. Another old, crippled friend, this 1969 Fargo is on its third engine, fourth transmission, the equivalent of replacement hips, knees, and internal organs, but costlier, not covered by Medicare. This may be the old girl's last year.

He turns the ignition key again, and the Fargo seems to take a deep breath, summoning all its dwindling strength, and it fires up and holds. "Good on you." That's intended for the truck but Homer hears it as a compliment, gives him a lick.

Arthur is on his way to Quarry Park, feeling a need to pay his last respects, admire its rough-hewn majesty before it is jackhammered into desecration. Bizarrely, inexplicably, Garibaldi elected two numbskulls last winter as Island Trustees: the self-aggrandizing Kurt Zoller, a tour-boat operator and self-proclaimed libertarian, and Ida Shewfelt, the holiest of rollers, who believes God created the world

5,700 years ago in six twenty-four-hour shifts. Together they control the three-member Local Trust Committee.

British Columbia's Islands Trust Act was intended to shield the Southern Gulf Islands from over-development, but the statute is fuzzily worded, poorly enforced, and subject to the whims of local Trustees. Zoller and Shewfelt are determined to upend Garibaldi's pro-conservation Community Plan as they trumpet their vision to "grow Garibaldi." How Arthur despises that use of the verb. One grows vegetables, not islands.

It's the Trustees' latest initiative that has Arthur roiled up. The island's old limestone quarry, abandoned several decades ago and deeded to the community as a park, would be rezoned to industrial. TexAmerica Stoneworks, headquartered in Fort Worth, seeks to reopen the quarry. Limestone prices have skyrocketed. This is being hailed as exciting news.

Arthur's route takes him from winding Centre Road, the island's east-west connector, to a paved lane that climbs steeply to the quarry. It abuts Gwendolyn National Park — Margaret has beat her brains out trying to persuade Parks Canada to extend its boundaries to encompass the quarry. But the bureaucrats decry its lack of "natural values."

The Fargo lurches onto the quarry's white, dusty entrance road, where Arthur parks near a towering limestone seam, thrust from the ocean floor in eons past. It was well worked before the pits were ceded, leaving steep-sided gullies in the hill and a maze of alleyways and cul-de-sacs and caves. Families take their kids here on weekends to explore and watch with awe the peregrine falcons that soar from nests high above. And here's one now, diving like a missile and snatching a hapless snake that dared wriggle from its hole.

Falcons have been seen to capture lumbering game birds, and robins in mid-air, but are rarely successful against the agile, darting cliff swallows that nest in narrow crevices. There are scores of them in the air, their nestlings out, fattening before fall migration. Higher still, floating on thermal drafts, are a few vultures and eagles, patient, patrolling.

Arthur lets Homer out and warns him to stay in the shade of the truck. His arthritic limbs would find it a test too severe to manage the steep, wonky steps that lead to the viewpoint near the summit. Reluctant but ever-obedient, the pooch sits, and watches with sad, watery eyes as Arthur takes up his walking stick and begins his climb.

He rests, panting, taking in a view. He envisions giant excavators and bulldozers cleaving off slabs of rock, dump trucks ravaging the island's quiet country roads, the brutal reports of dynamite blasts, the island's winged and four-footed citizens fleeing their nests and dens.

Finally, he attains the flat ridge atop the escarpment that locals call Bob's End, in honour of a popular local who ventured too close to the edge in a downpour. He enjoys a visual feast: the islet-dotted Salish Sea, the Coast Range to the north, the Olympics shining white to the south, snow-capped even in August. Nearer is Garibaldi's smaller and wilder neighbour, mountainous Ponsonby Island, untamed by the blight of civilization, its few dozen residents eking a living off the land: loners and New Agers.

In more immediate view, to the north, are a few farms and artist studios snuggled into the valleys bordering Gwendolyn National Park. The north island is otherwise unpeopled except for the remote hamlet known as Bleak Creek. To the southwest is Breadloaf Hill and its homely little subdivision and scatter of shops, and to the east, Ferryboat Landing, where the *Queen of Prince George* has nestled into the dock, excreting little toylike vehicles. Swallows swoop and flutter above and below.

Arthur has endured unhappiness in this life — unloved and, he suspects, unwanted as a child, friendless and awkward socially as a bookish student of the classics and the law. Then, as a young lawyer, he took a wife, alluring Annabelle, artistic director of the Vancouver

Opera Society, who turned out to be voraciously unfaithful, and he nosedived into the depths of alcohol addiction. Twenty years of that, thirty more in AA.

But this island, this placid sanctuary to which he retired from the grind of the courtroom, has brought him peace and fulfillment and joy, a caring life partner, a sense of belonging. That is something he'd never known.

He lies on the sun-dried moss and watches the clouds drift by. High on a limestone crag a bald eagle coaxes two fledglings onto a branch of a gnarled oak rooted in a seam. They take wing, led by their mom, to the scavenging grounds on the rock-strewn beaches. TexAmerica Stoneworks plans a massive loading dock down there, where the seals and otters play.

No, this will not happen. The quarry and its park will be saved.

Fortified by this vow, he makes his way back down, not limping anymore, the pain unfelt, ignored. The wasps are forgiven — they were merely protecting their home, as Arthur aims to protect his.

Homer gets to his feet, ungainly, overcoming his own pain, tail wagging. Arthur embraces him and lifts him up into the truck. The Fargo too has found new strength, and rumbles into life with a throaty growl.

3

The Community Hall is packed — three hundred islanders on fold-up chairs, Arthur near the back with Margaret and Reverend Al and Zoë, his wife. A syrupy-voiced pitchman for TexAmerica Stoneworks is answering questions while extolling the largesse his company is offering. There would be a job for every able-bodied worker who cares to join this exciting endeavour. They will build sheds and lifts and warehouses and quarters for workers. They will grow the island's economy.

Kurt Zoller and Ida Shewfelt are sitting up front nodding with approval. The third Trustee, a realtor representing the Outer Islands, sits numbly acquiescent.

The hack for TexAmerica rests his case. Objections are made loudly and passionately by the conservation-minded, but Zoller gavels them into silence. Question period is over. They are out of order. The democratically elected Trustees will not be dictated to by a noisy minority.

Zoller delivers a barely coherent ramble about the company owning surface mining rights and they can do what they want, it's the law, and the Trustees' hands are tied. Margaret leans to Arthur's ear. "What is he talking about?"

"I have no idea."

A taunt from Hamish McCoy, directed at Zoller: "How much did they pay you off, you scheming barnacle?" An aging leprechaun with a round face framed by a halo of white hair and beard, the scrappy sculptor has a waterfront studio next to the quarry. The old Newfoundlander has been on a rampage.

"I resent that inference." Zoller slaps the table, papers go flying. "This here meeting is getting out of hand due to the no-growth attitude of doomsayers. Motion to pass the bylaw."

"May I have a moment to pray on it?" says Ida Shewfelt.

"Okay, we will adjourn to make our decision."

The Supreme Being takes all of two minutes to stamp approval, and they are back with their decision, two to nil, the third Trustee cowardly abstaining.

§

Afterwards, Reverend Al invites leading doomsayers to a strategy session in his sunny backyard, over tea and beer. The two dozen attendees form the nucleus of the Save Our Quarry committee, with the feisty acronym of SOQ.

Arthur has parked himself as far as possible from local potter Tabatha Jones — Taba, as she's known — a lusty, busty redhead with whom Arthur had shared a single, vigorous conjugal episode last year, a tryst in the woods, impetuous, witless. He'd shocked himself — at his age!

An attractive woman of middling years, Taba never remarried after her faithless husband ran away two decades ago, but has enjoyed the company of many island men, long-term and short, single and not. But Arthur had never been unfaithful and still can't quite account for his behaviour. It was no excuse that Taba had bluntly propositioned him. Other factors were in play: his spells of loneliness during Margaret's long absences and her own admitted affair, also last year, with a smarmy psychologist.

Arthur confessed in turn, overcome with shame. There was hurt, there was lamentation, but also forgiveness. Not for Taba, though, whose long friendship with Margaret is now strained, their encounters marked by cool civility. Taba's gaily decorated pots and vases once adorned their home but most have disappeared into basement storage. Arthur wishes he had held his tongue — yet how could he have lived with such guilt?

Beside him, Margaret is scrolling through her phone. He chances a look at Taba. When she smiles a greeting, he drops his eyes and studies the pattern of tea leaves in his mug.

As soon as everyone has settled upon the lawn, the question of seeking legal redress is raised. All eyes go to Arthur. "You'll save the day, old son!" Hamish McCoy shouts.

Municipal law is not Arthur's forte. He's unsure about how mining rights might trump the preserve-and-protect mandate of the Islands Trust. Zoller isn't smart enough to have figured that out for himself, so it's likely TexAmerica armed him with a legal opinion. They have enormous resources, a division of Koch Industries.

"I shall get on it," Arthur says, with an effort at enthusiasm. Maybe he can conscript someone from Tragger, Inglis to work through the maze of law, regulations, and precedent. Old Roy Bullingham, the scion of the firm, will not be thrilled to know Arthur has undertaken a pro bono defence of an obscure limestone formation. The old skinflint is piqued that Arthur has been turning down lucrative criminal files. He's ninety-four and *he's* still working, ten hours a day, six days a week.

The Save Our Quarry members debate other options. Submissions will be made to the government. A petition will be circulated for the recall of the two Trustees. Meanwhile, a statement will be composed for the press. Margaret will beat the political bushes, lining up prominent allies.

Someone mentions "direct action." Arthur is not comfortable with that bold concept. It seems open to too many interpretations, including unlawful acts. He is a stubborn believer that civil society is founded on the rule of law.

§

Margaret wants a drink after that, and they carry on to the bar at Hopeless Bay, the Fargo burping and farting all the way. The shocks are gone, it's like driving a wonky Mixmaster. Margaret tries to tighten her seat belt but it's stuck in the door. "When are you going to put this clunker out of its misery?"

Arthur's noncommittal response isn't heard over the roar from the loose muffler. He would like to go green when his beloved old chariot gives up the ghost, but electric pickups are still on the drawing board.

He hollers: "I'll have to go to the city to do some research. Probably Monday."

"I'll hold the fort for a few days. But I have to pack for Ottawa."

To help organize a concert fundraiser for the defenders of Brazil's honeybees, for the legal costs. Several name performers have already signed on. David Suzuki has agreed to emcee. They hope to have it televised, with a plea for donations.

Hopeless Bay is a sheltered inlet with a community dock and an old General Store that sells everything from oranges to whisk brooms and dusty copies of *A Thirst for Justice*. It's perched on a small rise and from it a wooden footbridge over a narrow inlet gives easy access to the pub, the Brig.

They take a table for two on the open-air patio, which is cantilevered over the rocky shoreline. It offers a pretty view, waves lapping up a finger of the inlet, starfish clinging to wet rocks. But that doesn't allay Arthur's depression. SOQ is counting on him, but he's not sure if he's got the gumph. He tells himself to buck up, remembers his vow to save Quarry Park.

It's well into evening, and they're hungry, but they have half a chicken waiting in their fridge, so they settle for soup and crackers with Margaret's wine and Arthur's tea.

A couple of tables away is a foursome of local loafers with their splits of beer. Baldy Johansson, who'd been at the bylaw hearing but slipped away early, is holding the floor. "There's good times ahead, boys." He's well in his cups. "Jobs for every able-bodied worker."

Arthur can't remember Baldy ever having a job that lasted more than three days.

"Nobody goes to that park anyway," says Gomer Goulet.

"I've never been," says Ernie Priposki.

"We got to grow the economy," Baldy announces.

§

Arthur's funk deepens on their return home; a heaviness suffuses the air as clouds bulk up and blot the setting sun. He has premonitions of worse to come, and they aren't dampened as they pull in. From the chicken coop, they hear a loud, cackling commotion, punctuated by barking and human shouts. Arthur knows immediately what this is: mink attack.

He and Margaret scramble from the truck, run to the coop. The shouts are coming from Solara, standing outside its gate. "Oh, my Lord, that sorry creature's on a killing spree! It's a fucking hen holocaust! Help!"

Stefan holds Homer, restraining him. Normally, mink are on Homer's job resumé, but Stefan is doing the right thing — with his disabilities, Homer could be mauled by that furry little tyrant. Arthur sees at least ten dead bodies strewn about, a killing frenzy, an infrequent but dreaded island horror.

Stefan releases Homer to Arthur, then steps carefully toward the back of the coop and bears down on the mink. It's cornered between the fence and the shed, its eyes glowing, fangs bared.

Margaret silences Arthur with a tug. Solara calms down. Homer's barking fades into a whine. Stefan is without a weapon, no shovel or hoe. This gangling young man is now squatting, calmly staring back at the mink, speaking to it, his words too soft for Arthur to make out in all the clucking. Maybe a dozen or more hens had survived.

Whatever Stefan is vocalizing has a soothing if not hypnotic effect, and the animal curls into its long tail as if to sleep. Stefan picks it up by the scruff and strolls out to the apple orchard and sets it down, waits till it darts off, then returns to the witnesses by the chicken coop: pretty, elf-like Solara with her wide, shocked eyes, and Margaret with her quizzical smile. Arthur, feeling unsteady, lowers himself onto the chopping stump by the woodpile.

"I just couldn't . . . couldn't destroy her," Stefan says. "Can't fault her, she has babies to feed."

"That's fine," Arthur says numbly.

"Please get some empty feed sacks, Solara," Margaret says. "Make sure you use gloves."

Arthur follows Margaret to the house, changes into overalls, and prevails on her to sit tight while he attends to the obsequies.

Three of the hens are too mangled to survive, and Arthur takes on the dismal task of fetching each in turn to the woodpile and the chopping block. The not-so-elegiac side of rural life.

The farm's two incompetent mousers, Shiftless and Underfoot, have finally screwed up the courage to give in to their curiosity, and follow Solara as she brings the body bags. Stefan has found the hole in the chicken wire where the invader entered, and is already twisting it shut. Solara watches with awe.

Arthur has heard of people exercising semi-magical powers over fellow mammals, but it's not a faculty he'd ever expected to behold in practice. A rara avis, this Stefan. He has trained juncos and chickadees to eat from his hands. The geese often follow him around. So do the cats. A puzzling fellow, taciturn, self-contained, distant. A rapport with animals is just one of his many talents — he also has a gift for music, plays classical guitar.

After the carcasses are gathered, Arthur powers up the tractor and scoops a grave from under the invading blackberries in the west pasture. Solara throws meadow flowers after the bodies, then Arthur lowers the blade and fills in the hole. Stefan watches, casually chewing on a grass stem — he's a vegan, likes to graze. The mink whisperer.

It has begun to rain as Arthur returns to the house. He's intent on having a good, hot, pounding shower, but then realizes he's hungry, and studies the offerings of the fridge. He looks at the platter, white meat on one side, dark on the other, a drumstick left. He decides to make a salad instead.

But just then, Solara rushes in.

"Oh, I'm terribly sorry, Arthur, I truly don't want to be the bearer of even worse news to y'all . . . I don't know how to say it."

Almost instinctively, Arthur knows.

"You've lost . . ."

"Homer." Arthur races outside to the supine form of his lifeless dog lying under a pear tree in the orchard. Stefan is kneeling there, mute and sad. "Heart attack," he says. "He just keeled over. The uproar caught up to him."

Arthur takes the furry old fellow in his arms, overcome. This has turned out to be about the worst day in his life.

4
Saturday, August 25

The funeral service is held early in the morning around a shallow grave in the pasture where Homer reigned in the days when they had sheep: his favourite spot, on a bluff with a view. A dozen friends and neighbours attend, umbrellas unfurled in a steady rain. Barney the horse, two cats, and four geese show up as well, out of respect for their former comrade. Reverend Al delivers the eulogy, taking over from Arthur, who is in too much despair. Then they all repair to Arthur's house for tea and sympathy.

Arthur's funk continues through the weekend. He goes about his chores listlessly, incommunicative, his mind foggy. He forces himself to take his daily health walk, despite the rain, and he often pauses, looks around: Where is his old companion? Homer liked to scamper ahead, reconnoitering, sleuthing, urging him on with impatient glances.

Returning from one such walk, late on this Saturday, he veers off onto a deer trail that meanders across his north pasture. Descending into a vale of bracken and alder, a part of his domain rarely visited, he spots a form moving among the trees, another walker, a skinny man in coveralls carrying a jug. When Arthur looks again he seems to have vanished into the bush. A mirage? The island ghost, Jeremiah Blunder, whose spirit levitated from the well into which he'd drunkenly plunged in 1895. Maybe Arthur needs to have his eyes checked. Or his brain.

Arthur has a collection of Jeremiah artifacts — cups and bottles, rusted tools, a jar of buckshot, a pee potty, the workings of abandoned stills — but despite his many days scouring these forty acres of meadow, pasture, and forest, he has found no remnants of the infamous well.

Back home, he tells Margaret of the Jeremiah sighting. "Strolling across the north pasture with a jug of moonshine."

She says, "Are you sure you recognized him, given he's been dead for well over a century?"

Solara, rummaging through their library for something to read, barely smothers laughter.

Arthur flops into his old club chair and leafs through his library's dog atlas. Someone — Solara, he suspects — has left it lying open on the armrest. He can't quite focus on the pictures of border collies, too many memories — it's too soon to consider replacing Homer. When he's ready, he might choose a different breed, so he wouldn't be constantly reminded of his old pal.

"Maybe an Australian shepherd," says Margaret, who has sneaked up behind him, with Solara. They're leaning over his shoulder.

"Maybe." Or something more imposing, grander, like that Irish wolfhound pictured here, handsome and noble. Described as loyal, generous, sweet-tempered, dignified, thoughtful. Possibly the most devoted pet in the animal kingdom. A regal beast who, in centuries past, guarded the thrones of the Irish kings.

"Beautiful dog," Arthur mumbles. "Aristocratic."

"Their specialty is killing wolves, dear. No one has seen a wolf on Garibaldi for decades. You want a herder, a farm dog, not a hunter. Says here these guys aren't great guard dogs either. Too friendly to strangers."

"Nonsense, any dog can be trained."

Arthur reads on. The breed is older than ancient Rome; wolf-hounds were remarked upon by Caesar. Coursing hounds, hard-wired for the chase, blessed with keen eyesight, they were bred to be ferocious fighters, known as "war dogs," but over the centuries were transformed into the tame and trusted companions of the nobility of the British Isles. Everything about this dog, its looks, its temper, its glorious history, commend it to Arthur.

Dream on. He must settle on something more commonplace, with proven farm skills. A different type of collie, maybe smooth-coated this time. Or one of these English shepherd dogs, here hand-somely illustrated. Maybe one of the European herding dogs.

He sighs, closes the book, wipes a tear.

5
Sunday, August 26

The sun has returned, pulling mists into the air. Margaret is off to a meet-and-greet in the Cowichan Valley, so Arthur must attend church service alone. He dons his suit of funereal black and coaxes his pickup to transport him to Mary's Landing, a batch of homes bordering a pebble beach with a public dock, a nearby islet where sea lions bask and grunt.

Overlooking all is cozy, cedar-shaked St. Mary's Anglican, on a shoreline bluff above the island cemetery, its graves hidden from view by big-leaf maples and weeping willows.

After greeting friends and settling in a pew, he tries to be mindful of Reverend Al's counsel from the pulpit to accept loss, to find inspiration from the tribulations of Job. But he can't focus, refuses to believe Job's torment is any worse than his own.

He gazes sadly out the window, then blinks: Has he just seen another vision, a humanoid form? Hovering behind his truck, then vanishing. Job, seeking forgiveness and charity from the Lord. Maybe just rising mist, sculpted by the breeze. Maybe a ghost, because the path to the cemetery leads from there. Jeremiah Blunder, returning to his grave? Or is it more proof that Arthur is succumbing to dementia?

After service, he praises Al for his splendid sermon, then mingles with other parishioners in the parking lot, among them elephantine Nelson Forbish, editor of the weekly *Island Bleat*, who is sniffing around for items for his "News Nuggets" column.

"I'm closing in on deadline. You got anything for me?"

"One of my farmhands hypnotized a mink in the chicken pen."

"Save it for Facebook, I don't do animal stories."

Arthur dallies while the lot empties, intrigued by the mist-blurred form that evanesced near the path to the cemetery, and finds himself propelled there, past the lumbering trees, down a slope studded with crosses and stones, bottoming out at Pioneers' Row.

Arthur has always enjoyed visiting this lovely little graveyard with its quiet and privacy, and he aims himself toward his favourite bench, the bronze three-seater dedicated to "Dear Ethel T. Wiltby, Our Loving Grandmother." Dear old Mrs. Wiltby, offering comfort from the afterlife. "Thank you, Ethel," Arthur says, sitting.

This is a place of many buried memories, but also some that survived in lore. The quarry master who died under the massive block of granite that is his grave marker. The despotic wife-beater gunned down in his Model T Ford, with his widow — acquitted after a one-day trial — lying beside him. Major J.R. (No-Nuts) Nelson, who returned home in disgrace from the Great War, having accidentally shot himself.

But of more interest, almost abutting the Wiltby bench, is the headstone of Jeremiah Blunder, unreadable after a hundred West Coast winters, his remains identified by a plaque from the Garibaldi Historical Society.

Here, it is said, lies Jeremiah Blunder. Or maybe not. Maybe he's too busy making guest appearances on country roads. Maybe there has never been a body in this grave; maybe Jeremiah Blunder is still in an old stone well somewhere on Blunder Bay Farm, still clutching his jug. No papers or journals exist from those days, no death records. Some bits of old correspondence hint he bootlegged his moonshine off-island, by rowboat.

That evening Arthur packs for Vancouver. He must learn something about subsurface mining rights. Would they apply to limestone formations? Would such rights precede parkland zoning, or was Kurt Zoller talking nonsense? Arthur has already contacted the firm's savant, old Riley, a fixture in the law library, where he practically lives. He will have the answers.

6
Monday, August 27

Arthur alights from a taxi at the entrance to the bank tower where Tragger, Inglis occupies floors thirty-nine to forty-three. He hopes he can sneak in without alerting Bullingham, though the old fellow, sharp of eye and ear, too often manages to find him.

He enters the vast atrium and contemplates the bank of elevators. The thirty-ninth floor is to be avoided, with its bustle and gab at reception and in the secretarial pool. And he won't carry on to the forty-third, the partners' floor, where Bully presides. Arthur's office is there too, preserved, empty, Bully refusing to accept that Arthur is a full-time tiller of the soil.

Politeness requires him to hold the door for a Tragger, Inglis file clerk, a chatty fellow eager to engage with him. "Good to have you back, sir. How were your holidays? That was quite a little rain we had, lovely now."

Arthur nods and smiles, punches the button for forty-one, the library. The elevator stops on thirty-nine, and the clerk rushes off, presumably to announce a rare sighting of the firm's senior counsel.

The library is cathedral-like, bookshelves to the ceiling, walkways, ladders: all artifacts of long past — most of the research is done these days online, an art even Arthur has finally mastered. Several young lawyers are hunched over laptops and copying machines. And there is Riley, half hidden by a computer monitor, a grizzled, bespectacled gnome scribbling notes.

He looks up, his greeting a simple nod, as if Arthur, whom Riley hasn't seen for a year, is still routinely popping in.

He waves off Arthur's how-are-you and his compliments, and advises, in his clipped, no-nonsense way, that he is embroiled in a monstrous copyright action set for two months beginning in September. However, he has done a quick review of the quarry issue and could give an oral summation.

Arthur is still in mourning, slow of mind, and can't grab onto much of what Riley is relating. What he gathers is that a search through government records shows rights to the quarry were never extinguished, even after the park rezoning, and were assigned to TexAmerica Stoneworks three years ago. Those rights appear to defeat any local bylaw. It's unlikely though not settled that the Islands Trust's preserve-and-protect mandate will be of avail.

"There is no authority exactly on point. I can show you the leading cases. *Canada Cement Lafarge v. Manitoba* holds that industrial-grade limestone is included in any grant of minerals."

Arthur is dismayed by the bleak prognosis, and is about to slump into a chair when a voice too familiar intrudes.

"Ah, Beauchamp. We're most grateful for your visit." Roy Bullingham has, predictably, materialized at the door. "Do you think we can we have a few minutes?"

§

They are in Bully's sumptuous, mahogany-panelled office, Arthur standing at the window, taking in a view of Stanley Park, the inlet, the North Shore peaks, the suspension bridge sweeping over the First Narrows. His persuasions have not moved the old man.

"I shall have to be blunt." Bully, leaning back in a swivel chair, stern, disapproving. "I see no upside to this business with your quarry that would profit our firm. We do not go gambolling off to take on every picayune cause of action that pops up in some remote corner of the hinterland."

Arthur reminds him that the firm has a proud history of pro bono service to deserving causes.

"Are lives or livelihoods at stake? I think not. No, Beauchamp, we have exceeded our pro bono budget for the year. You are on your own."

"Surely you can give me a junior. It's no simple matter."

"That's what I'm afraid of. We cannot afford a junior. Nor can we afford Riley — he's needed for a copyright claim. Something about computer language. Beyond me. You are welcome to use the stationery and the staples." A pause. "However . . ."

"What?"

"If you were to agree to get back in the saddle, handle a trial or two, we might be able to offer some consideration. We have the Williger homicide coming up. Logging company CEO. Shot his wife with a hunting rifle. Accident, of course, though there's some issue about her having had a lover. Set down for ten days in October."

Ten days . . . plus a month of prep. Impossible. Arthur will not give in to this extortionate proposal. He will have to do without Riley. The judicial review of the rezoning of Quarry Park cannot wait.

He thanks Bully for his kind offer and returns to the library and opens a text: *Mining Law in Canada*. The words swirl before him, blurred, incomprehensible.

7
Tuesday, August 28

Syd-Air runs a scheduled half-hour flight to the Gulf Islands, and when Arthur, as today, is the sole Garibaldi-bound passenger Syd is generous about dropping him off at Blunder Bay's dock. So on this early evening he is quickly back home.

He alights on his dock with his overnight bag and a thickly packed briefcase. Margaret appears at the veranda door, waving delightedly while talking on her phone. Solara emerges from behind Stefan's van, races to meet him, relieves him of his bag. A mischievous look. "We have a surprise for you."

From behind the van the surprise comes bounding toward him, trailing its leash. Stefan comes running in pursuit. The dog, thickly furred, frisky but clumsy on its massive paws, stops ten feet away to assess this new stranger.

Arthur stares back. The dog is twice Homer's size. A male. Handsome. "What do we have here?"

"Irish wolfhound pup," Solara says.

"He's a *pup*?"

"Six months old. Y'all was admiring them. In that book."

"Yes, that's, um . . . wonderful, but how . . ."

"Wolfhound group on Facebook. Stefan and me, we drove up to the Comics Valley on the weekend."

"Comox Valley."

"Co-mox, I got it. Anyway, very nice lady, on in years, and now she's been diagnosed with stage two cancer. She wanted next to nothing, just wanted to make sure he had a loving home."

"What did she name him?"

"Wolfy."

"Absurd. I will not vulgarize him with that name."

Stefan draws beside him. "He's playing strange." He passes Arthur a couple of dog biscuits.

Arthur bends low, offering one. "Come here, fella." The dog temporarily called Wolfy approaches warily, snaps up the biscuit, backs away, gobbles it up. A second is offered. This time the pup doesn't shy away, instead gives Arthur a big, wet slurp on his face. Arthur laughs, then embraces him.

"Ulysses. That shall be your name. Hero of the *Odyssey*, king of Ithaca." Worthy successor to his own Homer, named after the great Greek poet who immortalized Ulysses. And to honour the Irishness of his wolfhound, one must also celebrate James Joyce's masterwork. Arthur is suddenly energized.

Margaret joins him. "You won't want to see inside the house. He knocked over the spice rack and chewed up one of your slippers."

Stefan seems embarrassed. "My mistake. He has to be watched until he learns inside manners."

Solara tosses an inflated rubber ball, and Ulysses bounds after it. In less than a minute it's in shreds. Then he spots a wandering chicken, which flees, flapping and squawking, as Stefan and Solara run for the trailing leash. The chicken somehow makes it over the henhouse gate, and Ulysses doubles back, leaps at Solara, sending her on her rear.

Everyone is laughing. Arthur hopes this over-energized, impetuous pup is trainable. He retrieves the leash. "Let's go for a stroll, Ulysses." The pup leaps ahead, Arthur staggering after him.

CHAPTER 3 » RIVIE

1

Saturday, September 1

Clustered around the antique oak table back of Ivor's, our core group tweaks the final inning of Operation Seduction. As usual, Helmut Knutsen presides, though nobody ever elected him. We aren't into power rankings, but the old activist has been chairing meetings for eons, and the role fits him like his ratty pair of Birks.

Okie Joe is only vaguely with us, he's focussed on his MacBook, code scrolling up the screen. He's pulled some emails from the U.S. federal pesticide lab that hint of negligent testing of neonics like Vigor-Gro but hasn't been able to punch a hole in Chemican-International's firewall. That bugs him. He has underground fame to live up to, post-Google, as a star hacker with Anonymous.

To my right sits Lucy, all honey-tongued and supportive. The hot body to my left belongs to Chase D'Amato, newly arrived from the Peace River dam site. Chase does a lot of the high-wire acts you see in the news clips, swinging and rappelling, suspending

Greenpeace banners from bridges and derricks. He's been arrested on four continents.

For all that, he's loose and easy, an almost stereotypical hunk: lanky, lean, bunned brown hair. Likes to pretend he's not conceited. Currently, he's tanned all over, except his ass. I know that because I conjugated with him last night.

We had a fling once and maintain a tradition of getting it on when he sashays into town, and that worked out spectacularly, a home run with bases loaded. I'm still tingling.

Lust has been sated, putting me in a more soothed mood just as I'm about to encounter Howell J. Griffin again. He texted me to say he'll be flying in this afternoon and has reservations tonight for Paramour, a French restaurant so expensive that nobody I know has ever been there. He'll call me when he lands.

"What if he insists on picking you up at home?" Doc asks.

I've been coy about telling Howie where I live. Out in Scarborough, I claimed.

Lucy's solution: "Tell him you're working late and you'll meet him outside my pharmacy when you get off." Her North York Rexall. Good plan. I'll explain I changed from my work clothes in the staff room.

"You sure he'll invite you up?" Doc asks.

"The odds against are infinitesimal."

"You bringing some safes, right?" Lucy said. "It's not like really fucking if you rubberize him."

Chase laughs. He wants to sympathize with my touchy situation, but can't help finding it funny. I do have condoms. Lucy slipped me some morning-after pills too.

I still wonder, though, if I can avoid his penis going into me. It's not that I hold any puritanical views. I'll prostitute myself for the cause if I have to, but I'm just not into Howell J. Griffin. It's not his phony urbanity or his male superiority presumption disorder, or even the panting, tail-wagging doggie love. It's his loyalty to his corporate master.

And here he is, my Becky phone is chirping. I put it on speaker. The room goes silent.

"Hi, Becky, it's me."

"You made it. Awesome. What's up?"

Chase makes a gag-me face.

"TripAdvisor has the Paramour as number two in T.O. Hope you're hungry. I have to warn you I won't be my usual bright-eyed self. Flying all night and day is a unique modern-day form of torture. But I will overcome."

I tell him where to pick me up. That he's wrecked is a plus: he may be so bagged he'll pass out.

2

It's Stage, whatever, Eight? Anyway, here I am on my totally-not-hot date with Howie, who is in meltdown after his nightmare overnight from Brazil. I told him he should've taken a day to recover, but I guess he couldn't break free of his manic obsession over the object of his desire.

The atmosphere in this über-expensive restaurant is dark and moody, and I'm beating back the butterflies. Tonight's the night, it's the Last Chance Saloon, I either pull it off or get fucked for nothing.

I'm in sandals not heels but in the same mini I wore first time we met, in the Beaver's Tail — it's the only garb I own that didn't come off the recycled racks — and I'm getting lots of looks: How come that bag-eyed boozer scored such a dishy date? This somehow flatters Howie more than me.

He is working on a sirloin while my alter ego, Becky McLean, picks at a Caesar salad. Between us is a bottle of champagne that probably costs more than half a year of welfare cheques. That came after his two martinis. I passed on the cocktail but am into my third flute of fizz, I can't help it, it's too pricey to waste. Stay sober, comes the warning voice.

I assume Howie found time to shower, but I still get heady whiffs of something, maybe fatigue sweat. He's been entertaining me with rambling tales of his triumph over the peasant farmers of Brazil, who had shamelessly tried to stop Chemican from dumping tons of neonics on the big, mechanized farms they dare to compete with.

"Had to do some fiscal favours under the table with selected bureaucrats, plus the state governor and a judge, but it's the cost of doing business. I brought you a little something."

A small gift-wrapped box. I go, "Wow, you shouldn't have." I slowly open it with a sickly school-girlish smile — it had better not be an engagement ring. Nope — a pair of scuzzy earrings. Cavities lined with crystals, some kind of serpent entwined around them.

"Brazilian snake earrings," he explains. "Gold and druse."

"Boy, that's . . . unique." I have to scramble for that adjective. "I can hardly wait to try them on." I pack them away, press my fingers to my lips, and schlep the kiss to his cheek.

We talk baseball awhile — me going, "What about those Jays, eh?" — but he's been following them online and knows the scores, the blowout last week with the four home runs, yesterday's walk-off double.

Plates are taken away. I decline dessert, ask for a coffee. He orders a Baileys. He's freaky, this guy, the way he can put it away. Not even slurring.

He'd really like to know more about me, about my family. I don't explain that my mains are living an organic garden-to-table existence up north, a little burg called Golden Valley. I follow the script: Becky's folks are disunited, re-partnered, her dad in Hamilton, her mom in Buffalo. "I really don't want to think about them right now."

Keep things simple, Doc said. Your life has been boring and sad. You've had to struggle, you're saving up for college, you had to abandon dreams of, for example, being a famous figure skater or ballet dancer or model. (For Howie, I chose figure skating, because in high school I was seen as a comer, though I never arrived.)

Howie orders a second Baileys. He has superpowers, bullets bounce off, even Lucy's Mix may not make a dent.

Finally: "Well, I could drive you home, or . . . what about popping over for a while? A little shot of Remy to top off the night?"

"I'd love to," I say.

3

Stage Nine. I'm in his roomy apartment, strolling with my cognac, being agile, avoiding his hands, stopping to admire the painting of breaching sperm whales, thinking of sperm, of condoms, of my jeopardized cunt. I peer through the glass of the inner office, locked and unlit except for the LED lights on his electro-devices, and I wonder how I'll get access in there.

"Wow, is that what they call a bank of computers?" I worry about myself, I'm getting too good at playing the simple-minded waif. "Had an old laptop once. Guess it died of old age."

This turns out to be another sharp move from Agent Levitsky. Howie pulls a clump of keys from a pocket, unlocks the office. As he ushers me in he wrong-foots himself on the shiny tile floor, grabs his desk for balance, recovers, drains his glass. He's half in the bag with juice and fatigue.

He can still talk, though, and rambles on about the setup in what he calls his war room, a big screen and a dozen small ones, internet feeds from security cameras in plants, labs, warehouses. Computers recording all this, terabytes of video.

I ask: Terabyte? He has to explain to me what that is. Meanwhile, I'm more interested in the big desktop, his main machine. There'll be a password.

"I'm going to give you this baby here." A thin Dell notebook, pulled from a shelf. "Packs a punch, so don't be conceived." Surely he means deceived. He taps in a password. It doesn't take. Another try, careful and slow enough for me to read. Krj791. The screen lights up with icons. "Two months old. I'll clean it out for you."

"Thank you, that's awesome."

He staggers out with the notebook, and I follow him. The door to the war room swings shut and locks.

It's time. "You are such a kind, generous man." A deep breath, and I embrace him, getting the full blast of his man smell, but my lips just miss his because he stumbles backward with surprise, nearly drops the notebook.

"I'm crazy about you, Becky," he gasps. "I want you."

I take his arm. "I think you need some fresh air, Howie. I've got something that will pick you up."

I perch close beside him on the balcony divan. The lights of Toronto sparkle, the stars unseen. Lots of Saturday night activity on the street below, partying noise from a bar. The buzz of traffic, and a distant siren. Howie's right hand settles on my upper left thigh, his left hand on my shoulder, and he pulls me into an awkward cuddle. The right hand crawls crotchward.

Now or never. Time to throw my secret strikeout pitch. "Whoa, Howie, let me warm up to it. I brought some of that elixir I told you about. Enhances the romance, if you know what I mean."

"Yeah?" Nuzzling me. "Like ecstasy? Tried it once, it was mellow."

"This has ten times more pop. Drove me wild last time I used. Also gives you a lift here." Becky does what Rivie just can't get down for — she fingers the formidable bulge in his pants. Clearly, Howie doesn't need much of a lift.

This immodest gesture is taken as an invitation, and the response is a handful of Howie between my legs, like I imagine a catcher's mitt might feel. I have to tug him away. The message: if I come across, it's on my terms.

I go back in for my bag, palm two of Lucy's Mix in my right hand, the two placebos in my left. Howie staggers after me, pours himself another cognac, studies the offering in my hand. "What's this magic potion called?"

"Passionata." Lucy and I came up with that while stoned. "I heard it's called Leg Opener on the street. Isn't that awful?"

I borrow his glass and make a production of popping and washing down the two safe caps. The pinched-end ones, so I avoid making the blooper of the century.

Howie hesitates. He tries to stifle a yawn. Then: "Yeah, let's go!" He gulps back his two caps. Stage Ten. That was too easy.

And now he is all over me, hands on my bum, his boner prodding my lower abdomen, his lips meshing with mine, a thrust of tongue. I gag a little, unpeel from him. I need to buy time, this chemical cocktail was slow to kick in on my test drive, so I ask if he'll do me the favour of having a shower. That gets him apologetic and fumble-tongued.

I go to his ear with a husky whisper. "I'll be waiting for you in there." The bedroom, door open, a bed lamp glowing. He starts scrambling from his clothes, sends his shirt flying, kicks his pants off, and heads for the main bathroom.

There's a bedroom ensuite, and I peel off there, assemble my clothes and sandals for a quick getaway, and slip within his crisp, washed sheets. It's a king, roomy. In a few minutes, Howie staggers in, a towel knotted around his midriff.

"I am so hot for you, baby." Demonstrating that by dropping the towel, revealing a club you could maim someone with. He catches himself, as if dizzy, revolves, falls backward onto the covers, barely missing me, his dick like a pink-nosed gopher sniffing the air. "Man, this . . . what do you call it?"

"Passionata."

"What a blast. You feel it?"

"Yeah, getting there. Hang on a sec, Howie, there's something we need to talk about. When you were in Brazil did you get bit by any mosquitoes?"

"Mosquitoes?"

"The Zika virus. Transmitted sexually. Babies with shrunken heads."

"No problem. There's Trojans in the drawer. Grab one, roll it on. I'm dying, I'm going to explode."

"Oh, you poor thing." The PT-141, the testosterone — why did Lucy think that was such a good idea?

He's still supine, splayed across the bed, waiting, I guess, for me to sheath his joint. "Don't move, Howie, I'm going to help you out."

Change of plan. Forget the prophylactic. I shimmy from the sheets, make a gymnastic dive between his legs, kneel there.

"Do it, baby!" He's totally wired for the expected blow job, but instead I grasp his supersized dong with both hands and pull. He roars as I jack him, like a charging beast of prey, and his hips rise a foot off the bed, and before I can duck away he emits a geyser of semen right in my face, in my hair, all over my tits.

"Holy fucking shit!" I yell, scrambling off him, off the bed, and bolt for the ensuite, wiping the come off me.

As I toss him a bath towel, he mumbles, "Sorry, didn't mean to. Jus' happened."

"No problem. I'll be right back for round two, sweetie. I'm going to fix myself up." I close the door, turn on the shower.

§

Holy fucking shit? "Language!" Mom used to say. I'm kicking myself for not staying in character, for reverting to Rivie Levitsky. Howie is used to being Wowed.

I'm under the shower for fifteen minutes. I shampoo three times. As I towel off, I listen for sounds from the bedroom. The quiet is unsettling. I'm wondering if he maintained enough mental capacity to change the bedding. Maybe he just crawled under it.

I crack open the door. He hasn't moved, is still supine on the bed, legs and arms splayed, his cock like a deflated party balloon. Snoring.

I approach carefully. There's sperm all over, a puddle on the floor that I almost slip on. I nudge his foot. Definitely out. The fuckless Howell J. Griffin.

I have nearly five hours, but I'm aiming for four. I get dressed but leave my sandals off, so I can pad about barefoot, noiselessly. Retrieve my camera from my handbag, unclasp the pocket with the two-terabyte hard drive, slip on thin rubber gloves. Howie's pants hang from an armchair. The left pocket yields up a thicket of keys.

As I pass by the bedroom door, I see Howie sprawled naked, still snoring, and I bring a quilt from a shelf and gently drape it over him. I don't want him stirring in discomfort.

The key to the war room is sturdy, and so is the lock, but it clicks open. The desk computer is a Sony workhorse, and of course it wants a password. I rummage in the drawers, examine loose papers, look for lists hidden under the envelopes and writing pads. Nothing. Would this security bot have memorized his multiple passwords? Probably not. The gift Dell notebook is also on his desk. I tap in Krj791 on the Sony and hit Enter. The computer roars into action.

My external soon begins filling up from his C drive. It's a fast machine but close to data overload. Two-plus hours, says the message window.

One of the two filing cabinets is unlocked and yields up mostly bumph: travel brochures, airline schedules, receipts, tax returns, photos of Howie, some of his ex, who is pretty. The other cabinet is keyed, the small one on the ring. Its four drawers are dedicated to Chemican records, a bonanza. Photographs, layouts, diagrams of alarm systems, codes to open doors, it's all here, maybe hacking the computer was superfluous. No scientific stuff, though, no files labelled Vigor-Gro. Those goodies must be in their lab in Sarnia.

The process of taking close-ups of security plans and diagrams, letters, memos, incident reports, an entire Brazil folder, takes three hours and three SD cards and two recharges. Meanwhile, my hard drive has sucked up everything from his big Sony. Just under four hours. I take a last tour of this electronic vault, make sure everything is in its original order, and then slip out, lock up, return the keys to Howie's left pocket.

I pause to check he's still breathing. He is and he's smiling. I hope his bladder holds out.

I scribble out a note. *Sweet dreams. Had a lovely time. Becky.* I pick up my shoes and head out the door.

4
Sunday, September 2

From somewhere, a familiar voice: "Motherlode. It's the codes for the alarm system." A printer whirrs and clicks.

"We'll have to disable the backup system too."

It's half past morning, and I'm in the fog of arousal from deep sleep, bumfuzzled as to where I am, couching somewhere. Right, I crashed on a late nineteenth-century divan.

Memory expands. I'm hotfooting from the scene of the crime, not a free taxi anywhere, sticking to the bright streets, ignoring cat-calls, holding my bag tight to my body. I fast-tracked to Ivor's all the way, decompressing in the cool night air, arrived after midnight, and they were waiting in the backroom, all jumpy, stressed out.

I finally crashed at around three. None of my fellow accomplices clustered around Okie Joe's workstation look like they've slept at all. Joe and Doc, Ivor and Amy, Chase D'Amato, Lucy. Off by himself is Rockin' Ray Wozniak, who doesn't sleep much anyway, at least at night. Head encased in Sennheisers, air drumming.

Okie Joe has finished downloading everything, and my digital photos are rolling across two of his monitors. "Stop," Doc says. "Grab that one." The printer burps out an image. A metre-tall pile of these.

I flap around in the bed in an oversized nightie Amy found for me, throw off a blanket, stretch, announce myself with a bright "Go-o-od morning!" She's back, folks. The queen bee of Operation Beekeeper.

I'm still jacked from last night's high-fives, but tense, waiting for Howie to call with his abject apology for falling asleep on me.

I'd set my phone to Do Not Disturb. Powered on, it shows one missed call, from my mom, her usual Sunday morning check-in. Howie is either still asleep or too wrecked to make contact.

"I'm bagged," Ivor says.

"Let's break for the day," Doc says. To Joe: "How you doing?"

"All backed up and encrypted."

Lucy bounces over to wrap her arms around me, her dozenth hug. "I had Ray bring your essentials." My hiking pack with comb and toothbrush, cut-offs and tops and underwear, socks and runners.

I tog up in the washroom, then join the troops.

Doc gives me the poop on the work assignments culled from Howie's emails and staff records. Three men do night shift at the Sarnia plant, one stationed in a booth at the gate, an outside guy who patrols the grounds, the third stationed inside — his remit is to do hourly patrols but stay out of the lab upstairs.

Of particular interest to Doc is a memo that works out a staffing issue: the outside guy will be off work on September 9, following dental surgery, and since the regular replacement will be on holiday they're bringing in an untrained temp as fill. Master ejaculator Howell J. Griffin signed off on that.

"So that's the target date," Doc says. "A week Monday." Eight nights hence. "Meanwhile, Chase will go to Sarnia overnight for a grounds surveillance." Turning to him. "Your pickup still runs?"

"Just needs an oil and lube."

"I'll go with him," I announce. The prospect of spying in the tall grass all night with Chase sounds orgasmic.

There's a chorus of no ways. Rivie is needed here. The nays have it, except that Chase voted for me. I ask Doc: "Who's doing the main event?"

"Me, Lucy, Chase, maybe Ray. You have done enough, Rivie. Lay low. You have an open ticket to Stockholm if the bottom falls out." Doc was born there, lived his teen years there, visits often, maintains close friendships.

I stand my ground. "I'm going to Sarnia with Chase. And I'm not going to miss the show. I've earned that. And you need my superpowers."

As if to add emphasis, my phone chirps.

"Good morning, Howie. How are you feeling?"

"Like a fool. I assume you've consigned me to your slash pile of failed suitors."

"You were exhausted. Things happen." Cool, not too severe.

"Passing out like that. Christ."

"We'll laugh about it one day."

"Well, *that* gives me hope. Thanks for being so damn empathetic, Becky. By the way, I cleaned out that notebook computer. Where can I drop it off?"

"How about when I get back? Jays are hosting Boston next Sunday. I'd kill to go."

"A *week* from today? Excuse me, you're going somewhere?"

"The thing is, my mom just called from Buffalo. She's having some kind of nervous breakdown. Have to take time from work, but . . . I'd really like to catch the Red Sox series."

"Well . . . Sure, absolutely. Terrific. Maybe between innings we can laugh about it."

"Hey, Howie, it happens to the best of us. Especially men."

He laughs. The guy actually has a good side to him.

"Goddamn, I'm going to repair the damage, I promise."

"I'll call."

"I love you."

"You're sweet." And I'm a bitch. I feel like shit.

CHAPTER 4 » ARTHUR

1
Monday, September 3

In the dog bowl sit great clumps of grey and mottled contents of dead cows' innards that smell like untreated sewage. Arthur watches with awe as Ulysses literally wolfs it down: a pound of tripe, which little resembles the delicacy offered by fine French restaurants.

Stefan has done extensive wolfhound research. Store-bought dog food might be okay for some lesser beast, but the good health of this kingly breed demands raw food. This comes in frozen blocks from a mainland cattle farm and costs a prince's ransom. It's complemented by various meats, fish, veggies.

"Energy for the chase, young fella." What Ulysses chases are the deer that occasionally jump the fence, but he has never caught one, and probably wouldn't know what to do if he did. Ulysses began by annoying the goats, then befriended them under Stefan's tutelage, and now gets it that all the animals of Blunder Bay, including the fowl, are part of the family.

As companionable as Ulysses is, he seems to feel that normal dog-like behaviour is beneath him. He rarely barks, which is a blessing, for it's a sonic boom. Nor does he herd, fetch, swim, or high-jump a tall fence — but he can perform Olympian long jumps over ditches. He has also been seen to escape the friendly confines of Blunder Bay by dislodging split rails. Twice, Stefan had to track him down outside the farm's perimeter. A couple of days ago, Ulysses sent prospective buyers fleeing from Blunder Bay's roadside stand. Not that he was at all unfriendly — it was just the sight of him.

Otherwise, he doesn't do much but race about and sleep and eat and lick people's faces and smell their bottoms and dig holes — Arthur nearly twisted an ankle stepping in one — and create general carnage. Anything in the house that is breakable is now on high shelves. Arthur has been left with two right-foot slippers and a chess set with a missing rook, bishop, and two pawns.

But such a handsome, noble hound. Arthur forgives him, indeed admires his independent spirit — Ulysses is no master's obedient slave. There is something soul-satisfying having this majestic animal at his feet of an evening as he lounges in his club chair reading the *Meditations* of Marcus Aurelius.

Ulysses's imposing presence helps dilute the loneliness that regularly sets in after Margaret's departures — she is in Toronto now, putting together the concert fundraiser for the Brazilian bee defenders. A more difficult cause now that Chemican-International has broken the protest. By bribing officialdom, according to Selwyn Loo, whose angry allegations got him a quick ticket back to Canada.

The dish licked clean, Ulysses stands at the door, letting his so-called master know it's time for his afternoon walk. Arthur stuffs the leash into his day pack, and Ulysses bolts past the open door, racing with great bounds, like a mighty jackrabbit, toward Stefan and Solara, who are shoring up a snake fence that the rambunctious pup knocked over. Ulysses is fond of Solara but adores Stefan, who talks dog to him, roughhouses with him.

Ulysses pauses to commune with the goats across the fence, several of which gather and touch noses with him. Now he tears back toward Arthur, who has learned to dodge these rushes. The pup screeches to a halt ten feet past him, returns for a lick and a muzzle nuzzle, and they set off. These are blessed times, his twice-daily dog walks, peaceful and meditative and companionable, as they were with Homer, the pain of whose loss is now beginning to dull.

The sky is streaked with filmy cloud, a pleasant late summer day, so Arthur takes a break from his dull-eyed poring over mining laws that seem arcane, almost impenetrable. He is out of his element in the civil courts — give him a good old-fashioned murder any day — and feels ill prepared for tomorrow's judicial review of the Quarry Park rezoning. It's first on the docket at the Victoria courthouse, so Arthur must catch the early ferry.

Solicitors for TexAmerica had clamoured for a prompt hearing — delay was costing many thousands of dollars a day, heavy equipment was waiting to be ferried over, hardrock miners were standing by, payroll costs soaring.

Arthur is weighted down by the burden of high expectations. Yesterday, after church service, Reverend Al convened a Save Our Quarry session, lauding Arthur's courtroom prowess, predicting he would bring TexAmerica Stoneworks to its corporate knees. An embarrassing standing ovation.

Arthur leashes Ulysses before they exit the driveway gate to Potters Road. The gate is usually open — it's a nuisance keeping it closed for the dog, but Arthur lives in hope the pup will grow out of his wandering ways. Homer never wandered.

Roadside cornflowers are in azure boom, blackberry tangles are heavy with fruit, and so are the branches of plum trees that have multiplied past the orchard fence. Potters Road is a popular stroll for long-weekenders from the city, and here are two couples grazing on plums and berries. Their yappy little dog sets off an alarm on spotting Ulysses, and the tourists freeze. "Poppy, come here!"

But Poppy either knows no fear or is blinded by it because she races straight for Ulysses and leaps at him, clamping on the loose folds below his neck, dangling there for a moment before Ulysses, with a powerful shake of his head, sends the little dog tumbling head over paws into the weeds. Ulysses tugs at the leash — he isn't interested in Poppy but wants to meet these interesting humans.

"He's very friendly," Arthur calls as he ambles past the fearful foursome, Ulysses straining all the way. "Just a pup. Enjoy the day."

With his thick grey coat, Ulysses doesn't do well in the heat of the day, so on reaching the far boundary of his farm, Arthur opens a small gate and they enter the forest — fir and cedar and thirsty maples, already yellowing at the top. Unleashed, Ulysses gallops merrily off, down an alder bottom thick with bracken.

Arthur loses sight of him, and his calls go unheeded. No sound of him crashing through the bushes after another deer — with his growing strength and speed, he may well be capable of running one to ground.

Arthur blinks. He could have sworn he had caught another glimpse of the island's infamous wandering ghost, spindly Jeremiah in his coveralls. But it was just the play of shadows in the trees.

He finally spots Ulysses, pawing among the ferns. Not pawing, digging — with a focussed intensity. Approaching, Arthur sees that Ulysses's powerful scoops have uncovered several clumps of cemented rocks around a depression, apparently some kind of cave-in. Ulysses looks up proudly at his master, panting heavily.

"What have we here, then? Good dog. *Very* good dog." Rewarded with biscuits from Arthur's pack, Ulysses proudly saunters off.

Arthur bends low. Two of the cemented rocks have broken off but the others can't be budged. Definitely the remnants of a man-made structure, the rocks cemented tightly together. As he pulls out some bracken bunches, he sees that the depression forms a five-foot-diameter circle. Surely Jeremiah Blunder's storied well has finally been discovered.

The interior is packed with thirteen decades of silt and dirt. Arthur is thrilled with this archaeological find, delighted with his scalawag pup's detective skills. Ulysses's many trespasses are forgiven.

Now he must hire someone to excavate this long-sought antiquity. Dare he enter into negotiations with Robert Stonewell? Known locally as Stoney, the self-proclaimed master mechanic also runs a business called Island Landscraping. A scoundrel, but Arthur is oddly attached to him, however masochistically, and he owns a backhoe with enough oomph to do the job.

Had Ulysses also seen the ghost? Has Jeremiah led them here? Arthur laughs at that silly notion. He marks the site with a tepee of branches.

2

Tuesday, September 4

As expected, it is heavy plodding in the blocky, seven-storey utilitarian structure known as the Victoria courthouse. Arthur's passionate defence of parkland is falling flat. His thrashing of Zoller and Shewfelt for ignoring their sworn environmental duties has the judge smothering yawns.

Mr. Justice R.B. Innes is a new face to Arthur: round and pink and bland of expression except for the occasional condescending smile. Specialized in property law, Arthur has heard, and hence was assigned this file.

"Anything else, Mr. Beauchamp?" Bo-chomp, he pronounces it, in bastardized French.

As a last gasp, Arthur pulls out one of the maxims they drummed into him in law school half a century ago. "It has been the dictum of the English law since the Magna Carta that the owner of an estate in fee simple owns everything up to the sky and down to the centre of the earth."

"Does not the Mining Act make a clear exception to that rule?"

Arthur resorts to bluster. "Whether or not the bylaw is valid, the Garibaldi Parks Commission has clear title to the land and therefore it also owns its minerals."

"Unless they've been granted elsewhere. What's your position, Mr. Shawcross?"

TexAmerica's relaxed, rotund lawyer is a senior partner in one of Vancouver's big firms. He seems embarrassed by Arthur's floundering and argues his case briskly and succinctly, as if to put him out of his pain. "Rights of the surface owner are subordinate to those of the owner of mining rights. Section 50, Land Act. When the quarry's previous owner went bankrupt, those rights were returned to the provincial government, then conveyed to TexAmerica. Exhibits A through J of our evidence folder."

"In the form of *profit à prendre*, I believe."

"As a matter of interest, m'lord, the concept of *profit à prendre* is canvassed in a paper I recently wrote for the *Real Property Law Journal*."

"Yes, I happened upon it. Admirable piece of work, Mr. Shawcross. Right on point."

Arthur attacks his laptop, vainly searching for that admirable piece of work. The term *profit à prendre* is gibberish to him.

Shawcross sums up: the zoning bylaw issue is moot; the current park zoning cannot impair his client's rights.

"Well put," says Innes. Arthur waits patiently for this chummy pas de deux to run its course. Innes then asks Arthur if he has any reply.

Arthur is inspired to offer up an amended line of popular verse: *I will arise and go now, and go from Innes, free.* But he stays on track. "Nowhere does the Mining Act condone destruction of key habitats of cliff swallows and peregrine falcons."

"I suspect there are many other places for your swallows to nest, Mr. Beauchamp. People have rights. Corporate entities have rights. Birds don't. Mining rights trump the stated purpose of the Islands Trust Act. I so rule."

3
Wednesday, September 5

The evening finds Arthur and about two hundred others at an emergency town meeting in the Hall. A special sailing of the gender-confused vessel known as the *Queen of Prince George* is due tomorrow: excavators, bulldozers, dump trucks, fuel trucks, semis with tools and materials.

On the stage, Reverend Al is fielding questions about SOQ's proposed blockade at Ferryboat Landing. The plan is for a human wall of protesters to stay the *Queen George*, as she's locally known, from discharging its cargo. There is an air of excitement and purpose, shouted calls to arms, especially from the dozen late arrivals who'd been celebrating Baldy Johansson's sixtieth at the local pub, all lit up, exchanging high-fives with every verbal sally.

Not so merry is Arthur, who sits at the back, alone, wounded, and morose, unable to look fellow SOQers in the eye. Several had attended the debacle in the Victoria courthouse and seen Arthur at his worst. He is on the cusp of senility, the fat-witted Falstaff of the Law Courts. He can picture Judge Innes entertaining his cronies over the inept effort by that poor poop of a counsel, old Beauchamp.

Taba Jones drags over a chair and settles beside him, too close — with Margaret away, the generously endowed potter tends to become teasingly bold. She lays a hand on his thigh. "You look like a nuclear meltdown. You'll appeal, right?"

"Yes." With minimal expectations.

"You've got to get out of this funk. I'm having some really cool friends from Vancouver over on Saturday for a barbecue. A couple who run a gallery where I show and two of their artists. Hip. Discreet. They'd love to meet the famous barrister."

Discreet. That seems a loaded word, hinting of concealment of sinful pleasures, maybe involving the heated pool by her kiln. "I'm not sure, Taba."

She goes to his ear. "Arthur, let's stop this pretence of being blind to each other's existence. It's fucking dumb and it's risky. It signals we had an affair."

An affair? It was a single, mindless rut on a hidden mossy meadow. But how alive he'd felt, nakedly mounting her, and even now the memory of it gets his libido churning. It had not been like that with Margaret, not for many years. But his wife has a temper easily ignited — he dares not risk word getting out that he shared a barbecue with Taba and her hip and doubtless libertine intimates.

"I may have something set for Saturday." What's his problem — why can't he pronounce a blunt no? "I'll check."

"Do that. Let's be real." Taba releases her grip on his thigh.

Arthur takes a deep breath, focuses on Al, who is firing up the troops. "Let's show them what Garibaldians are made of. Are we all together on this?"

"Together we stand!" cries Baldy Johansson, who is actually sitting. He gets a round of slapped palms from his birthday celebrants. The loudest of this cheering squad is Cudworth Brown, the ribald beatnik poet, a retired ironworker. "Occupy the ferry dock!" he cries. "They shall not pass!"

"Save the park!" Mattie Miller calls from across the room, pumping a fist in the air. "Save our beautiful island!" She earns a spirited ovation. A feisty exhibition from the normally mild-mannered grandmother — she raises alpacas just below Quarry Park. Her animals face imminent threats from the noise and dust from the nearby quarry.

Beside her is her neighbour, Hamish McCoy, the sculptor. "Kick their dorty arses off to Texas, by's."

That generates more cheers, more shouts. "Stand together!" "Never surrender!" Taba calls, "Impeach Zoller!"

Who is conspicuously absent, as is his cohort, Ida Shewfelt. But RCMP Constable Irwin Dugald, the island's tall, beetle-browed law enforcer, a man with a poor sense of humour, is standing at the back, making notes, probably jotting down names of the malcontents. Nelson

Forbish is also scribbling, furiously. A hot item for the mainstream media for which the porcine local newsman occasionally strings.

Cud Brown, who is fairly potted, begins a rambling ode to bravery. "Long will be remembered those who stood tall at the siege of Ferryboat Landing . . ." His words are buried by voices raised in song: "We shall not, we shall not be moved . . ."

Arthur's depression is allayed. He is proud of his fellow islanders, who have shown themselves unafraid to assemble in a grand, brave act of civil disobedience. He is one with them.

4
Thursday, September 6

A steady rain has dampened spirits at Ferryboat Landing, and the expected vast throng has not materialized. About a hundred have shown up, standing ten deep at the ferry slip, their arms linked, many awkwardly holding umbrellas, like a patch of giant mushrooms.

Arthur's only protection is a felt hat. He is in the middle of the pack, elbow to elbow with Mattie Miller and leprechaunish Hamish McCoy. This pair have had their quarrels, mostly about McCoy's roaming old pooch, Shannon, but are united in a greater cause.

Stefan and Solara are minding the farm. They'd been keen to join the demonstration, but were leery of jeopardizing their immigration status. Only one of yesterday's high-fivers has roused from their hangovers: Cud Brown, an armchair Marxist who has never been known to miss a demonstration. The muscular poet seems not to have heard Reverend Al's caution to be mute and civil — he serves as self-anointed spokesman for SOQ, giving loud, gruff face time to the mainland press, whose several vans and mobile units arrived by morning ferry. Cud has now joined the front of the line, taking up a position between Taba and Reverend Al.

The *Queen George* berthed half an hour ago, and the landing gate is down. Loaded trucks idle on the car deck. The first mate and other senior officers have given up trying to confront and persuade, and are conferring with Constable Dugald, who shouldered his way through the line, jostling Cud. The two are not the best of friends.

Dugald checks his watch, makes a radio call, presumably to his superiors, then strides across the landing gate, plunking himself in front of the bank of dripping umbrellas.

"All right, let's break this up. This is an unlawful assembly. I can think of a dozen laws that are being broken here."

"We shall not be moved," Cud says.

"Yeah, well, you're busted, pal."

"Okay, I'm busted. Now what? You gonna take me in?"

Arthur shares Al's obvious annoyance. There were to be no confrontations.

"Damn right I am." Dugald unclips his handcuffs. "Your regular cell is waiting."

"I hope you got room for two hundred more in your birdcage 'cause none of us are leaving."

"No problem, Cud. We're using the school auditorium as a holding centre."

"Who's we?"

"Me and them." Dugald gestures at the RCMP launch coming full throttle around Ferryboat Point toward the public dock. "Listen up, everyone. You have two minutes to get the hell gone from here or you're *all* busted and you'll be spending the night on a hard wooden floor." His voice rising with every syllable. "You want your kids seeing you locked up like common criminals? You want records? Mug shots and fingerprints?"

A voice behind Arthur: "I got family at home." Arthur turns to see Luke the plumber sidle off into the rain and mist.

"I have to take my cat to the vet tomorrow." Hattie Cooper breaks ranks, pulling her husband with her. A collision of umbrellas.

"I got sixty kids I have to drive home." The school bus driver follows them.

Dugald hollers after him, "Hey, Bjorn, bring the bus back afterwards. I may need it for the prisoners."

The exodus of the faint-hearted continues.

"I have to feed the dogs."

"My patio furniture is out in the rain."

"I have to take my meds."

By now, a dozen uniformed officers have trooped into the ferry compound. Arthur is dismayed — the siege of Ferryboat Landing is self-destructing. But he thinks of that smarmy judge, Innes, and his flip dismissal of the rights of nesting swallows. He takes up an empty position at the front of the line.

Grandmotherly Mattie Miller, who is as shy and mild-mannered as the alpacas she raises, pulls up her skirts, steps over a puddle, and joins him. So does Hamish McCoy, who despite the occasional muttered profanity has somehow managed to keep his temper.

The police squad is led by a glum, thickset staff sergeant whom Arthur vaguely remembers from some trial or other. The officer slips past the thinning front lines and confers with Dugald.

A boom mike appears overhead as the press gather, led by Nelson Forbish who cheerfully identifies the main perpetrators. "That's the ever popular parish priest, Al Noggins, and that's the world-renowned sculptor, Hamish McCoy, and over there that's our very own Arthur Beauchamp, the distinguished criminal lawyer."

Shouts from the press corps: "Mr. Beauchamp, a comment, please." "Tell us how you feel right now, sir." "Mr. Beauchamp, why have you joined this protest?"

Arthur faces the cameras. "To save this island from the depredations of a soulless mining corporation."

"Are you prepared to resist arrest?"

Arthur suppresses an impulse to make light of the matter, to jest about how he's been arrested before — twice for contempt of court. But the impromptu interview is cut short as the staff sergeant returns to address the thirty remaining protesters.

"Ladies and gentlemen, you are blocking a highway. That's an offence under the *Criminal Code*, section 423. You could do up to two years."

Quickly their numbers are halved, down to a brave baker's dozen. "Everyone sit," Al calls. Arthur squats, trying to avoid a puddle.

The senior officer glumly reads them their rights. Handcuffs are clicked open. A pair are snapped onto Arthur's wrists. He feels ridiculous.

"Let's help you up, old-timer," says a husky female officer, grasping him under the armpits, raising him to his feet. Only Cud Brown and Hamish McCoy resist, and are limply carried off, protesting police-state tactics.

"I think we can do this in two trips," Dugald says as he fetches his Ford Explorer SUV from the drop-off lane.

One by one, the handcuffs are removed as Arthur squeezes into the back of the SUV with six others, so tight with Taba that he can't find a place for his arm, and it ends up awkwardly around her shoulders, hovering above her breast. Both are soaking wet.

"Well, isn't this cozy," she says. "They can't keep us locked up through the weekend, can they?" She whispers, "You up for Saturday?" A tremor of arousal as she squeezes his thigh. "Come by a little late if you like, after dusk."

Arthur removes Taba's hand. He feels ridiculous, afflicted by lust amid despair. As the SUV jolts ahead, he hears the TexAmerica trucks grinding off the ferry. What a shambles.

§

Arthur sneezes. "Excuse me." He sneezes again. He has changed into dry clothes, and is sitting by his blazing fireplace as he chats on the phone with Margaret.

"Don't tell me you've also caught a cold."

"I'm fine."

"You looked awfully miserable on the evening news. How come you're home? Didn't they arrest you?"

"They just wanted us out of the way. Irwin Dugald drove us all to our homes. He handled the situation with remarkable aplomb, I have to say."

Ulysses makes a lunge for the hem of his robe, takes a mighty tug, nearly causing Arthur to eject from his club chair. "Down, boy!" The pup stares at Arthur with seeming disappointment: Why doesn't his master want to play? How come no afternoon walk? What's with the bad vibes?

"Ulysses is full of energy."

"I thought Stefan was training him."

"He may have met his match."

"Has he been talking to any more wild animals?"

Arthur looks out the window. "As we speak." Stefan is out in the rain, ambling along on the rock beach, in apparent conversation with two ravens walking beside him. All three pause occasionally to examine a shell or some wiggling thing in a tidal pool.

"I think that was a very brave thing you did, Arthur, if that's any consolation. Is there any recourse?"

"Hamish and Mattie may have an action in nuisance. A dim hope, but nothing ventured." He scribbles one of his notes, adds it to his pile: "Research law of nuisance."

Margaret has to get back to planning her fundraising event, set for this weekend. They sign off with long-distance kisses.

Ulysses stares at him expectantly, his tail wagging.

"All right, all right, let's go."

Arthur puts on a rain poncho and snaps on the leash. Ulysses gives him a wet kiss and pulls him out the door.

CHAPTER 5 » RIVIE

1
Monday, September 10

So we're all still revved up from Saturday's brilliant Save-the-Bees funder that a bunch of leading greenies put together. A Bee-In, they called it, an open-air event at Ontario Place emceed by David Suzuki. Six name bands headlined by Blue Rodeo and Broken Social Scene. Guest spot by Neil Young! Sixty dollars a pop, six thousand bums on chairs and more standing, plus thirty grand for the silent auction and forty-five more from outside donors.

A big chunk of which will go to Brazil's bee defenders, but there's surplus booty to help out with protests breaking out all over the freaking planet, now that Chemican is starting to be seen as an international pariah.

Lucy and I kind of paid our way by volunteering backstage. Personal highlight: Selwyn Loo intro'd me to Margaret Blake, who is a good hugger and radically cool.

And so now it's the turn for us eco-guerrillas to show our stuff. It's Bee-Day, or at least late evening, and here we are, the partisans of

Operation Beekeeper, all in a nervous tingle, standing in a patch of woods, on the fringe of what city planners like to call, oxymoronically, an industrial park. It's south of the busy border town of Sarnia, and from between the trees we can glimpse the St. Clair River and, on the other side, a rural snapshot of the thumb of mitten-shaped Michigan. Detroit is a hundred kilometres downriver, and its lights suffuse the southern horizon as the last rays of sunset dim into a mauve wash.

The day had been hot, the air's still heavy. The woods sparkle with fireflies but annoy with mosquitoes. We are six: Doc, Joe, Lucy, Rockin' Ray, Chase, and the imperious Jewish princess who whined and bitched when they tried to leave me behind. Chase and I scoped out the scene a few days ago, tenting here in the woods, about which I'll spare the details except we didn't get much sleep.

Doc drove us in Ivor's big unmarked van, the rest of us splayed on foamies and mattresses in the seatless back. The old fossil burner is parked a hundred metres down the street that borders this area of scraggly forest, which surveyors' ribbons have earmarked for a warehouse site. Across the way, and fifty metres down, is the entrance gate of the Chemican plant.

Its compound is surrounded by a three-metre-tall fence of thick woven wire. Several transport trucks and vans are parked in there. A rail spur with two tanker cars.

Okie Joe has all the codes. Everything else that I poached from Howie's war room has either been erased from his computers or stored in the Cloud with a password as long as his arm that he snail-mailed to his girlfriend in Oklahoma.

I pass Doc the high-powered binocs. "Take a boo at the guardhouse." A glassed-in shelter, maybe two metres square. "That paunchy guy in the grey uniform pretty well stays put, but wanders out for an occasional smoke or piss."

"Irwin Fleiger," says Doc. "Suspended for a week in May for drinking on the job." Doc must have memorized the relevant employee records. He's so sharp. "Age forty-one, five years with

Chemican. After secondary school, he did a six-month course in security work."

I direct his attention to the character coming around the corner of the sprawling two-storey structure. "That's got to be the temp they've got doing ground patrol." In a uniform, like Fleiger, but baggy, a couple of sizes too large. His flashlight does a full arc, and we duck.

"Archie Gooch, thirty-three, single, had to repeat grade nine, spotty work record, three arrests — shoplifting, hit and run, dealing amphetamines. Apparently that doesn't disqualify him from guarding a top-secret chemical lab. His ex-girlfriend sought and got a no-harassment order."

Gooch checks a ground-floor window, finds it secure, casts his light around, sends a beam at Fleiger in the guard shack, who calls out something joshing or profane. Gooch shuffles up to the front door, buzzes, bringing out the third member of this stellar team, the inside man. They confer.

"Barney Wilson," says Doc. "Twenty-eight. Eighteen months on the job. Took some kind of surveillance training. Also a Boy Scout leader."

"Every hour or so he comes out for a smoke," says Chase.

On cue, the Boy Scout leader tamps out a pair of cigarettes and he and Archie Gooch light up. After a minute of chit-chat, Gooch carries on, then stops to shake something out of an envelope, a pill or capsule that he pops into his mouth. Could be a cough drop. Could be his daily multivitamin. Could be dope of some kind. Speed, for which he already has a sheet.

Or maybe it's one of the drugs du jour, a high-test opiate like Oxycodone. That's what Rockin' Ray is guessing: "Oxy, maybe fentanyl, dope for dopes. Dangerous and disgusting, man." Even Ray has limits. "Hey, Doc," he says, "are we sure none of these bubbas are armed?"

"This isn't America," Doc says. "Yet." He takes a turn with the binocs, wiping the germs off first with a wet wipe.

"Average time of a circuit was seven and a half minutes for the regular guy, the dental patient," Chase says. "But this Gooch dude is no Speedy Gonzales."

Ten minutes and forty seconds later Gooch reappears, joins the guardhouse guy for another gasper — these boys are total chimneys — then checks the parked trucks before beginning another tour. Again he pauses, tongues another small item from his envelope.

Doc goes, "Let's give it another hour, say about midnight, less ambient light." The main sources of illumination will be a street lamp, four yard lights, the glow from the guardhouse, and a dimmer glow from the barred windows of the plant. Its laboratory is on the second floor, and totally dark.

We hunker down, swatting mosquitoes, praying for a breeze. I pull my black jacket over my head — we're all wearing dark clothes — and squat under a poplar tree with Lucy and Ray. For about the fifth time I check my phone, my regular one, to make sure it's on mute. I scrapped the Becky phone after texting Howie a couple of days ago with, "Sorry missed your call. Mom needs total rest. Back Sun for Sox game. Jays need our help!!" A grinning emoji.

Bummer. I really wanted to catch that series.

Lucy has a cap on, with flaps, to cover her magenta hair. She's leaning against Ray, who is crouched over a lit cigarette, trying to shield it from view. From its glow I see him slipping something into his mouth.

I go, "Tell me that's some kind of vitamin supplement."

"Waker-upper. I didn't sleep all day."

"What was it, Ray?"

"Fank you, little darlin', for being so concerned about my habits and needs. It was just a dot, a cursmidgen. Not more than a hundred micros."

Lucy goes, "Oh, shit. Houston, we got a problem."

"Acid? You just did a hit of acid?" Keeping my voice low, though I want to scream. Doc and the others are out of earshot.

"Chill. Hey, ladies, it's a picayune hundred micrograms. To tune me up, heighten the awareness. A little lightness of being, man."

"Shut up," Lucy says. "Now what? Doc will go ballistic."

"You sure it's just a hundred?" I've done a few trips, one with double that, and managed okay.

"Absotootly."

Lucy curses. I clap my hand over her mouth. "How do you know it's not four hundred?"

"I was told."

"Who, by the guy you scored it off?"

"Totally chill dude who looks after the band."

"T. J. Gully." Lucy groans. "A drunk. A garbage head."

"Never done me wrong. He deals pure."

Lucy hushes him again and we do a feverish tête-à-tête. Do we tell Doc? But we don't want him calling this off, we're too ready, too primed. Do we leave Ray behind? What if he goes bizarro? Mind you, Ray is almost always on some kind of dope and never seems to lose it. But he has a role in this caper. He's supposed to hide downstairs, below the second-floor lab, with a view of both doors, send a text alert if anyone enters. A hundred micrograms might not impair that simple function — we've practised it a dozen times. But can we take that chance?

"Okay, let me babysit," Lucy says. "I'll text the alerts. We'll tell Doc that Ray is so bagged he could fall asleep."

So Lucy and I find Doc, both of us feeling crappy for leaving out one little detail. Doc thanks us. He'd seen Ray yawning with fatigue.

2

"Phones on vibrate," Doc says. "Gloves on." And he leads us across the road while Fleiger, the guardhouse guy, is focussed on taking a piss into a bed of nasturtiums.

We crawl on all fours to the fence, Chase taking up position there with a pair of industrial wire cutters. We stay low while Archie Gooch, taking a break from his labours, perches on a ramp at the back door of the plant and pulls from his cigarette pack not a straight but a spliff. We can smell it from fifty metres away, a billowing of smoke — he almost disappears in the fog of his exhaust fumes.

He takes a couple more hits, dinches the roach, flicks it, gets up, steadies himself, aims for the corner of the building, and weaves off around it.

Lucy can't help herself: "And the employee-of-the-year award goes to . . ." Almost too loud, and there is choked laughter and, from Doc, "Shush. Let's move it."

Chase clips the bottom two strands, then we scurry into the compound, dart behind a tanker truck, then lope to the back entrance. The ramp where Gooch had been smoking his face off leads to a loading bay and a wide steel gate, and a regular door next to it, accessed by a keypad.

Okie Joe opens his notebook, a pen flashlight between his teeth, and he clicks a couple of multi-digit codes that he has assured us will unlock the door and disarm the security system. Open sesame. We are in. Noiselessly.

Barney Wilson, the inside guy, is presumably parked at his desk near the front door, out of view, a hundred metres away. A light glows from that direction. He has a radio tuned to a country music station, a distant complaint of sliding guitar. Assuming he follows protocol he won't be doing his next walkabout for half an hour, at midnight.

A few windowed offices, a coffee lounge, otherwise it's all open space. Massive tanks, tubes, conduits, crates, an assembly line for packaging Vigor-Gro in ten-litre containers. Cranes and hoists, fork stackers. A wall of shelves with hand tools: drills and bits and clamps and crowbars. Conveniently close to our back door is a wide staircase to the chemical lab. No surprises, all according to the diagrams and photos in Howie's files.

There's a dark recess behind the metal racks of protective gear —
that will be Lucy's and Ray's lookout. So far, Rockin' Ray is fairly
dormant, not tripping but he's only an hour into it. But then as the
rest of us race upstairs, there's a clatter and a soft curse, and it looks
like Ray has tipped something over, a helmet maybe or ear protectors.

He emerges on knees and elbows to retrieve a hard hat, and I
get this wiggle of worry over his playful act of strapping it on and
saluting like a soldier. He's too close to the rack, the whole thing
could go down. But he crawls back safely.

We wait in silence until we're sure the guard, Wilson, heard
nothing over the hillbilly lament on his radio, and then we carry
on up to the lab, which is thick-walled but with two high windows
cracked open, maybe because it gets hot in there. Again, a keypad
lock, and again Joe does his magic. Totally dark except for various LEDs, some blinking, and dim light from windows. Doc does
a survey by pen flashlight: long metal tables, beakers, flasks, tubes.
Lockers, refrigeration equipment, machines for mixing, I guess, or
analyzing or quality control or whatever they do.

An interior door, unlocked, takes us into Chemican's records
storage and library. Several computers. Shelves with manuals and
texts, cabinets and drawers, folders of multicoloured files. As Doc
dives into those, Joe hacks the computers, gets them regurgitating
data into his externals. I return to the front door of the lab, where
I've been assigned to watch for activity below.

Everything is cool for about half an hour, then my cell wobbles,
and I duck as Barney Wilson appears below. The guys in the lab
got Lucy's alert too, because the computer fans stop whirring. An
overhead light goes on. I find a hidden corner and listen to Boy
Scout leader Barney Wilson hum-sing "Oh! Susanna" as he does the
rounds, probing with a flashlight.

After several minutes, I hear him closer, climbing the stairs,
coming from Alabama with his banjo on his knee. A rattle of the
door handle. But he leaves it at that and returns downstairs and I

breathe out slowly. The front door clicks open. Wilson has gone out for his hourly smoke.

Another couple of hours pass. The same routine: going into suspended animation as Wilson walks about singing Boy Scout campfire songs. Occasionally we spot Archie Gooch from a rear window, a lighter flaring, sucking up tobacco or more reefer, topping off with one of his mystery pills.

I hate this spooky lab, this Vigor-Gro death house, its poisons. Not touching anything though still wearing my clammy rubber gloves. So far, no activity from the acid freak below, though he must be squirrelly with the silence and darkness. Unless he's so bagged he couldn't stay awake, or maybe the LSD hasn't kicked in.

Finally, Doc motions me over to the library to confer. He's got a full backpack of files. The copying of hard drives is complete, everyone's packing up their gear, pen lights, cameras, external drives.

"Get anything good?" I ask.

"Suspicious test results for starters. At least one blatantly made-up survey, so there's likely more. Some junk science. It'll take a day or two to sort it out for the media."

The material is to be bundled out over the net to major dailies in Canada, the U.S., and Europe, plus the TV networks and progressive journals and webzines.

"We'll wait for Wilson to make another pass," Doc says. "As soon as he's out the front, we're out the back."

We return to our stations. I'm ecstatic. This has gone like silk.

§

The minutes creep by. It's three a.m. Finally, Wilson reappears again. Phones vibrate. We hide.

From his repertoire of campfire songs, Wilson has chosen "Home on the Range." What's next? "Old MacDonald Had a Farm"? He seems in an amiable mood. But maybe he sings because he's nervous in the dark.

"'Where seldom is heard a discouraging word.'" I'm guessing he's maybe only a hundred feet from the staircase.

Then, suddenly, a loud, ragged snore, causing Wilson to go wildly off key. Another snore from Ray, then a gagging sound, a snort, maybe from Lucy clapping her hand over his mouth.

"Who's there?" Wilson yells.

"I am the avenger!" Ray calls in a ghostly voice. The rack collapses, helmets and ear protectors crashing to the floor.

I am at a window now, Doc too, all of us. "Let's fucking go," Chase says in a fierce whisper.

"Wait," says Doc.

Ray shows himself, a hostile from deep outer space, a wild explosion of hair, and he's decked out in hard hat, safety glasses, two sets of ear protectors, red rubber gloves. He grabs a pry bar and starts smashing the levers and faucets at a bank of huge storage tanks. A stinky fluid gushes out.

Wilson is goggle-eyed with panic, frozen in place as the first wave of Vigor-Gro sweeps over his feet. Turning to flee, he slips, takes a face-forward splat on the mucky floor, gags as a second wave hits, and gets up drooling, spitting, his legs spinning as he takes flight for the front door. Ray drops the crowbar, races after him, screaming: "You are the archfiend, the spirit of evil! I am the avenger, the enchanter!"

We fly down the stairs. Lucy is standing there in the slop of Vigor-Gro, her mouth hanging open, like a zombie. Chase slings her over his shoulder like a sack of potatoes. As we scramble out the back door, I glimpse Rockin' Ray gaining on Wilson as they slip and slide in the wash of poisonous neonics. As they barrel out the main door, Ray yells, "Lower the life rafts, this ship is going fucking down!"

For what it's worth, he has created a diversion that lets us scurry unseen to the fence. A last glimpse of the avenger shows him with his head still encased in all that gear, and he's no longer pursuing Wilson but super-stoner Archie Gooch, who is screaming in terror.

I get another glimpse as we're taking turns crawling through the fence hole. Wilson has scrambled into the guardhouse with Fleiger. Ray is still yelling incoherently about the fires of hell as he sprints past Gooch, who staggers, as if caught in Ray's slipstream, then collapses on the road in a faint.

Ray disappears into the woods. Neither Fleiger or Wilson seem interested in pursuing, though they race out the gate and down the road, ignoring Gooch, who is sprawled prone on the pavement.

We all pile into the van but Chase, who streaks across the street into the bush, hoping maybe to use his wilderness tracking skills and bring down the Devil's Enchanter. I go up front with Doc, who jams the shift into drive and pulls away. He looks like the wrath of God.

"What's he hallucinating on?"

"Acid." A hundred micrograms. But I don't tell him that, because he won't believe it. I don't believe it. More like six hundred.

§

The planned exit route is Highway 40 south, staying clear of Sarnia, connecting to the 80 east to Toronto. But we're still on the local roads. There's little traffic, no sirens so far. Doc is not one to leave comrades behind, and I know he's in turmoil over whether to hang or cut and run.

We're not far along before Doc hands me his phone so I can read out a text from Chase. It says, "Scott Road near Christopher. Two blinks."

Google Maps locates us eight hundred metres away from there. Doc turns off a side road while I navigate. Fastest route, two minutes, says the screen, but we're heading north again, perilously close to the scene of the crime.

Semi-rural Scott Road is in deep slumber and we slow to a rolling crawl as we near Christopher Drive. From the bushes to the left, two flashes, and it's Chase with his phone flashlight. I leap out to help him wrestle Ray into the back, sans helmet, earmuffs, and eye protectors. But babbling. "Save the bees. To bee or not to be a bee. Bee happy. Happy bee."

"He was crashing through the bush like a snake-bitten moose," says Chase. "Let's be gone."

"Be loose, man. Be there or be square."

"Be quiet," Lucy commands, hugging him, tearful, because she loves that goof, and we are rolling down the road.

Aside from Ray's continued soft mumbling, we remain silent for a long while, the van reeking of our anxious sweat. Then Lucy says, "Archie Gooch may want to lay off the ganja after this."

I can't help but chime in: "Maybe Ray scared him to death."

We're all laughing now, even Doc. As a further mood lightener, I start singing a tune I can't get out of my head. Chase joins in, then Lucy and Joe. "Oh, give me a home where the buffalo roam, where the deer and the antelope play . . ."

CHAPTER 6 » MAGUIRE

1
Tuesday, September 11

Inspector Jake Maguire hefts his bulk from his cruiser, moving slow, weary from a long drive and an interrupted sleep. His breadbasket is roiling. He's got to do something about his intake, too many sneak attacks into fridge and pantry, too many furtive visits to the food dispensers. He can barely look in a mirror at that paunch, his baldness, his florid face poorly decorated with a woolly, untamed moustache. He used to be called handsome.

He makes his way to the open doorway of the sprawling Chemican plant. It's an old building, thick wooden posts, wood doors, wood siding, a fire trap. He watches sourly as a cleanup crew swabs the floor. Gauze masks, rubber boots. "Is that stuff toxic?" he asks.

"Only to bugs, apparently." Gaylene is her name, Detective Gaylene something, Sarnia PD. She's been briefing him, all efficient and over-eager. Tall, with blond hair, an unruly thatch that doesn't want to stay in place.

"Smells like cat piss. Can someone get me a coffee?" They dragged Maguire out of bed for this. He arrived at dawn after a bleary-eyed hour's drive from London, the coffee shops still closed.

Gaylene doesn't exactly jump to it. "They have coffee in the lounge. We've got Fleiger in there."

"Which one is he?"

"Guardhouse duty."

"Where are the other two guys?" Wilson and Gooch. They hired hysterical cowards to guard this joint. First responders had to waste two hours looking for a bomb because of them.

"They're both in Sarnia General."

"For what?"

"Shock."

"*Shock*? Fuck."

"Gooch keeled over in a faint. He's still out. They can't seem to wake him. Wilson's hooked up to a dripper, some kind of sedative. That nutter came after him with a crowbar, so—"

"Get him down to the detachment."

"Which detachment?"

"Mine. Lambton County OPP." He spells it out: "Ontario Provincial Police. Our show." In case she has any ideas.

"Yeah, well, meanwhile those are our Ident people." Half a dozen from Sarnia PD in there, doing prints, taking pictures. "Want them to stop?"

Already, Maguire doesn't like her attitude. In the good old days, you'd never see a lady cop. Now they're everywhere. It's the influence of all those TV cop shows, where they have to demonstrate gender equality. "They'll work with a team we got coming in from London." OPP's regional HQ. "Where's this coffee lounge?"

"We can go in the back door. They've got boards to walk on."

Gaylene detours him to the wire fence to show where it was cut. Lots of scuffle marks on either side. An officer is on knee pads, poking around for butts and buttons.

"Any wire cutters found inside?"

"Yeah, one," she says, "but identified as company property."

"The crowbar?"

"He abandoned that, it was lying on the floor, in the goop."

The delivery bay at the back of the plant is open, as is the door, to alleviate the stink. "This how he got in?"

"Has to be," Gaylene says. "No forced entry. The plant super swears it was locked. "

A keypad. "They must've had the code."

"They?" she says.

"The nutter wasn't alone. Maybe he wasn't so crazy. Performing. Creating a diversion."

Gaylene shrugs, brushes the strands of straw from her eyes. "Maybe a stoner. One of my guys picked up a fresh marijuana butt in the grass over here."

"Fresh?"

"Clean. Smelled fresh."

Amazing that she can tell. Must have a nose for pot. He walks stiffly over the two-by-tens laid out as a walkway to the lounge. Vigor-Gro: he remembers something about it from the TV news. A demonstration in Brazil, a protester chaining herself to a truck or something. Mass arrests. A talking head interviewed about bees.

This shit-show guarantees Maguire all sorts of pain. He's six weeks from retirement. They're going to bully him into hanging in long enough to close the file. He and Sonia have their thirtieth coming up. They have plans for Hawaii, her idea, not his, to celebrate three decades of marriage. Maguire has to go along with it but shudders at being trapped in a tube in the sky for umpteen hours for the reward of a sunburn, sand in his crotch, and the horrors of the ukulele.

Gaylene goes to the coffee maker. "Cream and sugar?"

"Just enough milk to lighten it. Thanks." He's hungry, but there's only a chocolate bar dispenser in here. Sonia will kill him if she finds another Oh Henry! wrapper in his pocket. She's a retired nurse and is always on him about his health.

"Service with a smile, sir," says Gaylene as she passes him a filled mug. The smile is sardonic. Why would someone name a girl Gaylene? They'd call her Gay. Gay Gaylene, which she probably is, the way she doesn't groom her hair. Pretty good to look at just the same, despite the smallish boobs. Kind of a waste.

Irwin Fleiger is a flabby, pallid dude in a kind of uniform with a security tag. A loaded ashtray in front of him, smoke curling from a cigarette which Maguire butts out. He sits across the plastic table from him, turns on the little recorder he carries everywhere, and introduces himself.

"From the top, Mr. Fleiger."

"I already told . . ."

"From the top, please."

"Well, this terrorist . . ."

"Terrorist?"

"One of them environmental activists is my bet."

"I don't need you to bet." Maguire sips his coffee, makes a face. Bottom-shelf Nabob.

"Okay, he came out the front door chasing Barney Wilson, and just then the fill-in guy came around the corner. Gooch — Archie Gooch. Anyway, when Barney piled right into the guardhouse with me, this freak went after Gooch, right out the gate to the road, and I saw him collapse there, in the middle of the road."

"You saw who collapse?"

"Gooch. The freak just ran past him."

"Describe him."

"Who? Gooch?"

"The freak."

"He was wearing all this gear from the shop, helmet, goggles. Tall, skinny, long blond hair, that's about all I can say. Dark clothes. Gloves."

They all wore gloves, Maguire assumes. Ident can forget about prints. "You had a camera? Take any pictures?"

"I got distracted because I had a handful with Barney, he kind of cracked up."

"Was this skinny longhair carrying anything?"

"Like what?"

"Like wire cutters."

"No, he was waving his arms, shouting."

"Shouting what?"

"He yelled, 'It's going up!'"

"What did you take that to mean?"

"Explosives. I figured a time bomb. I got the hell out of there, practically had to drag Barney, and we split down the road."

Maguire wouldn't hire these clowns to guard his dog. "You saw the perp run into the bush out there?" He points out the window.

"Yeah, where that black-and-white just parked."

An OPP cruiser. They finally got here, two members heading into the scrub with a sniffer on a leash.

"See anything else? Any vehicles?"

"No." Fleiger's nicotine-stained hands are getting all fidgety. Maguire quit twenty years ago, Sonia always on him. Now he's a crusader.

"What else did you do?"

"Called 911."

"No other Chemican employees around?"

"Just the three of us. Like I say, Archie Gooch was filling in. The normal guy got a tooth pulled yesterday."

"Any idea how our long-haired friend got in here?"

"That's the mystery of the century."

A uniformed constable leads in a civilian in a lab coat. They confer with Gaylene.

"What?" Maguire says.

"They got into the laboratory upstairs," Gaylene says. "Whole bunch of files are missing."

"Means of entry?"

"Unknown. Access is by a keypad code."

Inside job, Maguire decides. "Who's the director of security for this hillbilly fire drill?"

"That'll be Mr. Griffin," Fleiger says. "Howell Griffin."

To Gaylene: "Bring him in."

2

It's just after ten a.m. as Jake Maguire rolls into the Lambton County OPP office, which sits forlornly out in the farmland north of Sarnia, your basic one-storey detachment you could mistake for a turnip farmer's ranch house except for the black-and-white sitting outside.

The day shift has been taken off traffic duty to help out at the Chemican plant, leaving only a constable shuffling paper back of the counter while keeping an eye on Barney Wilson in the waiting area. Still in his grey Chemican uniform, looking rattled, jumpy.

"He's all yours, Inspector," says the constable. "There's coffee and tea in the back."

"I'm good." Maguire had stopped on the way to grab bacon and eggs and a proper coffee and was feeling more human, less stressed. His heart was last clocked at one-forty-five over ninety-five, and he has ordered himself to gear down.

Gaylene, whose last name is Roberts, Detective Sergeant Roberts, is supposed to join him here but is, thankfully, late. Can't be much over thirty, how does she get the three stripes? Maybe it's regarded as politically correct to promote the token lesbian.

Wilson's rumpled uniform is stained yellow, maybe from slipping in the Vigor-Gro, maybe from pissing himself. He's staring into space, and for no accountable reason has taken off his boots. "Morning,

Barney. I guess it's been a long night. I'm Inspector Maguire, I'll be serving you today." Not a crack of a smile. "How're you feeling?"

"I got a headache. I get dizzy when I walk. My feet are swollen. I think I got some kind of allergy."

Those feet had run through the slop. Maguire wonders if the Vigor-Gro was a factor. "Grow Fast with Vigor-Gro" said a sign in the Chemican lab.

Wilson limps on sock feet as he follows along to the CO's office, but somehow misjudges the doorway, and ricochets from the frame, stumbling sideways. Maguire grabs him by the arm, carefully deposits him on a padded chair.

He tries to get him at ease with chit-chat about his security background and his job. But that doesn't work — the Boy Scout leader is robotic, needs a brain enema to help him excrete an account of the night's events. About all he remembers is hearing a crash and the intruder coming at him out of nowhere with a bar. Yelling he was the avenger and Wilson was the archfiend from hell.

Finally, Gaylene wanders in. "Sorry I'm late. Had to get my kids to school, my husband is on a job out of town."

Husband. Kids. Maguire does a quick reassessment. Okay, occasionally he's wrong. "This is Barney Wilson. Barney has memory issues. Sometimes that's because people aren't trying hard enough. Or they're holding back." He leans into him. "How did you let them in, Barney? Through the back door?"

It takes a while for him to pick up the implication. "No way, man!"

Gaylene shakes her head. Maguire has to agree — this hoser is too dumb to pull off something like that.

"There's a Howie Griffin out there waiting to see you," Gaylene says.

"Let him sit." He works at Wilson a bit more. Gets out that he finds the plant creepy, doesn't like being the inside guy. Sings campfire songs as he does his circuit. "Home on the Range" that night. When pressed he kind of remembers hearing someone snore, which

Maguire finds off-the-wall implausible. Can't remember how his uniform got stained in front, vaguely remembers taking a nosedive into the flow of Vigor-Gro, can't remotely identify the perp, except he concurs with the long blond hair.

He recalls seeking refuge in the guardhouse, and the freak chasing Gooch and shouting something about a bomb, the exact words he doesn't remember, and then not much more, just running.

"Can I smoke in here?" Fiddling with a pack of Winstons.

"Outside. Don't forget your boots and don't wander too far. We'll arrange a ride." Maguire sends the stiff away, and again he bumps into the door frame. The constable has to help him to the front door.

"Jesus fuck, Chemican hired Curly, Moe, and Larry."

"Who?" says Gaylene.

"Never mind. How did this Griffin guy get here?"

"Flew in from Toronto, picked up a renta."

"What's he like?"

"Kind of a dork."

§

"So what's your take, Howie?" That's what he wants to be called. Big, hale, glad-handing guy halfway through his forties. Appropriately pissed off at what happened, but maybe masking nervousness behind the bravado, the way he keeps shifting and sniffing.

"Can't be an inside job," Howie says. "The pass codes are only given out to six plant staff, all highly vetted. We change the codes every Friday. Front entry, back door, and lab."

"Who are the six?"

"Plant supervisor, crew boss, his foreman, the three night security guys."

"Names, addresses, phones, emails."

Gaylene, who's sitting beside Howie, gets him to text her all this stuff from his phone.

That done, Maguire asks, "They all happy in their work?"

"What do you mean?"

"You got a disgruntled crew boss maybe? Grievances? Issues about overtime or back pay."

"Not that I'm aware of." Another shift and sniff. He looks disapprovingly at Maguire's little voice recorder.

"Maybe you can check your personnel records," says Gaylene. "Someone may have an attitude about Vigor-Gro. It's controversial. I heard it kills bees."

"What you heard is concocted, it's propaganda. Vigor-Gro has been certified safe by U.S. and Canadian government testing labs."

"You keep a record of these pass codes?" Maguire asks.

"On my computer at headquarters, and I keep a copy in my home office. No one else has access."

Maguire still has a niggle that he's covering up somehow. "Kind of weird that this happens when one of your regulars got replaced by a temp with a dirty sheet, three convictions. It's like they knew you were undermanned last night."

"Archie Gooch has been coming in on call almost six months. No complaints. He's on a drug rehab program. My company likes to give a helping hand."

"They did blood and urine tests," Gaylene says. "A ton of THC, but the bigger deal is opioids. He was wired to the hilt on oxycodone, and now nobody can wake him."

"Maybe he's faking it," Maguire says. "What's on his blotter? Let's see . . ." He passes Howie a printout: "Lifting a leather jacket — that shows balls — hit and run on a cyclist, a meth lab in his girlfriend's basement, and beating on that girlfriend. What do you think, Howie, is Archie the susceptible kind of guy who'd take a bribe?" Greeted with a shrug. "I want your files on him. We want to know who he hangs with. Anarchists, maybe."

He turns to Gaylene. "I want all the guys who have the key codes brought in here today." She leaves, already punching a number into her cell.

"Don't want to get personal, Howie, but where do you live?"

"High-rise on Adelaide."

"Who lives there with you?"

"Me, myself, and I. Since this spring when my wife decided we had irreconcilable differences."

"She keep a key to the apartment?"

"I had the locks changed."

"You ever have friends over?"

Hesitation. A tell. "Not recently. I was in Brazil for a week. We had some issues down there."

"Okay, but you ever have guests over to your apartment?"

"A few guys from my office occasionally for poker. I keep my home office locked."

"Give us their names."

Howie goes to his phone again, texts these contacts. Gaylene returns. "The plant super will assemble everyone here for four p.m., sir."

Maguire worries that she's going to make herself indispensable. He returns to Howie. "Any other visitors?"

Another tell: a delay, a shrug. "I've been seeing a young lady."

"She stay over?"

"Yes, sort of."

"When?" Maguire should call the outside man's dentist, get some pointers on pulling teeth.

"Let's see. Weekend before last. Saturday, I think. I just got back from Sao Paolo."

"Name, phone, address."

"I don't want to get her involved. Real innocent gal, she's in the States right now with her sick mom . . ."

"Name, phone, address."

"Well, okay. Jesus. Becky McLean. Works at a Rexall in North York. Not sure of her address." He gives them a 647 number.

"Got her photo?"

"Thought I did. Couldn't find it." He goes into his phone again, scrolling. "Still not here. It didn't take, I guess."

Maguire wonders why he would lie about that. He goes at him a little more, how he picked Becky up outside her pharmacy, their dates, dinners, a Jays game, a boat trip on Georgian Bay. Howie uncomfortable, perspiring a little, weirdly vague about the Saturday night sleepover. "We kind of made out, no big deal. We have a date Sunday at the Dome, Jays and the Red Sox." He shows his season's pass for two. Maguire writes down the seat numbers.

"Mind if we come by this week and have a look at your security setup?"

"Our Canadian head office, you mean? That's in T.O."

"Yeah. Your home office too."

"Sure, Inspector. Be my guest."

"And we'll need to take prints from you."

"No problem."

After Maguire lets him go Gaylene gives him a fist bump, a kind of salute to the old fart, he's still got jism. "Like I say, Jake, a dork. What's he hiding?"

"Coke habit, for one."

3
Thursday, September 13

Operation Vigorous, they named this, from Vigor-Gro, but the Chief Superintendent likes to call it Operation Vigorish, maybe because of all the overtime he's griping about even though they've hardly got started. As if it's dirty money. But Jake Maguire's crew has taken to call it that too, or Operation Vig, in jest. Or The Vig.

Maguire wanted to run the case from the London detachment,

so he could come home to a good wife and good cooking. But he's stuck in Toronto, self-proclaimed Centre of the Universe, more aptly called Hogtown. For the unforeseeable future, he's in a Best Western in North York with a short taxi commute to the Toronto OPP, near Keele and the 401. Operation Vig works out of a cramped space on the third floor — it's barely able to contain Maguire plus two guys and one female, the total personnel they pried loose for him.

The Vig has got a little complicated because material witness Archie Gooch is being fed through a tube and is now formally diagnosed as being in a coma though there's nothing physically amiss — the heart still pumping oxygen to the brain, occasional spasms and twitches, but the eyes won't open. The accepted theory is he got so stoned on his potent weed he stopped counting how many hits of oxycodone he was doing. Gooch was probably too stupid to look up the death stats.

The Vig has seen little progress over the last two days. The theory of an inside job didn't pan out. All of the six with access to the key codes were easy to clear. None could remotely be considered environmentalists or particularly corrupt. Bribery seemed out of the question anyway — the perps wouldn't have had that kind of money. What they had was a pretty smart spy.

Gaylene Roberts is doing the footwork on Howie's little popsy, Becky McLean, or whatever her real name is. Maguire has kind of adapted to Gaylene since she got less snarky, plus she's looking much hotter now that he knows she's not a lesbian. So he got the Chief Super to assign her to help run the file.

First thing she did is check with the manager of the North York Rexall where Howie picked Becky up. The manager never heard of any Becky McLean. No one by that moniker in the employment records.

And of course she hasn't called Howie after disappearing to wherever to see her allegedly sick mom. The number Howie gave them for Becky McLean was dead. Telephone records at Bell had a phony address. Not strictly phony, a nursing home in Scarborough where no one had heard of her.

Amazingly, Howie is still confident she'll show for their date at the Red Sox game Sunday night. Poor bastard.

This morning Maguire is up in Howie's suite on Adelaide, with Gaylene and a couple from Ident, lifting prints. Good luck to them because Howie's cleaning lady scrubbed everything down pretty good, except for his office which he insists he keeps locked. Spacious, expensive digs, no female frills. Lots of CDs, a wall of books. A man cave in the current lingo, which is what Sonia calls Maguire's own homely woodworking shed back of the garage.

The dork is on a sofa looking like he got swallowed up in an earthquake. Even though Howie's not talking to reporters he's all over the news. Him and Chemican. After a media deluge yesterday, the press demanding answers from them over suspect test results on their Vigor-Gro and its effects on bugs and birds. Also some hanky-panky involving a Chemican-friendly Congressman with ties to the director of the Environmental Protection Agency. Making the evildoers look not so evil. Still, crime is crime. B and E and conspiracy, ten years max for each.

One of the Ident guys calls from the entrance to Howie's inner office. "Think we got a partial of a bare foot, sir."

Maguire goes in to where they've chalked around an impression being dusted on the tile floor, near a filing cabinet. About a size six. Eliminates Howie. Left foot, toes to heel, minus the arch. Imprinted on some kind of whitish, hardened liquid surface. There are other dabs and spots too, leading from the bedroom to the inner office, that shine in the light of camera flashes.

The Ident guy bends low, scrapes a couple of samples into a plastic bag, bends lower, takes a sniff. "Some kind of congealed liquid. Not alcohol, I don't think."

Gaylene brushes a strand of hair from her nose, takes a turn, flakes a bit of the white stuff away, puts it to her nose. "Semen."

Maguire grins. He wasn't expecting such expertise from this olfactory ace. He can't fight off an image of her going down on her sweetie, taking a snort of come up her nose.

He looks back at Howie, wondering how he got his pecker tracks all over his office floor. He's staring blankly at a painting on the wall. Whales breaching. Time to put this nature lover on the grill again. Turn up the heat.

CHAPTER 7 » ARTHUR

1
Saturday, September 15

Arthur's Fargo runs faultlessly, the old girl pleased with her new battery, determined to prove she isn't ready for the scrap heap. But Arthur won't get to the church on time, because he and Stefan spent half an hour clipping Ulysses's way out of a thick tangle of black-berries — the reckless pup had plowed into it while chasing a robin. Another lesson learned.

It's a pleasant, warm morning, with only a few wisps of cloud as Arthur pulls into the lot of St. Mary's Church, where a dozen vehicles sit. The Save Our Quarry's core group has gathered here for a session called on short notice.

It was learned only late yesterday that Selwyn Loo would be arriving this morning, on Syd-Air from Vancouver. Much to Arthur's delight, the famed environmental lawyer has agreed to take on the cause of Quarry Park, with pro bono aid from West Coast Environmental Law, with whom he serves as lead counsel. He has done his homework and has a report to make.

Selwyn came on board after TexAmerica Stoneworks issued a writ against SOQ and its lead activists claiming general damages and an injunction to prohibit blocking, impeding, tampering, demonstrating, or in any other way interfering with its operations. A classic SLAPP suit. Arthur was served at his front door on Tuesday.

About twenty stalwarts have assembled up front, and Selwyn is at the pulpit. "Sorry, I'm late," Arthur says, hurrying up the aisle.

"Find a comfortable pew, Arthur, and I'll sum up," says Selwyn, who has an uncanny ear for voices. A slender, handsome man. Dark glasses, a thin, white cane. Vancouver-born, tracing his roots four generations back to Hong Kong. He knows Garibaldi well — years ago he'd helped save the old-growth forests on the north end of the island: Gwendolyn Bay, now a national park.

The ever-unavoidable Taba Jones moves down to make room for Arthur. It would seem an insult to take a less crowded pew, and once again they are tightly joined at the hip. He has already apologized to her for weaseling out (though that's not how he put it) from her party last Saturday. He explained he'd got caught up watching TV coverage of the Bee-In at the Toronto lakeshore, where Garibaldi's very own Margaret Blake shared the spotlight.

Arthur and Taba have reached a kind of truce. She will stop vamping him if he stops pretending he can't see her through his fog of denial. Arthur isn't sure how that's going to work out.

Selwyn uses the pulpit as a leaning post — there are no notes on it, of course. He wouldn't use them even if he had the gift of vision. He is almost off the Mensa scale, with what would normally be called — were he not sightless — a photographic memory.

"Time is pressing," Selwyn says. "Structures are going up at the quarry, all equipment is in place, and blasting begins in a week. On Wednesday we will be moving to quash their SLAPP suit and opposing their motion for an injunction. I will also argue my own motion to restrain *them* — until the appeal is heard of the bylaw issue that Arthur so valiantly fought."

Giving Arthur credit where none is due.

"Hamish McCoy and Mattie Miller will support that restraining application by bringing an action in nuisance to prevent serious risk to their properties, their livelihood, and to McCoy's works of art and Mrs. Miller's alpacas. This course was wisely suggested by my eminent colleague, Arthur Beauchamp."

Arthur feels embarrassed by these inapt plaudits. He still feels a staggering loss of confidence from his poor showing in court. That patronizing judge, treating him like a senescent dimwit. Then getting busted at the ferry landing, a vaudeville show, Arthur playing the donkey.

"Any questions?" Selwyn asks.

Many hands are raised. Arthur settles back with a sigh of relief. A great burden has been lifted. He'd phoned Selwyn out of desperation early this week, was astonished to hear these golden words: "I'll get right on it, my friend." Arthur would have gone out of his mind trying to grapple with writs and restraining orders.

Lost in his thoughts, he's unaware the meeting has finished until Taba gives him a nudge. "Hey, space case. How about introducing me."

Selwyn, she means, who taps his way down a few steps to greet and embrace Arthur. Selwyn says he's pleased to find him in such robust health — a deduction somehow reached by simple physical touch. Arthur returns the compliment, thanks him effusively for stepping in, and introduces Taba.

"You're fantastic," she says, hugging him.

"Well, you seem pretty fantastic yourself," he says, lingering into the embrace.

Arthur understood he was gay. Maybe not.

"We'll have some fun with these Texas jackboots," he says. "Arthur, I'm hoping you can spare some private time."

"Of course. My day is free. In fact, I'd like to invite you to stay the night at Blunder Bay." Selwyn has always enjoyed his times there.

"If it doesn't put you out, I'd be delighted. We can pick each other's brains."

§

As the Fargo rolls into Blunder Bay, Selwyn finally concludes a long conference call with West Coast Environmental staff about the SLAPP suit and the nuts and bolts of the multiple restraining orders. "Sorry, just clearing the decks," he says.

BC's new anti-SLAPP legislation has given Selwyn all the ordnance he needs but he also seeks a declaration that TexAmerica's attempts to silence the protesters be declared frivolous, vexatious, and contrary to Canada's Charter of Rights.

Arthur hears distressed calls from a dozen Canada geese in the near pasture — Stefan is there with Ulysses, trying to persuade the invasive flock to shit elsewhere. These big, arrogant destroyers are protected under the Migratory Birds Convention Act, though few seem to migrate anymore. But there's no protection from the wolfhound speeding toward them like a dog possessed, and in panic several fleeing geese crash through the treetops beyond the fence line. None seem to suffer more than a loss of pride.

Arthur describes the scene to Selwyn, who expresses eagerness to meet Ulysses. The pup, elated with his triumph, is already bounding toward them with those amazing long strides. Typically, he can't find the brakes until he's past them, sending up clumps of grass and dirt. Stefan hurries along behind, with his latest companion, Mouser, a one-eyed feral cat he's tamed.

Selwyn seems a little awed as he and Ulysses inspect each other, the dog's nose probing in the usual inappropriate places.

Arthur parts them, gives Ulysses a rub. "Good dog. Well done, boy."

"Majestic animal," says Selwyn, then recites from William Robert Spencer's paean to a brave wolfhound: "'Oh, where does faithful Gelert roam, the flower of his race.'"

Arthur completes the stanza: "'So true, so brave, a lamb at home, a lion in the chase.'" It is not the first time he has bonded poetically with Selwyn, a lover of nineteenth-century romantics.

Selwyn clasps Stefan's hand. "Arthur tells me you have an amazing rapport with animals."

"It's a little talent I have."

Solara hollers from the deck of her house: "I'm making us a picnic lunch. Y'all got half an hour."

2

After Arthur shows Selwyn to his room and makes tea, they move to the parlour, sharing the sofa.

"Selwyn, the bylaw issue you alleged that I fought so valiantly was actually a majestic flop, and I think you know it. You have not buttered me up without good reason."

"You see through me. Yes, you may not be completely at home in the civil courts but that pales against your mastery of the criminal side. Hear me out. You're aware of the unusual event a few nights ago at Chemican's plant in Sarnia?"

"Of course." Margaret had been on the phone about that break-in, which came almost on the heels of her successful bee funder.

News reports had described a bizarre scene: a lithe, long-haired young man had sneaked into the plant, opened valves that emptied the tanks of Chemican's infamous bee killer, Vigor-Gro, then raced past security masked in helmet, safety goggles, and two sets of ear protectors. He has not been found or identified. It complicates matters that one of the night watchmen collapsed while running away in fright, and is in a coma.

Police believe the perpetrator did not act alone — a great many files were stolen from the testing lab at the Sarnia plant.

Then, on Wednesday, a torrent of Chemican testing results for Vigor-Gro inundated the media, along with internal memos suggesting that much of the company's science was at best careless, at worst deceitful. Tests done on bee populations — some showing significant die-offs from Vigor-Gro — appeared to have been altered or, in some cases, buried. Other test results had somehow disappeared.

Chemican-International has been ducking and dodging, declining to respond to the media while police pursue their criminal investigation, yet making vague claims about being victimized by lies, fraud, and conspiracy. They insist the raid cost them multiple millions of dollars in product and cleanup costs.

That's all Arthur knows, but clearly Selwyn knows much more. There's no mystery now about the boon Selwyn seeks from the master of the criminal side.

"They call themselves the Earth Survival Rebellion, which is allied with a deep underground network, Europe-based, Résistance Planétaire. I confess, in entire confidence, that I am privy to a project called Operation Beekeeper. The participants may not elude detection forever. They could face serious charges. Ten years maximum for conspiracy, breaking and entering, theft, and wilful damage, or worse if sentences are consecutive. There also may be an issue over that fellow in a coma."

Arthur sips his tea. He sighs. "The rust has set in, Selwyn. I haven't done criminal work for three years."

"You're a member of the Ontario bar. You did some celebrated cases there."

"Many years ago."

"These are good people, Arthur. Bright, caring people. Committed to the preservation of our planet. A little impetuous, a little crazy, and very brave. The damage is regrettable, as is the fact that a guard may have injured himself. But they have pulled off a great feat. They deserve our undying gratitude, not imprisonment."

Arthur wants to say he has lost confidence in his courtroom skills. He wants to explain that he is over the hill and accelerating down it. He wants to tell Selwyn there are others more able, more nimble of mind. Ontario lawyers, familiar with the terrain, with the courts, the judges. He has a farm to run, and would miss Ulysses unbearably.

But he can't bring himself to bluntly reject Selwyn's petition — he would seem an ingrate. He'll stall for time before letting him down gently. Meanwhile, he'll seek advice from Toronto's Nancy Faulk, a friend, a top criminal counsel, a warrior.

"No arrests have been made," he says, "and hopefully none will be. I'll ask Margaret for her thoughts, of course."

"Good. Talk to Margaret."

§

After the picnic, Arthur and Selwyn roost on the beach logs, enjoying the sun, talking about law and life and poetry, while Solara gathers the leavings, listening, fascinated by their handsome, erudite guest.

Stefan has wandered off to the wooden dock, is crouching there, tuning his guitar, staring into the water, possibly talking to a seal or a porpoise. With Ulysses at his side, maybe translating.

Suddenly, a flurry of fleeing herring breaks the water, followed by Blunder Bay's resident seal, which snaffles two of them, an agile catch. Stefan rises to applaud. It almost seems he was waiting for the moment, that it was somehow orchestrated by him.

Arthur senses Selwyn imagining the scene as he describes it. "How beautiful," he says.

Sightless since his early teens, this man is still capable of constructing visions of beauty unseen — Arthur is in awe of that. In past years, Selwyn suffered from a depressive disorder, but that seems gone as he compensates ever more fully for his loss of sight. He makes approving sounds as they listen to Stefan strum his guitar: something classical and languorous.

Stefan will be moving on once his landed immigrant status is approved. He's been offered work at a wildlife refuge in the rainforest on north Vancouver Island. Arthur is torn by that prospect

— he'll miss this mystical young man who shoots the breeze with animals. Yet another reason not to go to Ontario — Solara can't be expected to carry the load by herself.

3
Monday, September 17

A movement in the forest causes Arthur a visual warping, a hazy snapshot of a lanky form raising a jug to his lips: another perplexing Jeremiah mirage. But it's a black-tailed doe popping up from the salal, her ears perked, and now she's bounding off, with Ulysses in pursuit. When the deer clears a dense thicket of bracken, Ulysses screeches to a halt, remembering the blackberries, not taking any chances.

By the time Ulysses gets his gears going again, the deer has disappeared into the forest. The pup soon returns, panting, defeated but unbowed, and gets back to his task of digging around the exposed stones of Jeremiah's well. Arthur shares this labour, working with a trowel. They have already unearthed a complete circle of rocks, two deep, and cemented around a slight depression. The well's innards are clogged with soil from 125 years of runoff from the surrounding hills.

It's close to eleven, another fair day, and Arthur has been at the well for an hour, waiting for the CEO of Island Landscaping, Robert Stonewell, who has been tasked to excavate the site. Arthur has reached out to the Garibaldi Historical Society, which has agreed to erect a monument here, with a covered display case for Arthur's small collection of found artifacts.

Stoney has either slept in, which is distinctly possible, or forgotten about the planned rendezvous, which is just as likely. He is nicknamed Stoney for good reason.

Arthur is confounded by his latest Jeremiah sighting — more proof that his senses are distorted by stress. The rational part of his mind strives to reject the notion of Jeremiah's ghost taking on the form of a deer. Yet it also seems a paranormal message, a plea from the beyond to set matters right, expunge the indignity of having been written off by history as a drunken, stumbling fool.

Maybe in the course of his archaeological dig Arthur will find some answers to the mystery of Jeremiah Blunder. He feels an obligation to him. It's his AA training kicking in, his sense of brotherly feelings toward a fellow addict.

What is his ghost trying to tell Arthur? That the accepted theory of a drunken fall was grossly false? There are island tales, doubtless skewed by many tongues over many decades, of fierce rivalries between the early settlers, over land claims and horse thievery.

"Were you murdered, Jeremiah?" Arthur asks the unreadable rocks. "Is that why you can't sleep?"

Arthur's sleep has been almost as patchy, with much tossing in bed, rising at night for tea or a read or a moonlit stroll. Much of his tension stems from anxiety over Selwyn Loo's forthcoming duel against the crack team of counsel for TexAmerica. He's also oppressed by a sense of guilt over his inability to level with Selwyn, to admit to his qualms about taking on an explosive, taxing defence of a group of headstrong eco-mavericks who deliberately broke the law. "A little crazy," Selwyn called them.

Arthur rests his rear on a mound of excavated dirt and rubble, and Ulysses sits beside him, gazing at him consolingly — he can sense his master's anxiety.

"We're a team, pal. They're not going to separate us."

In confirmation, Ulysses awards him a sloppy kiss.

§

An approaching growl of machinery. Ulysses races off to investigate and returns romping alongside his quarry, a lumbering backhoe.

Stoney is at the controls, a scrawny, unshaven fellow with long, lank hair. Sitting perilously in the raised scoop, cradling a heavy-duty chainsaw, is his loyal retainer, Dog, a squat little man about as tall as his saw is long.

Stoney's navigational skills seem compromised by the effects of the joint he's smoking, because the backhoe veers off the trail and stops in a tangle of willows. He remembers to cut the engine; then, abandoning Dog to alight as best he can, gives Ulysses a rub and follows him to the well site.

"And where, good sire, is this here grave you want dug up?"

"It's a well, Stoney. Jeremiah Blunder's old stone well."

Stoney pinches his joint and flicks it, finally noticing the circle of cemented rocks. "Oh, yeah. It's coming back."

Arthur isn't pleased that Stoney has managed to get so high so early in the day. It's mid-September, cannabis harvest time, and he's likely been sampling from the grow he keeps on his small acreage, amid the rusting hulks of the many old vehicles he collects, an eyesore so infamous that no one ventures near.

"Stoney, this dig must be done with utter care and precision. No drugs will be allowed on site. No booze, no pot."

Stoney tries to look shocked. "I deny the inference that I am under the inference . . . the influence."

"You reek of pot."

"Yeah, he's guilty, Mr. Beauchamp," says Dog, who has joined them and is having a friendly wrestle with Ulysses. Dog, at least, seems bright-eyed, unimpaired.

"I only took a little hit to enhance my creative powers," Stoney says. "Helps me see the big picture." He looks about, as if visualizing that picture. "Okay, I got it, I got the logistics figured out, it's chicken soup, man. This baby probably goes down seven, eight feet. Couple of tons of dirt to move, and so we don't have a problem with the walls collapsing we'll buttress them with timbers."

Arthur sees merit in this plan. Maybe marijuana does somehow tweak the brain.

Stoney continues: "The rest will have to be hand shovelling. That's where Dog's expertise comes into play." Stoney puts a brotherly arm around his shoulders. "But first, all them alder must fall to the mighty slices of his chainsaw — right, Dog?"

"No problem."

"And how long will the entire operation take?" Arthur asks.

A dismissive wave of Stoney's hand. "A week, seven days, no more. We'll want to get to it while the good weather holds."

"And when can you get started?"

"I got to tend to my garden, just a day or two, but Dog can get going right now. We can fast-track this sucker, eh, Dog?"

"No problem."

"How much, Stoney?"

He ponders, finally comes up with the preposterous figure of ten thousand dollars.

Arthur shows shock and dismay — faked, but he has bargained too many times with Stoney to be played the sucker. He points out that the Garibaldi Historical Society is sponsoring the project. "A charitable society, doing good works for the community. Our budget is four thousand dollars."

Stoney goes down to $7,500. Arthur informs him that, sadly, he must seek a second bid from Island Excavating. Stoney counters by wishing him good luck. "They'll send a whole crew, one Dog is worth seven of them lazy goofs."

A further flurry of counter-offers concludes with an agreement for $5,500 with a cash advance for what Stoney calls start-up costs. A good deal — Arthur is proud of himself, though a bit ashamed at taking advantage of his contractor's stoned condition.

Stoney checks his watch. "Meanwhile, I see it's past noon, time to take a break. I'll leave my rig here, and maybe you can lift me home. I'll be back soon as I get my crop in."

Arthur leads him off, Ulysses galloping ahead while Dog revs up his saw. Soon, distantly, come the welcome sounds of next year's firewood being felled. Arthur's mood has lightened with this brief, rewarding respite from his low spirits.

CHAPTER 8 » MAGUIRE

1

Monday, September 17

Jake Maguire can't find much to do this morning but exercise his flat feet, even though there's not much pacing space in a squad room the size of a walk-in closet. Occasionally he pauses to look over shoulders hunkered above computers. Most of the vigour of Operation Vigorish is spent Googling or whatever they do, a task at which Jake Maguire is not adept. He'd rather be working stakeouts or phone taps, casing stiffs, building a collar, stuff he knows upside down. But he can't find anyone to stake out or wire into. They still haven't got any IDs.

Maguire was kind of hoping Howie Griffin was involved, an inside job. But he was polygraphed and cleared — the needles didn't jump when he kept saying, "I don't remember," referring to the night he got it on with Becky. Or didn't. How is it the dork doesn't recall banging her when he woke up and found his sheets soaked in semen?

Becky had left him a morning-after note, which he couldn't find until he retrieved it from a pair of exercise pants in a locker at

Molloy's Gym: *Sweet dreams. Had a lovely time. Becky.* A handwriting expert will be called in if they can find a comparable.

Griffin walked out of his last interview, when Maguire sweated him too hard about the night in question. He claimed he needed a break, a holiday. Still, it's hard not to feel sorry for the patsy — his bosses decided he was not making a positive contribution and pink-slipped him. You don't sleep with the enemy, and you don't go bonkers over them. Cold-hauled, doped up, snoring off to la-la land while his playmate cheerfully strolls into his office with his jism on her feet.

She wore gloves but not socks. A little slip-up there, doll. The prints came out good, all Maguire needed now was a foot.

You can't call it a breakthrough, but they're inching close to Becky McLean. Surprise, surprise, she didn't show up for the Red Sox game yesterday. Maguire confirmed that because he was in the stands — a terrific seat, over third base, several rows back of Howie and the empty seat beside him. Hell of a game, Jays pulling it out in extra innings with a pair of doubles.

Maguire observed how the network cameras followed several fouls hooking into the stands near him. He figured what the hell, a shot in the dark but maybe Howie and his foxy little lady were caught on film at the Rangers game. So he and Gaylene spent last evening viewing a tape of that August 13 game, courtesy of the Sports Network.

Bingo. Bottom of the eighth, there was Howie jumping for one screaming over his head. Pause, rewind, copy, Exhibit One. Beside Howie, looking up at the arc of the ball, was a dark-eyed cutie in cut-offs, didn't look much over twenty. No one in his right mind would imagine this doll being hot for Howie Griffin. Except maybe Howie Griffin.

One of the constables, Lorne Ling — Long Ling, they call him, because he's short and stubby — has a blow-up in front of his screen of Becky looking up at the foul. It was somebody's idea — Gaylene's in fact — that Howie's little popsy might have attended a rally for a cause close to her heart. Ontario Place, a week ago Saturday, a Bee-In, they called it, to help out Brazil's farmers. Big-name bands, speeches dissing Chemican and Vigor-Gro.

Most cops of Chinese heritage, at least those Maguire has worked with, demonstrate infinite patience, though he wouldn't say that publicly because he's not sure if it's somehow racist. Anyway, Long Ling gets top marks for his doggedness. He is reviewing YouTube videos taken at the Bee-In, trying to spot Becky among the New Age fluffy bunnies gathered there. He's found hundreds of the little vids, from thirty seconds long to three hours. He's in headphones, tapping his foot to the music.

Ling makes room for Maguire to lean in for a view: on the outdoor stage, a rock and roll band, a gyrating girl whose thin, bare legs straddle a floor mike like a penis. Long Ling pretends he's not interested, fast-forwards to the end, goes on to the next clip: the stage again, Dr. Suzuki at the mike. Ling listens awhile, takes off his muffs.

"I got nothing, except I'm learning about colony collapse. The general theme is if the bees perish, we go down with them."

"Doom and gloom, pal. There's two sides to every story. I read the bees are getting hit by some kind of mites that lay their eggs in the beehives. Plus we had a hard winter."

"Yeah, but their studies—"

"It ain't our job to save the world, Long Ling. That's what we got politicians for. Our job is to clean up the mess."

Maguire has been getting pressure from some in government to call this a terrorist attack. Chemican's people are begging him not to, because a terrorist attack voids their insurance. Nobody seems to give a shit about Archie Gooch, who's been in a coma for a week.

Gaylene beckons Maguire over to her computer, whose search window reads, "Bees neonicotinoid protest." She clicks on a photo of a scholarly-looking gentleman behind a desk.

"This pissed-off brainiac keeps cropping up. Papers, lectures, interviews, stats and graphs and equations. Field tests with neonics. Six-syllable words. I got at least thirty hits on him."

"Who is this genius?"

"Dr. Helmut Knutsen, a biochemist."

"So what about him?"

"He kind of disappeared off the academic map a couple of years ago. Born Stockholm, three years at the Sorbonne, Ph.D. from McGill, taught there, went on to UC San Diego, got into a flap over his activism, for making noise about grants from Bayer and Monsanto. He was demoted from department head, quit teaching, returned to Canada. But not a peep from him since."

"Doesn't look like a break-in artist." Mussed grey hair, a penetrating gaze through wire-rim specs. About fifty, though the picture could be old.

"I'll make some phone calls," Gaylene says.

§

The coffee in the OPP lounge is predictably blah, so on returning from lunch Maguire grabs a takeout grande at a corner Starbucks. Nicotine junkies cluster outside the OPP building's no-smoke perimeter, some in uniform. Maguire can't help sermonizing: "Save your lungs, gentlemen. Try sucking a dick instead, they're not carcinogenic." He gets hoots and raised middle fingers.

Inside, he can't resist stopping at the dispenser for an Oh Henry! He munches half of it, furtively, out of habit, hiding the rest in a deep pocket before he enters the squad room. One chocolate bar won't show up on the scales, especially with all the exercise he gets from pacing.

Long Ling is still looking at YouTube videos. Sean Wiggens is on the phone with the forensics lab. He's the fourth and least useful member of Maguire's team, and is known on the Force as Wiggie, probably because he's scatterbrained, zoned out half the time. He's a six-and-a-half-foot uncoordinated beanpole who likes to loom over people, especially shrimpy Long Ling.

Gaylene finishes off a sandwich from the canteen, announces she just got off the line with someone in the president's office at UC San Diego.

"There was a confrontation over an op-ed Knutsen wrote, mocking neonics. They blame him for Monsanto revoking a hefty grant they promised. No contact with him since he checked out of California, but he left a forwarding address in Montreal, where they mailed him a severance cheque. I'm on it."

Maguire sits down with his coffee, feeling useless. They've got sweet dick. A crafty young trickster and a bitter scientist, that's all they've come up with. The trail is getting cold — the perps could be anywhere, the other side of the country. Latin America, Europe.

Meanwhile he's stuck in Toronto with no end game in sight, with only an occasional day off. That will happen tomorrow, a short-haul flight to London. When he phoned Sonia to tell her to expect him, she seemed to hide concern, maybe impatience. Their thirtieth coming up. Hawaii. Maguire had sworn he would take her.

"No problem, honey," he said. "We're gonna wrap this up at hypersonic speed."

Gaylene is on the blower, to Montreal, tracking down Professor Knutsen's forwarding address. Doing it in fluent French. Annoyingly cocky, for sure, but she's the best female cop he's ever worked with. She too is away from home, and missing her partner and her boy and girl. Maguire has got to stop feeling sorry for himself.

There comes a sudden shout from Long Ling: "Got her!"

Wiggie, the squad-room skyscraper, knocks over his chair as he rushes to Ling's monitor, followed by Gaylene, still talking on the phone, "Call you back, sorry, emergency." They form a tight pack around Long Ling, so Maguire has to crane over Gaylene's head, barely managing to avoid contact with her extended butt.

"I'm backing up," Long Ling says. "It was uploaded from a phone."

The opening shot is of a band tuning up, ambient crowd noise, people shuffling about in front of the camera. The lens then moves to the side of the stage, behind the curtain, several crew bustling about backstage. A blur of activity, then the camera pans right, and holds on a pair of young females bent over clipboards, like they're comparing notes.

Long Ling freezes on them. One is definitely the pseudo–baseball fan known as Becky McLean: dark, petite, and pretty as a kitten, brown hair cut shorter than in the photo from the SkyDome. Jeans and floppy shirt. Her confederate is taller, with a mop of magenta hair, also hot-looking in a kind of witchy way, all mascaraed up, and wearing a T-shirt promoting the 2017 Ontario Tour of a band called Panic Disorder. Both have badges that say "Staff."

Gaylene bends closer to the screen, and her bum thumps Maguire's groin. Embarrassed, he backs off. But she bumps him again, teasingly, and again he jerks back, flustered. He wants to think she's not being indelicate or risqué — it was kind of like high-fives, just lower down.

The tail end of the video is brief: the girl in the Panic Disorder T-shirt sees they are being filmed, and says, "Get the fuck out of here," and the camera clicks off and that's the end.

Still rattled by Gaylene's immodesty, Maguire covers up by barking orders. "Okay, we need a master for evidence and copies for each of us. Find out who organized this carnival, who they hired, who volunteered. Addresses, phones, backgrounds, where they hang, their friends. When you show photos of these two ladies you'll get questions. Explain we got a missing persons report, it may be nothing, we don't want to alarm family and friends. Say no more. And let's check out Panic Disorder."

That last task doesn't take long. Gaylene pulls up several links: reviews, comments, photos, none from mainstream publications, most from counter-culture media. A lanky, long-haired bozo on guitar; another string bean alternating on guitar and keyboards; a black, wild-haired woman on bass; and a fat, hairy freak on drums. A barely-making-it bar band, Maguire decides, with a slim but loyal following. Maybe Becky's girlfriend is a groupie.

No website, but here's a Facebook posting from a week ago about their next gig — they're opening two nights from now, Wednesday, in an east-side tavern called Squirrelly Moe's.

"You want to send someone?" Gaylene asks.

"Yeah, me."

"Get real. It's a hipster bar. You'll stand out like a grizzly bear at a New Age picnic. May as well wear a uniform."

"I'm checking it out. You guys work the fucking Bee-In. Fast, before these jokers get lawyered up." Maguire has an attitude about lawyers — meddlers, gumming up the system with their tricks and technicalities.

2

Wednesday, September 19

It wasn't easy, but Maguire found the mojo to tell Sonia he'd have to postpone his one-day furlough because of some hot new leads in the case. "We're going to wind this up lickety-split," he said with fake enthusiasm. "Guaranteed. Hawaii calls."

Guaranteed if they can scoop the young lady flagging herself as Becky McLean. How hard could that be? They've now got a list of Bee-In organizers, seven of them, greenies, eco-obsessives. They'll have info on employees and volunteers. Surely someone will recognize Becky and her punk-haired friend.

Last evening, after divvying up the interview list, Maguire picked up a car from the pool and visited Squirrelly Moe's, on Queen East, near Broadview. A poster in the window: *Panic Disorder, 7 to 10 wednsday and thursday, 8 to whenever Friday, No Cover.* A blow-up of them on a stage, three characters stomping around the fat drummer with his braided beard.

Maguire had stepped inside for half a minute to scope the layout: a dark dive smelling of spilled beer, walls plastered with posters and graffiti, a dozen patrons, mostly young, capacity for maybe forty more, but also a few older guys at the long bar, ordering up before happy hour ends. His best lookout would be from the last barstool, in the shadows with a 270 view.

The bartender was squinting at him, probably making him for a cop, and he looked like one. Others turned his way as he sauntered off. Grizzly bear at a picnic, Gaylene warned. He's got to work smarter.

That was yesterday, and Maguire spends much of today wandering among thrift shops for appropriate gear. At five, he's back in the squad room. Long Ling and Wiggie are still away on their interviews, Gaylene holding the fort, working the phones. Proudly, he lays out his uniform for the night: ragged jeans, a denim jacket a size too small with patches, a peace symbol and a cannabis leaf; the jacket open over a T-shirt urging "Save the Birmingham Eight," whoever they are, all topped off with smoked grannie glasses and a Che Guevara cap. Gaylene roars with laughter.

Undeterred, he goes to the can to change. He studies his bushy stache, hopes it's hip enough. On leaving he nearly collides with ungainly Wiggie, who says, "Excuse me, sir, but this here men's room is only for personnel . . ." He does a double take. "Hey, Inspector, that's perfect."

"So what did you get?"

"Okay, I got a list of about two hundred volunteers, none named Becky McLean. The lady who signed them up works for the Green Party. The list has phone numbers, some emails, no addresses. She remembers Becky from the pictures I showed her, but not her name or anything about her or Becky's friend. She kind of got uncooperative, and was like, 'Who says they're missing? Do you even know their names? What's this really about?' I don't think she believed the cover about alarming the families."

Maguire holds his temper. Somehow, predictably, Wiggie has cocked this up, he's a lousy actor. This is threatening to become a big, noisy effort to nail down these dames. If word gets back to Becky, she'll be getting out of Dodge fast. Bye-bye Becky, bye-bye chances of a fast collar, bye-bye Hawaii.

"I'm honing them down," Wiggie says, cowed by the glaring old dude in his sixties peacenik gear. "Thirty volunteers worked backstage. I'm gonna start phoning, set up interviews. Hey, Inspector, that outfit really works."

Back in the squad room, Wiggie advocates so loyally for Maguire that Gaylene relents: "Okay, maybe you'll pass for a sixties freak. At worst, a dope dealer." She works him over with makeup, darkens his stubble, combs back what's left of his hair into a rubber-banded ponytail.

"So what about Professor Knutsen's mail drop in Montreal?"

"It's the apartment of a former girlfriend of his, a biologist. He picked up his severance cheque and other correspondence, and that was it. She has no idea where he is. Didn't leave a number, email address, or contacts. He has no kids, no siblings, no ex-wives, just a couple of live-together partners, including her, a five-year run."

"Cagey character, guilt written all over him. He's lurking somewhere."

"And working. CBC says they just uploaded another burst to the media." Gaylene picks up her ringing phone. "Thank you so much for the call-back. I'm Detective Sergeant Roberts, OPP. It's about a missing person, and I'm trying to set up some interviews with the Green Party staff. Would Margaret Blake be available?"

3

Maguire has use of a squad car, but takes public transportation when undercover, a bus today, then the Queen streetcar. None of his fellow travellers gives the old sixties relic much of a look, they're used to characters in Toronto. He doesn't want any unsightly bulges showing so he isn't armed, has no radio, just his smartphone.

He gets off at Broadview and walks to Squirrelly Moe's. It's just after six, a little early but Maguire hopes to grab that view stool when happy hour lets out, as it's doing now. He slips inside, lowers his granny glasses, sees his lookout spot is empty, and commandeers it.

On the wall beside him, some sad loser has written with a red marking pen: "Everything I've loved became everything I lost." Another graffiti next to it: "Suck it up, loser." A second response: "Piss on pity!" Maguire's dark corner has negative vibes, a worrying omen.

He swivels for a see. The pub is about a third full, mostly hippie types, some likely underage. Half of them staring at their Facebook pages or on Snapchat, or whatever they do these days, others taking selfies, hugging and mugging.

At the back is a wooden stage, raised two feet, tall speakers on either side, audio equipment, drum set, keyboards, propped-up guitars. The stage abuts a stairwell leading down to WCs and, presumably, storage, and maybe a room for the entertainers. On the other side of the stage is a door to the alley, smokers occasionally drifting out there to tar their lungs.

Pouring shots behind the bar is a surly-looking guy with a dome as shiny as a peeled onion. Maguire doesn't get a nod or even a look, in the dim light here, so he pulls out his phone and thumbs a text to Gaylene: "Made it for Hippie Hour" and a smiley face.

The bartender finally discovers him. Maguire orders a pint of honey ale and gets a long, disapproving study. "Cash not credit."

"Business has been good." Maguire fans some bills.

"What you selling?"

"Whatever you want. Top shelf."

"You ain't doing your business here, pal. Keep your nose clean."

"Cool, man."

When the barkeep returns with the ale, he tips him a sawsky, to make friends. He's feeling pretty smug, give old Jake Maguire a pat on the back — all those years in undercover narcotics are paying off.

Everything flows easy for a fair stretch of time, Maguire nursing his brew, not wanting to get looped on the job. More customers are wandering in, the place filling. No sign yet of the vampish young lady with the Panic Disorder T-shirt, maybe she's downstairs with the band, giving blow jobs. Or maybe this could turn out to be a washout. Maybe he was too optimistic with Sonia.

A weirdo in a Mexican sombrero with a face full of grizzled hair climbs aboard the stool next to Maguire and says, belatedly but politely: "Would anyone be sitting here?"

"Just you, pal."

"Are you from around here, brother?" He doffs the hat, sets it on the bar.

"Just came up from the States. It's getting weird down there, man."

"Welcome to the true north strong and free." He takes in the Che Guevara cap, the slogan on his T-shirt. "Whom, might I inquire, are the Birmingham Eight?"

Maguire wasn't expected this hairball to speak in complete sentences, however ungrammatically. "Freedom fighters, man. And whom the fuck are you?"

"The gentleman you are talking to is a musical impresario. This is my band here. T.J. Gully." He offers his hand.

Maguire regrets having been curt. Gully, manager of Panic Disorder: he remembers that from the internet bumph Gaylene pulled up. "Tony Calhoun," he says, accepting Gully's hand. "I heard your guys really rock out."

"We're an inch from stardom, my good man." He calls the grouchy bartender over. "Kindly refill this fine fellow's mug, Baldy, and I'll have the usual."

"Cash not credit, Gully."

"I believe, sir, our contract provides for complimentary liquid refreshment for the band and its entourage. I am the entourage."

"Liquid refreshment means a coffee or a Coke."

Gully's pink alcoholic's nose wriggles with distress.

"On me," says Maguire, handing Baldy a fifty. "I'll get my change later, stick it behind the cash register." Gully's whiskers part in a grateful smile.

Maguire waits until his new best friend gets his drink, a double martini with olives, then says: "Tell me about these future stars, Mr. Gully."

He is pleased to do so. Maguire learns three of them started off as a busker band working the subways, but they "lacked firepower" and only took off when Rockin' Ray Wozniak crossed the border on the American Refugee Program. Introduced them to "the Oakland sound, post-punk heavy-metal." But the glue that holds them together, says Gully, is Mary Bumpo, from Alabama, who also does vocals.

Maguire isn't interested in Mary Bumpo. "Back up a bit. Rockin' Ray, the American refugee. He's political?"

"We're all a little political these days, friend." Gully hovers over his martini, enjoying the fumes, then closes his eyes while he sips. "Imperfect, but what can one expect from that uncouth billiard ball." He pulls a deck of Dunhills from his shirt pocket, fiddles with a cigarette.

Maguire keeps talking to stall him from going out for a break. "I was wondering if maybe Rockin' Ray Wozniak is from the Left. A brother refugee. Peace and justice, man."

"I cannot verify he is a warrior for peace, sir. Ray has a brief history of minor violence, having laid low an admirer of The Donald in a bar in Fresno."

"Right on. Cool. Maybe you could introduce us after the show. How's your drink? Like a freshie?"

"I don't mind if I do, sir. I shall return forthwith." He sticks the cigarette in his mouth, makes for the front door. There's a lineup out there, impatient faces at the windows.

Maguire sees his own pint is almost empty. He's been tilting it mindlessly, over-excited. He raises two fingers to Baldy, then does some fast calculating about his follow-through with Gully. Does he ask about groupies, about Becky McLean's magenta-haired friend? He itches to show him their photos, but that could explode in his face.

Gully returns, smelling of smoke. Just as Maguire is framing another question, the band troops up the stairs to loud applause that continues until, after some tuning, they rip into their first piece. A screechingly discordant wailing that checks further conversation, but the kids are into it, a couple of chicks standing, wiggling their bottoms.

Rockin' Ray, the lead guitarist, gyrates like a madman during a solo, his fingers whanging at the strings, then Mary Bumpo takes a turn, screaming indecipherable lyrics into a mike.

Gully excuses himself again, grabs his sombrero, and works his way to the back, placing the hat brim-up on the stage. He throws in a few bills for starters, then disappears down the stairs, presumably for a leak.

Maguire feels his own pressing need, but sticks it out, saving Gully's seat and ordering him a fresh martini. On his return, the impresario gives Maguire a smelly little shoulder hug.

Maguire had planned on a sobering coffee but when he finishes draining his second pint, Baldy is there with a third. "What a great band," he yells to Gully before heading off for a piss, weaving among the tables, dodging bodies, pausing at the sombrero to drop in a twenty, then aiming for the stairs. He's a little wobbly, he's got to slow the intake.

He was expecting gender-equal privies in a joint like this but there's a men's and a ladies'. He's third in line, now second, a coke-head just exiting, rubbing remnants into his gums. Of more interest to Maguire is what's behind a green door on the other side. It's labelled "employees and guests only" and it's ajar, lights on within.

Maguire's need is great, he doesn't want to miss his turn, so he says, "Coming right back," and quickly slips over to that door and takes a narrow view inside. Lounge chairs, a table supporting several empty beer bottles, an ashtray, scattered newspapers, that's all he can see until he widens the door a titch. Two gay wankers on a settee, laughing at some joke.

He pokes his head in quick: against the far wall is a young blond, her back to him, sitting in front of a makeup counter and a mirror, doing something with her hair. He sees her mirror image now, and bingo it's the dame who was with Becky, painted up like a witchy harlot, only no longer magenta-haired but honey-yellow. He darts back, hoping she didn't catch his reflection.

In the can, he triumphantly texts Gaylene again, more detailed, a full paragraph about Rockin' Ray and the newly blond-haired dish, a friend of the band.

She returns with, "Need backup?"

"Just stay handy, gorgeous."

He waits, embarrassed by his cheek. She finally comes back with, "Are you sober?"

"All good. Stay tuned."

§

Back at his base station, nursing a mug of alleged coffee, finishing off a burger as hard as a rock, Maguire keeps an eye on the stairwell and the back door, just in case the honey-blond makeup artist decides to break camp.

He has abandoned hope of getting more out of T.J. Gully tonight. He's corked, mumbling to himself, and the decibels in here are brutal. But Maguire does manage, through hand signals, to get his business card.

Ray Wozniak has soaked through his T-shirt, and peels it off without missing a beat. A dexterous dude, this tall, blond political refugee, probably one of those anarchists that infest the body politic. Maguire would bet his life savings on him being the masked man who scared the piss out of those doozy night guards. Maybe making Archie Gooch more brain-dead than he ever was.

He turns to the wall, squinting for graffiti more uplifting than the last sampling. In marking pen: "Don't die wondering." That's a thought to make you think. A twist on that: "Don't die wandering." Then: "Not all who wander are lost."

Thought processes of the millennials, the hip generation. Maguire is finding it tougher and tougher to relate to the young. Maybe if he and Sonia had had kids. They wanted, couldn't.

He balefully studies his coffee, rejects it in favour of another sip from his shot glass. Baldy had brought him a double of Maker's Mark with the coffee, a gift of the house. Maguire has been tipping too liberally. He holds his booze well, has always taken some pride in that.

Gin-sodden T.J. Gully wobbles from his stool and somehow finds his way to the back, down the stairs, either to ralph or grab some kip in the Green Room. He's left half a pack of his Dunhills on the bar, and Maguire pockets them. He can return them to Gully as a goodwill gesture, when he interviews him more formally, in an OPP interview room.

Finally, around nine, there's a break between sets, and Maguire decides it's time for another whiz. He finds himself tottering as he makes his way down to the can, following Rockin' Ray and his band. Someone opens the green door for them, wide enough so that Maguire gets a blast of cannabis fumes as he sneaks a peek. He makes out Gully passed out on a couch. Rockin' Ray Wozniak gets a hug from the makeup artist, calls her Lucy.

The door closes. Maguire gets in line for the john, starts texting.

4

Panic Disorder was supposed to wrap half an hour ago, at ten, so Maguire hopes this is the last encore — it's a weekday after all, most people have jobs. After their gig finally ends he'll wait for Ray and

Lucy to take off, then tail them, maybe even collar them. He's exhilarated by that prospect, entertaining dreams — enhanced by four shots of bourbon — of making the catch solo. Old Jake is going to wrap this baby up with pretty red ribbons, retire from the Force with a bang. He doesn't need backup, he's Frank Colombo, he's Starsky *and* Hutch.

Distracted as he is by his dreams of glory, it slowly dawns in his hazy brain that he may not have thought this through. How *does* he tail them? On the streetcar? What if they have wheels? Maguire doesn't, and even if he did, he's twice over the limit.

He almost does a nosedive jumping off his stool, regains his balance, makes aim for the front door, manages not to trip over his own legs, or anyone else's. Outside, he attacks his phone with fat-fingered clumsiness. From inside he hears a last skirl of guitar, a closing barrage of drums and cymbals.

He gets a wrong number, dials again, fighting off his own panic disorder as he sees the band gathering their instruments. Up the stairs comes T.J. Gully, being held upright by the two gay-looking dudes. Up comes Lucy behind them with what looks like a bag of laundry.

Gaylene comes on finally, anxious: "Check out my texts, for God's sake."

"Yeah, shorry, didn't look."

"You're *shorry*? You're plastered."

"Baldy's fault."

"What?"

"Never mind. Hang on." He steadies himself against the window frame as Squirrelly Moe's begins to empty. Somehow, Gully has regained his feet, is staggering about with the sombrero, hitting up the lingerers. Lucy hands Rockin' Ray a towel and a fresh shirt, then helps him pack guitars into their cases.

"I need backup real fast."

"You got it."

"What's that mean?"

"It means I'm across the street. Unmarked Buick LeSabre."

Maguire sees it, a late nineties model, Gaylene frowning behind the wheel. "Where'd you percure . . . get that?"

"Drug squad. A seizure. You're tanked, Jake."

"It's my cover. I'm in total control."

"Yeah, I'll bet. Okay, there's a green Aerostar van out front. See it?"

"Green . . . Got it."

"I think it's their band van. That's a definite, there's a fat-assed ghoul heading for it, packing out the drums."

Maguire quickly pockets his phone as the drummer passes by, dripping sweat. He's followed out by Mary Bumpo, with her bass guitar.

Maguire stays put, lowers his cap to give himself shade, pulls out the half pack of Dunhills, sticks one in his mouth, making like he's an ordinary Joe getting his nic hit — which would work better if he had a match. But here's Mary Bumpo, pausing to take her own smoke, a little brown stogey. As he paws through his pockets, she extends a lighter. He mumbles his thanks, takes a little puff.

"'Save the Birmingham Eight,'" she says. "They already got saved, brother."

"Far out." That's all he can come up with.

She looks at him oddly. He grins stupidly. That puff felt good, and he can't help himself, takes a drag. It hits him right away, a bracing, tasty jolt, bringing remembrance of past pleasures, his decades-long habit, two packs of Sweet Caps a day.

Bumpo makes for the Aerostar van, following her Panic Disorder mates through the sliding side door, hauling Gully in with them. The drummer squeezes into the driver's seat, starts the engine. Maguire waits anxiously for a break in the traffic, finally manages to wobble across the street to the Buick, just as the van pulls out. He takes another drag, butts out, climbs in.

§

Maguire has to concede Gaylene is a slick wheelman for a woman, she keeps eyes on the Aerostar all the way to the west side, and now it has stopped fifty feet ahead, in front of a rundown two-storey office building. She switches off the headlights, pulls into a parking space, and kills the engine.

"Where are we?" He's drunk, bagged, half-awake.

"Lower Dufferin. Stay down."

He is down already, the seat tilted back, but from over the dashboard he can see the old building. His vision is distorted, he's seeing double, but it's dark, a derelict structure, all but a few windows boarded up, maybe some kind of hippie squat. Painted on the wall, the anarchist symbol, a capital A circled. Two of them, but they come together when he focuses.

Now he sees Rockin' Ray and Lucy exit from the van's sliding side door. They embrace. She hands him two guitars. Wozniak looks about, then manoeuvres through a large hole cut into the front door. Lucy climbs back into the van.

"Shit," Gaylene says. "Stay or follow?"

Maguire has to think, it's hard. "Follow."

Gaylene gets on the horn, calls in the address. "Roger. Got it. Thanks." To Maguire: "It's a teardown, a squat, eviction order being held up by the lawyers."

He mumbles: "The lawyers, always the lawyers."

They follow the van as it takes a left on King, moving west, Gaylene keeping it in view as she thumbs Wiggie's number. "Wakey, wakey," she says, and gives him the squatters' location, tells him to hustle his ass over to cover it.

Maguire fidgets, struggles to hold back a burger fart. He feels the pack of Dunhills burning a hole in his pocket — that second cigarette was a big mistake, the need is back, big time.

His eyes close. He has a sense of losing it . . .

CHAPTER 9 » ARTHUR

1
Wednesday, September 19

Selwyn Loo's blitzkrieg against TexAmerica's gutting of Quarry Park is to be heard today not in Victoria but Vancouver, to convenience counsel, so Arthur rises early, to the summons of his bedside alarm, so he can catch the early ferry. He dons his favourite old three-piece suit — unfashionable but it's his comfort-zone uniform. A visiting barrister does not go to court in jeans and boots.

Nor does one show up in a beat-up old pickup, so he'll be parking the Fargo in the lot at Ferryboat Landing. A taxi will meet him on the mainland after a three-hour milk run — he'll be lucky to make it to the Law Courts by noon. He spoons down some oatmeal, and, briefcase in hand, slips out quietly, hoping not to arouse Ulysses, sprawled asleep on his dog bed just inside the mud room.

It's only dawn, but Stefan, as usual, is already up, clucking to the chickens while tossing feed and stealing their eggs. Solara, with coffee in hand, still in pyjamas, is watching him from the deck of their house. She appears to have become overly fond of her housemate, but there's been no indication that they've slept together. Her feelings for Stefan seem not to be fully shared.

Arthur hurries to his truck, keeping an eye on Ulysses. Even while sleeping, his ears seem tuned to the sound of the engine starting up, and his habit is to race down the driveway after him before the gate swings closed. Occasionally, he makes it out to Potters Road and has to be led back into the farmyard.

Predictably, as the engine ignites, Ulysses is already up on all fours and moving. Arthur gets on the gas and zooms past Stefan, who stands there grinning with his booty from the coop. At the driveway gate, Arthur hops out, swings it open, then jumps back in and accelerates out. The gate swings back and latches shut, forcing Ulysses to pull up.

From his rear-view, Arthur catches his determined hound clearing a fallen rail of the snake fence in a majestic bound. The wily pup has outsmarted the boss, has found a shortcut to the road. He emerges from between the trees, forcing Arthur to brake hard, his heart in his mouth. But Ulysses keeps going, challenging the Fargo to a race, which Arthur lets him win by gearing down to a crawl, then stopping and alighting. Ulysses does a U-turn and returns to old grey-haired human friend who is making loud, unhappy bad-dog sounds.

Stefan finally comes running up with a leash. Arthur gives his pet a farewell hug and wrestle and apologizes for his scolding tone. He will make it up on his return late tomorrow, with a big knuckle bone and a long evening ramble up their favourite trail.

He frets that the delay will make him miss his boat, but pulls into the ferry parking lot just as the *Queen George* slides into the slip. At the ramp, he gets stares and smiles from the locals disembarking: there's stodgy old Beauchamp in his ancient suit, now severely rumpled.

§

Arthur has had limited experience with the civil courts and it's a struggle to grasp the labyrinthine phrases being tossed about in room 30 of the Vancouver Law Courts. The argot of torts vaguely remembered from law school: anticipated harm, collateral effects, reasonable use, invasion of interests in land.

Selwyn Loo and Nathaniel Shawcross, TexAmerica's mining hotshot, bandy about these concepts with ease, as does the chambers judge: R.B. Innes. Yes, the same smarmy, moon-faced judge who shot Arthur down in flames two weeks ago has been appointed to hear this tussle over a limestone formation. Arthur should have expected that — the Chief Justice would have decided Innes was the go-to guy on Quarry Park issues.

They scrapped all morning, affidavits read, law argued, facts disputed, but Arthur got here just as the court adjourned for lunch. Over sandwiches, Selwyn brought Arthur up to speed. Innes had debated with him affably, in his condescending manner, congratulated him for his superb presentation, dismissed his motion to quash the corporation's SLAPP suit, and granted TexAmerica an injunction against any blocking or impeding of its operations. Selwyn had expected nothing else. His crew from West Coast Environmental is already preparing a notice of appeal.

Now, this afternoon, they are dealing with the restraining order sought by Mattie Miller and Hamish McCoy, both of whom are in court, as are several SOQers, including Al and Zoë Noggins and Taba Jones. All arrived last night, bunking in a short-term rental.

Arthur is slouched on the counsel row almost directly behind Selwyn, so can't see his play of expression as he recites selected passages from his clients' affidavits. But Arthur can read Shawcross's confident body language as he basks in the warm glow emanating from Judge Innes, his devotee. *Admirable piece of work, Mr. Shawcross.*

Innes listens to Selwyn with an occasional raised eyebrow, a clue to the disdain he holds for the petitioners' claim of anticipated nuisance. Occasionally he turns to Arthur, beaming at him, as if they are old comrades fortuitously brought together.

Selwyn continues to amaze: he describes photos he has never seen. "Exhibits Twelve to Eighteen depict Mr. McCoy's grounds, the charming, whimsical home he built for himself in the manner of a hobbit house, which doubles as a gallery; his sculpture studio, clay oven, workbench, and tools. As you see, most of his work is done outside. The next three photographs display some of his art."

Because of their colossal size, McCoy's abstract and often risqué creations appeal to a narrow market. Several international galleries were brave enough to exhibit him, but few public museums. Towering, naked, humanoid figures, some birdlike with wings or four-footed like bears, Hamish in grinning pose beside one of them, with his big old mongrel Shannon.

Innes looks at the photos askance. "You say he sells these for substantial amounts? This lopsided, beaked giant with the erect penis?"

Arthur had urged Hamish not to include that one, but the combative elf insisted.

Arthur starts as he hears Hamish declaim: "That rubs me right raw, b'y." Arthur turns to see him standing in the third row. "I put eight months into this gorgeous crayture."

The judge tries to break in. "Mr. McCoy—"

"It's the way I makes my livin', your worship. If their limestone dust and dort gets into me plaster, I'm just about skinned."

"Mr. McCoy, you have no standing."

"I'm standing as big as I can. I got a million dollars wort' of me works in that yard."

"Mr. Sheriff, please remove that gentleman."

Hamish looks confused, peers about trying to spot the gentleman referred to.

Many in the audience are laughing. Innes turns from pink to scarlet. "This court is recessed. We will have order!"

Hamish continues to act out during the break, fuming and cursing, attracting stares from the Great Hall of the Vancouver Law Courts building. Rain slicks down the vast transparent ceiling, a massive angled skylight. A sudden downpour after a fair day, it adds to Arthur's blues about how the hearing is going.

Selwyn and Reverend Al team up to try to talk Hamish down: his courtroom outburst was understandable, and may have actually helped the cause. The TexAmericans, Selwyn explains, are now alert to the costly damages that may ultimately be due to McCoy and Mattie Miller; indeed, they may be having second thoughts about the project's financial viability as legal costs bleed them.

Taba now joins in, embracing Hamish, praising him for his heroics. Other SOQers surround the little sparkplug, giving him love. Soon, he is beaming. "I did the right t'ing, b'ys. Gave that horse's ass an earful."

Behind him stands one of the court sheriffs, ready to grab him if he tries re-entering room 30.

§

When the hearing resumes, Selwyn goes to work for another twenty minutes, then calmly sits, awaiting the inevitable.

"I don't need to hear from you, Mr. Shawcross." Innes glares at Arthur as he renders judgment, as if assuming he was the inspiring force behind the effrontery displayed by the pernicious little Newfoundlander.

"Ruling. There is no proof of existing harm. No nuisance exists or has been proven likely. Plaintiffs will have a further opportunity to bring the matter before this court should damage occur or be imminent. Case dismissed."

Selwyn rises, unperturbed, icy. "I thank Your Lordship for the deep consideration you have given the matter."

Innes regains his faux-genial air with a stiff smile. "Tomorrow, Mr. Loo, a justice of the Appeal Court will hear your application for a stop-work order until a full court hears your appeal of my earlier decision." That being his slap-down of Arthur's fumbled attempt to quash the Quarry Park bylaw.

"It's not beyond the realm of possibility that you may get your stay." Innes rolls his eyes: the prospect is laughable. "In which case today's rulings may be moot. Good luck. This court is adjourned."

2

As an honorary member of Vancouver's staid Confederation Club, a haunt of overpaid CEOs and their avaricious lawyers, Arthur gets a rate, though he never pays it — the bills are forwarded to Tragger, Inglis. For some reason Bullingham tolerates these excesses, maybe as a lever to entice him back to work.

He's in his preferred suite tonight: well appointed, a king-size bed affording ample room on which to toss and turn while fuming over today's washout. He feels bad for Selwyn, who fought with Sisyphean grit. Tomorrow, he will make a last-gasp effort before an appeal judge.

After showering away the body sweat — he'd heated up with anger at that irritating excuse for a judge — Arthur heads to the dining room. He picks up a *Globe*, takes a small table by the window, the view suiting his mood: rain squalling down on Howe Street. He has deliberately chosen to sit as far away as possible from Nathaniel Shawcross, who is across the room, entertaining a pair of TexAmerica directors. They are jolly. They are drinking champagne.

They haven't noticed Arthur hiding behind his newspaper. Their view is also hampered by four large men seated next to him, retired industry leaders, in their cups, loudly solving the world's terrorism problem.

"We've got them right here in Canada."

"Those hippie degenerates got away scot-free." The Chemican invaders, Arthur assumes.

"Marxist revolutionaries. We coddle them in our universities."

Leafing through the front section of the *Globe*, Arthur finds a brief account of the aftermath of the Chemican break-in, the company making a lot of noise about smears and distortions as its secrets continue to pour through the busy portals of the internet. None of the hippie degenerates arrested yet, the authorities tight-lipped. "Our inquiries are continuing." A terse rebuff to the press from Inspector Jake Maguire, of the OPP.

Jake Maguire. Arthur thinks back. Wasn't he the lead investigator in the Ciccini mob hit in London, Ontario? A few decades ago. A double homicide that fell apart when a key witness recanted. Arthur remembers buying Maguire — a detective sergeant then — a few consolation drinks after the trial. More than a few. Maguire seemed a likeable guy, despite his considerable animus toward the courts and the legal profession. Arthur had stood his ground, and they departed, drunkenly, on good terms. That was a year or so before Arthur went on the wagon.

Arthur retrieves his phone. For what it's worth, he'd promised Selwyn he would seek Margaret's advice about representing the Earth Survival people. "I'm fine with whatever you decide," that's her mantra, that's what he wants to hear. She'll surely understand his reluctance — she worries about his atrophying brain: his many lapses, his foggy memory, his scribbled reminders scattered about the house. His Jeremiah hallucinations.

It's close to ten in Ottawa, but she's at her desk, dissecting the Budget Speech.

"Any good news in it?"

"More moolah for scientific research. The Pest Management

Regulatory Agency relied on an American contractor for the Vigor-Gro testing, and the Health Minister is scrambling for excuses and fixes. What's your good news?"

A sardonic snort prefaces his tale of Innes's fawning over a bullying corporation, his enjoining the protesters, his caustic dismissals of Selwyn's every line of attack.

He dares not mention Selwyn's risky relationship with the Earth Survival Rebellion and simply explains that Selwyn had inquired whether Arthur would be available in case any of these rebels were arrested.

"He inquired?"

"Importuned might be the better word. Impossible, of course, given the toll the years have taken. I'm . . . let's accept it, devolving into quite the scatterbrain."

"Don't be ridiculous, dear. Maybe you've mislaid a few marbles temporarily, but that's because your mind is so active elsewhere that you've stopped being observant. You're still quick-witted and perceptive behind that lazy charade of pretending you have half your wits. I've seen you do a *Times* crossword in ten minutes."

Arthur is stunned by this exaggerated bill of health, based on flimsy evidence. "I am quick-witted enough to know that such a trial would be better fought by someone else. There are several extremely sharp criminal counsel in Toronto."

His favourite, Nancy Faulk, is embroiled in her own nasty divorce action, and advised, in her acerbic way: "Arthur, I'd drop everything, including my pants, to work with you again — you lead, I'll follow, Astaire and Rogers — but I ain't fucking doing it without you. I'm in a domestic crisis."

So Arthur had to give up on her. He has been on the horn to several others, but all are tied up.

Margaret is relentless: "The activists who did that raid are heroes. And they may be in trouble — some over-height beanpole of a cop has been showing photos of two young women they suspect are involved — they were volunteers at the Bee-In. Staff have been instructed to keep mum. I hope no one gets arrested but if they do I believe you need to take them on. I know you. Once you get your teeth into it, you'll get your focus back. And your self-confidence."

"Do I understand you're suggesting I need that trial?"

"I am. So you can be proud of yourself again."

That hurts. "Well, I'm sorry. I don't need the strain. I have a farm to run. Ulysses threatened to follow me to the ferry yesterday, for God's sake. I absolutely have to spend more time with him. And we're losing Stefan at some point, so I'll be sorely needed at the farm."

A long sigh. "Okay. Sorry, darling, I shouldn't push you."

"Anyway, they're probably in some safe haven in Latin America or somewhere. Hiding out with comrades in the Brazilian jungle." He concludes, weakly: "I love you."

"Love you back." They disconnect.

Arthur watches a server approach Shawcross's table with another bottle of Mumm's. Meanwhile, the tycoons next table down are worried about their investments.

"Our adviser says cut and run. Chemican has an image problem. Growing worse."

"I'm staying in, old boy. Once this bee business blows over, they'll be back up there with Bayer."

"It's mites, I read that they lay eggs in the beehives and the baby mites bore into the bees' brains and suck them dry until they're too disoriented to find the hive."

A menu is placed in front of Arthur. He no longer feels hungry. "The mushroom soup will do, I think." Surely they can't enhance mushroom growth with Vigor-Gro.

He opens his newspaper to the *Times* crossword.

Across from the bustling harbour, the North Shore Mountains emerge wet and shining from the shrinking fluffs of cotton that once were rain clouds. The sun has burst forth, drawing Arthur from his gloom, propelling him down to the Seawall at eight a.m. to join the joggers and cyclists hastening to Stanley Park.

The pleasant day brings at least feeble hope. Maybe Selwyn will make a lucky draw in the lottery that is the daily docket at the Law Courts. A liberal justice who abominates the Koch brothers and their ilk. A birder, a fancier of cliff swallows and peregrine falcons. *Imagine, m'lord, a mining company being permitted to tear up Stanley Park . . .*

An unlikely fancy. They'll get some antediluvian sourpuss with a portfolio of mining stocks.

He slings his suit jacket over a shoulder as the day continues to warm, and enters the vast, forested peninsula that adorns the towered city like an emerald tiara. Malkin Bowl, Hallelujah Point, the totems, these familiar sights barely registering as he replays Margaret's diagnosis. Has he really been performing a lazy charade of being addle-brained? Has he invented an excuse for his waning confidence? And is that born of the dread of being too sorely tested, of ending his career in failure? Maybe so, but he dares not risk making a mess of things, losing these brave mavericks to a long term in a federal penitentiary.

He makes it all the way to Brockton Oval, then circles back by Lumbermen's Arch. He is sorely missing Ulysses, who ought to be proudly at his side among the many dog walkers with their everyday little spaniels and terriers.

He exits the park at Nelson Street for the long trudge to the Law Courts. Selwyn's hearing is set for ten, and Arthur is a few minutes late, but he stops outside the registry to read the docket. *Noggins et al v. Garibaldi Island Trust Council and TexAmerica Stoneworks Ltd.*, Court 41, Madam Justice M. Pearl presiding.

Mandy Pearl? He blinks, focuses — it's no hallucination. Mandy Pearl, the wise, thoughtful trial lawyer with whom he'd shared not only courtrooms but rooms more intimate, whom he'd feted at a bar dinner on her appointment to the bench three years ago. She was elevated to the Court of Appeal just this spring.

He hastens to the escalator, then up the stairs, avoiding the elevators — too slow for him — and on reaching the door to the Appeal Court chambers, takes a deep breath and enters, depositing himself in the back row, unobtrusive, unnoticed.

Selwyn is decrying the projected pillaging of parkland that has long served as a favourite playground for Garibaldians, for their children. Shawcross is staring balefully at him, looking wan, hungover. Sitting behind him are the two TexAmerica directors with whom he was making merry last night, looking equally discomposed. Members of SOQ have returned in force, augmented by several parents, teachers, and children, a school outing. Hamish McCoy sits beside Taba with arms folded, scowling but behaved. Kurt Zoller has turned up too, alone, friendless.

And there on her dais is Madam Justice Mandy Pearl, listening intently, making notes. A petite, dimpled, grey-streaked blond no less pleasing to the eye than three decades ago when she rescued Arthur from alcoholic despair.

She is either not aware of Arthur's presence, or is pretending not to be.

Memories flood. It was 1987. He had just finished a tense, ugly murder case while on the wagon, desperately trying to break his addiction. Mandy, in her late twenties, had been junior counsel on the opposite side, and for no reason he could divine seemed to be keen on him.

After the trial, on returning to his car, he found Annabelle, his perfidious first wife, in its back seat under a thrusting, bellowing

Wagnerian tenor. Arthur fled, in search of strong drink. Mandy traced him to a restaurant where he was powering through multiple martinis.

She made a citizen's arrest, bundled him into her car, bedded him down in her condo, and they made love for a week until he was on the dry again.

He has not had a drink since. Mandy saved his career, maybe his life, even though Arthur did return to Annabelle, his other cruel addiction. Mandy remained single, gave her full devotion to the law, but she and Arthur remained friends. No one knew of their short, intense *affaire d'amour*.

Mandy is obviously aware that Arthur R. Beauchamp is a party to this action — he is named as such. Ought she to have recused herself? There's still no sign of recognition from her — but he's slouching behind a large, half-asleep retiree, the type of fellow who wanders about the courts looking for drama. Likely, he'll find none here.

Shawcross has become alert to the judge's obvious interest in Selwyn's argument, his attack on the concept that mining rights defeat all comers: the legislation was archaic, unsuited to modern times. Selwyn answers Mandy's questions succinctly and with clarity. She is clearly intrigued by his uncanny ability to quote precedent verbatim without eyesight.

As Selwyn concludes, the bulky fellow in front of Arthur gets up to leave, and Mandy takes a quick glance their way, then down, expressionless. That she dared not look him in the eye could bode ill, he fears. That she seemed so encouraging to Selwyn could be a way of letting him down easy.

Why must Arthur always retreat to the dark side? Mandy does not play games. That is demonstrated when Shawcross, taking his turn, gets into tough going.

"But as I understand it, Mr. Shawcross, this land was deeded as a community park long before your client obtained mining rights. That was only three years ago."

"Mining rights have prevailed in this province since 1891, M'Lady."

"Is a nineteenth-century act appropriate for the twenty-first century?"

Shawcross seems shocked by the boldness of that question. His ambiguous response is delivered in a frantic tone of disbelief — could a stay-work order actually be in the cards? A full appeal could not be heard for many months. He complains that TexAmerica would lose half a million dollars for each week their operations are held up — an obvious exaggeration.

"Well, that's too bad," Her Ladyship says. "But doesn't the fault lay with the company for rushing ahead without a proper environmental study? For lack of due diligence? For failing to properly consult with the community?"

"That is simply not the case, with respect. The island's two elected Trustees were fully briefed and are enthusiastically in accord with this project."

"Yet the petition filed by Mr. Loo bears four hundred signatures — two-thirds of the island's population."

"Your Ladyship may note that a substantial number of those are children."

"And children have no right to be heard?"

"The issue, M'Lady, is the supremacy of mining rights under long-settled law."

"As I read the Islands Trust Act, its object is to preserve and protect the unique amenities and environment for the benefit of everyone in the province. That's a sweeping mandate. Do you not agree there is at least an appealable issue here? Do we allow mining corporations to run rampant over sensitive areas protected by law?"

Shawcross may be wishing he hadn't overdone it last night. He is palpably in physical pain, and muffs the wording of precedents relied on. Finally, cornered, he is forced to concede there is no case on point involving the primacy of the Mining Act over the Trust Act. He has no answer as to why no environmental assessment was made.

The lawyer for the Garibaldi Islands Trust, aware of how the wind is blowing, says he has nothing to add.

Mandy rules: "All operations of the respondent with respect to Quarry Park will cease until this court meets in full session to hear the appeal."

Zoller stalks out. The room applauds.

"Order!" cries the sheriff.

Mirabile visu. It was wonderful to behold.

§

Taba scampishly locks elbows with Arthur as Selwyn leads them unerringly to the Robson Square exit and into this benign end-of-summer day, tap-tapping along the walkway among the rushing waterfalls and floral gardens. Arthur and Taba are on their way to the Pacific Centre parkade to meet Herman Schloss, a wealthy retiree and the treasurer of SOQ, who will be taking them to the island ferry in his hybrid SUV.

"You were on top of your game," says Arthur.

"I had not imagined it would be so easy. Incredible judge, Ms. Pearl. Have you had previous dealings with her?"

Arthur frames a careful answer. "Long ago we did some things together."

"Like what?" says Taba. "Did you fuck her?"

Selwyn seems a little shocked at Taba's earthy humour, then he laughs. So does Arthur, though with a hoarse rasp.

§

Herman Schloss has invited a full complement of boisterous friends into his commodious SUV, into which Arthur secures a position midway in the back seat. He fully expects Taba to squeeze in beside him or even perch on his lap. But instead she accepts Schloss's invitation to join him up front.

Arthur isn't sure why he feels miffed by that. Or by the hug and kiss she bestows on Schloss, a ruddy, handsome man in his sixties. He's currently on marriage sabbatical, his actress wife doing a bit part in Hollywood. A generous fellow, he'd forked out for the group's multi-room Airbnb.

As they work their way through city traffic, Arthur pretends to ignore Taba's coquettish deportment — leaning toward Schloss, touching, pulling her blouse tight over those heroic breasts. The thought is laughable that he might feel jealousy, a pitiable emotion to whom only those of feeble character fall prey. After all, he and Taba have solemnly agreed on a truce from her flirtatious advances. He is pleased, he tells himself, that she has honoured their pact.

§

While his fellow SOQers celebrate over a twenty-six of rum in a stateroom of the *Queen George*, Arthur settles into a secluded nook and phones Margaret, pulling her away briefly from a staff meeting.

"Brilliant," she says. "Congratulations."

"All credit to Selwyn Loo."

"Give him a smooch for me. You owe him big time, buddy."

§

Arthur's Fargo is waiting for him in Ferryboat Landing's upper lot, so he goes ashore on foot. As he strides across the ramp, he stops short, frozen with shock at seeing Ulysses waiting, furiously wagging his tail, now racing to him gleefully.

"Been here a couple of hours, Mr. Beauchamp," says one of the local ferrymen. "But he's been good. Gave him water and a ham sandwich, hope you don't mind."

Arthur is nonplussed — how did Ulysses again break out of Blunder Bay? He'd given strict instructions to Stefan and Solara to shore up the snake fence and keep the driveway gate closed. And how, except through some arcane doggy instinct, did Ulysses know Arthur would be arriving on this boat?

But here comes bad news — Constable Dugald pulling up in his Ford Explorer. He steps out, scowling. "Your goddamn wolfhound has been running loose."

"I regret that, Irwin. The gate must not have been latched. He's just a pup. Quite harmless."

Dugald lurches back as Ulysses leaps at him. Arthur has to grab him around the neck to pull them apart. "He's just being playful," Arthur says, wincing. "See? He likes you. Good dog. Sit."

But Ulysses is too excited to sit. He wants to play with his new friend, and dances behind him for a rear-end sniff. Again, Arthur must corral him.

Dugald brushes a dusty paw print from his uniform. "I got nothing against dogs. Used to have one. But you don't secure this hound, I'm looking to laying charges under the Animals Bylaw. That means the pound. He's a hunting dog, right? We got livestock all over this island, and if he takes down a sheep there'll be hell to pay. Any farmer has a right to shoot him. We don't want to have to put him down."

Such prospects cause Arthur icy shivers. He must keep his temper. "I have farm animals. They're his pals. He lets the goats climb all over him."

"You been warned. Keep him fenced."

Ulysses picks up the harshness of tone, backs away, confused. Dugald stalks off. Arthur bends to give Ulysses a scratch behind the ears. "Don't worry about him, boy — he's a bonehead." Ulysses likes the sound of that word, and charges ahead, up the hill to the parking lot.

§

Arthur doesn't dare put his errant pup into the back of his truck, and squeezes him into the cab, his upper body resting on his lap as he enjoys the passing views. On arrival at Blunder Bay, Arthur finds the driveway gate latched shut. "So how did you get out, buddy?"

Scanning the fence line, he finds the answer. Once again, two top rails have been knocked askew near the apple orchard. Ulysses stays in the truck, whining, as Arthur doffs his suit jacket and heads to the orchard to lift the heavy cedar rails back into place.

Solara sprints down the hill from the goat pen, looking both relieved and guilty as she finds Arthur struggling with the fence. "Oh, my Lord, I reckon he gone and did it again. He is super strong. We been looking all over. Let me help." She hoists one end of the top rail, still babbling nervously. "Stefan has been traipsing all over the island. Where did you find him? Is he okay?"

"He's in the truck. Please fetch some spikes." Snake fences are not to be hammered together — that's one of the rules of rustic architecture — but emergencies call for exceptions.

Ulysses appears behind them, looking triumphant. Either cleverly or accidentally, he must have pressed against the handle to push open the driver's door.

"You bloody rascal," Arthur says, roughing his fur, looking for ticks, and finding none gives his muzzle a playful shake. "Give me a chance to change, Ulysses." What a character. So different from Homer. But equally loved.

"How did the court action go?" Solara asks.

"Court action?" It comes back, as if from a century ago. "Yes, of course. The enemy was routed."

CHAPTER 10 » MAGUIRE

1
Thursday, September 20

Maguire awakes with a banging head, and is disoriented by sunlight pouring through a window. If the bedside clock isn't malfunctioning, it's almost noon. He's under clean sheets, in his skivvies. He sits up, looks around — he's in his goddamn hotel room, and can't remember getting here. His last memory is riding shotgun with Gaylene as they followed the Panic Disorder van from Rockin' Ray Wozniak's squat.

He scrambles up, finds his phone. Gaylene answers cheerily. "All woke up? You were sleeping like a baby when I left you."

"Goddamn hell!"

"You're welcome. You could barely stand, Jake. You've had at least twelve hours, I've had maybe three."

"The perps!"

"Relax. All bases are covered. Wiggens is still on the stake at Wozniak's squat."

"Who's Wiggens?" Maguire's short-term memory is still clouded.

"Sean. Tall, skinny, dumb? He works with us? Operation Vigorish?"

"Oh, Wiggie, right."

"He spotted Wozniak once at a second-floor window, bare-assed. Maybe got up to pee. Meanwhile, Lucy got dropped off at a converted warehouse on Sorauren Avenue in Roncesvalles — she has a loft there, a house-sit. I dug out the name of the owner, Dr. Wenz, a professor on sabbatical in Europe. I sent Long Ling to cover her, got you back to our hotel, and parked you in your room — you were like the walking dead."

"Jeez, Gaylene, I hope that's not going in your report."

"That you were in the coop? Hey, I got your back, but roses would be nice."

"You're an angel. What else?"

"Eight twelve a.m., Lucy, full name Lucy Wales, leaves her digs, dressed for work. Long Ling follows on foot, subway, bus, and at eight fifty-eight he's standing in a mall in North York watching her enter the Rexall where she works. Where Becky McLean claimed *she* works. Long Ling got a little conspicuous during his follow, so I traded places with him. When Wales was on break I sneaked in for a quiet talk with the manager. Wales works part-time, off at three, not due back for two days. She's taking some courses in chemical science at Ryerson, so I suspect she concocted the Mickey Finn that put Howie Griffin out."

"You did good." Maguire wants to kick himself. This was supposed to be his catch, it was slipping away. "I'm going to see if we can borrow a SWAT team."

"Um, maybe hold off on that? Wait till we get them all together? They're still posting from somewhere."

"Okay, but I'll get the ball rolling, then call you from head office."

He rehydrates his dry throat and mouth by draining half of a bottled water. But that doesn't resolve a different, more nagging need. He can't figure out why or for what. Not food, though he's hungry. Coffee maybe, but not the shit the hotel offers in its ridiculous pods.

Finally, he gets it. He retrieves the pack of Dunhills from a jacket pocket. He stares at it longingly but also with dread. "Fuck you!" he cries, and crumples the pack, tossing it, a three-pointer into the wastebasket.

He pops a couple of Advils and heads for the shower.

§

Chief Superintendent Lafriere has a long afternoon budget meeting with a junta of Queen's Park bureaucrats, so Maguire is forced to fiddle about in the Operation Vig room, chewing on mint Nicorettes, kicking himself for getting snockered last night, acting the fool and passing out.

He contemplates using the dead time to haul in Gully, the band manager. But he decides against — the furball can't be trusted to check his busy tongue. Operation Vig may be leaking like a sieve already, thanks mostly to Wiggie's poor interview techniques with the Bee-In volunteers — the giraffe got nothing, they were skeptical, asking too many questions. A bad idea, Maguire has put a hold on it.

He uses his lag time to catch up on his reports. The Super will be grumpy when he reads them, after his session with the cost-cutters. Grumpier if he learns Maguire was plastered last night, so he minimizes his alcohol intake to a couple of beer and a shot of bourbon, praying no one checks with Baldy the bartender.

His boss will not be enthusiastic about his pitch for search warrants and a flying squad, so he embroiders his case, inflates it with a sense of urgency — the perps may have got alerts from the Bee-In volunteers and must be nailed before they head for the hills. Maguire will be in doo-doo if he loses this collar.

At three fifteen Gaylene calls in, sounding weary — she's at the Finch subway station, eyes on Lucy Wales as they wait for the train. "She just gave a sharp elbow to a drip who crowded her. Feisty gal."

Wiggie reports in too. There've been casual comings and goings at the hippie squat, none by Wozniak, though someone unseen picked up a delivery pizza at the smashed-in front door. Meanwhile, Long Ling is still on lookout outside Lucy's loft. But where is her buddy, the conniving cutie known as Becky McLean? He adds another Nicorette to the one in his mouth.

§

Chief Super Lafriere spends ten minutes frowning over Maguire's report, then removes his reading glasses, gives him a sour look. "You couldn't convict a dog with what you got. Not even enough ammo for a search warrant."

"We're zoning in on them, Chief. Getting close to their operations centre. Either Lucy Wales or her boyfriend is going to take us there. We're going to need manpower to roust them. A SWAT team, Ident members to frisk the joint."

"Good undercover work, Jake, I'll give you that. But by your own admission your eager beavers may have set off alarms by interrogating an assortment of unreliables and sympathizers. You're running out of time. Maybe you need to bring Lucy Wales in. Sweat her."

"I can't see her giving her pals up, sir. I don't think she sweats much."

"Well, you better locate their safe place before they run like rabbits. You do that and you'll have your warrant and a full crew. I'm guessing you've got maybe one more day before your leaks turn into a flood. Pull it off, and you can retire happy and proud. That's coming up, isn't it?"

"I can hardly wait."

Back in the Operation Vig room, Maguire gets his updates. Wozniak finally showed, and was picked up by the band van. Wiggie followed it to Squirrelly Moe's and is keeping watch outside. Gaylene tailed Lucy on the Bloor line to Dundas West Station, then on foot, the target stopping at the Loblaws for a bag of groceries before heading to her loft.

Gaylene sounds totally bagged. He tells her to hang on until he joins her.

§

Armed with a double grande latte, Maguire finds Gaylene slouched in the Buick a few car lengths north of Lucy's loft building.

"You're a real trooper," he says.

"I'm about to conk off."

"Sure, grab some sack duty."

She eases over to the passenger seat and kicks off her shoes. He climbs in beside her, checks the view from the windshield — there's a clear channel between the trees to the target building's front door.

Gaylene quickly falls asleep, still sitting up. It's a roomy car, and with the middle armrest pulled up he reaches around her to tilt back her seat. But she slides toward him, her head resting on his shoulder. As he tries to brace her with his right arm, her head slips, descends, coming to rest on his lap, her face hidden by her mussed hair. Not daring to wake her, Maguire sips his double latte, feeling unwanted twinges in his groin.

§

For an agonizing three hours, Maguire stays frozen, Gaylene snoozing on his lap, one leg tucked in, the other foot braced against the dashboard, her left ear pressed to his crotch. He'd had to undertake a delicate manoeuvre, undoing his belt so he could relocate his penis from under the area of her nose. He has no place to put his hands, so keeps them folded, not daring to touch her body. So far, thank God, no one strolling by has taken notice.

He's praying Gaylene will not suddenly awake — he'd have a tough time assuring her the bulge in his trousers is his service weapon. Just as he's wondering if he can take it any longer, Lucy Wales appears at her door, hauling out a bicycle.

He does a quick calculation. Arousing Gaylene could cause her to startle and give them away. Wales is approaching, wheeling her bike, her phone to her ear. Windbreaker, a pack on her back, no helmet. It's eight thirty and the sun has set but there's far too much street light.

Suddenly she halts, still on the sidewalk, just beside the passenger door. He's staring straight ahead, but senses her glancing at his loose belt and the thatch of blond hair hiding his groin. "Enjoying a little street penilingus? Yolo."

She jumps on her bike, but before pedalling off turns and aims the cell phone lens at him, through the windshield. A camera flash. She accelerates away, her legs pumping.

If there was a hole nearby, Maguire would crawl into it. "Sweet fucking Jesus," he sputters.

That arouses Gaylene, who propels up suddenly. "Oh, God, sorry. Did I just collapse on you?"

Crimson with embarrassment, he can't find words, dares not mention Lucy Wales's passing encounter. *Enjoying a little street penilingus?* He hides his loose belt under his jacket, grips the wheel, starts the engine.

"Oh, shit," Gaylene says, watching Wales pedal away, north on Sorauren. A bike light and reflectors. No rear-view mirror.

He waits until she's half a block away, then pulls out, still shaking from that mortifying interlude at the curb. Driving at half the speed limit, he allows vehicles to pass him, occasionally pulls over to let her stay well ahead. She turns left on Dundas, then up to St. Clair, along a stretch of small retail shops, then zips into a darkened alley. Maguire rolls past it, then parks in front of a shop. Ivor Antiques, its sign says.

Gaylene bolts from the car, disappears down the lane. Maguire huffs after her, hitching up his pants, fastening his belt, stumbling in the dark before getting a glimpse of light from the rear open door of Ivor Antiques, Lucy hauling her bike in, the door clicking shut.

Maguire works his way around a trash bin, finds Gaylene with her ear pressed to that door. "Voices," she whispers. "Jackpot."

2
Friday, September 21

It's a quarter to three in the morning, and Maguire has his search warrant and a crew of six, armed and in full gear. He has posted three at the alley door to await a radio command to ram it open. He and three others are inside the antique store — the front door easily jimmied, your basic Yale lock.

Maguire is focussing hard on the tasks at hand as he struggles to achieve a state of denial over his awkward encounter with Lucy Wales. Her attempt to photograph him from a moving bike — surely that was a flubbed shot. He is frazzled nonetheless, was bumping into things in this crowded space, with all its furniture and bric-a-brac and art. But he made minimal noise and now keeps out of the way as his team quietly frisks the place, treading carefully, using pen flashlights.

Clearly, it's a front for a secret society of eco-activists. A member found paperwork and photos in the sales desk that revealed the owners to be Ivor Trebiloff and Amy Snider, husband and wife, white guy, black woman, big smiles. A quick pedigree check has them both with a few summary convictions, plus a felony in the States, while demonstrating for various noble causes. In case they're not in the backroom with the others, Maguire has sent Long Ling and Wiggie to their address in Islington to pick them up.

They've already got Wozniak, found him at the illegal squat at midnight, drinking beer, smoking weed, and plucking on an acoustic guitar. Gaylene is at HQ, cutting his papers, sitting him down for a little workout. Two other officers are in Lucy Wales's loft in Roncesvalles, shaking it.

Lucy Wales. Who led them here. After making a hideously wrong assumption with possibly mortifying consequences.

Yolo. You only live once. How can he possibly face that young snip? What could her shot through his windshield show? Probably just his head and shoulders, a guy behind a steering wheel. From the angle she took it, Gaylene's head and body would — hopefully — be hidden by the dashboard. But his insides are roiling with anxiety. That takeout slice the guys brought him doesn't help. Spicy salami with anchovies. Nor does the chocolate bar he ordered. He would kill for a cigarette.

The door to the backroom is not fastened by much more than an eye hook, and there's a gap atop it, emitting a bar of light. An electronic tech has stuck a miniature camera up there and set up a wireless monitor. Sound is off but you can see three individuals close together. One is Dr. Helmut Knutsen, likely the ringmaster, scrolling through a long document. Another is a tall, skinny, sharp-featured guy, about thirty, working the keyboard of a second computer. They are fuelling on coffee.

Lucy Wales is running both a printer and a copier, chatting, laughing. Is she regaling them about the old dude she saw getting head in the front seat of an old Buick? Maguire actually considers borrowing a helmet and visor to go in there. But how odd would that look? — he's still in his civvies. All he can do is pray to the Lord Almighty she will not recognize him.

Several minutes pass without much happening. It doesn't look like anyone else in the gang is dropping in. "Okay, stow the camera," Maguire says. A tech reaches up and puts it carefully in a pouch.

Maguire radios the team in the alley. "One, two, three, open sesame."

He puts his boot to the door, which crashes open. The lock on the back door splinters simultaneously, as cops pour in from both sides. A coffee pot spills, mugs clatter to the floor.

"Freeze! Nobody move!" Maguire's bellow is ignored by the tall, skinny dude, who is banging something out on his keyboard, maybe a self-destruct code. A SWAT guy tackles him roughly, and spins him to the floor.

Lucy Wales is on her feet, wide-eyed with shock, but capturing the action on her phone camera.

Knutsen has swivelled in his chair, is looking sadly at the helmeted men, the Smith and Wessons pointed at him. "Take it easy, officers," he says. "We're not armed."

"Get that tall fellow on his feet," Maguire says. "Cuff them."

Lucy Wales, prayers answered, shows no recognition of Maguire as a female officer clicks the mitts on her — she looks dazed, unfocussed. The officer pats her down, takes her phone. Maguire wants that phone, but right now it's going into an exhibit bag.

He clears his throat, introduces himself as Inspector Maguire, OPP, and announces they are under arrest for possession of stolen documents and conspiracy to break and enter. He narrates the standard police caution, then asks, "Anything you wish to say?"

No responses.

"All right, let's holster the arms. We're going to be friendly here. Professor Knutsen, we've had eyes on you folks for some time, so let's do this the easy way. You can help yourselves by telling us where you got these documents. We know you've been putting them online."

"I have nothing to say, Inspector."

Maguire ups the ante. "One of the security people at the plant was under attack and now he's in a state of suspended animation. If he doesn't make it we're looking at a homicide here. We can nip that in the bud if you tell me right now none of you meant to hurt anyone."

Maguire gets nothing. The average dumb-ass perp might go, "Honest, sir, I never meant to," but these guys are prepared, lawyered up.

Lucy is now staring at Maguire, and her eyes widen. "You followed me, didn't you?"

"Lucy," Knutsen says, a cautioning tone.

She shuts up, her dark, shadowed eyes still fixed on Maguire. A sneaky smile.

CHAPTER 11 » RIVIE

1
Friday, September 21

It's like a Tom Thompson painting but with the colours right in your face, coming at you in three dimensions, maybe four if you count the mind-bending effect of the karmic flower tops we're smoking. Bursts of crimson and fluorescent yellow from sugar maples and tamaracks, the redolent, oxygen-rich breezes from the piny forest, sunlight dappling the rushing stream and its swirling ponds.

I'm squatting beside our little dome tent, wholly gaged after a wee toke, my brain racing like a hamster on a wheel, buzzing with colour and confusion and errant thoughts and memories. It's an indica-based strain called Dance of Shiva — Chase scored it trekking in the Himalayas, just a couple of grams but a pinch trips you right out. Beats the piss out of the bud you get at your local pot shop.

I think it's late afternoonish, though time seems irrelevant. I don't know what day it is. I can't even count the days I've been here, at least a week since Doc sent me into exile. I'm Enemy Number

One, the Mata Hari of Operation Beekeeper, the cops are turning Toronto upside out and inside down. We heard on the radio they're flashing around photos of Lucy and me.

We're somewhere, only God and Chase know exactly, in the vastness of Algonquin Park, a two-day paddle from the last civilized outpost, where Chase parked his pickup and launched his canoe. Our kit includes tent, sleeping bags — two joined into one — a chess board, a deck of cards, several books, and a dwindling supply of condoms.

We kill time over Chase's portable chess set — he usually wins — and a few novels I brought, and Chase's thick history of Northwest explorers, complete with fold-out maps. He's totally into that kind of stuff, a wannabe Pierre Radisson or David Thompson. We sustain ourselves on granola and a wilderness survival diet of edible plants (Chase knows them all), roots, berries, fresh-caught trout, and something that seems close to love.

A flash of raspberry red, fluttering above, diving into the forest. "What's that?"

"Pine grosbeak." Chase is lying on his back on a bed of pine needles, resting after his twice-daily yoga routine. "Male. Common resident. Winters over."

I'm not sure I should be falling in love with Chase D'Amato. The pluses are he's handsome and physical and sexy and smart and resourceful and totally in tune with his universe. But it's his universe, the wilderness, the beyond. I'm a metro mouse, I'm not at my best here — it's kind of spooky. I need bustle, I need people, action, conflict. I need to join a demonstration once in a while.

And I don't like being dependent on a man, on anyone, to tell the truth.

It feels sort of like Stockholm syndrome. Though to get the full effect, I guess I have to go to Stockholm. Rivke Levitsky's bolthole.

I'm not her anymore, by the way. Nor Becky. I'm Marigold Bright. Such a cheerful name, bound to charm the immigration officers. Marigold Bright has a passport, a birth certificate, a Mastercard, a wallet full of jack in dollars, euros, and krona, and an open one-way ticket to Stockholm on Finnair. All tucked away in a trekkers' backpack, with my clothes, toiletries, blond wig, and black-framed, clear-lens specs — to match my passport photo — and a Lonely Planet guide to Sweden.

Chase doesn't want me to split. He thinks the idea of Europe is all kinds of stupid, that I can learn to tough it out in the Canadian woods. He has other lairs we can retreat to, farther north, isolated cabins, cottages owned by summer people, friends who'll let us crash for the winter months.

I'm torn. Doc warned that if "things blow up" — meaning if he and the others get busted — I've got to grab the first flight out of Pearson. Friends of Earth Survival Rebellion will meet me in Stockholm. I'll get working papers. I'll blend in, get Swedenized.

If things do blow up, how am I to know? There's zero phone reception here, and anyway my battery is almost dead. Our sole communication with the outside is a windup radio that gets a couple of signals, the CBC, a Pembroke station.

We tune in to the news at night, when there's better reception. We learn that Archie Gooch is still comatose. I am praying, in my way, for the poor schmendrick, sending vibes: *Wake up! Wake up! It was only a nightmare, Archie, none of it really happened.*

We also learn that more documents are being leaked, so the guys are still operating from the back of Ivor's. I miss them real bad. I miss the camaraderie, the love, the cool, wise comfort of Doc Knutsen. I miss Amy and Ivor and Okie Joe, crazy Ray and quirky, lovely, sloppy Lucy. I'm freaking at the thought I may never see them again.

A couple more winged visitors, white and grey, clicking and chuckling in the tree above, unafraid. A whiskey jack, Chase calls them, a grey jay. Different from the blue jays I've seen. (And speaking of which, they're nowhere in the pennant chase. Go Jays next year!)

Poor Howie. The CBC says he got dumped by Chemican. A reporter learned his apartment was taken apart. How he must hate me. A sacrifice to the greater good, I get that, but it doesn't ease the guilt. One day I may write him a letter, explain how he inadvertently helped save the planet.

Chase rises, picks up his fishing line, wades barefooted into the stream, casting for protein. Trout every day. Brook trout, lake trout, roasted over coals, with edible nuts and mushrooms that Chase insists are safe. He keeps a small fire going, which is sort of illegal out here, but it's mostly hot coals, fairly smokeless, near the water.

I think a lot of my mom and dad, how they must be worrying. I miss Mom's weekend calls. The cops must have traced them to their little socialist commune — it's only two hundred klicks due west of here, a burg called Golden Valley — and they've probably been grilled hard. But they're cool, my mains, especially Dad, a former director of the Civil Liberties Association. He'll have given them an earful.

I am spooked by the eerie call of a loon on a distant lake. Across the stream, a big fuzzy form moving between the poplar trees. I yell to Chase: "Bear!"

He calls back: "That look like a bear?"

It's a moose. Spooked by our shouts, it retreats back into the bush. But there are bears, black bears, we saw a couple while canoeing. And there are wolves too. I don't tell Chase about my bad dreams, generated by their nightly distant howling. Chase has a Bowie knife he keeps in a sheath, he doesn't believe in guns. Because I'm such a scaredy-cat he's rigged up ropes for easier access up a nearby climbing tree, a thick-waisted pine. But don't bears climb trees?

Evening is approaching with its autumn bite. The weed is wearing off. I throw some kindling on the fire and ready the bed of coals for the two sleek trout Chase is proudly holding by the gills.

§

The stars dazzle in a cloudless, moonless night. I am awed by their countless numbers, feel dwarfed into insignificance by the unknowable, infinite universe. The distant, strident calls of a wolf pack.

Nearer, an owl hoots. I shiver with cold and anxiety as I clamber from my clothes, don pyjamas, crawl into the sleeping bag, awaiting the warmth of Chase's body, wanting him close, inside me.

He is working the radio, a tiny flashlight in his teeth — it's time for the hourly news. A bombing in Marseilles, a school shooting in Texas, another crazy, racist tweet from Trump, and . . . news that causes me to shriek: the arrest last night of six persons charged with conspiracy and B and E'ing a Sarnia chemical plant!

"Oh, my God!"

"Be cool."

A blur of words on the radio. Former professor arrested with two others at St. Clair antique store. Three more picked up at their homes. All remanded for two days. Crown opposing bail. Voice clip from OPP Inspector Maguire. Culmination of ten days of intensive investigation. Computers seized. Stolen documents found. Search continuing for remaining suspects. Suspects! Plural. Means they're looking for Chase too.

Rivke Levitsky, alias Marigold Bright, must now dematerialize. Like, biggety bang.

2

We are out of the wilderness, and by late evening have settled into a crowded campground just off Highway 60. Though it's dark I don't want to be seen — my smug mug is all over the media — so I'm in a sleeping bag in the bed of Chase's old Chev pickup. That's where we'll crash until dawn. Meanwhile, Chase is off hunting for an outlet to power up our phones.

I'm spazzed. We paddled like demons on fire half last night and all day long under a searing Indian summer sun, me sitting forward, trying to match my *coureur de bois*'s fierce strokes, my arms aching, muscles screaming. Bears, moose, and beavers hurriedly made way. At sunset we beached onto the south shore of Opeongo Lake, tied up the canoe, fast-tracked to the camp's parking lot and Chase's truck.

The Northwest explorer finally returns, shaking his head. "The park office has power, but they won't let me in. There's a working pay phone outside, though."

The nearby tents have grown dark, the last Bunsen light doused. A soft squeal and grunt: a sharing of carnal knowledge. But there's no one wandering about. I pull my Jays cap down to shadow my eyes as Chase helps me from the truck. "Hold the fort," I say, and ache my way up the trail to the park office, where a yard light glows.

It's after ten. I'm hoping Selwyn Loo is a late-nighter. But he isn't and answers the operator groggily. "Yes, I'll accept," he says.

"It's me," I say. "I'm in—"

"Don't say. I have a safe line, but for the record we have solicitor-client privilege. We'll keep this short. You've heard?"

"Yes."

"You're well?"

"Bagged. Scared. Well enough."

"Okay. Sunday night at Pearson. Is that doable?"

"Doable . . ." My brain is in slow gear. "Okay, but . . ."

"No buts. You're ticketed. Finnair 5998, departs at ten p.m. You'll be met on arrival. Then we'll connect."

Awareness hits hard — there's no turning back. "Tell them I love them."

"Bless up. Be good. Be happy. And be careful."

3
Sunday, September 23

A soft kiss as Chase lets me out at Terminal 3. He has been my valiant knight. I will miss him, but we would never have made it past the soulmate level. We are wed to others — he to the starry skies of the great outdoors, Ms. Bright to brighter lights. Yet I tell him, as our lips part, that I love him, and to stay safe.

"And I love you. *Bon voyage.*"

I feel a vast void as I enter the terminal, collar up, cap down, bowed by my heavy pack, faux-blond bangs hanging over the spectacled eyes of my sunburned face. I'm praying that I look like the average young grad student off on a well-earned trekker's holiday to Scandinavia.

It's eight thirty, well past peak hour, but there are still too many people about for comfort. The ticketing machine whirrs, pauses, finally recognizes Marigold Bright and her reservation, spits out a boarding pass.

I don't fly much, on principle, but when I do, getting through security always brings butterflies. But I'm toting no gels, liquids, guns, or revolutionary handbooks. I've stuck my ticket and passport in my *Lonely Planet*, which I pretend to read, for effect, as we inch along. But the line is short, and soon I lower my pack and bag into a plastic basket.

At which point I feel the unwanted nearness of the dude behind me, bending by my ass as he pulls a laptop from his roller bag.

"First trip to Sweden?" he goes as he straightens beside me, looking at my guidebook. Swarthy, red-faced fellow, all eyeballs, an obvious cheeser the way he goofs at me.

"Thought I'd try it out."

"Fourth time for me. Doing a little buying. I'm in farm equipment. You'll like Stockholm. Forget the stodgy reputation. Lots of action if you know where to go."

"Yeah, that's what my boyfriend says. He's meeting me there."

That has the desired effect. "Enjoy," he says, and shuts up.

My goods pass inspection. I get a green light from the X-ray. Smooth. I'm in.

I make it swiftly to the Finnair boarding lounge, where I take a back seat and hide behind an abandoned *Toronto Star*. I flip through the pages with dread, grimace as I come upon the account of the bust, informing the masses that "the search continues for alleged co-conspirator Rivke Levitsky, alias Becky McLean." A grainy photo of Lucy and me backstage at the Bee-In. They might have found a better likeness had Doc not warned us to ditch all personal pix. He's depicted too, being ushered from a police van in handcuffs. My guru in tousled hair, sombre, brave.

The flight is called. I wait for my group to be called, then sidle forward. The airline attendant glances at the passport photo, at me, at my boarding pass, sends me cheerily on my way. I am shaking with relief as I head down the overhead tunnel, phone out, thumbing a text to Selwyn Loo: "Colour me gone."

But why is that smarmy farm equipment buyer standing there at the aircraft's door? Smiling at me. Blocking my way. Showing a badge.

"I regret to tell you, Ms. Levitsky, that you are under arrest."

§

Somehow, I have no tears. I'm not shaking. I'm beyond numb, anaesthetized by my despair. I have short-term memory loss, can't bring back my hour-long journey from the departure lounge to this police station. The last thing I remember was walking out, wedged in between a woman from the Peel Regional Police and Constable . . . Jensen? No, Jayson, him saying, "Just smile, we don't want to disturb the passengers," and then his smarmy, "Would you like me to call your boyfriend in Stockholm to tell him you'll be late?"

Actually, there is something else I remember: I quickly corrected my text-in-progress to Selwyn Loo. "Colour me BUSTED!" And hitting Send before Jayson confiscated the phone.

Then what? An airport security room, Jayson radioing his HQ. I can't remember when they cuffed me, or took them off. It's like a dream patchily remembered: leaving the airport by a back door, a squad car waiting, a quick, silent drive to Peel Regional Police Headquarters.

Now I'm in a glassed-in room, square and bare and oppressive, two chairs on each side of a long table on which the contents of my rucksack are spread. I'm sitting up straight, trying to look defiant, unbowed. I haven't shed a tear. I will not.

Two detectives are seated across from me: an old, overweight bull with a shaggy moustache, frowning at me over the rim of a takeout Starbucks. An OPP Inspector, Maguire. He showed me my arrest warrant: fraud, conspiracy, B and E, knowingly using a forged passport, false pretences, the list goes on. He then gave me a warning about my right to remain silent, which I am stubbornly invoking.

His companion is Sergeant Gaylene Roberts, thirtyish, genial, respectful. The good cop to Maguire's bad.

"Sorry we had to wait for the last minute to pull you in," she says. "We hoped to catch you with some of your confederates. No such luck. What should we call you? Rivie, as in your emails?"

"I have a right to see a lawyer, I believe."

"She talks," Maguire says. "It's a quarter after eleven, Rivie. Some folks might not think so, but lawyers are human, they need their sleep."

"I'd like to phone my lawyer, please." Selwyn Loo. He sleeps by his phone. *Be ultra cool.*

Sergeant Roberts: "You'll have loads of time before you're arraigned tomorrow to confer with counsel. Meantime, you can help yourself by answering a few simple questions. The courts can be very lenient to those who cooperate."

"I'll cooperate with my counsel, thank you."

Maguire: "Well, young lady, we better tell you we have a complete book on you. Had a good look around the loft you share with Lucy Wales. Cleaned the mess up while we were at it. Fed the cats even."

"Very kind of you."

"Maybe you were too stoned to remember to wipe your computer. Your Finnair open-date confirmation was in your trash folder. It just took a couple of calls to learn you reserved for tonight's flight."

I almost choke. I am my own worst enemy. "I'm not saying anything until I see my lawyer."

"By the way," he says, "Howie passes on his regards. You did a real nice job on him except you left your footprints in his discharge. Gives the concept of pecker tracks a new meaning."

Great undercover work, Levitsky. Like, fubar. "When can I see my lawyer?"

"Soon as we mug and print you at the OPP office," Maguire says. "That's where we're headed, so don't expect some damn lawyer is gonna appear out of the blue tonight."

"Can I have my phone?"

He bangs the table. "Goddamn, let's get serious here. There's a guy could turn into a vegetable for what you and your pals pulled off . . ."

A knock on the door. Jayson pokes his head in. "Need to confer, sir."

The three of them huddle by the door, speak low. Maguire swears. Looks at Roberts. Looks at me. "Son of a . . . How did he find us?"

"Phoned the desk sergeant here. Said he knows you, sir."

"Well, he can't come in. Unless he's a real dumb lawyer he knows the rules."

The door swings open, and a tall, beak-nosed septuagenarian coolly invites himself in. "Well, what do we have here?" Big, sonorous voice, big smile. Dark suit, white shirt, loosened tie.

"I'll be damned," says Maguire. "Arthur Beauchamp." The air seems to go out of him, but he manages a weary smile, offers his hand, introduces Gaylene Roberts, who looks ruffled, and waves Jayson from the room.

"You're looking well, Jake," Arthur says. "Thirty years ago, wasn't it? The Ciccini double homicide. We had drinks after."

"Yeah, I remember unloading on you about your so-called profession. No hard feelings, I hope. I've been following your career. Read somewhere you retired."

"I wish. What about you?"

"On the cusp. So they brought you all the way from Vancouver just to cop a plea? Because that's what you're looking at. This sucker is a wrap, counsellor."

"*Dum vita est spes est.* While I breathe, I hope."

This weird chit-chat has me sitting there with my mouth hanging open. Arthur Beauchamp, out of the blue. Did he parachute from the heavens? I've heard about him, Margaret Blake's husband, he's sort of famous. Bee-chem.

Finally, he turns to me, swallows my hand with a leathery, warm grip as he studies me with clear-eyed intensity. Somehow he feels like a long-lost favourite uncle.

"How are you feeling?"

"Pissed. They wouldn't let me call a lawyer."

"I'm sure they feel bad about that. Well, you have a lawyer now." He turns to Maguire. "You won't mind if my client and I have a few minutes?"

"Five minutes, then we take her in for processing." Maguire leads Roberts out.

It's chilly in here, so why is Mr. Beauchamp taking off his suit jacket? To impress me with his red suspenders? I finally get it. "This will serve nicely as a coat hanger," he says, and drapes the jacket over the lens of a security camera.

He draws up a chair, close, confiding, and explains the miracle of his sudden arrival. He flew in from Vancouver late this afternoon, was met by Selwyn Loo, and their first stop was a remand jail. He was interviewing Doc and the gang when my SOS came in. A few phone inquiries, a taxi ride, and he was here within the hour.

"I blew it," I say. "They found my plane ticket in my trash folder."

"I assumed it was something like that. This is no doubt a very harrowing experience, Rivie. But I'm told you're a tough, resilient young woman, and you seem to have yourself remarkably together.

Take a deep breath and relax as best you can. Now, have you said anything to them?"

"Only about wanting a lawyer, Mr. Beauchamp. Said it a hundred times, a mantra."

"Okay, good. They're going to take you to the OPP building for photographs and prints, and you'll be in a cell overnight. Be pleasant with them, talk about the weather if you like, or movies or music, but otherwise keep your thoughts to yourself. That goes for everyone, other persons you may meet, prisoners too. They often like to set one up as an informant."

I nod. "What about the night duty guard who won't wake up? Gooch. What if he dies?"

"Let us hope he doesn't. In any event, no blame can attach to you or your friends for a mishap suffered by a fellow so poorly trained by his employer."

I find that comforting. Blame Chemican. "I hope it's not crass to ask who's looking after your fees."

He frowns, as if confused by the question. "I'm not sure if anyone is. Scratch that off your worry list."

I'm assuming he's pro bono — he's a friend of Selwyn Loo, who's a friend of Margaret Blake. "Okay, thank you — really, I'm grateful. But please level with me. I'm guilty. I did it and I'm glad, but they're laying a whole bunch of shit on me, it's like I blew up the Parliament Buildings. Plus there's a prime witness who wants to crucify me. So maybe it's easier for him, me, you, the judge, the Crown, the system, the Canadian taxpayer, if I just plead guilty and do my time."

He looks at me severely. "That is an utterly ridiculous thought, if I may be blunt." He rises with a sigh, reclaims his jacket. "We'll have time to talk at more length before remand court tomorrow. You will also meet your alleged confederates there. I'll be seeking what we call Judicial Interim Release — legalese for bail. We'll have to see where that goes."

"Where that goes" doesn't sound too encouraging. But I take a deep breath and the tension releases its grip. I smile and thank him. I fight off an urge to hug him.

Bee-chem. *Bee*-chem.

4
Monday, September 24

I spend a lonely, sleepless night in an OPP cell that reeks of disinfectant, a pillow wrapped around my ears to muffle a morbid soundtrack of metallic clanks and obscene jokes from the cops watching that I don't hang myself. I struggle to come to grips with a shitty future: lost freedom, lost youth, lost hope.

They let me have some clothes from my pack to change into. And they provided room service. How delightful: an Egg McMuffin, canned juice, and coffee that could have been brewed in a septic tank.

It can't possibly get any worse than this. I make a vow to get on top of myself. Accept facts, get real. So I fucked up. So we got busted, too bad, so sad. Now we just ride it out. We're going to do time, I'm tough, I can get my head into that. An extended holiday, I'll read books, take courses. Ten years, fourteen? Nelson Mandela did nearly thirty.

After breakfast, I'm fetched downtown to the courthouse, Old City Hall, to the women's lockup in the basement, and they put me in an interview room where Mr. Beauchamp waits, doing a crossword puzzle. He is in a funereal suit, but with his flashy red suspenders. He abruptly rises and welcomes me, in his courtly, old-school manner. He tells me he has spoken to my mom and dad, and they are on the way.

"They both impressed me as thoughtful and caring and wise." He adds, "They love you dearly," and I am doomed, I go to pieces, a tropical downpour.

He knows I've been fighting against this moment, this loss of defences, and he goes: "Courage, Rivie." He takes my hand, the one not grasping a wet ball of Kleenex, and tells me a sad-funny story about the small island he calls home, and his own recent arrest during a protest that fizzled in the rain. This coaxes a smile, even a raspy, feeble laugh.

I expect him to put on his grave face and instruct me about my criminal charges and my chances, but he prefers to entertain me with the escapades of a giant dog called Ulysses. It's an almost superhuman task to picture this straight old dude, with his vaguely Victorian manner, as his apparent alter ego: a grass-stem chewer who raises goats on a funky nowhere island and gets busted with the yokel locals. The sixties must have skipped right past him, and maybe he's trying to make up. Which is kind of cool and lovable.

Through all this, he holds my hand, and I remind myself this is a professional relationship, it's business, however unprofitable for him, and I unclasp. I want to tell him I'll work off my debt on his farm. Bumble Bay? Bungle Bay? I'll feed the goats, harvest the arugula, shovel the chicken manure.

He knows, from Selwyn Loo, about my junket to Algonquin Park with Chase D'Amato, who is named in the indictment as a co-conspirator, along with "divers others." Beauchamp doubts they can link Chase to Operation Beekeeper, even though his prints may be found in Ivor Antiques.

I think about choices. I could have buggered off with Chase. I could be snuggling with him right now in a log cabin somewhere in the True North. Oh, well.

Mr. Beauchamp says no pleas will be entered today, no trial date set, but there'll be a tussle over bail. A "show cause" hearing, he calls it, and the cause the Crown may show is that I'm a flight risk. I go, "Me? Marigold Bright?" His face crinkles handsomely when he laughs.

He has enough dope on me, from Lucy and Doc, I guess, and my folks, to make a pitch for my interim release. I don't have great answers for the few questions he asks.

Career aspirations: "Something to do with words and concepts. Teaching? Journalism? Escape fiction?" (I dare not say I harbour the pretentious notion of writing the Great Canadian Novel. I'm too embarrassed to admit I'm several chapters into it.) Religion: "Faithless Jew." (I know he wants me to say I'm into God and the whole shtick, but I can't.) Games, hobbies, sports, pastimes? "Chess, hiking, cycling, reading, dreaming of a better world, and, um, Major League Baseball."

§

I'm escorted to a lockup area locally called the "bullpen," and am accosted by a character with boozy breath, in a suit he must have slept in. "What do you say, honey, you look like you could use a little legal aid. You're in luck, I'm on a hot streak."

I assume he's some kind of excuse for a lawyer who snuck in here to blatantly hustle clients. I tell him I have a real lawyer, the world's best, then make a beeline for my buds, the six other members of the Sarnia Seven, as the media are already calling us.

While police guards watch, I am swept up in a mass hug. We're together again! Doc Knutsen and Lucy and Okie Joe, Rockin' Ray and Amy and Ivor, your friendly neighbourhood eco-terrorists.

Doc looks gothically bagged but insists he is fine, he is proud: "Our current discomforts are dwarfed by our great accomplishment. We have won, Rivie, we have alerted the world. No matter what happens now or next day or next year, we have won. We have done something memorable for humankind and for all living things on this planet."

And suddenly, during this stirring sermon, I find myself going, Hey, girl, you whiny bitch, quit moaning over your mistakes and petty pains, you should feel proud and happy — like Ivor Trebiloff and Amy Snider over there, both of them smiling and composed, tested warriors who've done protest time, six months in one case in

North Dakota, and have lived lives of no regrets. They were arrested in their pyjamas on Friday night and carried bodily to a bun wagon.

They have their arms around Okie Joe, who also looks totally serene in the knowledge that he has done good and important work.

Right on, Dr. Helmut Knutsen. Thanks for reminding me what this was all about. The Earth Survival Rebellion rang loud the gong, warning the world they're killing our bugs and birds. We exposed monstrous lies. Chemican is flailing, blaming everything on bad apples among their scientists who did faulty tests or lied about the results. Several have been fired, and are being welcomed into the offices of litigation lawyers.

These latest panic reactions, says Doc, prove indelibly that we have won. And it is not out of the question, he adds, that we will win at a more tangible level. Like how, I wonder. Some technicality?

And what about poor Archie Gooch, still surviving in tubes and diapers? "Shit happens," says Doc. Does that sound insensitive? I'm not sure.

The sleazy lawyer, who is the kind they make jokes about — *so they threw the lawyer off the plane instead* — holds out a business card to Rockin' Ray. "Yo, hombre, here's your ticket to freedom. I do legal aid on the taxpayer's dime. A hole in my calendar just opened up this morning. You wanna fill it?"

Though off his drugs, Ray looks spacey, maybe because he's confused by the previously unknown condition of being straight. He focuses on the lawyer, then goes, "Definotly."

Lucy and I laugh. Here we are, besties again, different setting, different plot, cracking up over a scumbag lawyer. She's gold-haired still, but without the audacious makeup, which somehow makes her look nymph-like and forlorn. But she's all about facing the inevitable and seeking the bright side. "It's not like the old movies, sweetie, modern jail is almost cushy. We're first-timers. Go directly to medium security, take workshops in behaviour adjustment."

She's less worried about herself than her lover. Ray is the only one of the Sarnia Seven they can physically tie to the raid at the Vigor-Gro plant. His DNA has to be all over the safety equipment he tossed in the bush.

"They nabbed him naked in his room in the squat," Lucy says. "Along with his hash pipe, a pound of bud, two grams of whiff, and ten hits of acid."

So he faces this additional array of drug charges, plus the likelihood of being deported to the States, where he's looking at an assault charge for putting out the lights of a vocal fascist at a Donald Trump event in Fresno. He came up here on the new North America Refugee Act but never got around to filling out all the forms. I'm guessing Ray is not a solid candidate for bail.

Oklahoma Joe, who has his working papers but not immigrant status, could also be deported. I'd almost forgotten he has a real name — when I looked at the list of conspirators, I went: Who is Joe Meekes?

We continue to huddle and exchange recent adventures, pumping each other up as we get ready to make our first public appearance since reuniting, like an old eighties punk band. We expect a full house, we expect fans, heartening vibes, pumped fists.

I like our label, the Sarnia Seven — the rhythm, the alliteration, the good-luck numeral. The Sarnia Eight doesn't work as well, so I'm glad the media are ignoring unindicted conspirator Chase D'Amato. They haven't clued into our proper underground name either, the Earth Survival Rebellion, or connected us to Résistance Planétaire. Which is good, we're not seen as part of some intergalactic conspiracy.

Lucy takes me aside, cups my ear, launches into a whispered, hilarious side story from just before she got busted — about Inspector Maguire getting his nob sucked in the front seat of a big old Buick by his sidekick Sergeant Gaylene Roberts.

I am stifling laughter, but also wondering if Lucy embellished. But she insists she saw his belt undone, Roberts's bramble of hair obscuring the activity below. Also, she has — or had — circumstantial evidence, a photo taken through the windshield showing only his head, presumably as Gaylene was giving head below.

But her phone was seized, and doubtless the photo erased. We work through the implications of that — falsification of evidence, could that poison the Crown's case?

An overweight creep decorated with swastika tattoos is escorted into the bullpen and relieved of his handcuffs. As he's led toward the stairs up to bail court he gives Ray a Nazi salute — they've obviously exchanged a few discourtesies in the male lockup. The freak calls, "My mouthpiece says I'm gonna get bailed, suckers."

Rockin' Ray yells, "Stick it, you scumsucking pus bag."

This prompts him to shoot back at us, with, "They're gonna lock your asses up, you nigger-loving commie shits." I give him a middle finger. Unfortunately for him, he looks at me, salaciously, making a slurp sound, when he should be looking at his Indo-Canadian police escort and the half-open door he's led into.

A court officer comes in to announce that we have to wait for our debut until after the mid-morning break, and we're being moved to a bigger court. Apparently we're of higher status than other prisoners because we'll be in front of a real judge, not a justice of the peace. I don't know if that's bad or good.

CHAPTER 12 » ARTHUR

1
Monday, September 24

Arthur has found it a rare delight to defend those who are actually innocent, as opposed to not provably guilty, and rarer still to defend those like Rivke Levitsky who defy the law on justifiable moral grounds and want proudly to be seen as guilty. *I did it and I'm glad.*

But it concerns him that this spunky rebel is at serious risk of a lengthy term in the penitentiary. He'd felt unable to say that this morning — she was unhappy enough, surrendering to tears at the mention of her parents' love.

Sharon and Holden Levitsky don't own a vehicle, so are coming in by bus. Sharon is a botanist, and excels in identifying the wild edibles they thrive on; Holden taught literature at a community college before taking early retirement. Arthur finds much to admire about their low-impact, back-to-the-land lifestyle — an achievement he himself strives for when he is not flying across the continent, living in hotel rooms, and dining in fine restaurants.

Their daughter is worthy of the best defence Arthur can muster, as are her half-dozen confederates. Arthur would have felt like a coward had he not taken them on, and an ingrate given what he owed Selwyn for his toil and generosity in thwarting the despoilers of Quarry Park. So Arthur had no choice but to saddle up and strap on his guns one last time.

He'd spent much of Saturday running through a checklist of essential chores with Stefan and Solara, and the rest of the day rambling through the woods with Ulysses. On Sunday morning, after making him promise not to run off again — "or that bad man will put you in a cage" — Ulysses stood as tall as his master to give him a loving goodbye hug. Arthur headed off wet-eyed to catch his flight.

These memories and musings carry him from the downstairs lockup to the grand lobby of Old City Hall, an ornate nineteenth-century Romanesque structure of debatable beauty that is adorned with a clock tower with a five-ton bell. A National Historic Site, yet for the last half century it has been the busiest courthouse in Canada, a judicial beehive. It houses the Ontario Court of Justice, better known as the provincial courts, where the multitudes are judged, where Legal Aid lawyers toil, and where bored young prosecutors direct traffic.

After admiring the flamboyant lobby Arthur carries on to the lawyers' lounge, where he finds Nancy Faulk making notes from Operation Vigorous's skimpy investigation reports.

Arthur had needed a co-counsel familiar with local waters, and Nancy kept her promise by dropping everything — except her own divorce proceedings — to help him navigate them. A Toronto native with a working-class upbringing, she's savvy, tough, but abrasive, and has fought and mostly won in the local courts for over twenty years.

Her firm is Faulk, Quan, Dubois, three radical feminists. That would have made Arthur uncomfortable in years past, but he has been well trained on how to behave by Margaret's many critiques of a failing she calls his "old-fashionedness." Liberated of false values, Arthur has lately been confiding to male friends that he himself is a feminist.

The boardroom of Faulk, Quan, Dubois will be home base for the defence in *Regina v. Knutsen et al*. Nancy Faulk will be on the record for Ivor Trebiloff and Amy Snider, who though charged with breaking and entering the Sarnia plant have the best of defences: they weren't there. Nor do they face overwhelming proof that they joined a criminal conspiracy.

Arthur and Nancy have time to chat before they're due in bail court, 101. "I assume you've met the Levitskys," he says.

"And aren't they the upbeat, über-self-reliant, nineteenth-century Utopians. I'm taking them to the Vanier lockup, then to my place, and I'm giving them my king bed. The one on which I used to open my pussy to a prick named Stanley." Her husband, also a lawyer. Nancy has shorter hair and wider hips and more worry lines but is still lovely and just as bouncy and irreverent as when they last shared a courtroom, over a decade ago, the Island Airport gold heist.

She tends to ramble on, cynical, with a soupçon of self-pity. "The Levitskys have been hippily married for almost forty of their sixty years. Drop out, live sustainably, grow your own pot, is that the answer? I'm forty-five and I've struck out three times. Delete that — I walked three times. Backed out. Now I've got a reputation as anti-commitment, and only married guys will sleep with me." She smiles, sensing Arthur's unease. "Relax, you're not my type. I go for the weak egos."

"Clearly you have left a trail of broken hearts made stuporous by your radiant charm and beauty."

She laughs. "You're still a total fraud. What's with the uncool red braces?"

"A fetish. They can also be used as a weapon of distraction. Who will be our judge?"

"God, ultimately. Not funny, sorry. They're planning a special bail hearing in the old council chambers, and we'll be before Chuck Tchobanian. Started off as a streetwise storefront lawyer, then got straight or got religion or some fucking thing, became a Crown, now on his third year on the provincial bench. Unpredictable, cynical, teeming with sellout guilt, no patience with bullshit."

"Do we want him doing bail?"

"If he's in a good mood. Otherwise he's a pain. So keep it light."

"Crown Counsel?"

"Magnus Curlbotham, anal, harmless, but he's instructed to oppose bail all the way down the line."

"By whom?"

"Deputy A.G. Azra Khan. Cunning, combative, conservative. Charming, though. And sexy."

"I know him only by reputation. He set some manner of record, did he not?"

"Thirty-eight straight convictions. Half of them homicides. Ontario record."

"Lucky for us he's now a bureaucrat. When do we get discovery?"

"I'm trying to nail down Magnus for tomorrow, after we're done with bail. The two chief investigating officers are available. Did you hear about their presumed blow job?"

"Indeed." He'd interviewed Lucy Wales in the women's remand centre on Sunday. She claimed to have seen Gaylene Roberts's face buried in Maguire's crotch, pants open, belt undone. She'd captured him on her iPhone camera through the windshield as she pedalled away.

Lucy had impressed him as a bawdy but forthright young woman, saying: "Tell the old bull I got nothing against blow jobs. In fact I'm all in favour. He wants to drop his pants *and* the charges I'll give him one to remember for life."

2

"T.J. Gully," says the well-whiskered little man. "I manage Panic Disorder."

"And you seem to be managing it very well," Arthur says. He got corralled by this odd, bushy-bearded fellow outside the old council chambers, while waiting for it to be put in order for the bail hearing.

He had emerged from a throng of young champions of the accused. Arthur assumes the cotton mills were busy over the weekend churning out slogan-wear for their yellow T-shirts: "To Bee or Not to Bee," "Bee-Dazzle," "Chemican Kills," "Save the Sarnia 7." Several tops are decorated with black-and-yellow honeybee stripes.

"Panic Disorder, my good fellow, is a musical ensemble that is standing on the very doorstep of stardom. Your client, Mr. Wozniak, is its resident genius, its heart, mind, and soul. I have just engaged them to open for the Frank Zappa Revival Band."

Arthur backs up a step, away from the sour alcohol breath. "We will do our best for Mr. Wozniak."

Gully closes the gap. "If they don't let him back on the street, sir, it's a disaster of catastrophic dimension. Cancelled dates. No tours, not even bar gigs for his four fellow musical artists, who will be thrown on the mercies of the welfare system. My own career as impresario would be severely damaged, though that is my least concern."

He carries on in this vein for some time. Arthur thanks him, tells him to stick around. Despite his florid manner of speech, T.J. Gully might have some use as a character witness.

§

The former council chambers, reformatted as a grand courtroom, are crowded and busy, almost Hogarthian with bustle: lawyers, clerks, court officers, dozens of reporters. In the public gallery, amid the hoi polloi of Toronto citizenry, sit the costumed young radicals.

These hypothetical disrupters of order are being watched by flinty-eyed court officers, stationed at doors and about the room. The Crown Attorney, Magnus Curlbotham — middle-aged, thin, slicked hair — seems nervous, maybe because of all the bee venom being directed his way.

Arthur turns to see Inspector Jake Maguire and Sergeant Gaylene Roberts take seats behind him. She waves, but he acknowledges Arthur with only a nod. Arthur returns a wink intended as a message: *I know about you two.* Proof of fellatio is only on Lucy's say-so but upsetting enough that Jake may have been prompted to wipe the photo from her phone. Tampering with evidence has been known to cause mistrials. Arthur will bank that one, hoping to earn interest.

The Sarnia Seven aren't heavily guarded when fetched to court — a sign that security doesn't see them posing much risk. As they assemble in the prisoners' dock, they are greeted with claps and cheers. Arthur is piqued to see Rivie Levitsky waving back and Rockin' Ray bowing theatrically to his fans. The clerk seems unsettled by such untoward behaviour, and her calls for order issue from a dry throat.

Judge Tchobanian, however, shows unexpected patience, and waits for the noise to peter out before warning that courts are solemn institutions, not to be treated as cheap carnivals. Then he adds, "Anyone who acts up again will be booted out of here." He's enjoying himself, playing to the media.

Arthur goes on record for his five clients and Nancy for her two. The judge gives Rivie Levitsky an especially long look — she's attractive, an alleged seductress, already a counter-culture star. "Okay, looks like we have seven candidates for interim release. Mr. Curlbotham, I'd like an overview of the Crown's case."

The Crown Attorney weeds through his notes. "Overview, yes, give me a moment, please, Your Honour." Finally, he beckons Maguire, who leans over the barristers' rail and hands him a summary. Curlbotham has not done his homework. Arthur dislikes lazy prosecutors; they make one dull, overconfident.

The gist of the script is this: Chemican's Security Chief was "compromised" by the accused Levitsky, who obtained access to its Sarnia plant's security codes through false pretences, enabling her confederates to make secret entry and steal important documents and digitized information and cause the company multiple millions in losses. Their illegal acts led to a security guard's near demise and he remains in a coma. The police caught three of them "red-handed with the fruits of their crime," three others at their homes, and one while attempting to flee the country with a forged passport. Fingerprints, DNA matching, boot imprints, seized documents, and hard drives are all to be introduced as proof, along with "matters still being investigated."

He sits. Arthur rises. "My overview will be succinct, Your Honour. Whatever the Crown proves or fails to prove, we are not dealing with hardened criminals driven by avarice or any other wrong-headed motive." He moves closer to the dock, where the prisoners are still on their feet. "These men and women with whom I stand are idealists who are guilty only of seeking to alert humankind to an environmental threat of global concern. But none are guilty of a criminal conspiracy, and I want to announce that loudly, clearly, and confidently."

Proclaimed with a snap of his suspenders. A morsel of bravado for the press, who serve the eyes and ears of the Toronto public, from whom a twelve-person jury may be chosen some months from now. Arthur's little speech prompts muffled concurrence from the gallery, and one "Whoop." But security officers can't pick out the whooper from the sympathizers' ranks, and Tchobanian seems willing to let this one go.

"Ms. Faulk?" he says.

Nancy doesn't bother to rise. "I'll be even more succinct. There is no evidence that either of my clients did anything wrong."

"Okay, let's arraign them one by one. Mr. Curlbotham, who do you want to call first?"

"Helmut Knutsen."

The judge invites the other six to sit, and they do. The clerk recites the charges against Knutsen without faltering: counts of conspiracy, breaking and entering, theft, and possession of stolen property. This will be a template for all accused, with minor variations.

"My client will reserve his election and his not-guilty plea," Arthur says with a nod to the press table. He's undecided whether to elect a trial by jury or judge alone. A judge like Tchobanian, for instance, who seems quick and smart and doesn't truckle to the Crown.

But getting the accused out on bail is a vital first step. It makes everything safer and easier — conversations are strained in the barren interview rooms of prisons. When a client is remanded in custody there's often too much rush to get the trial on.

Curlbotham finds the police notes about Knutsen. They're subtly designed to portray him as a kind of chronic obsessive, an academic renegade with a chip on his shoulder, citing his many "inflammatory" writings on neonics and other pesticides and his dismissal by UC San Diego. Since then, he "appears to have been hiding out."

"What's that mean?" Tchobanian asks.

Curlbotham glances again at his sheet. "No listed phone number or mailing address, just a box number. The Crown believes he is the inspirational leader for this attack on private property and that he also engineered Ms. Levitsky's attempt to flee the jurisdiction with a false passport. So he too could be a flight risk." He stops reading, takes flight on his own: "These are serious crimes involving vast financial and property damage. The Crown has met its onus. Bail should be denied."

Knutsen continues to present as calm, dignified, pleasant, interested, and he has managed to fight off his tendency toward a sardonic tilt of eyebrow. A well-spoken and engaging fellow, he had listened carefully to Arthur's advice on the proprieties of the courtroom. Obviously brilliant as a scientist but maybe Curlbotham's allusion to an obsessive tendency was not off the mark.

Arthur rises. "My friend seems to feel that living a quiet, private, contemplative life is somehow suspicious, if not altogether sinful. Dr. Knutsen rents a studio room. He is working on a book to be published next year. Please give these to His Honour." He passes a folder to the clerk. "There are more on their way but this is a selection of letters commenting on his character and repute, mostly from academics but also one from a United Church minister and another from his publisher."

Arthur's manner is businesslike, get-it-done. This judge had seemed impatient with clever words and displeased when Arthur played to the media. "The Crown can offer no proof Dr. Knutsen was among the group that entered the Sarnia plant on the night of September eleven. Yes, he was present when allegedly stolen documents were being posted online, but who's to say he wasn't merely invited to witness that?"

Curlbotham rises in an effort to respond, but Tchobanian waves him down. He has merely glanced at the letters. "Dr. Knutsen will be released on ten thousand dollars, one surety."

Arthur is deadpan but delighted: a token form of bail, requiring only a friend's signature.

Curlbotham seems to shrug it off. He can at least tell the Deputy A.G. he tried. "I call Joe Meekes."

Oklahoma Joe, as his mates know him, takes his turn standing while the several counts are recited. Arthur had not found him easy to talk to: shy, taciturn, a loner, a Bernie Sanders socialist, and the ultimate cyber wonk.

Curlbotham turns to another page of his police notes: "Mr. Meekes is an American citizen who came to Canada some fourteen months ago under the new North American Refugee Act, and has not found gainful employment. We believe he has a degree in computer technology and specializes in breaking security codes. The Crown will be alleging he hacked and disarmed Chemican's locks and alarm systems. He was caught in the act of uploading documents stolen from them and had to be physically restrained. There is no reason to believe he will remain in Canada for his trial. Crown strongly opposes bail."

Tchobanian nods approvingly — in this contest of brevity, Curlbotham is threatening to out-duel his opponent.

Arthur replies: "Yes, Mr. Meekes is an expert in hacking, and in fact worked for the Google Corporation in Mountain View, California, for three years developing code that would detect and block criminal hacking activity. He makes a living as an international computer consultant, working online from his Toronto apartment. He has no criminal record. He pays his taxes, and supports his widowed mother in Tulsa, though he is committed to Canada. He loves this, his new, welcoming home."

Curlbotham sags a little. He makes no effort to reply. The judge lets Oklahoma Joe out on a ten-thousand surety but he must render up his passport and remain within the Greater Toronto Area.

"Ivor Trebiloff and Amy Snider, I'm calling them together." Curlbotham knows the gods do not favour him today, but he has his instructions and he plows on, describing this married couple as running an antique business as a cover for nefarious activities. Each has histories of radical protest and criminal records for contempt of court, trespassing, causing a disturbance, and resisting arrest.

Ivor and Amy stand tall during this, holding hands: in their sixties, veteran lefties doubtless with prized collections of peace buttons. Those four convictions are dwarfed by the scores of times they'd gotten arrested but not charged at a myriad other protests, which they attend as some do whist nights or flower shows, almost compulsively.

Nancy Faulk takes a turn. Her clients were solid senior citizens who'd owned their Toronto home for thirty years and their business for twenty. The resisting arrest charge occurred forty years ago in Biloxi, Mississippi, outside the church of a racist preacher who was inciting lynch mobs. That's where Amy and Ivor met and fell in love. The other arrests occurred at a protest on behalf of the Sioux Nation of North Dakota, a Detroit rally against the invasion of Iraq, and an event outside the Turkish embassy in Ottawa. There was no evidence they entered into a conspiracy or did anything wrong in relation to Chemican-International.

Arthur is proud of Nancy. The Turkish Embassy event was an artful touch, Tchobanian's roots being Armenian.

"They'll be released on their personal bond," the judge says. "Who's next?"

"Call Lucy Wales."

She looks slightly amused as the charges are read, maybe because she finally noticed the couple sitting nearby: Sergeant Roberts, reputed penilinguist, and her reputed felatee. Curlbotham makes a point of how this twenty-two-year-old student just got fired as a part-time pharmacy employee. As he carries on about how her apartment was festooned with anarchist posters and leaflets, Jake Maguire motions him to pause.

They huddle for a second, then Curlbotham announces: "The Crown does not oppose the accused's release on her own undertaking."

The gung-ho Deputy Attorney General will wonder what caused this cowardly surrender. Maguire's motive doesn't escape Arthur, though. Or Nancy, whom he catches grinning.

Tchobanian simply shrugs. "I expect you're fine with that, Mr. Beauchamp?"

"My learned friend has a kind heart. I trust he will be similarly generous to my remaining clients." Rockin' Ray and Rivie.

But Curlbotham proclaims, "Those two cases cry out for pre-trial incarceration." He has decided to put some effort into this. "The evidence against them is exceptionally strong. Both are flight risks. I call the case of Raymond Wozniak."

The lanky young musician stands wearily, scratches his stubble, tosses back his long blond tresses, takes a look back at his adoring fans, then smiles patronizingly down at Curlbotham, as if challenging him to do his worst.

The case against Wozniak is in fact blacker than Arthur had hoped. Helmet, goggles, ear protectors, and the red plastic gloves he'd abandoned in the bush near the plant all bore his DNA. Curlbotham is able to trumpet the unassailable proof that Ray was the wild-haired ghoul who smashed open the Vigor-Gro tanks with a crowbar, then pursued two guards in turn, screaming, "You are the archfiend, I am the avenger!" causing one of the guards to collapse and be put on life support.

Judge Tchobanian has obviously followed media reports of the incident and of Archie Gooch's plight. "This accused never touched him, though, right? You haven't charged him with any kind of assault, so why is this relevant?"

Curlbotham falls back on the potpourri of six drug charges Ray faces: various quantities of hash oil, opium, cocaine, LSD, and mescaline, not to mention "an unlawfully excessive amount of marijuana," were found in his illegal flat. That alone, he says, should keep him sequestered. As well, he still faces an assault indictment in California and is now charged with assaulting a Canadian peace officer. This relates to an allegation that he urinated on a constable from the upstairs window of his squat while other officers were bursting into his room.

His Honour appears to be struggling to suppress mirth. "He seems a menace to society, Mr. Beauchamp — are you sure you want him out?"

Arthur maintains a straight face. As to the assault PC, he says Wozniak had no idea the officer was standing beneath a vision-obscuring maple tree. He is wanted in the U.S. for scuffling with a pro-Trump demonstrator, so he's hardly likely to make a run for the border. He plays lead guitar in a popular local rock band, whose four other members will be forced onto the dole if he's not freed. The band is committed to a coming event to raise funds for cerebral palsy. Their manager, Mr. Gully, is here and can attest to that.

The hairy little man rises from several rows back. Tchobanian looks at him for a long moment, then waves him back to his seat.

"Thirty thousand, cash or property bond. Passport to be surrendered. Prior approval for travel outside Toronto. Report twice weekly to Fourteen Division for drug test. No drugs or alcohol or this bail order will be revoked."

Ray responds with a sound like "Whoa" or maybe "Woe."

Tchobanian, looking at him severely: "You have a problem with that?"

"No, man, Your Honour, I just had a stomach cramp."

Arthur gets him to sit before more damage is done, and Rivie quickly takes his place, even before her name is called.

Her particulars, as recited by the Crown, are widely known: the seduction of Howell Griffin, her arrest at the Toronto airport. She faces a bundle of charges.

"A conniving Mata Hari," says Curlbotham. "Our records show she is single, college educated, and practically a full-time agitator. She has no possible answer to the forged passport charge, which by itself merits a custodial sentence. She is at extreme risk of running."

Arthur lacks a strong response but does what he can. There was no proof she was party to the break-in. No proof she committed any offence relating to Mr. Griffin or his property. Mere seduction was not listed in the Code as a crime. Curlbotham seeks to deny her the presumption of innocence on the passport charge. No prior record. Lived all her twenty-three years in Toronto. Loving, supportive parents. Her ambition was to become a writer.

Arthur can tell he's losing Tchobanian. He may be reflecting on the shame he might suffer were this slippery actor to turn up suddenly in Stockholm. Many judges try overcautiously to balance the scales — if they give too much to the defence they have to toss a bone to the Crown.

Arthur works harder. He warns that with the backlog in Ontario courts this trial might not come on for at least a year, maybe two. A jury trial could take several weeks. It was a complex case, with many side issues — for instance, the true role of the Crown's prime witness, Mr. Howell Griffin: Was he duped or did he collaborate?

The latter is a fat, gleaming red herring, but Arthur casts for it anyway. It will help feed the press.

"So it would seem quite unfair, Your Honour, that Ms. Levitsky could face lengthy interim custody, given a backlog that is no fault of hers, while presumed innocent of these charges."

Tchobanian studies her with frowning intensity. She looks right back at him, unflinching, Saint Joan daring her interlocutor. Arthur imagines him wondering if a famous but mellowed version of this young radical could one day write a memoir about having been wrongfully martyred by a small-time provincial judge.

"Fifty thousand surety, no passport, no access to any airport, no straying beyond the City of Toronto, standard terms apply. Ms. Levitsky will wear an ankle monitor twenty-four-seven until this court otherwise orders."

"Even when I shower?" Rivie says.

If she's teasing Tchobanian it works: he colours. Almost everyone in the room, including the judge, is either imagining her naked or trying not to. Except Arthur, who has quickly developed a grandfatherly affection for his client.

The judge regains his composure. "Transmitting bracelets, Ms. Levitsky, are not only waterproof but tamper-proof."

"Your Honour, won't that impede me? I ride a bicycle everywhere, and I'm sponsored for the Cycle Against Cystic Fibrosis Rally next month."

Arthur can't suppress a smile. Curlbotham makes a weak effort to complain but Tchobanian waves him off. "Okay, Ms. Levitsky, cancel the monitor but you'd better be prepared to bike twice a week to sign in at Fourteen Division." To counsel: "Can we adjourn a week to fix? I'll be in 126 Court that day, and I'm assigning this case to my list."

Arthur and Nancy chime their glad consent. Curlbotham rolls his eyes before assenting: this judge has shown himself too cozy with the enemies of the state.

The clerk calls out, "Case adjourned to Monday, September twenty-eight."

As the room empties, Inspector Maguire beckons Arthur to join him behind the witness stand.

"What was that big, fat wink about, counsellor?"

"Merely a friendly message, Jake."

"She told you, right? Lucy Wales, about being on her bike, taking a boo at me in my car. With Gaylene."

"And making an offhand remark about penilingus. Street jargon, I suppose."

"She's got a dirty mind. It's fake news, things got lost in translation."

"Really, Jake? Well, I thought you were exceedingly generous in telling Curlbotham not to seek terms of bail."

Maguire lacks words but reddens. Arthur can't quite work out how to reap some advantage from this. "The photo she took on her phone — does that still exist?"

"I'm a month from retirement, I'm not going to dirty a thirty-five-year clean record by tampering. But it's totally misconstrued and has potential for being fucking damaging if it gets on the street, especially cruel to the woman I've been loyal to for three decades. Gaylene fell asleep on me — she'd been going full tilt for two days on three hours sleep. That's all. I swear. Ask her. No, don't ask her, I haven't told her about the, ah . . . Lucy incident. It's embarrassing. She's married, got two kids, she doesn't need this."

"May I see a copy of that photo?" That's met with hesitation. "It will have to be produced on discovery, Jake."

He pulls a folder from his briefcase, passes Arthur a four-by-six glossy. A flash has caught Maguire through the windshield, bright-eyed with shock and dismay, one hand raised as if in protest, no sign of a partner. But what is this? Just above the lower right border of the shot, a little round nub near the passenger door. It looks like a big toe in a brown sock.

Arthur asks Maguire his view of it. He studies it, seemingly for the first time.

"Yeah, okay, it's her big toe." It dawns that this may actually aid his cause. "If she was going down on me you'd only see her heel."

"Lucy says your belt wasn't buckled."

"You wanna know, I had to do some hasty readjustments. You're a guy, Arthur, you're human, do I have to spell it out?"

"Have you discussed this with Curlbotham?"

"No. I was hoping they wouldn't notice it, I guess."

Arthur pockets the print. "I'll give some serious thought about how to deal with this at discovery, my friend."

"Please for fuck's sake do."

"Jake, I have no reason to doubt your word. This may come as a shock, given your stubbornly negative view of my profession, but I am dismayed that you think I might enjoy embarrassing you."

"Thanks. I'm sorry, I . . ."

Arthur puts a hand on his shoulder, squeezes it. "I'll have to take my client's instructions. I'll explain it to Lucy. And to her co-accused, whom I'm sure she regaled. They have kind hearts, Jake. They're really not criminals, are they?"

A pause. Maguire, cooled out now, obviously isn't keen to argue the point. "What I will say is, okay, there's an element of altruism, they weren't in it for themselves."

"I'll tell them you said that." Arthur shakes his hand, a gesture implying they've made a pact, however vaguely drafted. He handled that as best he could. There may be profit down the road.

3

Arthur had left the courts for a quick, relaxing but celebratory walk and now has to manoeuvre through a thicket of press to reach the bail counter. He finds Nancy Faulk there, directing traffic. She is aided by Selwyn Loo, who had popped into the bail hearing, quickly measured the direction of the wind, and popped right out to get his sureties lined up. These are solid citizens, without wordy Bee-Wear T-shirts.

Lucy Wales is already out, on her signed undertaking. Cameras are forbidden here, so Arthur will not be embarrassed by public images of Lucy wrapping her arms around him and delivering a big smack on the lips. She retreats to mingle with friends.

"Magnificent work, Arthur," Selwyn says as he deftly flicks his cane to ward off a snooping reporter.

"Aspirat primo fortuna labori."

"Fortune smiles on this first effort." Selwyn knows his Virgil.

"The luck was in drawing an excellent judge. Tchobanian is now seized of the file, and I've grown keen on him." Arthur has always been at his best with juries but they can be finicky. Nancy Faulk too may favour electing to go to trial before this fine fellow. They must huddle over it.

Right now, Nancy is busy with Ivor and Amy, getting them signed out. More hugs. Arthur gets squeezed hard by both — this is a very huggy group. Nancy reminds her clients that all alleged conspirators are to gather at her office, tomorrow, two p.m., then sends them off home.

"Where they're going to make orgasm-rich love while, back in my lonely office, I sweat over a reply to a fucking divorce petition." She sighs. "How do you suppose they do it?"

"What?"

"Stick together. Stay in love. Forty fucking years of unbroken happiness."

Arthur feels sorry for her. She needs someone to love, and to love her.

Nancy points out Rivie's parents, standing by a pillar, smiling at Arthur. He'd noticed them earlier, in a hug-fest with Ivor and Amy: old friends, obviously, fellow veterans of civil rights campaigns.

Arthur asks her to carry on at the bail counter — Doc Knutsen is next — while he exchanges a few words with Holden and Sharon Levitsky.

Both are tanned, rugged, and hale. Outdoors people. Early-retired, living off small pensions. Sharing a large acreage on a lake with six other Old Left couples. Sharing the chores of communal gardens and woods, of raising chickens and ducks. Pinochle and board games instead of TV. Off the grid.

Neither of them hug, a welcome relief, especially as Holden has a bushy beard. But they are generous with their thanks, delighted to meet the lawyer so entertainingly portrayed in *A Thirst for Justice*.

They chat awhile about the gentle pleasures of country life, then Holden says: "We assume this will be a difficult defence. We can put together twenty thousand dollars, and hopefully more later."

"It's from our co-op's building fund," says Sharon.

"Very generous, but you folks will not be allowed to deplete the building fund. We will have sufficient resources. Unfortunately, Rivie will not be able to visit you up north. She is confined to Toronto unless with a police escort." He adds, "She's quite the gal."

"We're aware of that," Holden says with a helpless shrug.

Here she is now, at the counter, greeting her surety, Richard Dewilliger-James, pink of complexion but green of politics, a young, well-heeled money manager. She waves gaily to her parents, who respond with vigour.

Professor Knutsen is about to leave with Selwyn Loo, but pauses to confer with Arthur: "I have some ideas to make this case relatively painless. Perhaps we can talk about that when we gather tomorrow." He turns away, takes a couple of steps, then briefly turns back. "By the way, thank you. That was impressive."

The saccharine band manager, T.J. Gully, waddles by, trailing alcohol fumes that tickle Arthur's nose, and bellies up to the counter. He pulls a wad from a bag, presumably Rockin' Ray's thirty-thousand cash bail. Arthur doesn't care to ask where he got that from.

Rivie hurtles past him into her parents' arms.

4

Tragger, Inglis, Bullingham has a thriving commercial branch in Toronto, to which Arthur repaired after the bail hearing — a courtesy call merely, coffee and a cruller — after which he set out by foot to the offices of Faulk, Quan, Dubois, above Chinatown. He'd promised to join Nancy for dinner to discuss the next event: tomorrow's sifting through the Crown's exhibits, the process known as discovery.

With all defendants on the street, with preliminary hearing and trial many months away, he can divert his mind to matters more agreeable. Such as Blunder Bay Farm — its garden must be exploding with fall bounty — and his rascally pal Ulysses, whom he misses and needs. His more pressing want, however, is to hold Margaret in his arms awhile, to sleep with her, make love, to share their triumphs, hopes, and worries, to enjoy her tales of political intrigue and scandalous Ottawa affairs.

She's only an hour away by air but Parliament is in session and her evenings are jammed with committee meetings. So they've made do with a program on his new iPhone called FaceTime, which somehow, miraculously, he figured out — after confusing it with Facebook, which he is *not* on, and never will be, along with Twitter and whatever else the profiteers of vanity come up with.

When he reached her, she was in the Parliamentary dining room, and he apologized for interrupting her shrimp salad. She was pleased at this proof he was not a technological Luddite, and proud of her wonderful husband for getting the Sarnia Seven out.

She looked beautiful, especially when she airmailed a playful kiss. They made plans to unite at Thanksgiving, three weeks hence.

Arthur turns the corner at Spadina. It's seven o'clock, the sun setting soon upon a balmy autumn day. Lots of fellow walkers but too many lazy fools in big cars circling about for parking spaces. The busy city: even on Monday there are lineups at the better restaurants in ever-expanding Chinatown.

Faulk, Quan, Dubois has the second floor of a six-storey art deco building, the ground floor given over to two restaurants. The one called, disloyally, Montreal Bagels is closed and dark but the Mongolian place is open and busy, the outside tables filled.

Across the street are an obviously struggling bookstore, a shop vaguely called "Spirituality," and a Chinese venture named Fu-King Supplies, which Nancy has explained sells items to enhance love-making.

Nancy buzzes him into an attractive suite of offices: framed photos from the 1920s emphasizing the art deco motif, a cubist print by Picasso, a flowery Matisse. Reception area, secretarial pool in the middle, four junior lawyers in the back, overlooking a garage and an alley, the three partners with views of Spadina Avenue, each with a balcony.

Nancy yells: "Fucker!"

That startles Arthur, who has just strolled into her office — he wonders what he's done wrong.

"Fuck you, you faithless fuck!"

She slams a telephone receiver onto its cradle, then mimics a haughty male voice: "My lawyer prefers that you raise your concerns directly with him. Ta-ra." Fiercely: "The slimy toad. No, toads aren't slimy. They're all warty."

She's been tippling — open on her desk is a bottle of Beefeaters gin, Arthur's favourite beverage of yore. Early-twentieth-century feminists stare reprovingly from her walls, Nellie McClung, Henrietta Edwards, Thérèse Casgrain, all perhaps wondering how such a modern woman can be so rattled by a typically pompous male.

"Bad news?"

She takes a few moments to cool off. "He wants to evict me from my home. His lawyer is applying for an order for sale. She's a bitch." She picks up the gin bottle, hides it behind her Ontario Reports. "You don't need to see this."

He lies: "It doesn't bother me."

"Sit down. Take the soft chair. Buckle your seat belt, because the road gets bumpy. Magnus Curlbotham has been fired off the case."

Arthur stiffens as he goes down on the soft chair, his ass hovering for a few moments before landing.

"Azra Khan is steaming over Magnus's poor showing in bail court. He's personally taking over the file."

Charming, cunning, combative, Azra Khan, Deputy Attorney General of Ontario. Thirty-eight straight convictions. Arthur holds a similar record working the other side: thirty-seven without a loss.

"And he's going by direct indictment to a jury."

Meaning they lose Chuck Tchobanian. Arthur plays with this scenario, finds it grossly unfair.

"We're cordially invited to his office in the McMurtry Building tomorrow at ten. Detectives Maguire and Roberts will be present to answer any questions. I may be tempted to ask if Maguire came in her mouth. Speaking of which, I'm famished. Do you like Mongolian?"

"I don't know."

"I recommend the tail of sheep in mutton soup, dried curds on the side."

Arthur follows her out. "Mr. Khan must have many able, experienced counsel to choose from. Why is he choosing to lead this prosecution?"

"The trial will be a media event. A win cinches a high court judgeship — there'll be four openings next year. Knowing Azra, I'm also damn fucking sure he wants to take you on. It's Rocky Balboa returning to the ring against the West Coast title holder."

"You two seem well acquainted."

"A dozen trials against him. Four murders. Two of them hung juries, then he won the last two."

"'Sexy,' you told me. Is your knowledge of him also carnal?"

"You're shameless. Yes, we got it on after one of the mistrials. We were both married, so no romantic expectations — it seemed less sinful that way. He was almost as hung as the jury, by the way."

"Thank you for sharing."

5
Tuesday, September 25

Azra Khan seems young, though he is fifty-seven. But to Arthur everyone under seventy seems young. Tall and fit, clad in a well-cut grey suit, his longish hair coiffed, no beard to hide the squarely sculpted chin, a friendly, confident air. The only impairment: a poorly suppressed patrician hauteur, presumably bequeathed by his parents, British-educated Pakistanis who came over during Partition.

For no obvious reason, except to pre-empt friction by introducing a foreign issue, Khan mentions the upcoming mid-term American election, expressing himself as fearful that the "self-admiring, boorish felon" who is president may continue to control Congress.

This excoriation of Donald Trump takes place over coffee and tea in Khan's commodious book-lined office, with chamber music playing softly from speakers on a shelf. Arthur and Nancy are in comfortable chairs; Khan is standing within easy reach of the coffee pot, ready to pounce on any opportunity to pour a refill. A screen has been set up in front of a video projector. Inspector Maguire and Sergeant Roberts are in view outside, guarding boxes of Crown exhibits.

Declining to hear protests, Khan tops up their mugs. "Another touch of milk, Arthur?"

"It's fine as is, thank you very much."

"You may be pleased to know, Arthur, that I hold your co-counsel, the irreverent Nancy Faulk, to be among the most gifted in her field. It almost seems unfair that she is also among the most attractive. I hope that doesn't sound sexist."

"It does, Azra," she says.

Khan has Arthur smiling as he mimics shooting himself in the head.

"I feel particularly honoured to finally meet Western Canada's most widely heralded criminal trial lawyer. I have encountered the best of the East so I am thrilled to be able to oppose you, sir. In anticipation of that, I reread *A Thirst for Justice* on Sunday while I was up at the cottage, supposedly fishing."

The book is on his desk, as if for show, Arthur's face in profile on the dust jacket, his eagle's beak dominant.

Arthur seeks to frame an equally generous response, but Nancy butts in: "That's why you pinched this file. This is an ego trip, isn't it, Azra, you want to add a trial against Arthur Beauchamp to the memoir you'll write when you retire from the Supreme Court of Canada."

Khan laughs ruefully, in the manner of one caught in the act. "I erred in assigning the case to the usually reliable Magnus Curlbotham, and I must pay the price." He holds aloft a transcript of the bail hearing. "You two took him to the cleaners. With great panache, you managed to persuade Chuck Tchobanian that conspiring to attack and destroy a multi-billion-dollar business and causing it ruinous damage and the near-death of an inept guard was all a merry lark."

He smiles at Arthur during this hearty rhetoric, as if assessing him, testing him. Arthur senses trouble if he rises to this sport fisherman's bait.

Nancy, however, is fearless: "Yeah, you want to sidestep Tchobanian, so you're indicting directly. Which is kind of sneaky — it's judge-shopping in reverse. Is your case that weak, Azra, that you have to tilt the scales?"

"His Honour showed extravagant gall in appropriating rights to a trial after having presided over the bail hearing. Unheard of. Rather greedy of him as well. Actually, our case is stronger than we knew." Khan seems not to want to sit. He wanders to a window that looks out over bustling Bay Street. "Curlbotham didn't have all the information." He draws the shades, turns off the background music, points to the screen. "We want to show you a little video from the night of the takedown."

The police particulars had mentioned a micro-camera in a gap above Ivor Antiques's backroom door. Arthur assumes technicians worked overtime on sound levels and image improvement and that the detectives have just got around to viewing it.

"So let me invite in Jake Maguire and Gaylene Roberts." Khan goes to the door. "Come in, come in, and bring your booty with you. And please join us for a coffee, tea, or juice before you set up."

The two plebeians are shown the serving table, but are on their own. Maguire doesn't hesitate to pour his own coffee. He swirls it, sniffs it, sips, then nods, as if finding it reasonably tolerable. Arthur remembers him as a heavy smoker. Now he has a healthier addiction.

Gaylene Roberts passes on both coffee and tea, produces a laptop, plugs in a USB drive.

"Question them at will," says Khan. "We shall be as transparent as the cloudless sky. And afterwards, we three can have another chat to help us resolve some issues."

§

The camera's pinhole lens has captured Ivor's backroom in startling detail, at least in the area of Okie Joe's computer station. He is seated at one monitor, typing commands, Helmut Knutsen beside him at another, scrolling through documents. Lucy is working at a printer.

Arthur makes out soft music from somewhere, then spots a small radio near a copier. The music obscures low conversation. But when Knutsen approaches the camera with an empty coffee mug his voice is magnified.

"I would much rather she leave Canada altogether." Responding to Lucy, it appears. "As I firmly advised her to do."

Khan lifts an eyebrow at Arthur. Proof, ladies and gentlemen of the jury, that our brilliant scientist is running this show.

Lucy, her voice raised: "And what about Chase? Shouldn't he go with her?"

"No way they'll ever nab him," Okie Joe shouts. "He knows that park upside down and backwards."

Arthur stifles a groan at this unexpected mention of Rivie's sometime lover. Chase D'Amato, ex-Greenpeace stuntman, hadn't made contact since dropping Rivie off at the airport — had he gone back to Algonquin Park?

Knutsen returns to the computers with a filled coffee mug. Arthur makes out: "Why are these data taking so long?"

Joe says something about "heavy traffic."

"This is one they want suppressed," Knutsen says. He calls to Lucy: "Check the news."

Sergeant Roberts presses the pause button. The screen freezes on Lucy reaching across to the radio.

"They're about to listen to the three a.m. 680 newscast," Roberts says. "We have the clip directly from the station, if you'd like to hear the relevant bits more clearly."

"Like what?" Nancy asks.

"There's a sound bite from a city councillor, opining that the investigation has stalled, and another from a doctor who's at a loss to explain why Archie Gooch is in a coma, given the lack of apparent damage to his heart. Or what passes for his brain."

Arthur nods in agreement to Nancy's suggestion that they get back to the video. It runs for only twenty seconds more, but they are awkward seconds for the defence: Lucy says something about "the oxy-head" smoking "super skookum shit, you could smell it from a hundred metres."

"Amazing that he stayed on his feet," says Knutsen, who then refers to Gooch as a "casualty of war" with what seems an uncaring shrug.

At which point the camera was removed. Seconds later the door was kicked open.

Roberts passes them USB drives. "Copies of the video. And some security cam footage taken elsewhere."

"Let's see the wiretap authorization," Nancy says.

With a beaming smile, Khan hands each counsel a copy. "All in order. Judge Gerlach was available to sign it."

"In what sleazy backroom did you find him at a quarter after two in the morning?"

Khan ignores her, flips a page of the bail hearing transcript, quotes from Arthur's pitch to Tchobanian: "'The Crown can offer no proof Dr. Knutsen was among the group that entered the Sarnia plant.'"

What is Arthur supposed to say? "Touché"? He is dismayed. That video, when played for a jury, could torpedo any reasonable chance of acquittal on the conspiracy and the breaking and entering.

"Lest you think we booby-trapped you, the OPP's digital sound technician was away for the weekend and only got to it late yesterday."

"What else has been inadvertently kept from us?" Nancy asks. "What's this security cam shit?"

"Ivor Trebiloff's white van was recorded gassing up at Hickory Corner," Sergeant Roberts says. "Tuesday, September eleventh, early morning. Knutsen pumping and paying cash, Lucy Wales dashing out for, I guess, a pee."

Jake Maguire hands out copies of photos and expert analyses of shoe and boot prints near the cut in the fence. Some matches were found with footwear seized from the defendants' dwellings. No positives from soil particle analysis.

Roberts passes out the fingerprint charts. Matches to all Sarnia Seven were lifted from the backroom of Ivor Antiques. Similar matches were found in Ivor's white van. An eighth person's prints were also found in both locations.

"The mystery man is Chase D'Amato," she says. "He's been booked several times, most recently for decorating Calgary's Husky Tower with a banner saying 'Oil Sucks.'"

"So now it's the Sarnia Eight," says Khan. "Or will be when our stellar investigative team collars Mr. D'Amato. We suspect there may be others."

Arthur hopes Selwyn Loo has not been traced to the Earth Survival Rebellion's war room — he'd paid it a few visits. As a lawyer, Arthur wants to believe, not a tactical adviser.

Now Roberts is laying out various physical exhibits on Khan's wide desk, which, except for Arthur's biography, has been cleared to permit this display. Among them, the crowbar — Rockin' Ray's instrument of destruction — and his improvised masked-avenger gear. Rivie's false passport. Various cell phones, tablets, and laptops.

And more paperwork: binders are handed out with copies of relevant documents, texts, emails, notes, photos, and calendars printed from seized computers. Arthur will have something to say to the jury about his clients' ineptness: true terrorists know enough to wipe everything clean.

Khan riffles through his copies: "You'll find several references to Operation Beekeeper and some to ESR, or Earth Survival Rebellion. Your allegedly well-meaning idealists are allied with an international subversive organization that condones violent action. *La Résistance Planétaire.*"

He wanders again to his outlook over Queen's Park, the heart of the government that he serves. "Resistance. Rebellion. This is not the language pacifists use, my friends."

Arthur senses worse to come. Khan wants to regain Curlbotham's lost ground, and more, with a quick counter-offensive. That seems imminent, as he asks the two officers to wait outside again, escorting them, expressing the kind of indulgent gratitude one offers for excellent service.

Arthur says to Nancy, *sotto voce*: "Is he trying to set us up for a plea?"

"He's about to shit on us. Watch this."

"A line has to be drawn," Khan says, returning to the table, refilling his own mug. "It's terrorism, my friends. That they don't wear Nazi tattoos or taunt with the black flag of ISIS doesn't make them good terrorists. In the government's view, there are no subcategories of good and bad terrorists. Our solemn duty is to set an example, to deter others who may be inclined to more monstrous evils."

He smiles, realizing he's being florid, as if rehearsing for a jury.

"And our solemn duty," says Arthur, "is to defend our clients from the audacious imputation that they are terrorists of any shape or cut. A conviction on that basis would set a frightening precedent, equating acts of civil protest with mass murder. Is that where you wish this country to go? Down the road paved by Mr. Trump?"

That taste of Arthurian rhetoric catches Khan up, and he hesitates too long before framing a response, allowing Nancy to butt in: "What's your game, Azra? Where is this leading us?"

"To a judicial review, my dear. I will be urging the high court to reverse the interim release orders for Helmut Knutsen, Ray Wozniak, and Rivke Levitsky. They're likely to get rapped hard, up to ten or even fourteen years, so they may as well start doing their time now. I may decide to add to the mix Joe Meekes and Lucy Wales — God knows how that scheming young anarchist got out on her mere undertaking."

He pauses, as if expecting a response. He doesn't earn one and carries on: "Knutsen ought to be held at Her Majesty's pleasure because he's clearly the prime mover and a powerful influence on lesser minds. Levitsky for obvious reasons. She's lucky she hasn't been charged under Section 246(b). A conviction attracts a life sentence."

Arthur struggles. He used to know the Code backwards and forwards. Khan helps him out: "Administering a stupefying drug."

"Ah, yes, of course. And where are your proofs of that?"

"Currently unavailable, but a logical presumption. Hopefully, Mr. Howell Griffin will decide to be more candid with us so we can add that count to the indictment."

Arthur tries not to show discomfort. Griffin claimed to have no memory for what transpired in his apartment on that critical night. What if his memory miraculously improved?

Khan continues: "Now, as to the alleged enchanter, Mr. Wozniak, let us eliminate some surplus items. His varied collection of narcotics doesn't interest us, and we can dispense with the comic relief of the accusation that he took a whizz on the head of one of Her Majesty's finest. However, he may be guilty of homicide. I am given to understand Archie Gooch could be on his way out. If that happens, we shall be indicting Mr. Wozniak for manslaughter and seeking a term of life imprisonment."

Arthur stifles a profanity. Surely no sane judge would see a probable manslaughter here. This judicial review will delay his return home to harvest his beans and cukes.

Nancy is seething. "And when will these appeals take place?"

"Friday. I am bound by law to give two clear days' notice. Documents are being prepared for service as we speak. I shall be showing His or Her Lordship the incriminating video."

"Azra, you seriously think that when all our clients show up on Friday, His or Her Ladyship won't wonder why all these security risks haven't already fled for the hills?"

Arthur rises, strolls to the desk, looks over the cell phones, locates the one tagged "Lucy Wales." He doesn't touch it, but asks Khan if her photos were reproduced.

He seems unsure, and puzzled. "I can ask the detectives."

"It would be better not to," says Arthur. He doesn't want Khan to learn Arthur had hinted to Maguire he was amenable to suppressing this evidence.

"Binder eight," says Nancy, quick to sense where this might lead. "Under the Wales tab." Arthur flips through his copy of the binder, locates several ten-by-eights printed from Lucy's phone. Khan flips through his own binder, even more puzzled.

Lucy had bought the phone, used, via Craigslist, to replace the one she garbaged after the Sarnia raid. She'd taken only six photos: a cat treed by a dog, a takeout menu from a pizza parlour, a selfie of her left nipple, a shady character looking lasciviously at her in a subway car, and, next to last, Maguire in the Buick, gaping wide-eyed at a camera flash through the windshield, and finally a shot of the police pouring into the backroom of Ivor Antiques.

Arthur explains that Lucy snapped the second-last picture just as she passed the officers' surveillance car. Khan studies it, then finally sits.

"She'd already had a good look into the front seat," Arthur says. "That's when she made a comment to Jake."

"This has not been mentioned to me." Khan's face muscles have tensed.

"The comment," says Arthur, "had to do with an act of fellatio. His belt was undone, his pants open, and Sergeant Roberts's face was in his groin. In the lower right is her toe in a brown sock. I can see why they never mentioned it to you, though it's undeniably relevant to the chain of events leading to the arrests."

"I am gobsmacked." Khan slumps but remains fixed on the photo, on Maguire's face, which might indeed suggest he was in the throes of sexual ecstasy. He is not as good a detective as Maguire, doesn't grasp the significance of the upraised toe. Still, Arthur is unsure whether this game can be won.

He continues: "It would be tragic if this were to go public — both officers are married, she with young children, he with a loving wife of three decades and on the eve of a well-deserved retirement."

Khan looks out the glass partition, sees the two officers glancing in. He quickly closes the exhibit binder, then screws up his face as if in pain.

Nancy finds her gentler voice: "We have to cross-examine them on this, Azra. If they come up with something totally lame, like she was only having a nap on his lap, the jury isn't going to believe them. Your two prime witnesses will have lost all credibility."

Khan hunches forward on his chair, locking eyes with Arthur. Finally, a little smile of resignation. "Surely we can find a way to withhold this from a jury. And the press, of course. What solutions do you see, my friend?"

"It bothers me, Azra, that the Crown may be burdening the courts, and the honest taxpayers of Ontario, with futile appeals against the several orders for judicial release."

Khan's smile widens. "Would Ms. Wales instruct you not to tender this photo in the course of these proceedings?"

"Quite so, Azra. In writing, if you like."

"And the act she observed would not be canvassed should she take the witness stand?"

"Provided the bail conditions stand."

"We are all three in accord?"

"Of course," says Nancy. "You have a good heart, Azra."

"Please understand that an indictment against Wozniak for manslaughter is not foreclosed even though he remains on bail." Khan again looks out at the two detectives. "Those long surveillance shifts must be deadly boring. Attractive woman, Officer Roberts. I'm not sure how the old boy wangled that but he did well for himself, didn't he?"

6

Arthur and Nancy take turns briefing the Earth Survival Rebels about the newly disclosed video and the Crown's more muscular approach to the trial. In summary, Arthur advises, Ontario's most feared prosecutor has entered the arena and seeks long prison terms by painting them as terrorists.

"Azra loves headlines," Nancy says. "You don't get headlines playing softball."

This takes some air out of the accused, who are gathered this afternoon in the boardroom of Faulk, Quan, Dubois. Selwyn Loo is at the head of the table, directing traffic, and he seems tired or hungover. Perhaps he'd celebrated too well yesterday with their clients. Or maybe he's been working too hard at devising some kind of workable defence.

Arthur's hopes for acquittal deflated as he watched those several minutes of micro-camera surveillance. He fears that the defence is left with merely a vague, sneered-at principle called justification: the forgiveness of criminal behaviour. A defence mainly notable for its near-total lack of support in the courts.

Given that these activists are guilty — in the strict, unforgiving language of the *Criminal Code* — the battle to be fought may only be for minimal jail times, as against the ten-year maximums the Crown will seek. Or more in the case of Rivie, who faces fourteen on her fraudulent passport count.

"To amp up the pressure," Nancy says, "Khan wants to turn the screws on Ray Wozniak. He's hoping Archie Gooch will cop it so he can indict Ray for manslaughter."

Rockin' Ray, who has been edgy and hyperactive while detoxifying, nearly falls off his chair. He scrambles to his feet, yelling: "Manslaughter? Of who, that dweeb, Gooch? — he OD'd, man, he slaughtered himself. Guy was a total junkie, smoking oxy-laced weed, a fucking belching volcano of second-hand smoke. My glasses had fogged, I never even seen him. What's my crime? Like, I scared him to death? I was maxed out myself, tripping, man. I didn't make re-entry until the afternoon. Goddamn Gully." Suddenly he grins, a mood switch. He does a riff on an air guitar, invents lyrics:"When your dealer's a souse get him outta the house."

"Shut up," says Lucy Wales, though she joins in the laughter.

Arthur pooh-poohs the manslaughter charge, assures Ray that Khan's threat is a typical prosecutorial ploy to extort a guilty plea to a lesser charge.

"Like what?" says Ray. "Pissing on a constable?"

More laughter. Arthur can't help but join in — the charge of assaulting a peace officer has become a source of much mean humour on social media, a viral knee-slapper. He assures the assemblage that Khan intends to stay it, along with the drug charges.

"My head is banging," Selwyn says. "Can we have some order, please."

Arthur continues: "It is only by dint of some delicate maneuvering that Mr. Khan shelved his plan to appeal your interim releases. On that issue, I must have your ear, Lucy."

"You can have both of them." Leaning against a wall, dark glasses, green hair and matching lipstick. Braless under a Bee-Dazzle T-shirt. Rivie wears one too. And Amy and Ivor. The Sarnia Seven seem to have decided to exploit their sudden fame, legally and loudly, taking it to the streets.

Nancy is dubious about that strategy. Her earlier warning to Arthur: "Some of these characters may enjoy the camera too much." Now she hammers that point home: "Ditch your Bee-Dazzle T-shirts, people — beware, bee wary. The media are going to be all over you like black flies in June. Just like yesterday."

A media mob scene, Selwyn Loo tapping his way through them, creating a channel to the waiting van-sized taxi, Arthur and Nancy silencing their troops while tossing out platitudes about Canada's fair and progressive justice system.

"What you're not going to say," says Nancy, "is I did it and I'm fucking proud. You're not going to talk about the case. That includes talking off the record."

Selwyn solemnly shakes his head. "I am no criminal lawyer, so this may sound heretical, but talking about the case, educating the citizenry from whom a jury panel is selected, may be exactly the right thing to do. Our little group will then seem — to the press, to the public — more authentic, true to themselves. Not trying to wiggle out of anything."

Nancy announces: "Okay, hold that thought, everyone. We'll get back to you after we have our story straight."

As they break for coffee, carrot sticks, and gluten-free items from Montreal Bagels, Arthur gives thought to Selwyn's aperçu. It strikes him as astonishingly risky. A rule of almost biblical severity decrees that clients must be told to shut up; it's the First Commandment of the criminal bar. Yet the point of the Sarnia Seven's action was to make a loud statement. Should they now be silent?

Arthur takes Lucy aside. She quickly mutes him by pressing a slender forefinger to his mouth.

"I got it," she says. "We stay out of jail if I shut up about the blow job. My lips are sealed. Maybe a lot tighter than Gaylene Roberts's were." She laughs, heads for the coffee pot.

Helmut Knutsen, looking purposeful and grave, replaces her, asking to meet alone with Arthur, who leads him into Nancy's office.

"If I'm Joe the plumber and I'm on the jury," Knutsen says, "I'm going to convict."

The door is open to the balcony, a view of busy, eclectic Spadina Avenue, a couple of customers furtively exiting Fu-King Supplies.

"I have some ideas to make this case relatively painless," Knutsen says. "It's me that they truly want. I'm the mad scientist who corrupted the minds of the well-meaning but gullible others. I can do the time. I've already lived long — they haven't. Rivie, Lucy, Okie Joe, all of them — incarceration would scar and embitter them."

He is stiff, like a soldier at attention. Or a prisoner of war. He seems to want to be a martyr.

"So you would plead guilty if the Crown declined to pursue jail time for the others?"

"It would be the honest thing. I am guilty. Proudly guilty."

"You will be of no use to your comrades, Helmut, or to me, from behind bars. We need you to help prepare our defence for a trial that may be many months away."

"What defence?"

Selwyn, who has been at the door, listening: "The defence of necessity."

PART TWO / DEAD OF WINTER

CHAPTER 13 » RIVIE

1

Tuesday, February 12, 2019

"You may find her opinions hard to take but she's easy on the eyes.
I'll be back with my feisty young guest after a word from my good
buddies down at Etobicoke Dodge-Chrysler."

I snatch off my headphones to protect my ears from yet another
inane commercial. Forty minutes more of this ordeal — live talk radio,
a concept designed by the same creative minds who brought you the
rack and thumbscrews. It sucks but we've got to do this media shit.

It was Selwyn Loo who proposed that we not hide behind a
wall of silence. Arthur and Nancy disagreed: it's risky, it's not done,
defendants should be seen and not heard. But the whole point of our
action was to raise awareness. And now we have an audience, it's big
and it's growing — how can we waste this opportunity?

So we're waving banners, blitzing the press, posting on social
media, and going on talk fucking radio. All but Ivor Trebiloff and
Amy Snider — Nancy had told them there was no point in fanning
the embers of the relatively weak case against them.

The rest of us, caught red-handed, have little to lose by admitting we did the dastardly deed. But there are boundaries. We don't mention Lucy's Mix, or what went on, exactly, in Howie's king bed on September 1, or my stealth attack in Howie's so-called war room. We don't mention Chase D'Amato at all, or the tryst in Algonquin Park. We focus on the bee holocaust. That trumps everything, including the risk of self-incrimination.

"You're listening to Open Mike with Mike Busco, AM with an attitude, on CXLR, the voice of West Metro. In my studio on this cold, cold morning, we've been discoursing with Rivke Levitsky, as she currently likes to be called, the femme fatale who—"

"Just Rivie."

"Rivie? That's the name you prefer today? You've been Rivke, Becky, and Marigold, and now it's Rivie, so it's a little confusing."

He's fiftyish, a stout, bearded loud-talker, lacking couth and cool. His preferred debating tool is cheap sarcasm. For this, I dragged my ass out of bed in the dark and bitter cold.

"Not as confusing as your last commercial. How can they claim to sell the car of the future? Cars are of the past. They're last-century, they've done their damage."

"Yeah, I almost forgot, you're one of those. Rule number one on my station — you don't diss my sponsors. So how did you get here at six a.m.? By dogsled?"

"Pedal power."

"Pedal power? Is that like pedalling propaganda? Oh, oh, she doesn't look so pretty when she wears a scowl. Joke, Rivie, sometimes I can't help myself."

"No, honestly, Mike, I love your sense of humour. But seriously, back to bees, I assume you heard about the huge colony collapse in Africa. Humongous dump of Vigor-Gro on Ethiopian soya fields—"

"Whoa, what's that got to do with your case — last I heard, we're not broadcasting to Ethiopia."

"This is a global catastrophe. Bees pollinate the plants we eat.

Without pollination, Earth cannot sustain itself. Hundreds of millions will starve. Billions. That is why we went after the Chemican plant. So we could alert the world, this country, the government, the media, you, Mike Busco. That is why we rely on the defence called necessity. Any harm we did, any laws we broke, these are infinitesimal wrongs as against the good we did for planetary survival."

I machine-gun this speech, not giving him a millisecond to interrupt. Scripted, sure, but it's our bullet-point message to the media, to the public, to the people of Toronto the Good, twelve of whom will try us.

"So essentially you're saying your crimes should be forgiven. But why is it so necessary to B and E some legitimate business and cause millions in damage and the layoff of three hundred hard-working men and women? Couldn't you have put up a billboard? A full-page ad? Hey, wouldn't a Super Bowl commercial get more attention? With all the funds you're raising . . ."

I break in before he gets into full rant mode. "I'm glad you mentioned that, Mike. Check out OperationBeekeeper, one word, dot org, you'll find various ways to donate. Every cent goes into bringing in expert witnesses from five continents—"

"Okay, that's your free ad for the day. But let's bring this home, here, southern Ontario. What about *our* bees? Where are they?"

"It's the middle of February, Mike."

"Right. There's none around, so they must have had a huge colony collapse like in Ethiopia, except caused by the cold weather."

"It's not colony collapse. The hives are still—"

"What do bees do in the winter anyway? Do they hibernate like bears? Do they go south like . . . what's that butterfly's name?"

"Monarch. You nailed it, Mike — bees are definitely going south, in the hundreds of millions, thanks to poisonous pesticides like Vigor-Gro."

"So if there's a big die-off because of the weather, you want to blame Vigor-Gro? And keep on doing that even though Chemican is suing you for umpteen millions? They say it's the weather, hotter summers, colder winters, that's what's causing the die-off."

"That's fake science, Mike, and I'll tell you why."

"Right after this word from the guys and dolls over at Chicken Little on Dundas in downtown Etobicoke. Traffic report coming up, news, and weather, then stay with us, folks, we'll keep the lines open."

He flicks an off-air switch, sits back, examines me. "You wanna wait till after my show, we could throw your bike in my van and I'll make you a gluten-free breakfast and you can seduce me and steal my secrets."

I look about — where did I hang my down jacket? "What's the audience rating for this shit-show? Point zero zero two percent? Maybe half a dozen lonely dolts plus your mom and your brother-in-law?"

He jerks back like I brushed him with a high slider. Guests aren't supposed to show attitude. A woman in the control room, probably his producer, is frowning, listening.

"Hey, sweetheart, in the last GTA survey we ranked eight in a crowded field. This may be your last chance to pitch your goods, because everyone in the media is bored with you guys."

"Not as bored as your audience. I haven't seen a single one of your call lights go on. Like, *hello*, is anyone out there?"

"They're waiting for me to get you worked up, you arrogant skank. That's when they like to pounce, when they smell blood."

"Do the dolls at Chicken Little know they're advertised by a misogynist prick?"

"When you get booked for a ten-spot, sweetie, you better pray your cellmate ain't some sadistic bull dyke lifer."

This douchebag ranks up there with the flamers and troll-holes who infest my social media feeds. Colour me gone. The woman from the control room has anticipated that and is in the studio, holding my jacket and helmet.

§

I'm not even vaguely astounded that Richard Dewilliger-James is outside in his electric muscle car, a Tesla Model-X. Richard is my friendly ghost — omnipresent, clingy, dweebish — and because he's also my surety he has to protect me, like an investment. He works for his family's financial firm, runs their greenish-ethical funds. He yearns to be hip, a task that ranks up there with the cow jumping over the moon.

A gullwing door opens to reveal, from behind a burst of condensation from the heater, a plump, pink-skinned nebbish wearing pyjamas under a coat. His complete name is Richard Dewilliger-James the Second, so of course that's how we refer to him: Richard the Second, or often, Dick Two. Ponytail and earring, scared-rabbit eyes, a stupefying eagerness to please.

"Mother rang me up twenty minutes ago to say you were on Open Mike with Mike Busco. Sorry, I didn't have time to change. It was a kind of knee-jerk thing, but it's minus twelve and there's snow coming and it's still dark. I hope you don't think I'm being weird."

I am barely able to spin my bike lock's combination. My fingers are about to freeze and drop off. The Tesla's bike rack tempts, but I'd have to endure Richard's sticky, heroine-worshipping neediness for at least half an hour, plus he'll want to buy me breakfast and talk about how the world needs more love.

Wait. Under his coat he's in purple flannel pyjamas. He's not taking me anywhere but to my building's front door.

"I was worried you could run into some bad characters. You probably think I'm overreacting, but one never knows."

That's not Richard's worst habit, questioning himself, but it's up there. His major idiosyncrasy is he thinks he's in love with me.

"Okay, let's blow this dump." I hook up the bike and step in and the wing comes down and we are off.

There's no escape from Mike Busco, the radio on, the bearded brownshirt ranting: "... the Sarnia plant closed, maybe four hundred workers laid off, one brave young man dead, maybe from foul play — it's no wonder Levitsky freaked out and ran, she can't take the heat ..."

"Turn it off."

"Oh, yes, that's gross. I'm sorry."

One brave young man dead . . . Three weeks ago they finally stopped tube-feeding Archie Gooch. His beater just petered out. When diced, sliced, and magnified, his heart appeared to have been normal, healthy. Also, the pathologist said he'd likely been brain-dead, literally, for several days before his heart stopped. As a result of some arcane reaction, his life force was extinguished by an opiate overload or fright or both.

And, yeah, the prosecution has laid a manslaughter charge on Ray the avenger, whose unerringly stupid reaction to that has him seeking his own personal Jesus. In an effort to stay drug-free in this time of crisis he has joined a holy roller church on the Danforth called the Assembly of the Lord Saviour Divine.

"I blew it," I announce.

"Oh, good gosh, no," Richard goes, "Busco was the one got blown. Totally." He reddens, embarrassed by his phrasing. "I mean you were all over him. Verbally, I mean." Panic setting in.

I succumb to my mean streak: "He offered to buy me breakfast for a fuck."

His cherubic face blooms like a red, red rose. "Oh, my good Lord, how did you handle that?"

"I ordered poached eggs on multigrain."

He jerks a look at me to see if I'm only kidding. Then he has to correct his steering as the Tesla announces it's too close to the cycling lane.

"I love your sense of humour. I love everything about you."

"Just drive, Richard."

Why does this continually happen to me? I'm a love magnet, if you don't count Chase D'Amato (and where in hell is *he?*).

But I'm not lovable. Even Lucy, my best bud, says that. An aggravating Joan of Arc complex is on display. I *am* an arrogant skank, I pulled a skanky number on poor Howie Griffin. Whom I carefully avoided last week when I saw him slouch down Harbourfront Park, thinner, worn, haggard, leaning into the cold wind off the lake.

"I checked today's schedule," Richard says. "You have to sign a bunch of thank-you letters to donors. Then there's the Writers' Union All-You-Can-Read Book Auction at the Arts Centre. That's a mouthful, isn't it? You're expected to say a few words."

He's like having a personal secretary. A very glutinous personal secretary.

"Oh, yeah, and tomorrow you have to remember to sign in with the police." Twice weekly, it's a drag. "I can drive you there."

When we pull up to our building on Sorauren, I give him a dirty big smooch. He earned that, Dear Diary, so don't call me a teasing bitch.

2

Lucy's morning mess includes underwear on the bathroom floor, wet towel on a kitchen stool, cold toast in the popper, half-consumed mug of coffee, the pot still warm, all combining to create a sense of her having run sprints around the flat after getting up late for her eight-thirty chem class.

An empty sardine can in the sink probably means she fed the cats, though Sinbad still looks hungry — he's on a window ledge, staring rapaciously at the house sparrows. Sleepy is, as ever, sleeping.

I spend twenty minutes straightening, though I don't have time to clean — these are precious morning hours, when Lucy is out, when I get a chance to write. I do this in our only bedroom, which I have claimed for the final two months of our house-sit — coincidentally the last three months before jury trial, verdict, and probable imprisonment. *Ms. Levitsky, I sentence you to ten years in an institution for the criminally sane.*

I have lost my job, and the peanuts it paid, of teaching English to Syrians. Some tight-ass bureaucrat freaked out at the prospect of my instilling these refugees with revolutionary fervour. I don't crowd-fund but I get online support, I get contributions. Just in: $500 from Muslims for a Carbon-Free Planet. A couple of my former language students were behind it. Cool.

So this is my shtick, mostly, when I'm not out trying to save the world. I process words. I get in three hours a day on an old desktop Okie Joe restored for me. He set up some kind of program that backs up my daily output into the deep, deep Cloud and erases it from my hard drive. In case the law comes sniffing by again.

I rarely go on social media — it's a trollercoaster out there, the capslock warriors at the controls. Never fire back is the rule. Don't feed the trolls.

I never learned to type, so I peck. Magically, words appear. Sentences. Pages. Images. Suspense. Witty dialogue. Pot helps.

Often I scroll back to the beginning, a year ago, when Operation Beekeeper was hatched. I reread and reread, fascinated: Was this me? Have I truly done something so wicked and glamorous?

I've no idea what kind of literary animal this is: a diary, a journal, an autobiography, a non-fiction, thinly disguised fiction? Whatever, I am driven to get it all down, my memories, imagining myself back there, being there.

When I'm not sure, I have guessed. Or used a little imagination. For instance, I had Chase D'Amato in the Arctic tundra, pining for me while eating moose steak by his fire and throwing the bones to his team of huskies. That was in an early draft, from three months ago. Now, as I light up a crumbled bud of sativa, I find that image stiff, sterile, unsatisfying.

So instead shall I export my lover — my *occasional* lover — to ... how about New Zealand? The mechanics of his getting there can be worked out later. He is on a beach surrounded by admiring women. A topless beach. Maybe bottomless. Why am I doing this to myself? Delete paragraph.

The postcard Chase sent me was of fishing boats in the Bay of Biscay, in a kind of 1950s style, that he must have found in some collectibles store. It was postmarked January 4, Yellowknife, NWT. "Happy New Year to All Bee-ings!" No signature, his muscular, blocky handwriting.

Chase probably had a friend mail it from Yellowknife. He knows the cops read my mail. Maybe he *is* in New Zealand. Or southern France. What he sent me was reassurance. *I'm somewhere cool, I'm okay.*

I'm almost sure, again, that I'm in love with him. But what I feel could be something more basic: my old nemesis, fornication deficit. It's been five months if you don't count the performance poet with whom I did a drunken, fumbling one-nighter.

After I spotted Howie last week, so sad and hunched over, so lonely and betrayed, I had a pornoroid dream, gripping a bat, ready to stroke one into the stands. But what I grip turns out to be Howie's big, hard, pulsing cock. I woke up horny for him. Is that sick or just weird?

My middle fingers start to peck: *Howell J. Griffin looks so forlorn and lonely and betrayed that I feel yet another surge of guilt. But something aberrant too: desire. I feel I owe him love.*

§

"Fucking cats."

Lucy is home, shouting, banging around, letting me know she needs to vent. My muse chides: *Hey, stupid, don't forget to back up this time.* I copy to a USB drive, pocket it, rise, stretch, turn my phone's ringer back on, and emerge.

Sinbad is on the sofa, grooming himself. What prompted Lucy's expletive was he'd pulled down Kropotkin's portrait and rent it into shreds. An ironic gesture of defiance to the anarchist icon.

"Can't we just kill this cat?" she says. "We'll tell Dr. Wenz he died of something. Cancer. Was in horrible pain. Had to put him down."

"Maybe you should show him a little love."

"I'm all out of love. Tank is empty. Fucking cat. Fucking Wozniak. He's fucking a fucking Jesus freak."

She has lost Rockin' Ray to a drug-free, booze-free existence as an adherent of the Assembly of the Lord Saviour Divine, a retro-hippie sect for those who saw God while doing — or at least recovering from — psychedelics. Lucy believes he adheres mostly to a sultry, holy-rolling Korean-Canadian whom he calls, ickily, Sooky-Sue.

"And now he's fucking moved in with her."

A third-floor walkup on Ossington, above her uncle's Rapid-Loans franchise, catering to the poor and desperate. Ray still plays local taverns with Panic Disorder but has lost his chops. He looked shaky last I saw him, wasted, hollow-eyed. But that was before he found Jesus and Sooky-Sue.

Lucy flops onto her fold-out couch. "How was that phone-in show?"

"It shit the bed. I walked out on the slob. For that, I got up at five a.m.?"

I tell her about Richard the Second picking me up in his flannel pyjamas, and how I'm worried I raised his expectations. "I gave him tongue. He got all flustered and red."

"Did he get a bone on?"

"I never thought to check."

"He's in pyjamas and it didn't jump right up at you? I think he's queer."

"I can't do tonight's book auction thing. Richard wants to pick me up for it. Do me one favour and I'll never ask another for as long as I live. Please go with him."

"No way. He's your surety. Your problem. I've got an organic chemistry paper to write." Lucy lost her job too, but scored a student loan, is taking a full load this term, five classes.

"You pick up the mail?" I ask.

She gestures at the pile of flyers and envelopes on the dining table. "Nothing from Chase, sorry. A notice from Chemican's attorneys basically telling us to shut the fuck up or they'll charge us with criminal libel. Forwarded from Tragger, Inglis, Bullingham, which is where our big-shot lawyer supposedly works. Arthur What's-his-name, I haven't seen him for so long I forgot his name. Beauchamp. Pronounced Beech'm. Arthur Beauchamp. I've maybe seen him twice since we got busted. What's he doing out there in his little hillbilly island except playing with his dong?"

I too am wondering about Arthur Beauchamp's commitment. He came on like he cared, cool, in control. He got us bailed, then he bolted at the first snowfall. Typical West Coaster.

CHAPTER 14 » ARTHUR

1
Saturday, February 23

"Why are you holding a roll of paper towels?" Margaret asks. She's dressed to go out. Off to a state reception of some kind. It's five p.m. in Ottawa, cocktail time.

"I forgot to get toilet paper," Arthur says. "I forgot to write it down." Or he did write it down, on one of the scribbled scraps that festoon the farmhouse, but forgot he'd done so. At his current rate of deterioration he'll be in diapers soon, babbling.

"Your phone has an app for reminders . . . Forget it." Likely, she's telling herself: don't waste your breath; the dotard lacks the skills to run such an app.

"I assume you're sitting on the can as we speak."

"Exactly." The lens of his FaceTime camera has him in a cold-weather plaid shirt with his suspenders down. It's embarrassing. It doesn't feel as private as the phone. What if he's hacked, the image going out to millions, a Facebook joke?

Margaret's call came as he studied the forecast on this iPhone. More rain. He hopes that won't slow up Stoney and Dog.

She says, "By the way, I'm trying to reach Selwyn Loo. I'd give him a kiss, but I don't know where he is."

"Berlin, dear. Trying to charm Professor Hoff to come out of hiding, and to bring his Nobel. The microbiologist."

"Dieter Hoff. I saw him on TV last summer, hyping his book. In excellent English, by the way."

Arthur is aware of that, and thankful — testimony through an interpreter causes jurors' faces to go blank.

Dr. Hoff, author of *De-Pollination: Why Chemistry May Kill Life on Earth*, is needed to square off against an equally famous scholar whom the Crown is likely to call: Stanford's Jerod Easling, entomologist, author of multiple books about bugs, and a popular talking head on science shows. The Crown has already sent the defence a copy of his written opinion, and to Arthur's dismay its exoneration of neonics was telling and lucid.

"Handsome, your Dr. Hoff," Margaret says, "and I think he knows it. The lovely young thing doing the interview was about ready to go down on him. Anyway, he doesn't seem shy, so why would he hide, and from whom?"

"Maybe he's just hiding from us. Not sure why. Not long ago he was eager to assist, and even gave us a rough draft of his opinion."

"So I imagine the SOQers have been wildly celebrating Selwyn's triumph."

"There was an event at Al and Zoë's last evening, so there will be a few hangovers today. They're planning a more sober event tomorrow, after church gets out."

"Give everyone a hug for me. Even Taba."

Arthur is taken aback by the lack of vitriol. Maybe, just maybe, she is summoning the grace to forgive.

The Appeal Court ruling came down yesterday morning. A narrow, qualified victory for Selwyn Loo and Quarry Park, a blow to TexAmerica Stoneworks. By three to two, the Appeal Court quashed the rezoning bylaw, holding that the Trustees, while not accused of improper motives, acted despite "a total lack of environmental assessment." The dissenters held that mining rights trumped conservation rights, bylaw or no bylaw.

"It's more of a reprieve than a victory," Arthur says. "Now TexAmerica and its two puppet Trustees must at least pretend to do due diligence. For the right price they may find a wildlife biologist to say the swallows and falcons aren't threatened. Our backup strategy should be a recall petition, to quickly replace the two Trustees. That's on tomorrow's agenda."

Arthur would like to wipe, flush, and rise, but can't imagine how to do that and maintain any semblance of decorum. It doesn't help that his sense of balance is impaired — he twisted an ankle yesterday by stepping into the latest Ulysses hole, a cavern near the garden gate.

"Meantime, my dear, we are soon to have a manpower deficit. Stefan will leave in April for his wildlife refuge."

Both know Solara can't handle the extra burden, especially with the Sarnia Seven trial upcoming. So Arthur will retain Stoney and Dog for odd jobs, and a neighbour will help with the animals.

"How's the dig? Found Jeremiah's body yet?" Visible merriment on the screen. If all goes well at the well, he will pay her back for all her needling.

"Stoney promised to work through the weekend. He and Dog should be at the site now. Ulysses and I shall be on our way presently."

They came by yesterday to borrow his tractor with its narrow scoop — "for the fine work," Stoney said. Arthur couldn't get up there, because of his ankle, but could hear the grunts of the backhoe from the house.

"I hope this isn't a fool's errand, Arthur." A frown to mask her teasing smile.

Arthur harrumphs. "The Historical Society is keen on the project. Unveiling island history. I don't think I'm obsessive."

"Of course you are, darling. You keep seeing Jeremiah Blunder."

"A couple of locals have seen him too."

"Local drunks."

"I like to think he's trying to tell us his body is still in the well — he's never been properly buried."

"Uh-huh. And why is he always clutching a jug of his homebrew?"

Arthur doesn't know. A warning from a fellow alcoholic of the perils of drink? He conjures a picture of skeletal fingers gripping his jug to the bitter end.

After they disconnect, Arthur reflects on Margaret's seeming change of heart: *Give everyone a hug for me. Even Taba.* Was she mocking him? No, that sounded sincere, an acceptance that Arthur's seductress is a leading comrade in the struggle, and deserves a hug equal to the others.

In fact, he had already hugged Taba, last night, at Al's and Zoë's. Or, more passively, he was hugged by her. He'd gone behind a tree for a pee. Taba spotted him as he zipped up, gave him not just an embrace but a boozy kiss.

But everyone was hugging and kissing. And anyway she has a more reliable married boyfriend now in Herman Schloss. At the party, she clearly relished her role as the handsome tycoon's steady. She flashed Arthur an occasional grin that seemed to say: "I offered — I bet you're sorry now."

Why does that annoy him? He's free now, he has fought temptation and won. She has moved on to greener pastures.

2

As Ulysses races into the house to accept the leash, he skids on the kitchen tiles and topples a pile of folders from the table. Spilling from them, decorated with large, dirty paw prints, are expert reports and studies, correspondence, opinions on the law, maps, charts, surveys, and graphs — Selwyn sends him a packet of these each week.

Arthur will unsnarl the mess of files later. He'll have to read them one of these days. He knows they are important, feels like a child avoiding homework, but he just can't find the strength. Yet the trial of the Sarnia Seven is only three months hence.

Thinking about it oppresses him. He frets over Nancy Faulk's conspiracy theory — she has learned that Azra Khan is a curling buddy of the Chief of the Superior Court of Justice; they're in the same club in Rosedale. The Chief has power to choose a judge for *Regina v. Knutsen et al* from a rota of ninety in Toronto. "We may end up in front of some crazy conservative ideologue," Nancy said in one of her occasional phone calls.

Arthur said, "Then we will be glad to have twelve sane jurors."

Meanwhile, he has no clear understanding of the necessity defence. He's not sure how to raise it, or how it works. Only once in his five decades at the bar has he heard it argued.

That was in 1975. Performing an abortion was then a crime, and Henry Morgentaler had defied that law. As a young barrister, Arthur had sat in on the famed abortion doctor's appeal to the Supreme Court of Canada. The issue was whether an abortion was necessary to preserve the patient's health.

Astonishingly, Morgentaler, acquitted by a Quebec jury, was convicted on appeal. Even more astonishingly, the Supreme Court upheld that reversal, an insult to that great democratic institution, the jury system. The majority court sneered at the necessity defence as an "ill-defined and elusive concept."

However elusive, the defence seems applicable, for instance, to avail a mother who steals to feed her starving baby. It was used in the nineteenth century to defend shipwrecked mariners who resorted to cannibalism. Less sensationally, the defence has been used in traffic court, where a speeder may plead he was taking an injured friend to hospital.

But how it might apply to a well-planned break-in and theft from a chemical plant? The defence doesn't operate when a lawful course of action is available or when the defendant isn't in direct, immediate peril. The test comes down to this: Was there any way out?

He grabs a walking stick to take weight off his ankle, sticks the leash in his pocket, and opens the door for Ulysses, who romps away.

Someone — probably Solara, who is forgetful — left the driveway gate unlatched, and it has swung open. Ulysses notices that, then looks proudly at Arthur, letting him know he has pulled himself together, is no longer tempted by an open gate. Stefan has worked hard to check his wandering ways: talking dog to him, teaching him obedience, rewarding him with meaty bones.

Ulysses divines they are heading to the big dig, and takes off up the north pasture. Arthur follows, through the orchard. The rain has given way to occasional showers and, in defiance of the sombre forecast, a slice of blue has appeared to the southwest. It widens as they amble up the pasture toward the woods. Apollo, that rare winter visitor, bashfully peeks out, blinks, then covers up.

A single ray of sunshine makes one's day at Blunder Bay in February, especially after weeks of sopping rain, the winters made ever wetter by the inexorable march of climate change. Still, there has been no snow, and no toe got frozen. He feels sorry for his fellow countrymen who must brave the biting cold of, say, Toronto, where it is well below zero. Nothing will seduce him into going there until he is absolutely needed.

As Ulysses leads him down into the bracken-thick bottomland, the sun sends more darts, through leafless alders and willows, sketching the almost inevitable caricature of a grizzled old-timer doing his ghostly rounds with a jug. Arthur laughs it off this time; he no longer wants to play this game. He has created these images because he enjoys the notion that Jeremiah sends clues from the afterlife, he wants to be the great detective who solves a great murder mystery.

At which point his wife will apologize for mocking him.

Something is bothering him. It comes to him suddenly: it's the missing sound effects from the direction of the well site. He prays they are on mid-afternoon beer break.

Ulysses has gone ahead, as scout. That he doesn't soon return suggests he doesn't want to bear bad news.

Arthur urges himself on, his ankle throbbing, finds Stoney's backhoe near a stack of neatly fallen alder trees, branches bucked and piled. Dog's two chainsaws are under a tarp, along with two twelve-packs of empties. Ulysses busily chews on a leather work glove.

The backhoe's engine compartment is open, wrenches and tool bits lying in rain puddles. Arthur closes it. Sunk into the ground near the well site, its rear wheels half hidden in the mud, is Arthur's tractor.

§

The sun has quit trying but the day remains pleasant, so Arthur decides to do a proper hike, exiting by the north gate. Ulysses takes the lead up a well-trod shortcut toward Centre Road, then races ahead, alarming Arthur — Garibaldi's main connector can be dangerous for unleashed dogs. He calls, whistles, but Ulysses disappears from view where the trail hooks to the left.

Arthur hurries as fast as his game ankle will allow, arrives roadside just as Irwin Dugald's Explorer squeals to a stop only five feet from Ulysses, who had wandered onto the pavement and now, scared, races back to join old human friend with unhappy face making angry bad-dog sounds while holding leash.

"Caught in the act," Dugald hollers from his window, as Arthur snaps the leash on Ulysses's collar. "That dog is on probation, and now I see you've been letting him run loose."

"Thank you for the reminder, Irwin." Arthur doesn't want to argue. But Ulysses remembers this unfriendly human in uniform and voices a soft, wary ruff.

"You been keeping your gate locked, Arthur?" Dugald makes no move to exit his vehicle.

"Of course." A bald lie.

"I hope so, because a sheep got killed last night. A yearling, one of the Shropshires they're raising at Gwendolyn Valley Farms. Some of the hippies living up there found it. Dragged five hundred feet from the kill site. Had to be a damn big dog."

"That's terrible. Has to be an off-islander. It's happened a few times. Tourists bring over dogs that have never seen a sheep or a deer, and some can go a little haywire. Some breeds. Not wolfhounds."

"Maybe. Pass the word around." Dugald gives Ulysses a long, musing look, then drives off. He has obviously not bought Arthur's defence; Ulysses remains a canine of interest.

They march on, Ulysses tugging at the leash, pausing occasionally for a sniff break, and finally they arrive at Robert Stonewell's centre of operations. His driveway entrance is festooned with signs promoting his diverse trades: mechanic, builder, taxi driver, dirt mover, and provider of septic systems and emergency towing. A freshly painted sign advertises his latest venture: the witching of wells.

Not the excavation of wells, the witching of them. *A week, seven days, no more.* That promise was made in September, almost exactly five months ago.

The driveway curls around a hill studded with abandoned cars and trucks, skeletons mostly, the small acreage resembling a bombed-out war zone taken over by broom, salal, and blackberries. His funky two-floor cabin crowns a small hill, and nearby is his garage and a work shed.

Arthur finds him, along with Dog, under a tarp strung between those two structures. Tools and parts are scattered about. They are drinking beer, apparently taking a break from dismantling a riding mower.

Greetings are exchanged and Dog makes room for Ulysses beside an old barrel stove that creates a little warmth and a lot of smoke.

"Offer you something?" Stoney says, cracking open another can.

"No, I'm here on business."

"I could have used your services ten minutes ago, counsellor. The head of the Gestapo was up here on a pretext so he could hassle my livelihood. According to Dugald I need a licence to be a septic installer. I told him I been putting in fields and tanks for all my life without no licence, so I'm grandfathered. That's the law, I told him."

"What was the pretext?"

"Asking if we know anything about Gwendolyn Farm's sheep that got killed by a dog. He knows I don't have a dog, except Dog here, and I ain't about to squeal on nobody's else's dog, neither."

"Very noble of you."

"I'm starting a water witching service. Only thing you don't need a licence for. What happened to the days of free enterprise? But I digress. What is the item of business, good sire?"

"It's about the dig, Stoney."

"Oh, yeah, well, Mother Nature ain't cooperating. With this rain we had—"

"It's dry today. It was dry in September, when you told me you wanted to get to it while the good weather holds."

"Events conspired against us, Your Honour. Equipment issues. Manpower issues. Dog and me were needed for the harvest. It was like the last big year before they legalize reefer, man. This fall the government takes over."

"My tractor is mired in the mud."

"We're gonna haul it out soon as we get the backhoe fixed."

"Why aren't you fixing the backhoe now?"

"Well, I have to do this here crap mower which I promised last July. To be fair, it has precedence."

"It's the middle of February, Stoney. No one is mowing grass."

"Arthur, pray have pity for the working class. Dog, what day is this?"

"Saturday."

236

"Exactly. It's Saturday, a traditional weekly holiday, and here we are busting our asses, eh, Dog?"

"Meanwhile my tractor is halfway down a sinkhole."

"Okay, I'm just pulling your leg, and now I'm almost afraid to tell you the truth, because we're at the point where you won't trust anything I say, but the backhoe is missing a part, and it's on order. The dig is number one priority when that arrives."

"What is the part?"

"Left-hand differential side gear."

Arthur has been applauded as one of the great cross-examiners, but as usual, in his dealings with Robert Stonewell, his powers have failed. He doesn't know if he's telling the truth or still bluffing. He feels stymied.

3

On this fourth week of February the island has enjoyed a string of sharp, sunny days, as snowdrops bloom in clumps among the apple trees, whose buds are fattening. Crocuses bravely raise tousled heads of purple and yellow. Daffodil bulbs push up green spikes, and sparrows and thrushes rehearse their arias for the coming sold-out season.

This is a day that ought to be enjoyed in the garden, preparing spring planting, or hiking with Ulysses, but groceries are running low and Arthur has driven to the General Store. He could have sent Solara or Stefan but they left this morning to the city for feed for the animals.

As the Fargo noses into a parking stall, Arthur observes that Abraham Makepeace, owner of the General Store, has installed a cork bulletin board on posts near the front door, as a community service.

Only a few notices have been posted so far: for sale are a cord of firewood, a "barley used" wood chipper, and a rider mower ("Needs work"), plus there's a photo of a well-fed orange tabby whose distraught owner asks, "Has Any One Seen Fluffy?"

Abraham Makepeace is also the postmaster at the store's Canada Post outlet. The spindly old bachelor is a font of local knowledge, partly because he likes to gab with everyone, partly because he feels empowered, in his important government role, to read postcards and letters that have somehow come unsealed.

"Your box is full," he says reproachfully as Arthur bellies up to the counter.

"I'm sorry." Arthur always feels ridiculous uttering this typically Canadian knee-jerk phrase. Why should he feel sorry?

Makepeace pulls out a batch of envelopes, passes them one by one across the counter. "This here will be an overdue notice for your house insurance. You better get on top of that. Revenue Canada too, because they're questioning your farm status. One of your law partners is retiring, so there's an event for him a week Friday at the Point Grey Golf and Country Club."

"Thank you, Abraham, I think I can manage the rest."

With a weary shrug, he passes Arthur two weightier items, Priority Post packets from Toronto. These contain documents from Nancy Faulk and files from Selwyn Loo — presumably new and amended expert reports, more photos, videos.

Arthur must set aside time to get into this stuff. Maybe, if he lays in enough provisions, he can batten down in his study over the next two weeks. The trial is set to start May 13, so he expects to be in Toronto by late April, about two months from now. Nancy wants him there much earlier. So does Selwyn, who temporarily denies himself the gentle winter climate of his West Coast home — he must soon return to argue a major pipeline reference.

Selwyn wants Arthur to travel to Germany to work on Dr. Dieter Hoff, who was originally enthusiastic about testifying but now is balking.

"He declined to say why," Selwyn told him.

"Don't tell me he's been bought."

Selwyn viewed that as absurd — they had already bought Dr. Jerod Easling, the entomologist and professional witness, regarded as charming by his fans and as glib by his detractors. As well, Hoff in his writings and appearances has expressed contempt for Chemican-International and the other agrochemical giants. "He's up in the air about it and wants to meet you before he decides. He read *A Thirst for Justice* and has decided he wants to be your best friend."

The government's courtesy ballpoint pen is out of ink, foiling Arthur's attempt to sign for the two packets. He digs out his own pen as Makepeace gestures at the window. Arthur observes Constable Dugald getting out of his Explorer.

"In case you haven't heard," says Makepeace, "we had another dog attack last night. Yearling alpaca from Mattie Miller's herd."

An alpaca? Arthur could see a pair of wolves taking down such an animal, but a dog? He is dismayed: poor, shy Mattie Miller, who stood arm in arm with Arthur at the Battle of Ferryboat Landing. Who has joined with her neighbour, the redoubtable Hamish McCoy, to sue the despoilers of Quarry Park for threatening their livelihoods.

"Animal Control Officer came over from Victoria this morning," Makepeace says. "He is up there now."

"I just got a report from him." It's Irwin Dugald, coming from behind. "He has a photo of the suspect canine." He moves closer, behind Arthur's left ear. "Can we have a quiet talk?"

Arthur is suddenly on edge, decides he needs strong coffee. He shoves his mail into a shopping bag and leads the officer across the walkway to the Brig pub.

The midday sunshine has propelled several hardy drinkers to its outdoor patio. Heroic poet Cud Brown is shirtless, showing off a hairy, flabby chest to Felicity Jones, the server. Beside him is Hamish McCoy, slugging back a hot toddy, looking even more agitated than usual, maybe because of the nearby alpaca kill. He might think blame will fall on Shannon, his big, old wandering bitch, a mix of big-dog breeds: Labrador, German shepherd, others that can only be guessed at.

As Dugald takes a barstool, Emily LeMay greets him with, "A horseman walked into a bar," and laughs at her take on the stale joke. But Dugald does have a long face, seems about to spread gloom. Arthur doesn't sit, just leans against the bar, impatient — he has store chores.

Dugald waits until Emily comes with their coffees, then looks about to make sure they can't be overheard. "First Gwendolyn Valley Farm's ewe and now an alpaca. This time, Leroy has paw prints. Leroy Letkow, the Animal Control Officer. Big paw prints. This wasn't no Chihuahua."

Dugald has had it in for Ulysses for some time, so Arthur is emphatic: "I can assure you it wasn't an Irish wolfhound."

"How would you know unless you were there?" He's not smiling; he's serious about this.

"I was there in the middle of the night?"

"I ought to caution you here, Arthur. You have a right to remain silent—"

"Stop this, Irwin. What is this business about a photograph?"

Dugald waits, sulking at the reproof, while Emily refills their mugs, then relates what Letkow reported to him by phone. This Animal Control Officer — new at his job, on his first visit to Garibaldi — was looking at the alpaca's disembowelled remains when he spotted the alleged perpetrator advancing across the field, as if returning for a morning snack.

"The dog ran away, but Leroy got it on camera. Pretty much looks like a wolfhound."

"Who says?"

"Leroy Letkow says. He's on his way here."

"Well, that's all very interesting. I have some extensive shopping to do, Irwin, and I must obviously stop by and see Mattie, she must be distraught." He checks his shopping list, then drains his coffee.

"Where's Ulysses right now, Arthur?"

"At home."

"Do you know where he was last night?"

"At home." Had Arthur fed him dinner? No, because Stefan has insisted on taking on that task, as part of the training regimen.

"Did you see Ulysses this morning?"

Arthur resents being cross-examined as if he's a common criminal. But he's forced to hesitate — does he actually remember seeing Ulysses this morning? Does he even remember if the gate was open before he drove out?

"Of course he was there." Stefan had probably taken him for a run.

Dugald sighs. "This is hard, Arthur, but I was by your place a couple of evenings ago, and I saw your driveway gate had swung open. I'm taking the blame, I should have alerted you."

"My good fellow, Ulysses has been carefully and successfully trained not to go anywhere near that gate."

The constable leans toward Arthur, gives him a shoulder squeeze. "My friend, I know how you love that dog. I'm a dog man myself, would be, except Roberta . . . I had a dog that . . . Never mind." A rueful head shake. "But it looks to me, Arthur, to be honest, that you're carrying a heavy burden, and maybe it's time to let go, to open up with me. You'll feel better if—"

Arthur cuts him off. "I'll feel better if you stop reciting from a police interview manual." He wants to get back to the store, get on with his day. He also has a powerful need to see Ulysses.

But here comes further delay, in the form, presumably, of Animal Control Officer Leroy Letkow, a vigorous young fellow whose khaki uniform and dark aviator glasses suggest he's of authoritarian bent. Dugald does introductions. Letkow declines coffee, asks Emily for a tomato juice.

"I want Mr. Beauchamp to see the photograph, Leroy. I'd like to see it myself."

"Yes, sir." Out comes his camera. "The dog depicted was observed at ten-oh-eight hours by myself after having returned to the scene of the crime."

Arthur has to work through that ill-conceived sentence before he's able to focus on the image of a retreating rear end. "This is not a picture of a dog. It's a picture of a dog's ass."

"He turned tail pretty fast," says Letkow. "He was big and had a dark coat, just like your wolfhound."

"As described to you by my good friend here, Constable Dugald."

"Yes, sir."

"If you take your sunglasses off, you'll see the dog's coat looks more yellow than black."

Letkow nudges the glasses onto his forehead. He appears startled to realize it's sunny outside and that he was in the dark, so to speak, when he observed the suspect dog. Arthur doubts that he has ever seen a wolfhound.

"It's not Arthur's dog," Dugald mumbles, embarrassed that his building of a case against Ulysses has been exposed as a mean vendetta.

As Emily LeMay returns with the tomato juice, she can't keep herself from peering around Arthur's shoulder at the camera's screen.

"That's Shannon," she says, demonstrating an uncanny ability to identify a dog from a long-distance shot of its rump.

She is likely right, though: Hamish McCoy's big, old, yellow pooch often goes where not invited — Mattie has complained about that, though Shannon has never bothered her alpacas. Shannon is normally a lumbering old gal, but the photo seems to capture her taking it on the lam. That could be evidence of *mens rea*, a guilty mind.

"If that's Shannon," Dugald says, "she belongs to Hamish McCoy, who's out on the patio." He directs Letkow's attention to the half-dozen men at a shared table. "Meanwhile, I've got some papers to process. When you finish up here, Leroy, give me a call and we'll figure out the next step."

Dugald has learned to avoid encounters with the hot-tempered Newfoundlander, and especially wants to avoid tangling with him over his dog. Without a parting word, he takes flight out the front door and down to his Explorer.

Leroy Letkow, unaware of the leprechaun's fearsome reputation, lowers his shades and advances upon the sextet of sunshine-loving beer drinkers. Arthur follows, his phone to his ear, talking to Solara, who is on the road with Stefan in his van. She confidently confirms Ulysses was home all last night and when they left this morning.

Arthur pauses on the patio to study his shopping list, wanting to get going on it, but is torn, curious to see this picaresque scene play out.

Letkow introduces himself. Baldy Johansson, who is already drunk, moves to make room on his bench, offers to pour some beer into Letkow's tomato juice. "Have a Red Eye, pal."

Letkow says he doesn't drink alcohol, remains stiffly standing.

Cudworth Brown, the bare-chested heavyweight poet, asks, "What can we do you for, Leroy?"

"Well, it looks like a certain local dog enjoyed an exotic South American banquet at Mrs. Miller's alpaca ranch. The victim had its neck broken and its stomach torn open."

"We don't know nothing." Gomer Goulet volunteers this on behalf of the entire table. Hamish McCoy is like a coiled spring.

"We have identified a large dog named Shannon as having been at or near the scene of the crime. I have reason to believe the dog in question is a second offender that also took down a sheep and is owned by one Hamish McCoy, who I am instructed is sitting here. Which one of you is Hamish McCoy?"

Cud Brown rises. "Right here, sir, I'm Hamish McCoy."

"Well, Mr. McCoy—"

Honk Gilmore calls out, "No, I'm Hamish!"

"I'm Hamish," says Gomer.

The others chime in similarly until Cud ups the ante: "Don't listen to these pugs, officer. I'm the *real* McCoy."

Everyone succumbs to helpless laughter except Letkow and Hamish, who, though the island's most instantly recognizable character, seems invisible to this humourless dogcatcher.

"Okay, losers, have your fun," says Letkow. "RCMP Constable Dugald and me will be taking Shannon in for further investigation including paw print analysis which may lead to her termination—"

Hamish roars to his feet. "*Termination*? You bleedin' fart-hole, bugger off afore I dig you a extra arse with the point of my boot!"

Letkow retreats a step, looks pleadingly for support to Arthur, who steps between them, slowing Hamish's advance but not his tongue: "I get through wit' you, b'y, you scrawny, pompous, two-bit civil servant, won't be enough of you to pray over!"

Letkow backs up a few more feet, bumping into an empty table, knocking over a chair.

Hamish tries to pursue, but Arthur has a fistful of his wool sweater. "You touch me dog, I'll beat the livin' Jaysus out of you and serve up your nuts to her for breakfast."

Letkow has made it to the exterior steps, and is on his phone, presumably calling 911.

Finally, Hamish's mates help Arthur wrestle the fiery little sculptor back to their table, but he continues to shout at the defeated, retreating foe: "Get off me island, you fart-mouth chucklehead."

As Letkow escapes out to the parking lot, Hamish turns to Arthur: "Promise me, counsellor, you ain't gonna let that stun barnacle terminate me dog."

"You have my word." He urges Hamish to go home and keep Shannon restrained. He will be available for further consultation tomorrow after church service.

"Okay, b'y, but I ain't no churchgoer." His temper much soothed, Hamish tosses back his Jameson's and heads down to his truck.

Arthur has qualms about taking on such a difficult client, but it seemed the swiftest way to cool him out.

§

On leaving the store, shopping done, Arthur again stops at the bulletin board, oddly troubled by a question that somehow demands contemplation, as if deep and philosophical: "Has Any One Seen Fluffy?"

4

Sunday, February 24

Saturday's sun has given birth to the mists of Sunday, and at ten o'clock they are so thick that Arthur can barely see homely little St. Mary's Church from its lower driveway. There are forms in this mist, and irate human sounds that rise above the grunts of his Fargo.

Soon, he makes out that a score of the faithful are gathered around Reverend Al Noggins on the grass out front; he is engaged in loud debate with someone.

Arthur isn't inclined to believe a rebellion is brewing against the country pastor. More likely the issue has to do with the discovery late yesterday, in Gwendolyn Park, of the bloody carcass of a feral goat. What manner of dog would have the agility and hunting skills to take down a wild goat among the park's crags and steep declines? Even a hungry wolf would hesitate — and there've been no wolves on Garibaldi since pioneer days.

Arthur decides to park away from the action, by the path to the cemetery, in case he is called upon to spirit Al away from this seemingly unruly demonstration. Unruly because of the string of loud and profane epithets that rend the air.

But it turns out to be a one-man demonstration, its provocateur low to the ground, unseen above the surrounding heads and shoulders. The deep, gravelly, Irish-accented voice easily identifies the rowdy sculptor.

From what Arthur can make out, Shannon was dognapped during the night by the fart-mouth chucklehead with the aid of Constable Dugald, and is in the RCMP pound. Reverend Al tries in vain to subdue the grizzled elf, while Zoë tries to subdue Al. He shouts something about McCoy profaning this holy ground. That sets Hamish off.

"Lard thunderin' Jaysus, I don't give a damn we're on holy ground! There'll be holy hell to pay if they put Shannon down! I want me lawyer! Where's me lawyer? He promised to be here!"

Al sees Arthur emerge from the greyness. "I shall ask God to deliver him to you."

On cue, Arthur says, "I believe Shannon is innocent."

That causes Hamish to turn a half-circle, to find that God has apparently delivered. "You're damn tooting, counsellor." He turns to address the wider jury. "My Shannon ain't no killer. And me lawyer's gonna prove that. And he's gonna sue the dorty cops who done this, for false arrest and slander of me dog. Ain'tcha, Arthur?"

To Arthur's gratitude, Al seeks to head off that dire prospect: "No need to bother Arthur with this." He pulls out his phone. "I shall go directly to the top. And to help me get my message heard, Hamish, I'll need you to join everyone inside to pray for Shannon's safety."

McCoy looks incredulous. "If you ain't noticed, me ol' cock, Hamish McCoy don't do church, don't have time for all the folderol, don't credit your biblical fairy stories. I'se a full-time practising atheist, and proud of it."

"Our Lord may have infinite patience with stubborn mules, Hamish, but in my weakness I do not. This is the deal. You go inside and join in prayer for the release of our beloved sister Shannon, or you cannot expect intervention, divine or otherwise."

"Balderdash!" McCoy begins to sputter, out of words.

"What have you got to lose?" says Zoë Noggins, gently taking his arm.

Zoë and the parishioners somehow manage to get Hamish into the church, sort of carrying him, or at least lifting him off his feet, as he profanes and blasphemes. He doesn't otherwise resist.

"Now what?" says Arthur. He has stayed outside with Al, who presses buttons on his old flip-top phone — either in an effort to reach the receptionist for the Lord Almighty or, more likely, someone far lower in the chain of command.

"Alas, Arthur, news travels slow among our small, ingrown islands. What goes on in the world's remotest hot spots arrives faster. Anyway, this morning, Ned Bailey, over on Ponsonby — retired deacon, you may know him — called me to confirm . . . Just a minute." Into his phone: "Hello, Irwin? Yes it's Al Noggins. And how are you on this foggy Sunday morning?"

There follow a few moments of light chatter with Irwin Dugald, co-napper of Hamish's dog. Inside, Zoë is at the piano, leading the assemblage into song: "What a Friend We Have in Jesus."

"Very good, Irwin. And were you able to reach anyone from the Conservation Service? Ah, good, good. They looked at that paw print then?" A wink for Arthur. "First spotted on Ponsonby, Irwin, that's what I heard this morning. Couple of messy deer kills. It must have swum over."

A cougar, Arthur realizes. A mountain lion. Island dogs don't kill goats, they don't kill alpacas, and they don't kill cats. Big cats kill little cats. Like Fluffy. Whose owner resides two miles north of here, where it's sparsely populated.

"Okay, I shall spread the word. One more thing — Hamish is in a snit . . . Ah, very good, and he can just go down there and claim her?"

Al leads Arthur to the church door. "Wildlife Conservation Officers are on their way from Victoria. They say it's likely a young male visiting from the big island. Well, let's see if Hamish continues to reject the Saviour."

Heads rise from prayer as they walk in. Hamish, in a back row, sits sternly, arms folded.

"Shannon is a free dog," Al announces, ascending to the pulpit. "Let us thank the Lord for answering our prayers."

Someone shouts a hallelujah. Hamish has the wary look of one who's not sure if he's being ribbed.

Thanks to those prayers, says Al, Constable Dugald has been shown the light: Shannon was wrongly accused, the perp is a cougar. "Our brother Hamish has the choice of running off to collect Shannon straight away or expressing his thanks by staying for the service."

Hamish grumbles and shifts but doesn't rise, and eventually smiles, cynically, knowing he's been bested. "This better be good, b'y. Fill your boots."

5

Wednesday, February 27

Arthur chooses the sturdiest of his collection of walking sticks — it's made of hard, knobbly western yew and can double as a defensive weapon. When he steps outside Ulysses perks up his ears at the sight of familiar human friend with backpack and walking stick.

Arthur gives him a rub. "Sorry, old boy. You're no longer a pup. You have a job now." He kneels to Ulysses's eye level, directs his attention to the livestock. "Your job is to protect the chickens, geese, goats, cats, and Barney over there."

He points to their old horse, who chats with Stefan in the orchard. Stefan whistles to Ulysses, who gives up on old human, races off to join young human and grass-eating animal friend.

The weather is still pleasant this morning, as balmy as spring. Yet Arthur may well be the only Garibaldian hiking today. Islanders are sticking to their homes and cars as the cougar roams free.

A panic reaction has spread like a contagion on Garibaldi, though Arthur considers it overdone and illogical — the cougar is holed out in Gwendolyn National Park, well north of where the vast majority live. Mattie and Hamish are among only a few dozen farmers, artists, and hippies up there and they're all staying put, sheltering their animals. A squad of Conservation Officers are there too, with their tranquilizer guns, hoping to trap, immobilize, and relocate the big cat far away from the encroaching human tide.

Arthur gets no more than three hundred metres up Potters Road when a neighbour comes by in his van and offers a lift. Arthur thanks him but spurns the offer.

"You heard about the lion?"

"Of course, Harvey."

"An alpaca and a goat on the weekend, and now a couple of what used to be free-run chickens up at the Clegghornes' near Bleak Creek."

"I hadn't heard that. Good Lord, the cougar must have been starving. Let's hope its hunger is sated."

"They say this animal is a killing machine. If it can take down a wild goat maybe you want to worry about your tame ones."

"Ulysses comes from a long line of warrior dogs."

"That big galoot? Could have fooled me."

Were Arthur's phone not ringing in his pocket he would have responded sharply to that unkind assessment. Instead, he lets Harvey drive off.

"How are you?" It's Nancy Faulk, in Toronto.

"I'm quite well, my dear. I'm out on my ritual hike to the post office to pick up more of your depressing case law on the necessity defence." Arthur wishes he hadn't answered — she's going to pester him: he's not doing his homework, he's needed in Toronto.

"So what did you think of Chernikoff's analysis?"

"Chernikoff?"

"Crim law professor, Dalhousie. We gave him our set of facts."

"I presume he says we're facing desperate odds with our necessity defence. It's what they all say."

"So you haven't read it."

"It's probably at the post office."

"Which suggests you haven't been collecting your mail."

"This is not the city, Nancy. The mail comes by boat. You have to add an extra three or four days."

"Wow. How nineteenth century."

Arthur has scorned the new digital shortcuts, regards emailing as the work of the Devil, and defines an attachment as holding affection for another. His official excuse is that he doesn't have a working printer and suffers an optical handicap that prevents him from reading from a screen. He is too proud to admit he is a total klutz with all but the most basic computer tasks.

"I'm going crazy here, Arthur. We're heading into arbitration next week to see who gets the Toni Onley watercolour his mother gave us and the antique Swiss cuckoo clock he bought on my credit card. He's claiming visiting rights to the fucking wine cellar because he can't afford his own."

Arthur sighs. "When do you absolutely need me to be there?"

"Yesterday."

"We're having a bit of an issue here with a mountain lion."

"Oh, dear. Has it eaten anyone?"

"A few domestic animals."

"Well, that's terrible, Arthur. It puts into perspective the disappearing bees and the destruction of ecosystems and the very existence of life on this planet."

Arthur endures the sting of her mockery for a few silent moments, waiting for her apology. It doesn't come, so she obviously means business. He promises he will bury himself in the reports all week and be caught up by Saturday.

"Good, because I'm booking you a flight to Berlin for a week from now. You are to put your famous honeyed tongue to work on Dr. Dieter Hoff."

De-Pollination: Why Chemistry May Kill Life on Earth, Hoff's book, sits unopened in the den. A wintry trip overseas is not high on Arthur's wish list, but they need this vital yet curiously reluctant witness — and he feels guilty about his slack-assed approach to the impending trial.

It's age. He just can't get the steam up the way he did when young. Or is it something else? Is his brain frozen by fear of failure? That last effort, about mining rights, had shown him at his fumbling worst; he'd had no idea what anyone, including himself, was talking about.

A slightly quivering need, a sexual tension, also beguiles him. He gets this way after several weeks of missing Margaret, and he's not been with her since the Christmas holidays. He's hoping hard mental work will burn the need off.

He is not far up Centre Road, almost at the lumberyard, when an old VW van pulls over, another neighbour, with four romping kids in back. She explains she picked them up early from school, not trusting the school bus. Many other parents were doing the same.

"Where's Tigger?" an eight-year-old asks.

"I love Tigger," says her little brother.

Their mother explains: "That's what the kids in school have taken to calling the mountain lion."

The young of Garibaldi have obviously been reared on A.A. Milne, or else inundated by the Disney version. Arthur hopes this will not build into a Garibaldi meme. He thanks her for her ride offer and sends her on her way.

He wonders if Jeremiah's ghost will show up. In pioneer days there were cougars and wolves here, and all manner of lesser predators. It would not have been easy keeping sheep or fowl or even horses. Maybe the effort, the losses suffered, drove Jeremiah to drink, and his demise wasn't due to a drunken fall, but suicide.

The third offer comes from Baldy Johansson, who has just pulled out of the lumberyard in his rusty long-bed pickup. He is hauling tall posts and spools of barbed wire, presumably to fence his shack from the cougar.

He wants to tell Arthur all about the lion, in case he hadn't heard. His neighbour's cat, Fluffy, has been added to the victims list as a probable. All owners of pets are being warned to keep them indoors. They're saying the cougar may have rabies.

Arthur's earlier robust confidence about his safety has waned under this bombardment. But he hefts his stick and carries on, though more warily now, as the road curls steeply into heavy forest.

6

It is with a sense of relief that Arthur makes it to Hopeless Bay without having seen Tigger the cougar or, for that matter, Jeremiah Blunder. Arthur doesn't plan to tarry — he hopes to pick up Professor Chernikoff's analysis of the necessity defence, buy some groceries, a writing pad, and some pens and pencils, and get home and start reading and analyzing and understanding. And in the effort, suppress the wriggling discomfort he's been feeling, the roiling of testicles distracting him from the intricacies of admissible evidence.

The Fluffy leaflet has been removed from the outdoor bulletin board, along with, one assumes, all hopes for the cat's survival. Newly posted is a sheet headed *Cougar Warning!* — multiple exclamation marks and a number to call if anyone makes a sighting. *Locals are advised not to venture to the north end! Children should be kept indoors! Gwendolyn Park is closed to the public!*

Arthur turns to see Norman Forbish's all-terrain vehicle rumble toward him — the newshound drives it out of necessity not choice: no ordinary car can accommodate his bulk. He claims that he's dieting and is down to three hundred and thirty pounds.

As the ATV pulls up, Arthur sees it's laden with several hundred copies of the *Bleat*, which is published — or at least mailed — every other Wednesday. Though often Thursday, even Friday. But today Forbish has made deadline.

"Anxious times," Arthur says, helping him unload the twined bundles. "A lot of the fear is irrational, but I worry about those young people up at Bleak Creek." Six couples, three toddlers, in a tiny community next to Gwendolyn Park. They bought there last year: seven organic acres, a rambling old house with two old cabins and a new tepee. A commune of city-bred naïfs, struggling through their second winter here. They're off the grid, powerless except for a few solar panels. No cars but several bicycles. They mostly hitchhike.

Forbish stares at Arthur, not getting his drift. "So why should we worry about them? They aren't as poor as they look. I was up there in summer, doing a feature. Where they come from, in Tennessee, the local businesses started a crowd-funding campaign to get them out of town, they were ruining the tourist business. They bought the old Gillespie place for a song, and have got lots left over."

"Why I worry is they have preschool kids. Are their parents watching them or are they doing . . . whatever they do. Drugs, I suppose."

"So what? So they let the kids play outside, it's healthy, all the fresh air. They're all running around naked, kids, adults. They're hippies. I don't judge their lifestyle, they don't judge mine."

"Nelson, where have you been for the last three days?"

"Putting this here edition to bed."

Arthur checks the *Bleat*'s headline: "Local dog busted for alpacacide." A photo of Shannon.

"Have you not heard about the cougar?"

"What cougar?"

Save it for Facebook, I don't do animal stories. That now becomes ironic. Forbish has trouble grasping the essence of the *Cougar Warning!* leaflet. He blinks, and the words remain. He turns red. He's a proud man, and Arthur feels sorry for him.

§

Arthur fills his pack with oranges, oatmeal, olive oil, and various other edibles that Blunder Bay's fields do not yield. He buys few vegetables — garden kale abounds in February, and carrots and potatoes can be dug fresh and crispy until spring.

What else? An essential item, but what? This latest forgetfulness attack finds him poking into his pockets for a shopping list he forgot to bring. He scans the shelves for clues. Coffee! He'll be going through buckets of coffee. Dutifully, he goes for the high-priced organic fair-trade medium-roast beans from Ethiopia, hoping he's not being conned.

Nelson Forbish is behind the post office counter stuffing *Bleats* into subscribers' boxes. He crowds Abraham Makepeace, making him irritable as he deals with Tug Cooley, a hairy bear, foreman of the team that keeps TexAmerica's machinery oiled and ready at the quarry. He's a Yank with a work permit. He wears a "Make America Great" cap.

Makepeace weighs a shoebox-size parcel. "Eleven pounds, three ounces — what have you got in here? Rocks?"

"Yeah, post office guy. Exactly. Limestone samples for quality analysis in Fort Worth, Texas, if you wanna know. Any more questions? I got a friggin' drink waiting. They want this in three days."

Arthur stands close enough behind him to detect his alcohol exhalations. Cooley is often in the Brig on his off-hours, with a few of his crew, a sullen group, paranoid, locally unpopular. Graffiti is inscribed, in large letters, above the pub's main entrance: "no miners allowed."

"I can't promise three days," Makepeace says. "We are the people's post office, we are not some rip-off overnight courier. Can't even promise five days."

"What kind of friggin' bureaucratic bullshit is this? The sign says, 'Expedited Priority, Three Days.'"

"That doesn't apply to Garibaldi Island. Sign here and here."

Cooley does so grudgingly.

"A cougar," Forbish mutters. "How come I'm the last to know?"

"Maybe you ought to listen to the radio, Nelson," Makepeace says. "It was on the CBC. It's even got a name now. Tigger."

Tug Cooley chimes in: "Hey, editor guy, that lion gets you we can all relax, he won't be hungry for months."

Hurrying off to his waiting drink, Cooley pretends not to notice Arthur, another limestone-hugging adversary. His only island friends are the few thirsty regulars he buys for and the two Trustees, hopefully soon to be deposed.

"I can barely breathe." Makepeace wheezes like an accordion as Forbish gives him a bump while bending. The postmaster is too agitated to examine Arthur's mail, and without comment hands over a *Harper's*, some letters and bills, Nancy Faulk's latest packet of case law and opinions, and Dr. Dieter Hoff's freshly revised German edition of *De-Pollination*. The new English version has yet to go to press.

§

En route home, Arthur turns down two offers of rides, but hesitates over the third, from Taba Jones in her canopied Chev pickup. She is heading down to Potters Road anyway, she explains. She's collecting signatures to recall Trustees Shewfelt and Zoller.

"You signed this yet?" She holds a clipboard with the petition, which already bears a couple of pages of names.

"Not yet. Shall I do so now?"

"When I get you home. It's cold. Climb in and shut the door, for Christ's sake. I'm not going to eat you."

By now, Arthur has hesitated too long. Taba looks unusually attractive today, especially in full-breasted profile, and, rarely seen, in makeup and a dress, her russet hair under rare control, in a clip.

He slings off his pack, climbs in. "I wanted the exercise, but those clouds look threatening."

"Say hello to Arthur, Rosie."

Her neighbour's Labrador retriever — whom Taba often dog-sits — offers a friendly sniff from the king cab.

Arthur tells himself he must stop being scared of Taba. They'd been good chums, pre-coitus: reserved Arthur, earthy Tabatha, fighting common causes, sharing cynical jests. They flirted. It went too far. She has a new lover now. Life goes on.

He wants to ask how that's working out, her affair with Herman Schloss: the environmentally friendly gentleman of means who feels no shame in so publicly cheating on his lovely actress wife. They're from Los Angeles, where that may be excusable behaviour. But not on Garibaldi. Here, affairs are properly furtive.

Arthur can't seem to frame an appropriate question about Schloss, so the obvious fallback topic is the mountain lion. Taba shares his view that islanders are inflating the threat but she also shares his concern about the hippie back-to-the-landers at the island's northwest crown, in the area called Bleak Creek.

Taba had given a lift earlier today to a pair of them, hitchhiking to the mall. "Obviously mated to each other, but neither looked over twenty. Naive, earnest escapees from the rat race. We all went through that phase, right?"

"I didn't." A matter of some pride to Arthur.

"A cougar with the cute name of Tigger isn't going to spoil their off-the-grid lifestyle experiment. They're more thrilled than scared. It's a spiritual thing — the cougar's coming is a sign, a message. They *hope* such a beautiful animal will visit and bless them."

She parks outside Arthur's gate, hands him a pen, holds out her clipboard. "Sign with a big flourish — I want your neighbours to see." She plans what she calls a "walk and knock" — up one side of Potters Road, back the other, fifteen doors. In the meantime, could Rosie play with Ulysses?

"Splendid suggestion." The dogs have already sniffed each other out during a couple of outings, and Ulysses, who impatiently waits at the gate, seems eager to refresh their friendship.

Taba takes off, blowing him a kiss. Arthur hefts his backpack and leads Rosie into the farmyard. The dogs romp off. He would love to join in their play, or at least sit on his front step and watch them, but he has made a vow, a promise to Nancy Faulk.

Crack those books. Start learning about neonics and honeybees, start reading the several hundred cryptic pages of law reports piled up in his study.

He casts one long, yearning look at the dogs chasing each other's tails, then takes his groceries to the kitchen and grinds a batch of coffee beans.

7

It has taken Arthur an hour to snip open various bulky envelopes and sort their contents chronologically in four neat piles on his old oak desk. The smallest pile is correspondence from Nancy and Selwyn, mostly about tactics and procedures and other boring forensic matters. The biggest pile collects articles about bees and neonics from popular journals and scholarly reports. Witness statements and expert opinions comprise a third pile, and the fourth is law reports. Which shall he attack first?

His inability to focus seems an increasingly chronic condition and it's complicated by the same tension he felt earlier today, that insistent phallic itch, amplified by the recent nearness of Tabatha Jones.

He supposes he should invite her in for coffee when she returns for Rosie. Or a real drink — Arthur keeps a supply of the better brands for guests. He wonders if he should start a fire. No, alcohol and a fire would seem too inviting. He doesn't want her misreading his attentions. Or lack thereof.

He sips his coffee, checks the weather on his iPhone — wind and rain expected: good, that will keep him cocooned here. He rises from his desk, puts on some Chopin études to help him relax.

Finally, he picks up Professor Chernikoff's analysis of the necessity defence, the one touted by Nancy Faulk. Thirty pages plus footnotes and references. Arthur takes a deep breath and plows ahead.

Chernikoff kicks off with Aristotle, whose *Nicomachean Ethics* lays it down that one ought to be excused for a wrongful act done under pressure which "overstrains human nature and which no one could withstand."

Chernikoff then draws on the wisdom of another philosopher, two millennia later. Back in the days when life was nasty, brutish, and short, Hobbes wrote, in *Leviathan*: "If a man by the terror of present death be compelled to do a fact against the law, he is totally excused, because no law can oblige a man to abandon his own preservation."

Terror of present death — that's the hitch, the test that the Sarnia Seven seem bound to fail. The test that failed Morgentaler when Canada's highest court belittled the necessity defence as an elusive concept.

If one acts to save one's own life under immediate pressure, the law may forgive. But if one acts to warn against planetary suicide — that doesn't seem defensible. It would take a brave judge to loosen the necessity defence from the bonds of precedent. It should be called the impossibility defence, because it so rarely succeeds.

Arthur is up again, pacing. This is hard work, this thinking. What has happened to his ability to concentrate? Maybe his brain rebels at the illiberal, depressing law on this issue. The whole case is depressing. The holocaust of honeybees, the dire consequences to humankind — it's all too impossible to deal with; too much is being asked of him.

Defending crimes of murder was easier. No one cared if he won or lost except the client. Arthur wasn't fighting for a cause; he wasn't afraid of letting anyone down.

This will be his last trial — no question about that, given his age and the apparent slowing of his brain. It seems almost inconceivable that the most important trial of his life will be his curtain call.

He wonders if he's suffering a kind of stage fright over it, and it's blocking him, keeping him from buckling down.

Three thirty. He suspects Taba has often been detained over tea and nibbles — the people of Potters Road are overly friendly. From the porch he waves to Solara and Stefan, who are taking the dogs for a walk along the shore. They have a concert tonight, bluegrass at the Legion.

He decides to start a fire, a small, cozy one in his den's airtight woodstove. He'll be working late in this room, so may as well be comfortable.

He puts Chernikoff away, picks up Hoff's preliminary report. It's in German but with an English translation which, on comparing texts, seems done inexpertly. Arthur takes some pride in his German — studied in his youth so he could read Goethe and Schiller — and he hopes to impress the Nobel Laureate with his fluency.

Hoff's popular book, *De-Pollination: Why Chemistry May Kill Life on Earth*, has been published in many languages. Arthur will take his recently updated German version to bed with him tonight.

The author photo on the flyleaf depicts a handsome, robust hiker in an alpine meadow in bloom. A soft-brimmed bush hat, a hiking pole. Arthur worries the man may come across in court as *pompös und aufgeblasen*.

8

It's after six, so Arthur has survived the first few hours of the ordeal known as trial preparation. He feels brain-dead, like one of those lost, poisoned bees. Their sense of direction is corrupted, they can't find their way to the hive.

Their assassins, known as *Varroa destructor*, are mites once isolated to the Far East that have now spread to Europe and the Americas, where they are ubiquitous. They lay eggs in the hives, and when the eggs hatch the young mites feed on the bee pupae.

These parasites are helped along by pesticides that impair immune responses. Which leads back to neonics. Such chemicals not only make bees more susceptible to the mites, according to this study from *Science Magazine*, but cause overstimulation, paralysis, and death, and, short of that, loss of learning, foraging, and homing ability. They persist for years in soil and water, and spread to wildflowers near treated fields. Even the homely dandelion is a suspect carrier.

Arthur flips through several pages. Here is a coloured illustration of a bumblebee. He wonders: How can you not love a bumblebee, so fuzzy and colourful and playful? More laid-back than the honeybee, less driven, but under an even graver threat.

He takes a break, succumbs to the mesmerizing display of flames flickering from the window of his woodstove. The alternative view, outside, is too sombre now in the darkening twilight. The third option is to return to grappling with the tables of dosages and bee deaths drafted by a scientist at the University of Sussex.

But now a fourth option opens up: the dogs bark a welcome to Taba Jones as she enters by the gate.

It would be impolite not to ask her to come in awhile. He remembers she occasionally enjoys a bit of brandy with her coffee.

As he takes her coat, he tries to recall if he's ever seen her in a dress. Certainly not in such a hip-hugging skirt. Better than those baggy pants she prefers. He restrains himself from complimenting her, fearing that might be heard as a flirtation.

She takes off her shoes, replaces them with slip-ons from her bag before being shown into his den, where she pauses, goggling at the stacks of documents and case reports. Arthur admits he's finding little joy in his role as a weary, overworked warrior for justice. "It's a struggle gearing up."

To his offer of something to eat, she says, "If I have another piece of pie I'll die." Taba is pleased with herself, having collected nineteen signatures from thirteen families on Potters Road. "Even old Gullivan, who doesn't much fancy all the Goody Two-Shoes environmentalist stuff going on."

In the kitchen, Arthur digs out a decorative coffee mug he rarely uses. It came off Taba's potting wheel a decade ago, Margaret's birthday gift to Arthur. It's the only one of Taba's creations not to have been banished by his life companion; the rest are imprisoned in a basement storage room.

Her back is to him as he returns to the parlour — she's almost hugging the woodstove. "Perfect," she purrs, upon sampling the brandy-laced fair-trade Ethiopian in her artisanal mug. Without turning, Taba, a gossip sponge, entertains him with the affairs of the day, and the night, on Potters Road. Mrs. Tucker, according to a neighbour, gets it on with her gardener in the potting shed. Mr. Gullivan's daily health walks often have him sneaking up Mrs. Rodlee's driveway.

Arthur sips his own coffee, just half a cup, to be polite, as he stands awkwardly by the bay window. He would prefer to sit, but suspects it's proper etiquette to stand until a lady guest seats herself. She's not budging, so he stays on his feet.

In an effort not to stare at her snugly wrapped rear, he looks outside — and starts, spilling hot coffee on his hand. Ulysses is trying to mount Rosie. But making a botch of it, being shunned. Arthur decides it's unwise to describe the scene to Taba, jokingly or otherwise — it would come off suggestive, a libidinous hint.

She continues to offer her back to him, her well-rounded bum. If she's doing that to arouse him, it's working; he feels himself heating up. He needs to sit, to avoid a male mating display through the thin material of his slacks, and finally parks himself in his old club chair.

At which point she turns to him with a bright smile. Somehow, Arthur notices, a blouse button has come undone, allowing for a more abundant display of cleavage. She salutes him with the coffee mug. "I remember this. Your birthday. Did she throw out everything else?"

"It's in storage." The awkward topic causes him to tense.

"Along with her husband, eh?" Grinning, as if to persuade him she's joking. "I guess I ought to get Rosie back. Am I keeping you from work?"

She seems in no hurry to leave. And anyway Arthur can't deny he's enjoying her coquettish company, enjoying this break from his labours. "I'll get a fresh start in the morning. There's still coffee in the pot. And a good splash of Courvoisier." The threat of an erection has faded, and he rises.

"I'd love another." She departs the hearth, shoves him gently back into the chair. "After I pee. Don't get up." She pads off.

Doubts creep in during the several minutes he's out of range of her magnetic field. He really ought not to have asked her to linger. Is it the testosterone talking, trying to seduce him into doing something stupid and dangerous? Is this some kind of test of strength?

The mere thought of Margaret's reaction to this little coffee klatch causes the air to hiss from his inflated libido. Margaret will not be pleased to hear that Taba had warmed herself with coffee, brandy, and a roaring fire in his parlour. He ought to tell her before she hears it from the neighbours. Taba's old Chev sits outside the gate, so the whole of Garibaldi Island may soon know. Arthur can only hope she will be gone by the time Stefan and Solara leave for their bluegrass event.

He gets up, wanders over to his desk, laughs at himself. Such paranoid nonsense. His is just one of a dozen homes Taba visited on Potters Road. No island scandal is being played out here, other than that she has something going with Herman Schloss, who is handsome and rich and quite a catch. Arthur is happy she has someone else. Now they can get back to being friends and confidants.

On returning with her refilled mug, Taba gets close, invading the neutral zone he'd intended to enforce. She smells very good, of perfume and something else, glandular maybe, that causes him to go into full breast-fetish mode. Fearful she will detect his returning erection, he backs up and sits back on the thickly panelled oak desk.

Taba eyes him mischievously over the rim of her fortified coffee, takes a healthy swallow — she's already a little high — then sets the mug on the desk. "I'm so glad we're friends again, Arthur. And by the way, I get that you love Margaret. Whom I also love. But it's complicated, because I also love you. Differently. As you've guessed."

No, he hadn't guessed. She reads the surprise on his face, breaks eye contact, turns pink. It's the first time Arthur has ever seen her embarrassed. He is shaken by that casual confession of love, though vaguely flattered. He blurts, "What about Herman?"

"Temporary relief. He's a snore. He doesn't recite from Keats and Milton."

Though Arthur did — on a mossy bluff under an arbutus tree. Arthur had underestimated the aphrodisiac power of great poetry, hadn't expected it would get him so energetically laid.

She has him surrounded now, one hand resting on the desk, the other on his knee. He seeks a reprieve, twists about, riffles through the legal briefs. "I'm expected to have this all mastered by the weekend. I feel like a college student, procrastinating as exams loom."

Message received, Taba backs off, just a step. "I'm sorry, I'll stop teasing." Then: "By the way, I can help you."

"How?"

"You're having trouble concentrating. I can help you with that."

Again she moves closer, her hands on his thighs. In retreating, he finds himself in an awkward and indefensible position: leaning back, his elbows on the desktop, and he can't sit upright, can't find leverage. He feels a tug: emboldened by the bulge below, Taba has unhitched his belt.

She slides down, her face lost behind a thick crop of red hair, her nimble, muscular fingers working with astonishing speed, snapping open belt, button, and fly, and stroking his engorged member as one might throw a vase on a potter's wheel. There comes a tickle, a touch of tongue, and in a panic he lurches up, breaking the connection, and grasps Taba's arms and gently, firmly, leverages her back.

"I can't," he says. "I'm truly, truly sorry."

"You're *sorry*?" She withdraws, straightens, eyes wide with disbelief. "How truly, truly Canadian of you."

§

Taba's departure was swift, with Arthur in a red-faced fluster, getting her coat, then retrieving Rosie and seeing them to her truck, as all the while they emitted shared croaks of strained laughter and apology over their respective roles in a clumsily improvised bedroom farce.

Now, in the bathroom, standing naked under a hot, cleansing torrent, aghast that he'd skirted so close to a disaster of orgasmic magnitude, hardly able to fathom how, God knows how, he'd found the strength to deny the primitive urgings of his id, desperate to believe he had not encouraged what nearly happened, feeling shame but still flushed and quivering with carnal heat, Arthur takes matters into his own hands.

CHAPTER 15 » RIVIE

1

Friday, March 29

Panic Disorder opens tonight for Bryan Adams on his Never Say Never Tour — the iconic rocker will donate tonight's net to the Earth Survival Rebellion defence fund.

It's in Roy Thomson Hall, and we scored prime seats, as is our right, Lucy and me at the end of the third row, other Rebellionairs here and there but not Doc, who avoids crowds like the plague he's afraid he's going to catch.

We have to stand and kick back our seats as a stunning Asian woman, with the bored expression of a model or princess, wiggles past and claims a seat a little ways down, advertising her perfect legs as she shrugs from her coat. Hair the colour of seaweed. Braless under a top that doesn't pretend to hide her nips.

"It's Sooky-Sue," Lucy hisses. The holy roller who stole the heart of Rockin' Ray. You wonder what really goes on at the Assembly of the Lord Saviour Divine. They claim to be post-psychedelic, in recovery, but maybe it's a cover for something shifty, maybe a tax scam. They have their own house of worship, a former Jehovah's Witnesses' Hall that was too square to survive on the Danforth. They chant, they sing.

Lucy says, "Do you think that bitch is beautiful?"

"Well, striking. It's the beauty inside that counts."

"Please. You know how I hate nostrums."

"Okay, she's mousey and unoriginal but faking it just for you, sweetie, because she knows you'll be staring at her all night."

"Did you see her dilated pupils? She's supposed to be a recovering trip-head. Not."

"Ray loves you. He'll be back. He doesn't want you to see him in pain as he dries out."

"Where's your minder?"

"Who?"

"Richard the Second. Richard Dewilliger-James. Why isn't he sitting on your lap?"

"He's somewhere back there sulking. I had to tell him my heart belongs to another."

"You told him after or before you fucked him?"

"He's still a virgin. This is your chance, Luce."

"Maybe I will." Looking again at Sooky-Sue.

I made a mistake several weeks ago putting my tongue in Richard's mouth. My bad, because he rightly got the wrong idea. Yesterday, invited for lattes and appies in his solar-powered rooftop condo, I panicked when he seemed about to propose and told him I was secretly engaged. Not mentioning to whom. He knows about Chase D'Amato, that there's an arrest warrant out, but he doesn't know about *me* and Chase D'Amato.

Even I don't know about me and Chase D'Amato.

House lights dim. Darkness except for the exit signs. A rustling and rumble of anticipation. A thinly focussed spotlight spears the stage. Standing under that spot, audaciously, zanily, is Rockin' Ray Wozniak, in a safety helmet, goggles, and ear protectors, guitar raised above his head like a warrior's shield. He flings the ear protectors into the crowd, whirls his axe, and blasts a triumphant ascending chord as his bandmates emerge from the darkness behind him.

Roy Thomson Hall explodes in a kind of joyful delirium, every woman and man capable of standing is jumping and stomping and screaming and whistling. Including me, Dear Diary.

2
Tuesday, April 2

It's mid-morning and we've all been rounded up like stray cats into Nancy Faulk's boardroom. We're seated around an oval table, my co-conspirators and me, with Nancy and Selwyn Loo at the head, who explain that a judge wants us to show up in court tomorrow so she can observe us in the flesh. Apparently, she's pissed off because some kind of pretrial hearing should have happened long ago, before the trial date was set.

Missing from the room is my occasional lawyer, the avuncular Arthur Beauchamp, who is somewhere above Greenland on his way to cajole Dr. Dieter Hoff, the microbiologist. The judge is too antsy to wait for him to return, so tomorrow Nancy Faulk will represent us all.

Alas, she's in a totally fubar divorce situation and looks wretched. One of her associates is filling for her at some kind of mediation thing in some other boardroom. At stake in this tug-of-war, among other salient matters, is an antique, yes, *cuckoo* clock.

"When *will* my allegedly legendary lawyer return?" I ask.

"Arthur has a flight back on Friday," says Nancy.

"Well, it'll be good to have him drop by." That was too obviously snarky so I add, "Really."

Nancy says she expects that on his return he'll stop overnight in Toronto but then will go on to the West Coast. "He has a situation involving a cougar named Tigger. Don't ask."

Lucy, beside me, goes, "What's with this cougar that's so vital? Is it sleeping in his house? Did it eat his dog? Is my lawyer also the local Animal Control Officer?"

"Goats," Nancy croaks. "He's got goats. Chickens."

Clearly, Nancy is overly hungover. She was leaning on her elbows but now wilts, groaning as she passes the baton to Selwyn. He stands, cool, calm, taking charge, begins with an update on the Queen v. us.

Happily, our necessity defence is shaping up. Hopes are high that Dr. Dieter Hoff will get retained. Experts who have come aboard include a microbiologist, climatologist, statistician, and a professional beekeeper.

Selwyn has met with them all but is too modest to say he awed them with his almost extrasensory genius. Enough funding is in to pay their fees. Donors, Bryan Adams, various good-works orgs, others like the Beekeepers' Association, have been generous.

So while the great Arthur Beauchamp is missing in action and hotshot feminist throat Nancy Faulk gets shitfaced every night because she stupidly married a dick, it's up to a sightless chess master to allay confusions and sooth worries.

So attractive too, so racked. The mystery continues: Is he gay? Dual? He's got to be situated somewhere in the LGBT queue. Surely he could get it up for randy Rivie Levitsky. But he doesn't give off signals.

I am so primed. Chase D'Amato is available only in my self-abusing dreams. Richard Dewilliger-James was a potential desperate measure before he was claimed on waivers by Lucy Wales. She practically abducted him Friday night at the concert after-party, swarming him while Rockin' Ray and Sooky-Sue looked on.

Richard the Second, who only had eyes for me, is now addled over an anarchist with green hair who espouses direct action as a way to ignite the spirit of revolt among the downtrodden. She'd banged him in his Tesla X then twice more in his penthouse. Turns out he isn't gay buy crazy shy, and so naive and awkward he had no idea what to do. Lucy says he comes from snoresville but is taking him on as a kind of project in sexual therapy.

Meanwhile, as Selwyn continues to outline the case for the defence, Lucy and Ray are diligently not looking at each other from opposite sides of this oval table. But I suspect the revenge sex may not be working because he seems calm and spaced. We know he's not on drugs, because they test him weekly. Could be hooked on meditation.

Ivor Trebiloff is beside him, then Amy Snider. So totally in love. Sharing every good cause as it come along. Childless, they spend part of their evenings helping out at a hospice for kids with terminal cancer.

Why can't Rivie Levitsky find such companionship? Why can't I even get laid? My only offers are from internet trolls who want to rape me. *I know where you live.* I've seen that more than once.

Selwyn says he's a little baffled over tomorrow's appearance in what they call chambers court. The judge apparently wants to look us over, maybe expecting a freak show for her entertainment. Following that, she will be closeted with counsel for a pretrial, at which issues of law and procedure are supposed to be resolved in the absence of public, press, and us.

Lucy nudges me, whispers: "Woman judge is good, right? As opposed to a misogynist prick."

To my other side, Okie Joe inputs Selwyn's briefing with a virtual keyboard. Joe Meekes. Now that I know his full name he somehow seems more distant, less of a pal. Or maybe that's because of his changes: he's more settled, his mood softer, he smiles more. Can't figure out why. Hmm, is it because his girlfriend came up from Tulsa in December and has moved into his flat?

She's a chiphead too, and together they're running an online network for the American Refugee Society, keeping them connected, helping with immigration, red tape, finding jobs.

So that's everyone up to date but Dr. Helmut Knutsen, who sits as far away from me as possible because he saw me sniffle. It's just a

cold, it came on after the Bryan Adams benefit and is mostly gone.
Anyway, I've given up trying to get seduced by him, I can't even get
within range.

However shy, he does have an ego, with overtones of the messianic. Lucy and I have decided his *raison d'être* is all about creating his
legacy, even if it costs him a decade in the brig.

Selwyn sits. "Nancy?" He has to give a little nudge to rouse her
from her torpor.

She slugs back some aspirin with a gulp of water, then looks
sorrowfully about the room. A raspy, croaky speech: "We have been
kicked in the butt by Deputy A.G. Azra Khan. He has conspired to
put us in front of a vain, sociopathic birth accident. Madam Justice
Colleen Donahue, former go-to gal for the insurance industry,
fighting claims by the crippled and the flooded out. A leftover from
the Harper regime, bitter because the Liberals have kept her stuck at
the trial court level."

Groans around the table.

"Even worse, she's smart. Taught insurance and constitutional
law at Osgoode. Former talk-show pundit and essayist for the right-
wing media."

More groans.

"Also, she hates me from a confrontation at a bar retreat when I
called her a fascist cunt."

Ironic cheers.

3
Wednesday, April 3

When I come from the shower, towelling off, Lucy is pondering
what to wear for court. She's also smoking pot, which she never used
to do in the morning. Until Ray got into religion and Sooky-Sue.

"I've got to be myself today," says Lucy as she tries on a T-shirt
inscribed "My Vagina, My Rules."

This is not normcore attire. I go, "So I guess marijuana *does* cause brain damage. You heard Nancy. The judge is a sociopathic birth accident, and I'll bet she's a pro-life Irish papist whose Bible says you do not hold exclusive rights to your own vagina."

Lucy whips off the shirt, tosses it like a stripper would, with a whirl, a windup, and a fling, aiming for Sinbad, who spills a bowl of granola as he jumps off a table. He yowls back at her in anger.

"Fucking cat," says Lucy, getting a rag.

The flat, as usual, is a total slum. Lucy is the main perpetrator of this but likes to blame the cats. We have to clear out the rubble soon, attack with mops, borrow a vacuum somewhere — Professor Wenz returns on Easter weekend.

Whereupon Lucy will move in with Richard the Second and I'll be on the street. How fair is that? He's *my* bondsman. But the bashful nerd isn't offering me a spare room in his vast solar eyrie.

Right now I'm more worried about today, about things somehow going awry in court. Nancy Faulk, with her hangovers and her harried vibes, doesn't give me confidence.

I open my laptop and search for *Garibaldi Island Cougar*, scroll down, click on a headline from the Garibaldi *Island Bleat*. "Cougar Runs A Mock" — I can't tell whether that's a typo or ironic. An alpaca. A Shropshire sheep. Various chickens and pets. A goat. Okay, Beauchamp's excuse isn't so flimsy. He raises goats. Their need for safety trumps mine. I'll see him when I see him.

While I'm at it, I check my messages. Some illiterate toad has found my text address. I NOW WHERE U LIVE COMMIE JEW CUNT. Sorry, scumsucker, you don't scare me.

Lucy holds up another T-shirt. "This will make the judge happy. Poached it off a guy at the beach last July, he was selling this shit off a wagon." It reads, "Pro-Life. Pro-Gun. Pro-God."

I finally remember how clever Lucy is at faking me out. I observe how her hair is its natural brunette, no face paint, no black outlining. She'll obey Nancy's dress code: clean, neat, casual.

I too will suck up — with leggings, neat blouse, long skirt. Maybe I ought to go all the way: a cowl, like Atwood's Offred.

§

The Superior Court of Justice, at 361 University Avenue, is a boring, blocky rectangle, seven storeys of courtrooms strung out along corridors that radiate from the building's dominant feature: a pair of giant escalators. A utilitarian touch, but ugly. They're lifting Lucy and me to the fourth level, where we are to attend in room 4-8 for what they call a pretrial hearing.

The courts don't open for twenty minutes but there's already heavy traffic on our upscalator, with slick-combed lawyers in black robes taking meetings on the go. Some reporters in their off-the-racks and permanent presses have hustled up past us and are bugging a lawyer in a pinstripe suit and flashy fuchsia tie. They want to know what's going on, why the secrecy.

"It's our prosecutor," Lucy says. "He's gorgeous."

Deputy Attorney General Azra Khan has turned to banter with the press but looks over their heads at Lucy and me, appraises us unblinkingly. He's disturbingly handsome. Dark, magnetic eyes. Longish black hair, grey at the temples. Laugh wrinkles.

A reporter asks if he made a deal with the defence.

"Ms. Stevens, the Crown has zero interest in backroom deals with anyone. The Crown is interested solely in justice being done in a public court of law. Let the bright light of the free press freely shine on this case." A rueful grin. "Except, sadly, today, when we shall be in camera."

Protests erupt.

"I shall dutifully convey your concerns to Her Ladyship." He returns his gaze to Lucy and me. I lock onto his eyes, let him know his jaunty sound bites don't impress me. He still ascends backwards on being delivered to the fourth floor, but does a nimble little dance and alights safely. His bag-toter, what they call a junior, stumbles along after him.

The reporters join other media milling outside our courtroom, along with a fair number of the curious public, all barred from entering by a court officer.

"Don't turn to look over your left shoulder," says Lucy.

I do so and see Nancy Faulk talking with someone facing away from me. That broad, muscled back seems eerily familiar. The slumped shoulders.

It's Howie. Howell J. Griffin. Now his rugged, sad features come into profile. His belly flab, his least attractive feature, has gone. What the hell is *he* doing here? Has he discovered reading? He holds a couple of library books.

Before he can turn and see me, I am ushered into chambers court.

4

The only difference I can see between a regular and a chambers court is the lawyers don't wear robes. In fact, room 4-8 is actually fitted out for jury trials, with a glassed-in prisoners' box that can barely accommodate all seven of us. The court officers must endure Nancy's wrath as they hustle us into it: she maintains we're free on bail and can sit anywhere.

The Court Clerk, last name Pucket — *Miss* Pucket she wants to be called, not Ms. — regrets to advise that Justice Donahue prefers the traditional practice of "defendants being in their proper place."

She's a cliché, this Miss Pucket: the prissy bureaucrat who has served the system with obsessive loyalty from time immemorial.

Nancy is in better shape today, though far from peak, smelling of breath mints as she goes to my ear: "Howie Griffin buttonholed me. He hoped to talk to Arthur. I said no. I'm setting him up with counsel."

"If he wants to meet with me, no way. He could be armed and dangerous."

"Wrong concept. This is more of a romantic comedy. He's bitter, yeah — at Chemican for kicking his ass summarily out the door. But he made it clear he'd be happy to see you get off. Have you ever considered the big goof may still be in love with you?"

I can't, won't accept that twist in the plot.

Madam Justice Colleen Donahue, already scowling, enters energetically from the wings. Severely cut grey hair, squat, dense, muscular, like a wrestler. A perky nose that twitches right and left, like a bunny's, as she looks us over in the prisoners' box. Her expression turns to disappointment as she sees no fangs or devil's horns. Doc wears a tie. So does Ivor, his trademark bow tie. Rockin' Ray has pulled his hair into a neat ponytail. He looks a little dozy, though.

Khan makes his promised pitch for the journalists outside, with a barb at us defendants "who doubtless will join me in welcoming the press given their penchant for eagerly basking in media attention."

Nancy punches back: "My learned friend's shyness, on the other hand, is legendary. I assume we're appearing on a pretrial motion, so I have no objection to this court being open to the public. But first may I voice a complaint that this hearing was brought on with unprecedented abruptness. As a result, Mr. Beauchamp could not be here."

Donahue twitches her bunny nose. "And why is Mr. Beauchamp not here?" A strong, deep voice, as muscular as her build. I think I remember her now, from before she was a judge, punditting on the tube, clever and sardonic.

Nancy says, "Because he was on a plane to Berlin yesterday, when notice of this hearing went out."

Khan responds. "I had no role in setting the matter down for today, and learned counsel knows that."

Donahue's expressive nostrils widen. "I set the date, *sua sponte*. You may wish to regard that as crisis intervention. A jury trial is six weeks away from being on top of us, and it's scheduled for a full month, and there has been no pretrial hearing and no preliminary issues have been raised, argued, or resolved. I don't know why that's so, but I don't want anyone bringing any last-minute motions that will delay this trial."

Khan rises. "M'Lady, with respect, the Crown made several overtures to my learned friends to suggest a pretrial date. Each was answered with unfulfilled promises to get back to us."

I figure Nancy would prefer to postpone things until Arthur shows up, but she confidently announces she's ready to answer any of the judge's concerns. I'm learning about trial lawyers. You can't ever come across as timid or unprepared.

The judge puts everything on pause, directing a court officer to open the door for the public. She makes a spirited speech of welcome, particularly aimed at journalists — she's not shy about buttering them up.

Once everyone has settled in, she surveys the press rows, and begins in a stern, teacherly tone: "Please understand that though this is a formal court appearance a publication ban is in effect until the trial has concluded. I will meet with counsel afterwards for a conventional pretrial hearing that ought to have occurred months ago." Her decibels rising sharply. This lady is either profoundly irritated or acting out for the media. "And yet, somehow, inconceivably, by some back-door means, without the court having been consulted, a trial date of May thirteenth, barely forty days from now, has shown up on the court calendar."

In what sounds like a rehearsed duet, Nancy and Azra Khan express regrets at a slip-up. A month-long drug conspiracy had got postponed. Counsel had arranged with the court registry "to fill the hole in the court calendar with the case at bar." Regrettably, due to "administrative oversight," Her Ladyship was not informed immediately.

Proving, I guess, that the machinery of the justice system is as well oiled as any bureaucracy.

Madam Justice Donahue accepts their grovelling apologies, then launches into a roll-call thing, right out of kindergarten, turning first to Doc, asking if he understands the charges and how he intends to plead, and when Nancy interrupts and says she'll talk for us Donahue snaps that this is her courtroom and she'll do it her way. Nancy rolls her eyes theatrically. The presence of the press has amped up the vibe in here.

We all respond, calmly and clearly, yes, we understand, yes, we plan to plead not guilty. Rockin' Ray is almost *too* calm, spacy, his voice vaguely haunted.

Judge Donahue then explains we'll be asked to make our pleas formally on May 13. I wonder if that's it, we're done, like a pain-free trip to the dentist, then Donahue asks the prosecutor: "The manslaughter charge against the accused Wozniak, how is it alleged the death came about?"

She's been looking at Ray, who is still zoned out, returning a wide-eyed zombie stare. I worry that he's off the wagon, in breach of his bail conditions.

Khan explains about Archie Gooch's collapse outside the Sarnia plant, then being in a coma for four and a half months before expiring. "The Crown avers that Mr. Wozniak deliberately committed an assault as defined in Code Section 265 in that he threatened to apply force to Mr. Gooch while pursuing him with a weapon. That led directly to the coma and ultimately to heart failure."

A snort of laughter from the gallery has Donahue looking about in vain for the culprit.

Nancy jumps in: "Evidence will show Gooch had enough Oxycodone in him to addict a herd of elephants."

"Counsel, I didn't ask you to comment, but since you're up, please correct me if I'm wrong — I understand the defence seeks to raise a necessity defence."

"We are quite excited over it, M'Lady. We have engaged several expert witnesses, many from afar, and Mr. Khan is responding in kind."

"Only out of an abundance of caution," says Khan. "We maintain my friends are reaching for the moon for a defence not available in law."

The judge then says she wants another hearing, a full day, in open court (with a nod to the press), to test the admissibility "of this extremely rare and difficult defence." She makes a face, wrinkling up her nose, as if smelling something putrid. "I will ask counsel to agree on a date that is also suitable for Mr. Beauchamp. It must be well in advance of May thirteenth, to allow counsel, if necessary, to change course — we don't want experts flying in from all over the world if, ah . . ."

Her Ladyship stalls, her nose keeping beat to the sound of snores from the prisoners' box. It's Ray, and he is asleep, though leaning on Okie Joe, who nudges him awake.

A titter of laughter is a trite phrase I adore, and that's what runs through the courtroom, amplifying the judge's irritation at Wozniak. She complains to Nancy: "He was staring at the wall like a dead man. I need to know if he's on a prohibited substance."

Ray seems to snap to attention. "I'm clean, ma'am, Your Honour. I sometimes fall asleep when I'm in prayerful meditation."

The judge doesn't seem to have an answer for that, and waits while Khan consults with his junior. Khan then explains that Wozniak has honoured all his bail conditions and has consistently passed regular tests for alcohol and drugs.

Donahue ponders that, and sneaks a glance at the media — whose smiles warn her they may depict this hearing as a scene from a Broadway comedy. She decides to cut it short, announces, "Counsel will meet me in chambers," and rises without a further word. Miss Pucket calls, "Order in court."

I wait while the room empties, watching Nancy head off with the prosecutors for their pretrial. I wouldn't mind talking to her about what just went down, especially the judge's snide view of the

necessity defence, but she makes hand signals telling me not to wait
— she'll be joining Khan for lunch.

To talk about what?

§

We're dim summing in Chinatown, all seven of us, joking, speculating, lingering over cheung fun, as we wait for Nancy to get
back to us. I feel sorry for her — she's taken on extra burdens in
Beauchamp's absence.

I can't help but express a niggling worry she could offer a plea
bargain, and they go, "No, no way, not Nancy." But she has to be
dispirited by the naked hostility she got from the judge and her bad
vibes about the necessity defence.

"Anyway," says Lucy, "the Crown doesn't do deals with terrorists." Khan, on the escalator: *The Crown has zero interest in backroom
deals with anyone.*

So there's this frisson of paranoia in the Smiling Dragon
Restaurant when Nancy finally phones in. Doc listens. His eyebrows
go up. Now a wry smile. He puts her on hold.

"Mr. Khan was only bluffing — he *does* deal with terrorists. If
each of us agrees to plead guilty to one count of conspiracy, all other
charges will be dropped. Including Ray's manslaughter. Nancy wants
to know our instructions."

We all groan and boo.

"LOL," says Lucy.

I go: "Does she recommend that?"

"The offer came from the other side. She just listened."

Everyone joins in a vigorous rejection, except Ray, who stares
into space.

Lucy throws her fortune cookie at him. He comes awake.
"Unpossible," he says.

CHAPTER 16 » ARTHUR

1
Wednesday, April 3

Arthur wakes up dazed, disoriented, his inner clock still on Pacific Time. But on arrival in Berlin he'd set his watch to local time, and it reads a quarter to six, so he has slept fourteen hours. Through his fourth-storey window he can see strips of rosy cloud, the promise of a vibrant sunrise.

He'd needed that long sleep — it had been a murderous flight, fifteen hours including time spent in airports. It was mid-afternoon when Arthur checked into this hotel, the Französische, near the opera house, in the city's cultural heart. He'd had a bite to eat and headed directly to bed. But somehow, despite his restorative sleep, he still feels fagged.

He rises quickly, hurries through his ablutions. He has decided on a brisk, cold walk before breakfast, to get his benumbed legs working again. He will have time to visit a couple of museums before joining Dieter Hoff tonight for dinner, when, hopefully, Arthur will persuade him not to chicken out.

He's a little astonished at the bustle on the streets at six a.m. Are Berliners so fond of work that they get to their desks and shops before the roosters crow? That must be, because many of the shops are already open. Oddly, here is a tavern, loud with laughter and music.

Now the sky turns dark. Arthur feels prickles; something evil and portentous is occurring. He's afraid he has suffered some kind of stroke, an aneurism that has altered his perception, caused a time warp.

As he watches a procession of formally dressed musicians, all bearing instruments, disappear into the Opernhaus for a performance of *Rigoletto*, he speculates that he has been propelled into future time. Finally it descends on him that it's still Wednesday, and it's six ten p.m. He had slept not fourteen hours but two.

He lacerates himself mercilessly as he makes his way back to his hotel, to his room, to his bed. *You* are Rigoletto, you are the clown. Your brain cells have calcified. You belong in a care facility, not a courtroom. You pose a menace to your clients.

Or maybe it's because he's still rattled over having been so sorely tempted into sin by Taba Jones. *You're having trouble concentrating. I can help you with that.* The invitee at war with himself, Good Arthur versus Bad Arthur, his conscience versus his cock, and even though the good guy won there's no escaping the fact he'd practically asked for it: the warm fire and warmed brandy, his obvious ogling, his tented pants.

The most guilt-provoking facet of Taba's near fellatery was its aftermath: mere minutes later, in the shower, enjoying a great, shuddering, spouting orgasm while evoking her receiving him. However, the upside was that he regained his ability to concentrate — spectacularly, in that he absorbed all those forbidding precedents, opinions, and scientific studies in ten days. And as he focussed on the plight of bees, and the knock-on effect of planetary disaster, his private concerns faded for a while.

But they bloomed again when Margaret, on Sunday, called to chat, mostly about Arthur, his health, his stress level, her worries about the rigours of an overseas flight in economy class — which in fact turned out to be an ordeal beyond imagining. But this had already been an expensive defence, and it was mostly funded by small donors. Arthur's conscience refused to fly business class.

"Why does he have to see *you*?" she'd asked. "How arrogant of him to demand you come to him. After Selwyn did his best."

"He'll be more comfortable with me. Selwyn, frankly, has not mastered the art of putting strangers at ease."

Her call had come just as Arthur concluded yet another week of reading, absorbing, collating, working out how Chemican's vast environmental threat should be presented to the jury, how it would be best understood, how to get maximum impact. So his head was full of that, and he wasn't tuned in when she mentioned she'd be in Toronto for some kind of LGBTQ event, and that they should get together. If she specified a date, he didn't catch it. He would call her this Saturday, before his return flight, to confirm time and place.

So far, in the weeks since Taba's visit, he hasn't found the courage to mention it to Margaret. Or even that she was in the neighbourhood with her door-to-door petition. But why should he have raised a matter of such microscopic importance? When Margaret asked, on Sunday, "So what's the latest gossip?" Arthur turned the topic to the futile hunt for Tigger. But he'll have to give her the bowdlerized version of how Taba popped in before she returns to Garibaldi and hears it from the neighbours.

Such thoughts tumble through his head until sleep finally comes.

2
Thursday, April 4

Again Arthur wakes up at twilight, but this time on the real Thursday morning, at six-forty hours. Just to make sure, as a sanity check, he hurries to his window: a few joggers and cyclists, a delivery truck — Berlin is yawning awake.

He rises, ravenous, and as he readies for the day he pores over a map of the Mitte. Arthur has only two more days here, so he will be a busy tourist. But he hasn't had a nourishing meal since his travels began, so his first stop will be the hotel restaurant.

He last visited Berlin before the Holocaust Memorial was completed; it will warrant a brief morning stroll and some sombre reflections about the extraordinary evils that humans are capable of. He must also try to stop by Humboldt University, where he once gave a lecture and where Dieter Hoff teaches doctoral students. This evening they are to meet at a Turkish restaurant the scientist favours. On the phone, he sounded pleasant and engaging, eager to meet the famous advocate. Flattered, Arthur replied just as effusively.

In the hotel restaurant, while piling into his eggs and sausages, he remembers to turn up his phone, muted and ignored since he was first airborne.

He puzzles over a voice message from Nancy Faulk about Justice Donahue signalling, at a pretrial hearing, that she threatens to torpedo the necessity defence before the jury gets sworn. Azra Khan, emboldened, "offered to put us out of our misery."

No fuller explanation by email. Arthur's callback must wait; it's the middle of the night in Toronto.

His phone nags at him to check his text messages, a medium he has yet to master, and he finally locates worrisome information from Solara Lang: Tigger has killed a deer near Centre Road, only a mile from Blunder Bay and not far from Evergreen Estates. Residents there "are freaking." Stefan is doing night watch with Ulysses.

Arthur suspects the deer was one of those semi-tame ones that folks in that small subdivision attract by spoiling them with handouts. In any event, by venturing to the populated south, Tigger has grown bolder. And more dangerous, particularly to himself. Locals with hunting rifles won't wait much longer for Conservation Officers to find and deport it.

It would be a tragedy if that rare and magnificent wild creature were to be killed. Arthur needs to do his business here quickly and get back.

§

As he wanders about the maze-like lanes of the Holocaust Memorial he feels an ominous vibration in the area of his heart. He fears this is it, the big one, the stress of travel has killed him. But it's his phone, in the breast pocket of his suit. He fumbles it free, and is greeted rudely: "The great man deigns to answer! I'll try to make this brief."

Arthur grows glummer by the second as Nancy fills him in: Justice Colleen Donahue's snap pretrial hearing, her apparent distaste for the necessity defence, her order that its legitimacy be tested at a second hearing — it's set for eleven days from now, Monday, April 15. "She wants to cut us off at the pass, Arthur. She won't allow *necessity* to be whispered to the jury. It's the new n-word."

Arthur's in shock. That would strip their clients of their only defence. Everything they've invested would be wasted, all the mental toil, the travel, the costs, this mission to Berlin. The trial would be all but a formality, convictions all but mandatory.

"Khan left that courtroom smelling blood. He'll take a plea to conspiracy, no offer of leniency. The Seven voted unanimously to tell him to fuck himself."

"Justice Donahue: Did she do any criminal work as a lawyer?"

"Oh, yes, five years as a Crown, to get her training, then getting the big bucks as an insurance litigator, leg-off claims, screwing widows, the usual."

Arthur heaves a shuddering sigh. "Is there any way we can get this judge moved from the case?"

"Not short of a drive-by shooting, and even then no one will pry this trial from her cold, dead hands. Did I tell you she was vain? *The Guardian* was in court. *Le Monde*. She made sure *they* got notice."

Arthur thinks aloud. "Then that's our edge. If she forestalls our only defence, they'll quickly head back to their newsrooms in London and Paris. She will lose the limelight she apparently prizes. We have to do our subtle worst to persuade her not to lose a chance to referee a historic debate among renowned scientists."

"Then it's *really* important that you land Hoff."

3

"To me, they are great heroes, your clients," says Dieter Hoff. "For their effrontery alone, they deserve medals. But for such bravado first prize must go to the Chemican corporation, yes? — for their lies and SLAPP actions and their falsified tests. Here, in the EU, the directors would be in prison."

In the U.S. and Canada, Arthur complains, no one at Chemican has even been investigated, let alone charged with a crime. The governments share culpability; their regulatory bodies having failed at due diligence.

Arthur and Hoff have been at this for an hour, roasting the enemy over kebabs and squid and fried eggplant. And, for Hoff, too much wine. Arthur sips soda water with lemon, but Hoff is on his second half-litre of Merlot. It seems to have coloured his face, though maybe he has somehow retained through the winter the ruddy outdoors look that graces the back of his dust jacket. He wears a similar bush hat, even while dining — circumstantial proof of both baldness and pretension.

After the waiter tops up his Merlot, Hoff raises his glass in a slightly unsteady salute. "I am happy to know that observing me over-consume alcohol doesn't make you uncomfortable. It does comfort me. Especially lately."

He seems unready to expand on his afterthought, so Arthur just says, "It bothers me not in the least, Dieter."

Hoff reaches into a bag and hauls out a hardcover copy of *A Thirst for Justice*. "I feel I know you, Arthur. Because your life is an open book." He laughs at his jest, and extends his pen.

On the title page Arthur describes Hoff as "*Ein neu gefunden freund.*"

"I had a tumultuous first marriage also. Berthe was like your Annabelle. Also in the opera business, but as a singer. Not a great one — she exercised her vagina more than her vocal cords."

Arthur winces. The wine is getting to this newfound *freund*. Presumably, it will ultimately give him the courage to explain his unforeseen reluctance to testify.

"But she was much in demand. Mostly because she was fucking the booking agent. On tour, her exertions were heroic — everyone from the lighting director to the entire woodwind section and at least two of the Three Tenors. Pavarotti for sure, she boasted of it. But it is I who got sued for divorce. I assume you are aware of that."

"I am only aware you were divorced." Ten years ago, according the profile Selwyn's team prepared. They must not have looked beyond the fact of the divorce. There were no children of that union but he is remarried and they have a daughter.

"The grounds were cruelty. Like you, I felt emasculated, and had a long period of impotence. Berthe mocked my poor efforts without mercy, and one evening I swung blindly at her and broke her jaw."

The restaurant is noisy, so Hoff has raised his voice, causing nearby diners to glance their way. Arthur cautions him with a raised hand. Hoff lowers the volume: "Obviously this is news to you."

"I'm afraid so." Arthur, who has never struck a woman, is shocked by this confession from a brilliant scientist.

Hoff moves his chair closer to Arthur. "Probably it is not news to your prosecutor, or to the Canadian police, your famed Mounties. I had not such a good lawyer as you, and in family court I was found guilty of assault."

He dabs a wetness below his eyes. "I hoped to be brave, like your Sarnia Seven. I was ready to risk a hostile cross-examination about my bad marriage, even if I had to explain she was a lying whore."

Arthur assures him that his marital history is irrelevant and would not be mentioned to a jury trying the Sarnia Seven. "An act done in anger does not diminish your expertise or your credibility. An act involving deceit — perjury, forgery, theft — that would be another matter."

"That's what I most fear." Hoff finishes his glass, calls loudly to the waiter: *"Mehr wein, bitte."*

His glass replenished, he says, "Yes, there is a second troubling matter that I hesitated to raise with your remarkable colleague, Selwyn Loo. I was afraid he would judge me harshly." He glances down at Arthur's scribble in *Thirst for Justice.* "My newfound friend. It helps me to share my anxieties with you, who has been through your own struggles and pain."

Arthur nods, waits, hiding his discomfort.

"I am now, recently, accused of plagiarism."

A rambling account ensues involving a graduate student, her studies of honeybee depopulation in Eastern Europe, her prognosis of an impending collapse of fruit and berry production, her concluding, stirring words of warning in a paper she revised and submitted for publication, and the mysterious reappearance of those words, intact and unedited, in Chapter Twenty-Seven of the updated edition of *De-Pollination.*

"You can see how this can happen, Arthur. Katerina was my student, and her work — which has earned her a position at Cambridge — got mingled with mine. So much paperwork, so many studies, so many accreditations to so many fine scientists. I *believed* I had composed that passage. A mere hundred and fifty words, but the vindictive bitch threatens action, exposure, my public shaming."

A vision flares in Arthur's mind of Azra Khan rising with a gleeful look to begin his evisceration of the defence's main witness.

Hoff continues: "If it goes to a disciplinary hearing, or worse, a suit in damages, it is all over. My career is over, kaput. You know how these things go, Arthur, with the opposite sex. They are so unforgiving, so unrelenting, *ja?*"

"Have you acknowledged her contribution in any way?"

"*Nein*, no . . . It is hard to explain . . ."

"Please try."

"You see . . . this was two years ago . . . there was also a romantic aspect."

"With Katerina, your student?"

"Let us say she studied under me." A hoarse laugh. "My wife found out, of course, as women tend to, and of course that ended my little *liebschaft.*"

Arthur has trouble accepting that he has flown from the Pacific shores of North America to Central Europe just to learn this Nobel winner is a plagiarist and a misogynist. He waits until Hoff heads to the WC before phoning Lufthansa to book an early morning flight back.

4
Saturday, April 6

Arthur slept in till nearly ten, after yesterday's long, dismal flight and the slow, crowded boat to the Southern Gulf Islands. Now, over oatmeal and coffee, he ponders his agenda for the weekend, which will feature much garden time, much vigorous hiking with Ulysses, and not much agonizing over the *Queen v. the Sarnia Seven.*

That matter goes back on the shelf. A mountain lion is on the loose and, warns the latest *Bleat*, is running "A Mock." It has certainly become bolder, coming closer to home. Many of his fellow small farmers on Potters Road have livestock and own rifles. The casual killing of a cougar is a serious offence — unless you find one in your sheep pasture. Then, the defence of necessity kicks in, by law.

Stefan and Solara, alternating long, wearying shifts, weren't able to exercise the farm's rambunctious Irish wolfhound, so today Arthur will take Ulysses for a long trek into the hills. The dog seems confident this will happen, because, having finished his own morning porridge of tripe, eggs, yogurt, and vitamins, he waits impatiently at the door.

It's sunny out, but Arthur stuffs a rain poncho into his rucksack, just in case. A chicken sandwich, a flask of water, a bone for Ulysses. His sturdy yew walking stick. Into the pocket of his down vest go his phone and his reliable but rarely used Leica, already on video setting in case he glimpses the cougar.

Ulysses bursts free out the veranda door, sending a covey of juncos into the air, then races over to greet Solara, setting up mason bee houses, then to Stefan, hosing down the muddy tractor. Stoney and Dog had managed to excavate it from its hole without getting the backhoe stuck too — miraculously, the backhoe is back in action with a new left-hand differential side gear. According to Stefan, it was in use for several hours. Arthur will want to see proof of that.

Recent sunny days have teased daffodils to bloom, but have also encouraged the horsetail and creeping buttercup, so tomorrow their advance scouts must be ambushed with hoe and trowel. Spring is definitely icumen in: last night he heard the first tentative voices of courting frogs.

Arthur waves the leash at Ulysses, who obeys reluctantly, his hopes dashed that friendly old man will take him on his favourite route, the muddy north pasture, an off-leash zone. But that would mean passing Jeremiah's well site and confirming suspicions that the two sandlot archaeologists did little more this week than lean on their shovels..

So it's off up Potters and Centre Roads, and then where? The day is fair, the far hills beckon: it's time to revisit Quarry Park. Before closing the gate, Arthur takes a view of his funky waterfront farm, his *angulus terrarum*. He fills his lungs with the sweet, moist air of the Salish Sea. Berlin is a distant memory. Toronto seems just as far away.

§

It's slow going up Centre Road, mostly because Arthur often has to pull Ulysses into the weeds to dodge the cars, trucks, and campervans pouring from the ferries — weekenders hurrying to their cottages, desperate to escape from urban toil and tension. Finally, he can see, from a rise, the turnoff to Old Quarry Road. Descending it, raising dust, are two government vehicles, the Conservation Service crew cab followed by Irwin Dugald's Explorer SUV.

The truck's driver and its four passengers swivel to look at the character with the giant dog. They look tired, defeated. Arthur half expects to see Tigger's corpse in the back, but it's full of tools and tents and tarps.

Curious about where everyone is going, and even more curious about the apparent bullet hole in the SUV's windshield, Arthur signals Dugald to pull over. The hole is high on the driver's side of the windshield, a web of glass blossoming from it. Arthur can't dismiss the notion this has something to do with Dugald's sole passenger, the mistake-prone Animal Control Officer, Leroy Letkow. Both roll down their windows.

Ulysses recognizes the RCMP constable, whom his master's voice once described as a bonehead, and growls at him. "Be nice," Arthur says.

Dugald gives Ulysses a loud "Woof!" and the dog backs up a step. "Real brave hound, isn't he? We're on a call down to Mary's Cove. We just got word Mrs. Rollicks's pet pot-bellied pig went missing. Hers is that yellow bungalow near the church."

"She left her gate open, is what I heard," says Letkow. "That's just asking for it. She impressed me as senile."

"*You're* senile." Dugald is in a foul mood. "The cat's on the move, Arthur. The north island doesn't do it for him anymore. Here, down south, is where the easy prey hangs out."

"Fish in a barrel," says Letkow, who is eager to share his research on cougars: "This dude is trying to establish his territory here, for which males need up to fifty square kilometres, bigger than this whole island. So he kind of owns it, from a nature perspective." He adds, dramatically: "He controls the night."

"Shut up, Leroy. Our orders, Arthur, are if we can't bring it in, we do it in, it's that simple. Right, Leroy? Isn't that why you were practising your gun skills in the parking lot this morning?"

"Nobody told me it was loaded. No damage except to the windshield. No one got killed."

"The wildlife task force aren't willing to work with him. I'm taking him back to his B and B. Should be taking him in."

"I am the Animal Control Officer. Some people seem to forget that." Letkow makes his plea directly to Arthur, as if presuming he has some kind of authority. "There's an animal loose that I need to control. I am being inhibited in my duties."

Dugald continues to pretend he can't hear or see Letkow. He is focussed on Ulysses, whose mood has improved — he sits on his haunches, enjoying the scene. "I'm sorry I suspected your wussy dog, Arthur. Can't see him harming a bug, except accidentally stepping on one, so I don't expect he'll be your best friend when a rogue mountain lion decides to grab a quick lawyer for dinner."

This provokes a roar of laughter from Letkow that seems an effort to get on the cop's good side.

"Put a sock in it, Leroy. I used to own a *useful* dog, Arthur. A German shepherd. They guard. They bark at assholes instead of sticking their nose up them."

"Irwin, I think you're jealous that I have such a spirited, handsome companion. What happened to your German shepherd?"

"It was Roberta or him."

Though Old Quarry Road is narrow, steep, and unpaved, federal funding has kept it well maintained — it's the sole land route to a national park. But the colossal trucks and other rolling stock of TexAmerica Stoneworks will reduce it to four-wheel-only rubble if they ultimately get their way in court. This is a very nasty company — Arthur can see them destroy or poison nesting grounds of the swallows and falcons.

They've had biologists up there, hirelings paid to play down the extent of wildlife losses. They've located and counted old nests and collected feathers, bird droppings, and other avian evidence. Armed with their reports, the two current Trustees would be free to again rezone this parkland for industrial use. The recall petition, which Zoller calls a witch hunt, is still collecting names. TexAmerica claims it's not funding the incumbent Trustees' "Stay the Course" campaign.

There's a lot to worry about on Garibaldi. That's good. It keeps Arthur from worrying about the Toronto case. It is internationally important, yet he has somehow developed a kind of grudge over it, a resentment.

As the road coils higher he puffs harder, leaning into his walking stick, staggering a bit as Ulysses jerks him along. The pup begins to resist — this wasn't what he'd bargained for, hauling slow, wimpy human friend — so Arthur unsnaps the leash. Ulysses romps ahead, finding a shortcut through the high dry forest of fir, oak, and arbutus.

A few hundred metres farther along, they come upon the first limestone seams, from which blocks have broken — they lie helter-skelter by the roadside. Ahead, a dog yaps, prompting Ulysses to race around a rock pile. He races back quickly, spurred by profane and frightened yells from unhappy male human. Arthur recognizes him as one of the young fellows who often drop into the Brig. There's no gate or fence here, just the TexAmerica guard hut and the yappy dog.

The guard stammers on seeing Arthur: "You can't come here with . . . What kind of animal is that?"

Arthur puts Ulysses back on leash. Tug Cooley, the bearlike foreman, exits a trailer parked among the trucks and heavy equipment, sleeping giants that have sat on their wheels and tracks for the last six months. The yapping dog, Cooley's famously annoying corgi, is baiting Ulysses, a mock-bravado response to the leashed interloper.

"That animal's a donkey, Cal, you dumb-ass. You wanna donkey ride, I'm sure Mr. Beauchamp will oblige. What can I do you for, Mr. Famous Trial Attorney?"

"You can do nothing for me, thank you, Tug. We intend to wander about awhile in our lovely community-owned park and enjoy a lunch from our favourite viewpoint." He looks at the rubbish strewn about. "We will pack out our wrappers."

"I'm supposed to tell everyone we ain't taking blame if there's an accident — you're at your own risk. Shut up, Dumbbell."

His corgi's name is Dumbbell? Why would one do that to a dog? But the command works, and Dumbbell shuts up.

"Sign here," Cooley says. It's a legal document releasing TexAmerica from all claims from any event, past, present, or future, occurring at this site, or for that matter anywhere in the universe. A signatory is granted the one-time right to enter described lands for which the party of the first part holds mining rights.

"Only an imbecile would sign this."

"I have orders from the top. We got to protect ourselves from mischief and thievery—"

"Tug, if you hinder Ulysses and me in any way I will sue you and your company for five and a half million dollars in punitive and exemplary damages."

Cooley is silenced, clearly unsure how much to credit a threat made with such lawyerly specificity. "Okay, look, the release is obviously not intended for normal established residents like you. We got problems with those freaks at Bleak Creek, they're here practically every weekend, and days between, camping overnight. They think it's a playground."

"It is." Arthur assumes they come in the back way, a walking trail across Gwendolyn Park that connects Bleak Creek to the quarry.

"A thieves' playground. They don't respect property. Tools have gone missing."

Naive, earnest escapees from the rat race. Who said that? Ah, yes, the potter with the Amazonian bosom. *It's complicated, because I also love you. Differently.* He still hasn't decided how to tell Margaret about Taba's visit — or how much to say. Should he make light of it? *Arthur, I don't find this funny at all. She'd already collected your signature, so why was she knocking back brandy in our parlour? What else did she want, as if I didn't know?*

Distracted by these thoughts, Arthur interrupts Cooley's harangue about "this friggin' island" with a wave and an adieu, and lets Ulysses pull him toward the forested path that climbs the ridge to the top of the limestone cliffs — to the escarpment that locals still call Bob's End, sixty years after Bob went over.

Man and beast finally arrive there, exhausted, and slump onto a bed of moss. Arthur keeps Ulysses leashed, to restrain him from following in Bob's footsteps, and goes into his pack for his sandwich and the bone, and he and Ulysses set to.

The panorama on this crisply sunny day is spectacular: the archipelago of islands in the Salish Sea, the distant rings of snowy peaks to north and south, the lone majesty of Mount Baker to the east. The sole view-blocker is a high, long crag, only a stone's throw away but on the other side of a deep crevasse.

Spreading out below him, to the north, is Gwendolyn National Park, its thick primal forest, its lake and stream, its ocean inlet. Beyond it, out of view, is Bleak Creek. In clear view, just below the quarry, are Mattie Miller's alpaca ranch and Hamish McCoy's waterfront hobbit house. With good binoculars one can see his tall humanoid art forms with beaks, wings, breasts, and a penis erectus.

The bald eagle's nest from which Arthur had seen fledglings try their wings last summer is deserted. No sign of cliff swallows, but maybe it's early. Peregrine falcons usually overwinter, however, and he has seen a couple wing quickly by, a good sign.

Arthur has kept his body and brain occupied since his flight from Berlin, and this is his first opportunity to relax and empty the mind. But unwanted thoughts of the looming jury trial in Toronto dribble in, and soon the taps are full on. He can no longer blind himself to the crisis created by the loss of an eminent, powerful voice for the bees, of a witness who could stand toe to toe with the savvy communicator, Dr. Jerod Easling.

It finally dawns on him why he resents this trial — the chances of a win were always marginal, but now it's a sure loser. Their Nobel winner crossed off. Madam Justice Donahue threatening to slam the door shut on the necessity defence. Arthur hates losing. It's selfish, an ego thing, but he can't help it.

"Surely, you are aware," said Dieter Hoff before they parted, "of the work of your own Dr. Ariana Van Doorn." Arthur had seen the name several times in the scientific reports he'd powered through.

After Hoff dropped him at his hotel, he'd immediately phoned Selwyn Loo, with a lugubrious account of the professor's sins of arrogance, theft, and infidelity.

Selwyn simply said, "I sensed there might be an issue of character," and went on to express his respect for Dr. Ariana Van Doorn and his qualms about how she would handle the rough-and-tumble of court. She had little experience testifying. Brilliant, yes, but a relative rookie in her field. At the precocious age of twenty she'd earned a Ph.D. from the University of Saskatchewan's Faculty of Agriculture. Now, at thirty-three, she was a tenured professor at Simon Fraser University and a well-published rising star among entomologists.

But Selwyn had heard she was uncomfortable in public and social events, and shied away from speaking at them. Such a wallflower, he feared, would be outgunned by Dr. Easling. Selwyn has returned to

Vancouver to prepare for a pipeline reference and will arrange to meet with her in the next few days, assess her, sound her out.

Arthur's phone erupts, shattering the stillness, slamming the brakes on his buzzing mind. "Where the hell are you, Arthur?" It's his wife, and she's not on the phone but FaceTime, not in Ottawa but Toronto. He can't see her yet, though — his view is of shelves of law books and a window through which he can read a familiar business sign: Fu-King Supplies. It's Nancy Faulk's office on Spadina Avenue.

Margaret adjusts her laptop screen, sits on a desk chair. Her face shows strain, confusion.

"How delightful," Arthur exclaims. "I was just thinking about you, darling." Before she can get a word in he blurts out an apology for not having called promptly, as promised, on his return from Germany. "I had no idea you'd be in Toronto."

"Yes, you did. I told you on the phone a week ago. Guest speech to the LGBTQ Political Action Forum. I assumed — as did your legal team, by the way — that you'd stop off here. This very day. I have a hotel room. With a king bed."

Arthur now remembers her mention of Toronto but not that she'd be staying overnight. A disaster is unfolding. It's out of Rockin' Ray's acid trip: *Lower the life rafts, this ship is going fucking down.* In contrast, Ulysses is in heaven with his bone, oblivious to unhappy human friend holding inedible tiny screen with moving pictures.

Arthur stammers out excuses: "I'm devastated, my mind was entirely elsewhere. I've truly been missing you, darling, so I must have been massively distracted when you mentioned we might have a night together. Had I remembered, of course I would have, ah, turned heaven and earth . . ." He's dying. "I confess that I had a powerful need to be here, home, Garibaldi. I had to clear my mind. We had a setback."

"I know. Hoff. I talked to Selwyn." She stands, leans over her computer for something. A tissue — Arthur hears her blow into it. She comes into view again, looking out onto Spadina, another tissue at her eyes. "Okay, let it go, Arthur. There are more important things to worry about. Nancy tells me there's a hearing soon at which the judge could eviscerate your only defence." She finally faces her laptop camera. "I hope you're ready for it. Nancy seems to think you don't have your heart in this trial."

Margaret's poorly masked show of emotion has Arthur shaken, despairing, helpless — somehow life has failed to equip him with the tools to deal with distress of those he loves. His response is staccato, machine-like: "Please reassure them I am pumped for it. We may have a new star witness. Dr. Ariana Van Doorn. At the top of her field, and she's been right under our nose all this time. Please tell Nancy I shall be in Toronto in plenty of time for the pretrial issue on the fifteenth. I'm already preparing for it. Not this very minute, but—"

Margaret interrupts his frantic babbling: "Exactly where are you right now, Arthur?" On the screen, she bends, squints.

"Up on the mesa at Quarry Park. Bob's End. With Ulysses. He's just over here torturing a cow's knee bone." He aims the lens at Ulysses, who, shockingly, has dropped that bone and stands at stiff-tailed attention, hackles raised.

Margaret's voice comes breathlessly. "Oh, my God. Hold onto Ulysses's leash with all your might, Arthur, and look up, follow his eyes."

Arthur freezes for a moment, overcome by fear of the unknown — maybe Jeremiah has finally been revealed to Margaret. But what she glimpsed, in the far background, on a ledge of the crag that thrusts from the view-blocking limestone mesa, is a large, handsome, well-fed cougar, crouched, staring, still.

Ulysses, sensing Arthur's sudden tension as a call to action, surges forward, tugging the leash so hard that Arthur slides on his bum a few feet before he gains control. Tigger watches this scene with indifference, then jumps from the crag and disappears before Arthur can take its picture.

He and Margaret talk excitedly over each other. The cougar has a hideaway in the quarry, she insists, a den. Arthur is gratified that

Tigger appears not to have moved his base to the populated south. "Just think," he says, "if I hadn't been here . . ." He pauses to rethink and censor. *If I'd been in Toronto* is what he was about to say.

Margaret isn't listening to him anyway. She is congratulating herself — she'd managed to preserve her FaceTime image as a photo, and has a shot of Tigger sauntering away.

He says, "The media will love that."

"Get a grip, Arthur. I won't turn informer, nor will you. We have to protect that beautiful wild animal."

"Surely we should alert the wildlife people."

"I don't trust them. They have a licence to kill."

She's right. Arthur thinks of Leroy Letkow and his bullet hole in the windshield.

"I trust Stefan," Margaret says. "Talk to him." She shouts: "I'll be right there!" To Arthur: "I have a cab waiting. I'll see you when I see you."

"I love you." But Arthur is talking into the void.

6
Wednesday, April 10

Laid low for three days with yet another cold, Arthur has had to stay indoors, so of course the fates decreed that the weather would be constantly, delightfully brisk and sunny. It continues so this morning, and despite his drippy nose he is determined to get out with Ulysses, a trip to the store for mail and missing essentials. Like tissues — he's carrying around a roll of toilet paper.

They will visit Jeremiah's well, where Island Landscraping has allegedly been hard at it for the last week. If so, and if Phase One has been completed as Stoney maintains, he is owed a draw on his contract. Fat chance.

Arthur's plans for an early start are spoiled when Nancy Faulk phones to ask if this is a good time to have a chat about the hearing on the necessity issue on Monday, five days hence. It is not a good time, but Arthur puts down his walking stick, fixes himself another pot of tea, and for nearly an hour they hash over how to dissuade Madam Justice Donahue from gutting the Sarnia Seven's only hope of a defence.

Nancy has already drafted her own argument, which she has sent to him as a "pdf," a form of electronic document — he has no idea what the initials stand for. She pelts him with case citations back to 1754, which she promises to send as links.

"I'll give it my best, but as you know—"

"Yeah, you're a computer illiterate."

"My dear Ms. Faulk, I do not need cases to tell me it's fundamental to the rule of law that a judge may not usurp a jury's right to decide on guilt or innocence."

"Tell it to the judge. I printed out the leading cases and my brief. You'll find everything in a Priority envelope at your local post office."

Yet another fat chance. She doesn't know the local post office.

Nancy feels it necessary to update him on the saga of her divorce — obscenities exchanged in a law firm's boardroom, her wannabe ex storming out over an issue with a money-losing timeshare unit in a ski lodge.

The rant consumes several minutes, and she concludes with, "Speaking of divorce, your wife is totally pissed at you for breaking your date on the weekend."

"I am aware. One of those domestic mix-ups that occasionally flare up and quickly burn out. I wired her flowers with a contrite note affirming my unyielding, eternal love. Thankfully, Margaret is not without friends in Toronto, and I of course include you, my dear Nancy, so I'm sure she wasn't lonely."

"Not in that convention hotel. Famous for the action in its pickup bar. All those handsome men breaking free of domestic constraints."

"Don't be ridiculous."

"He says, frothing with unrepressed jealous fear."

Arthur remembers: Margaret spoke at some gay and lesbian event. His leg is being pulled.

"Get it together. Read the case law. Hustle your bloody arse out here."

§

Ulysses looks on, detached, uninvolved, as Stefan and Solara struggle to fix the north pasture's tractor gate, which somehow, with unintended brute force, Ulysses has dislodged from its hinges.

Arthur gives a hand, holding the gate steady while they try to fit it back on. Solara calls: "Must have happened when he was roughhousing with Tabatha Jones's dog."

"Ah, yes, I remember — Taba popped in out of the blue with a petition." Arthur quickly rolls out some toilet paper and loudly applies it to his nose. "Damn cold. Must've got it on the plane."

Arthur remains in turmoil over his dawdling failure to put things straight with his life companion. Were he to admit, in a mindless eruption of honesty, that he and Taba had made even the slightest erotic contact (that grasping of fingers, the touch of tongue), or conjured her up for an onanistic workout in the shower, his divorce proceedings would dwarf even Nancy's in ferocity.

Margaret won't be back on Garibaldi for a week and a half, the start of Parliament's Easter break. She will not mix it up with friends and neighbours; she'll want peace, a private time, a chance to rejuvenate. Anyway, no one will talk about Taba. The cougar. They'll still be talking about Tigger the cougar.

After the pasture gate can finally swing freely on its hinges, Arthur detains Stefan for a consultation: "I've been thinking about your idea of going it alone with Ulysses."

Stefan had offered his aid, and his uncanny ease with wild animals, to the BC Conservation Service, but the cougar hunt was a closed shop, best left to "our qualified experts." Feeling slighted but also challenged, Stefan now wants to take Ulysses before dawn, unseen, to where Arthur saw Tigger. Stefan thinks its den is a nearby cave or recess, and if he can locate this hideout, he'll phone the Conservation Service and seek a guarantee for the cat's safe conduct off the island.

"I might let Ulysses go with you," Arthur says, "if I'm allowed to toddle along."

"Excellent." Expressed without enthusiasm, as if he feels Arthur may not be up to the hard scrabbling. "Let's set it up after I do a scouting trip up there."

When Stefan first approached him with the idea, Arthur had demurred, fearful of exposing Ulysses to danger. But the young wolfhound is needed less for safety than for his traits as a sight-hound and his reliable nose for the spoor of fellow beasts. Wildlife Conservation has resisted hiring bloodhounds for this job because of the cost — they are handled by a third-party contractor.

In any event, there's no guarantee Tigger is still on the island. No domestic animals have been lost for a week. Mrs. Rollicks's pot-bellied pig was found yesterday plowing up the flower beds of St. Mary's graveyard.

7

While traversing the north pasture, Arthur heard hammering from the well site, and an occasional curse or shout, but now the only sound is of ravens hoarsely heckling from the cedars, so Stoney and Dog have likely taken their mid-morning beer break.

Arthur suspects Stoney is financially distressed — a frequent plight — and is putting on a show to extort a quick partial payment before he sits on the job for another year. Arthur stopped visiting the site long ago — the lack of progress was too depressing. The malingerers took down an alder grove to create a clearing, they got Arthur's tractor stuck in the mud, and the backhoe broke down. That's about it.

Ulysses senses that his two favourite local layabouts are down there in the alder bottom, and he sprints that way. Several seconds later, hammers start up again, prompted by the foreseen arrival of the dog's owner.

The path opens up between the trees, revealing a circular clearing bathed in sun and surrounded by hills of newly dug soil and clay. Gone is the backhoe, but it has done estimable work, excavating around the well to a depth of seven feet. Arthur could be looking at a New Age meditation circle — at midpoint is the shrine: Jeremiah's well, a sturdy, round structure of cemented rocks held up by angled timber braces and surrounded by a moat. Stoney and Dog, who have buttressed the braces with crossbeams, greet Arthur, lay down their tools, and pick up their beer cans.

"I have underestimated you fellows."

"Dog and me accept your apology. We're used to being underestimated, aren't we, Dog?" A rhetorical flourish that goes unanswered. "As you see, sire, on-time completion of Phase One is done, the heavy machinery phase."

Arthur has to bite his tongue not to take issue with the alleged on-time completion. Dog, sensing his partner is in negotiations mode, takes Ulysses aside, to share a sandwich from his lunch bucket.

Arthur stares over the edge of the pit, at the moat — at least two feet of water cover the lower part of the well.

"That's gonna be an issue," Stoney says.

A non-issue, however, had the dig been done in dry season. Arthur ought to have reduced the agreement to writing, the way a lawyer would.

"Seeps right back in after you pump it out," Stoney says. "So there'll be a slight delay while the water table lowers."

Arthur will want "slight delay" defined. He listens patiently to Stoney's explication of Stage Two, which will involve extensive hand-digging. Doing so within the clogged well could be dangerous, so the plan is to use a spade until they hit the foundation stones, and break and enter from there.

"If there's a human skeleton, like you suspect, that's where it'll be."

The Historical Society's plans for a ceremonial unveiling will be a bust, Arthur fears, if Jeremiah's bones aren't here. But the many sightings of his ghost, however ephemeral and mystic, have to mean something, a silent cry for a proper burial. Could he have been chased into his well by a cougar? And drowned there? Arthur adds that to his hobby collection of morbid theories about Jeremiah's demise.

The stones forming the well's spherical walls seem snugly fitted. Hardly a dribble of excess cement. Arthur is awed by the mastery of the creator of this rustic oeuvre, by the artistry and effort of a lone bachelor pioneer. The quality of his homemade spirits was also said to be superb, according to scraps of information passed down. Perhaps he was a genius unrecognized in his time.

"Luckily we got the right man for this labour-intensive job — Dog over there is a digging machine. But we're talking unaccountable man-hours — there's a seam of heavy marine clay down there. I've run some numbers and my best estimate for Stage Two is an even ten grand. That's on top of the five you already owe, of course."

"We have an agreement, Stoney."

"We do? Jeez, sorry, I don't remember seeing it."

"A verbal contract is valid in law. The total agreed price is fifty-five hundred."

"Yeah, but I understood that was only for Phase One."

"No, Phase One was three thousand. Plus I gave you a thousand for start-up. Plus I paid for your left-hand side gear." Arthur gets a headache. He's losing all dignity here, haggling with Stoney while honking into balls of toilet paper.

"I recollect it was five K for the backhoeing and then we'd work out a deal for the hand-digging phase. Now maybe I was stoned at the time and forgot I was dealing with one of the sharpest legal minds in North America, and if it's your word against mine I'm obviously doomed, but I honestly never thought this would happen between us after all the years we been—"

"Stop." If Arthur doesn't accept defeat he'll be seen by the whole island as a shyster ripping off a guileless local tradesperson. He pulls out his chequebook.

§

Arthur kicks himself all the way to Hopeless Bay, riled at having been outduelled once again by the crafty stoner. Operation Jeremiah has now doubled in cost. The bleeding, he solemnly vows, stops here. The Stage Two contract will be printed and signed this time, and witnessed. The party of the second part will be required to adhere to strict deadlines. The completion date of the thirty-first day of August shall be strictly enforced. Only acts of God, war, or insurrection will annul this formal indenture.

Arthur tugs Ulysses off the road as Mattie Miller's farm truck overtakes them at the rise looking over Hopeless Bay's wharf, store, and bar. While normally she might haul feed or tools, today her cargo is a herd of hitchhiking hippies from Bleak Creek, with their packs and bags and children, all on a shopping trip.

Mattie has obviously noticed the RCMP cruiser in the lot, and lets out her dozen non-wearers of seat belts on a private, secluded driveway. Arthur stops to engage with her, mostly about Tigger: even though he took down one of her alpacas, she forgives and hopes he has swum off.

Meanwhile, the Bleak Creekers have found Ulysses a great curiosity and mob him. He mobs them back, excited by the attentions of a pack of whiskery, long-haired young humans with interesting odours. A couple of preschoolers take a special shine to Ulysses, and pet and hug him and get licks that have them squealing with laughter.

The new bulletin board provides an excellent hitching post for Ulysses. The cougar warning is still posted there, as is a photo of the once-missing pot-bellied pig. The "barley used" wood chipper is still for sale. A psychedelic-design leaflet about a "solstice midnight party" in Quarry Park reads: "Celebrate the Equinox under the Sign of Aries!!" Arthur finds this wondrously confusing, given the spring equinox was three weeks ago and the summer solstice is over two months away.

His first purchase is a box of tissues, quickly put to use. Then a brand of pills that promises to dry him out. He adds some fruit and sundries to his basket, then steps outside to see if Ulysses is okay. A four-year-old boy hugs him around the neck. Another toddler trips over his prone form and is scooped up by a Bleak Creek mom. Arthur is proud of his maturing pup. When he is not making mischief, he is remarkably gentle, especially with the young.

Ulysses's sole known enemy, Constable Dugald, is in the pub. From what Arthur can make out, through its windows, he's having words with a table of TexAmericans: Tug Cooley and his crew of watchdogs. They seem in a sullen mood, especially Cooley. Maybe he's in a snit about the belated equinox party planned for the quarry.

Arthur will wander over there presently, for his tea, but first must summon courage to wrestle with Abraham Makepeace for the rights to his mail. The postmaster is not at his post, however — he is in the utensil section with the Bleak Creek families, either helping them or guarding against their presumptive urge to shoplift.

Or he may have been crowded out by Nelson Forbish, who is again behind the counter, stuffing his *Bleats* into the boxes.

"Nelson, could you do me a favour and fish out my mail? Box ninety-two." Arthur sneezes and honks into a tissue, gets a "Gesundheit" but no sympathy.

"That would be highly irregular," says Forbish, "plus Abraham would kill me. This will keep you busy." He passes Arthur a copy of the *Bleat*. "I found out too late about how Mrs. Rollick's pig survived by hiding in the graveyard, but I can't be a hundred percent perfect all the time."

Pet Porker Latest Cougar Cuisine, says the headline. "The actual latest cougar meal," says Forbish, "was Tug Cooley's corgi. That's why he's knocking back the bourbon."

Those at Cooley's table have got very loud now that Dugald is no longer a calming influence — he has gone down to his vehicle and appears to be radioing for instructions.

Poor Dumbbell. Arthur remembers how he snarled and barked at Ulysses. A similar show of false bravery may not have impressed Tigger. As Forbish pieced the story together, Cooley and a few of his crew, armed and boozed up, went cougar hunting last night in Gwendolyn Park, leaving Dumbbell alone to guard the TexAmerica work site. The dog's remains were found this morning in a nearby gulley.

Forbish has a theory: "Maybe if the damn cat wasn't being chased all over the island it wouldn't always be so hungry. If I had hunters pursuing me, I'd need all that extra protein too."

Their attention is again diverted to the Brig, where obscenities are being exchanged between Cooley's mates and Emily LeMay, who appears to be cutting them off. One of them is impaired enough to poke her in the chest. She cuffs him so hard he nearly ejects from his chair. This brings Dugald racing back up from the lot.

Makepeace too is absorbed in this scene, so Arthur leans over the counter and steals his own mail. Just a few bills. No Priority Post from Nancy as promised, but none expected. Maybe tomorrow.

Crossing the ramp to the Brig, he watches Dugald escort Tug Cooley and his boys to his big SUV. He's a good guy at heart, this island cop, and Arthur expects he'll take them back to the quarry. As for Cooley, he's an annoying loudmouth, and so was his dog, but he loved his pet, and that counts for something. Arthur feels bad about his loss.

Settling down with his afternoon tea and antihistamine, Arthur opens the *Bleat* and turns to his favourite column, Nelson Forbish's "News Nuggets," the second-last of which salutes "our ever popular ravishing redhead Tabatha (Taba) Jones" for collecting nineteen recall signatures "while going door-to-door all the way to Blunder Bay on Potters Road, which she says is her favourite road on our island. Not surprising because she's our favourite potter!"

Arthur's headache returns.

Arthur wakes up to a wet slurp across his face. It's the giant, four-footed alarm clock. Someone had opened the bedroom door to allow Ulysses entry. Probably Solara — he can hear her chatter away to Stefan in the kitchen.

He wants to go back to sleep and finish his dream, to parse it: Arthur was in divorce court, beltless, holding up his pants with both hands. Taba Jones was in the witness stand, stroking what looked like a candle holder as Azra Khan huddled in a corner with his client, Margaret Blake.

His duty done, Ulysses abandons muttering old man on bed, returns to the happier humans in the kitchen, Solara laughing. The smell of fresh-brewed coffee finally pulls Arthur upright; he swings his legs off the bed, lets his feet search for his slippers in the darkness.

It's just after five o'clock; sunrise is at seven twenty-five. The plan is to be at the quarry in an hour. Tigger, who prefers to hunt at night, returns to his hidey-hole in the twilight — so Stefan theorizes. Yesterday, he'd spent a few hours up there, and found enough prints and scat across the chasm from Bob's Leap to satisfy him that its den was close by.

Still in his pyjamas, armed with a coffee, Arthur joins his two co-conspirators as they hover over an aerial map spread on the kitchen table. Stefan has highlighted a path from Bleak Creek — it cuts through Gwendolyn Park and crosses Hamish McCoy's driveway, then enters the quarry well away from TexAmerica's grumpy gatekeepers.

Arthur knows that trail well. "It isn't marked and isn't often used — except, apparently, by the youthful denizens of Bleak Creek."

While Arthur climbs into his clothes, Solara coaxes Ulysses into Stefan's van, then returns with a weather report. "Mostly clear. Half a moon. Chilly. Y'all bundled up, Arthur?"

He has extra layers on, topped off by a jacket with many pockets.

He has a Thermos of tea in his pack. Water, flashlight, granola bars, dog biscuits. Walking stick. Pepper spray. Cell phone fully charged. He spoons up his oatmeal. He is ready.

Stefan folds the map into a pouch, tells Solara: "Stay close to your phone, okay?"

"Yes, sir, massa." With a smile, but Arthur has sensed an impatience with Stefan. Maybe because of a bruised heart from feelings unshared. Maybe because she has detected an imperious air. She wanted to join them but was needed here. Should they locate Tigger's lair, she would relay the coordinates to the Conservation Service tip line — but not before exacting a promise that Tigger would be freed unharmed in the northern wilds.

§

It's well before six as they near the quarry turnoff. Stefan motors past it slowly, following instructions from his back-seat driver. "The road narrows here," Arthur says. "Ends at the national park. There'll be a few downhill hairpins."

Arthur is in fact in the back seat, serving as comfort human to a nervous passenger. Ulysses stopped whining when Arthur switched from the front, but he's clearly not at ease being taken for a ride at this dark and spooky hour.

Arthur still has reservations about bringing his pup into this — Ulysses has never harmed another animal, while the cougar survives by doing so. Arthur worries that his carefree pet may have gotten too cat-friendly, hanging with Underfoot and Shiftless and one-eyed Mouser.

"In about two hundred yards the road trifurcates. Take the right." That leads to Hamish McCoy's hobbit house. Mattie Miller's alpaca ranch is to the left, Gwendolyn National Park half a kilometre ahead.

Stefan's headlights pick up a staked cedar sign: "McCOY STUDIO AND GALLERY, WEEKENDS ONLY," and in smaller print,

"Parental Advisory." As they turn onto Hamish's gravelled driveway, Arthur's phone rings with a repulsive jingle that he hasn't figured out how to de-select. He wonders who could be calling this early.

"Fucking hell, Arthur!" It's Nancy Faulk, with some kind of bad news.

"Hang on a second, please. Pull off here for the moment, Stefan. Yes, Nancy? Is there a problem?"

"Damn right there's a problem. You're the problem." She's practically shouting.

"Nancy, it's not quite six a.m."

"It's almost nine, you mean — you better get used to eastern time. Damn it, I don't care what the time is. Selwyn and I need to speak to you right *now*. Why aren't you fucking *here*?"

Selwyn picks up. "Nancy, may I cut in? Go meditate. I asked her not to call you, Arthur, but she claims to have reached her limit. Did we wake you?"

"Not at all. As it happens, Stefan and Ulysses and I are up early on a quest to find our visiting mountain lion. If you'll excuse me . . ." To Stefan: "That's the layby, we can disembark there." Back to Selwyn, heartily: "How did it go with Professor Van Doorn?"

"She's in. I don't know how I got the impression she was timid. Quite the reverse, very confident and forthright. She regards the opposition's Jerod Easling as less a scientist than a professional talking head."

Selwyn Loo offers a striking contrast to Nancy's frantic and antagonizing manner, though Arthur sees it as a good-cop, bad-cop routine. He mimes to Stefan to let Ulysses out. This call is holding them up.

"She's flying to Toronto for the weekend," Selwyn says.

"Who?"

"Dr. Van Doorn. I'll be in BC Appeal Court next week, but you'll have a chance to share time with her. Assuming you have time to spare, given the critical pretrial issue you'll argue on Monday."

"One second." Arthur mutes his phone, hefts his backpack on, gestures with his flashlight. "The path intersects the driveway about fifteen feet up. Some second-growth fir and cedar, then we go by an old barn. Quietly." It's just a few hundred feet from there to McCoy's bedroom. It wouldn't do to awaken the excitable old runt, or his dog Shannon.

Unmuted, Selwyn continues with an edge of ill-temper: "If I may speak directly, Arthur, we expected you to be in Toronto by now. I am trying to restrain any irritation I ought to feel. Nancy, however, is berserk. I feel she might be on the verge of an emotional collapse."

She shouts: "Tell him he blows this, he wears it forever."

Arthur has never met a lawyer quite as excitable as Nancy, but of course the convergence of this major trial with her divorce has rendered her especially vulnerable. Arthur knows he has to do better. "Tell her that if all goes well, I'll fly out tomorrow."

Nancy comes on another line: "All goes well means exactly what?"

"All's well that ends well. Wherein the king is dismayed by the stealth of the inaudible and noiseless foot of time."

"This scene is more *King Lear*, with you in the lead role, buddy. I am on my knees begging you to show up tomorrow at seven a.m. at the Victoria airport for your reserved eight a.m. one-way nonstop to Toronto. The only excuse I want to hear is you got mauled by a cougar and are at death's fucking door!"

§

As they trudge off, Stefan asks, "Everything all right with your case back east?"

"Emotions are on display. It typically happens to barristers readying for an important trial. Happily, my associate is at her best when rattled."

"But not you."

"I am not. I'm at my best when I find the still point." Advice from a guru known as Shiva, long, long ago.

Once into the grove of tall trees they lose the moon. Arthur holds the leash, Stefan the flashlight. Ulysses, whose excellent eyesight has earned him the lead, strides along with the confidence of one who has memorized the route. And maybe he has, with his specialized hunting-dog brain, having thrice travelled this way in fall and winter.

With the last clump of Douglas firs behind them, they trudge past McCoy's old barn. The path takes a right turn at the shoreline, where the star-glittered sky fully opens and moonlight dances on the saltchuck. Ahead, the rising limestone cliffs seem luminescent too. Soon the path morphs into wide limestone slabs, a staircase created by the Parks Commission several years ago.

Arthur pants harder than Ulysses as they breach the wall through a narrow passage and attain the long flat ridge that Stefan aimed for. On this ridge, maybe sixty metres away, is the dark outline of the crag on which Arthur spotted Tigger on Saturday.

Their mossy ridge, where they will camp, is slightly higher than Bob's End, which is to the east, across the steep gorge. It's shadowed from the moon down there, and Arthur can barely make out the dim outlines of the long gulley. Eventually it yawns open to a gently sloped grassy meadow: a popular spot before TexAmerica moved in. Families often picnicked there and tossed Frisbees and played hide-and-seek in the nearby caves.

The only signs of human habitation are to the north, where McCoy's porch light gives off the merest glow, and, to the south, the brighter shine of security lights from the limestone company's encampment, whose structures, trailers, and heavy machinery hide behind a weed- and moss-encrusted hill of scrap limestone.

They settle themselves on their ledge, bringing out a tarp, flasks of water, and dog biscuits for Ulysses, who gobbles them and lies down to sleep. Arthur joins him, nestling between his paws.

Disoriented by the suddenness of his waking, the cold twilight air, and the strange locale, Arthur sits up abruptly. Stefan, who has just nudged him with his boot, lowers his binoculars and raises a finger to his lips: maintain silence, let Ulysses sleep.

The eastern sky is rosy; Arthur's watch says ten minutes after seven. Rising on his elbows, he sees an almost languorous form lying on the crag, surveying his domain.

Stefan kneels, whispers: "He can make us out too." He straps on his rucksack. "I'll try to persuade him to trust me."

That's not the plan Arthur remembers. They were to have followed Tigger to his den while staying out of sight, relying on Ulysses to pick up the spoor. If the cougar has indeed gone rogue, and kills for sport — an entertainment normally reserved to humans — Stefan risks his life.

Arthur tries to make that point as he follows Stefan to the lip of the gorge for a pee, but Stefan is insistent. Arthur has brought pepper spray; Stefan hasn't — he believes its painful effects should be reserved for humans.

"Take the spray, Stefan. I read that it conditions predators to avoid people."

"It conditions them to fear and hate us."

So that's it. There is silence except for the spatters of urine on the rocks below as they watch the sun surmount the horizon over the San Juan Islands and the Salish Sea.

Engrossed in the sunrise, Arthur is startled when Stefan, who rarely swears, says, "Shit!" He stares, or glares, at the grassy meadow where the gully spreads open, the picnic area. There are scrappy tents and awnings there, unseen last night. One of the Bleak Creekers stands in the meadow, naked, his skinny arms stretched to greet the dawn. Others emerge, in nightwear.

Meanwhile, Tigger dismounts from his lookout and pads off into the maze of cliffs and caves and twisting alleys. Stefan looks helplessly down at the hippie campsite, then hurries off in pursuit.

Arthur is astonished at Stefan's confidence, his recklessness, but expects he's on a Quixotic conquest — the activity below could scare the cougar into the thickly treed Gwendolyn forests. The urban innocents have scuttled a well-laid plan by their mere presence, but for their children's sake they have to be warned about the cougar and persuaded to pack out.

Ulysses yawns and stretches; Arthur picks up his pack and walking stick, and they begin a descent down a well-beaten zigzag path, into the shadow of the sun.

§

They are met by the formerly naked man, who now wears a blanket. It seems unlikely he was overcome by a sudden fit of modesty; he probably got cold waiting to celebrate the sun, which still hasn't risen above the ridge. He introduces himself as Krishna, bows, and says "Namaste," and adds, "I guess this is a bust."

Arthur is confused. "No one's being busted." He remembers this fellow Krishna from Hopeless Bay and the health food store, has seen him cycle down Centre Road. Thin as a stick bug, bronze complexion, beard with a comb stuck in it, facial rings and studs. Guru-like, possibly holding some kind of leadership role.

"I mean the night was a bust, man, the solstice party."

Arthur makes a connection: the confusing leaflet on the bulletin board — "Solstice midnight party. Celebrate the Equinox under the Sign of Aries!!" Krishna may have been doing that to the hilt — he still seems stoned. Maybe coming out of a magic mushroom trip.

Others join them, scrambling into clothes. An odd bunch these, not your typical American refugees. Apolitical, turned on, tuned out, all from a tourist town in Tennessee. Not ridden out of town but bribed to leave. One of them wears a Trump University sweater. Arthur's not sure if that's ironic.

He says, "Today isn't the solstice, I'm afraid. You might have meant the equinox, but that was nearly a month ago."

Krishna's partner has joined him, tattoo vines crawling up her neck, a blizzard of dark hair, a four-year-old hugging her thin legs. "I told you, Krish, it's usually on March the twenty-first, that's a week from now. Hi, I'm Glow. We love your dog."

Krishna rambles on obstinately. "I know for a fact the solstice is always the second weekend of March, no matter what. Like New Year's is always on the first of January."

They are all out now, the entire commune, twelve adults and three little kids. Two of the women look pregnant. Arthur had encountered a group of them only two days ago, near the General Store. Ulysses was the magnet then and still is; wolfhounds must be rare in their former Tennessee hometown.

Arthur displays an iPhone calendar to help persuade Krishna and Glow that today is the twelfth of April, that the equinox is long past, and that the solstice not till June.

"So, okay," says Glow, "I guess that's why no one came. We advertised it all over the island."

Arthur's phone vibrates in his hand. "Excuse me one second."

Stefan breathes hard from exertion, his voice weak, barely audible, as he tells of catching views of Tigger steadily moving downhill.

"What direction?" Arthur asks.

"Away from his den. We both stopped a while ago to look each other over. He knows I'm not his enemy. But I haven't proved to be a friend. Right now he thinks he's leading me astray. It's a game we have to play."

"Yes, but in what direction is he going?"

"Yours."

Arthur looks up at the direction he himself came from, peers about the crags and buttes, sees no sign of life except a soaring eagle.

He regards it as unlikely that Tigger will dare come near this convergence of hippies. The fact that he has eluded capture and detection has to mean he's people-shy.

"Ladies and gentlemen, please gather around." They shuffle forward, the twelve adults, now fully awake, eager to hear words of wisdom from this grizzled old seer who has arrived just as, behind him, the sun is about to breach the eastern wall. Ulysses, now unleashed, and the three children chase each other around the tents.

"Don't be alarmed but I've just learned our visiting cougar may be nearby."

"We love Tigger," says a young man in a U.S. army jacket and a red beret.

"We welcome all life," says a tasselled young woman.

Arthur feels like he's trapped in one of his ridiculous dreams. He should lecture them — Tigger is not from Pooh Corner! — but he can't find the words.

They're not listening anyway — they're welcoming the rise of the fiery sun god, now bursting like a volcano from the pinnacle of the tallest hill. A ritual has been planned for this moment, this first ray of sunshine on the supposed first day of spring, and must be performed even though they are three weeks late. A ritual from which he can't escape: they drag him into a circle of linked arms. He feels foolish, impotent — he has shown himself to be totally ineffective, has been silenced, kidnapped to play a role in some hokey astrological ceremony.

Arthur stumbles sideways as they move in a slow circle, counter-clockwise, muttering something he recognizes as an attempt at Sanskrit, the *Bhagavad Gita*.

Their eyes are closed. No one's watching the kids but Arthur. Two of them are near the tents, with Ulysses, who is lying down. The third, the toddler sired by Krishna and Glow, has gone from view.

There he is, an energetic climber, crawling up a few short steps carved into the limestone. A wanderer who has wandered too far, sixty or so yards in the wrong direction. Again Arthur takes a long scan of the snaggled hills above, and though he sees no cougar he does see Stefan on an outcropping, wildly waving, miming a phone to his ear.

Arthur hadn't noticed the thrumming in his pocket, but it's too late to answer — the boy calls: "Mommy, Mommy, come and see, it's Tigger!"

Arthur has already broken from the circle, and dashes toward the youngster.

His mother screams: "Cosmos! You come right down from there!"

Stefan struggles down a steep slope, a shortcut.

The cougar emerges from behind a boulder, and pauses fifteen feet behind Cosmos, who scrambles down the steps, starts to run. The cougar pauses, then launches forward, and Arthur's heart almost stops — indeed, everything slows: Arthur feels himself run sluggishly, as in his nightmare, watches helplessly as Tigger takes menacing slow-motion bounds in the direction of the fleeing four-year-old. But that's also the direction of his fastest escape route, the long flat runway of the meadow, so it's not clear which instinct has kicked in: pursuit or flight.

Cosmos's parents overtake Arthur, as do a few others with younger lungs and legs. Shrieks of horror as little Cosmos stumbles over a clump of grass and goes sprawling.

Bursting into this slow-motion tableau comes a lanky, leggy, furry missile who shoots past Arthur on the starboard side as his loud, ferocious barks echo and re-echo between the canyon's walls.

Tigger sees Ulysses coming as he is in mid-leap, paws extended, and makes an acrobatic spin in the air of nearly a hundred and eighty degrees before he lands, skids, then makes a beeline for the man-made steps and up the trail that had brought Arthur down here.

Ulysses, who knows that route, isn't content with sending the cougar fleeing. He pounds up the trail in pursuit, as if determined to bring the offender to justice.

Arthur's shouted commands don't call him back.

And now the search is not just for a cougar. It's for Arthur's brave and maybe foolish young dog. He wonders if some ancient gene had kicked in. After all, Ulysses's Irish ancestors took down wolves for a living. Coursing hounds, running machines. The war dogs of ancient days.

He and Stefan have again climbed up and over the northern flanks of the limestone towers, following what Stefan predicted as the most likely route for a cat chased by a dog: a path with no dead ends.

Arthur wants, of course, to believe his brave pup saved the life of the boy called Cosmos. But Stefan, who captured the climactic seconds on video, argues in favour of Tigger intending a fast downhill exit from the valley, a plan foiled when he saw Ulysses had an angle on him.

Arthur suspects Stefan is overprotective of Tigger, too eager to portray a wild animal as not dangerous to humans. It's not a point worth arguing. Cosmos is safe — he had got up quickly and into his dad's arms and Ulysses will surely be celebrated as a great hero.

Stefan's assumption that they're taking the right direction proves accurate, because they can now pick up barks from below: Ulysses's deep woofs, music to Arthur's ears. But a second dog is also being very vocal: it's Hamish McCoy's Shannon, once falsely charged with alpacacide.

It's just before nine o'clock when they emerge from the woods and jog the remaining way to Stefan's van. The canine duet comes louder, and has awakened Hamish McCoy — Arthur can hear bursts of profanity, welcome proof he's his usual robust self. Arthur expects Tigger has taken advantage of this clamour to slip away into the Gwendolyn wilds.

The van twists down a descent between old-growth firs to a sunny high bank that glows golden from scattered clumps of daffodils. A path leads thirty feet below to a crescent beach clogged with driftwood. The driveway curves back toward McCoy's home-cum-gallery-and-studio, and peters out among a cluster of his towering humanoids.

The barking continues, but behind them now, somewhere near the shoreline. Stefan brakes, alights, and sprints that way.

The profanity seems to come from the cold blue sky. "Weepin' bloody fuckin' Jaysus, b'y, help get me down off here."

Arthur looks up. McCoy, in his work coveralls, is perched atop an abstract bronze figure.

"I'se got no memory how I shimmied up, exceptin' an act of God."

Indeed, it did seem that McCoy had climbed this ten-foot-tall erection by means of superhuman effort. A vertical, smooth, veined penis, with a set of small, ornamental wings that he may have used as handholds. Chicken-claw legs. McCoy lies athwart the tip of the penis, his arms and legs hugging its bulbous glans.

"Don't just stand there, b'y, I got me a bad case of the collywobbles."

Across the driveway, slightly downhill, is an aluminum scaffolding on wheels. As Arthur rolls it up toward the winged erection he hears yet another ghostly male voice: "Hello? Hello?" It comes from a portable phone on a grating of the scaffolding.

"It's the b'ys from the fire hall. Call them off, Arthur, so's I don't look like the fool I am. That there rigging saved me loif, as I remember now. Then your hound and my Shannon clummed together to chase off the cat."

Arthur pieces it together: McCoy had been on the scaffolding when Tigger barrelled through the yard toward him. The old leprechaun dropped his phone as he escaped to the penis from the scaffolding, which he kicked away. Ulysses then zipped by, and he and Shannon either treed the cougar or chased it into the saltchuk. They're still making a racket.

As McCoy scrambles down, Arthur reaches for the phone. "Good morning, this is Arthur Beauchamp. There is no emergency."

"Well, that's good, because the ladder truck won't start, even though we charged the battery."

Stefan comes up the stone steps from the beach flashing a victory sign. "Yay," he calls, "they treed him."

Arthur phones Solara to initiate Stage Two of Operation Tigger: ensuring his safe passage from the islands of the Salish Sea.

10

The tide finally ebbs, after crawling almost to Arthur's feet. He has a good seat, a front-row drift log with a clear view of an old, sprawling arbutus that leans over the waves lapping the shoreline. He can catch glimpses of Tigger on a long, stout branch that curls high over half-submerged rocks.

The wildlife officers, who have again rejected Stefan's offer to help, to coax him down, clearly have a problem working out a plan. Several of them stand at the base of the tree, which clings to the rim of a steep, rocky escarpment twenty feet above high-tide line. Were they to immobilize the cougar with a tranquilizer rifle, he would likely not survive a fall onto the rocks.

Among that group is the maladroit dogcatcher Leroy Letkow, a hunting rifle holstered at his back. Arthur hopes it's not loaded. A few other Conservation Officers puzzle over matters from the shoreline, one of them in waders.

Annoyingly, a quartet of TexAmericans has also shown up, and they are sprawled like seals over bleached cedar logs. Typically, they appear hungover — they were likely awakened by the rumble of the government convoy grinding past the quarry's entrance road. Tug Cooley, their relentlessly hostile foreman, is not among them.

Meanwhile, Ulysses and Shannon have retired from the field like honoured soldiers and have been medalled with treats and bones. Both rest on McCoy's porch.

Constable Dugald approaches Arthur, stepping from log to log.

"Hey, Arthur, I saw on the national news about a dog-of-the-year thing for bravery. I want to nominate your hound for it." He sits, lowers his voice, less hearty, more sincere: "Sorry I dissed your wolf-hound. I got endless respect now. Man, I'd kill to have a big bruiser like that. I'm a dog man, you know. Used to be."

"I know. A pity Roberta isn't a dog woman."

"Yeah."

He looks so sad that Arthur wants to hug him.

Dugald comes out of his reverie. "Those wildlife guys better get a move on, before the whole island shows up."

That seems prompted by the sound of an ATV grumbling to a halt on the bankside road above. Nelson Forbish soon appears, two cameras slung about his neck, and wobbles ponderously down the stone steps.

Dugald gets up to go. "That cat keeps moving farther out, that branch is going to break."

Or bend low enough for him to jump safely into the water — that's what Arthur hopes he'll do. Swim away, Tigger.

Now the animal is out of view, behind a leafy bough. Arthur rises to find a better viewpoint on the pebble beach. It's squishy under-foot, where the high tide had reached.

Tigger inches farther out, testing his chances for a safe, wet landing that might avoid the sharp, protruding rocks.

An explosively loud crack. Arthur's first thought is that the arbutus branch broke, because Tigger falls, catlike, feet first. But the blast came from above. A rifle shot, he realizes, and he whips around, looking for Leroy Letkow, and there he is, rifle still sheathed, standing among his fellow animal rescuers, all agog, gaping at the man at the top of the steps, jubilantly raising a high-powered rifle.

"That's for Dumbbell!" Tug Cooley roars.

Tigger's corpse lies broken and bloodied on the shoreline rocks of the Salish Sea.

CHAPTER 17 » RIVIE

1
Monday, April 15

Picture this: A wife put a bullet through her husband's head as he drunkenly snored in bed, exhausted after having beaten her black and blue with fist and boot. Again. He'd done this umpteen times, a ritual. *Crap, it's almost bedtime, and I haven't beat the shit out of Ginnie.* Typically, this would give him a hard-on, and he'd rape her.

He also introduced her to smack, and made her a junkie. Begging for it even as she lay crumpled on the kitchen floor. *I'll never call the cops, please give me a hit.*

She is in the prisoners' box, this poor soul named Ginnie Littledear, awaiting sentence for manslaughter. It's today's opening act, we're next on Madam Justice Colleen Donahue's day calendar. With or without Beauchamp.

Donahue is delivering her judgment on sentence. The range is anywhere from a suspended sentence to life. The defence counsel must have done a crack job last week getting her client down from murder one to manslaughter, given the open-and-shut case, so I'm pleased to report that sympathy does factor into jury verdicts.

We'll need all the jury softheartedness we can get, we of the Sarnia Seven, we who sit here bum to bum in the back row. Nancy Faulk settled us here before racing back to the hallway — she is having a bird over the great Beauchamp being missing in action, and is probably on her phone. The pews are packed: comrades in their Bee-Dazzle ware, diverse greenies, old radicals, lawyers, cops, about two dozen press.

And Sooky-Sue. She is in the front row, just behind the prosecution table. Dressed down today, in a Panic Disorder T-shirt a size too small that calls public attention to her pointy, benippled boobs.

This burns Lucy, of course, especially since she insists that's an old T-shirt she'd left in Rockin' Ray's squat, pre-Sooky. The born-again bitch, Lucy contends, is laughing at her, rubbing it in.

That's because she spotted us yesterday peeking through a window of their alleged church during their paganesque Sunday service. I confess to this childish spying, though I only played a supporting role. As a lame excuse, we're both stressed because Dr. Wenz returns in a couple of weeks. Lucy will be forced to sleep with Dick Two in his opulent penthouse. I will be homeless.

Lucy says it's time to move anyway. Easy for her to say. A couple of times, coming back from a night class, she'd spotted a lurker outside our building. Heavy dude. Toque and padded jacket.

I know where you live. In two weeks you won't.

Anyway, yesterday: Lucy and I subwayed out to the Danforth to the former Kingdom Hall, which is sandwiched between a Greek tavern and a tobacconist. When the front door opened for a couple of late-arriving worshippers wearing, yes, spacesuits, you could hear chants and songs and tom-toms. It looked dark in there, with maybe only candles going. Spooky.

I totally get it that this sounds like a weird dream, the kind caused by smoking too much weed. And, in confession, Dear Diary, Lucy and I had shared a pipe of some locally, organically grown skunk just before this caper. During which the anarchist queen got so maudlin she needed windshield wipers. Two streams came together to create this deluge: she's bored to tears with Richard Dewilliger-James and is still crazy in love with Ray Wozniak.

So, anyway, we scooched around to the rear lane where one window didn't have its blinds down all the way — the last six inches were open for the air. We had a dim view, from the flickering glow of a mega-widescreen TV, of about thirty recovering acid freaks dressed as if embarking for the moon. The chanting had ended, but the tom-tom guy with the Viking horns kept a steady, ominous beat. Looked like Rockin' Ray, but I wasn't sure.

A high priestess in white, the Empress Sooky-Sue, fiddled with a balky remote, and here's where it looked more stupid than spooky, as she finally profaned the Lord's name, bent to the TV controls, turned the volume up. "To boldly go," intoned young Bill Shatner, splitting his famous infinitive, "where no man (sic) has ever gone before." Sooky tossed the remote's batteries into a recycle bin, and that's when she saw four eyes stare at her. She might have got to the window in time to see our fleeing asses.

She knows it was us anyway, because Lucy texted her ex last night: Star Trek? *How seriously fucked up is that?*

Meanwhile, Madam Justice Donahue carries on ("Regrettably, the jury tacked on to its verdict a recommendation of mercy, which I explained I could not legally countenance, let alone consider . . ."), often glancing at the gallery as if seeking appreciation: not from the Bee-Dazzle vulgarians, of course, but from the throng of reporters. Methinks she likes to see herself in print over coffee in the morning. Her vibrating nose makes you wonder if an itchy little creature nests in her nostrils.

Old bull Jake Maguire is just back from Hawaii. Third row, left, with his sidekick Gaylene Roberts, now a Detective Inspector, promoted for busting us. Maguire looks tanned but not relaxed, very stiff in fact, maybe still freaked over Lucy's penilingus photo and the prospect of the press getting hold of it. Or maybe he's just grumpy about having to tie up loose ends before he can fully retire. The deadly duo, I gather, are back in town to prep their team of witnesses for next month's trial.

Their star hitter is, of course, Howie Griffin, batting cleanup despite last year's slump. (The Jays' opening day is only a couple of weeks away. Do they let you watch the games in prison?) I'm still spinning after Nancy Faulk threw this curve: *Have you ever considered the big goof may still be in love with you?*

Howie isn't here today, but he's been subpoenaed for May 13, first day of our trial. I won't be able to look at him when he testifies. My eyes will be downcast in shame.

I am near the entrance, and as a court officer slips inside I see Nancy pacing out there. She is on the dry, her divorce proceedings on hold. But if it's not one thing it's another, and high-strung Nancy Faulk is tearing out her hair over Arthur Beauchamp's nonattendance.

He was supposed to do the talking today because, unfortunately for Nancy (and us), she'd called this judge a fascist cunt at a bar retreat several years ago. Nancy was smashed, a mitigating factor that, along with a formal apology, saved her from disbarment. Her backup position, if it turns out Beauchamp has absconded to Bolivia with the defence fund, is asking Donahue to recuse herself by reason of their mutual loathing. No one sees her pulling that off.

We have yet to file a Missing Persons Advisory for Beauchamp, but there has been total loss of contact since late yesterday. His last words, to Nancy, were that he'd just missed an afternoon departure from Vancouver and hoped to catch the Midnight Express, the flight from hell, he called it. He should have landed two hours ago. There have been no reports of airline crashes. Maybe his phone went dead.

There was much media ado over the bravery of his mahoosive dog, Ulysses, in rescuing a child, and over the assassination of Tigger, a cougar whom the kind-hearted islanders loved despite its faults.

The demands made of Beauchamp kept him tied to the island all Friday and Saturday. He was on the weekend news, railing against an evil mining company. The assassination of Tigger was symbolic "of how these heartless invaders plan to ravage our island." He pressed for a company henchman — Tug McCool? — to be charged. It was a spirited rant. I thought: save some for us.

Colleen Donahue sees she may lose the media, accelerates her delivery, a sprint for home: "Victims of severe abuse must not be allowed to assume they have licences to kill, either in cold blood or hot. Leniency in this case would send a wrong message. I impose on you a sentence of life imprisonment."

She *is* a fascist cunt. The Earth Survival Rebellion is at the mercy of a heartless judge.

Tearful Ginnie is led out in handcuffs to murmurs of disapproval when there should be calls for outright rebellion. Lucy and I tightly hold hands.

Donahue gives the press a moment to capture this climactic moment, as Ginnie's lawyer stalks out, muttering about an appeal. Then the judge asks, "Are counsel here for *Regina versus Knutsen and Six Others*, and can they identify themselves for the record?"

A rhetorical question because she can see that no defence counsel are here. The urbane, dreamy-eyed Deputy A.G. rises, and says, "Azra Khan for the Crown."

He introduces his juniors: a bland-faced person with slicked-down hair, apparently male though possibly a cyborg, and a gawky, enraptured female student-at-law who has been leering lasciviously at Khan all morning. "My learned friends from the defence side seem not to be here."

Donahue asks a court officer to take a peek in the hallway. Assuming the judge will order a break, half the reporters leave, hoping, I guess, to phone in the Littledeer weeper.

But suddenly there's gridlock at the courtroom doorway. Exiting journalists return, some walking backwards. They form an unruly honour guard for man of the hour, who strides in like an angry Moses, unshaven, rumpled hair, revealing a flash of bright red suspenders as he shrugs into his robes.

"Arthur Beauchamp for the defence," he announces.

2

Judge Donahue has directed her senior clerk, Miss Pucket, to remind us we belong in the prisoners' box. Our lawyers have decided this is not an issue they want to waste energy on. Arthur Beauchamp told us to imagine ourselves as royalty, with uniformed ushers escorting us to the best seats in the house, front and centre.

It's almost twelve and a half minutes since Beauchamp's theatrical arrival. If I deciphered Donahue's twitches correctly, she couldn't tell if his entrance was spontaneous or staged and so wasn't sure whether to tangle with him. All she said was, "Very well. Resume in twelve and a half minutes."

Such exactness. Why not ten or fifteen? I wonder if she's seeing anyone for her OCD.

So it turns out Beauchamp's plane was an hour late, he didn't know enough to take the train in, his cab got stalled on the 401, and he forgot to bring a charger for his phone. It wasn't much of a mystery after all. As I get to know him better I'm learning such lapses aren't rare. Hope they won't impair his performance this morning. Already he doesn't look ready, with his sour expression and baggy eyes — he can't have had much sleep.

With Arthur on the case, Nancy has chilled, or at least lowered her hysteria to a manageable level. At the defence table, to our left, they study her laptop screen, some legal precedent or maybe, for all I know, cat videos on YouTube. At the table to our right sits Azra Khan, next to the student who wants to fuck him, who's next to the cyborg.

Barrel-shaped Madam Justice Donahue bounds up to her dais, glances at the clock, checking it against her watch, then puts her glasses on, wrinkles her bunny nose, and finally speaks: "The issue is whether the defence of necessity is available to the accused. Since this is a motion from the court, it behooves me to offer some initial comments.

"As I understand it, both defence and prosecution have engaged the services of numerous expert witnesses travelling from afar. It would be a waste of their valuable time, and, similarly, the court's time and resources, if their evidence is ultimately ruled inadmissible. I am bound, as I see it, by this language from the Supreme Court of Canada in *Regina v. Osolin* — 'Speculative defences that are unfounded should not be presented to the jury. To do so would be wrong, confusing, and unnecessarily lengthen jury trials.'"

And she goes on like that, literally making the case for the prosecution: plug the defendants' only escape hole, whisk them off to the pokey, let's not waste the court's time. But Azra Khan doesn't seem offended at being usurped, or even interested in her spiel — in fact he has turned to look at us. Or more particularly, me. I remember that look from the escalator: appraising me as he bantered with the press, a look I gave right back at him, letting him know I was uncowed by the famous prosecutor, unflattered by his interest.

Does a smile tug at his lips? Impulsively, the mischief imp takes over the cockpit controls: I wink. The merest flick of an eyelid, but it causes him to turn away, as if caught being naughty. Score one for Rivie.

Donahue continues, "I do not seek to denigrate a rare but important defence. But before necessity can be put to the jury, I must be persuaded there's an air of reality to it on the facts, given it is available only in urgent situations of clear and imminent peril when there's no lawful way out."

She looks up, removes her specs. "I see you are standing, Mr. Beauchamp."

He is, with his thumbs under his red suspenders. Donahue seems to have more to say, maybe a final punchline, but brings the matter to a head: "Very well, counsel, please persuade me that the necessity defence is applicable to the facts of this case."

"If I may be so bold, M'Lady, what facts are those?"

Hesitation. "The facts alleged against your clients, Mr. Beauchamp."

"With due respect, M'Lady, facts that are alleged aren't facts. They are not facts until they pass the courtroom smell test." Spoken in the rich, reverberating voice that I guess he saves for the court, Olivier playing Hamlet. Or Gielgud. Voices remembered from my year of Shakespeare.

A lovely titter running through the Bee-Dazzle section gets a glare from the judge but no sound escapes those clamped lips.

Arthur stays with his condescending tone, as if to a student, which I suspect is deliberate, to piss her off: "It is not the judge but the jury, as the trier of fact, that, according to centuries of British and Canadian law, must decide whether an urgent situation of imminent peril exists and whether all other avenues to meet it are closed. When all the evidence is in we propose to argue that the defendants' actions saved human lives that were in immediate peril."

With that he snaps his red braces for emphasis, and carries on:

"It would be a clear error of law to close off a defence before it has been raised. That would result in long, costly, and needless delay, because an appeal based on that error of law would likely succeed and a new trial would follow before a different judge and jury."

Right back at you, Donahue. He's saying, Hey, lady, don't be a schmuck and risk an appeal, you could blow this chance to bathe in the bubble bath of this front-page trial. She seems pretty stubborn, though, hard to tell if his pitch to ego will pay off. Especially since he's being so curt and frank.

They haven't got off to a great start, these two. I can't figure why he wants to inflame this judge so early in the game. Maybe he's just grumpy over having had to rush sleepless into this tense courtroom. Maybe it's round one of a battle to decide who owns this court.

"In my submission a dangerous precedent is set — a threat to civil rights and the rule of law — if a court denies an accused the right to raise a defence without having heard its full nature. Especially if a judge makes up her or his mind from pretrial hearsay and press reports."

An icy stillness prevails. Donahue's voice finally forces its way through clenched teeth: "I hope, Mr. Beauchamp, that you have recovered from what I understand was a long travel ordeal. Do you wish to have a break to reconsider the words just spoken?"

Arthur spurns her thinly disguised demand for an apology: "Not at all, M'Lady, I am raring to go."

He's not kidding. This is something I noticed about him from the bail hearing: the court transforms him, becomes his theatre, he its star performer, eloquent and sly, with great marksmanship.

"Let me state my concern clearly: the Toronto public, from whom a jury will be chosen, will perceive that you have belittled the necessity defence, only weeks before the trial is to open, with remarks like 'waste of valuable time,' 'extremely rare and difficult defence,' or, last week, 'we don't want experts flying in from all over the world.' The very fact that you have brought this motion *sua sponte* suggests a bias."

Major points for Arthur Beauchamp. He has taunted Donahue to shoot back: "You will find, here in Toronto, that our public are not obedient sheep. Those who will be empanelled can invariably be trusted to make up their own minds." Point for the judge.

"In which case they should be trusted to hear our defence." Point for my guy.

"Counsel, you overstate and distort a simple procedural issue. And I take offence to your imputation that I have made up my mind."

I get it. Arthur wants to drive her off the case somehow, make her quit, get her recused, or whatever they do. I remember Selwyn Loo musing over that strategy. He's missing the fun today, his pipeline case in BC dragging on.

There's murmuring in the court, and Miss Pucket calls for silence while staring aghast at this interloper from Canada's western shores. I had expected a different movie: Beauchamp against Khan, the old gunslinger against the suave federal marshal. But Khan just sits there, suppressing a smile, staying out of this barroom brawl.

Donahue can no longer look at the media, whose reviews may not look so hot over tomorrow's coffee and paper. The hard thrower drafted from Vancouver is throwing strikes not against the prosecution team — those three silent spectators — but at the umpire. She digs her cleats in, takes a swing: "I expect you to respond, Counsel. Do you accuse me of already having decided this issue?"

"I very much want to believe that is not the case, despite views expressed in the national media, including one from a CBC newscaster who predicted we would merely go through the motions today. I can only hope these commentators were wildly off the mark and that Your Ladyship shows an open mind on the necessity issue."

That's evil. He's boxed her into a corner where she'll look like a shit if she strips us naked and leaves us defenceless. *Judge Rebuked for Pre-Judging*. It finally dawns on me that Beauchamp's threat of an appeal and a new trial also looms large. New trial, new judge, she's off the case, no more clippings for her scrapbook.

"I shall make my point as succinctly as I can, M'Lady: you cannot make a pre-emptive attack on a defence until you have heard all the evidence. With all due deference, you have jumped the gun."

Again he snaps his suspenders. After that, all you can hear is the hum of air ventilation. Nancy passes him a heavy casebook that he opens to a bookmarked page.

"Your Ladyship relies on *Osolin*. So do I. This could not be clearer: 'It is only when the totality of the evidence rendered at the trial has been taken into account and considered in the light of all the relevant circumstances that the trial judge will be in a position to make a ruling.'"

"What page is that?"

"Six hundred and fifty-one, *Supreme Court Reports*."

A long pause to read and reflect, then: "Mr. Khan, what is your position?"

"I'm pleased to be asked, M'Lady," he says with a smile, though his words seem acerbic. "The Crown doesn't wish to tempt the defence with grounds for appeal. We can argue about the necessity defence at the appropriate time. This, I submit, is not the appropriate time. I side with my learned friend, though I urge him not to assume that will become a habit."

He has earned a murmur of approval for his light touch, everyone in the room decompressing except the judge. She is in a fury, betrayed. "The motion of the court is withdrawn. I believe that is all the business we have."

Khan has sat, but bounces up as she barrels her way out. "No, M'Lady, my friends have filed two contested motions to exclude evidence—"

"We'll deal with them when I decide to deal with them. This court is *adjourned*."

3

Sooky-Sue gives Ray a squeeze as they join the horde making for the door. Lucy glares at her. "She's an *agent provocateur*."

I go, "What? Where does *that* come from?"

"She's a secret agent. The police state hired her to infiltrate Ray Wozniak."

"Oh, yeah, that's credible."

"I'm serious. The church thing with the *Star Trek* motif is just her cover. He's her entry to the Earth Survival Rebellion. To Résistance Planétaire. She might even be a cop."

She continues to develop this cockamamie conspiracy theory, so I shut down, take a boo at Azra Khan as he holds the door for his two useless appendages. He gives a last look around and for a moment we are again eyeball to eyeball. I'm not sure what his face is saying to me: something close, personal, like, *We're in this together, Levitsky.*

What does he want from me? A reaction to his subtle upstaging of the two combatants? Okay, you notched one. Three points.

Richard Dewilliger-James, my surety, Lucy's sex trainee, waits for her, so she gives me a "See you later, masturbator," and follows him out, looking dispirited, as if thinking, *What have I got myself into?*

I hang here, waiting to be introduced to Professor Ariana Van Doorn, who just now is getting to know Arthur Beauchamp. This statuesque, unruly-haired blond had been in the bleachers, enjoying the back-and-forth. A farm girl from Saskatchewan, precocious, kept beehives since she was seven. "Famously reclusive" is a phrase that recurs when you Google her. Or "publicity-shy."

Nancy Faulk meanders up to me, all smiley for a change. I tell her I figured Beauchamp was trying to goad the judge to quit this gig.

"That ain't gonna happen, kid."

"Then why the happy face?"

"The jury will hear our experts. We have a shoe in the door."

"For how long? Doesn't this just postpone the inevitable?"

"Not if we wear them down. All we need is one holdout to get a mistrial. Then the A.G. has to start all over. New judge, new jury."

I ask her about the contested motions the judge brushed aside.

"Has to do with your footprint in Howie's office and a video of the bust. We want to exclude them."

The court officers try to clear the room, and while Nancy and Arthur stuff their briefcases I grab Van Doorn who, Google confided, had been captain of her college basketball team. I'm five-four, so I have to look up, way up.

Introductions made ("Ah, the audacious young enchantress"), we stroll out together and wait near the escalator for the lawyers, who have trouble breaking through a phalanx of demanding reporters. I'll have to catch up later with my gang, they're off to a sushi place for lunch.

"You don't seem famously shy to me."

"I don't know how they got that wrong. I think I'm quite out-going. What I famously do, I suppose, is shy *away* from publicity. I abhor the role of a talking head debating some hired goon for the pesticide industry. Giving him airtime so the network can boast it presents both sides."

She'll do just fine.

§

Nancy Faulk drives, Ariana Van Doorn is beside her, and they talk about the German Nobel winner, Hoff, who didn't make the team. Something about plagiarizing a student's work. I'm in the back seat with my travel-weary lawyer and because of all the rain and the honking I can't catch all their words, so I lean forward.

"It took some gall," Ariana says, "given he was also making out with her. His wife is filing for divorce. It's pretty bloody awful."

"Yeah, tell me about it," Nancy says.

Nancy's husband stole their Audi, allegedly, so we are in her smaller Leaf. Beauchamp's battered brown suitcase is in the trunk. We are taking him for a ride, though it's slow going to the point of immobility — we're jammed behind a Queen streetcar in the cold, driving rain, as emergency vehicles roar by, an ambulance, cops, screaming around the corner and up Bathurst.

"Where are we going?" Arthur demands, grumpy despite having won the day. He's definitely ready for bed, and, to be honest, a shower. (No offence intended, Dear Diary, should he ever read you.)

"Semi-detached in Parkdale," says Nancy. "Lovely old street called Beaconsfield, a brisk half hour by foot to my office. Owner's a swindler, or was. Punky Kiefer. Owes me for getting him off with two years on eight counts of bank fraud. Not due for parole until summer — the trial can't go *that* long."

With opening day less than a month away, Nancy obviously doesn't want any more last-minute theatrics, and plans to keep Arthur around, sort of like a truant on strict terms of bail. I guess that's why his glum face: he doesn't find Toronto electric and fun. Misses his best friend, the hero of Quarry Park, still viral on the web. Why does a dog get to be man's best friend? Who's a *woman's* best friend? Why shouldn't man's best friend be a woman?

How is Beauchamp faring with his wife anyway? It's known he blew her off on a hotel date last week here in Toronto. Makes you wonder why. He doesn't give off that goatish vibe that many older guys do, and the concept of him getting nookie on the side seems inconceivable.

"I shall return to Garibaldi Island for Easter." This is Arthur's growly voice that he'd used in court. "This weekend. Friday through Monday. Margaret will join me. We have been apart all year!"

I know what it's like. I have Technicolor dreams of Chase joining me, which is why Lucy went, "See you later, masturbator." Not a word from him since his postcard: *Happy New Year to All Bee-ings!* My loving him, my needing him, is stupid and a waste of energy. We're different animals. He's the Arctic fox, I'm the city raccoon.

Nancy promises Arthur his Easter break and he pledges to be back well before the curtain opens on May 13. Bargain made, Nancy wiggles her Leaf past the streetcar, the jam breaks, and we move again. Beauchamp stares bleakly out his window, as if finding confirmations everywhere of his resolve to live on his rustic nowhere island.

The conversation turns to the more agreeable matter of how things went today in court. At one point, Ariana says to Arthur, "You came in there wanting a fight. I think you're a rogue." She has this big, throaty laugh.

"Always stand up to a bully." Said with his eyes closed.

"He likes to soften them up early," says Nancy.

Arthur: "I actually wanted to see how taking a run at her might work with a jury."

This is totally cool, being in close quarters with these two eagle beagles, getting the inside poop on how to work judges over.

Arthur is still talking with his eyes closed. "Sometimes they forget their role, and you have to remind them. This one seems to want to get her nose into things."

"Her twitchy nose," says Nancy.

"Liberal judges bore me, they're too accommodating. I actually prefer the bloody-minded ones. You don't get lazy, you stay on your toes. The first task is to teach jurors that judges aren't anointed by the gods, they're prone to error like any human, and ought not to be followed blindly, like some charismatic faith healer."

I ask, "Were you surprised when the prosecutor agreed with you?"

A long moment, and I wonder if my question put him to sleep. Then: "He hopes to disarm me. He knows I prefer Crowns who either toady to the bench or come on like gangbusters. He's biding his time, waiting like a cobra for the moment to strike."

I want to ask *Could you be a little more melodramatic?* Nancy, who is laughing, obviously gets it that he's playing with me. She has a more gentlemanly view of Khan's purpose: "He wants Donahue to back off so they can have a fair fight. He wants to go mano-a-mano with the Left Coast champ."

Turn on Beaconsfield, and halfway up the block on the right is a three-storey heritage red-bricker with veranda and yard space. This château has got to have at least three bedrooms, three baths. I grab Arthur's suitcase and ignore his protests as I lug it to the door. I want to look inside. How do I finagle a spare room?

4

Friday, April 19

On this the first day of Passover, as the observant celebrate freedom (Let my people go!), it's business as usual at Fourteen Division, on Dovercourt Road, where Constable Louella Baker presides over the bail sign-in counter and constantly complains about being a human word processor — she wants to be out busting bad people.

I tell her she could start with the trolls who want to send me to the ovens. She listens with sympathy but I know the cops can't do much. Some of these drama Nazis claim to want to get it on with me, though they mean rape. Others come right out and say it, if they can get past the censors. The full-blown psychopaths prefer penetration by large or sharp instruments. I've finally renounced all social media. I mostly use my iPhone as a phone.

"You're a day late, and you missed Monday." Louella phoned a short while ago, demanding I get my bony white ass down here.

"Hey, I was in court Monday."

"Doesn't matter, it's another stupid rule. I can give you some leeway if you apply in advance, otherwise I get crucified."

She lets me sign the Thursday page. I don't want her crucified, because she gives me a "You go, girl," whenever we talk about my case. Her stepdad, a farm worker, died of cancer from pesticide spraying.

I ask, "Any news?"

"Yeah, finally — a duty roster next month riding shotgun on patrol. See you Monday. Show up. Make me look good."

The heavy late-winter rains have ebbed at last, but I keep my poncho on for the drizzle as I mount my faithful steed and Hi Ho my way to my new digs on Beaconsfield, a quick trip away.

I wasn't sure how to approach Beauchamp. Maybe something like, I am but a penniless waif, dear sir, and have nowhere to go. Or this: the trolls know where I live and are causing me paroxysms of paranoia.

But I couldn't get up the nerve to lie to him, because I don't fear these sewer rats *that* much, they're all bluster, misfits with their repressed sense of inadequacy. I did the weaselly thing and told Nancy I was stranded and did she think Arthur would mind if I crashed at her client's house until I had to go to jail. No loud music. No wild parties. I'd make granola and he could share.

Beauchamp told her he would welcome company.

I've got a second-floor room, he the master bedroom on the main floor. The house is ponderously furnished in a style that may have been popular sixty years ago, fat chairs, tasselled hassocks, tubular desk, porcelain counters, clanky radiators, a moose head sticking out of a wall above a Naugahyde armchair.

I have the place to myself for the long weekend. Arthur flew off this morning to his Gulf Islands. Margaret Blake is there now. *We have been apart all year!* Sounds like Arthur's horny, but I can't somehow visualize the aging barrister having sex. Not that I'm trying to.

I reckon that during the trial I can bike from Beaconsfield to the courthouse far faster than going by streetcar. Lucy, who is already getting out of shape, will be chauffeured there by Dick Two. I worry that she has started to enjoy the life, the comforts.

Yesterday, as Richard helped her gather up her shit at the Sorauren loft, he couldn't look me in the eye — what, just because I didn't share his feelings? He offered to come back in his U-Haul and move my stuff too, but I said it's looked after, which it wasn't — until Okie Joe phoned and said he'd like to grab a coffee with me.

Joe's girlfriend, country-cool Arlene, drove up here three months ago in an old pickup that still has valid Oklahoma plates, and we loaded it up this morning with my meagre possessions: clothes, toiletries, music, laptop, cables, miscellaneous electronics and gewgaws, more books than anything. Espresso maker. Hash pipe. A little bit of weed. Manuscript.

And, oh, yeah, the ghastly Brazilian snake earrings that Howie gave me on the night of our last, climactic date. I'd forgotten about them.

Joe and Arlene were helping pack my heavy cardboard boxes down from the loft this morning just as Louella phoned. I raced off before I could ask Joe why he needed to talk to me. I assume it's something personal. Maybe he wants my advice on whether to propose to Arlene. What am I, an expert?

There they are, out front, by the truck, and they've already toted all the boxes up to the porch. A couple across the street and two houses up are doing Neighbourhood Watch with binocs, checking out the hippie freaks with the mysterious boxes from a beat-up truck with Oklahoma plates.

It doesn't take long to move everything up to the large bedroom I commandeered — a queen bed, I haven't been in one of those for years.

Nancy Faulk gifted me several bottles of fine wine from her husband's cellar (it's in her house), so I'm able to thank them over a $250 bottle, to wit, a 2008 Domaine Leflaive Puligny-Montrachet Les Folatières Premier Cru. Nancy knows I live off donations and loans — I should crowd-fund myself — and has also stocked cupboards, fridge, and freezer with eats.

So we fix up a snack lunch and chat, under the rheumy gaze of the moose, about their tech business, which flourishes — they design websites, do programming, and are working on a games app they think is bound to sell. They still network for the American Refugee Society, helping others become good Canadians while they themselves apply for status.

Okie Joe shifts uncomfortably with his apparent need to talk privately with me, so I invite him out for a toke of Purple Kush that I recently bought at a nearby Canna-Bliss outlet. Arlene gets the message, she doesn't smoke anyway, and busies herself by setting up my electronics and running some kind of spyware probe to see who reads my texts and emails. And maybe even this journal. If so, fuck you.

It's nice now, sunny. The backyard shows evidence of a former garden and dog, and there's a covered barbecue, a bird feeder, a basketball hoop, and the patio chairs we're on, the whole middle-class megillah. I have a picture of the money-managing swindler as very straight and normcore, divorced, alone, the ex has custody of the boys.

The yard is well fenced and well treed, and neighbours would have to crane to see us smoking dope, though I shouldn't assume they're all as nosy as the couple with the binocs. But who cares, really — pot is legal in Canada. Though it's not as much fun without that delightful frisson of paranoia and the self-righteous joy of stink-fingering the system.

Even though Okie Joe takes a hit, he can't seem to loosen up, and eventually I say, with that tight holding-it-in voice, "Come out with it, for Christ's sake."

"Chase D'Amato called."

I blow out a cumulous cloud of the Kush, choke on it, and have to lube my throat with a fifty-dollar swallow of wine. "Why?" I rasp. "I mean, why you?" To myself: Why not me?

"He knows I have a secure connection."

"So you don't know where he called from?"

"He's somewhere."

"That's reassuring."

"That's why he called. To reassure us. You, in particular. He's fine. In good health. In a good place. He's got a job. A new identity."

When comes the reveal?

"He said to give you a hug." And he puts an arm around me — awkwardly.

"He found someone else." I hear myself and want to vomit. I'm the abandoned heroine of a shitty soft-porn romance novel.

"Nothing like that," Joe says. "He loves you, but . . ." Deep breath. "Hey, Rivie, I kind of resent being the messenger. I told him that."

"Fine. Spell it out."

"Basically he wants you to live your own life. Not wait for him. He doesn't want your feelings for him to distract you from the causes we share. He wants you, all of us, to focus on our trial, to win, to make a statement that will have more impact than all his Greenpeace campaigns rolled into one. End quote. He also said he will always be your friend, however many miles apart."

How cowardly was my hero, breaking it off through an agent. He was afraid of dealing directly with me, didn't want me asking who she is, the bitch who connived him into her bunk. Some wilderness whore.

"Anyway, I hate being thrust into the middle of this. I told him you'd probably like to hear from him directly."

"How?"

"I have a safe mail drop."

This is not a high. This is a classic marijuana downer.

5

Eventually, the Purple Kush and wine power down, leaving only a headache. Anger and jealousy are replaced by melancholy and self-recrimination. What am I moaning about? I gave up on Chase D'Amato months ago, among the wolves, squirrels, and pine grosbeaks of Algonquin Park. We hadn't made any pledges to each other. We had an excellent physical thing going. Not much else. Politics. Cerebral stuff. Chess. At which I usually lost.

So it's not as if I was jilted, but it hurts the same way, except that the ego takes more of a beating than the heart. I feel stupid that I let pride rule my emotions. If he's found someone to love, that's good. Good for her too, especially if she doesn't mind living in a tent and shitting in a bucket.

I ponder all this while I arrange my room, put my stuff in closet and drawers. Eventually, aided by another, gentler puff, I decide my heart isn't broken. I'm a survivor. In three weeks the world will watch our trial. I can't allow myself to be distracted by something so trivial as love.

This evening, I am to meet with Lucy at the old place: finish cleaning up, feed the cats one last time. I'm sure Lucy will find some excuse to show up late or not at all. I feel fucking friendless.

§

But when I arrive, just after six, she's there. With a mop and pail, doing the floors with a sullen vehemence, barely acknowledging her best friend. The borrowed vacuum is out, the washer and drier going, the anarchist heroes are down from the wall, replaced by Dr. Wenz's German expressionists. The cats, banished to the roof deck, glower at us from the windows.

I want to ask Lucy if she's on speed or something, and if not, what's biting her. I need to unload my heavy heart but she pantomimes this not-interested look, pulls back her hair to show me she's plugged into earbuds, and points to the walls lined with books. There are cobwebs up there among the essays of Schopenhauer and Maeterlinck. I stick a bottle of rare muscatel into the fridge and dutifully retrieve the long-handle duster and the three-step ladder.

§

Mopping done, furnishings back in place, Lucy ruefully contemplates her next task, the bathroom. I indicate with hand signals: if you do the bathroom I'll do the bedroom. Its door is closed, and I head that way, but she bars my progress, pulls off her buds, and says, "I need a drink, I've had a berserk day." She plonks down on a chair by the dining table.

I open the muscatel. "Where's Richard?"

"I ran off, told him not to wait. But he will wait till death do us part. He's unbearable. I'm dying, Rivie. I can't survive this trial if I have to come home to him every night. You conned me into this. Help me find some way to tell him it's over."

Oh, poor you. Forced to live in the lap of luxury. I have just had my heart broken, but do you hear me wailing? Anyway, I don't want your sympathy. It would be like grovelling for it. I decline to share these thoughts, and instead suck it up enough to be supportive. "Tell him you need to live alone. You don't want your feelings for him to distract you from the cause of saving the planet. Don't tell him you're still in love with Ray."

Lucy takes a gulp of muscatel. "That brings up a problem."

"With Ray?"

"I got this extremely garbled text about how he got beamed up and can't come down."

Shockingly, I'm capable of laughter. She says she's not joking. She reads from her phone: "She beamed me up, baby, and I'm stuck." He added, "Rapid-Loans." Sooky-Sue's uncle runs a loan shark franchise by that name out of a building he owns on Ossington, and she and her beamed-up boyfriend stay in a one-bedroom on the third floor doing whatever recovering acidheads do.

Which turns out to be heavier than LSD. "Yagé," Rockin' Ray mumbled over and over as Lucy led the wild-haired, wild-eyed, sleep-deprived freak down the stairs and out to a waiting taxi. Yagé. Ayahuasca, from the Amazonian jungle. Trips for ultra-hips.

Lucy had found him on the third-floor landing, apparently evicted by his lover, incoherent, hearing voices — which he actually was, his cell tuned to a live podcast by a surgeon describing a heart bypass.

I look at the bedroom door. "He's in there sleeping it off?"

"All day. The bad news is he has to go in for his weekly test tomorrow. Blood, breath, and piss."

The bad news apparently has occult power because the bedroom door swings open and Rockin' Ray, wearing only his Stanfield's, makes a beeline for the bathroom. Sinbad, startled, nearly jumps from the roof.

Ray calls, hoarsely: "Why am I here?"

Lucy goes, "Because God beamed you to me. She commanded you to stop fucking Sooky-Sue."

"We don't call it fucking. We call it worshipping."

"Does she let you worship her in the ass?" Lucy tosses off her wine, pours another. So do I.

"Again, I ask: How did I get here?"

"Because you called me, you sap. Because if I didn't save your butt you'd've gone stumbling down the street and got run over by a truck or got picked up and busted for breaking your bail terms and right now you'd be staring out a steel cage wondering how you ended up there."

By the time this speech is over, Ray is out, two dripping hands raised. "What happened to the towels? Something weird is going on, there's no shit lying around. Man, I must have done more crystals than I planned."

As he dresses, we ask about how such excess came about. All he remembers, from last evening, is Sooky-Sue seeking to "elevate her raptures," which I assume is their church's euphemism for orgasms, by overdoing the ayahuasca. He's absonotly worried about tomorrow's drug test.

"Yagé is legal, man, it's our religious sacrament. Sooky is a trained shaman and she has a connection in Barranquilla. To keep me sane, I been doing it since just after I got bail, all tests negative, no alerts, no bells, no flashing lights." He checks his phone. "Sooky's worried."

"Tell her to worship herself," Lucy says, as Ray taps out a message.

I'm staying out of this, but I don't blame Lucy for feeling betrayed, having raced off to rescue him. "So why did Sucky-Sue kick you out? Because you couldn't get it up anymore? Couldn't satiate her need for elevated raptures?"

"It got a little weird last night. Even for me." He pulls on his boots.

"So she's just as goofy in bed as she is in real life, eh?"

Ray has his jacket and boots on, and is at the front door. He seems about to open it, then slumps, looks down, then up, and I see tears.

"I miss you, babe. I'm an assoholic, I know, and I've treated you wrong. But I'm a junkie for you, I'm hooked, you make me high. I can't help it. I love you."

She flies to him, attaches herself to him like cling wrap. He lifts her into his arms.

I'm into my jacket and helmet and out the door before they make it into the bedroom.

§

The pitiful, wine-soaked supporting actor to this weeper stumbles down the stairs desperately trying to be happy for Lucy while she drowns in sorrow for herself. That touching scene has completely done me in. I have never felt so abysmally alone. So unloved. So mate-less. Passover is happening, Easter is happening, a long weekend and no one has invited me anywhere.

I want my mother.

She also wants me. She'd called earlier, an hour of loving chatter. My folks are beyond secular but tradition is tradition and there will be matzo soup and brisket tomorrow. It was unintentionally cruel of her to invite me — she knows my bail conditions restrict me to Greater Toronto. Golden Valley is a four-hour drive away, up near North Bay.

As I push my bike out the doorway I spot a tall human shape across the street. Just standing on the sidewalk, looking at me, though I can't make out his face. It's dark now, after eight. *Heavy man. Toque and padded jacket.* Thus Lucy had described the night lurker. But this dude is in a parka. He's hidden for a moment by a passing truck, and next seen is striding north, toward Dundas.

I mount up and pump after him, still clutching my iPhone, hoping to get a shot of him under a streetlight. He sees me come and ducks into an alley. I'm not stupid enough to follow a hatemongering fascist douche into the dark, and do a wheelie south to Queen.

I pause by the Drake to look up Constable Louella's cell in my contacts. She answers, gasping for breath, and I remember she works out most nights at her local gym. "This better be unimportant," she says.

I laugh, promise to be short. I fill her in on the lurker and how I kind of chased him and she tells me I've got balls. I give her my change of address and she says, cool, she's in the area, she's off work this weekend, we could have coffee.

Then I ask her if I can get a day pass to visit my family to help them celebrate Passover.

"As I recall, doll, the formal conditions are you can't leave town without a police escort."

"What about making the conditions less formal? You can do that."

"Can't, Rivke."

"Mom plans a big Passover feed tomorrow. They don't keep strict kosher but she's a brilliant cook. They're very welcoming, Mom and Dad, I told them about how you—"

"How long does it take to drive up there?"

"Three and a half to four hours."

"I'll be by at half past eight in the morning."

§

That night, between the cool cotton sheets of my too-roomy bed, I have another dream of Howie Griffin. "I'm not that kind of guy," he says. But I'm all over him.

CHAPTER 18 » ARTHUR

1

Saturday, April 20

"Okay, Glow, let's try again," says the producer-director known as Big Boris, who is hippo-sized, thickly bearded, adorned by a cowboy's hat, and specializes in documentaries, or in this case, a dogumentary, as he calls it. "A lot more panicky this time. A cougar is chasing your toddler. You're scared shitless."

Glow yells: "Baby Cosmos, come here, or Tigger's gonna get you. Right now!"

The four-year-old, who seems to enjoy these re-enactments, descends the limestone steps on cue but scampers the wrong way, not toward his parents, Glow and Krishna, but to the lead actor, Ulysses the Wonder Dog. This is the third take, and the third time Cosmos has run to Ulysses.

The pup gives him a lick as he waits for his own cue. Arthur and Stefan are supposed to restrain him until he gets a signal. Then Ulysses, according to the script, will sprint off in pursuit of an imaginary cougar.

The problem is that Ulysses is not some trained circus dog; he's above doing tricks for applause. He does it his way.

The media hailed Ulysses, making him odds-on favourite to win the SPCA Hero Award. Yet it's still unclear, at least to Arthur, whether the cougar intended to snatch Cosmos or was taking the fastest route of escape.

Arthur can't see how Big Boris will pull off this *cinéma-sans-vérité*. He had told Arthur, "Guy I know, in the Rockies, he's got a pet cougar, so we're going to splice it in." He and his crew of five work out of Edmonton and have been on Garibaldi two days, setting up. The Bleak Creekers were easily persuaded to resurrect their faux-equinox tableau of tents and tarps here in the vale between the cliffs of Quarry Park.

TexAmerica made no complaint. The company has announced they are "re-addressing the situation," which seems a euphemism for giving up — most of their heavy equipment has been hauled away already. It's as if their energy has been sapped, like invaders succumbing to a war of attrition. The company's good name, if it ever had one, has been further blackened by their local foreman's vengeful murder of Tigger. Tug Cooley is back in Fort Worth, having avoided arrest for a string of non-extraditable offences, including careless use of a firearm.

"Let's try it again," says Big Boris, who's in no rush — it's a pleasant morning, the sky is clear. His three camera operators have already replicated skinny Krishna nakedly exhorting the sun to surmount the limestone ridge, and they have also filmed the sunrise ceremony: the rotating, chanting circle.

When Boris had the effrontery to ask Arthur to re-enact his bit part, he responded: "I'd as soon jump into a nest of writhing pit vipers."

Krishna fetches his son, horsey-backs him to the starting point, Boris shouting encouragement, promising Cosmos's future stardom, as if he assumes that's every four-year-old's dream.

"This is ridiculous," says Stefan.

"But in an eerie way engrossing," says Arthur. They stand well away from the action, leaning against a sun-warmed slab.

"It's not how I planned to spend my last day." Stefan has finally achieved legal immigrant status, and is to depart tomorrow, Easter Sunday, to manage a wildlife refuge on remote Quatsino Sound. Lovelorn Solara, though not in a celebratory mood, is preparing a farewell vegan dinner for him, with Margaret as sous-chef.

Arthur's life companion arrived late last night on a crowded ferry after an even more claustrophobic five-hour flight. She almost swooned with relief on disembarking into the relaxed ambience of Garibaldi Island. Her hug was tight. But it was after eleven and they had little chance to catch up — she went quickly off to bathtub and bed.

They made love on waking this morning, though it was no barn-burner. Negative factors included his tension over the upcoming trial and her exhaustion in opposing the Trans-Mountain pipe-line. As well, she has led a campaign to have the quarry annexed to Gwendolyn National Park.

But libido letdowns occur almost every time they reunite — they seem to have trouble finding each other after being apart so long. After a couple of days together, the process becomes more fluid, oiled by sharing and closeness.

Arthur hasn't found the right oh-by-the-way moment to men-tion he'd invited Taba into his private parlour for brandy-laced coffee by a blazing fire on a cold winter evening. Confiding the truth — or at least parts of it — is job one, he must face up to that. Ignoring it will cause marital grief. Worrying about it will cloud his mind for the trial — he must be at his best against the likes of Azra Khan and Madam Justice Colleen Donahue.

So he'd better raise the matter with Margaret today, before she looks through the back issues of the *Island Bleat* and comes upon a News Nugget about how "our ever popular ravishing redhead Tabatha (Taba) Jones" went "all the way to Blunder Bay."

"That-a-boy," Big Boris shouts.

Cosmos, finally tiring, stumbles during the latest take, then scrambles up crying and races into Glow's arms. Surely the director would now wrap things up. But no.

"He's a major movie star now, ma'am. So okay, I want you to ask him to do it just one more time. This time with the dog. Mr. Beauchamp, is he ready to fly?"

"Not exactly." In fact, Ulysses has lost interest after being held back for so long and is focussed on a propane grill on which wieners are sizzling and buns warming.

Boris claps his hands. "Take a break. Lunch is on Prairie Dog Productions!"

§

"Namaste, namaste," Arthur mouths as he works his way through the swarm at the food table. He has a double-barrelled hot dog for Ulysses; a single for himself, slathered with mustard. There are also celery and carrot sticks and apples, so Stefan doesn't go without, though he wanders off by himself with his plate.

Arthur has to hustle back to Toronto soon for three weeks of forensic spadework before the trial begins. He will have a house-mate: Rivke Levitsky, a high energy person. He feels an avuncular fondness for her but worries she'll want to chatter about the trial, bugging him with questions while he does his homework.

When she's not talking, she's at her phone's keyboard, typing notes, or voice recording, as if maintaining some manner of sponta-neous journal. She was an English literature major, so may suffer the common delusion of writing a novel.

Internet trolls, a scourge of modern times, have made her the subject of their base attentions. All the Earth Survival Rebels endure such insults and threats, but Rivie seems the main target. Threatened male egos. Fear of forceful women. That's what the behaviour experts say. Conversely, Arthur has always been attracted to forceful women, but can't say why.

Ulysses devours his lunch and, of course, wants more. Arthur thinks of sharing his own hot dog but is loath to give him any more chemically enhanced quasi-meat, and eats it himself.

§

After lunch, Ulysses remains uncooperative, peeved at his second-rate status: all humans had extra wieners and the fat male human who shouts ate four. But the local dog gets treated as if he's some inferior species. And they expect him to perform.

Big Boris has apparently devised a plan to solve Ulysses's camera shyness: he strolls a hundred metres away, down the grassy meadow and up the exit trail, then dangles something that looks to Arthur like a thick, braided rope. He yells, "Roll 'em!"

Ulysses, a sighthound, has no trouble identifying Boris's offering as a string of leftover wieners, and is quickly on his feet — he accelerates to warp speed, flies over holes and bumps, goes straight as an arrow for Boris.

"Don't move!" Stefan calls to him. He and Arthur know, from close experience, that Ulysses loves racing full speed ahead at humans — he will veer at the last second, usually to the right, missing by inches, then hit the brakes, leaving the target human shaken but safe.

Unfortunately, Big Boris's ill-considered choice is to veer to his left, and he takes the full brunt of the collision, sprawling into the tall grass as Ulysses deftly snatches the wieners from his flailing hand.

One camera stays on Ulysses as he continues up the trail with his loot and disappears into a hiding place. Meanwhile, another camera was on little Cosmos, who, prodded into one more scamper, stops and wails on seeing his beloved wolfhound vanish. The third camera watches Boris, supine, stare at the blue sky. "Cool, baby," he calls. "That's a wrap."

"Let's blow this scene," Stefan says. Arthur is in accord. Stefan whistles. Ulysses reappears, looking innocent.

On seeing Ulysses leashed and about to be led away, Boris complains: "Wait, we got the scene at the midget sculptor's, what's his name, McKee, McKay, where he climbed that phallus."

Arthur says that they won't need Ulysses for that sequence, though they might want to splice in a cougar. At any rate, he adds, Hamish McCoy is at the Hall today, setting up for the annual Easter Sunday Art Show.

He urges Boris to bring his cameras to this grand spectacle, an event hoary with tradition, going back eighty years, pronounced dead many times but just as often revived. "It would add a soothing, bucolic background to your stirring dogumentary. You could open with it."

"You just earned a producer credit," Boris says.

Arthur doesn't know where Prairie Dog Productions hopes to show this film, but if by some miracle it goes viral on, say, YouTube, the painters, potters, and craftpersons of Garibaldi might finally enjoy a boom year.

§

Stefan unexpectedly opens up as they return home in his van. He speaks of how comfortably he has adapted to Canada, to a new life, of his many pleasant months at Blunder Bay, of how thankful he is to Margaret and Arthur, his admiration for them.

"We will miss you equally," Arthur says. "Solara will miss you much more."

Stefan nods, his expression set, as if he's trying to avoid a show of emotion. "I'm sorry about that. I'm fond of her. I'm also afraid of commitment. I'm not good with people generally, as you've noticed. It's the famous Scandinavian genes — we're typically a private people, repressed, really, not very good at hugging. I am better with animals. Right, Ulysses?"

The pup responds by licking his ear. Stefan laughs.

2
Sunday, April 21

The Easter Art Show gets underway late, after a shower sends the Garibaldi League of Artists hustling their paintings into the Hall. Arthur and Margaret wait until they've set up, then do a quick tour, tarrying awhile at the Animal Section where they are compelled to marvel at four heroic portraits of Ulysses. Arthur supposes he'll have to buy one. But only one? Wouldn't that, he asks Margaret, hurt the others' feelings?

"Don't be ridiculous. That abstract by Marcia makes Ulysses look like a pompous tin-star sheriff. Don't encourage her."

Arthur figures he'll take two, the acrylic and the pen, one of which he'll send to Stefan — who drove off on the ferry this morning after he'd spent his last hour at Bungle Bay romping with Ulysses and exchanging goodbyes in dog lexicon. Ulysses returned to the house literally looking hangdog.

Solara had too much wine last evening at Stefan's farewell dinner, and got weepy as he serenaded them on his guitar with something baroque and sprightly. But Margaret was wet-eyed too, despite Arthur's efforts to keep things jovial. Stefan, allegedly unskilled at the art of the hug, performed with surprising gusto.

Predictably, somehow, Arthur still hasn't had his sit-down with Margaret. During waking hours they never seemed to be alone and when he joined her in bed the subject of Taba Jones felt massively inappropriate. In any event, Margaret again succumbed quickly to her weariness, abetted by the effects of Nancy Faulk's gift of an excellent ten-year-old Bordeaux.

The rain shower is in pause when they return outside the Hall, where a dozen sculptors and potters remain, displaying their works under awnings and beach umbrellas. Soon to join them, apparently, is Hamish McCoy: an old flatbed truck grunts up the driveway, Stoney at the wheel, Hamish and Dog peering over the dashboard. The thickly veined, erect penis with the useless, flapping wings is prone on the truck's bed, on foam, a red flag tied to its claw-like toes.

They park at a high point a hundred feet from the other exhibitors. Big Boris and his film crew are already there, already set up. Stoney is abundantly aware of the cameras because he hams it up while he helps raise the twelve-foot bronze. McCoy has devised a complex lifting crane from pulleys, cables, guy wires, and stakes pounded into the lawn.

It's unprecedented for Hamish McCoy to show up at the Easter Art Show. The rude fellow is cynical about what he calls the Sunday artists, "with their pretty pansies and moonlit ripples on the bay." They in turn put up with his snobbery, because of his fame. Clearly, Hamish has arranged with Prairie Dog Productions to do a shoot here today. He loves the media, loves to shock the public.

Arthur likes to believe many of Garibaldi's artists are quite talented and original; otherwise their creations would not be stacked up in his commodious basement. Almost every Easter show has seen him or Margaret buy canvases, though there's no more room on the walls of either house. So they're stored, along with Taba Jones's pottery.

Arthur pretends not to notice Taba, even though she and her bowls and vases are only a few tables away. Arthur particularly tries not to observe that Margaret is chatting with her. Instead he concentrates on McCoy and his crew as they wrestle with the penis. It is thirty degrees from the horizontal, and is wobbling. McCoy and Stoney pull taut lines and Dog has his shoulder to it. Exhibitors and attendees gather around, and occasionally applaud or heckle.

Meanwhile, shockingly, the conversation between Margaret and Taba continues for several minutes. There are smiles. At one point they turn to look at Arthur, who ducks his eyes. Good grief — are they comparing notes?

Maybe this is an elaborate practical joke. Not maybe — probably, because Margaret bends toward Taba and they buss each other's cheeks.

A cheer goes up as the penis stabilizes — proudly erect. A jokester hugs it. The cameras roll. Viewers of this documentary will wonder how a community as bizarre as Garibaldi came to exist.

§

Arthur and Margaret are finally alone, at their dining table, eating celery, beets, and artichokes left over from last evening. Solara has just left to put the animals to bed. They talk about her for a while, her brave smile, how she was unafraid to talk about Stefan. "Win some, lose some," she'd said.

"I guess you saw me talking with Tabatha."

"Yes, I glanced over. I was watching the erection's erection, of course." Arthur rises, pours her a second wine, refills his tea. "I couldn't imagine what you were discussing."

"Oh, the petition to recall Zoller and Shewfelt. She did an incredible job. Got two hundred more signatures than needed. Nineteen alone on our road. Where did I read that? Nelson Forbish's column."

"Ah, yes, the recall count was last week, I'd completely forgot. Too preoccupied with other bees-ness." His joke falls flat. "I should have congratulated Taba. And while we're on the topic, ah . . ."

"She came visiting. I know. She told me."

"Came in from the cold to warm up. Nineteen signatures! Even old Gullivan, who thinks climate change is fake science. She had brandy and coffee, it was the least I could do."

Arthur's hopes to leave it at that are dashed when Margaret says, "Did she come on to you?"

Arthur's teacup rattles. "Did she tell you that?"

"She did, didn't she?"

He's trapped. How much did Taba tell her? Surely not the nitty-gritty. They were smiling, they exchanged kisses! "Well, I did have quite an odd experience. So awkward that I hesitated mentioning it to you. Not that anything actually *happened*, really; it might have been the brandy, but she—"

"Oh, for God's sake, what did you do?"

"I did nothing, my dear. She, ah, offered herself, made a slight move in that direction . . ."

She flares. "That cow. Always after your ass."

He's in it deep now, and opts to fashion the event as a merry tale in which he played the innocent, fumbling fool. That doesn't work, lacking the verisimilitude a story demands if it's to hold water — Margaret finds little humour from the stripped-down version: her husband backed against his desk, rejecting Taba's advances.

Arthur does admit to having been slightly aroused, as he believes any man would be, but edits out the unbuckled belt, unzipped fly, the upright, finger-encircled cock, and the climactic event in the shower. Clearly, she suspects there's more to his story. Women, in his experience, can invariably tell.

Margaret drains her wine, stands, studies him as if he were some creature dredged from the ocean depths. "I'm going to bed. I'll see you in the morning." She gathers up some dishes, heads to the kitchen. "That scheming *bitch*!"

PART THREE / RITES OF SPRING

CHAPTER 19 » MAGUIRE

1
Monday, May 13

It took Jake Maguire five escalators to get up to the biggest courtroom in Canada, 6-1, it's like a football field if you can imagine goalposts on the left and right, the judge's bench at the midfield sidelines. Here is where famous trials are held, serial killers, celebrity defendants, international conspiracies with multiple defendants represented by multiple lawyers elbowing each other for the limelight.

Maguire is at about the forty-yard line just behind the prosecutors, in a new suit for this occasion because his old ones barely fit. He has a sore neck — a legacy from his Hawaii so-called holiday — so he has to twist his body around to see to the back.

The gallery is filling fast with the non-working public: a full platoon of lawyers who apparently have nothing else to do, students, media, and maybe a hundred Bee-hippies and Bee-beatniks, some wearing honeybee stripes but muted, not as ridiculous as at the bail hearing. Someone must have coached them: no plastic wings, no Bee-Dazzle T-shirts, because no jury's going to be wowed by clown acts.

A block of about a hundred and fifty seats has been allocated to the jury panel — less about twenty excused for illness or late pregnancy or severe disabilities — from which twelve will get conscripted this morning. The court sheriffs checked them out: all citizens, local residents, eighteen and over, no red cards for misbehaviour. Maguire dug a little deeper — Facebook was a kick-ass resource — and weeded out a bunch of names the prosecution might want to challenge. Environmentalists and lefties, do-gooders like social workers and community advocates. He doesn't feel guilty or sneaky about that because defence lawyers all do it too.

Maguire is officially retired but doesn't feel that way because the Sarnia Seven case is still his baby, or to put it another way he's chief babysitter, responsible for last-minute briefings and debriefings of Crown witnesses, catering to their needs, giving them courses in how to not fuck up on the witness stand.

Deputy A.G. Azra Khan gave Maguire that job because he doesn't trust his unseasoned underlings: a robot hooked on Brylcream and an articling student who's gawky as a flamingo and hooked on Azra Khan. Both sit there staring like zombies at their open laptops, while Khan chats with the lady known around here as Miss Pucket, the Court Clerk. Khan has worked with Maguire on some big ones, murders, kidnappings, and he made sure Jake is looked after, with an extra weekly stipend.

That will help pay off the bloodsucking credit card company, whose last bill gave him such a jolt that he thought, finally it's the heart attack Sonia keeps worrying about. Hawaii was three times as expensive as he'd roughly estimated, he hadn't factored in the cruise or the beachfront villa upgrade. Never mind. All good. Sonia was happy, that's all that counts.

Maguire overnights in an upscale uptown hotel except for weekends in London. Sometimes Sonia stays over with him and they go out for dinner or a show, like *Come from Away*, which was okay, but nothing beats a live performance in a courtroom. Khan versus Beauchamp, it'll be like Ali versus Frazier.

Maguire winces as he turns; somehow he kinked his sunburned neck on the flight from Honolulu in a midget-sized middle seat. Here comes Gaylene Roberts, Inspector Roberts now, down the middle aisle — she's also helping orchestrate this production, staying in the same hotel as him.

The boys in the OPP clubhouse bought out Gaylene's rights from the Sarnia PD, so she'll soon be on her way up the totem pole. Maguire hopes to still be around when she makes it to top raven. If he's not, he will raise a glass from the graveyard. She saved his ass that night he got looped at Squirrelly Moe's. He still hasn't mentioned the penilingus incident to her, and never will. It's buried now.

The deal with the defence lawyers ensures it won't be mentioned during testimony. It is to be considered irrelevant. Deputy A.G. Azra Khan had also promised that the photo of Maguire in wide-eyed shock will somehow disappear. They'd met in private, "man to man," as Khan put it, with a wink and a grin, jovially skeptical, unwilling to believe Maguire didn't get a head job. Khan seemed peeved he wasn't being showered with gratitude for making Maguire's problem go away.

Gaylene settles in beside him. "I'm glad you're going before me. So I can correct all your bloopers."

"I've a memory like a steel trap."

"One that's rusted shut."

They regularly joust like this, a friendly game, upsmanship. They've had only one verbal shootout — over Maguire's perhaps ill-considered remark that men tend to make better jurors than women. He meant that men are better jurors because they don't get all weak-kneed over reasonable doubt and such. But he let her win that one.

There's a rustling in the room that, he guesses, announces the entrance of the defence team. Maguire must endure neck pain again as he turns to see Arthur Beauchamp chatting with a law student back in the pews, then another fan, the old pro working the room. Finally, he makes his way forward, smiling, swinging his heavy briefcase onto the table, merrily greeting Khan and his team.

In his wake comes Nancy Faulk, also looking confident today, and not hungover. This feminist brawler is not a favourite of Toronto coppers, male ones anyway, but Maguire feels sorry for her — he would rather take a bullet between the eyes than go through a divorce like hers.

She's followed in by her clients Ivor Trebiloff and Amy Snider, the demonstration junkies, then mastermind Helmut Knutsen, who they call Doc, and their sad-eyed cyber guy they call Okie Joe, then Rockin' Ray Wozniak, looking like he pulled an all-nighter and is ready for bed. This dude lives in a different time zone from normal people.

Rivke Levitsky and Lucy Wales break ranks, stopping to engage with supporters, exchanging pats and hugs and fists. Miss Pucket takes this as a breach of decorum and rises in alarm, but relaxes when a court officer collects the two little hotties and ushers them into the prisoners' box.

How do these seven wannabe saviours of the world expect to get off? Except for one weak manslaughter count, there's no chance of any acquittals. They've been all over the media boasting about their burglary like it's a great political coup. Maguire's theory is they want to be martyrs, to use the trial as a political platform, and go down in flames.

"I stopped in the witness room," Gaylene says. "No Howie."

"He's not on till tomorrow at the earliest."

"You sure he's going to be all right?"

Maguire shrugs. "As long as he stays on his antidepressants. He threw up last time I pushed him for details."

"He's jerking you around. You said you were going to lay into him."

"Look at his side — head of security, thinking with his dick, gets shitfaced, gets shucked, and gets fired after giving away the crown jewels without even a piece of her ass as a consolation prize. I'm through forcing him to relive it. It's bad enough he'll have to regurgitate everything in front of a jury, then do a perp march in front of the TV cameras. I feel sorry for the dork."

Sharp at ten, not a second later, Justice Donahue swaggers in like a wrestler climbing into the ring. Miss Pucket calls, "Order in court," too late — the judge is already on her throne, surveying her kingdom. Maguire has never appeared before her, but Azra Khan told him she's strictly by-the-book. "Anal retentive," is how he put it. "That's her weak spot and Beauchamp knows it." Maguire assumes Beauchamp will keep picking at that weak spot, like an infected sore, hoping to get her rattled, making appealable mistakes.

Checking that everyone's in place, Donahue asks the accused to stand and they go through the formality of everyone pleading not guilty to everything. They do it straight, no speeches, no gestures, no embellishments, until they get to Wozniak, who pleads to the manslaughter charge "Definotly guilty," getting laughter from the partisans and even from some in the jury pool. Judge Donahue is not amused. She tells Beauchamp to remind his client "this is not a comic opera," following which there's a testy exchange about an accused's right to be emphatic in making his plea.

She's still smarting, after all the pleas are made, and lets counsel know there's not going to be any screwing around in her courtroom, though not in those words.

One of her things is not letting counsel ask questions of the jury panel. "This isn't the U.S., where they seem to revel in that annoying ritual." But even so, the jury selection is slow, prosecutors and defence challenging a dozen before making their first picks. Basically, the Crown rejects anyone who isn't straight and safe, the defence challenges those who are. Half an hour in, only two guys and two women have got seated in the jury box.

The process consumes the morning, a cat-and-mouse game where both sides try not to burn through their quotas of challenges

— Crown and defence each have eighty-four. Khan may not have been looking ahead — he's running out of bodies, and has only one challenge left, and all but three seats on the jury are filled. Faulk also has one challenge left and Beauchamp has hoarded his last two.

It's like the NHL draft, Beauchamp's team hoping that two prospects farther down the list — a social studies teacher and a college student — will be available to play defence for them. But first they have to stickhandle past four other prospects: an auditor named Mabel Sims, a well-dressed woman who's obviously rolling in it named Joyce Evans, and two scowling businessmen.

Beauchamp and Faulk have a long whispered conversation about Mabel Sims, who audits for the provincial tax branch and is an unknown quantity. Not a Facebooker anyway. Flinty-looking, as you'd expect an auditor to be. Finally, Beauchamp gambles on her, says, "Content," which surprises Maguire. But then he gets it — the wily old lawyer wants to save a challenge for the last dude in line, a petroleum engineer with Exxon.

Khan also says he's content, and Mabel Sims gets sworn. Just as much time is spent worrying over Mrs. Evans, and again Beauchamp finally says, "Content." Khan wins a smile from her as he welcomes her to the jury.

Now the jury box awaits a final bum to occupy its twelfth chair. The two businessmen, one in finance, the other in property development, get culled quickly by the defence, and now both Khan and Beauchamp are down to their last challenge.

The defence lawyers go into a sham huddle over the social studies teacher, a longhair who they've got to know gave Facebook likes to the David Suzuki Foundation. The prosecutors don't like him, but they're also not keen on the nineteen-year-old knockout who's next, a U of T pre-med student, Abbie Lee-Yeung, whose Facebook saves were mostly feminist and pro-lesbian.

Beauchamp says he's content with the teacher. Now Khan has to decide who he's going to spend his last challenge on. He doesn't agonize much — the teacher gets a failing grade, the pretty student gets a pass, with Khan taking a long, fond look at her lovely legs. With no sign of smugness, Beauchamp graciously says he welcomes the youthful energy she will bring to the deliberations.

And that's it, that's the jury. The Exxon engineer never got a look.

The judge recites an upbeat civics lesson to the jury about their historic role et cetera et cetera, and asks Azra Khan if he has any opening remarks. He's brief, a ten-minute summary of the plot and how it was carried out, a few bullet points about the manslaughter, and a promise to lay everything out chronologically "with as much clarity as the Crown can muster."

Donahue tells the jury they're not allowed to talk with anyone about the case, except jurors always do. She announces she won't "countenance any unnecessary delays." Her court will sit from ten to twelve thirty and two to four thirty and there will be no breaks mid-morning or mid-afternoon, and everyone should keep that in mind "by anticipating physical needs." She wants everyone back here at two p.m. on the dot.

2

Maguire suggested a nearby tavern. Gaylene suggested a sushi place. Maguire explained he only had a coffee this morning, mediocre at that, and no amount of sushi would fill the void. He finally got his way on something, and they are in the tavern and he's working on a quarter-pounder with fries.

"You could at least have gone for the salad option." Gaylene is being holier-than-thou with her tomato and lettuce on multigrain. "A big, sopping, high-cholesterol burger — I thought you were on a diet plan."

"Hey, I already got a wife to nag me about food. She's got me on a sixty-day diet that only a fanatic would get through to the end. It allows for exceptions, however, like special occasions."

She pretends confusion as she looks around this Ye Olde England cliché pub with its Union-Jacketed staff. "This is a special occasion?"

"Day one of the trial that you and me wrapped up for Azra Khan with a red ribbon on it. Except I don't see him putting much oomph into it." Maguire has a whole lot of time for Khan, as a professional, even though he's vain and snobby and an addicted womanizer.

Gaylene says, "It's too easy for him. He's bored. Or easily distracted. Maybe he's got issues at home, the wife or the kids."

Maguire wonders what's with her sad face. Maybe *she* has issues at home. "He's *distracted*? That's why he runs out of challenges and gets stuck with a militant feminist?"

"Oh, God, a feminist on the jury? We're doomed." She steals a fry from his plate.

"Maybe, Gaylene, you ought to appreciate I have some experience about juries. Feminists make bad jurors, they're quarrelsome, always arguing the other side. That's where you get your hung juries. Everyone's unanimous but them." He holds up his hand, commanding her to silence as he swallows the last of the burger. "Now normally you want Oriental jurors, they're old-fashioned, they actually believe in law and order, but this one, Abbie something, she's third-generation, a millennial, probably a socialist — it's all the rage. Also she's a freaking chemistry major, an honours student. I wrote a big red X next to her name."

"What's *your* degree in, Jake? Gender, racial, and cultural stereotyping?"

"Hey, do me a favour. I want to be in court this afternoon. I'm an essential member of the Crown's team, so I don't have to be excluded, counsel okayed that. I want to see the two surviving eyewitnesses in action."

"You're assigned to them. You prepped them. And you can babysit them. I've got my own stable." She's handling most of the experts.

Today's two eyewitnesses are Barney Wilson and Irwin Fleiger, the boneheaded night watchmen. They keep sneaking out of the witness room for a smoke, and dawdle coming back through security. They *need* babysitting. "Please? This judge is itching to bust someone for being late."

"All right, enjoy, you owe me one."

Maguire winces from his strained neck as he glances to the right. "Don't turn around. Rockin' Ray Wozniak has parked himself two tables behind you with his new groupie." Another stereotype-defying Asian, the sexy mystery woman known as Sooky-Sue. Probably one of the gang, the Earth Survival Rebellion.

He'd heard cop-talk that Wozniak's ex, Lucy Wales, had left him for some rich money manager. Good luck to her, is Maguire's attitude. He remembers from the bust in the antique store how she winked at him, like they were sharing a shameful secret. *Enjoying a little street penilingus? Yolo.* Maguire had got aroused by Gaylene's head on his crotch, but what man wouldn't? Forget it. Ancient history.

Rockin' Ray Wozniak doesn't seem aware he's accidentally under surveillance, in fact doesn't seem aware of anything. Panic Disorder have been doing regular late-night gigs in a club, so he's got to be among the walking dead. Astoundingly, this super-stoner has stayed clean since he got busted eight months ago.

It bugs Maguire that Khan laid that manslaughter on Wozniak, because the jury's going to think the prosecution is reaching. Now there'll be a sideshow over Wozniak being so wrecked on hallucinogens he was mentally incapable of a criminal act.

Gaylene resists turning around. "What's going on over there?"

"Sooky's doing all the talking. Ray looks sullen. Maybe she's cutting him off."

"Of what?"

"Sex."

"Or drugs?"

Maguire shakes his head. "T.J. Gully looks after him, his manager. But he's not using, he knows he can't order a beer without getting thrown in the nick. Right now he's being served a fizzy water."

"Ready to go?"

"I was thinking of coffee. And maybe dessert."

"Get your coat on, bub." She goes off to pay.

He winces again as he grabs his coat, then remembers he kept half an Oh Henry! in its left pocket for emergencies.

§

The court doesn't reassemble at two on the dot because the first witness, Barney Wilson, the Sarnia plant's inside guy, had a last-minute need to pee. Maguire visualizes him dribbling into the urinal while singing "Home on the Range" to get up his courage.

Barney has been on the dole for the entire six months since he got fired, and at age twenty-nine he's washed up in the security business he trained for. He thinks Chemican blackballed him, but Maguire told him not to say that in court, it only muddies the waters.

Minutes pass. Gaylene will come after Maguire's nuts with a carving knife for dumping this hoser on her. There's nothing he can do. He'll stay right here. Five of the Sarnia Seven sit there just shrugging and smiling, but Rivie Levitsky is busy with pen and notepad. She looks up in thought, then down, scribbling away again.

At five minutes after two, the judge gets Miss Pucket on the horn and tells her to bring in the jury, and they troop in from their door, Justice Donahue from hers, bristling, demanding to know the cause of the delay.

Khan calmly explains his first witness had to respond unexpectedly to "a physical necessity." He and the defence counsel mollify the judge by using the gap time to file a bunch of admissions of fact, minor matters like continuity of exhibits and dates and times and locations, plus entering a pile of ten-by-eight photographs that aren't being contested.

That doesn't kill enough time, and Donahue scans the big room, the court staff, the Crowns, as if looking for someone to blame, finally settling on Maguire.

Beauchamp notices that and pretends to be helpful: "Inspector Maguire seems ready and eager to brave the witness stand."

"Let us see if that can work," says Khan, falsely enthusiastic. He bends to Maguire's ear: "Well, we're off to an excellent start, aren't we? If that moron isn't here in twenty seconds, we'll have to start with Fleiger, so let's make sure *he* hasn't wandered . . ."

He trails off, swivels to see two court officers march in Barney Wilson, once again not making a good impression, unshaven, shirt not tucked in, having trouble locating the witness stand, and, on finally being led there, mumbling his answers so he has to repeat them.

The jurors aren't paying attention anyway, they're either looking at a big screen showing the design of the plant or at photos taken inside and out. Aluminum cladding, thick, square posts and beams, asphalt roof. It was built in the seventies, started off its life as a lumberyard warehouse, then an adhesives factory, a partial upper floor added when Chemican took it over.

The foreman, a sixty-year-old architect, hogs the interior layout. He designs suburban mini-malls, so Khan decided he isn't likely to be an environmentalist. The pre-med student, Abbie Lee-Yeung, is about the only one listening to Wilson describe his nightly routines.

Barney seems to have suffered permanent memory damage about the post-midnight hours of September 12. There came a loud crash. Then, pursued by a giant, pry-bar-wielding maniac, he frantically sloshed through the Vigor-Gro while an alleged time bomb ticked off the last deadly seconds. There's no chance Barney will ID Wozniak as the maniac, so Khan does what he can with this unsatisfactory so-called eyewitness, then turns him over to the defence.

Beauchamp strolls over to the jury box, and he says, "Now, Mr. Wilson, my hearing isn't as sharp as it used to be, and sometimes that's a blessing, but not today. So I want you to speak into that microphone loud and clear. If I can hear you over here, the jury can for sure."

Judge's bench, counsel table, and witness box are all miked, but Beauchamp doesn't need any electronic help. He has this deep baritone that's clear and resonant without seeming stretched or even loud.

"Yes, sir," says Wilson, "I'll do my best."

"Excellent. Can I call you Barney? I have an old trusted friend called Barney."

Maguire suspects Beauchamp's old friend is more blarney than Barney, but he admires the smiling old fraud's folksy technique, getting the witness all relaxed before pouncing. Praising Barney for his good deeds with the Boy Scouts and his work ethic, his eighteen months of loyal service to Chemican, leaving the impression he got screwed when they axed him over this one incident. "And now you can't find work."

"Because they blackballed me."

"I would assume your union has filed a grievance over your firing."

"No, they don't have no union at that plant."

The lead actor for the defence obviously knows that already, this was mainly for Juror Six, treasurer of a Steamfitters local in North York.

"Okay, you were taken on by Chemican two years ago. Who actually did the hiring?"

"Mr. Griffin. Howell Griffin. Director of Security."

"He interviewed you, and liked you, and hired you, yes?"

"Yes, sir."

"And when did he put you on the night shift?"

"About maybe four months in, after I did a training course."

"And who instructed you how to do an hourly walkabout inside the plant?"

"That would be Mr. Griffin."

"And these hourly patrols would take you how long?"

"Twelve minutes on average. I kept a log, it's all in there."

"I assume it shows your last log-in was midnight on Tuesday, September tenth."

"Yeah, I guess. Had to be."

"You always started exactly on the hour?"

"Pretty much."

"Why?"

"I dunno. Mr. Griffin told me to."

"And who gave you instructions to stay out of the upstairs laboratory?"

"That would be Mr. Griffin again."

And it's also Mr. Griffin who gave the night crew the codes to the plant's lockable doors from week to week. And of course Mr. Griffin hired the dead temp, Archie Gooch. And did Griffin also give Gooch the codes for his one-night stand? Barney says he must have.

Maguire can't figure why Beauchamp is throwing all these darts at Howie Griffin, as if trying to blame the whole thing on him. Maybe it's a red herring. Azra Khan's squinty look suggests he's wondering too. Judge Donahue is hunched forward, waiting for someone to go off track so she can assert authority.

The Sarnia Seven remain serene, except for Rivie Levitsky, still toiling over her notepad. What's she writing? Poetry? Rants for Facebook? Letters to her lover? Azra Khan must wonder too, because he gives her lots of looks. Probably wondering what it would be like with her.

Beauchamp keeps stirring Archie Gooch into the mix: "So if he had the code for the back door, and he unlocked that door, would you be aware from your workstation that that door was open and accessible?"

"No, because of all the tanks and machinery in between. We didn't have a security camera setup."

"Why not?"

"Well, there was talk of it, but Mr. Griffin put it off."

Beauchamp pretends he's shocked: "Mr. Griffin, your head of security, didn't want security cameras?"

"Yeah. Because of the cost, I think."

"You were listening to western music on the radio?"

"A station I like."

"And with that radio on, you wouldn't hear the back door being shut?"

"Not unless it was slammed. I always checked it every tour, and it was always locked."

Beauchamp seems about to conclude, half sits, but when Nancy Faulk whispers something he bounces up again, rummages for a document. "I forgot to ask, Barney, how are your feet?"

"My feet?"

"I'm looking at Inspector Maguire's report — you remember his interview, later that same morning at the OPP detachment?"

"Okay, yeah, sort of."

"You walked into his office in your socks. Your feet were swollen."

"Oh, yeah, my ankles too. I think I told him it was an allergy but I'm not sure."

"Well, what do you think caused the swelling?"

"Objection," says Khan, finally getting off his butt. "What he thinks has no probative value."

"Let's go at it another way," Beauchamp says. "Ten hours earlier you were wading ankle-deep through a rushing stream of Vigor-Gro?"

"More like running. So fast I slipped, head first, I was gagging on it."

"You gulped some down, right?"

"A pint at least."

"How long did that swelling last?"

"About a week."

"Any lasting damage?"

"Um, well, some of my toes went crooked."

"No more questions."

Nancy Faulk doesn't have any either. Khan seems tempted to re-examine about those toes or even have Barney show them to the jury, but decides to let the poor bugger go. Wilson stalls, not sure how to get out of here, aims first for the jury room door before finally being led out by a court officer.

Maguire wonders if the crooked toes are his only lasting damage.

3

Gaylene has Irwin Fleiger parked right outside the courtroom door, she's not letting this fish get away, and when his name is called he bustles to the stand like he's been kicked in the ass. Wears a shiny suit that may have fit him two decades ago when he wasn't as porky.

Like many cheesers Maguire has known, Fleiger gives off an air of resentment about the way the world has treated him, and that comes across early in his testimony, about how he'd been doing security for Chemican with a spotless record for five years and even had a title, Guardhouse Security Officer. Now he's a doorman and lives off tips.

Khan takes him through the plans and pictures, like with Wilson, except Fleiger doesn't mumble and is clearer about tasks and staffing issues. You can see his contempt for the late Archie Gooch, maybe not so much in words as in his face, which puckers up like someone just farted when Gooch's name comes up.

He describes how Gooch came around the corner of the building, "kind of staggering," as Barney Wilson barrelled out the door followed by "this alien like from a space movie, a seven-foot-tall insect with big bug eyes because of all those goggles and ear protectors."

Khan sees he has a live one and encourages Fleiger to describe without prompting about how Barney Wilson panicked his way into the guardhouse, and how the space alien was yelling about being the enchanter and the avenger and they were all going to die in the fires from hell. He also heard him yell, "This ship is going effing down!"

That gets Justice Donahue's nose vibrating. "Effing? Did he say effing?"

"No, ma'am, the other word."

"We're all adults here, what did he say?"

"The F-word."

"His exact words, please."

"'This ship is going fucking down.'"

"Thank you."

Chuckles from the back pews muffle Maguire's own grunt of laughter. What is funny is not Donahue's attention to accuracy but the way she wiggles her nose like she's congratulating herself for making the witness say a naughty word. Maguire wouldn't be surprised if she has a little hang-up thing about dirty talk.

Fleiger gets back on track. "He was screaming, 'It's going up!' I wasn't going to take a chance there was a bomb in there, and I grabbed Barney and we took off out the gate."

"And what happened to Archie Gooch?"

"Well, he ran out before we did, and the terrorist guy went after him, and he was catching up, and then Gooch just fell flat on his face, and the guy chasing him raced on past and into the bush. We had already took off by that time."

"Would you say the man in the goggles was definitely pursuing Mr. Gooch?"

Beauchamp bounces up, claiming Khan is "flagrantly" leading, and the judge asks him to rephrase, and Khan comes back with, "What was your impression as you watched Mr. Gooch running?"

Beauchamp isn't happy with that either. "Not an hour ago, my learned friend was arguing that one's thoughts have no probative value."

Khan kind of shrugs, and tries again. "What did you see Archie Gooch doing?"

"I saw him running for his life."

"Your witness."

Maguire knows Beauchamp is seething. But he doesn't show it, he's an Oscar-winning lawyer, and he's actually smiling as he rises. Kind of like a crocodile.

"Mr. Fleiger, you told us you had a spotless record with Chemican-International."

"Yes, sir, and they wouldn't even give me a letter of recommendation."

"A spotless record, yet you were suspended for a week in May of last year. Why was that?"

Fleiger reddens. So does Maguire, actually, but in his case with anger. Nobody told him about this, including, especially, Irwin Fleiger.

"It was over, ah . . . they accused me of drinking on the job."

"According to the morning supervisor's written report, as of seven thirty a.m. you were actually drunk on the job."

These specifics obviously came from the personnel files Rivie Levitsky copied while Howie Griffin was snoring. Operation Vig never found those copies, so they had to have been deleted, burned, or garbaged.

Levitsky has taken a break from her pen and paper so she can enjoy watching Beauchamp reduce Fleiger to the level of stammering fool. He denies he was pie-eyed but admits they found an empty mickey of Seagram's in the guardhouse that he'd bought as a birthday gift to himself and thought he'd left it in his car, and so on.

The sly old barrister circles for the kill. "You understand, Mr. Fleiger, that perjury is a serious crime?"

"I understand but I honestly forgot all about it until you asked."

"Your memory can play games, eh?"

"It was a mistake, no one's perfect."

"So let me take you back to Tuesday, September eleventh. You watched Mr. Gooch running out the gate?"

"Yes."

"He was running oddly, wasn't he? Kind of staggering?"

"Yeah, to be honest, he looked like he was high on something."

"Then you saw the man who looked like a giant insect running out the gate?"

"Yes, sir."

"And he was running faster than Gooch, right?"

"Yeah, definitely faster."

"So fast that he overtook Gooch?"

"Yeah . . . No, wait. Overtook means . . ."

"He went right past him, without touching him."

"I never saw no contact, to be honest."

"When Gooch, as you put it, fell on his face, the so-called enchanter was five feet ahead of him, yes?"

"I can't say it was five feet, things were real hectic."

"Okay, a few feet anyway."

"Maybe a few feet."

"So when you said Gooch fell flat on his face, then the other guy raced past him, you had it exactly backward, right? No one was chasing Gooch when he fell. I'm not accusing you of lying, you just made a mistake, right?"

Fleiger looks to the prosecutors for help, gets blank stares. "I must have. It was very confusing at the time."

"I assume that when you saw Gooch sprawled unconscious on the road, you hurried over to give him aid."

"Not exactly right away. I had my hands full with Barney and I was calling 911."

"Well, when did you check as to his well-being?"

"I didn't see no blood and it looked like he was breathing, so we kind of left him there until the ambulance came. It was only like ten minutes."

Beauchamp owns Fleiger by now, and gets out of him that he once saw Gooch take a couple of pills and that he reeked of marijuana.

Beauchamp acts like he's shocked. "My Lord," he goes and then resumes a familiar line of questioning. "Who hired this Gooch fellow?"

"Mr. Howie Griffin."

"And did Mr. Griffin give him the keypad codes for the doors of the plant?"

"That's company policy for all night watchmen, so, yeah, that would have happened, but they change the code every week."

"And so Gooch could have unlocked the back door without being seen, right?"

"I don't think he . . ." He reflects. "Yeah, I guess that's possible."

"In your initial interview with Inspector Maguire you called Gooch a loser. What did you mean by that?"

"Well, it looked to me he had a big drug habit, and he wouldn't be a guy I would hire as a security watchman."

"Do you know why Mr. Griffin hired him?"

"Something about outreach. I understood he was on drug rehab. It was a company policy to take on unskilled workers as trainees. Keeps the wage costs down, I guess."

"You knew Gooch had a criminal record—"

"Objection!"

Beauchamp raises his hands in mock surrender. "Quite right. It's not Mr. Fleiger's department. We'll wait until Inspector Maguire takes the stand."

That's it from Beauchamp. Nancy Faulk again declines to cross, obviously lying low because her two veteran lefties aren't charged with doing the B and E.

Before court adjourns for the day, Justice Donahue reminds the jury about not reading, listening, or watching the news about the case and not talking to friends and family about it, as if that's humanly possible, and to report anyone who seeks to influence them.

Maguire has to give round one to Beauchamp on points, but the jury will soon realize he was bullshitting them about Howie Griffin and Archie Gooch being the real conspirators. But that's what lawyers do best, sling the bullshit.

Maguire reminds himself to have a sit-down with Howie real soon. Not tonight, because Maguire needs his sleep — he's on tomorrow, it's his last stand on the witness stand, last stop on his farewell tour.

4
Tuesday, May 14

Wearing his best brown suit, feeling sharp after a good sleep, ready to take on the mighty Beauchamp, Maguire is met at the court-house door by Khan's student, the flamingo, who hustles him up to the sixth floor for a corridor conference with the prosecutors. The topic is Beauchamp's theory of a con game between Howie Griffin and Gooch.

Azra Khan is cynical. "He's just digging around in the mud to see what worms he might stir up." A pause while his adoring student laughs. "Mainly, it's an effort to distract us."

A successful effort, in Maguire's case. Maybe it's his old phobia about defence lawyers acting up, but he can see Beauchamp and Faulk pulling something out of their asses with the fragrant aroma of reasonable doubt. Just in case, Maguire has put out an all-points bulletin for Howie Griffin, who has not been receiving calls.

"Still," says Khan, "it would be interesting to know what other jobs Howie gave Gooch."

The nerdy, expressionless junior finally speaks: "Like how tight they were."

Maguire says he's on it, he'll check into the company's outreach program. He's about to follow them into court when Gaylene waves him down. She finishes a phone call with, "Late-model BMW. Also, Wiggie, check his cottage on Georgian Bay."

She looks Maguire over, straightens his suit jacket, fills him in. "Howie Griffin may have done a bunk. He moved out of his apart-ment when the lease expired. We tried to phone, email, text, we even tried Skype, and no Howell J. Griffin. He hasn't cut his services off, so maybe we should worry about finding him in some deadbeat motel hanging from a beam with a chair tipped over."

Maguire doesn't want to hear that kind of speculation just before testifying — he's prepped, he's primed, he doesn't need the distraction.

§

But he does okay, even better than. The jury warms to him quickly, this easygoing, straight-talking chief investigating officer who shruggingly confesses to his thirty-five years of service to the people of Ontario as a peace officer, thirty as a detective, the last ten as Inspector.

Khan looks pleased the way Maguire motors along, negotiating the curves, avoiding the potholes as he describes the scene of the crime, the Vigor-Gro mess and mop-up, questioning witnesses, collecting exhibits, giving orders, then moving smoothly on to the next day, and the day after that, all without having to even glance at his notes. Standing tall throughout, to give the jury an impression of confidence.

Nor are there any glitches over the exhibits, no fumbled hand-offs, which often happens in court, especially with photographs out of chronological order or otherwise mixed up, but today everyone, including judge and jury, is on the same page, picture-wise.

There's a hiccup, though, when Khan tries to introduce an exhibit labelled *I-33 for Identification*, a blow-up of Howie's ejaculate on the tile floor of his office-in-home, its partial impression of Rivie Levitsky's left foot. Before the jury can look at it, Justice Donahue sends them away early for lunch because Beauchamp wants to argue it isn't admissible.

The judge is livid. "Why wasn't this raised as a pretrial motion?"

Beauchamp looks at Azra Khan. Khan looks at Beauchamp. Finally, Nancy Faulk steps up. "During the pretrial hearing last month on the court's motion to exclude necessity, our footprint motion was also on the list. Along with a motion to exclude a wiretap. The transcript has you saying, 'We'll deal with them when I decide to deal with them.'"

Silence. Maguire remembers how she stormed out, pissed that Khan sided with the defence. Now she's red-faced, looking for someone to blame. She chooses Miss Pucket. "Madam Clerk, please see me in my chambers after we break."

Miss Pucket goes white. "Thank you, M'Lady, yes."

Maguire sits, massages his neck, as Beauchamp carries on. "Hopefully, we can run through our motions quite smoothly," and he launches into his argument to exclude the footprint evidence.

Maguire expects the judge to give it short shrift, but Beauchamp comes up with a pretty good argument. Under the Identification of Criminals Act, offenders can't refuse to be fingerprinted, but the Act doesn't mention feet; it's specific to fingers. It follows, Beauchamp says, that his client was denied her right not to be footprinted.

He's got case law from Manitoba to support this, so Maguire can see this one going to the defence, allowing Beauchamp to claim there's no proof Levitsky ever snuck into the dork's inner office. Nice try, except Howie will testify all she had to do was dig the keys out of the pants he wasn't wearing. But hold on — will Howie testify? His Spanish is good, what if he skipped to Peru where the coca plant grows? What if he *is* suicidal, and jumps in front of a GO train?

Azra Khan's reply is technical, about DNA and the intention of Parliament. Meanwhile, it's getting close to half past twelve, and the judge finally interrupts him in mid-flow wanting to know how long this will take. Khan needs another half hour.

"Which probably means an hour." Her Ladyship is still in a bitchy mood. "And then there'll be a reply. And then *I'll* need time to consider. We will take the noon break."

§

Not that he doesn't enjoy Gaylene's company, but Maguire wants to be alone over lunch, he doesn't need all her carping over his food choices. So he takes a healthy, long walk to a rib house on Bloor, and does justice to a pile of glistening, succulent, meaty pork ribs with fries, fuel for getting through an afternoon of legal technicalities.

He returns to court to find the public gallery has thinned out except for a scattering of press and lawyers and a few dogged Bee-Dazzlers. The jury has been sent away for the day. Maguire settles into a back pew, valiantly trying to grasp the Latin phrases being tossed around by counsel. Soon, his stomach begins voicing loud objections that he has trouble overruling.

The judge interrupts Khan: "In a nutshell, as I see it, you're saying that when the Act was passed Parliament must be presumed to have contemplated feet and toes."

That is punctuated by a dissent from the back row, hopefully audible and smellable only to those in Maguire's immediate neighbourhood. He does a show of looking about for an alleged perpetrator, his anus clenched against another threatened eruption. He holds on for another few minutes, then slinks out as a grinning court officer holds the door for him.

§

Maguire tells himself that's it, lesson learned. No more mindlessly packing away all those carbs and fats. Partly it's the tension of being on stage, he reckons, but mostly it's a reaction to Sonia's starvation diet based on Dr. Wendy's Ninety-Day Foolproof Diet Plan that she saw on TV and bought the book. It's a form of marital abuse.

He reminds himself to call her, to tell her how he did in court, and she should watch the evening news — CTV had a camera on him a little while ago when he went out to get some Soothe Digest capsules.

Gaylene had texted him to meet her, and he locates her in the courthouse café, downstairs, nursing a mug of tea. He goes for one of their so-so coffees, proudly ignores the pastries, and sits down beside her, carefully, his gut still settling.

She's got the latest dope on Howie. "He was up at his cottage on the weekend, in Pentangoo . . . I never get that right."

"Penetanguishene." Finally getting the best of her, he'd done patrols there.

"One of our members interviewed the neighbours. They said he looked like doom, so they didn't try talking to him, but they saw him spring clean his cottage and tune up his launch — the ice is gone. Then yesterday morning he drove off in his BMW X3 and hasn't returned."

"Okay, let's stop playing pat-a-cake with this doofus, he's under subpoena, get a bench warrant."

"Already done."

§

Maguire is back in 6-1 and it's half past two and the judge is ready with her footprint verdict. The room is fairly empty, only a few media stragglers. The Sarnia Seven look bored and weary.

Maguire has to give Justice Donahue credit, she's no slouch, doesn't even use notes as she rules the footprint admissible no matter what. Maguire feels good about that — Operation Vig did no wrong.

They go on to the next motion, to exclude the mini-camera video of the perps in the backroom of Ivor Antiques. Maguire suffers through it until almost five, the judge going overtime. She reserves her ruling until the morning.

5
Wednesday, May 15

For breakfast, Maguire kept it down to just a stack of pancakes, no meat, easy on the butter and syrup, and as part of his new fitness regime, went out for a hike up to Queen's Park and around the University Annex area. He even thought about taking the stairs to the courts' sixth floor but decided not to be extreme about it on his first day.

He slept okay, feels on top of things, and is determined to maintain his rapport with the jury — competent, casual, not your typical stiff-necked law enforcer. A pleasant surprise greets him when, as he steps off the escalator, he sees Mrs. Sonia Maguire down the hall, chatting with Gaylene, now waving as she works her way to him through the media pack.

Uncomfortable with public shows of affection, he responds to her hug awkwardly, but with a big grin. She gives him a peck, pats him on the belly.

"You can stop sucking it in," she says.

Sonia always sees through him so he admits to some weakness of will, and begs absolution — this is the last case of his career, his last time on the witness stand, hunger pangs were distracting him, but he woke up today full of resolve. She says it's not resolve he's full of.

But she laughs, and he relaxes. She didn't want to miss his last day in court, she says, and just jumped into the Corolla. She's looking great in the tropical blouse she scored in Honolulu, still got her shape at fifty-eight, maybe a little more ample than thirty years ago, plus she has also retained the personality of a college cheerleader, which she was. Retired RN, who Maguire met in Emergency over an exit wound in his inner upper left thigh, three inches from his balls. She got to know his junk pretty good even before their first date.

"Bridge is cancelled tonight so I can stay over. I won't make you nervous?"

"Nah, you make me proud. You always bring good luck, because justice gets done."

"How's the neck, dear?"

"I don't turn suddenly, I don't notice it."

"I'll give you one of my special massages tonight."

He arranges with one of the court officers to escort her to a seat up close, watches as the press follows them in.

He stays in the hall because Gaylene Roberts has been hovering. "Boy, thirty years," she says. "I'll be lucky to make it to fifteen."

"Having a little rough patch?"

"He hates Toronto. Career versus family, it's the old story."

"You want to talk, I can be your emergency responder."

"It's okay, we'll work it out. I don't know why I mentioned it. Okay, Howie Griffin. He's made contact. Through a lawyer. I'm holding off on the warrant."

§

Maguire struggles to retain his good humour as he slips into court. Another lawyer gumming up the works, advising Howie to honour the subpoena but keep his yap shut. Azra Khan will be pissed, but they can't confer right now because 6-1 is in session, except the jury is still out.

Maguire waves at Sonia, who gives him a bright smile. She's nestled in the middle of the accredited press. Their pens are working, Justice Donahue giving reasons for upholding the wiretap order and search warrant for Ivor Antiques. She finds there was a "firm evidentiary basis for the authorities to proceed." Judge Gerlach made "an inadvertent slip" in signing the warrant on the wrong page.

"He's an inadvertent soak." That's from Nancy Faulk, intended for Beauchamp but loud enough for Maguire to hear as he takes his seat behind the counsel table. But maybe not loud enough to be heard by Justice Donahue, who twitches angrily as she concludes, then glares at Faulk.

"Did you have something to say for the record, counsel?"

"Sorry, M'Lady. I was repeating 'inadvertent slip' in my brain, trying to imagine a slip that wasn't inadvertent."

An icy pause. "I will assume for the moment, Ms. Faulk, that you are not mocking the court. If, later, I am forced to assume otherwise, please be on notice there will be repercussions."

"Thank you, M'Lady, I am much obliged."

Jaunty and not snide, though the mockery is loud and clear. Donahue is supposed to have it in for Faulk over a drunken insult using the c-word, but lawyers are always insulting one another, it's part of their job, then they get together over drinks and laugh about it. Usually. With these two it may be different.

"Bring the jury in," Justice Donahue commands.

§

Back on the stand, Maguire gets a chance to pretend he's modest about his coup of tracking down that eighth-inning TV footage, starring Howie Griffin and Rivie Levitsky. The jury like it, a true detective story. The media are lapping it up because it's news to them.

Sonia is like a talisman, proud of him, beaming him smiles from the second row. Before court was called she was gaily chatting with the reporters. *If you're wondering about his tan, we just celebrated our thirtieth in Hawaii. You should have seen his sunburn.* This is the way she talks to total strangers.

Maguire has a file folder of ten-by-eight prints in front of him, some of them already entered as exhibits, by consent of counsel, others what the Crowns call "potentially contentious." Khan asks him to look at I-44, an image captured from the Jays game, the foul ball video. "Do you recognize anyone in this picture, Inspector?"

The judge interrupts, scrambling through her ten-by-eights. "I don't seem to have that one." Khan's junior digs out another, and Miss Pucket relays it to the judge, who asks the foreman if the jury have copies, which they do, six to share.

Finally, Maguire gets to answer. "The male person leaping up is Howell J. Griffin. The young woman flinching is the accused Rivke Levitsky—"

"I was not flinching!"

Maguire immediately loses centre stage, all eyes turning to Levitsky as she slaps her hand to her mouth. People are laughing in the gallery, media section, even the jury — but not Miss Pucket or Justice Donahue.

Maguire's reaction is to forget he's holding his exhibits folder, and it slips and spills twenty ten-by-eights onto the floor of his cubicle. Thankfully, all attention is on the judge berating Levitsky as Maguire squats down and tries to reassemble them.

One is a slightly blurry snap of his SWAT team blasting into Ivor's backroom. Someone screwed up, because it should be in the reject folder, but it's marked as an exhibit, 93, so the judge and jury may have copies already. He can't remember who took it.

Here's an important one, from YouTube, Exhibit 67, Levitsky and Lucy Wales backstage at the Bee-In with their staff badges. This whole pile has to be re-sorted into chronological order.

Donahue concludes: "Your outburst, Ms. Levitsky, may have been more reflexive than deliberate, but nonetheless it was thoughtless and ill mannered. Your counsel will caution you that repetition could have serious consequences, including loss of liberty."

As Maguire straightens up, he feels tremors, the kind that come with impending danger. He's too shaky to stand, and he slumps onto the witness chair, fixated on Exhibit 92. It's the flash-lit shot of him gaping at Lucy Wales through the windshield! Here's Gaylene's hovering toe!

A majestic fuckup has occurred. This photo was buried and

forgotten — how did it rise rotting from the grave? He slips it back into the folder, afraid to look at Sonia, who will have read his anguish. As well, his neck is in agony with the stress.

Meanwhile, Khan is asking him something. He only catches the name Operation Vigorous, and launches into a thick-tongued tutorial on how they set up at OPP Toronto, the name being inspired by Vigor-Gro, then in the next breath refers to it as Operation Vigorish, then has to explain that's what everyone called it, or Vig, with a hollow laugh, then rambles about how Vig, or The Vig, is also called juice in underworld jargon, which means the cut of the take.

The judge looks as bewildered as the jury. Khan is curt: "We don't need to hear the whole etymology, Inspector. Tell us what Operation Vigorous did."

Maguire can't remember what it did. His brain is totally occupied with not seeing Sonia. Every time he looks from Khan to the jury, his eyes skip past her, past the scandal-tattling journalists surrounding her. Maguire needs to have an intense talk with Khan, but the noon break — half past twelve until two, by judicial edict — is an hour away, and Justice Donahue prods them on.

What did Operation Vigorous do? Yes, he has another detective story, how they caught Rivie and Lucy on amateur video at the Bee-In — he begins a ramble about it, the untold hours that Constable Ling watched YouTube videos, armed only by the image from the Jays game, then he goes on a side trip about Lorne Ling, who everyone called Long Ling though he's actually quite short . . .

"Mr. Prosecutor, please control your witness."

Khan yanks the leash, forcing Maguire to stop and catch his breath as he searches for and finds his copy of Exhibit 67, the two girls huddled over clipboards, one in a Panic Disorder T-shirt. He pulls in deep lungfuls of air, works on clearing his brain, focussing, avoiding panic. He can do this, get a grip on himself, spin it out till lunch. Khan and Beauchamp can fix this without a fuss. Of course they can.

The jury seems relieved that the old copper hasn't lost his mind after all, as he finds his groove, connecting the dots from Lucy's T-shirt to the Panic Disorder gig at Squirrelly Moe's, his undercover mission there, skipping over irrelevant details like how he drank too much and smoked half a pack of Dunhills.

He credits Gaylene Roberts for backing him up and tailing the van but doesn't mention how he passed out and woke up in his hotel room. He lets the jury know he was proud of her, and of his whole team, the job they did shadowing the perps.

He manages to keep his anxiety level down, even though his neck is killing him, as Khan leads him through the critical evening of Thursday, September 17, when he joined Gaylene in the Buick.

"And where was she parked?"

"At the curb, facing north, maybe fifty feet in front of the condo's entrance door. She was very weary, so I got behind the wheel. At eleven fourteen p.m. Lucy Wales exited by that door with a bicycle. She was talking on her phone as she pedalled north. I gave her some space and followed, keeping her in view as she proceeded northwest on Dundas Street, north to Runnymede, then left onto St. Clair Avenue."

As a map of that route gets entered as an exhibit, Maguire finds the jam to look at his wife. He smiles. She smiles too, but cautiously. So far so good, he has made it to Ivor Antiques, having nimbly fled the scene of a marriage-threatening scandal. But he'll only be safe when they deep-six that photo by Lucy Wales.

He chances a glance at Ms. Yolo. She is grinning. He feels a weird sense of partnership, like they're in this together. Her ex-boyfriend, Ray Wozniak, stares straight ahead, like a clothing-shop dummy. Rivie Levitsky is writing. Maguire wants to apologize to her: *You weren't flinching, sorry. You were just twisting to look up.*

In the jury box, nineteen-year-old Abbie Lee-Yeung, second row, last seat, also makes occasional notes, and otherwise follows everything intensely, and seems fascinated by Rivie Levitsky. Occasionally she also sneaks a look at Doc Knutsen, as if trying to figure him out. Probably looked him up online, which jurors aren't supposed to.

It's still a long while before the lunch break as he launches into how his flying squad took down the Earth Survival Rebellion. Setting up and playing the footage from the pinhole camera fills most of the time. Lucy was clearly audible: "And what about Chase. Shouldn't he go with her?" Then Okie Joe, "No way they'll ever nab him."

Chase D'Amato was smart, he didn't try to go with her. But he won't be doing stunts for Greenpeace for a while. Or doing Rivke Levitsky. There's an indication he's in the Northwest Territories, Yellowknife. Good luck to him, is Maguire's attitude, who doesn't want to go through another trial.

The jury has a few sour faces when Dr. Knutsen, with a casual shrug, calls Gooch a casualty of war. Others seem indifferent, finding it hard to mourn a small-time criminal junkie.

Finally it's twelve thirty. Maguire waits for the room to clear, then explains to Azra Khan that a couple of issues have cropped up.

6

"Let's deal first with the annoying case of Howell J. Griffin," says Khan. "My guess is Beauchamp's rubbish about him conspiring with the late Gooch has caused an anxiety attack. Beauchamp's massive red herring became the media's lead story. Now he has a lawyer. Name?"

Maguire says, "Adelsen, Gaylene told me. G.J. Adelsen."

"Anyone heard of him?"

Maguire, the clockwork junior, and the flamingo shake their heads. They're downstairs in the Crown Counsel offices, waiting for a takeout order to arrive, two sandwiches, a salad, and a Whopper and fries.

Maguire had to ask Gaylene to take Sonia for lunch because of this emergency session. Before they parted Sonia asked why he'd turned white on the stand, and he said heartburn, he had to lay off the strong coffee. She didn't seem very convinced of that.

"So, okay," says Maguire, "it's a simple matter of telling Mr. Adelsen that nobody's prosecuting his client. Howie was negligent up the yazoo, but thinking with your pecker ain't a crime."

Khan shakes his head. "I don't have time or patience to handle this Adelsen. You and Finley will have to sit down with him over a beer and find out what their game is."

As if Maguire would enjoy grabbing a beer with this machine. Finley — that's his first name, or second? Khan had overlooked making introductions. Maybe to him, lawyers, like royalty, are a class above, and don't shake hands with commoners.

A secretary comes in with the food orders, plus a Thermos of coffee. Maguire greedily fills a mug. Finley makes himself useful, looking up Adelsen on his phone. "G.J. Adelsen. Okay, looks like he's actually female. Greta Jane Adelsen."

"Good work, Finley," Khan says, kind of caustically. "Please reach out to her. Tell her we won't need Howie for another week or so while we consider obstruction of justice charges. I want him to stew. But if he's willing to sit down with us and be candid, we're prepared to lighten up on him."

Khan turns to Maguire. "As to the awkward photograph, Jake, that's highly regrettable." He repeats those last two words with a dry tone that says there's jack-all he can do about it. Except maybe place blame. "Who did you have collating these photos?"

"Constable Wiggens. Wiggie."

"Wiggie. Ah, yes, the human skyscraper. Not the brightest star in the firmament, is he?"

Wiggie has his failings but Maguire won't let him be scape-goated. "Your junior here, Finley, was supposed to have filtered out the extraneous ones."

All eyes settle on the junior Crown, who finally shows human emotion — a pained expression as he confesses he found what is now

Exhibit 92 in the discard pile with five other prints from the smartphone of Lucy Wales.

"I assumed its vital importance had been overlooked."

Left with the rejects were a cat in a tree, a pizza menu, a close-up of a nipple, and some dickhead leering in a subway car. But Maguire gaping wide-eyed in the Buick is already tagged as an exhibit. So is Lucy's last shot, Exhibit 93, her snap of Maguire's squad busting through the doors of Ivor's backroom.

"This is vexing," Khan says. "Maybe, Jake, it will go unnoticed in the blizzard of exhibits the jury will be engulfed in."

"No, whoa, Katie bar the door. How do you stop the press getting ahold of this and asking questions?" Maguire is agitated, getting loud. "My wife is in the courtroom. What about Gaylene, she'll be scarred for life and all she ever did was pass out with exhaustion after seventy-two hours on the go."

It seriously bothers him that he never mentioned the penilingus incident to her, not wanting to embarrass her, not wanting to lie about having to fight off a hard-on, and then it was all supposed to have been handled by the lawyers. Even Lucy Wales was okay with censoring it from the script.

Khan looks puzzled. "She passed out? Really, Jake? That's, ah, not the impression I was given when I met with defence counsel."

"What did they say?"

"They didn't offer any graphic detail, but—"

"We weren't fucking doing it, Azra! She was bagged. She slid over onto me. I wasn't going to wake her."

"That's what you told Arthur Beauchamp?"

"Exactly." Except for the loosened belt, the manual readjustment of his dick, which he can't bring himself to mention in this company — the flamingo has already gone from pink to crimson. And Khan is focussed on his roast beef on multigrain, it's occupying his mouth, preventing him from confessing Beauchamp conned him.

Maguire is stunned, immobile. He can't remember eating his Whopper but feels it lodged halfway down his food tube. The flamingo, however, has set her tofu salad aside and is poring through her exhibits folder, exhuming another copy of Exhibit 92.

Khan chews slowly, swallows. "Being practical, Jake, can we expect the sheriffs to sneak into the jury room and remove all *their* copies?" He turns to Finley. "How many of these prints are out there?"

"Six for the jury to share." He's sweating, aware he's carrying the can for this. "We have three, defence has two, the judge one." He stops himself, rattled, checks a list. "No, wait, they haven't been passed out to the jury in case there was an objection."

"How could the original be marked as an exhibit then?" Khan asks.

"I don't honestly know, sir. Constable Wiggens didn't raise an issue."

Khan sputters. "What a cockamamie . . . Never mind. I'll work things out with Beauchamp at the end of the day. Maybe we can agree on a simple consent order expunging the exhibit."

Maguire sees a rainbow forming in the mist of his despair.

§

As his examination-in-chief resumes, Maguire is back on his feet — literally, but also he's got his head screwed back on. The jury seem content to assume he's lucid again after his brain farts of this morning. Khan has just had a whispered conference with Beauchamp, and they were nodding in agreement. All is good. Sonia looks much less worried. He's looking forward to that massage tonight. Maybe that will morph into something even more rewarding.

There's not much more the jury needs to know about the bust, except that Maguire gave orders to take down the remaining conspirators, the antique dealer and his lady and Wozniak. Who pissed on the uniformed guy standing below his window and is lucky they didn't beat the shit out of him.

There's a last-minute flurry of exhibits, from Ivor's backroom and front desk, from the residences of all accused, their computers. And then he tells how they found Levitsky's poorly trashed Finnair confirmation and how that led to her being collared at Departures and taken to the Peel PD.

"And then," he concludes, "Mr. Beauchamp over there showed up out of the blue."

"Uninvited, I presume," says Khan drily, this exchange getting laughter. "Please answer his questions."

Beauchamp stands, grinning. "Uninvited but not unwelcome, I hope."

"You're always welcome, sir."

"I hope you don't mind my saying you did an admirable job on this case."

"To be honest most of the credit belongs to Inspector Roberts."

"Were you not required here, Inspector, you would now be enjoying your retirement, so please accept my good wishes for finally escaping the clutches of the law." More laughter. "Seriously, we all hope you and your wife, who I see sitting over there, will enjoy a long, active, and loving life together."

"Thank you, counsellor." Maguire doesn't want to be cynical but he suspects Beauchamp is buttering him up to bring his guard down. Thankfully, the old smoothie doesn't go so far as to ask Sonia to stand. She gives Maguire a little wave, blushing.

Beauchamp finally gets to work, starting with the night watchmen and their gong show. He reads out Maguire's recorded reference to them as the Three Stooges. He has him describe how Barney Wilson twice missed the door of the OPP interview room, how he walked around in stretchy socks, his feet swollen, as Beauchamp puts it, "from splashing through this poisonous pesticide." That earns an objection, sustained.

Beauchamp uses Maguire to acquaint the jury with Archie Gooch's record, the falls he took for theft, hit and run, and mixing and dealing lid proppers. Beauchamp then glances over a stapled report he's holding. "He also committed a bruising assault on his girlfriend in his meth lab, did he not?"

That gets Khan up again, complaining, "My learned friend is on a fishing expedition and he's casting for hearsay. It's also irrelevant. Mr. Gooch is not on trial. Mr. Gooch is dead."

Justice Donahue obviously also thinks he's fishing. "Mr. Beauchamp, I confess that I too can't see how reviling the dead advances the interests of anyone, especially your clients."

Beauchamp comes back hard. "I would be immensely grateful if Your Ladyship withholds judgment on that. We are early into the trial. The defence has a right to explore every reasonable defence. My client is facing a manslaughter charge for which the maximum penalty is life imprisonment. I beg to be allowed to do my job."

She glares at him, her nostrils flaring at this dressing-down. Maguire doesn't know how they're going to unlock horns, until Khan agrees the witness may be asked how Gooch's "behaviour toward his female partner" was handled in court.

Maguire answers carefully, about how an assault bodily harm was withdrawn in favour of a no-harassment order. Beauchamp is okay with that, and carries on. "Inspector, Mr. Gooch's criminal record was known to the company when they hired him?"

"It's in their personnel records, yes. He was supposed to be on drug rehab."

"And in those records, there's no indication he had any training for this job."

"The foreman for security showed him around the previous day, that's all."

"Company records also show that Howell Griffin personally posted Gooch for the September tenth night shift?"

"We have a memo to that effect."

"I'd appreciate being able to show it to Mr. Griffin when he testifies."

Khan interjects to say they'll fish it out for him, which prompts a ripple of laughter.

Beauchamp won't let Gooch rest in peace. He wants to know about the THC content in his blood, and how to interpret it. Maguire says he's not a doctor, then Beauchamp qualifies him as an expert anyway, because of his eight years on narcotics. And of course Maguire has to concede that high-THC-content weed mixed with overdose levels of oxycodone meant Gooch might have been out of touch with reality.

"Enough to put him into a fatal stupor, do you agree?"

Khan is sitting on his hands instead of objecting, so Maguire just says, "A toxicologist and the pathologist who examined Mr. Gooch have subpoenas for tomorrow."

"Suffice it to say Mr. Gooch was a serial abuser of drugs."

"Pretty much, yes."

"Grand larceny, drug trafficking, beating up a woman — what else? running over a cyclist and fleeing the scene — very odd that a fellow with that background would get hired on a security detail, don't you agree?"

Khan is baited to rise again. "That's rhetoric disguised as a question."

The judge, silent since her exchange with Beauchamp, comes out of her sulk. "For what it is worth, Mr. Beauchamp, your point has been abundantly made."

"Thank you, M'Lady. Inspector, you were suspicious of Gooch right from the get-go, weren't you?"

"I'm not sure what you mean."

"You felt he might have taken a bribe."

"I don't remember thinking that."

Beauchamp checks a transcript. "In your initial interview with Howell Griffin you asked, 'What do you think, Howie, is Archie the susceptible kind of guy who'd take a bribe?'"

"All that means is we were looking at all possible angles."

"What was Howie's answer?"

"He just shrugged."

"And to tell the truth, you also suspected Mr. Griffin may have played a nefarious role in this matter?"

"I felt he was covering something up."

"Like what?"

"Like something may have happened in his apartment he didn't want to talk about."

"And did you suspect he was also concealing his extensive use of cocaine?"

"Okay, I observed he was sniffing a lot, so I may have inferred that. Our Ident people found traces of cocaine in his apartment."

"Where exactly?"

"On a plastic cutting board in the kitchen."

"One final matter, Inspector. Do you remember us having a brief chat back in September, at the Old City Hall, just before the bail hearing?"

"Vaguely, yeah, the court was on break." Maguire actually remembers it well — it was about Lucy's photo. Why is Beauchamp getting into this?

"I said something to the effect that my clients had kind hearts, that they weren't criminals in the ordinary sense, and you said there was an element of altruism, that they weren't in it for themselves."

"That was the gist of it, yes, I don't disagree."

"And you have had no reason to change your mind?"

"Not really." He thinks of adding *You can be a good person and still be a bad criminal*, but reminds himself not to tempt fate.

"Those are all my questions."

"Any redirect?"

Khan taps his pen on his pad, pondering, then finally, "No, M'Lady."

"Inspector, before you go, there's one matter I'm curious about." Justice Donohue sorts through her folder of photo exhibits. "I don't know if it was somehow glossed over. Yes, this one." She displays it to the room. "Exhibit 92, it appears to be an image of yourself in a car, looking rather dumbfounded. I'm curious as to its provenance."

Maguire opens and closes his mouth like a fish. Though he's otherwise immobile, his heart beats wildly and his eyes dart left and right, at Sonia amid the press, at Lucy in the dock, at Beauchamp, at Khan. There is no rescue, no escape, no hole to crawl into and die. He feels a sharp pain, and buckles.

CHAPTER 20 » RIVIE

1

Friday, May 17

Early this morning I learned a lesson: always use the staircase railing when creeping down in the dark from the second floor of Arthur Beauchamp's borrowed hacienda. Do not slip, as I did this morning, landing on the landing on my bum with a loud "Jesus fuck!" that drew Arthur from his bedroom, in his pyjamas — which I can attest, because he turned the lights on, are of baby blue stripes.

I was in shorts and runners, off for a pre-breakfast Lake Shore run before gearing up for Day Five of *Queen v. Knutsen et al.* Arthur offered me his hand, which was warm and strong, and I did my best *pirouette en pointe* to show I was undamaged. I promised to make another batch of the granola that he'd overpraised as "ambrosial." He said, "Be safe," and watched from the window as I jogged off into the dusky dawn.

Other huffing early risers join me on the Humber Bay Shores, as a cool spring sun rises above the islands and sparkles the waves and makes the city golden. Leaves are bursting open, and blossoms. Eastern Canada's impetuous, glorious spring.

The downside to this brightly dawning day is my ass is sore and threatening mutiny if I insist on hauling it all the way to Mimico and back. I tell it to stop bitching, get a life, that stairway tumble was a bad-luck episode and now I'm vaccinated against further mishap.

I'm currently dealing with another pain in the ass, that being Lucy Wales, who is still living (but not sleeping) with Richard the Second, while using me as a cover ("I'm sorry, but I promised Rivie we would [fill in the gap] tonight"), so she can sneak around with Rockin' Ray, who is still overnighting with Spooky-Sue, God knows why — he can't seem to break from her even though he's off the ayahuasca.

But he hasn't gone back to weed and psychedelics either, though his bail conditions were altered once the trial got underway: Ray no longer has to sign in twice a week at Fourteen Division, and no one's asking him for urine samples. Lucy and I figure the yagé caused him some permanent kind of altered consciousness, a compulsive meditation disorder.

I likewise no longer have to sign in. I still shoot the shit with Constable Louella, mostly by phone — we bonded like superglue on that Passover trip to Golden Valley, my mains regarding it as so cool for me to arrive under escort by a black, feminist cop who helped in the kitchen and told ribald jokes. I'm meeting her for a coffee and gab this weekend and I know she's going to pester me about the rumours of a high-level blow job in the OPP. (More on that later, and the resulting disorder in court.)

Louella's on night shift, and occasionally patrols up Beaconsfield looking for my lurker — just in case he *still* knows where I live. Which seems unlikely given I've been there two weeks and seen no one skulking around or spying except the nosy neighbours across the street.

Lucy speculated the lurker was Howie Griffin. Obviously (she said in that cocksure voice of hers), he wants to strangle you for ruining his life. I called bullshit — the lumbering creep I chased on my bike didn't have Howie's height, broad-shouldered physique, or agility.

The traffic roar from the Gardiner deadens with distance as I turn into East Humber Park, and the robins' songs come clearer. I pause at a lookout, settle my tender rump on a shoreline rock. I squint across Lake Ontario, look over the curvature of the earth, to the mountainous southern tail of the continent. I draw from my fanny pack the letter from Chase D'Amato, postmarked Puerto Próspero, Costa Rica, on May 1.

It came via Okie Joe, from his "safe mail drop." A little handwritten page, letting me know he's well, congratulating the Rebellionairs for our forthcoming victory, expressing his unwavering (really?) love for me, and it's always summer where he's at, in the wild, and how he saw a tapir the other day, and a rare red-rumped antshrike, and I can't tell if he's bullshitting or not. Nice to hear from him anyway. ("He's got a job," Okie Joe said. "A new identity." The image comes of a zip-line Tarzan, adjusting Lola Lovelylegs's safety harness.)

§

I slip inside the house, hoping not to reawaken Arthur, but lights are on in the room he uses as a study, and the radio is playing, the CBC. And in the kitchen there's coffee in the maker, plenty for sharing. Thanks to my pratfall he never got back to bed so I hope he's not too pissed off.

Although, actually, he's never pissed off. At least I've never seen him so. He's such an extreme gentleman it feels eerie. Most of the men I've shared space with have been louts. Or self-centred. Or distant. Like what's-his-name. D'Amato.

Arthur and I have fallen into the genteel habit of having tea each evening in our fat chairs under the moose head. My impression is he's lonely, needs someone to talk to, to share with, and so he tested me and found me a good listener, an honourable person who would keep his secrets. (Little did he know.)

There's a burden he wants to let go, and I'm sure I'll eventually hear it, though from the way he drops hints about the challenges of his long-distance marriage it's likely to do with infidelity. I open up too, about me and D'Amato, who I am trying to stop loving.

Or we talk about books. Or current events or the state of the planet or what we'll have for dinner tomorrow. We rarely mention the trial, it's off-limits, tea and stress don't mix. Bach often plays in the background, or maybe it's Vivaldi.

I don't want to disturb him, so I creep upstairs with my granola and coffee, and warm up my computer. I try to pry some creative time out of every morning before racing off to court, playing Leonard or Joni or k.d., catching up on my memoir before brain-fade sets in.

Anyway, Dear Diary, here is my account of the imbroglio (is that the word?) caused when Madam Justice Colleen Donahue flashed Exhibit 92 to the jury. It was my first look at the photo, and I couldn't tell whether Jake Maguire's face registered ecstasy as he was being fellated or, assuming that's a vile rumour, shock and dismay at being outed as a cop.

When I finally escaped the hullabaloo, after they took Maguire away in a gurney, I found an empty interview room to dictate a meandering voice memo, an *aide-mémoire*. This is it:

So okay, Judge Donahue had a copy of the windshield pic and she was obviously out of the loop about the conspiracy to save two marriages, and so she asked why Maguire looked so dumbfounded in that picture. She wanted to know the picture's "provenance," which somehow seemed a condescending way to put it.

Maguire's face got pinker and pinker and only his eyeballs were moving, speedily, crying out for rescue. Arthur must have hoped the prosecutor would step up, but Khan seemed to be at a loss. It was Nancy who rose, it's always the woman who takes action in life-and-death crises like this. She was asking for a recess when Maguire gasped, and fell sort of sideways, and a court officer barely caught him before he hit the floor.

There was no physician in this crowded court, but there was a nurse: Sonia, his wife, who bolted from her seat to his limp, prostrate form, cradling him, frantically seeking a pulse, wailing, begging him not to die, then kissing him on the mouth, and his eyes opened and he took a breath, and said, "I love you."

I witnessed this dazzling moment because I was close by, and so were Lucy and Ivor and Amy, having deserted the dock, acting on humanitarian instinct, sensing a heart attack or a stroke. It was chaos, the jury stunned and gaping when shepherded out, Miss Pucket bawling, "Order in court!" senselessly, uselessly, as court officers tried to clear the room, the media resisting, the judge in a stop-action stall at her chambers door.

The only cool head among the lawyers was Khan's storky student, on her phone, instructing an emergency response crew how to find their way to the sixth floor, 361 University Avenue, and bring a gurney.

Meanwhile I wrote furiously and so did the reporters, even while being herded out, a few already phoning in to set up their live reports.

The ambulance crew came within minutes, and brought along an emergency doctor. As they wheeled Maguire out, Sonia at his side, word came from the judge via Miss Pucket that we were done for the day and would counsel kindly join Her Ladyship in her chambers.

We of the Sarnia Seven were the last ones out of the room, and I darted down the hall to find this quiet little room.

§

It was a coronary, as we learned later that evening, something about clogged arteries. Maguire is at Toronto General and the prognosis is good, provided he sticks to a healthy diet.

Earlier that same Tuesday — there's irony here — Gaylene Roberts and Sonia Maguire had a wet lunch and were overheard by a reliable source (sympathizers are everywhere) regaling each other with stories about oddly lovable Jake Maguire. There was much hilarity over

Gaylene's confession of passing out then waking up with her head between Jake's legs. The reliable source noted that the women shared a ribald sense of humour. That leaves me wondering if Jake felt guilty over something he didn't do, and the stress did him in.

Enough of that, I see Arthur below striding out for his daily walk downtown. I've only got half an hour to assemble myself for court.

But first, Dear Journal (or Diary or whatever you are), on the Howie Griffin front:

I had another dream of him the other night. I was being Becky and I awoke writhing and wet. These dreams have got to stop. Why are they recurring? Is it a punishment? Always, on awakening, I have a moment of (a) hating myself for what I did to him and (b) hating myself for being subconsciously horny for him.

Nancy Faulk's theory is he's enraptured by me, a concept I find confusing. He fell in love with brainless Becky McLean, not a cool, cunning, eco-guerrilla saboteur. He doesn't know me. He's never met me. Maybe he just wants to score some Passionata.

Howie started off as number five on the Crown's witness list, but there've been no sightings of this reclusive bird, and meanwhile about twenty others have paraded to the stand.

Someone overheard our lawyers wonder if he's suicidal. How would you live with *that*, Rivke Levitsky?

§

I step from the sixth-floor escalator into a vast herd of humanity: loud, robed barristers, clerks and paralegals, court officers looking for troublemakers among the Bee-Dazzled, witnesses, journalists, spectators queuing for seats in 6-1. Plus us wrongdoers — we are the job creators without whom this whole edifice would collapse.

The room has been sold out ever since the start of day three, with Facebook freaks and Twitterheads having orgasms over how an OPP Inspector expired after cross-examination by a hotshot criminal counsel and was brought back to life by a kiss on the lips from his wife.

The press corps has grown too, a mob of them over there stalking Gaylene Roberts, nagging her about why Exhibit 92 is being kept from them. She gives the official explanation: an error, an irrelevancy, nothing to do with this case, it accidentally found its way into an exhibits folder and is now withdrawn. With that, Roberts is let into the courtroom.

She has taken over Maguire's role and gets to stay in court now that she has testified. She was the first witness on Wednesday, and was sombre but crisp, expanding on how Operation Vig was so competent compared to us amateur saboteurs. She let it out that she conked out in the Olds after having slept only three hours in two days. Nobody pressed her on that one, the judge now a party to the backroom deal to suppress hints of scandal.

So we have the unreal situation of Lucy being in a pact of silence with three prosecutors, two defence counsel, and one judge to protect the asses of two dicks. That's got to help on her sentencing.

The other witnesses this week were mostly technicians and crime scene people and handlers of various exhibits like the pry bar, Ray's abandoned avenger outfit, Lucy's employment records at her old drug store, plus there was CCTV footage from the gas station where we refuelled Ivor's old van, plus proof the van was registered to Ivor Antiques Ltd. Hardly any cross-examination, a little bit from Nancy Faulk to establish the keys to the van were hanging just inside the alley door, accessible to anyone.

Nancy will be leading the necessity defence but otherwise has seen limited action, occasionally dropping hints that Ivor and Amy unwittingly believed their backroom colleagues were merely planning a demonstration.

Lucy tears herself away from a pair of punked-up comrades with anarchist tats, and joins me just as the crowd streams down the hall to 6-1's yawning doors.

"News bulletin," she says. "The guys I was talking to? One of them is a server in an intimate hole-in-the-wall in Little Italy. He looked after Nancy and Doc last night. They were pretty cozy together, which, for Doc, is saying something. Like he didn't seem worried about her germs? Maybe something's happening there? Do opposites really attract? Never mind, I see Miss Pucket tearing her hair out because we're two seconds late."

2

My bottom feels better, expressing discomfort only when I sit flat, so I perch at an angle as we, the Sarnia Seven, clump together in what they call, medievally, the dock.

Doc looks distracted, impatient, as he waits for the main event, when fellow scientists will grapple over the honeybee holocaust. Last night's dinner, I learned, was paid out of his publisher's first advance — his book, part science, part politics, is a call for direct action on environment issues.

He keeps glancing at Nancy. Has he finally been taken captive by the most merciless of human emotions and feeling palpitations of the lonely heart? It takes some effort to visualize moody, messianic Helmut Knutsen getting it on with blunt, quick-tempered Nancy Faulk. But *mazel tov*, couple up, enjoy, abandon me to spinsterhood, the Seven's sole surviving single-o.

Ivor and Amy are holding hands, as ever, and so are Lucy and Ray, more covertly. As everyone stood for the judge's entrance, Lucy turned to scan the gallery to satisfy herself that neither Dick Two or Sooky-Sue were present. I'd spotted them earlier in the melee but they'd failed to queue in time.

The man standing in the witness box is a leftover from yesterday, the last witness, name forgotten, the stone-faced toxicologist. He'd been cut off at four thirty while being cross-examined about Gooch's oxycodone level. On Gooch's admission to the Sarnia hospital that level had been 11,285 nanograms per millilitre of blood plasma.

Arthur, whose shtick with witnesses is endless amiability, welcomes him back to centre stage, gets a grunt of thanks. "You agreed yesterday, Doctor, that Gooch's reading was absurdly high. But you have no reason to doubt its accuracy?"

"No, since a sample tested six hours later was well over nine thousand nanograms."

"Such extreme levels must be unprecedented in the annals of toxicology, Doctor."

"There are several reports of higher oxycodone readings, but in each case the overdose victim did not survive."

"Overdosing can damage the central nervous system?"

"Indeed."

"And can turn a human being into a vegetable?"

"Oxycodone can be a factor inducing a coma, if that's what you mean."

"And it can cause death." Arthur sounds that line with a deep, funereal rumble that makes me shiver.

"Such a result is, sadly, becoming more common."

Arthur then asks him to consider the effects of LSD on "for example, a tall, robust young man" two hours after he'd ingested five hundred micrograms. "Is it fair to say that such a person, at peak level of LSD intoxication, could be out of his mind and wildly hallucinating?"

"That would depend on an individual's level of susceptibility, but hallucinatory disorders are common even at lesser degrees of impairment."

Jurors' eyeballs swivel toward Rockin' Ray Wozniak. He looks right back at them, then at the ceiling as if to say, "Man, was I high." Abbie Lee-Yeung, the U of T student, sends me a secret, sharing smile that gives me hope. I'm awarding Arthur five out of five for this cross-examination.

Judge Donahue is twitching like a bunny with a carrot as she excuses this witness. She makes a frowny face at Khan and asks: "Just how seriously is the Crown taking the count of manslaughter?"

Even this law-and-order judge smells something gamy about it. Khan looks aggrieved. "Does Your Ladyship want this issue debated in front of the jury?"

Arthur sits, he's going to let them duke it out.

"I can't see that it matters, Mr. Khan, unless I have somehow fallen asleep and missed evidence that points to Mr. Wozniak being the author of Mr. Gooch's death. Or is there more to come?"

Khan turns to Inspector Roberts, gets a blank, so he announces he'll consider the issue and consult with the Attorney General. I assume that's a formality and he has just folded like a cheap suit. That's confirmed by the body language of Arthur Beauchamp, calm and cool, like a veteran ace strolling off the mound after striking out the side. (The Jays' home opener is this weekend. I don't imagine Howie renewed his season tickets.)

§

Clarkson Wakeling is Chemican's executive vice-president for Canada, though he's a Yank, an implant from their head office in Kansas City, their former PR director. Big chest, bigger gut, vanity tan, baldish, has an MBA, also several public service awards, as if that somehow makes him a credible witness.

I'm not sure what Wakeling adds to the Crown's case except to exaggerate his company's losses. His answers often sound rehearsed, as when he hides behind corporate jargon. Boiled down, his complaint is that we defendants cost Chemican a hundred million dollars. And counting, because the plant still hasn't reopened.

He actually has kind words for Howie Griffin, a "fine fellow" who'd done "stellar" work for Chemican in Canada and internationally, particularly in Latin America, "handling various intrigues, defending the company's good name, and soothing commercial relationships."Yeah, Howie, like buying off a judge in Brazil. "Under the awkward circumstances of this case there was no option but to terminate him."

Khan asks him to specify those awkward circumstances.

"We were apprised he'd been deceived and victimized by a very clever young woman who stole vital company records."

From Juror Ten, back row, I get a look of reproach. Mabel Sims, sixty, an auditor for the provincial taxation branch, emits a prim, churchy vibe. She's on the jury because the defence had to hoard its last challenges. I felt Juror Eleven, Joyce Evans, was also a risky choice, a little too haute bourgeois, but our lawyers seem okay with her, and she's composed and attentive.

When Khan sits, Nancy pops up, finally taking a central role.

"Mr. Wakeling, the balance sheets of Chemican-International show you are down to just over seven hundred million U.S. dollars net profit from one point three billion three years ago."

"We regard that as a short-term effect of a period of readjustment related to a shrinkage in specified international markets."

"Let's see if I can translate that into common English. International sales of your pesticides are plunging."

"No, ma'am, not at all. Many of our products continue to enjoy robust sales in all markets, worldwide. We are encountering product-specific softness in the European Union, however. That's compelled by factors over which we have no control."

"In other words, after the EU banned neonicotinoids several years ago, that market collapsed for your signature product, Vigor-Gro. You don't dispute that?"

"I would put it less emphatically, but yes, most European agricultural markets have been closed to Vigor-Gro, along with neonicotinoid-based products from other major suppliers. That restraint is currently being contested in the courts on behalf of vast numbers of growers who are seeing their crops devastated by increasingly harmful insect invasions, but—"

"Let's see if we can avoid propaganda that isn't remotely evidence-based—"

"Let him complete his answer, counsel." Donahue's tone is sharp, she's probably looking for a fight with her *bête noir*.

Wakeling: "I merely wanted to add that we are turning our focus elsewhere."

Nancy was in a groove and now is riled. "To the third world, right? Africa. Latin America. Where dictators and legislators get fat off corporate bribes."

Khan is up. "The Crown strongly objects."

Nancy pretends to ignore him. "Just last year, in Brazil, you guys paid off three congressmen and a judge—"

Khan is calling her shameful, Donahue is talking over him about how Nancy is out of order, and Nancy is interjecting that Wakeling shouldn't be coddled. It's great theatre, Nancy nailing this fucker, letting loose after being such a back seat to Arthur for the whole week. Four and a half points out of five.

Things finally settle down after a lecture from the bench and an ill-intended apology from Nancy, who calmly digs out a document. "Mr. Wakeling, according to your auditors, your Canadian division is projected to go into the red in the current year."

"That should surprise no one, ma'am, given that our major asset, the plant in Sarnia, is still in shutdown six months after its pillaging last September."

Judge Donahue reacts with a little grin, an unspoken touché. Point for the witness.

Nancy hands the witness a copy of the auditors' report. "Look at the signature page, please. What's the date on it?"

Brow furrowed, he examines it. "Yes, it appears the report came out on June twenty-six. Sorry, yes, I erred."

"Six weeks before September eleven. Maybe the auditors made their gloomy projection after being tipped off the plant was a target, do you think that's possible?" Nancy is off the scoreboard, six out of five.

"Don't answer that question," Donahue says, surly.

Nancy has a certified copy marked as an exhibit, then leafs through it. "What you call a major asset, the Sarnia processing factory and lab, barely turned a profit the last two years and was predicted to lose money this year and for years to come."

"The plant is, let us say, somewhat antiquated, and we had plans for some major upgrading and remodelling."

"Mr. Wakeling, can you point to a single document that confirms those plans were adopted?"

"I'm sure there are records of discussions about the matter."

"As in this confidential email to you from last July." A copy to Wakeling, another to the student, who huddles with her boss over it, Nancy talking all the while: "Third paragraph, first line. 'We'd be better off if it burned down. Big insurance payout.'"

A torrent of prosecutorial complaint. Expressions like "booby-trapped" and "outrageously blatant hearsay." The jury gets the heave-ho and there's this truly complex debate about (a) is the email admissible given it was stolen from Chemican's computers, (b) is it hearsay from the company's CEO, or (c) did Wakeling, in forwarding it to other company officers, including Howell J. Griffin, render it not subject to the rule against hearsay.

In the end, Judge Donahue rules that Nancy is entitled to the time-honoured tools of cross-examination. Suddenly Her Ladyship is being more balanced, probably a reaction to intimations in the press that she has been sucking on the Crown's cock (I paraphrase). The jury troops back in.

Predictably, Wakeling characterizes the CEO's comment about insurance as a joke but Nancy is ready for that with, "It may be the kind of joke that puts ideas in people's heads." I'm into this, I can hardly feel my sore butt.

Nancy gets Wakeling to admit the email was sent only nine days after the auditors' pessimistic report. Then she gets him to read aloud one of the outlined options: mothballing the plant and transferring the laboratory functions to Chemican's new testing centre in Hyderabad.

"Was that also a joke, Mr. Wakeling?"

"Of course not." Wakeling glances at the wall clock, urging it toward lunch break. "It was one of many untested ideas thrown out. I personally urged the case for modernizing the plant. No resolution to the issue was reached before the September tenth vandalizing."

"Vandalizing. You don't care to call it a terrorist act?"

"We are not comfortable with that characterization."

"But your insurers are. They're resisting your claim for a hundred million dollars because acts of terrorism void the policy."

"I leave those matters to our legal people. Their advice is subject to attorney-client privilege."

"Mr. Wakeling, I hope I'm not the only person in this room who hears that as grossly evasive. Come on. Great West Assurance has denied your claim. Google it, you'll find it."

"Again, I cannot comment on sensitive negotiations involving counsel."

"Nor should you have to," says the judge, sharply.

Nancy gives her a look of mock repentance: "I bow to Your Ladyship's expertise in the field of insurance law." Back to Wakeling: "If Great West is relying on that terrorism loophole, it seems to me you'd want these accused acquitted."

Khan rises, but Donahue waves him down. "That doesn't merit a response, Mr. Wakeling."

Nancy plows doggedly ahead: "The insurance adjusters are probably wondering where this hundred-million-dollar number came from. Or why you haven't reopened the plant. Why *is* that?"

"That would be better asked of our engineers."

"But I'm asking you, their boss. Why can't you get the Sarnia plant running? Isn't it just a matter of mopping up, doing some welding, and mixing up another big batch of Vigor-Gro?"

"I'm afraid it's not so simple, ma'am. Our engineers are currently working with our production and finance teams on a cost-benefit analysis to assess the plant's long-term profitability expectations."

"Mr. Wakeling, if the Sarnia plant is such a money-loser aren't you better off leaving it shuttered?"

He hesitates. "That's a consideration that depends on the sustainability of our markets."

"Yeah, and frankly, you're losing those markets because people around the world are waking up to Vigor-Gro's carnage of bee populations."

"Ma'am, I suggest a far more significant factor is the worldwide campaign by organized factions, well represented in this courtroom, to defame our company and its products."

"Your company defames itself, Mr. Wakeling." Four points.

"It's twelve thirty," says the judge. "Mr. Wakeling, because you are under cross-examination you may not discuss this case with anyone during the break."

3

My comrades and I enjoy a mild euphoria as we line up for the exit. May 17 has been a good day, or half a day, and especially good for Rockin' Ray. Nancy Faulk, who plays the bad cop to Arthur's good cop, has boosted our hopes with her evisceration of a corporate toady.

Lucy and I are finally escorted out by a mob of Bee-lievers, which is what we've begun to call our regulars. Ray, who is dawdling behind, would prefer to celebrate with us rather than deal with possessive Sooky-Sue — and there she is, shooting the breeze with Richard the Second. She abruptly sends him off with a flutter of fingers and waits for Ray.

I tell Lucy to hang tight, and I get right in Sooky's face, which stays serene and lovely even close up. She doesn't step back, doesn't blink, just gives me her cool guru eyes.

"I'm Rivie, we haven't met."

"Lucy's friend. It is my pleasure." So formal. The Korean princess.

"That guy you were talking to — do you know who he is?"

"Lucy's other friend. A seller of mutual funds. He tried to interest me in a Registered Retirement Savings Account. I gave him my card and told him he needed therapy. He's not comfortable in himself."

"He's shy. He's also a bachelor and he's very, very rich. Richard Dewilliger-James the Second. His father handles eighty-three billion dollars' worth of investments. You should get to know him better. Just think, if it works out you could stop hustling for alms at your little sham church."

"Fuck you."

I part from her, join Lucy, and we get in line for the escalator. Rockin' Ray has got himself surrounded by a posse of hot wannabe groupies and is signing autographs. Sooky-Sue looks at Richard, standing forlornly by himself, then at Ray, then back at Richard, and we lose our view as the escalator carries us down.

§

Lucy and I escape out the revolving back door into the busy plaza that curls around City Hall, our plan being to go for a quick health hike, then cancel its benefits by grabbing something grilled in grease by one of the street vendors.

But there's Azra Khan, making his way south across the square, unaccompanied, in a seeming hurry, like he's got big plans, and so naturally, because we are compulsive snoops, we follow him, at a safe distance.

Lucy says, "Maybe we can track him to his secret love nest and you can score some carnal *kompromat* off him — he's been eye-fucking you all week."

"Juror Twelve gets more looks than me." Abbie Lee-Yeung, our nineteen-year-old best hope on the jury. I like the way she continues to slip me little smiles.

Lucy goes, "Isn't he married or something? He seems awfully needy, genitally speaking."

"I feel his pain."

"Okay, he's crossing Queen, and . . . he's going into the Sheraton Centre." Big convention hotel. We hurry so as not to lose him in there.

The hotel is full of people with plastic name tags and perma-smiles and booths displaying the latest in home design concepts. We catch sight of Khan as he pauses to watch a humanoid robot serve crackers and cheese bites. He hurries on, through the lobby, en route, we suspect, to join an important friend for lunch.

An assignation? No, he wouldn't do that publicly.

Instead, he goes straight to the bank of elevators and joins a handful of conventioneers going up. We witness this literally from behind a potted palm.

We return to the lobby, speculating. A nooner with his secretary? With his storky student? With the gorgeous designer who redid his upstairs study? His best friend's wife? Should we linger, to see if he comes down alone?

Lucy finds a house phone, confirms that an A. Khan is registered, but can't wheedle out his room number. Registering under his own name, that shows either balls or recklessness. Or maybe his wife knows he has affairs and has given up caring.

We decide to skip out quickly to take lunch at one of the wagons, giving him time to get his rocks off before we return to our potted palm. As we approach the front door, we see a young, attractive face peering wide-eyed through the glass. Lucy goes, "Oh, my God."

As we step outside, Abbie Lee-Yeung seems about to take flight but holds her ground, digging her phone from her handbag, pretending she hasn't seen us.

It seems silly to play her game, to ignore her, so I say, "Hello," and Lucy says, "Hi, you." Abbie does a little nervous jump as she looks up from her phone, recovers, smiles, says, "Oh, hello," and we pass on by.

We wait forever for the walk light, too stunned or embarrassed to turn around to peek at her until we reach the square and find a bench. And by then she has disappeared. Obviously into the Sheraton Centre, because there's no sign of her on Queen Street.

I am the first to break the silence. "She wants to see the home decor displays. She's looking for ideas to brighten her dorm."

"She's getting it on with the prosecutor."

"No, it's ridiculous, it's beyond the bounds of human possibility."

"He hypnotized her with those dark, haunting eyes." Lucy playing devil's advocate.

"He'd have to have supernormal powers to work that fast."

"She slipped a note to him somehow. With her number."

"She's a juror. He'd be triple cray-crazy. He'd be disbarred."

"But only we know. We could blackmail him. Subtly. With hints. Suspended sentences would be nice."

I'm suddenly overcome with a laughing jag, prompted by the absurdity of it all. Lucy can't keep her face straight either, cracks up.

4

Clarkson Wakeling returns to the stand looking sullen and tense after steeling himself for further enhanced interrogation techniques. Nancy begins by going after Chemican over their dubious research on Vigor-Gro in lab and field.

Wakeling's strategy is to employ the ever popular arts of stonewalling and buck passing. He's not an agronomist, not a chemist, not an entomologist, not a scientist. He is a businessman.

But Nancy perseveres, pointing to goofs and deceit in various research studies, getting them on the record. These studies date from 2001 to 2006, when Vigor-Gro was finally approved by the U.S. Environmental Protection Agency. Nancy's team of scientists, mostly volunteering professors, had found hundreds of nuggets when mining the files we filched.

Nancy focuses on a few prime examples, including a multi-year study in South Dakota: "From 2001 to 2005, varying potency levels of Vigor-Gro were applied to a two-hundred-acre plot of canola. Not included in the final report, but mentioned in a memo marked 'Do not distribute' is a seventy percent decline in the population of red-winged blackbirds in a marshy nesting ground bordering the test acreage. That was in the second year of the study. By the last year, all the blackbirds were gone."

"Again, you would have to talk to the expert who led that study."

"We have. Dr. Muir said the blackbirds were edited from her final report. So was mention of a chemical spill in the creek flowing to the nesting ground."

The judge: "Counsel, are you planning to ask a question some-where along the way?"

"It's hard to come up with one he's willing to answer." Nice.

Glowering. "Carry on, but make your point."

"Thank you, M'Lady. Mr. Wakeling, the South Dakota study was released to the public in 2007. At that time you were Chemican's director of public relations, were you not?"

"Yes, ma'am. Floor thirty-three of the Chemican Tower in Kansas City, Missouri."

"And you advised removing all mention of the blackbirds from the report, right? Bad PR."

"That's technically true, but I suggested a separate paper focus-sing on that issue be drafted by a professional ornithologist."

"And was that done?"

"I believe so."

"And when was the ornithologist's report published?"

Frowning, as if trying to remember, then capitulating: "I don't think it was ever actually published."

That's just one of several graphic examples Nancy pulls from her arsenal of Chemican's made-up facts and buried fuckups, mostly culled from intra-office emails. One of them, from a company executive, touts the "cost-saving benefits" of hiring academics to sign research papers ghostwritten by Chemican.

Wakeling denies that was a company practice, but he's dehydrating under the onslaught, the court officer wearing out the carpet with trips to fill his water glass. Occasionally, the judge will show impatience, like with, "Counsel, is this relevant to *anything?*" or threats to put her on short leash — which maybe Donahue literally would like to do, given the occasional hints of kinkiness emanating from the bench.

Wakeling has to admit to a score of faulty tests, unsubstantiated claims, and examples of fraudulent math and statistics, but he heaps blame on the "aberrant behaviour" of certain staff scientists and technicians who were too eager to curry corporate favour by "bending" the truth. Seven of these miscreants had been told to seek employment elsewhere.

One of the string of emails had to do with the EPA's demands for retesting of a new, milder "Home Gardener" version of Vigor-Gro in the U.S. The company had planned a big, corny launch for it last year, with TV ads featuring happy families that spray together.

Surprise, surprise: the EPA withdrew its retesting order after a Chemican-friendly Congressman — a Trump tub-thumper — worked some under-the-table magic in Washington with the acting administrator of the EPA.

Wakeling cannot be pinned down on this one. He was not involved. He was busy with new duties following his transfer to Toronto. Yes, he knew the Congressman, "a fighter for American farmers," but was not consulted about corporate donations to his

2020 re-election campaign. In his former PR capacity, he also had friendly relations with the Trump-appointed EPA acting administrator, name of Blugenhoff.

"So when did the EPA green-light this product, Vigor-Gro for the Home Gardener?"

"Late last year, I believe. In December."

"Just before Christmas?"

"Around then."

"Though you're no longer in public relations, head office still calls upon your expertise in that area from time to time?"

"I'm happy to offer input when asked."

"And you've offered input in matters relating to the EPA?"

"Where there is public interest, yes."

"So can you tell us how your company thanked the EPA's acting administrator for his services?"

Wakeling bristles. "I find that question quite insulting, ma'am."

The judge: "I suggest you be very careful, counsel."

"Thank you, M'Lady." She's *so* courteous. "Are you telling me, Mr. Wakeling, that you're not aware that Mr. Blugenhoff and his family spent the Christmas holidays in a palatial Cook Islands villa owned by a Chemican board member? All expenses paid, including first-class airfare?"

"I don't know where you might have heard that or why you would think I know anything about it."

"Because in an email of December fourteen, marked 'confidential,' you advised head office against flying the Blugenhoffs on a corporate jet."

She passes him a printout, a copy going to Miss Pucket for the judge, another for the Crown, talking all the while: "Sender is the Vice-President of Operations. The subject reads, 'Villa Shangri-La, Cook Islands, December 23, return January 7.'"

A pause to let the reporters catch up — they're enjoying this. "Quote: 'The Embraer is available both dates. Thoughts?' End quote. Your response: 'Potentially bad optics. Best to keep our prints off this.' If you'd like, Mr. Wakeling, I can show you the Air New Zealand travel voucher for those dates, two adult Blugenhoffs and their three kids."

Wakeling studies the email as he takes a long, slow drink, briefly raising his eyes to the rows of scribbling media. "This was several months ago, so . . . I'm assuming it must have slipped my mind."

Nancy has him hanging on the ropes, but her strategy is silence, waiting for this maestro of public relations to show his stuff. He studies the note again.

Finally: "I can see how a goodwill gesture might be seen as a . . ."

"Payoff," Nancy suggests.

"Well, as a thank-you. But not intended that way, merely offered as a means to, ah, maintain future relations." Another peek at the press. "Of course we didn't want the gesture misconstrued, so . . ."

Again he tails off, and again Nancy fills in for him: "So you didn't want your corporate fingerprints all over your sweetheart deal. I get it. Bad optics. I have no more questions. Thank you."

Wakeling goes limp with relief. I can see into his brain: he's mapping out the shortest route to the nearest saloon. But he only gets three steps in that direction before being hauled back by Donahue. "Excuse me, Mr. Wakeling, it seems counsel has further need of you."

She means Arthur Beauchamp, who is standing patiently, awaiting his turn. Wakeling will have to hang in a little longer before he can get drunk. It's just after four o'clock as he drags himself back to the stand.

§

Arthur does his trademark affable bit, which you'd think would ease Wakeling's tension but seems to make him even jumpier, maybe because he thinks Arthur's setting a trap. Nancy may have triggered a paranoid disorder.

Arthur commends Wakeling for saying kind words about Howie Griffin, the "fine fellow" who'd put out foreign fires for Chemican and who was reluctantly let go. "It surprises me therefore that he wasn't awarded any severance pay after nearly eighteen years of faithful service."

"I've been instructed that issue is being discussed as we speak."

"Are you involved in these discussions?"

"No, sir. They're being handled by our house lawyers, at head-quarters in Missouri."

"And who's acting for Mr. Griffin?"

"I don't know. I heard he has a lawyer."

"And what prompted this sudden act of corporate contrition?"

"I can't answer that. It was a board decision."

"Do you know what it sounds like to me, Mr. Wakeling? It sounds like Griffin threatened to blow the lid off Chemican's corrupt practices unless he got paid off—"

"You don't have to respond to Mr. Beauchamp's rhetoric." Judge Donahue has jumped in a little late — the rhetoric will make for juicy headlines. But why is she doing the prosecutor's work? Maybe because she used to be one, and prefers a more belligerent style than Khan's. He just sits there, thoughtful. As if he has other matters on his mind.

Arthur cools it, gets chummy with Wakeling, thanks him for being so helpful, regrets that this has been such a long day for him. He wants to know more about Howie's routines, his work ethic. Wakeling says he wasn't in the habit of looking over Howie's shoulder. Howie was a self-starter, reliable, no demerits on his sheet. Sarnia security was his show, from hirings to firings.

Wakeling was also proud of his company's outreach program, and was aware Archie Gooch was accepted for it and had a "minor" criminal record.

"Despite that record, your usually reliable Mr. Griffin put him on night security duty."

"It appears so. Just one night. We learned he mainly did equipment checks, deliveries, pickups, various things. Garbage, recycling."

"You learned that from whom?"

"Well, we retained a firm of investigators shortly after the incident."

"So out of the blue Gooch was given all the key codes to the plant and a highly sensitive night posting."

"We found that troubling, of course, after the fact."

"Mr. Griffin was not keen on installing security cameras in the plant. Did that concern you?"

"That has been a long-term budget item."

"You're aware from your private investigators that Griffin was a heavy user of cocaine?"

"Objection. Hearsay." Azra Khan finally heard from.

There's a tussle over this. Khan complains about "Mr. Beauchamp's habit of ignoring the rules of admissibility." Arthur urges the Crown to produce the report from Chemican's detective agency to confirm Inspector Maguire's surmise about "Mr. Griffin's coke habit." Judge Donahue seems either unaware or unconcerned that the jury is present through this, so the damage, if any, is already done.

"Where is Mr. Griffin anyway?" she asks.

"He is under subpoena," Khan says testily, "and will be here when we are ready for him."

"It seems most odd that we have not heard a word from a central witness whose name pops up almost monotonously." The jury also has to be wondering. Me too. I worry about Howie being a suicide risk.

Khan mouths something muted. Donahue says, sharply, "Please proceed, Mr. Beauchamp."

"Mr. Wakeling, may I put it simply — you are aware that Mr. Griffin, while employed by Chemican, was using cocaine."

"I actually found that out after he was terminated."

"And your investigators checked into whether Archie Gooch, in the course of his various deliveries and pickups, supplied cocaine to Mr. Griffin?"

"I don't think they concluded that. It was speculated."

Khan half-rises, then subsides, as if finding it an unbearable effort to restrain Arthur's misbehaviour.

It's almost four thirty. Arthur obviously hopes the jury will be fixated all long weekend (Monday is Victoria Day) on his weird (to me) diversionary tactic of incriminating poor Howie. Won't this ultimately be an exploding cigar? When I take the stand I'm not going to say Howie set this whole thing up and we were somehow entrapped. I'm not going to lie.

Donahue reminds Wakeling that he may not talk about the case during the three-day weekend, then sends him off. Miss Pucket is eager to call order in court, but the judge waves her back down.

"Mr. Khan, has the Attorney General had a chance to consider the manslaughter count?"

Smiles are shared among counsel and veteran court watchers. Obviously, Azra Khan, as Deputy A.G., calls such shots himself. He plays along. "Yes, M'Lady, the Attorney General prefers that we focus on the main issue, the conspiracy. I am directed to enter a stay of proceedings on the count of manslaughter."

We, the Seven Sarnians minus Doc, go off to our favourite public house to celebrate. One down, only thirty-eight charges to go.

5

After court, as Lucy and I hoof it west on Queen, I get a paranormal message: we're being followed. Sure enough, when I look back there's the follower, about a minute behind us: Abbie Lee-Yeung. Okay, coincidence, we're just a couples of blocks from the courthouse.

According to the jury list she lives nowhere near Queen West, but in the leafy enclave of Wychwood, probably with her parents, who have to be moneyed to live there.

Weird that she's going our direction. Is she on her way to meet the learned counsel for the Crown? Not likely, because the Sheraton is behind us. Lucy buzzes the hotel anyway, and asks if A. Khan is still registered. He is. The mystery deepens.

Lucy suggests we check out the latest spring styles of the bourgeoisie, and we stop at a shop window, commune awhile with the mannequins. As Abbie passes by there's a round of smiles and hellos. She half-pauses, as if there's more that needs to be said, then carries on at a quickened pace.

We dawdle behind her until she turns up Spadina toward Chinatown. Where we're heading is the Cameron, a dive favoured by proletarian artists and poets, to join our gang for an unwind over bar food and beer.

Lucy's in a mood to celebrate, obviously. Rockin' Ray's vindication was documented by the microphones, cameras, and notepads of the world. A bunch of Bee-lievers had to form a phalanx to break him from the scrum and get him safely into a cab.

Ray is no longer a free agent, he has signed back on with Lucy. They even have a place to shack up, T.J. Gully's snug in Cabbagetown, an illegal suite where he also keeps his office. The impresario-agent–human drugstore has been sent to a farm in Quebec for a month's rehab.

Predictably, Spooky Sooky is going for the gold. Last seen, outside the courts, she got picked up in a gullwing Tesla. Four out of five for me, who made that happen.

§

We've taken over a table in the Cameron's dark and smelly far reaches. Lucy is horsing around, awarding Ray with a knighthood — "I dub thee Lord Wozniak, the Count of Manslaughter."

Joining the applause is Nancy, who has popped in for a quick one en route to pick up our ringleader for yet another romantic dinner (they've been outed, but no one's taking bets it will last).

Just as she's about to split, Lucy and I draw her aside and eagerly share our circumstantial case against Azra Khan: his lunchtime tryst in the Sheraton, conceivably with Abbie Lee-Yeung.

Nancy laughs until she's hoarse and wiping tears. Finally, she recovers enough to explain: Khan has installed his seventy-eight-year-old mom in the Sheraton so she doesn't have to come in from the suburbs for radiation treatments.

"That's actually not funny, given his mother's condition. But you are."

Nancy leaves, and Lucy and I slink off soon after, feeling like two creepy, gossipy little schoolgirls.

6

Saturday, May 18

Dear Diary, a.k.a. Semi-Autobiographical Mystery,

It's half past ten on a lazy Saturday and I've just had a confessional chat with Arthur over coffee and scrambled eggs — though God knows I have more than enough egg on my face already from Nancy's revelation. I feel all the worse when Arthur confirms that Azra Khan's mom is terminally ill.

At least he doesn't chide me, though he asks me to keep my counsel about the matter. I shall so advise Lucy Wales, fellow snoopaholic.

I keep kicking myself: my God, I'm not sixteen, I'm twenty-four, an age at which I should have some idea of who I am and where I'm going. Aside from the clink, that is. It doesn't help that I have no idea how long I'll be in stir.

I'm probably not going to make a living as a diarist, or a novelist, or an author of anything except my own misfortunes, but I'm still toying with the idea of becoming a brilliant trial lawyer. The effective word is toying, since a criminal record may bar me from the bar.

Still, I can dream. Crack prosecutor Rivke Levitsky takes on the corporate crooks. Could I put up with the stuffy proprieties of the law, the medieval traditions, the flagrant hypocrisy? I don't know but I enjoy digging into Chemican's files, looking for crime and corruption.

Anyhow, Dear Diary, that's how I plan to spend most of this Saturday afternoon, ferreting through the enemy's files in the boardroom of Faulk, Quan, Dubois, with Ariana Van Doorn as my mentor.

Enough. I back up, shut down, hide the external in my underwear drawer, head down the trippy staircase.

§

We're looking for studies done on humans, Ariana and I. She's intrigued by the peculiar disorders endured by the singing watchman, Barney Wilson: his temporarily swollen feet, his crooked toes, his navigation problems.

Vigor-Gro was tested on rodents, with no apparent ill effects, though Ariana thinks something about Chemican's data doesn't add up. Research in Saskatchewan showed that white-crowned sparrows fed neonic-treated seeds became disoriented and lost so much weight they were on life support.

Several of Chemican's researchers went a brave step further, volunteering to ingest teaspoon-sized hits of Vigor-Gro. All came out of that unscathed, except for one case of the shits that was traced to an overripe crab salad.

Ariana and her team found hints — scraps of information buried in subfolders in a backup hard drive — that a much broader study was done with paid human volunteers. An internal email mentioned testing procedures "on individuals M 1-59 and F 1-44" that involved a range of dosages in millilitres. Another made reference to a return date "for a final physical." But no results showed up, no conclusions.

Dr. Van Doorn believes those findings have been erased. Nancy plans to confront Chemican's chief scientist over that. He's up next, on Monday.

We have two computers running, accessing Okie Joe's uploads to the internet. Ariana also brought in a wagonload of printouts, copied from booty from the Sarnia lab, categorized and labelled, and she's going through them one more time, looking for the overlooked, occasionally cross-checking on her computer.

I burrow through a smaller pile of printouts, from the files I photographed after Howie succumbed to Lucy's Mix. (Uploaded to the Cloud, accessed by Okie Joe's seventeen-digit password.) Business stuff. Staff memos. Security alerts. Reports to his bosses in Kansas City from overseas or Latin America. Oblique references to "expressing gratitude" or "reaching an understanding," had to be codes for bribery.

Howie sweated the small stuff too. An organic farmer's threats of bodily harm after his spinach was infected by windblown Vigor-Gro. A sign-carrying provocateur who picketed the Chemican Tower in Kansas City. An irate bird lover brandishing a jackknife.

I'm supposed to look for evidence of human testing, so have no reason to riffle through these files except that I have a dim memory from that night eons ago when I was padding around barefoot, photographing documents. A memory about something involving lawyers, a court action.

And here it is: one lonely document stamped "Legal —Volunteer Testing Program": a printout of a July, 8, 2005, fax to Chemican's lead lawyer from an attorney named W.W. Squirely, of Joplin, Missouri. It's titled "Re: Dover and Chemican-International Ltd." and advises that "settlement documents, duly executed, have been dispatched this date to the addressee by DHL Express," followed by a tracking number and the hope that "all is to your satisfaction."

That's it. An entire claim in damages has disappeared from Chemican's files, except this one orphan fax. The addressee, one Baylor Jessup, was Chemican's head of legal in 2005 but a quick check shows he's retired.

When I search the internet for "W.W. Squirely" I find him still listed as a practising attorney in Joplin, though according to

Google he's ninety-three. Local media described him as a well-loved country judge until he lost to a Democrat. Couldn't have been that well-loved.

What was the Volunteer Testing Program? Who was Dover? How had Chemican screwed him around? Presumably, they had a raft of lawyers to choose from, so why was this handled by their top beagle? Did Jessup take the old country lawyer to the cleaners?

I call Ariana over. An internet search fails to sniff out any court action between Dover and Chemican. A search through the docs stashed in the Cloud comes up with "Squirely not found." The only Dover is the white cliffs of.

§

It's time for our evening tea. Arthur has a Brandenburg concerto going downstairs. These lovely pieces get a lot of play, because he doesn't have many CDs and isn't keen on learning how to find old friends online, friends like Johann Sebastian, Ludwig, and Wolfgang.

While I was away for the day, Arthur evicted the fat chairs and dragged a sofa over. He rises from it, in his old-fashioned gallant way, as I enter with my tea. He motions toward the stereo. "Is it too loud?"

"No. I'm getting into Bach." The vigorous, driving melodies, the flow and complexity. I'd been raised on a diet of folk and jazz.

Arthur enjoys our rituals under the moose, enjoys regaling me with lighthearted tales from Garibaldi Island. I'm learning its whole history, its cast of characters, its current nemesis: a foreign corporation that threatens to blight a spectacular limestone formation in dedicated parkland.

Sometimes he turns sombre and talks about his youthful years in Vancouver, his cold, proper academic parents, his incarceration in a private boys' school, his social awkwardness. Especially with girls, is what I've picked up.

He closes *The Poems of Catullus* as I settle beside him, and asks how my day was.

Though we're not supposed to talk shop I tell him about the W.W. Squirely fax. Nancy is on it. She hopes to reach the old boy by phone tomorrow or Monday. If that doesn't pan out, she'll hire an agent in Missouri to poke around. I sound efficient, competent. Trying to impress him.

He responds in Latin, and it sounds lovely and rhythmical and perplexing.

"Catullus?"

"'Who scans the bright machinery of the skies and plots the hours of star-set and star-rise.' In Wigham's rather loose translation."

I get it. Talking about the case is against the rules. I ask about Margaret, and he brightens. She has next weekend free, no agenda. She's intrigued at the prospect of staying in the house of a swindler name Punky Kiefer. She (allegedly) is thankful that I'm here to give him a booster shot of youthful zest.

I offer to stay out of their way, but he says Margaret wants us to have meals together, like a family. "She's that way. A 1970s hippie and a founding member of the Earthseed Commune, long since disbanded." A melancholy, distant smile.

There's a long lag while we sip our tea. Finally, I go, "Is everything okay with you guys?" Another long pause. I feel stupid, I've been too bold.

A sound halfway between a sigh and a throat clearing. "It's my fault, really. There's a woman back home who is incorrigibly attracted to me. We had an episode. And then a recent close call. Margaret knows. Most, not all."

It comes out hesitantly at first, becomes a flow. He seems to have shocked himself, says he has never shared this with anyone, this episode, this infidelity. Not even with his buddy, the local preacher. But I guess the urge to confide sins was building up, it's bred into us, we all hunger for absolution.

The Other Woman is an environmentally friendly potter named Taba. I get the impression of sexy, immodest, brash, used to getting what she wants. What she wanted was him between her legs. She didn't have to work hard getting him there, is my impression. Factors included long-distance separations and Margaret Blake's own brief, regretted affair.

The close call had her between *his* legs, her face anyway — an act not consummated, so I don't know why the big deal. Except that he told his wife a cleaned-up version that she doesn't believe. Now he's caught in a tangled net of half-truths and false denials even though he's innocent, at least on the second count.

Is he just unloading or is he asking advice? I go, "You don't seem to be very good at lying, Arthur."

He barks a little sad laugh.

I rehash a self-help line I'd read somewhere: "We can forgive marital lapses by our partners as long as we know we are loved." True, I suspect, but what do I know? "I'm sure Margaret feels that way."

"I do love her. But she's furious. She called Taba a scheming bitch."

"Well, that's good. Her fury isn't directed at you. She knows you're a typical unthinking, libidinously subjugated male. You're normal."

That's pretty blunt, but he seems to take it okay. In fact, he can't help laughing at himself a little. I say, "Anything else bothering you?"

"I miss my dog."

I lean over and give him a hug. Then I leave him to his Latin poetry and clean up the kitchen and go upstairs, suddenly weary, wishing I had someone to love.

7

Tuesday, May 21

As I dictate this it's an hour and thirteen minutes after midnight. I arrived home an hour ago — angry and more scared than I care to admit, so scared that I sobered up with a bang.

I checked all the doors and windows before I showered, making sure not to disturb Arthur's sleep. I drank a lot of water. I set my alarm. I went to bed and tried to read. I got up and went to my desk, stared awhile at a blinking cursor, but my trembling fingers couldn't work the keys.

So instead, here's my Victoria Day podcast:

I remember waking late Monday morning, just shy of ten, still bummed out about having no lover, no partner. Wondering why, in the heat of young life, I was not having affairs and causing my lovers to writhe with guilt like Arthur. No one seems to want me but the trolls. And Azra Khan, though he has other matters on his mind right now, like his mother, with cancer — that's probably why he seems distracted and passive in court.

I had no agenda for the day, except a Panic Disorder benefit at eight p.m. But I did my run, to Harbourfront, a bad choice midday on a sunny long weekend when you must focus on finding openings between clumps of bare-legged walkers and joggers and avoiding head-on collisions.

In the afternoon, while Arthur was away strategizing with Nancy, I couch-potatoed a Jays game in the TV room. I hoped for a glimpse of Howie's reserved seats, but no foul balls went that way. The game was a disaster, eight-two for Boston.

After which I biked up to Cabbagetown to hang awhile with Lucy, in T.J. Gully's cozy illegal. You enter by the leafy backyard. Three rooms and a bath, wallpapered with sixties rock posters: the Band, Stones, Doors, Byrds, Cream, Janis, Zeppelin.

So after we get her water pipe going, Lucy goes, "I have a theory why Abbie Lee-Yeung is following you."

"Let me guess. She's an undercover cop, like Sooky-Sue."

"That was a joke. This is different."

"Sweetie, all your theories are jokes. Like a teen juror getting it on with Azra Khan. Abbie just happened to be walking behind us."

"Twice on Friday, she followed you. You, not us."

"The first time, we were leaving the Sheraton when she walked in. Big deal."

"She was standing outside. She had stalked us from the courthouse. She isn't interested in me. She wants to get you alone. She wants to proclaim her love for you."

This is why I love Lucy. She's such a fraud.

Ray was already at tonight's venue, rehearsing. Before T.J. Gully went on his rehab he booked Panic Disorder for Squirrelly Moe's, which is cashing in on the publicity from the trial. It is currently the most popular dive in town for the millennial-pseudo-hipster crowd. A fundraiser for the bees, with a substantial cover.

At sunset, Lucy and I ponied up for a cab to Queen and Broadview, to Moe's. I was so stoned by then I was at Paranoia Level Three, worried that Lucy was right: all those intense looks from the back row, from Juror Twelve. An idealistic young woman looking for a hero to love.

§

Bodies flying around, supposedly dancing. A woman whipping her T-shirt around, boobs flying. A couple getting it on under the staircase. Blow being openly snorted. A drunk guy bodily tossed from the stage by Mary Bumpo. The funder was oversold, overcrowded, the bouncers losing control.

I was outside at the back having yet another toke when I heard the approaching sirens. I texted Lucy: *I'm gone from this armpit.*

I lurched my way out to Queen through a smog of reefer, followed by others equally uninterested in a confrontation with the bylaw squad. We gathered at the streetcar stop as two flashing cruisers wheeled past us. Six or seven of us jumped on the first westbound 501.

We were comrades, all high, and we congregated at the stern, talking and laughing. They wanted to know about the trial, how's it going, who's winning, let's hear it for the bees, man, and what about that OPP dick who had a heart attack?

I wasn't paying attention to the big, hulking strap-hanger behind us, mainly because his back was to me, but when I got off at Beaconsfield I sensed him behind me — or put it this way, I smelled him, rancid and boozy, or maybe it was his padded jacket.

Nobody else got off there, and as I strode north up my poorly lit street I could tell he was plodding behind me. I quickened my pace, darted a look back, saw my pursuer ten feet behind, faceless in the dark, jogging now, calling out: "Hey, baby, I'm hot for you, you wanna ball?"

I was, like, freaking. "Crawl back to your cave, you creep."

He goes something like, "How do ya want it, Jew-girl, from the front or back?" Hoarse, slurred.

He's drunker than me, slow of foot, I figured he'll never catch up at the speed I'm going, even in sandals. I sprint up the middle of the street, pulling off my pack, fumbling through its pockets for my phone.

Interior lights are on at one house, upcoming, on my left. On my right, my darkened safe house looms.

I know where you live. But he doesn't, he has no idea that's my house. I speed past it, not wasting my strength by screaming but, as I think back on it now, mostly not wanting to wake Arthur up, not wanting to rattle him, ruin his sleep. And for that reason, I don't call 911, I don't want cops and sirens.

I had a better plan. Remember, I was pretty loaded. Anyway, I saw a chance for the nosy Neighbourhood Watchers across the street to be heroes, to actually catch a culprit, for it's their house that was lit.

So I dart left, open their wrought-iron gate, run up their walk, and, thank God, there's the wife at the window, in a robe, binoculars at hand. She has observed me through them many times, coming and going.

I pound on the door, ring the bell. Nobody comes. I'm frantic, the Nazi has seen me turn in here. There's a plaque on the door: "Mr. and Mrs. Willis White." I yell, "Mrs. White, help, let me in!"

She yells back, "You don't belong here! You belong across the road! Go away!" (Reflecting on this later, I was struck by the odd fixation on belonging. Were we, across the street, considered inferior?)

Anyway, after her "Go away!" I yell, "He's a rapist! A murderer!"

A male voice: "We know what your game is. Get off our property or I call the police!"

"Please fucking do!" But hadn't I just told myself no police? "Wait!" I holler, then venture back to the sidewalk, and the skunky ogre is in retreat, slouching back to Queen Street.

I take a circular backyard route to the swindler's, enter by the kitchen, and now here I am, at my desk, talking to my voice recorder, rehashing the night. The padded jacket. It's the guy Lucy spotted outside the Sorauren loft, sans toque. Same piece of rancid shit I chased on my bike, I'm sure. How was he able to hone in on me?

Elementary, Dear Journal. He'd heard about the Squirrelly Moe's funder, guessed I'd be there, hung around Moe's, spotted me, followed me, and the rest is hysteria.

8

I am baggy-eyed, my brain is splintering, and I'm wrapped in a film of sweat. I may have slept two hours. It didn't register until the caffeine and aspirins kicked in that I'd left my bike at Lucy's. I ran like stink all the way, and arrived on the sixth floor of the courthouse six minutes after ten o'clock.

And now, as I hustle into 6-1, I find it in session, everyone silently waiting for me, heads turned to stare at the pitiful wretch. Justice Donahue is deadpan as she looks up from whatever she's doodling. I'm required to do the walk of shame to the prisoners' dock before she deigns to address me.

"I'm hoping, Ms. Levitsky, that you were kidnapped by aliens. Because nothing short of that will satisfy me."

Arthur's expression asks, "Do you need help with this?" I shake him off. I'm going to lay it out for this anal arbiter. I stand, take a deep breath. "Last night, as I was returning from a benefit, walking alone down a dark street, I was pursued by a very large, inebriated Nazi who expressed a desire to have intercourse with me. He referred to me in a salacious manner as a Jew-girl. He used other language I don't care to repeat here. I was able to outrun him and find shelter. I slept for maybe ninety minutes. I apologize for being six minutes late."

I sit between Lucy and Amy, who jointly embrace me. Judge Donahue seems unsure whether to absolve my sin or challenge me: *Did you alert the police?* But would she risk sounding distrustful? As she glances at the media, her nose wiggles, scenting censure — bullying me was not going to endear her to them, her sarcasm had already rung a wrong note.

"Very well, I shall presume the authorities are dealing with the matter. Most regrettable indeed. Ah, Mr. Beauchamp, I believe you are still cross-examining. Can we bring Mr. Wakeling back in, please."

"A moment, please," Arthur says, then leans to my ear: "My dear, dear Rivie, I am shocked beyond belief. Where did this happen? Never mind, I shall demand we recess for the day."

"No, please, I'm fine." I'm not, but I don't want to seem the cringing victim. "Can we talk at lunch? You need to finish taking down that company goon." Clarkson Wakeling, he's waiting to be ushered to the witness stand.

Arthur pats my arm, walks off toward the jurors. I can't tell where their collective heads are at. Some seem distressed, either at the peril I'd faced or at Donahue's awkward reaction to it. Juror Ten, Mabel Sims, the tax branch auditor, is frowning, as if distrustful of the young Jezebel's wild claims.

Abbie Lee-Yeung, however, is sending vibes of compassion and solidarity. The eye contact is intense. Maybe scary. *She wants to proclaim her love for you.* All sorts of weird, awkward scenarios come to mind.

Lucy nudges me, whispers: "Please tell me you didn't make all that up."

"Hope to die. What happened last night?"

"Got shut down. No one busted. Got driven home. Got laid. You look like a wreck. Talk later."

Khan's student legs it out of the room, presumably to check on my alibi. I am a rival for Khan's affection, she's dying to discover I lied about the Nazi as a deceitful play for the jury's sympathy. To her disappointment, she'll find a complaint on file: I texted Constable Louella Baker last night and she'd answered over her morning coffee: "On it. Wish you'd phoned. Let's do lunch."

Arthur worries about my friendly relationship with a cop. Lunch will be his chance to size her up.

Corporate apologist and conscripted flak-catcher Clarkson Wakeling does a nervous sidestep as Nancy crosses paths with him, on her way out, dialling her phone. W.W. Squirely's number in Missouri, I'm guessing, as she continues her pursuit of the Dover file.

Arthur thanks the Crown for copying him with the report from Chemican's private investigators. He holds it aloft as he beams a smile at the witness. "Mr. Wakeling, when we broke on Friday, I think we'd established that Howell Griffin was a heavy cocaine user and that Archie Gooch was suspected to be his supplier and confidant. You have no issues with that?"

Wakeling: "I don't have all the facts, but I can't disagree."

Beauchamp: "That theory was put forward by your investigators, correct?"

"It was raised, yes."

"And you were shocked to learn that Griffin gave Gooch the entrance codes for the Sarnia plant."

"I still find that disturbing, sir."

"And the alleged break-in occurred on the one night Gooch was assigned to guard the plant. Your investigators suspect that was not coincidental."

"They raised that possibility."

"And it follows that Howie Griffin may have been in league with those who pilfered files from the laboratory."

"As I understand it, our detective agency was unable to confirm that. Mr. Griffin declined to talk to them."

"But they raised the possibility, as you've said. Indeed, it's possible that Mr. Griffin set the whole thing up."

"Why would he do that?"

"Because head office gave him a nod and a wink. Because the Sarnia factory was losing money. Because it was well insured."

Five points and a bonus to Arthur for whaling away at this dubious scenario that we were used as pawns in a nefarious scheme. I get it — he wants to give the jury something to latch onto as a backup to the necessity defence.

Khan, who has been patient, can take it no longer. "I am registering a continuing objection to my learned friend's tendency to pretend he's cross-examining when he's actually arguing his case. And doing so without evidentiary basis, just surmise and conjecture."

Donahue: "I'm afraid the witness asked for it, didn't he? Objection denied."

The gawky student returns. She won't look at me, though I shoot fire at her. She confers with Khan. He nods, glances my way. I return a cold stare — he disrespected me by doubting my word.

Arthur changes direction. "Mr. Wakeling, in your former role as PR director for Chemican, you were consulted when the company's reputation was under threat?"

"If you could be more specific, sir . . ."

"Major suits in damages. Threats to drag the company into court. Your advice was often sought, yes?"

"If the company's good name was at risk, yes."

"What good name is that?"

"Objection. Baiting the witness."

"Upheld."

"Mr. Wakeling, you often sought to tamp down complaints before they went to litigation." Pulling a paper from a file. "For instance this memo from 2015 about meeting with an organic farmer in California whose spinach fields became infected by Vigor-Gro."

"That, as I remember, was settled out of court."

"After you talked him into it. According to your memo, one of your levers was a threat to sue him for slander."

"That was a confidential memorandum, and so is the settlement agreement. It has a non-disclosure clause."

"Which can be overridden by the courts."

Donahue looks impatient. Khan rises. Arthur ducks. "Let's put that aside for the moment. Let's go back to 2005. What was your capacity with Chemican that year?"

"Well, I would have been thirty-five, so . . . yes, I had just been promoted to publicity director."

"And that was around the time Vigor-Gro won EPA approval?"

"Yes. I was part of a campaign team tasked with earning it market awareness."

"All your testing on Vigor-Gro had been completed by 2005?"

"Yes."

"And did Chemican-International settle any court actions that year?"

"You would have to ask our legal department."

"I may. But in the meantime are you personally aware of any civil actions in damages that year?"

"None in particular come to mind."

I'd found myself yawning, but now comes a spurt of wakefulness. Arthur has my memorandum about the Dover settlement in July, 2005. This is my baby, I found the fax sheet. Maybe it's nothing, but if so why has Ms. or Mr. Dover been scrubbed from the company records?

"Surely all settled damages claims against Chemican are filed somewhere."

"You would have to ask Legal, in Missouri."

"What was the Volunteer Testing Program?"

Wakeling's face kind of flinches, a threat reaction, but he's quickly back to form: bland, serious. "I'm afraid testing programs were not exactly in my bailiwick. Our science people might know. I believe Dr. Jinks, our head of science, is in the witness room." He shoots a look at us miscreants in the box. "Of course many of our files were stolen from the laboratory."

"But not destroyed, Mr. Wakeling. In fact, it's on record that they're extant." Arthur smiles over at Inspector Roberts, who nods in affirmation, then catches herself, and reddens.

"No more questions," Arthur says. He has decided to keep the Dover fax under his vest for now.

Donahue: "Redirect?"

Khan: "No, M'Lady."

Wakeling just sits there, as if needing a cattle prod to get him mobile. Finally, on the judge insisting he's free to go, he gains his feet, and make a beeline for the door.

9

Now begins the next phase of the prosecution case: expert evidence. The Crown has the burden of proof, so their experts go first, their job being to shield Vigor-Gro from blame for its role in the mass extinction of bees. Meanwhile, I'm enduring serious brain-fade. I need a pry bar to keep my eyelids open. I am kept upright only because I'm tightly bookended between Lucy and Amy, on whose soft, warm shoulder I long to doze.

Proceedings stall over a tedious effort to find seats in this packed courtroom for several of the experts subpoenaed by Crown and defence. Experts, being of a higher class, don't have to twiddle in the waiting room, they're supposed to get reserved front-row seating.

Finally, a bunch of lawyers with time to kill are rousted from the front, Donahue telling them they should return to work and get in some billable hours. Their places are taken by Dr. Ariana Van Doorn and some of her team: a wildlife ecologist, an agrologist, and a professional beekeeper. Dr. Jerod Easling, the slickly handsome TV star, enters last, looking around as if for news cameras, hiding his disappointment with a resigned smile as he sits behind the Crown table. Next to him is Dr. Owen Jinks, Chemican's chief scientist, a biochemist.

When everyone has settled, Jinks is called to the stand. He's half the size of the last witness, a wiry middle-aged jockey with weird hair that sticks straight up. He regurgitates his resumé in short, sharp sentences. A Kansas farm background, loyal to his roots and his employer. Been with the company since 1991. Ph.D. from Kansas State in 1994. Chief scientist at Chemican since early 2003. Oversees the Sarnia lab as well as others worldwide.

He's also a regular lecturer at agro events. Doc Knutsen, who looked him up, says he's mainly a courtroom warrior and defender of Vigor-Gro before boards and commissions.

Dr. Jinks extolls the prime features of Vigor-Gro: safe to use, easy to apply, and, yes, environmentally friendly. He buttresses these sweeping claims with a PowerPoint presentation intended to show Vigor-Gro was rigorously tested from inception through multiple lab and field studies before being met by universal acclaim from satisfied growers.

Dr. Jinks rambles on about how it took a decade and four hundred million dollars to bring Vigor-Gro to market. That involved "rigorous scrutiny" by "independent scientific experts" to ensure the product was safe for humans. Not so safe, however, for the bees they tested, thousands of them overdosed with pollen seasoned with Chemican's patented neonicotinoid, called ziegladoxin. My weary brain can't fight off a cynical image of Jinks as a mean little boy, squashing beetles and pulling wings off flies.

I'm yawning as he assures us Vigor-Gro isn't "the major stressor" causing colony death. "It should not be inferred," the transcript drearily reads, "that the mortality results are transferable to actual field exposure conditions." Field doses applied at a "typical" rate of five micrograms to a hundred kilograms of soil had "negligible effects on honeybee colony health."

And that's more or less when the lights go out. My last sensation is of Amy's healing warmth as I nestle against her.

§

"Earth to Levitsky. Come in." It's Lucy, into my right ear. "Judge is worried you're dead."

One eye pops open. Donahue is indeed studying me. When I open my other eye she decides I'm conscious, and turns back to the shock-haired gnome in the witness box. Dr. Jinks, that's his name.

How long have I been out? An hour? It's ten past noon. Nancy is crossing Jinks, and she's really going after him, about a series of field tests in Alberta, the results skewed, the math made up, micros and kilos pulled out of a hat to minimize the crashing of bee colonies. Chemican had fired a whistleblower whom they'd goaded to alter test results. One of the fallouts from Operation Beekeeper.

Jinks is flailing, red-faced, denying that those field tests helped wangle Vigor-Gro past Canada's Pest Management Regulatory Agency. The research team that produced those results had been "overly creative" and for that sin they had been "terminated." Which, in a literal sense, sounds like an extreme measure. A couple of jurors wince.

Nancy has timed this perfectly, it's twelve thirty. Over their cheeseburgers and western sandwiches, the jury will be wondering if there are limits to this company's depravity.

Donahue cautions Jinks not to talk about the case, and adjourns court. As the jury is let out, Lucy opens my hand and slips me a little yellow capsule. "A waker-upper. Worked for me."

I tuck it into my bra. I don't have time to ask about its origins, because here comes Constable Louella Baker, out of uniform, for our lunch date. While being herded out the door, curious reporters catch her shaking hands with Arthur, then embracing me.

They don't hear her growl to Arthur, "I'm gonna rip that motherfucker's balls out." I hope she means my unfriendly neighbourhood Nazi.

§

You can call it lunch but for me it's breakfast — a quiche, strong coffee, and Tylenol — in a crowded, loud bistro up on Dundas. Louella brazenly showed her badge to get a table for three.

Thanks to me, sort of, her career is taking off. She has parlayed our alliance into a posting with the Toronto Police Service's hate crimes unit, and is tasked to try to nail my stalker for criminal harassment.

Arthur listens quietly, over his bowl of crusty onion soup, as Louella takes me through Sunday's every seamy detail, from getting stoned with Lucy, abandoning the tawdry funder to grab a streetcar, then being chased by the slow-footed whack job.

Louella asks: "Who did you talk to on the streetcar?"

"There were a handful of us in the back. Bee-lievers, but nobody I knew, and most got off before I did."

"Any of them take any photos? Like with you? Selfies?"

"No, they were too cool."

"What about Mr. and Mrs. Willis White? Could they have seen him from their window?"

"Maybe. He saw me turn into their yard. You'll have to shout through the door. They have a heavy paranoia scene going. *Folie à deux*."

Louella fetches an iPad, turns it on. Arthur gives me a severe look. "I fail to understand, Rivie, why you didn't wake me."

"Yeah, and you run out of the house in your pyjamas, and he knows where we live and posts it on the White Christian Nationalist Brotherhood listserv. Also, Arthur, be real, you'd be up all night worrying, you needed your sleep. Me, not so much."

Arthur frowns. "Justice Donahue deserved your cutting excuse for being late, but your plight is all over the news, so this nasty character will be on alert. Given his apparent obsession over you, he may be deranged enough to return to our street so I urge you to refrain from jogging off God knows where in the middle of the night."

"Five a.m. is not the middle—"

"That's not the point. You ought not to be going out alone at any time. Anywhere."

"I'm not going to live in fear—"

Louella referees: "Hey, break it up, go to your corners. You got to take care, doll. I can't watch Beaconsfield around the clock. I'm going to show you some mug shots, our hate crimes collection."

"No way I'll recognize him. It was too dark."

"Let's try." She opens a tablet, six ugly faces stare from the screen.

I study them, shake my head. Louella scrolls to a second set of six. I start. "Whoa. Number three. Where have I seen him?" I concentrate, work through my weariness. It comes. "Oh, my God, the Nazi from the bail hearing. We had words in the hallway, he called us Commie nigger-lovers, Ray almost hammered him."

Arthur backs me up, he was in court when the judge granted bail. "It was something involving a cemetery."

"Donald Stumpit," Louella says. "Beat a charge of desecrating a grave. He did a couple of bits for vandalism and assaulting a couple of women in hijabs. Saddles up with a group called the Final Reich. Hush-hush on this until I track him down, okay?"

I'm excited, it feels like a breakthrough. "He gave me a dirty, drooling slurp as he headed into court. I think I may have given him the finger." Is that how a rapist's obsession is sparked? "Hey, maybe we can set a trap. Like, I slip out at midnight to buy some taco chips from the 7-Eleven—"

"That will not happen!" Arthur booms.

This doesn't sound like Arthur, the calm, courtly counsel. More like the stern family patriarch. I try to soothe him with an earnest promise to be a good girl. No reason to make him anxious, but I'm going to figure out a way, with a few friends, to trip up this cave person, catch him with his dick hanging out. No reason to tell grumpy old grandpa the details.

10

An hour into the afternoon, as Nancy continues to poke at Dr. Jinks, I start to flag again, the caffeine losing its bite, Lucy's Waker-Upper tempting me. When I pressed her about it, I got: "Home remedy, trust me." From her lab at Ryerson? Then maybe it's safe. From the personal pharmacy of T.J. Gully? Maybe not so.

Nancy accuses Jinks's research unit of multiple offences: exaggerated claims, distorted graphs and tables, tweaked statistics. But it's slow sledding, mathematically dense, and she occasionally has to consult Ariana or Doc on a technical or scientific issue. This irks the judge, who wants her to jack it up or "we'll be here till kingdom come."

I guess Nancy is trying to show that this junk science wouldn't have come to light if we hadn't pillaged their records, but some jurors are starting to stir and clock-watch. Except Abbie Lee-Yeung, who writes intently, as if covering for me by taking on my suspended role as memoirist — I'm too bagged to make notes.

A gentle bra adjustment drops the capsule into my free hand. I slug it down with water. Miss Pucket watches, suspiciously. Her frown prompts Azra Khan to turn and check me out. I give him my defiant look: I'm strong, unbroken. He's supposed to be this A-list prosecutor with his unbroken record of thirty-eight convictions, but so far he hasn't shot out any lights. His mom has cancer, so he's distracted, but it's like he's just along for the ride: Why bother spreading himself when Judge Donahue is sure to gut the necessity defence?

Interest perks when Nancy moves on to the testing on rats and rabbits. Jinks appears to take pride in the "lack of serious ill effects at moderate- to high-milligram dosage ranges." Fewer than twenty percent of these gentle, little mammals had to be put down, he's pleased to advise.

Nancy challenges that: "Lack of *serious* ill effects? And yet many of these animals had to be put down?"

"In most cases, to allow for laboratory analysis. Admittedly a few creatures suffered neurobehavioural impairments, but these were minor and short-lived."

The yellow capsule — let's call it Lucy's Mix Number Two — works its magic fast: I'm wide-eyed with alarm that it's considered okay for researchers to torture bunnies in order to sell a potion that kills pollen-seeking insects and starves swallows and flycatchers and warblers.

Ariana Van Doorn has armed Nancy with other animal studies, one of which she places in front of Jinks.

"I presume you're familiar with this report from the Bayer Corporation from 2008."

Jinks scans the first-page summary. "I recall looking at it."

"The experiment involved pregnant rats that were fed daily doses of Bayer's patented neonicotinoid. Their offspring matured poorly and showed disorientation during behavioural tests. Brain structures were altered. Do you not find that troubling?"

"Not at all. Those results were not replicated in similar studies we examined. More importantly, our patented compound, ziegladoxin, differs substantially in molecular makeup from Bayer's imidacloprid. It's apples and oranges."

"But both are nicotine-based, yes?"

"As are all neonics, of course."

All of this is a prelude to the experiments on humans, the Volunteer Testing Program. Jinks has obviously been warned this would arise because he has a spiel ready: "To be absolutely certain that Vigor-Gro could not be accused of having any harmful effects on, say, farmers or other users, we debated whether to develop a program of testing on humans — one that would be carefully calibrated, of course."

"And you followed through?"

"It came about this way — you might find this humorous — several of my colleagues dared me to serve as a human guinea pig, as it were, and I think I shamed them by imbibing fourteen point five millilitres of Vigor-Gro in a fruit drink, and suffered absolutely no ill consequences. If anything, I felt invigorated, and spent the following hour in the gym doing tumbling and floor exercises."

Sadly, almost no one finds this humorous, and Jinks breaks the awkward, shuffling silence by adding that he challenged his colleagues to spunk up and do the same. Five of them did so. All got high marks from their physical, blood, and urine tests. One of them, a smoker, claimed to have got a gentle nicotine boost.

The happy results from those impromptu experiments encouraged Jinks to undertake the larger test with paid volunteers. "We were spurred in that effort because the company eventually hoped to put out a home-and-garden version of Vigor-Gro and we wanted to be irrefutably certain it was safe for domestic use."

Nancy draws from him the history of this study. In late 2003, a call went out to several colleges in Missouri and Kansas, offering as bait three thousand dollars plus expenses to attend a few weekend trials. Several hundred applied, and after interviews that was winnowed to one hundred and three, the median age about twenty-one.

"You chose only men and women who were in robust health?"

"Basically so. All were given checkups. Some were more fit than others, of course. A true cross-section, I believe, of our region's undergraduate population."

As to the procedures, he recalls that Vigor-Gro was taken orally, with a chaser of juice, a few millilitres on first exposure, then a higher dosage the next weekend. I fight a vaguely hallucinatory sense of tasting it, a horrible green sludge sliding down my throat. Lucy's Mix Two has sharpened my sensations, it's definitely some kind of speed.

"Everyone had to sign a release, correct?"

"A form of release. Acknowledging they'd been fully informed about our testing procedures."

"Did the release limit the rights of these students to sue for negligence or malpractice?"

"Our legal team didn't . . . Well, let me be clear, we were a hundred percent confident in our product, so we didn't feel such a provision was necessary." Nancy just stares at him, demanding elaboration. "As well, our legal department felt that the courts might look askance at such a restriction."

"Sage advice," says Judge Donahue, dryly. Dr. Jinks looks startled by that interjection — he'd been assured the judge was onside.

Further probing reveals that records of the volunteer program remain at head office "under lock and seal and closed to the public to protect the identities of participants."

"Why the secrecy?"

"I'm afraid you would have to ask Legal."

"Surely the test results on these students are available?"

"I regret, counsellor, that I lack clearance to make them available. However, I recall these tests were conducted without any undesired consequences."

Nancy keeps after him, with an air of incredulity, but he claims not to recall any issues reported by the student volunteers, other than the occasional loose bowel, which staff physicians attributed to eating disorders unrelated to Vigor-Gro or their patented ziegl-adoxin.

"You had no complaints from any of the one hundred and three about side effects from these dosages?"

"None come to mind. These tests occurred in late 2003, through 2004, so that's fifteen years ago."

"Were no claims in damages against Chemican made by any of these students?" The circling lioness slowly closes in on her prey.

"You mean, like a court action? I'm not personally aware of any."

"I mean a claim that didn't become a court action. One that was settled. Please help me here, Dr. Jinks. Dover was the injured party's name. Charles Arnold Dover."

This is new. Nancy has dug up some background on him, his full name.

"I'm sorry. Charles Arnold Dover? It's not coming back." He has gone a little pale. "You might ask our legal team—"

"Right now I'm asking you." Nancy hands him a copy of the fax. Jinks's face kind of flinches, a threat reaction, but he's quickly back to form: alert, serious. Another copy goes to Khan, a third via Miss Pucket to the judge.

"This copy of a facsimile transmission, as you will note, is stamped 'Legal, Volunteer Testing Program,' and is dated July eight, 2005. The addressee is Baylor Jessup, Chemican's chief counsel at the time. You know him, of course."

"Mr. Jessup. Yes, retired now."

"And it's from His Honour W. W. Squirely, former judge, of Joplin, Missouri, and you see that it's headed 'Re: Dover and Chemican-International Ltd.'"

"Mm-hmm, yes."

"Please read us the text."

"It says, 'Sir, please be advised that settlement documents, duly executed, have been dispatched this date to the addressee by DHL Courier,' and I assume that's a tracking number."

"Surely, Dr. Jinks, this rings a bell?"

Jinks can't be sure if Nancy is armed with copies of the settlement papers, or some confidential memo that the document-shredding unit overlooked. So he screws up his face with mighty concentration. "I do recall now an issue arose involving one of the participants."

"Right. A student at Missouri Southern State University in Joplin?"

"Probably … yes, we had several volunteers from Southern State."

"And what was the issue that arose?"

"Thinking back, a young gentleman expressed some unhappiness with his test consequences. I honestly can't remember the specifics."

"Surely you remember that he hired counsel and threatened court proceedings against your company."

"Frankly, madam, I had no further involvement with that matter or with Mr. Dover. Mr. Jessup handled it. Legal tends to keep everything under wraps. I heard something about a settlement of a nuisance claim, but I don't know the terms."

Khan makes a show of rising with great effort. "If it please the court, why is this alleged fax being sprung upon us without forewarning?"

Nancy responds: "Because we came upon it only yesterday. The original resides among Chemican's legal files."

"More importantly," Khan continues, "why are we being asked to wade through a flood of hearsay?"

Donahue: "I wondered when you would ask. I am struggling, Ms. Faulk, to find this even remotely relevant to your stated defence of necessity."

Arthur gives Nancy an encouraging smile that suggests they prepped for such a challenge. "The tests on humans," she says, "are relevant because through their actions the accused will have shielded thousands, maybe tens of thousands — none of them volunteers — who are facing present danger from the crippling consequences of close contact with Vigor-Gro. I believe we can prove that statistically."

Donahue grapples with that slippery claim, in her peculiar nose-twitchy way. She seems torn about whether to send out the jury or cut this debate short. Khan doesn't wait for her to decide, amps up the rhetoric, accusing Nancy of a "glib *argumentum ad hominem*" to support not just a flood but a "tsunami of hearsay." The fax was hearsay, and so was Dover, and so were his complaints, whatever their nature.

Donahue swivels to the jury: "There are many exceptions to the rule against hearsay, but generally speaking statements made outside this courtroom, relayed to the witness, are inadmissible. So there is no proper evidence before you that a Mr. Dover or any person raised any issues or complaints relating to the human testing program described by Dr. Jinks. You are to disregard all testimony to that effect. The fax proffered by Ms. Faulk will not be marked as an exhibit."

Many would cave, but not our Nancy. She seeks an order allowing Dover to give "commission evidence" from his domicile in Missouri.

Judge Donahue's tone is sardonic: "Ms. Faulk, I presume you are aware that taking commission evidence from afar could result in this trial being delayed for weeks or even months. Perhaps you could offer a cogent reason why Mr. Dover can't just hop on a plane to come here to testify."

"Because, M'Lady, as a result of imbibing neonicotinoids during the Christmas holidays of 2003, in the course of Chemican's Volunteer Testing Program, he developed and still suffers severe nervous system complications. That's what his law office told me this morning, if you'll excuse the hearsay."

Maybe because of Lucy's Mix Two, I have to blink away an optical illusion of Donahue's nose twirling like a propeller on a beanie.

"Counsel's application to take commission evidence is denied. The court will not hear a further such motion in the absence of affidavit material attesting to the relevance of testimony to be sought. I see it is nearing the half hour. Are counsel finished with this witness?"

"Not quite, M'Lady," Nancy says. "For the purposes of further cross-examination I ask that Dr. Jinks be instructed to have all files relating to the Volunteer Testing Program couriered to him overnight from Kansas City."

"If that's a motion, it's denied. Adjourn to ten o'clock tomorrow."

I'm in the back seat of Nancy's Leaf, crashing again, fighting it, hoping to survive until I make it home. I protested, she insisted. "You're not walking home, kid. Or anywhere. Until that creep is off the streets." She now knows about Stumpit, has joined our pact of silence.

It's rush hour, we're crawling along to Parkdale. Nancy and Arthur are doing post-game analysis and I'm their silent audience, leaning forward between them.

Arthur asks, "What about their retired head of Legal?"

"Jessup. Moved to Palm Springs, where all rich lawyers go to die. Phone is listed but doesn't answer. A search for *Dover v. Chemican* came up empty, so it was settled before it got that far. Nothing in the media, so it was hushed up. One of us is going to have to talk to Mr. Charles Arnold Dover. Was nineteen then, now thirty-six. That's all I know, aside from he's in bad shape."

She had got through to the office of W.W. Squirely, but spoke only to his secretary, though he could be heard in background, loud and slurring. Nancy made out: "Our tongues are tied. 'Splain that to her."

The blunt-talking secretary, named Cherry, told the judge to shut up, and explained that he meant their hands were tied because of a non-disclosure clause.

Arthur groans over the prospect of a trip to Missouri, especially this weekend, with his wife coming. But he and Nancy are determined to work the angle that Vigor-Gro messes up some people.

We finally get to Beaconsfield, a one-way north, and to the semi-detached bricker of Nancy's jailed client, the swindler. As I alight I check across the street to see the curtains slightly part at the Willis Whites. *You belong across the road!*

Nancy comes in for a drink, which she earned, she had a big skookum day. While Arthur puts on tea, she opens one of her husband's two-hundred-dollar Cabs, splashes some for me, and toasts her wannabe ex with some select coarse language, but not with much zap, more out of habit. I want to ask how her thing with Doc is coming along, but decide it might embarrass her, and maybe Arthur doesn't know about it.

I also want to talk to her (not to Arthur, that feels awkward for some reason) about Abbie Lee-Yeung and Lucy's theory she's stuck on me. But it's a ticklish topic, better raised when I'm not so pooped.

Six o'clock. I'm gone. If I can get in ten hours I'll be up before dawn for my morning ritual run.

CHAPTER 21 » ARTHUR

1
Thursday, May 23

Arthur is on lunch break in the barristers' lounge, alone with his thoughts and a stale egg sandwich, avoiding company by pretending to be absorbed in a legal brief as he relaxes his mind for the contest ahead. A kind of meditation, though that's an art he's never mastered.

For the last few days Arthur has served no role whatsoever at this trial — he was a dispensable accessory, a ceremonial sword. He and Nancy divvied up the cross-examinations equally, but to her goes the greater glory: she takes on scientists while Arthur's specialty has been cops and muddled night watchmen.

But finally, today, he will be back in the ring, duking it out with Dr. Jerod Easling, the star player of this sellout show. The other evening, Nancy showed Arthur YouTube videos of Easling on panels and in debates. She did so to fortify her argument that her more brittle, needling style of cross-examination could back-fire when met with Dr. Easling's poise and cordiality. She thinks Arthur can out-affable him.

She added: "Also, Donahue abhors me, and she likes you. In fact, she's hot for you."

That seemed extreme hyperbole but he has sensed the judge's growing respect, the kind combatants hold for each other. At any rate, it was finally agreed they would both cross Easling, Arthur going first, to soften him up.

Hot for him or not, Arthur has zero hope Donahue will let the necessity defence go to the jury. She's a proud woman, unlikely to change a view so forcefully held. In which case a guilty verdict becomes almost obligatory — unless Arthur and Nancy can somehow tweak out a hung jury. In which case nineteen-year-old Abbie Lee-Yeung becomes key.

He feels rusty. He's been missing in action for so long that he expects he's little remembered by the jury — except for his cross of Jake Maguire. Dismayingly, he is still seen as responsible for sending the old bull away on a stretcher. Her Enigmatic Ladyship is off the hook because she'd merely followed up with an amiable question about a comical photograph. (Now unheeded, forgotten by media outlets with their short attention spans, their lust for the latest.)

Arthur has learned that Maguire had dietary problems, so he ought not to have accompanied his get-well card with chocolates — a gift prompted by having seen the fellow occasionally sneaking off with a candy bar. He's recuperating at home, and the word is he'll be back in court next week.

Still unaccounted for, unaccountably, is supposed star witness Howell J. Griffin. The Crown is either saving him for dessert or has decided not to risk calling him — in which case much of the evidence about the role played by Rivie Levitsky would be circumstantial.

As to Ms. Levitsky, his housemate, she continues to sneak out before daybreak for a run or a pedal, despite Arthur's warnings. Her attempts to tiptoe softly down the creaky stairs invariably wake him — often from recurrent dreams of Ulysses waiting across a yawning, bottomless chasm — and he frets until she returns. She lightly flouts danger: "Five thirty is not a typical lurking hour, especially for an out-of-shape hatemonger like Donald Stumpit who gets his courage up with drink."

Arthur is eager to impress her with his cross of Easling, though he isn't sure why her approval is important to him. He certainly won't be at his best; he fears he has lost his stuff, his fire, and will be seen as a doddering old actor making a pitiful return to the stage.

Dr. Easling was on the stand all this morning, confident and twinkle-eyed, charming jurors and reporters with what pundits describe as "charisma," which once meant a divinely inspired talent but has become a prosy triteness that makes Arthur want to throw up.

Easling went on the charm offensive right off the bat, while relating his credentials ("those Amazonian field studies persuaded me I loved bugs more than the bugs loved me"), and blushed as Azra Khan read out his many international honours, including his several honorary doctorates.

Easling then pitched his credentials as a conservationist, a lover of the great outdoors, its wildlife, its wild spaces. He hikes forest trails, he camps, he canoes, he *truly* cares about the planet, he's not some "Starbucks environmentalist."

Then he won the jury's respect by conceding Chemican had covered up faulty science and cannot escape culpability by scapegoating half a dozen employees. However inexcusable, these corporate lapses could not negate the "powerfully positive impact of neonicotinoids" and "the vastly improved crop yields earned by their judicious use."

He had backup for those claims, the sworn testimony yesterday of a few carefully chosen growers from afar: well-spoken, militantly non-organic farmers from Silesia, Gloucestershire County, and North Dakota. (Chemican had generously paid their fare and room and board and, presumably, a bonus, though Her Ladyship wouldn't let Nancy pry further.).

The Englishman bad-mouthed the EU for its ban on neonics: "We didn't use Vigor-Gro last year, and the flea beetle larvae made short work of the oilseed rape. The crop was hardly worth its harvest."

The Pole, a prosperous landholder, had a similar complaint about the EU ban: it cost him an additional forty thousand euros to apply several different licensed insecticides.

The Dakotan, a struggling widow and mother of five, had tried to break her neonics habit but found aphids had developed resistance to standard insecticides. When she went back to Vigor-Gro she claimed to have found bees thriving in a sea of neonic-infused canola.

Easling enlarged on that: studies showed that pre-neonic chemicals destroy beneficial insects while neonicotinoids systemically target aphids or beetles. "So, obviously, neonics are more environmentally friendly."

He scorned laboratory studies that pointed to neonics as the main culprit in colony collapse — they did not reflect realistic outdoor conditions. He derided many field studies too, as being scientifically weak, scoffed at a recent one from Harvard that warned that neonicotinoids were killing bees at an exponential rate. However, he applauded research done at a few universities of lesser renown — Wageningen, Ghent, Maryland — that gave neonics a pass.

At times, Easling resorted to scaremongering: as pesticide use drops, food prices rise — annual double-digit jumps must be expected wherever neonics are restricted, a crippling, maybe mortal blow to the poor and needy. Thus Vigor-Gro helps save humankind from wholesale starvation.

At times, he was conciliatory: it was essential to strike the right balance between protecting the environment and providing a reliable supply of healthy, affordable food. That could happen were growers to set aside tracts of land for untreated plants rich in pollen.

The main thrust of his argument was that neonics have been unfairly tried and convicted by the kangaroo court of espousers of the Brave New Green World. The true perpetrators were varroa mites and a fungal parasite called *Nosema ceranae* "and a host of other parasites and pathogens unwittingly spread about the planet by human action."

An additional culprit was that handy reason for all things dire, global climate change and its extremes: too much rain, too much drought, too much heat, too much cold.

Added to that, honeybees were losing access to flower-rich prairies that once flourished across the globe. They must now struggle to survive on "monotonous diets of mass-flowering crops" like canola. He likened such vast tracts to a green desert that blooms only two weeks a year, so bees have no food source for the remaining fifty. "It is no wonder our precious *Apis mellifera* has fallen on hard times."

Wild bees "like our beloved bumblebee" also suffered from habitat loss. Forced to spend more time foraging, facing longer commutes to their nests, they had less time to feed and produce offspring. These factors contributed to the die-out.

Dr. Easling spoke directly to the jury as he testified, and was rewarded with their rapt attention. He decorated his points with an occasional eloquent turn of phrase borrowed from his YouTube jousts. Arthur guesses that his self-effacing tendencies hide an overweening ego. That might be his weak spot.

"We shall see," he mutters to his half-eaten sandwich.

Azra Khan looked distracted this morning as he put Easling through his paces. Arthur feels sorry for the prosecutor, who is looking more wan and depressed every day. Quite a contrast from his jaunty air, at their first meeting in the fall, with his assurances that these arrogant activists would get the max. But weighing on him now is his mother's sudden, fast decline. She is in her final stages, and has been taken to a hospice in Richmond Hill, a long commute for him each evening.

So he is incapable of giving his best to this case, and has confided he regrets having taken it on. That admission came today at the noon break, with a sigh, as he drew Arthur aside to ask if they could have a quiet tête-à-tête at day's end. Arthur agreed, then Khan gathered his underlings and rushed off.

However preoccupied he is, however lacking in gusto, Azra Khan is a professional, and once committed to a task will do his best. Arthur knows that, he knows his type — because that is Arthur's type.

And for Arthur to do his job he must, tomorrow, Friday, take a day away from Toronto and this trial. Who would have dreamed this case would see him trotting off to southwestern Missouri to meet with an apparently irascible ninety-three-year-old former judge named W. W. Squirely?

He would have preferred not to abandon Nancy for the day but the weekend is unavailable. Margaret arrives on Saturday and woe to him if he jilts her once again.

2

Jerod Easling mounts the stand. The spectators and jurors settle in. Madam Justice Donahue muscles her way onto the bench. Arthur rises, and begins:

"Dr. Easling, this morning you relied on various studies to conclude that the neonic family of pesticides should not be blamed for honeybee colony collapse. I'd like to direct your attention to events in the spring of 2008, after an outbreak of corn rootworm in Europe. You are familiar with the dire events that followed?"

"Fully aware. In fact, I was retained to do some studies related to the outbreak."

"Retained by whom?"

"Bayer Crop Science."

"Okay. Some of us here may not remember it, so let me quote from an article in *The Guardian*: 'Dismayed beekeepers looked on as whole colonies collapsed. Millions of bees died. France, the Netherlands, and Italy reported big losses, but in Germany the incident took on the urgency of a national crisis. The government had to set up containers along the autobahn where beekeepers could dump their hives.'

"Dr. Easling, that mass poisoning was found to have been caused by a neonicotinoid called clothianidin — you'll be familiar with it because it's a Bayer product — which is said to be ten thousand times more potent than DDT. So please tell us how that disaster of 2008 squares with your view that neonics are environmentally friendly."

Easling turns to the jury. "There is another side to that story that didn't get as much press attention. Yes, European corn growers may have overreacted with excessive use of clothianidin, but from their perspective they were facing their own imminent disaster. Western corn rootworm is a hugely devastating pest and those little beasts have caused farmers billions of dollars of lost revenue. And by the way, Bayer generously compensated the European beekeepers even though it was not bound to."

"The upshot, I think you'll agree, is that the European Community banned neonics five years later."

"With little reported success, Mr. Beauchamp. Insect populations have still not recovered in any marked way. So I will have to say, if you'll forgive me, the jury is still out on that issue." Laughter all round.

The exchange did not work out as Arthur had hoped: he merely gave this fellow a megaphone. Easling's clever evasions and his manner of amiably lecturing the jury will have to be curbed.

"Let's see if we can find common ground on the basics, Dr. Easling. Neonicotinoids target the central nervous system and as a result bees lose their homing ability and their sense of direction, yes?"

"Those are often among the effects, but toxicity levels vary, depending on how much the bees are subject to chronic long-term exposure—"

"Thank you, but let's go one step at a time. The nicotine agent in these products can cause overstimulation and paralysis that leads to death?"

"While that is so, there are many other factors that effect the mortality of various species of bees."

"Dr. Easling, we'll speed along much faster if you just respond directly to my questions."

"I'm only here to help, Mr. Beauchamp."

"Of course. I don't mean to be brusque or discourteous."

"That never entered my mind." Big, sunny smile. "I'm too habituated to giving lectures, I guess, so please be patient with me."

"Okay, we have established that neonics cause our already busy bees to buzz about aimlessly and then they drop dead. But this nicotine-based substance has other qualities — for instance, it's water soluble, correct?"

"Neonicotinoids are water soluble."

"And they remain potent in soil and wet areas, do you agree?"

"Yes, though we don't know for how long they persist. May I add to that?"

Arthur waits too long, and Donahue intercedes: "Oh, just let him."

Easling grins — it's all a game to him. "As yet, I haven't heard of any unwanted effects on habitat as a result of neonics' long-term presence in the ground or anywhere."

"Dr. Nadia Tsvetkov, at York University here in Toronto, found spillover effects from treated crops in wildflowers, clover, dandelions, even maple trees. Have you read her report?"

"That may be a very recent report. I'm not in a position to dispute it, but, ah, maple trees? That might take some convincing."

"I'll make sure you get a copy of her report. Now, you relied on eight separate studies in support of your claim that neonics should not bear the brunt of blame for mass deaths of bees."

"I'm sorry, what studies were those?"

Nancy hands Arthur a marked document. "The ones in your written opinion, Exhibit 143, page forty-seven, footnotes thirty-three, thirty-five, and forty-five through forty-seven."

"I'll take your word for it, Mr. Beauchamp."

"And will you also agree that seven of those eight studies were financed by agrochemical giants: two by Syngenta, two by Bayer, three by Monsanto?"

"I have no doubt they were. Major corporations have a duty to ensure the safety of their products, and spend many hundreds of millions doing so."

"To little effect, I suggest, given Monsanto has been sued for billions because its infamous bestseller, Roundup, was proven to cause cancer—"

"Ob-*ject*," says Khan. "My friend is wandering very far afield."

"In my quest for flowering crops," Arthur says. Even Judge Donahue smiles. The merriment buoys Arthur. "I'm sorry, my mind has been on my untended, weedy garden back home."

"The sooner we finish," says Donahue, "the sooner you'll be getting your kohlrabi in."

She continues to confound Arthur. Is this ice lady melting, showing ordinary, warm human traits?

"Dr. Easling, surely you will concede that these studies are tainted by corporate funding."

"No, because the strict practice of sponsors is to hire respected, independent scientists, then to back off completely. Totally arm's length."

"These respected scientists get paid very well, I assume."

"To get the best, you have to pay the piper."

"I think the expression goes, 'He who pays the piper calls the tune.'"

Easling reddens. "My bad. Touché. My point is a research team has no incentive to fudge data or tweak the graphs. A contract has been signed. Payment is guaranteed even if they give a damning review."

"But wouldn't a damning review disincentive Syngenta, say, or Chemican, from hiring that scientist again?"

Again Khan, who is unusually active today, objects. "Calls for speculation."

"Let me put it this way, Dr. Easling — a researcher could not be blamed for softening his or her opinion when contemplating the prospect of further big paycheques—"

Donahue: "Can we move on, Mr. Beauchamp? I think the point has been made, for what it's worth."

"Let us turn, then, to studies reflecting data from organic, sustainable growers. I must assume, Doctor, you have read the written opinion by Dr. Ariana Van Doorn, which is . . . yes, Exhibit 156."

"I did. An admirable work by an emerging leader in the field, though I respectfully take issue with several of her analyses and conclusions."

"Hopefully not this one — after scouring hundreds of research papers she concludes that growers enjoy healthy profits and lower costs when spurning chemical-based pesticides. You have no reason to disagree, I assume."

"Nor do I have reason to agree, Mr. Beauchamp. I haven't analyzed her data. Many of the studies she relies on haven't been widely reported."

"Doubtless because you can barely hear them whispered behind the blare and clamour from agrochemical lobbyists. Organic growers don't spend millions on full-page ads and Super Bowl TV spots."

"Objection. My learned friend—"

"Thank you, Mr. Khan, objection allowed."

"My point is, Dr. Easling, that the agrochemical giants abhor an approach that reduces pests naturally, organically, and safely. That cuts into their bottom line—"

"Argumentative," says Khan.

"I'll move on." Arthur pauses to catch his breath. He is not making great headway here, instead is coming across as stubborn and preachy. The jury is giving away nothing — it's as if they're waiting for one or the other combatant to deliver a knock-down blow.

"Dr. Easling, you seem to put great store in the prospect of growers agreeing to set aside tracts of farmland for bee-friendly plants. I hope you will agree that the big industrial farms have snubbed that approach — less arable land, less income."

"I don't agree. The state of Bavaria, bowing to public demand, has just passed a law setting aside ten percent of green spaces into wildflower meadows. The idea is spreading across Germany and Europe and in my belief will soon be accepted worldwide."

Arthur dares not look at Nancy, or his clients or, especially, Rivie Levitsky, for fear of seeing their discomfort. He hadn't heard about this Bavarian initiative. "My point is that factory farms have refused to act voluntarily, so governments are being forced to create habitats for the bees."

That wasn't his point at all, but sometimes one has to bluff. "Dr. Easling, there was a study last year that found numbers of flying insects, pollinators, had fallen by three-quarters in twenty-five years."

"I have read it. Dr. Dieter Hoff led it. Brilliant scientist — I'm in awe of him."

"Then you've also read his best-known work? *De-Pollination: Why Chemistry May Kill Life on Earth.*"

"More than once."

"And do you agree with his thesis that agricultural chemicals may indeed kill life on earth?"

"I suspect Dieter doesn't believe in it himself. There is an element of hyperbole in that title that I'm sure helped him sell more books."

Chuckles in the gallery, grins in the jury box. Arthur must soft-shoe away from Dr. Hoff, whose plagiarism of his student's words may soon embroil him in deserved scandal.

"Following the 2008 disaster, Dr. Hoff became one of many in the scientific community who urged the European Community to ban neonics. That's fair to say?"

"He made submissions to the Commission tasked to review the matter."

Arthur recalls Rivie confiding that she keeps score during these fencing matches. Her card must show Arthur losing badly on points.

He decides to follow Nancy's advice: test Easling's objectivity, expose his role as a mercenary for the agrochemical industry.

"You also made submissions to that Commission?"

"Yes. I believed then, and still do, that the moratorium was short-sighted and was imposed without a scientific *raison d'*être or due regard for the rights and the welfare of the EU's farming community."

"Not to mention the welfare of the powerful agribusinesses you represented at those hearings."

"Businesses also have rights and legitimate concerns, Mr. Beauchamp."

"You've testified at many other governmental hearings and inquiries relating to the licensing of neonicotinoids, correct?"

"Scores of times, on behalf of the producers, sellers, and users of such products. As an aside, I wince every time I am referred to as a hired gun for those I represent. In fact I favour strict control of all guns — except spray guns, of course."

That gets a laugh, though to Arthur it sounds scripted, a tired joke he must often trot out at banquet speeches.

"Chemican, Bayer, Dow, DuPont — you've advised all the big ones."

"In my area of expertise as an entomologist, yes."

"And what were your average annual earnings from them over, say, the last ten years?"

"I don't sit around staring at balance sheets, Mr. Beauchamp. I wouldn't dare to guess." A resentful glance at Khan, then Donahue, inviting them to cut short this intrusive line of questioning. But financial bias affects credibility, and both judge and prosecutor are biting their tongues to avoid opening up avenues of appeal.

"Twenty million per year, would that be about right?" Prompting a gasp from the Bee-lievers in the back.

"That is wildly inaccurate."

"Then what is accurate? Please help me, Dr. Easling."

"I'm not going to hazard a guess. All I can say is I'm paid for my time, abilities, and expertise, sir, just as you are."

"I'm not even getting my expenses covered, Professor. How much are you getting paid for testifying here?"

"I shall submit a bill to the proper authorities in due time."

"Are your fees being topped up by Chemican-International?"

"Of course not. I appear as an independent witness. I am not on anyone's payroll."

"Are you not? Chemican does pay you an annual retainer, isn't that so?"

"Several firms do. I couldn't be sure about Chemican. You would have to ask my agent."

"You have an *agent?*"

"Rolfe Morgan Associates. Everyone in Los Angeles has an agent." This effort at humour clongs. People are no longer finding him funny and chummy.

Nancy, who looks relieved to see Arthur upping his game, hands him a thick volume of financial statements that has Chemican's logo on the cover. "Professional fees . . . here we are, Rolfe Morgan Associates. So on page thirty-eight, we see a nice round number of ten million dollars — that would represent your annual retainer with Chemican-International? Less agent commission, of course."

"Okay, I'm not going to quibble about fees. I'm well paid for the work I do. Because I'm well paid does not mean I've been bought. I have a reputation for the truth, and am damn proud of it." His voice quivering.

Easling is used to testifying before boards, not courts, and especially not criminal courts, with their more zealous and often cutting cross-examinations, and he has finally allowed Arthur to get under his skin. Khan knows that, a message he conveys to Arthur with a weary smile.

"This morning, Professor, you listed climate change as a factor in colony collapse."

"Bees don't like unpredictable weather any more than we do — storms, floods, smoke-filled skies, sudden freezes, all take their toll."

"It's odd to hear you say that, because wasn't it just six years ago that you proudly called yourself a climate change denier?"

"All the evidence wasn't in." His body language — shifting, tugging at a lapel — announces that this topic is no more agreeable than the implication that he pimps for Big Agro.

"So you are no longer among the one percent of scientist deniers."

"As of several years ago I felt that claims of man-made global warming were not supported by data. I've modified my position. I assume you're about to refer me to my controversial op-ed for the *Los Angeles Times.*"

"Yes." Arthur picks up the clipping. "In which you scorned the California government's support for solar and wind solutions. Quote: 'It is both shameful and idiotic to base public policy on a cocktail of iffy science, half-truths, and apocalyptic fear-mongering.' You also wrote that a study warning about species extinction was 'typical alarmist anti-corporate drivel.'"

"I wrote that from the point of view of a biologist not a climatologist. At the time insect populations were not seen as threatened."

"To be clear, Doctor, half a dozen years ago you denied this planet was undergoing climate change and global warming?"

"As I say, my views have, ah, matured."

"You were wrong. Can you admit that?"

"I was wrong. As it turned out."

"Thank you. Last year you appeared on a major U.S. network called Fox News, commenting on a United Nations report that excoriated the major pesticide manufacturers for their, quote, 'systematic denial of harms,' 'aggressive, unethical marketing tactics,' and heavy lobbying of governments, all of which 'have obstructed reforms and paralyzed global pesticide restrictions.' Do you recall how you characterized that report?"

"I may have used some firm language."

"Would you like us to play back your words?"

"I believe I described the UN report as alarmist anti-corporate propaganda from the bloated bureaucracy of a once respected international institution."

"And you're aware that caught the eye of the U.S. president?"

"I believe he tweeted his approval."

Arthur catches several jurors making faces, reflecting Mr. Trump's dismal approval rating in Canada.

"I assume, Dr. Easling, that you are familiar with *PLOS One*, the online journal of the Public Library of Science."

"It's well known, yes. Fairly well respected."

"You're familiar with its recently published study on neonics?"

"I can't say, to be honest . . . they publish thousands of studies."

Arthur hands him a printout. "Just last year. Surely you've read it." Said with a slight tone of astonishment.

"Well, my schedule has been hectic."

"Understandable, with all your appearances in public and on the media. Here's the abstract on the first page, you can read along with me. It says that since neonics became widely used in the mid-2000s, American agriculture has become forty-eight times more toxic to insect life. That's because neonics don't break down like other insecticides; they persist in the environment for years."

"Was this peer-reviewed?"

"It was."

"I'm afraid I can't comment without further study."

"But you wouldn't categorize it as typical alarmist anti-corporate drivel?"

"I suppose . . . No."

"Okay, maybe you can comment on the recent UN warning that unless we clean up our act insects will be extinct within a hundred years. Do you regard that as alarmist anti-corporate propaganda?"

"I regard that as an extreme view."

"You've been wrong before though, haven't you?"

Easling's struggle to respond is manifest, his face screwing into one massive frown. But it's four thirty, so Arthur will not get to hear his answer. His flight to Missouri leaves at nine a.m., so he's through with Easling, but Nancy will want to take a few more shots at him.

Donahue recites the mantra about not discussing the evidence, then bolts as if her bladder is on fire.

Easling straightens tie and jacket, reassembling himself, knowing he will have to survive the gauntlet of press outside. He catches Ariana Van Doorn's eye, and mimes getting his throat cut. Arthur finds that bravely non-egoistic for a change.

"I render him unto you, my dear," he tells Nancy. "Have at him."

"Nothing more to do but dispose of the remains. Never follow a dog act, they say." She collects the clients, boldly takes Doc's arm, places it around her waist. The alleged hypochondriac offers no resistance.

Rivie Levitsky turns on her way out, blows Arthur a kiss, and flashes five fingers. Five out of five. He knows she's exaggerating, but he held his own battling on the enemy's turf.

Now approaches Azra Khan, whose proposal for a quiet tête-à-tête has morphed into an offer for early dinner at his favourite restaurant before he visits his dying mother.

3

Khan barely seems aware of the fawning going on about him, the maître d' effusively escorting them to the best table, the servers scampering about them like puppies. In the fashion of a kindly prince, Khan asks after their health and their families. He can speak a passable Afghan Persian.

Arthur now understands why this restaurant, the Kabul, is his favourite. Not that the food is bad — the curried lamb is quite tasty.

Azra doesn't come quickly to the reason for this meeting but Arthur suspects he is angling for a deal, maybe on sentence, two or three years maximum. There's little chance his prideful crew of idealists would accept that. Or instruct him to negotiate.

But if it's about a deal, why isn't Khan bringing Nancy in on it? The answer to what he seeks may hide in the fat brown briefcase that sits by his feet.

"I must say, Arthur, you've done a superb job turning the trial into a prosecution of Chemican. It's rather like blaming the assault victim for the crime, isn't it? Then you left Jerod Easling sucking air. Now we must pull out the stops and plug all the holes."

"One of those holes seems to be your prime witness."

"Howie Griffin. He is indeed a hole."

"A clenched one, I gather."

Khan snorts into his tea, alarming the server picking up their plates. "He has a lawyer, as I suppose you know."

"I know Nancy advised him to retain counsel."

"Greta Adelsen, who articled under her five years ago. She has gagged him, but I have to put him on the stand nonetheless. I can have him declared a hostile witness, I suppose, if he claims head office instructed him to dupe some starry-eyed radicals into raiding the Sarnia plant for the insurance. Arthur, that has to rank as the reddest herring in the history of the criminal courts."

A tray of cakes and cheeses arrives. More tea is poured. Azra orders a brandy.

"I'm driving, so just one," he tells Arthur. "But it helps soften the pain."

"It's a difficult time for you, Azra. I'm so sorry. You have other family helping, I hope."

"Brother, sister, my wife. Her own sister has flown in from Lahore."

Khan clears a clogged throat. "Sorry, back to business. Clearly, we have three of your clients — Knutsen, Lucy Wales, Joe Meekes — in possession of stolen documents. Caught in the act of uploading them. The break and entry, however, offers problems—we may not be able to show beyond a reasonable doubt that each and every accused was actually in the plant. Except Wozniak, of course."

So it does appear Khan seeks a plea bargain. The trial and his mother's grave condition have worn him down. Arthur must now play hard to get. Probation, fines: Are they in the realm of possibility?

"Without a cooperating witness in Howie Griffin our case against Ms. Levitsky gets especially wobbly. Their computer nerd seems to have erased every image, every bit and byte she copied from Howie's office-in-home. We can't place her in Sarnia at all. She wasn't among those seen at the gas stop at Hickory Corner. Her footprint in Griffin's discharge means what? So she brought him off in his office. They went to it on the floor, who knows?"

Arthur finds that image most unsavoury. He refuses to imagine his spunky second-floor tenant in lewd coition with the enemy. Her true version is jarring enough.

Khan continues: "She's been coy in her public interviews about whether she drugged him, but that's obvious. She admits engaging with him physically, in the vaguest of terms, but that's more than Howie remembers, even though he woke up in a sea of sperm. You've seen Maguire's paltry interview notes — Howie gave him nothing. Maybe purposefully, maybe because he'd been stupefied by drink and testosterone."

"Do you really have anything on Rivie? She may have looked in Howie's drawers, as it were, but she stole nothing from him but his pride."

"We have her on uttering a forged passport." Khan shrugs. "Okay, small potatoes. You could solve my problem by calling her so I could have a go at her, but why would you?"

"A good question, Azra."

Arthur is in a dilemma over having his clients testify. Yes, they could enhance the necessity defence, give it focus, a personal touch. But they would have to admit they conspired. They would thereby supply the proof Khan seeks, proof beyond a reasonable doubt that they burgled the Chemican plant. As well, Khan's cross-examinations would cause the flimsy structures of Arthur's various red herrings to come crashing down.

Even worse, at least for Nancy's clients, those cross-examinations would yield proof that Ivor Trebiloff and Amy Snider had aided the conspiracy. Nancy has been pressing Arthur not to put the five others on the stand, to stick with the experts only.

"So what do you propose?" Arthur asks.

Khan goes into the brown briefcase, pulls out a thick binder. "Levitsky shot her mouth off all over town justifying her actions. So did a few others, particularly Knutsen."

Arthur has to wear that. It was Selwyn Loo's idea, to enhance the necessity issue, portray the clients as authentic, true to themselves, not cowards hiding behind their constitutional right to silence. The chickens have now come to roost.

The binder is full of clippings, maybe a hundred. From several international dailies and magazines — *New Yorker, Vanity Fair, The Walrus, Toronto Life* — and transcriptions from radio and TV broadcasts, plus a hard drive, presumably with video and audio interviews.

"I'm not comfortable subpoenaing journalists, Arthur. They resent the appearance of not being objective — the Crown is sensitive to that — and it also means extra days of trial. But let me tell you, my friend, I'll be damned if I'm going to crawl from the courtroom like a well-used doormat."

Arthur's bemused look as he tries to picture a crawling doormat seems to set Azra off: "Please don't suffer any misapprehension about my determination to see your clients not just fairly convicted but sentenced in a way that sends a loud message to wannabe do-gooders who arrogantly believe they're above the law. I intend to go flat out to win this goddamn trial."

The serving staff may not have heard Khan's words, but they seem disturbed by the force field he projected. So much for Arthur's notion that a deal was on the agenda.

Khan swallows the last of his brandy, ruefully shakes his head.

"Terribly sorry for the outburst, I'm under a bit of strain. It's an old briefcase, you can keep it." He returns the binder to it.

Arthur sees an upside to Khan's proposal, but keeps that to himself. "No one wants to rankle the media, Azra, and it would be impolite were I to say it's your problem . . ." Arthur raises a finger, announcing he has a thought. "Dare I propose a quid pro quo? Might you be willing to surrender your right to have last go at the jury?"

"The closing addresses?"

"It's not carved in stone that the Crown closes last. In any event the judge will have the last word with the jury, and she won't exactly be cheering our side on."

Khan manages a wry smile. "I think we can live with that."

"Then let's see if we can agree which interviews will be admitted."

"Yes. Yes." He's heartier now. "That's what I was hoping. Nothing in them diminishes your necessity defence. Oh, and you might tell Nancy that her two clients aren't affected. Mr. Trebiloff and Ms. Snider were circumspect about their roles, as well they should have been."

He picks up the bill, waving off Arthur's feeble protests. "Please allow me to drop you off."

Arthur declines, says he enjoys his twice-daily walks.

"I understand you're sheltering Ms. Levitsky in Punky Kiefer's house. Widely respected con artist, that fellow. Nancy did very well to get him two less a day."

"I'd rather it not be widely known we're there."

"Of course. The obnoxious fanatic who targeted Levitsky. I hear the Police Service have a make on him."

"Donald Stumpit, über-lieutenant in the Final Reich. He's on the run, but I worry. It's not in an obsessive's nature to give up, is it?"

By now they are outside, a crisp, bright evening. Khan pauses at the door of his Lexus.

"Sharing quarters with that young woman doesn't make you uncomfortable?"

"Why should it?"

"A bit of a conniver, isn't she? Levitsky and fellow traveller Lucy Wales think it's quite a lark to follow me around during lunch breaks. Up and down the escalator, out in the square."

"Maybe they've taken a fancy to you, Azra."

That is met with a sardonic grunt. Arthur heads off down Ossington with the brown briefcase. *Nothing in these interviews diminishes your necessity defence.* Could they even enhance it? More importantly, could they save the Sarnia Seven from the hazards of the witness stand?

Arthur will pore through the clippings tomorrow, Friday, on his hopscotch flight to Joplin, Missouri, to meet with Judge W.W. Squirely and, hopefully, Charles Arnold Dover.

4
Friday, May 24

After enduring the obstacle course that flying has become — lineups, multiple security checks — Arthur has arrived in the pleasant little city of Joplin in the heartland of the USA. It's early afternoon as his taxi drops him in front of a single-storey building with Doric columns. It looks like a minor Greek temple, or maybe a miniature courthouse.

It's actually the law office of W.W. Squirely, who's known locally as Judge Squirely, though he was voted out of office seventeen years ago. Admirably, he's still practising at ninety-three, though he's likely a souse — he was calling out drunkenly as Nancy spoke to Cherry, his bossy secretary. That was at three in the afternoon.

Cherry has since persuaded the judge, or bullied him, to give audience to Arthur. She seemed confident that Charles Dover will also agree to see him.

A sign inside the door window says the judge is in. An older couple in the waiting room nod and smile at him. There's no receptionist. Various awards and tributes from service clubs festoon a wall. Photos of Squirely presiding in court. This seems a man lost in the past.

A printer chatters from somewhere, and presently a large, shapeless woman emerges from an office with several stapled sheets, and loudly greets him. "I looked you up on Google, Arthur Ramsgate Bo-champ. Famous criminal counsel from up in Canada. Don't tell the judge you're a teetotaller, he won't respect you."

"If it will make him feel better I used to be an infamous drunk."

Cherry calls the couple over to the reception desk, hands them pens. "Sign here, here, and here."

"The judge says this is all right?" says the husband.

"Stanley, he wrote it out, why wouldn't it be all right? You take possession soon as you clear it with the bank." They hurry off.

Arthur asks, "How long have you been working for the judge?"

"Ever since he stopped being one in 2004."

"What is it he can do that you can't?"

"Write his signature, that's about it."

A loud, raspy query from down the hall: "Why are we working on Saturday?"

Cherry shouts back: "Because it's Friday, you dimwit. I'm gonna bring in that lawyer from Canada wants to meet you."

"Would I be guessing right, Cherry, that the judge may be suffering a little dementia?"

"Between you and me, his engine tends to miss a lot."

"Even though it's well lubricated? Fills his tank with premium, I gather."

She smiles, pleased that he can loosen up and banter with her. "You want to catch him before he wets his first whistle, and that's about now, after lunch. He's real good at nodding and smiling when I bring clients in. I do most of the talking."

She goes to a bank of old metal filing cabinets, bends with difficulty, pulls out a folder about six inches thick. "Charlie Dover. This was the judge's first big case after the voters gave him the boot. I was pretty green myself then — my only experience with the law was being his mistress for the previous ten years. Still help the old boy out sometimes. Anyway, I felt real bad about Charlie Dover. He got shafted. Doctors said his condition would go away and it never did. Settled for only two hundred grand, and that's all gone now."

She hefts the file onto the reception desk, then locks the front door and flips the sign so clients will know the judge is out.

"I need you to understand, Mr. Bo-Champ—"

"Please call me Arthur."

"I will, that's real friendly." She sizes him up. "We can get friendlier. You staying the night?"

"Ah, no, I have a flight to catch at eight."

"Charlie will be along at four when he's off work."

"That's fine. What work does he do?"

"Admitting office at the hospital. A desk job — he gets lost easy so he has to stay put. Lives with his twin sister, a radiologist."

The judge roars again: "Operator? Operator? Gaw-damn, get me long-distance!"

Cherry ignores that. "I'm leery to give you this file because of the non-disclosure, which as I read it means Chemican could sue me for double the two hundred thousand."

"Well, Cherry, I'm pretty sure the non-disclosure clause only applies to discussing the amount of the settlement." She has already breached it, but no matter, she means well. "Maybe you can let me have a quick peek just to confirm that."

A louder roar: "Where'd you hide my Jack?" From the office, scowling and brandishing a cane, steps a stooped old fellow with a bloom of snow-white whiskers.

Cherry yells: "You go set your scrawny ass back down and I'll get you your fucking Jack. We got a distinguished visitor here to talk about Charlie Dover's case."

Cherry shepherds him away, pausing to reach behind a bookshelf for a bottle of Jack Daniel's.

The Dover-Chemican file is conveniently open to the settlement deed, and Arthur can't avoid taking his quick peek. The $200,000 settlement and the $400,000 disclosure penalty are stated in clear language but there's no bar against discussing the claim in general. As well, the standard exception applies: "Subject to a ruling of a court of competent jurisdiction."

Cherry returns, retrieves the file, beckons Arthur to follow. "Counsel may now approach the bench."

Arthur takes a deep breath and goes in to meet the judge, who roosts on a high-back swivel chair behind a massive oak desk bearing several trophies, a gavel, and a phone off the hook.

Squirely rises and raises a full whiskey glass in greeting. "I am honoured, Mr. Beauregard. Sit, sit, we don't stand on ceremony here. A little tipple before we call proceedings to order?"

"There was a time, Your Honour, when I—"

Cherry nudges him into silence, seats him, pours him a short one. Arthur pretends, dutifully, to sip, his nostrils filling with the delicious, nagging aroma, then with shaking hand sets his glass on a window ledge.

Cherry takes over, briefing the judge as to why the illustrious Mr. Bo-Champ has come to pay his respects, explaining he's here to help poor Charlie Dover out of the goodness of his heart, and is suing the crooks running the Chemican corporation, and believes the settlement is null and void.

By the time she peters out, the judge is snoring.

Cherry retrieves Arthur's glass of whiskey and disappears, leaving him alone with the Charlie Dover file.

It was opened in February of 2004. An initial interview with him discloses that he and his twin sister, Tammy, were raised in a farming area near Joplin, where their dad is a veterinarian. Charlie considered himself lucky that he was among the 103 chosen for Chemican's testing program. Agrochemicals were widely used in rural Missouri and he had no fear of them. The $3,000 stipend was an impelling enticement for a nineteen-year-old sophomore working on a Bachelor of Science degree.

In September of 2003, he was administered a three-millilitre dose of ziegladoxin in a glass of apple juice, following which he felt a slight, transitory dizziness that the testers shrugged off as an anomaly — no one else among the 103 had shown adverse symptoms.

On a second go-round, during the Christmas break, Dover downed a juice containing eight point five millilitres of the neonic. A physical examination followed the next day, which he passed handily. Blood and urine tests showed no abnormalities. But a day later he began enduring not just dizziness but acute spatial disorientation. A physician attached to Chemican's research group prescribed a tranquilizer and told him to go home and rest. It was beyond any possibility, she said, that the dose of neonicotinoid was related to his condition.

Arthur is suffering a condition himself all of a sudden, the kind of tingling a lawyer gets when he is looking at a multi-million-dollar action in damages. Yet this was settled for $200,000.

Charlie Dover's difficulties continued unabated through the next several weeks, during which he was examined by his family doctor, then taken to see a neurologist, who wanted tests, and more tests, the bills mounting up while Chemican denied access to their medical records.

Enter W.W. Squirely, retained by the Dover family to seek redress for their son. A flurry of correspondence ensued, resulting in Chemican kindly offering to retain "independent specialists" — their quotes — to examine Charlie.

Bulking up the file is a battery of reports from these specialists — three neurologists, an internist, an allergist, a psychiatrist, all absolving Chemican, most expressing confidence that Charlie would recover, or, as one put it, "grow out of it."

§

The judge has an apartment back of his office, and that's where Cherry is making him dinner — Arthur hears a sizzle of frying through his open window. Despite all her down-putting of the senile judge, she must be devoted to him: she has created a credible façade behind which he can enjoy the pretence he's doing something more than knocking back the Jack.

Both Charlie Dover and his twin sister, Dr. Tammy Dover, seemed relieved when the judge left. The reason for that, it turned out, was they did not have kind things to say about his skills as a lawyer and negotiator.

In 2003, both siblings were taking courses at Missouri Southern to prepare them for medical school, though only Tammy got there, a radiologist now, at the still-young age of thirty-six. Squirely was referred to them by parents and friends of parents: he was respected, well known for his twenty years as a judge.

"He got bombarded," said Tammy, "by bullshit from the quacks Chemican hired. He actually believed their prognoses. Believed Charlie's symptoms would vanish with time. One of them claimed he had a pre-existing condition, another suggested substance abuse. The shrink said it was a mental disorder — like he was compulsive about bumping into walls? This case was way above the judge's pay grade, he should have referred it on."

That was her opening salvo. She was calmer during the next two hours, filling in gaps as her brother responded to Arthur's gentle grilling.

Despite his disability, Charlie is smart and alert and as well spoken as his sister, though more subdued. His blue eyes rove a lot, as if trying to judge distances and directions. He's a little hefty because of lack of exercise, while Tammy is slender with the weary look of one who worries excessively.

Both have followed the Toronto trial in the media and online — local coverage has been extensive.

"You've had interview requests?" Arthur asks.

"Maybe," says Charlie. "I don't answer my phone because I can never find it. I don't open the door, because I can't find it either."

Whenever they go out, Tammy takes·his arm. She or her husband drives him to and from work. He has a suite in their house full of stuffed furniture. In case of emergencies, his address is on a wristband with Tammy's cell number.

"It's best if you continue to keep the press at distance until we get you to Toronto."

"No problem," Charlie says. "When do you want me?"

Arthur calculates. Two more days of Crown evidence, then the defence begins. "Late in the week, maybe Thursday." He looks at Tammy.

She says, "We'll find the time."

Arthur stuffs the Dover file into the brown briefcase with Khan's binder of clippings. It's six thirty; he has a plane to catch.

5

On landing at Pearson International, a chirrupy, amplified voice reminds Arthur he may now use his cell phone, whereupon he realizes it was on airplane mode all day.

He finds two texts from Margaret: one four hours ago letting him know she's arriving in Toronto tonight, not the morning. *Surprise! Surprise!* A smiley face, a heart. The second message, sent from the Ottawa airport nearly two hours ago, urges him to turn on his phone. A voice mail offers similar advice. Rivie clocked in twenty minutes ago with another voice mail: "Hey, the leader of the Green Party is here. Stop being offline, and puh-*lease* don't still be in Missouri."

It's from the house phone. Jostling for position in the jammed aisle, clutching his briefcase with its precious goods, Arthur makes a couple of failed stabs at returning the call before he finally connects.

Rivie doesn't bother with a hello. "Margaret says your phone was probably in airplane mode all day. Tell me that's not true."

Arthur pleads guilty. He'll be there within the hour, hopes they'll wait up.

Margaret comes on, reminds him about his penchant for breaking dates with her, but in a lighthearted way. Arthur welcomes her to Chez Punky Kiefer and asks what she and Rivie have been doing.

"I'm regaling her about your absentmindedness, darling, over a lovely Spanish rosé."

Her jolly mood is fortified by good news from Garibaldi, where the results of the recall petition have just been certified. "It was signed by two-thirds of our residents, my love. Zoller and Shewfelt have been formally turfed and the by-election is set for the last Saturday in June."

By now, Arthur has made it to the arrivals lounge and can breathe again.

"The bad news," says Margaret, "is those two jerks are going to run again."

"And who will be on our team?"

"Zoë Noggins and your favourite female predator."

That was spoken with a cynical lightness, but Arthur grimaces nonetheless.

6

Saturday, May 25

Arthur sleeps in till almost eleven, blinking awake to the sound of female mirth and the smell of fresh-brewed coffee. Last night, after he went to bed — feeling like an outsider, Mr. Staid-and-Boring — Margaret and Rivie carried on in their merry way, to the smell of fresh-smoked cannabis.

He woke up when she finally slid in beside him at three a.m., and he wanted her, but pretended to sleep, fearing a rebuff, however gentle. There is always tomorrow, he told himself, and stayed awake for a long while before drifting off to dreams of Blunder Bay and a wolfhound named Ulysses.

He gets the sense, as he pauses at his washroom door, that Margaret and Rivie are sharing intimacies or bawdy anecdotes. They're getting along far too well, he decides. In a rash moment of weakness, of letting go, he'd told Rivie too many details about the episode with Taba, details not shared with Margaret. Rivie knows about Taba's offer to fellate him, and how she came within a hair of doing so.

To her credit, Rivie didn't blame him for leading Taba on. She couldn't understand why he carried such a weight of guilt, given "your local erotic potter" was the aggressor and he'd found the will to resist.

She also chided him for not being very good at lying to his wife. Arthur wonders: Is it that apparent? He has learned it's very hard to lie to someone you love. A dilemma — do you hurt her more by the truth or by leaving her in disbelief or doubt?

The chumminess between Margaret and Rivie, their sudden bonding, astonishes him. Is this the daughter that his childless wife has secretly longed for? With whom long-held secrets are shared? He doesn't want Rivie playing the role of hippie therapist. *If he takes a little break from the traditional scene, so what? Cool. Equal rights for women too.*

Still, Rivie is a refreshing diversion for the Green Party leader, a break from the plotting, glad-handing politicians she must deal with daily.

As he shaves he hears them planning their day, a photo exhibit, lunch, a Green Party drop-in hosted by a celebrity whom Arthur has never heard of. All of which allays the guilt of being unable to entertain Margaret, though he must at least take her out for dinner. But the afternoon will be spent with Nancy Faulk in her boardroom, going over the Charlie Dover file and Khan's binder of interviews.

Yesterday, Nancy was on her own in 6-1 court, pitching relief against Dr. Jerod Easling, as Rivie put it, and keeping him off the scoreboard. Also heard from were a bureaucrat from Canada's Pest Management Regulatory Agency and an analyst from the U.S. Environmental Protection Agency, both of whom denied hanky-panky over the Vigor-Gro approval process. A juror in the back row nodded off during this.

Arthur can't find his slippers but decides to make his grand entry into the kitchen anyway — then — pauses on hearing Rivie: "You have to take them by the hand."

As he steps inside, Margaret is mixing eggs, her back to him. "I *know*. He fumbles around — sometimes he even finds it."

"Here he is now," Rivie says quickly. "We were talking about how men always lose things."

They have zeroed in on Arthur's primary weakness, his early indicator of senile dementia. He loses stuff: shoes, keys, remotes, toiletries. But why are they so focussed on him? — they seem to take great pleasure talking about his foibles.

Rivie pours him a coffee. "Milk, no sugar, right?"

"Thank you. It's grand to see the two of you so perky." He looks about. "Has anyone seen my slippers?"

"They're on your feet," Margaret says.

Arthur looks down at his slippered feet and blushes. He *is* losing it.

§

Today celebrates Selwyn Loo's return to Toronto, on a week's furlough from the environmental wars in the West Coast courts. There is much catching up in Nancy's boardroom: about Rivie's close scrape with the Nazi — who has disappeared from his usual haunts, according to Constable Louella Baker — and the trial's many twists and turns, and the evolving defence of necessity.

Selwyn expresses disgust at Chemican's tactics to force a cheap settlement of Charlie Dover's claim: the ruthless battering of a country lawyer and, as Dr. Tammy Dover unsubtly put it, the barrage of bullshit from hired quacks.

Arthur knows only one other victim: hapless security guard Barney Wilson, who gulped down mouthfuls of Vigor-Gro while splashing around on the factory floor. It's hard to believe that of the 103 student volunteers only one fell victim to this condition. Presumably, the Vigor-Gro triggered some kind of allergic or immune disorder which affects only a small population.

Selwyn asks, "How are you two getting along with the judge?"

"She's been laying off me," Nancy says. "Not sure why. She still thinks I'm the spawn of Satan."

"Fear of the Court of Appeal," Selwyn suggests.

"She's being far too pleasant," says Arthur. "Prodded the Crown to drop the manslaughter. And now with Azra lying in the weeds, I have no foe to joust with. That's putting me off my game."

"Madam Justice Donahue has suddenly got a hard-on for Arthur. Ever since she flashed the photo that nearly paid off Jake Maguire. She fucked up, but Arthur took the hit."

After they unscramble that for Selwyn, he passes judgment: "She feels Arthur did an honourable thing in shielding two senior officers from scandal. Maybe that will pay off."

Arthur shakes his head. "She will not leave necessity with the jury. Despite Charlie Dover. Despite the health risks posed by ziegladoxin. As a strict matter of law, I fear she would be right."

Selwyn nods. "The common law has made us slaves to precedent. What are you picking up from the jury?"

Nancy says: "Foreman is a low-level architect, over-serious, rarely smiles, so he makes me nervous. The others are even harder to read, except for two. Juror Ten, Mabel Sims, a tax auditor, wants to nail these subversive hippie freaks to the cross. Juror Twelve, Abbie Lee-Yeung, could deadlock the jury if she doesn't buckle under pressure."

Arthur sighs. "So realistically our hopes depend on the pluck and tenacity of a single teenage student."

"So that's Plan B," says Selwyn. "Hang the jury."

Nancy spells it out. "Plan B-E-E."

§

They spend the remaining day winnowing Khan's list of media interviews, choosing those that best advance the necessity defence. This is something new for Arthur. He can't recall a single trial in which he didn't fight like a tiger to keep a client's inculpatory statements from the jury.

One interview stands out: an hour of video on TVO featuring Doc Knutsen, his points made dramatically and with clarity. A paean to pollinating insects, a bleak scenario of human life without them, the urgent need, as he put it, "to wake the world with a dynamic act of civil disobedience."

"No reason now to put Knutsen on the stand," says Nancy.

"An excellent reason to keep him off it," says Arthur. Khan would have a fine day needling Knutsen for his lack of humility, his occasional spurt of arrogance. And his bitterness. Yet he hungers for his day in court. "He will not be pleased at being sidelined."

"I'll handle him," Nancy says, confidently. "How about we don't call any of our guys, period?"

Arthur still wants to think about it.

A while later, Selwyn alerts them to another useful interview. Removing a set of headphones, he replays a piece on college radio: Rivie and Lucy blithely recounting Rockin' Ray's heroic, five-hundred-microgram acid trip.

"That's his defence, isn't it?" says Selwyn.

Arthur agrees. Intoxication, lack of awareness, of conscious intent. Armed with this, and what is already before the jury — the toxicologist's confident opinion that five hundred micrograms would bring on hallucinations — the loose cannon of the Extinction Rebellion need not be exposed to the perils of cross-examination.

That decides it for Arthur: there's little advantage and much risk in calling any of the Sarnia Seven to the stand. When he affirms that to Nancy, she hugs him. "You've had a rough go of it, partner. Why don't you go home and fuck your wife?"

Arthur's plans to take Margaret out for a romantic dinner are scotched when he arrives home to find Rivie has just returned from a fish market. She claims she's a master trout chef.

He and Margaret are ordered to "chill" while she heads off to the backyard barbecue with a tray with trout, berries, and pine nuts. Margaret was also surprised by the young rebel's insistence on treating them to dinner. She too had expected an evening out in a starred restaurant, and looks almost jarringly attractive: long, black slit skirt, freshly reddened lips, and she's done something to highlight the silver of her eyes.

She's in a frisky mood. Parliament is in short recess and she's off tomorrow for the West Coast to do stuff she enjoys: town halls, mingling with real people. She goes on and on about retiring, but remains a prisoner of Ottawa out of loyalty to those who sent her there.

Having retreated to the TV room to watch the six o'clock news, she and Arthur are on a fat sofa that he'd stored here. She has poured herself a flute of Prosecco and is not exactly nursing it. She nudges him. "Hello, stranger. Got any plans for the night?"

Made shy by her boldness, he can't quite formulate a response except to move closer. She extends a bared leg across his lap and pops a teasing kiss on his cheek —but further progress is interrupted by Rivie's entrance with a tray of crackers and cheese bites. Arthur quickly removes his hand from his wife's thigh, then feels foolish when Rivie grins. Still trapped in the puritanical web woven by his severe, loveless parents.

§

Rivie had exaggerated her talent with wilderness cuisine — the fillets were overdone and the nuts unevenly roasted — but Arthur praised her creation as fit for the gods.

She credits her erstwhile lover, Chase D'Amato, for the recipe, then glumly muses about him. "Last heard from? Costa Rica, maybe, if I can believe the stamp on his letter. Hanging with tapirs and red-rumped antshrikes. Working at what? Jungle treks, zip-line tours . . ."

Her voice fades into silence. Into memories, Arthur supposes.

Margaret, tipsy by now, says cheerily, "Hey, we're definitely going to the ballet tomorrow. I got the tickets." To Arthur: "*Firebird*. A matinee."

"I'm envious," says Arthur, who must spend Sunday with Khan's clippings and recordings.

Rivie tries to look pleased, but Arthur senses wistfulness. Lonely, unpartnered, missing her daredevil lover, only too aware that her housemates will be coupling tonight in the bedroom below hers . . .

§

Though Arthur hasn't found his own release, Margaret lies sprawled on the rumpled sheets, catching her breath, her legs splayed, her head nestling on Arthur's shoulder. "That was perfect, darling."

Arthur doesn't quite know how he pulled it off. The feat had mostly been performed by hand, with instructions. But now he thinks back to an overheard exchange. Rivie: *You have to take them by the hand.* Margaret: *He fumbles around — sometimes he even finds it.* Was Rivie giving tips to his mate? Is there no limit to the intimacies women share?

Margaret rolls over, begins a descent beneath the sheets. "I can do better than that cow." Her head disappears.

CHAPTER 22 » MAGUIRE

1

Tuesday, May 28

Tim Hortons coffee sucks. Second Cup is inconsistent and tends toward bland. Starbucks is often bitter but gets a passing grade because of freshness due to the huge turnover. Only a handful of small roasters get A's. What Maguire is drinking right now, according to his exclusive rating system, gets zero.

They're in their hotel restaurant, him and Gaylene Roberts, post-breakfast, killing time before court. Gaylene listens with a patronizing smile, humouring him over what she calls his coffee fanaticism.

Maguire carries on: "The problem with all these chains — Starbucks is the worst example — is all the folderol, all the fancy brews. Soy latte, caramel macciato, chocolate mocha, and they've got something called an iced lavender latte. Whatever happened to coffee that looks like coffee and, damn it, *tastes like* coffee?"

That is loud enough to fetch a waitress, or server as they now have to be called, who asks if everything's okay. Maguire says his coffee is castrated and he'd appreciate it if she would refill him with some freshly ground and brewed.

"Castrated?" Gaylene asks.

"No balls."

"In addition to being a grump you have an addictive personality. It was nicotine, now it's caffeine."

It was also chocolate bars. Maguire is beating that one, determined not to die twice, the next death permanent, you only get one chance at a life-saving kiss.

Breakfast was oatmeal and half a grapefruit. He's battling starvation. The hospital nutritionist, a health tyrant, would basically have him restricted to carrots and kale. But he's twenty pounds lighter, has been walking every day, and he's back in his old role of being OPP liaison with the Crown Attorney. Gaylene has pretty well got him up to speed, and now she's off the case.

"I'll miss you," he says. "I always enjoy the way you jerk my chain."

"I'll miss your rants. I had to get out of that courtroom, Jake, I was going crazy with paranoia — the seas are rising, the insects are vanishing, the birds and frogs are dying, we've only got two decades to turn it around or we go the way of the dinosaurs."

Maguire tells her that's nuts, but there's no persuading. The major reason she's stressed has to be her marriage.

"We've only got one witness left anyway," she says, "and I can't bear to watch what they're going to do to him."

Howie Griffin, security expert extraordinaire. An OPP patrol spotted him Sunday at his lakeside cottage in Penetanguishene, outside, reading. Wiggie Wiggens and another constable were dispatched up there yesterday to fetch him. They found him outside, in shorts, tinkering with his sixty-horse Merc. They spent some time convincing him resistance was futile and he could choose to be restrained or come along peacefully.

"He started an argument," Wiggie said. "Wanted to talk to his lawyer. He had to be cuffed right there in his shorts, shirt, and sandals. We didn't have a warrant to toss the house, or we would have."

"Very righteous of you."

"It was full of books. Nature. History. Politics. You wouldn't believe."

Anyway, Griffin spent last night in the cooler.

"The dork was offered a chance," Maguire says. "Could have been a good citizen and assisted us with our investigation." As usual, a lawyer is jamming the gears of justice. Greta Jane Adelsen has muzzled Howie.

"So, when are you heading out?" he asks.

"This afternoon. I've been given a nice little homicide in Elgin County."

"I expected that."

She looks surprised. "How? The body was just found yesterday. The Chief Super called me personally."

"Well, you want to know, I kind of bonded with Lafriere over my heart attack. Told him you earned yourself a juicy murder. You've got a love triangle, the victim stabbed forty times in a frenzy. Crime scene is twenty minutes south of London, so you can actually work out of my old office. I'll help you on the staffing, and it'll take your mind off things, a holiday in the country."

She smiles again, differently, warmly. "You are too much, Jake."

"And you don't need a hotel. Sonia would want you in the suite."

They've bonded too, Sonia and Gaylene. That grew over the last two weekends, when Gaylene stopped over on her trips to Sarnia. But it began early in the trial when the two women cracked each other up over that fake news blow job. Over that, he had a heart attack.

"And you'd be closer to your family. And who knows, they still haven't replaced me in the London regional HQ."

Maybe a career move to London would win back her husband,

who hates Toronto. It's an irony that he and Sonia had always wanted kids but are happily married. Gaylene and her partner have a boy and a girl, and their marriage is in meltdown.

"That close brush has made you kinder and gentler, Jake. I'm finding you . . . it's like the bees, it's disorienting."

Maguire can't finish his coffee refill. "No balls," he repeats. As they rise to leave, Gaylene gives him a big goodbye hug.

2

It's a bright spring day, and Maguire enjoys a slow stroll from his hotel to the courthouse — he's not going to overdo it on his first week of full parole from what his doctor jokingly called house arrest. This will be his second day back, and he's finally resuming his role as unseen courtroom fixture. On Monday, he had to brave the press and, worse, speeches from counsel and judge: quips about The Kiss and his return from the afterlife.

He'd missed a lot of testimony, nine days, nine rounds of bruising battle, only to return to a long, boring morning of listening to the perps' media interviews. Counsel wanted selected portions read aloud, so Khan gave speaking roles to his machine-like junior and his infatuated student, who droned on and on. Some of the magazine pieces, like the *New Yorker* profile of Helmut Knutsen, were too long, so were just filed as exhibits.

The afternoon was slightly more entertaining, tapes of radio and TV interviews and a couple of long podcasts, one of them very loud and lefty, a Q and A in which Levitsky, Wales, and Wozniak detailed the whole conspiracy, literally bragging about it — except for the bedroom scene with Howie Griffin, Levitsky was coy about what happened there. The total effect, though, as far as Maguire could see, was they hanged themselves with their own tongues.

Only Trebiloff and Snider, owners of Ivor Antiques Ltd., kept their yaps shut, so their role isn't quite so obvious. The unindicted co-conspirator, Chase D'Amato, was never discussed with the media, obviously to protect the ass of this shadowy, forgotten eighth perp.

What Maguire missed out on while recuperating was Arthur Beauchamp's exercise in creative fiction, portraying Howie as a coke-snorting mastermind who used the Sarnia Seven as puppets to get the plant shuttered for the insurance. Something like that. Like Howie suckered Rivie, not the other way around. The legal mind at work.

The defence has a new gambit — they're bringing up an American who claims he got crippled from drinking Vigor-Gro seventeen years ago. Another from Beauchamp's endless supply of red herrings. He wants to call a specialist too, to back him up.

As Maguire steps out of the elevator, he realizes he dallied too long — 6-1 is already filling up, it's close to ten. He casts about for a tall, buff, brown-haired prime witness, then remembers that Howie, who was in the city jail on a bench warrant, will be in the witness room, under escort by super-sleuth Wiggie Wiggens.

But that room is empty, no Howie, no Wiggie. Maguire's mood is suddenly grim as he hurries down an empty corridor and gets on the blower. He can't reach witless Wiggie and leaves a forceful voice mail, then radios an alert to OPP dispatch. "Get me Constable Wiggens!" He waits, gets nothing, then he texts.

From down the hall a court officer hollers: "Inspector Maguire, Court 6-1. Inspector Maguire, Court 6-1."

On arrival there, Maguire feels a tension, jurors uncomfortable, reporters' pens held stiffly over notepads, the prosecution team trying to look small. But Judge Donahue is smiling, a rare event. "No rush," she says, urging him forward. Khan and the robot make space for him.

"Inspector Maguire, I address you in your role as manager of the comings and goings of witnesses. I am not blaming you for this. The last thing I want, given your recent illness, is to cause you stress. No doubt a blunder has occurred at a non-supervisory level."

The phony sweetness grates on Maguire. "Thank you." That's all he can think to say.

"Counsel for Her Majesty says his final witness, Mr. Griffin, is nowhere to be found. Indications point to him being not only a reluctant witness but an uncooperative one. I thought you might help us out."

Maguire glances at his screen — Wiggie has sent a text.

"Don't let me tear you away from your tweets, Inspector." Still smiling.

"It's a message, Your Ladyship. Mr. Griffin was released from the lockup just after nine, he was in the company of his lawyer." Maguire is relieved that this is somebody else's fuckup.

"We will recess for fifteen minutes."

§

It takes Maguire ten of those minutes to catch up to Wiggie in the Eaton Centre mall, only two blocks away. Greta Adelsen finally answered her phone. She's in a menswear store, Moore's.

That's where Maguire also finds Wiggie, looking exasperated. He's getting an earful from Adelsen, a well-structured redhead who'd be cute if she weren't so pissed off. She's holding a greasy pair of men's work shorts. Griffin is in a changing room, trying on a suit.

The picture couldn't be clearer. Because Wiggie — who's too honest — didn't have a search warrant for the cottage he couldn't lawfully retrieve the arrestee's city clothing. Maguire would have done it.

3

Judge Donahue's fifteen-minute recess lasts half an hour, but she's okay about Maguire's explanation. A snafu at the lockup, nobody's fault really. The judge thanks Maguire for his service, gets sucky again about his return to health and how even in retirement he makes the Ontario Provincial Police proud.

She doesn't invite the jury in for this backslapping event. Nor does she admonish Griffin or his lawyer or make the point that Howie could've shown up on time in shorts and sandals — she probably doesn't want the press to think she's the time-obsessed crank she is.

Adelsen and Griffin are in the front row, she in her robes, he in a dark suit — nice classic cut but it hangs like drapes over what used to be a gut. White shirt, no tie. More grey in his hair than when last seen. His face more lined, but handsomely, and he's getting looks from the ladies.

Those don't include Rivie Levitsky, who studiously ignores him and whose expression seems contorted and stiff, as if she's struggling not to show her feelings. Howie doesn't look at her either, stares straight ahead.

His little redhead lawyer introduces herself for the record, advises she's concerned about "preposterous allegations" that her client was criminally involved in this case. That doesn't seem to bother Arthur Beauchamp, with his tranquil smile.

"My client is under subpoena and is prepared to testify," Adelsen says. "He wants to get this over with."

The judge thanks her and calls the jury in. As Howell J. Griffin takes the stand and swears to tell the truth he seems oddly relaxed. Serene may be the word, as if he's come to terms with stuff.

Azra Khan leads him through his career, from his master's in computing at York, being hired by Chemican out of college, a spell in their Mexican operation, a spell in Kansas City, then to Toronto, as head of Canadian security and the go-to guy for special missions in Latin America.

"Anything to add to that?"

"Unemployed. Divorced, living alone in a short-term flat. Running, reading, thinking, trying to stay sane." That odd, rambling footnote about a sad life causes murmurs of sympathy from the gallery. He won't look at any of the Seven, though he checks out the jury, judge, and counsel.

In a calm, composed way he explains he ran a cyber-security department for Chemican as well as being in charge of guarding offices, plants, delivery systems, you name it.

Khan asks, "Can we put on record that you hired Irwin Fleiger, Barney Wilson, and Archie Gooch?" The gang that couldn't guard straight.

"I recommended, Personnel hired."

Khan then barrels right ahead into the love story, starting with how Griffin and two guys from the cyber unit met for a cold drink after work on a hot August Friday in the Beaver's Tail. And did he meet someone there? He did. And how did she identify herself? As Becky McLean. And do you see her in this courtroom?

So finally he looks at her, and she at him, unhappily, probably feeling guilty at wrecking his life. Howie gets something in his throat, clears it. "Second from the left. Light brown hair, dark brown eyes."

You can see the possibility of an emotional scene here, maybe over her betrayal, how she used him and tossed him aside. Khan is aware of this because he moves Howie along briskly, skipping over how they bantered and shared their stories, reducing this first encounter to buying her dinner, inviting her up, showing her around, making plans, not having sex, sending her off in a cab.

He breezes through their subsequent dates — the Jays-Rangers game, the romantic strolls, the Georgian Bay boat ride and picnic. Given Howie's refusal to be prepped, Khan is doing a pretty good job. But soon he'll get into the murky stuff where Howie's memory drive is corrupted.

"During the final week of August, you were in Brazil?"

"Yes."

"Tell us about that."

"There was a protest. Millions of honeybees were disappearing and small farmers and beekeepers were going broke, so they block-aded Chemican's plant in Sao Paolo. I was sent down to try to fix things. And I guess I did. I fixed things, all right."

"We don't need to hear about your work down there." Khan's tone was brusque. "When did you return to Canada?"

"I left late Friday, August thirty-one, arrived the next afternoon, maybe slept for two of my twenty-four hours en route."

"All right, take it from there. Tell us what happened on September first."

"I had invited Becky, as I called her then, for dinner at Paramour. I had time to get home and shower and change, check messages, unpack, put away my electronics, laptop, some paperwork. Had a triple shot of espresso and drove to a drugstore in North York where Becky said she worked, and she was waiting for me outside. And we went off to dinner."

"How much alcohol was consumed during this dinner?" As if Khan doesn't know — Operation Vig scooped a copy of Griffin's bill from the restaurant. The total could have fed an Ethiopian family for six months.

"I can't remember. A lot, on my part. Becky just had a few glasses of champagne."

Khan has him identify Paramour's bill, which lists the champagne, a bottle of red wine, two martinis, three Baileys. There are gasps from the crowd as Howie admits driving home after swilling enough juice to float a yacht. It's another reason for Maguire to dislike Griffin, his blood alcohol had to be at least point eighteen, probably higher, he risked lives.

The bill goes in as an exhibit, and the scene moves to Howie's apartment. Poured himself yet another drink, a cognac. Maybe two or three — here is where his memory fails.

"Did you or she take any drugs that evening?"

"Not that I remember."

"Tell us how the evening progressed."

"I assume I went into my war room, as I called it. To get a notebook computer. I must have offered it to her."

"And did she take it?"

"It was still there the next day, on the dining table with her note." *Sweet dreams. Had a lovely time.* Exhibit 37.

"Was Ms. Levitsky in the war room with you that night?"

"I couldn't swear to that."

"Do you remember removing that notebook computer from the office?"

"Not really."

"Do you remember locking your office door?"

"It shuts and locks automatically."

"Did you leave your keys in that door?"

"I assume not."

"Why?"

"Because they were in my pants pocket the next morning."

"Okay, where did you find your pants?"

"On a chair by the bed."

"Do you remember placing them there?"

"I don't even remember taking them off."

Maguire hears chuckling behind him. He doesn't think Howie's faking his blackout. He thinks he was doped up. With rohypnol, for instance, the date rape drug, it causes brain blanks.

"Was anything stolen or removed from the apartment?"

"Nothing, no. Nada."

"What's the last thing you remember?"

"We kissed."

4

Khan putters about with several follow-ups about what he and Levitsky did next, what words were spoken, whether they had sex, and draws blanks — he's stuck with that lone, last memory of a kiss.

On rising from his sticky bed Sunday morning, Howie couldn't reconstruct the evening, and at around eleven he phoned Becky and apologized, though for exactly what he wasn't sure. Then came an exchange about her ill mom and a date for the Red Sox game the next Sunday.

Azra seems about ready to drop it there, then remembers a leftover. "Mr. Griffin, a theory has been bruited about in this room that you somehow conspired with various and sundry individuals to plan the September tenth burglary in Sarnia. What do you say to that?"

"I didn't. But I might have, had I known then what I know now."

It's definite — Howie has gone over to the enemy. Maguire sends a telepathic message to Khan: don't press the issue, it's a setup.

Khan's on top of it. "Your witness." He makes a sweeping gesture to the defence.

That's sardonic, but makes for a dramatic moment to launch Arthur Beauchamp to his feet. "I'm intrigued by your afterthought — 'had I known then what I know now.' Are we to understand, Mr. Griffin, that you are abandoning views previously held?"

"In a fundamental way. Significantly so."

Where does the dork suddenly come up with big words? Something has changed, all right. He's composed up there, clear-eyed. It's like he's achieved some kind of Buddhist clarity.

"I had a jolt back in September when this happened — the midnight raid in Sarnia, then the arrests. My getting the boot. I was embarrassed, but mainly confused, very confused. I couldn't understand why she . . . why they would do a thing so risky, without profit. And I guess somewhere along the line, thinking about them, thinking about me, ashamed about my role as a corporate enforcer . . . anyway, somewhere down the line I had a catharsis, an awakening. Enlightenment."

The judge lets him carry on like this. Maybe she can't figure out what's going on, or she's stunned, like a lot of people in here. Like Maguire.

"I've had a lot of downtime since then to do a lot of reading. Books. Online. I discovered I've been an idiot. I no longer want to be on the wrong side of history. If there is to be any history."

494

Howie carries on like this, unchecked. It's like he was blind and now he sees. He's with the bees, he's with the planet — all life is threatened by a climate change crisis caused by capitalist greed. "I was spreading this disease on behalf of the world's most corrupt agrochemical corp—"

This is finally too much for Judge Donahue. "Halt!" she says, glaring at Beauchamp, as if blaming him, though he only asked one question and let Howie preach. "The witness will kindly save his message of salvation for another time and another place. This is a court of law."

Beauchamp gives her an astonished look. "If it please the court, the credibility of this witness is an issue in this trial. The jury will want to know whether his stark change of mind is a belief honestly held."

Donahue can't bring herself to admit he's right. Her nose does its rabbit wiggle for a few seconds as she checks the wall clock — twenty minutes before the noon break. "Time is waning, Mr. Beauchamp. Please proceed."

"Mr. Griffin, you and I have never met, is that so?"

"This is the first time, yes, sir."

"And we have never talked to each other, or communicated with each other, directly or through any third party."

"No, sir. In early March, I did talk briefly with Nancy Faulk. She advised me to hire a lawyer."

"And before appearing here today, to whom have you mentioned your crisis of conscience?"

"My lawyer, Greta Adelsen. My ex-wife, Maxine, we met over drinks." For some reason he seems compelled to add: "In a wine bar. I haven't been consuming much. I don't like to drink alone, and I'm almost always alone."

"Drugs?"

"I was doing too much cocaine, it was my escape. I couldn't live with what I'd become, an accessory to crime—"

Khan is up. "Can we avoid the melodramatics?"

The judge: "You are being asked about cocaine use. Answer the question."

"I stopped dead six months ago."

Beauchamp asks, "When exactly?"

"When Chemican's fraudulent tests were leaked to the media, I realized their science was corrupt, the whole enterprise was corrupt. I felt revolted at what I'd done. And then . . . when I really straightened up was when Becky got pulled in. Rivie, I mean. Rivke."

He staggers his way to the finish line. On Maguire's first encounter with this character, at the Lambton County OPP, he'd been wired, wiggling his snout almost as bad as Justice Donahue. He's obviously clean now, in a weird spiritual way. But despite all his detective smarts Maguire can't tell if Howie is putting it on. Or was he pulling a dork act last September?

He doesn't like to drink alone. That's maybe true, Wiggie didn't see any booze in his lake cottage, or empties. It *was* full of books. Beauchamp asks him about these, the books that aided his reformation. Maguire is vaguely familiar with some of the titles and authors, *This Changes Everything*; *Oil and Honey*, *The End of Nature*; *Silent Spring*; *The Sixth Extinction*. Naomi Klein, Al Gore, James Hansen, Rachel Carson.

As he lists endless others, the judge looks more and more distrustful, wary, sensing trickery. The jury seems puzzled, withholding judgment. Several of the women are looking him over pretty good, though not Abbie Lee-Yeung, who's staring at Levitsky, as if wanting her reaction. But Rivie's head is down and she's writing.

"Let's return to the last week of last August. You were in Sao Paolo. You were assigned to tamp down a protest, or as you put it, to fix things. How did you do that?"

Howie catches the eye of his lawyer. She nods. He says he doesn't wish to incriminate himself. The judge goes through the traditional charade of giving him protection under the Evidence Act, then scowls at him. "Very well, Mr. Griffin, your answers can't be used against you on a criminal charge. Other than perjury."

In a nutshell, Howie tells how he was instructed by Kansas City to reach out "informally" to local decision makers. Chemican ultimately set up Panamanian accounts for three top public servants, plus the state governor and a judge. Nearly two million dollars got funnelled into those accounts.

"Do you have records to prove your superiors knowingly participated in the crime of bribery?"

"Voice recordings and captured WhatsApp texts."

Maguire picks up vibes of discomfort from the two Chemican representatives. Wakeling, their Canadian chief officer, is still here, with Jinks, their head scientist. Dr. Easling is long gone.

When the judge adjourns for lunch, the two Chemican guys bolt out of here, maybe to warm up their shredders and call their lawyers. The press follow them, and you can hear them hollering questions all down the corridor.

The accused, except Levitsky, scrum with their lawyers at the counsel table with volume down but in tense tones. Griffin chats amiably with Miss Pucket, then joins his lawyer in the exit queue. He doesn't look at Levitsky and she doesn't look at him — she's still in the dock, still focussed on her writing pad.

Khan breaks the huddle with his team and joins Maguire. He asks, "Can you keep an eye on Griffin?"

"Why? Maybe it's better he disappears. The loony bin van is outside waiting to take him back."

"He's been gotten to. I don't know how. I want him back here at two o'clock. I'm going to take him off at the neck."

Maguire ponders how he plans to do that as he follows Griffin and Adelsen out the back exit to the lunch wagons around the square. They're not supposed to talk about the case while he's under cross, but that probably doesn't stop them.

He watches in sorrow as they tuck into their thick, meaty takeaways, and unwraps his own lunch, a container of tomato salad, an apple, and two hard-boiled eggs.

The packed house hushes as the big hand creeps toward the top of the clock. Wakeling and Jinks are in their reserved seats, and have managed to squeeze in a stout lawyer. The Sarnia Seven are whispering and analyzing, glancing at Griffin, working on the same brainteaser as Maguire — is this guy for real or is he jacking us around?

Rivie Levitsky continues not to be aware of Howie's existence, but has finally recovered from her trance and is consulting with Lucy Wales, in whispers, but intensely. Wales has the kind of hiccups you get when you gulp a couple of cocktails over a fast lunch. Slowly sipping water isn't working.

. The jury returns, Miss Pucket bellows everyone to order, and Judge Donahue gallops in. Wales hiccups. Howie retakes the stand. Wales hiccups, drinks water. Beauchamp rises.

"Mr. Griffin, I have, perhaps regrettably, insinuated that you helped facilitate the Sarnia attack at the behest of your employer. You deny that."

"That is not on the list of shameful things I've done for them."

"This enlightenment, as you call it, hasn't really come out of the blue, has it? Your role with Chemican has bothered you for some time."

"Increasingly, for the last few years."

Wales's hiccups provide a soft background rhythm.

"You thought of whistleblowing."

"I didn't have the ammunition. Until Brazil."

"How did the protest get resolved?"

"An injunction was restored by the judge we bought. The state government sent the army in. There were arrests. The plant was reopened."

"Having done your business there, you returned to Toronto on Saturday, the first of September, dog-tired but determined to keep your date for dinner. At which you consumed half a bottle of champagne, a bottle of red wine, two double martinis, and three Baileys. I take it that would be more than your usual limit."

Punctuated by Lucy's "Hic," that gets laughter. Miss Pucket cries for order.

"Frankly, I got so drunk that I can't remember driving home. I don't know why I let myself go like that. I was exhausted. I was nervous. I was deeply in love, blindly but deeply, and I was afraid of rejection. I was also sitting on evidence that could implicate my employer in the crime of bribery. A confluence of factors bore down on me, and . . . I guess I just let myself go."

"You were sober enough earlier in the evening to engage with Ms. Levitsky. What did you talk about?"

"I griped about my flights, the delays, the security lines. I'm sure that didn't impress her. I went on about Brazil, a bit of a travelogue. I gave her a gift, a pair of artisan earrings, which I think she felt were bizarre and outré."

Prompting a slight eruption from the prisoners' box, more of a snicker than a snigger. Probably Levitsky, who strains to keep a straight face. Beside her, Lucy tries the water cure again. Then: "Hic."

Beauchamp asks, "What else was discussed?"

"Baseball. My former wife, my divorce. My parental background and what I assumed was hers."

"Did you talk about how you handled the blockade in Sao Paolo?"

He takes a while to compose an answer. "I confessed to her what I did, hiring the lawyers who set up the contacts and the payments. I told her about my thoughts, my doubts, my sense of guilt about the role I played in Brazil. And that I'd played elsewhere over the years, doing Chemican's dirty work. I told her that in doing so I felt corrupted as a human being."

"At your apartment later, after a couple of cognacs, it's likely you were still carrying on about Chemican?"

"Maybe. Probably. I don't know."

"And you brought Ms. Levitsky into your office, your war room, correct?"

"I don't remember but I'm sure I did."

"And at some point you gave her the keys, you gave her complete access to the room."

"I must have done that. I can't see any other possibility."

"Why?"

"Because to get the entry codes to the plant and the lab she had to know the password to the main computer. It was not written down anywhere in my apartment. So I either gave it to Rivie or turned on the computer for her."

"You could have said, 'It's all yours, take what you want.'"

"I might have. Anything was possible that night. I didn't care. I was up to here with my job. I was drunk. I was in love. I would have done anything for her."

Somehow, with that response, Lucy Wales stops hiccupping. But she looks distressed, maybe because her bladder's pretty full.

"How did you react when you learned she'd been stalked and threatened by a self-proclaimed Nazi?"

"As every normal, sane person would react, I imagine. With abhorrence. The guy is still walking around somewhere while these people" — his arm arcs toward the prisoners' box — "are on trial for trying to save the planet from mass starvation."

That's it, Beauchamp sits.

A shout from somewhere near the back: "Right on!"

The judge roars, "Remove that person!"

Rumblings of discontent as a court officer hustles off an old hippie. Then a deathly silence as Khan rises. "I have a few questions in re-examination."

Maguire suspects that behind the cheerful smile, Khan is seething. He probably thinks Howie — a bribemaster, an experienced schemer — was paid off and that this was all rehearsed and Beauchamp pulled a fast one, marginally ethical.

"Mr. Griffin, on Sunday you were so reluctant to testify we had to send two officers all the way to Georgian Bay to pick you up, and here you are today, eager to testify, words pouring forth as you bare your soul to the world. Can you explain this sudden transformation?"

"Mr. Khan, I had hoped against hope that you would not insist on bringing me here. I knew I would have to admit arranging bribes, and I would risk arrest. I have no option now but to simply tell the truth and take my chances."

That kind of boomeranged on Khan, but he doesn't lose his smile. "You're referring to the corrupt payments you engineered in Brazil. But were there others?"

"A lot, I suspect. I know of two others, to officials in Romania and South Africa, but I wasn't directly involved."

"And of course you reported these instances to the authorities."

"No, I didn't."

"You didn't call up the FBI or Interpol, and tell them you felt you were being corrupted as a human being."

Beauchamp, who has been moving ever closer to the edge of his seat, finally ejects from it. "I object. This isn't re-examination, it's sarcasm. My friend knows he can't attack his own witness."

Donahue merely urges Khan, nicely, to "stay within the bounds."

"You told Mr. Beauchamp that when the accused uploaded deceptive Vigor-Gro tests to the media, you suddenly decided their whole enterprise was corrupt. Did this catharsis or enlightenment, as you call it, occur before or after you were fired without severance?"

The long pause doesn't help Howie's case. "My suspicions about Chemican jelled a few days after I was fired, when I read about the faked research in the *Toronto Star*."

"Ah, your suspicions *jelled* after you were fired. And of course you weren't bitter about getting the boot, were you?"

Beauchamp doesn't rise to the bait this time. Maybe he doesn't want the jury to think he's coddling Griffin.

When Howie is slow to answer, Khan presses him: "Two decades of loyal service — for one little slip-up you deserved a lot more than a pink slip. Is that how you felt?"

"Frankly, I felt a huge sense of freedom."

"You were quite content not to have got compensation?"

"I was more unhappy with the way I was summarily let go. By a phone call from Mr. Wakefield's secretary." A glance at his former boss, who whispers something to his mouthpiece.

"And given you were determined to whistleblow on your employer, did you renounce a claim for compensation? Some might think that would be the high-minded approach."

Beauchamp can't take it any longer. "This doesn't arise from my cross-examination. My friend's rights to re-examine are narrowly restricted, and he knows it — they don't allow for bullying and rhetoric."

"That sounds rather odd coming from my learned friend, who has proved himself a master at those arts."

Sparks are flying finally. Maguire saw this building up, Khan getting crankier, realizing he underperformed while his opponents played fast and loose.

Beauchamp retorts: "I'm as eager as anyone in this room to hear everything Mr. Griffin has to say, but surely my friend doesn't have to rely on schoolyard taunts to elicit that information."

"May it please the court, I am seeking leeway in dealing with this witness. I am loath to accuse my friend of lying in the weeds with him, but—"

"That is a shocking—"

"Break it up!" Judge Donahue barks. She's the referee pulling the NHL stars apart before blows get exchanged. "Mr. Khan, you may explore the issue of Mr. Griffin's claim to have seen the light but you know better than to use the tools of cross-examination."

"Very well. Mr. Griffin, let me rephrase more gently: given your decision to blow the whistle on Chemican, did you renounce a claim to severance pay?"

"I received legal advice about my rights in that regard, and my lawyer is proceeding with a claim."

"Well, good luck with that. What do you expect to get, given your testimony today?"

"Hopefully enough to pay my lawyer."

That gets laugher, which blunts Khan's gains. "And she is here, Ms. Adelsen, the smiling young woman on the counsel seats behind the defence table. When did you hire her?"

"About six weeks ago."

"And did anyone recommend her?"

Beauchamp stays seated, smiling, pretending the question doesn't faze him.

"I spoke to Nancy Faulk in this courthouse. I told her I needed someone I could completely trust, a fighter."

"So though you never conferred with Mr. Beauchamp, you did with Ms. Faulk."

"I approached her because she knows who's who in the Toronto criminal bar."

"And you're aware that Ms. Adelsen formerly worked as counsel in Ms. Faulk's office."

"She knew Greta was a smart, skilled counsel, and that was good enough for me."

"Your miraculous awakening coincided with your loss of taste for cocaine. Or had you merely lost your connection?"

The quick shift seems to startle Howie. "I'm not sure what you mean."

"Your source was in a coma. Poor Archie Gooch."

Finally, an accusation rankles Griffin. "That is completely false. Only a fool would choose a misfit like that as his drug dealer."

"It's a theory that Mr. Beauchamp has been hammering away at for the last two weeks."

Beauchamp is up. "So what? With respect, M'Lady, how long is my friend to be allowed to mock the rules and procedures of the criminal law?"

"Mr. Khan, I'm not giving you any more freebies. If I hear another challenge to this witness, or even a leading question, I will shut you down."

For the next while Khan uses more finesse, but still manages to work Howie over, gets out he didn't know Gooch was on a big oxy habit and didn't think he could do much damage on a single overnight shift. Admits that was careless but insists the break-in would have happened even if the regular guy was there.

As to his actual source of coke, Howie checks with his lawyer and she gets the judge to affirm he's still protected from self-incrimination so he admits his pure flake travels from Latin America with his checked luggage.

Khan studies the wall clock — it's getting near the end of the day, he'll want to end on a high note. "You told Mr. Beauchamp you were in love with Ms. Levitsky. Is that still true?"

Howie deliberates over this, as if it's one of the great issues of our times. "I think . . . I'm not sure, but I think I'm in love with her more than ever. In the sense that I'm blown away by her, by what she has done."

A murmur of oohs and aws.

"You told Mr. Beauchamp, 'I would have done anything for her.' Is that still true?"

Another thoughtful moment, a quick glance at her, then he nods, as if the answer has suddenly come. "Pretty well anything, because I know she wouldn't ask me to lie for her."

"But you've already done that, haven't you?"

The judge, sharply: "Don't answer that. The witness may stand down."

Khan shrugs. "Very well. The Crown has completed its case."

Griffin makes a sound like "Whew," departs the stand, and joins Greta Adelsen, who rises and squeezes his hand. Levitsky stares at them, glassy-eyed, as they make for the exit.

Nancy Faulk gives notice she has a lengthy motion to make when they resume. Judge Donahue excuses the jury until two p.m. tomorrow.

Lucy Wales, in bladder agony, races from the room like a greyhound. Her comrades file out slowly, shepherded by their lawyers.

Khan's long-boned student flutters about her boss, applauding him, and when the room clears she can't hold back, and kisses him — a cheek shot, which Azra obviously doesn't mind because he gives her a pat on the ass.

Maguire can't quite decide if all this exhilaration is warranted. Azra Khan was going to take Griffin off at the neck. But at the end, no one carried him out on a stretcher.

Sushi tonight. At least once a week, it's one of Sonia's decrees. He shudders at the thought of sushi.

CHAPTER 23 » RIVIE

1

Wednesday, May 29

Despite a night to recover, it still feels like I've fallen down the rabbit hole (it's still brillig). It hasn't helped that I tied one on at the Cameron with Lucy and some Bee-lievers who kept buying rounds.

When I got home I tried to read my notes from court. They were barely decipherable. On one page, prompted by Howie proclaiming to the world his everlasting love for me, I lost control of my pen, there's a scrawl zigzagging down the page.

The Bee-lievers were sure that Howie underwent an eco-religious transformation, and why not? I can see him having his catharsis, his cleaning-out of false assumptions — ironically inspired by his love for Becky McLean. I can see him reading Klein and McKibben and Monbiot, and doing a big rethink. And hadn't Nancy Faulk told me in early March he'd be happy to see me get off? *Have you ever considered the big goof may still be in love with you?*

But Lucy, ever cynical, thinks he has a less principled motive: he's suing Chemican for wrongful dismissal, wants to come to court with clean hands as a reformed fixer. He's more in love with his own dick than you, sweetie. Did you catch the body language going on between him and his lawyer?

As if I could care. Though that was low, trying to make me jealous.

Anyway, here we are, back in court, a morning of legal wrangling to add an extra dose of throb to my headache. I notice the lawyers do less posturing when there's no jury, though there's still some chippiness going on between Beauchamp and Khan.

Nancy has launched into what they call a no-evidence motion. She wants all charges against Ivor and Amy dismissed, arguing there isn't a scrap of evidence to go to the jury. Even if a conspiracy was hatched in the backroom of Ivor Antiques it doesn't mean they were among the hatchers. There's no proof they even knew the Ivor Antiques van was used overnight on September 10. Its keys always hung in the backroom.

Azra Khan argues there's ample evidence against Ivor and Amy. Their prints were in the backroom and the van. The jury is entitled to infer they condoned the use of their premises and van for an illegal purpose. It would be laughable to suggest they didn't know what was going on back there. There was no rental agreement, everyone had keys, all were friends of long standing.

Ultimately, Donahue dismisses Nancy's motion because she's "loath to usurp the jury's function."

That adds to my malaise. I just want to suffer alone at lunch break, so I hike aimlessly through Queen's Park and the university and the Annex, kvetching to myself about this trial, our prospects, my future, or lack of it.

I can't kid myself about Howie anymore. Lucy is right, he was not an honest witness. That had to be transparent to the jury. *I told her about my thoughts, my doubts, my sense of guilt about the role I played in Brazil.* Bullshit, Howie. In fact, over dinner you *boasted* about the role you'd played. Still . . . He did sound sincere about his feelings for me.

When we resume, Arthur rises to address the jury: "You have heard several Crown witnesses praise a powerful, nicotine-based insecticide called Vigor-Gro. Witnesses paid by an agrochemical giant that earns billions from it. You are now about to hear the other side of the story, from witnesses who are not being paid, who owe allegiance not to Chemican-International but to the truth."

Thus begin Arthur's opening remarks, a summary of testimony to come from Ariana Van Doorn and the several other wise women and men sitting in the front row, most of whom, he points out, have generously waived expert witness fees "so their words cannot appear tainted by monetary bias."

These witnesses, he promises, will give effect to the "great, historic defence of necessity."

Our microbiologist uses up most of the afternoon, with a detailing of the history and structure of neonicotinoids, ziegladoxin in particular, and their interaction with bees. An expert in parasitology as well, he explains the roles of the other foes, *Nosema ceranae* and *Varroa destructor*. I barely stay awake through this, thanks to the banging in my head.

The other witness is a shy, stout woman about sixty, a professional beekeeper from the Niagara area. Arthur leads her through her training, her background, her business, its struggles to stay afloat selling honey at local markets.

A fifty-acre cornfield nearby had been planted with neonic-treated seeds — Vigor-Gro, as she found out later. She speaks of the shock she felt last summer when walking among her hives. "Piles of bees in front of them, dead and dying, the dying ones just shaking and vibrating."

I'm haunted by this insecticide holocaust, a ghastly death dance, bodies piling up. She lost more than a million honeybees. Her reaction: "I cried. It wasn't just the financial loss. You become attached . . . it's hard to explain."

Her struggle prompts sniffles from the gallery. The press laps it up. Jurors look troubled. ("Appeal first to the heart," Arthur told me, "then to their minds.") He probably wants more from his beekeeper, but sits. ("It's all about timing, never spoil the moment.")

Khan pretends confusion. "Madam, do I understand you blame a neighbour's cornfield for your loss of bees?"

"Not his field. Windblown neonic dust from when he was planting his seeds. We sent some of the dead bees to a lab."

"Did you ask the lab if you had a varroa infestation?"

"They tested for neonicotinoids."

"But not for parasites that commonly affect honeybee colonies?"

"No, sir."

"And you still have forty hives?"

"Yes, sir."

"And you were insured for your loss? You were compensated?"

"Not really, we're arguing."

"Is that because the provincial bee inspector blamed you for poor maintenance of hives?"

"He did, but . . ."

"Thank you, that's all I have."

Donahue snaps at Khan. "Let the witness finish her answer."

She does: "It was a difficult year, that's all. We tried . . . We tried so hard."

2

Thursday, May 30

I am back to being myself this morning, though I share the sadness that pervades room 6-1, hanging in the air like smog as Arthur leads Charlie Dover through the private hell he has endured for seventeen years. But no bitterness shows — he's comfortable on the stand, polite and convincing, earning sighs of empathy from the Bee-lievers, sympathetic looks from the jury.

I get that Dover's null sense of direction is heartbreaking, but if played by Chaplin it would be hilarious. His accounts include: spooking neighbours as he wanders into their yards, getting tangled in dog leashes on the street, his panic at the screeching of brakes and blowing of horns if, unattended, he steps off a curb.

But mostly, when in public, he was with his twin sister, Dr. Tammy Dover, who is here, front row, where Judge Donahue invited her to sit. They'd walked into court hand in hand.

Dover is put on pause while counsel debate the non-disclosure clause: whether the settlement amount can be disclosed publicly. Arthur gets in a barb about Chemican desperately wanting that clause "to give them cover for ripping off a teenaged college student."

Donahue admonishes him for playing to the jury, then takes her own shot at a sound bite: "The Superior Court of Ontario cannot be fettered by a contractual term in a foreign civil agreement." One out of five, M'Lady. Anyway, she orders the $200,000 settlement made public.

Arthur spends another fifteen minutes asking about how Dover copes, and gets out how he never gives up hope that someday he'll recover.

Abbie Lee-Yeung dabs at tears. Four out of five for compassion.

§

Khan flips through Charlie Dover's affidavit, frowning, as if finding his claims of dubious value. He looks at the clock — he has half an hour to take a run at him. "Despite your difficulties, you have held steady employment at the Joplin Hospital for eleven years."

"In the admitting department, at a desk, yes."

"Once you're home, you can find your way about."

"I have a system of railings installed in my suite."

"And despite this odd disability, your health is good?"

"I've broken a few bones in falls. Otherwise pretty good. I wish I could exercise more."

"You've testified to taking a dose of three millilitres of ziegladoxin as part of a test in September of 2003. Afterwards, you reported a dizzy spell?"

"Yes."

"How long after you imbibed the solution?"

"Maybe half an hour. The doctor who examined me said not to worry about it."

"You didn't have second thoughts about taking a second test on December twenty-eight?"

"I thought they knew what they were doing. They were scientists."

"During that second test you imbibed eight point five millilitres of ziegladoxin. You were examined the next day. Blood and urine tests showed no abnormalities, and it wasn't until a day later you had more dizzy spells."

"And I was disoriented."

"But it didn't come on for forty-eight hours after you consumed the potion, correct?"

"Give or take an hour or two."

"Had you consumed alcohol between the test and the onset of these symptoms?"

"I joined a few other test volunteers for a few beers after we were examined. We were making jokes about how nobody turned green or grew extra limbs."

The vision prompts nervous giggles behind me, makes me queasy.

"Did you take any drugs or narcotics during that time frame?"

"No."

"Marijuana? Amphetamines? Mushrooms?"

Dover reflects. "Months later I tried drugs. Psilocybin, MDA. I tried everything."

"After you developed these symptoms, you somehow got back home to Joplin?"

"Yes. They arranged a car for me."

"And you went to your family doctor and he referred you to a neurologist. Despite their best efforts your condition got no better."

"Correct."

"So you retained counsel. Mr. W. W. Squirely."

"He was recommended, yes."

"A former judge, widely respected. Many decades of experience."

"Yes, he told me—"

"Now I don't want to hear what your attorney said, but he made a claim for compensation from Chemican-International and entered into talks with their lawyers. Right?"

"Yes."

"And in the course of negotiations, you were examined by a host of medical experts. Your affidavit refers to three neurologists, an internist, an allergist, and, ah, what else . . . oh, yes, a psychiatrist." A verbal wink, intended for the jury. "And as I understand it, none could point to ziegladoxin as a causative factor in your problem with getting about."

"They were advertised to us as independent specialists. But they were all hired by Chemican, paid by them."

"Nonetheless, they were all distinguished professionals, academics. Their examinations of you were long and exhaustive. You were given dozens of tests, blood, CT scans, EEGs, neuroimaging, and they found no clear link between the Vigor-Gro you consumed—"

"Objection." Arthur is up. "I have been patient, M'Lady, but I give up waiting for my friend to ask a question. This isn't cross-examination, it's a harangue."

"You know better, Mr. Khan."

That was not even a glancing blow from Her Ladyship. Khan just carries on. "None of the other one hundred and two who consumed the same amounts of ziegladoxin showed any ill effects. Does that not surprise you, Mr. Dover?"

"Not really. I was unlucky — I was susceptible, they weren't."

"Did you suffer any physical abnormality after these ziegladoxin tests?"

"Nothing disabling, sir."

"No problem with your feet?"

He thinks about this. "I walk oddly, I can't bend my toes."

"Why? Never mind." Khan awkwardly pulls back from that knee-jerk follow-up. "Happily, you haven't suffered intellectually. Your mind seems very sharp indeed."

"Thank you."

I'm guessing Khan knows his efforts to discredit Dover are back-firing. So he suddenly becomes Dover's best friend and advocate, applauding his strength, his survival tools, his cool, the contentment he finds in his books and music, in photography and art magazines.

"Well, then, good luck." Khan sits, trying not to show he's frazzled by having asked the one question too many.

Obviously, Arthur had set him up so he could take advantage of the neat little tool called re-examination. "Mr. Dover, please don't leave us in the dark about why you can't bend your toes."

"It's as if my toe bones have turned to jelly. They flop about."

"Crookedly?"

"Yes."

And the judge and the jury and anyone who's been paying attention to this trial will remember directionless Barney Wilson, ex–security guard. *Some of my toes went crooked.*

§

Cuddling a nearly new laptop — I just got it today — I pause halfway down the stairs and listen to Arthur taunt Ariana Van Doorn in the moose room. She will make her debut tomorrow, and Arthur and Nancy are prepping her.

"Necessity? *Necessity?* My dear Professor Van Doorn, why was it so critical, so *necessary*, to commit a serious criminal offence, a surreptitious break and enter by night, when no one's life was in immediate peril?"

"Excuse me, my field is biology—"

"It's a simple question, madam, I'd like an answer, please." Arthur has Khan's slightly old-school accent down pat.

"Okay, in my opinion, people *have* been hurt, they *were* in immediate peril. According to the pesticide poisoning statistics we heard yesterday, one in 12,500 users accidentally imbibe insecticides in any given year—"

"*Immediate* peril, not some accident in the vague future . . ."

"Objection, counsel is baiting the witness, and is also being ridiculous." That's Nancy.

Ariana gives a throaty laugh. I carry on down to the back patio with the Dell notebook. Okie Joe will be stopping over to make sure it isn't rigged to explode in my face. I pack a pipe with pot.

I'm seeing criminal law in a new light. There's flexibility to it. I find it profoundly creative of Arthur and Nancy to have made adjustments on the fly to the frail defence of necessity. They've narrowed its focus to real people, like the unlikely duo of Barney Wilson and Charlie Dover.

Most people are deaf to the climate crisis, they don't want to hear about the bees, it's all too depressing and abstract. It was maybe asking too much of our jury to conclude we had to knock over an insecticide lab as a wake-up call against planetary collapse. But the poisoning of a fellow hominid brings it home.

Because we raided the Vigor-Gro plant, because we exposed their corrupted tests, because we spoke up, because of the publicity, *because of this very trial*, we have rescued farmers susceptible to what we now call the Dover-Wilson Syndrome.

That's the essence of today's testimony from an agricultural economist, a climatologist, and an actuarial scientist with a doctorate in statistics. Together, with reams of tables and stats and graphs and international sales figures for Vigor-Gro, they made a case that it's statistically likely that a "significant" number of pesticide users out there are allergic to ziegladoxin. And it's also statistically likely that our action has warned a "significant" number of accidental imbibers to get flushed out right away. Something like that.

It's a pretty stretchy theory, so taut it could easily snap as the jury tussles with it. But if they're desperate to find reasonable doubt . . . just, possibly, maybe?

Azra Khan attacked that proposition relentlessly, as a desperate ploy and phony guesswork. Hate to say it, but he did a damn good job. Four out of five.

§

It's a rosy-hued evening, and I'm still on the back patio, having a last puff from the bowl of Purple Kush I shared with Okie Joe — he has just biked off after digging through my little Dell. "Bugless," he said. "Pre-packed with goodies. I cleaned out some crap."

I had a laughing fit as I recalled to him Howie's drunken malapropism: "Packs a punch, so don't be conceived."

The laptop arrived by mail today at Nancy's office, in its original box with an envelope taped to it, a note inside: *Dear Rivie*, then four words: *As promised. Always believe.* Underneath that: *Howell*.

Always believe what?

There's a return address, a Penetanguishene box number. Should I reply? *Received.* Signed, *Conceived but deceived.* I think I've attained an excessive level of highness.

We also found a Word icon on the desktop titled *Rivie*. It opened to reveal the same edict: *Always believe.*

I reopen that document, start a new paragraph: *Good evening, Howie, I know you're there. You're listening. You outsmarted Okie Joe. You've heard every word I've said. Please advise: Are my thoughts also being transmitted?*

I wait for the magic phrase. Then, magically, slowly, it comes: *"Always believe."* But it is I who typed it.

"I think I'm in love with her more than ever." Did he actually say that under oath yesterday? What kind of love is this? Obsessive? Fanatical?

I'm too stoned. And I'm losing the light to the night and the mosquitoes. Also, one gets a little spooked as darkness creeps in, at least in this neighbourhood. Donald Stumpit is still hiding in some rathole waiting for the fuss to die down so he can come a-visiting again. This kind of stuff shouldn't be in your head when you get stoned.

I pack pipe and bud and laptop into the house, flop on my bed, hit the remote, check on the Jays at Fenway. Biggio's waiting at the plate, there's a conference on the mound.

I'm too loaded to focus on the screen. There's a conference in *my head*. Phrases flutter there like butterflies. *Packs a punch, so don't be conceived, conceived, deceived, always believe.*

Dear Howell,

Always doubt, never deceive.

Rivke

3
Friday, May 31

Ariana Van Doorn is relaxed, dry in manner, stating clearly and calmly what we have been shouting from the rooftops. Our howls of doom caused people to tune out — she's jargon-free, gets to the nut, makes sense of the complex, she's like everyone's favourite teacher from college.

Nancy Faulk asks few questions, lets her ace insectologist run the show, starting with taking apart Dr. Easling and his purchased opinions about the good that is done by pesticides.

During a TV interview, he'd scoffed at a UN report blasting the agrochemicals for their greed and lack of ethics. Ariana's comeback: "Condemning that study as alarmist anti-corporate propaganda is the irresponsible rhetoric one might expect on Fox News, not from a dispassionate, unbiased scientist."

You'd think that would get a rise from Mr. Khan, but he just doodles on his writing pad.

Easling had also pooh-poohed a Harvard study that concluded neonicotinoids were the main cause of colony collapse — not varroa mites or other parasites and pathogens, not climate change.

"Regrettably, Dr. Easling has ignored the evidence. The Harvard team examined eighteen bee colonies at three different apiaries for over a year. Twelve of the hives were regularly treated with neonics, and half of those were completely wiped out."

Ariana makes a terrific point about how neonics makers, "if they cared about the health of the planet, would invest their millions to modify crops organically so they don't require insecticides." Encouraging growers to use less chemicals "obviously isn't part of their business plan." She directs that to the stone-faced Chemican officers in their reserved seats.

Their business plan (if I may add a footnote) hadn't taken into account the Earth Survival Rebellion. Chemican's numbers continue to slump on the stock markets. We may destroy them yet. Direct action works.

I feel rosier today, slept well enough — though with vivid stoned dreams. My optimism chart has risen a few ticks since we began our defence. Nobody expects complete exoneration, but even if Justice Donahue takes away the necessity defence, we've still got Abbie Lee-Yeung to hang the jury (such a lovely, dark, ironic colloquialism).

I've been trying not to make eye contact with Abbie, I don't like the way she locks on to me. She's in my peripheral vision now though, staring at me, barely hiding a smile. This time I answer — with a blink she could take as a wink. You'll vote for us won't you, Abbie? I will love you if you do.

Sort of mockingly, Ariana applauds Easling's expressed concerns about monocultures, but then builds on them: vast fields of corn or canola or soya are "killing grounds for beneficial species." Monoculture demands more and more insecticide, pests grow resistant, pollinators accustomed to varied habitats and diets vanish. "And today, because of neonics' long lifetimes, vast landscapes are permeated with neurotoxins, accelerating the collapse of biodiversity."

I've heard this in rehearsal, of course, but in my ears it sounds true, unprepared, felt.

How true was Howie? *I was in love. I would have done anything for her . . .* What is his game? (Why must I cynically assume he has one?)

I think back upon that big, handsome, horny, fumbling, over-apologetic marriage rebounder, and wonder if that was the real Howell Griffin or a clever act. Had both of us been imposters? And had we somehow fallen into each other's trap?

When I come back to this world, Ariana is raising the stakes: Hummingbirds are in serious decline. A single neonic corn kernel can kill a songbird. She relates how white-crowned sparrows were fed four treated canola seeds for three days, just one percent of their diet. Then came severe weight loss, disorientation, they barely hung on.

New studies showed neonics are "an alarmingly major factor" in the plummeting numbers of birds. In Canada and the U.S. bird populations have fallen by three billion from ten billion over the last five decades.

Test rodents also showed brain abnormalities and spatial confusion. Pregnant rats fed neonics transmitted neural disorders to their offspring.

Nancy asks, "And what about humans?"

"We are at risk. These nicotine-based products target an insect's nervous system so there's real concern that chronic use or accidental ingestion may also damage the nervous systems and brain structures of our own species. That risk expands as neonics make their way into our food and contaminate groundwater and wells."

Khan continues to doodle. I can roughly make out his artwork: faces, I think. Unhappy faces. How will he go after Ariana?

Mockingly? Surgically? Full bore? He did a pretty good job on our witnesses yesterday.

I heard his mom is fading. He must be in agony as we approach the last days of the trial, the final speeches, the climactic verdict. One would have to be made of stone not to feel pity for him. It seems almost unfair that he has to carry this burden . . .

Not that I want him to win.

Ariana spends several minutes on U.S. government charts and stats that prove neonics are regularly found in common fruits and vegetables — and, shockingly, in thirty percent of all baby foods.

Anyone thinking of having a baby (which, Dear Diary, I am not) may want to look up some recent studies that Ariana scares us with: persistent neonic exposure to pregnant mothers can cause birth defects, deformities, autism.

Nancy lets that set in for several hushed seconds, as the clock closes in on twelve thirty. Donahue finally breaks the silence, sending the jury off to lunch to reflect on deformed babies.

§

Lucy and I get tacos from one of the wagons by the square and find a sunny bench. We critique the morning — which I feel good about, Ariana was brilliant. But Lucy is cynical, distrusting the jury, claiming to sense their negative vibes.

"The foreman, the mini-mall designer, he thinks we're pulling a fast one . . ." Hesitating, studying me. "What's with that shit hanging from your ears?"

"A joke. I found them in my pack when I was in the jane, thought I'd try them on."

"Holy shit, Howie's snake earrings."

I slip them off. "I forgot I was wearing them."

That causes Lucy to guffaw. "Like, you walked out of a court-house washroom unaware you're flaunting those two dangling modifiers which your boyfriend gave you as seduction bait after shafting the Brazilian natives?" A gasp for breath after that speech, then another scornful laugh.

"He was gathering evidence against his corporate masters."

"Bullshit. You're signalling, you're flashing like a bird of paradise, announcing you're ready to mate. Too bad the imposter didn't see you displaying or right now you'd be scarfing down his spermatozoa instead of a chicken taco."

When I told her about his gift laptop, it was the same song. Howie had turned the tables on me, it was his turn to hose me, to seduce the seductress.

Okay, maybe I'm not using my brain, I'm under the subconscious control of some other organ. Surely not the heart. Which pretty well narrows it down to a body part rarely active except in my fantasies.

"He's not into you, my sweet. 'Always believe,' that's what sham artists want us to do."

I don't buy that. He isn't asking me to believe in him. Or even the Lord Buddha. I think it's more conceptual. Always believe in truth. In life.

This is too heavy for me right now. It's been a tough week.

4

Azra Khan is cross-examining Ariana and I can't take it in, I'm imploring my memory cells to release some information. When did I stick those earrings in my day pack? Why did I? How come I put them on in the ladies' room? Am I having a nervous breakdown?

I return to the reality of Court 6-1. Khan is doing something unexpected — he's not challenging Ariana, he's not defending neonics, he's not denying the decimation of pollinating insects. "If all you say is true," he begins a question, or "Assuming neonics pose dangers to human health," then he concludes with various versions of "So what?"

520

"Let us get to the nut of this, Dr. Van Doorn. The defendants rely on the defence of necessity. They seek to be exonerated because no option was open, they had no alternative, no way out. I ask you, not in your capacity as an expert, just as an ordinary, rational human being: Does that make sense? Couldn't they have organized a boy-cott or a demonstration? A social media campaign?"

"I can't say. They may have done that, I don't know."

"Petitioned various governments, their regulatory agencies?"

"Those would be options only if there was more than an infini-tesimal chance of their being heard."

"Picketed the offices of neonics makers? Picketed Chemican's Sarnia plant, the head office in Kansas City?"

"Well, my answer would be similar. Where would it get them?"

"They could have brought a court action against the agrochem-ical industry. A class action."

"In my role as an ordinary, rational human, Mr. Khan, I can't believe that wouldn't take untold years. The crisis is happening now."

Bring it on, sister. Ariana has unshackled herself from the role of dispassionate expert, has become openly partisan. Arthur shows no eagerness to intervene. I can tell he likes her spunk.

"Nonetheless, Professor, the defence of necessity obviously doesn't operate when lawful courses of action are wide open."

"But if those lawful courses are all likely to fail, no options are realistically available. The proof is in the pudding. The form of direct action they chose has gained a worldwide audience and in fact is inspiring demonstrations and boycotts."

I wonder if she was in a debating club in college. Judge Donahue seems to be enjoying the to and fro, but with a skeptical twirling of her nose that says Ariana Van Doorn is reaching, it's all guff. Donahue will eventually pay back our lawyers for their saucy manners by denying the jury our only defence.

But who's to stop them in the privacy of the jury room? Their basic obedient Canadianness, I guess. Eleven of these good soldiers can be depended on not to mutiny — but it only takes one to hang the jury. Plan B double e, Nancy calls it.

Abbie has stopped gawking at me, is madly writing down Ariana's points, arming herself for the wrangling to come in the jury room. Ariana gets some smiles from other jurors but no eager nods of agreement.

Khan is unrelenting. "Another requirement of the defence is that there be direct, immediate peril. Tell me, Professor, how does plotting in a backroom of an antiques store in Toronto to commit a crime far away and months ahead meet that test?"

"When the crime, as you called it, was committed, the peril was still direct and immediate."

"And what particular individual was in immediate peril?"

"I heard evidence that it is statistically probable that many were in peril, especially those severely allergic to the ziegladoxin in Vigor-Gro. Like yesterday's witness, Charles Dover."

"But that wasn't the goal of these accused. Theirs was a much wider mission. To save the bees."

"And every other life form, including ours."

"They weren't directing their minds to the plight of any Charles Dovers out there, were they?"

Finally, Ariana looks kind of stumped. "I can't imagine they were, no."

Azra Khan says, "Thank you, ma'am," and sits.

And that's the case for the defence, our lawyers announce.

Then, with the jury out, Khan asks the judge: "Now that the evidence is all in, M'Lady, I should apprise you that I have discussed with my friends the sequence of closing arguments, and it is agreed that the Crown will sum up first."

"Unusual, but as you wish."

"As well, can Your Ladyship instruct us whether our addresses to the jury should touch on the necessity defence?"

Donahue looks down at the lawyers with a crafty smile. "No, that wouldn't be right. I don't dare make a ruling on necessity until I've heard the final speeches. My duty is to listen to both sides and keep an open mind."

I assume the lawyers know that's bullshit, and that she knows that they know that she knows it's bullshit. But Arthur looks relieved that she didn't immediately pull his only defence.

It also helps that Nancy and Arthur will get last kick at the can. That happens Monday.

Then on Tuesday, the judge will lay down the law to the jury. And then we're in their hands.

<h1 style="text-align:center">5</h1>

It's happy hour, stress-remission time, and the Cameron is our target, but halfway there a powerful magnetic force causes my bike to brake and skid to a stop. Lucy, close behind, almost piles into me.

She looks around. "Why are we here?"

"To case the joint. To contemplate how it all began."

Lucy picks up that we just cycled past the Beaver's Tail. "Seriously, have you gone crackers?"

"It's for the memoir I'm writing. For accuracy. I need another hit of this place."

"Not. You want to relive your conquest of Howie Griffin. No, worse, you're hoping he still comes down here every Friday."

We lock our bikes. She comes in just to humour me.

Inside, it's like August 10 last year, loud and clinking, full of nine-to-five sex-seeking missiles, the same exposed chest hairs and hastily applied makeup.

The bar stools, where Stage One played out, are filled, it's standees only, four deep. No empty tables either, but that doesn't deter Lucy, who spots a pair of junior execs ogling us from the mezzanine. She blows them a kiss on the way up, then goes, "If you cool gentlemen would like to buy us a drink, we'd be happy to keep your chairs."

After they scramble away to get us tequila shooters, Lucy snipes at me again. "Why don't you just call Howie up and say you want to fuck him? Or did you have a premonition he'd be here?"

"I'm *not* obsessing over him." He's cute, that's all. That lopsided grin . . . But what attracted him to brainless Becky McLean? That she was so adorably cute? *My mother told me never to accept drinks from strangers.* Immodestly, I get why he desired Becky physically. But was there enough to fall in love with?

Always believe . . . that I love you?

Lucy wants to split from this glitz saloon. I feel we are honour-bound to wait for our shooters. We debate the issue until a server drops off two flutes of champagne. "Table of five over there," she says. They're waving. We have been recognized. A minute later, another two glasses of bubbly. "Table near the door." A smiling young couple, hipsters.

When the capitalist trainees finally show up with the tequilas, they goggle at all the champagne, then study us more closely as we shoot the shooters.

"You are . . ."

"Yes," says Lucy. We tell them sorry, we have to rush off, please enjoy the champagne. We get hoots as well as applause as we work our way out, bumping fists here and there.

6

Saturday, June 1

It's after ten as I lock my bike outside Faulk, Quan, Dubois, so I'm a little late for our gathering of conspirators. Nancy called us in to catch us up on what happens after the speeches, after the judge's instructions, after the jury goes out.

I don't go in yet because I'm seduced by the fresh-baked aroma from this building's ground-floor tenant, Montreal Bagels. Arthur, who has set the weekend aside to work on his jury address, has a weakness for poppyseed bagels.

So I detour into the store and get in line. I'm number four, and they're selling fast, right off the baking trays. The decor celebrates Montreal with blow-ups of the mountain and river and the historic inner town. I'm absorbed in these as the customer behind me speaks softly into my ear. "Rivie, just tell me one thing."

I almost jump out of my sneakers. I know who it is without turning around. Out of the corner of my lips: "Abbie, I can't talk to you."

"After this is over, will there be any chance of seeing you? That's all I want to know."

"Don't do this. You're compromising both of us. I can't respond to you." I abandon all thoughts of bagels, turn toward the door, but Abbie is in lockstep.

She blocks my exit, her eyes intense, pulling, pleading. "I will never vote to convict. *Never.*"

Then she lets me pass by. I glance about outside: no security cameras, no one in hearing distance. But ten feet away there's Helmut Knutsen standing near the law office entrance as a taxi drives off. He looks at me, then at Abbie as she jaywalks this busy street and enters the shop called Spirituality.

He says nothing until we're inside. Then, very softly and firmly: "No one must know she spoke to you. Especially our lawyers."

"I didn't invite that. She ambushed me." We take the stairs, hurrying.

"No matter. She has a fixation on you. That's dangerous."

"She said—"

"Stop. I don't want to hear what was said."

That's it, I'm cut off. I follow him to the boardroom, where our squad mills about, and join Lucy at the coffee pot. She grabs my wrist as I pick up a mug. "Your hand is shaking. Maybe you don't need a coffee, you need a transfusion, you're white." But she pours for me.

"I'm fine. Just out of breath."

"Let's get going, gang," Nancy calls. "Won't take long. Arthur sends his regrets."

Everyone takes chairs but me — clutching my coffee, staring out at Spadina Avenue. No sign of Abbie. Is she still in the Spirituality store? Shopping for aids to achieve at-oneness? A talisman to bind me to her?

Nancy says, "I don't want to spoil your weekend but you may want to bring your jammies to court on Tuesday. Donahue has been known to keep defendants in custody while the jury's out."

No one must know she spoke to you. Especially our lawyers. Even the one Doc's making out with? Can he be right? Do I dare share with Lucy? No, not even, I need to think this through.

"The many possible verdicts range from total innocence to nobody walks. It's possible some could be convicted of conspiracy but not break and enter. Some may walk while others go down."

There goes Abbie, carrying on past Fu-King Supplies, then whirling, looking up, across the street, at my window — at me, I think. Or is that the delusion of an overwrought mind?

"I love you all, but I have a special duty to Amy and Ivor. They've got a shot — you all do, but not as clean a shot: with them it's a simple matter of reasonable doubt. Arthur will take the lead on the necessity defence, and I'll back him up."

My brain continues to boil as Abbie disappears toward Kensington Market. Why doesn't Doc want me to tell my lawyer? Anything I say to Arthur is privileged, so what's the problem? Could I be putting him on the spot somehow?

"For the rest of you, the best hope is Plan B, a mistrial and a do-over — unless Her Ladyship has her own catharsis and decides to save life on Planet Earth. Plan B will require at least one juror to turn rogue. You all know with whom our hopes reside."

I sense everyone looking at me. I wish I could tell them a mistrial is guaranteed, that Abbie will hang the jury. I just have to keep my mouth shut. What could go wrong?

§

Outside, everyone disperses except Lucy, who waits until I finally buy the bagels. I stick them into my pack, and we saddle up, and she says, "Okay, you are very definitely freaking out. Give."

I could fib, but she'd see through it. Or I could bluntly say I can't talk. But she would think I distrust her, she'd be insulted.

She follows as I bolt into the U of T campus — we're off to Queen's Park, yet another climate crisis rally. Suddenly, in front of Convocation Hall, I brake, and once again Lucy almost runs into me.

The thought that brought me to a halt: What if something *does* go wrong? If things go kerflooey and Arthur learns I kept the Abbie episode from him . . . too horrible to contemplate.

We perch on the curb. Lucy squeezes me and goes, "Okay, let's hear it — you've been secretly seeing Howie for the last two months. You missed your period."

Her genial expression fades to sour as I tell her everything, right down to Doc's *I don't want to hear.*

Lucy blames me. She'd seen this coming. She'd warned me about Abbie's infatuation. I was somehow at fault for not assuming she'd stalk me outside Nancy's building.

"I was dry-gulched, and thanks for your support and sympathy, but what matters right now is Doc's warning to button it."

Lucy's view is don't listen to Doc, his messianic complex skews his thinking. "And where does he get off giving legal advice? Talk to your fucking lawyer."

I am definitely going to do that. I feel a ton lighter.

§

The Queen's Park rally became a march down University Avenue, several thousand, banners high, traffic backing up, cops trying to keep us to the sidewalks. When it began to rain we dispersed — near the courthouse, justly — and Lucy and I subwayed our bikes to the

Summerhill Station for a birthday party near there, food and drinks supplied, otherwise BYOD.

And when I get home it's past eleven, and there are lights on, and Arthur is loudly orating to the moose and the Naugahyde chair. "The burden of proof, my friends, is on the Crown. And that burden is a weighty one, because the Crown must convince you beyond a reasonable doubt, *beyond* a reasonable doubt, ladies and gentlemen, that these accused are inexcusably guilty."

I glimpse him as I creep upstairs — he's in pyjamas and slippers, a forefinger stabbing out his points of emphasis. "Excusable. By that I mean lawfully excusable. And that brings us to the great, historic defence called necessity."

This won't be a good time to mention Abbie Lee-Yeung.

CHAPTER 24 » ARTHUR

1

Saturday, June 1

"And that, ladies and gentlemen, finally brings us to the great, historic task . . . no, a historic opportunity that has been granted to you, as this entire, anxious planet watches and listens . . . and hopes . . ."

Maybe something stronger than hopes. Prays? Beseeches? Enough. It's almost midnight. Arthur has to get back to sleep. He got about an hour in, then woke from a bad dream: he was tongue-tied, babbling incoherently to an impatient jury.

That drove him out of bed. In an effort to prove he wasn't befuddled and incoherent, he sounded out some lines. They seemed to make sense, so he relaxed and rehearsed his jury address for half an hour. He doesn't want to be over-prepared, though — he's at his best when he wings it.

He checks that all doors are locked, all lights out. The hanging lamp over the stairs is on, so one less thing to worry about: Rivie is safely back from wherever she was. Unhappily, it may be her last free Saturday night for many years. Arthur has allowed himself to become too fond of this impetuous young client — that has magnified the stress.

Once back under the covers he remains uneasy, the dream bothering him again, like a harbinger of misfortune. He forgot to pull the curtains, and senses a flicker of light through his street-facing bay window. He is used to car lights passing by but this was coming from a static position across the street.

Again, he abandons his bed, and takes in a street view from that window — it's raining lightly, and much is hidden by trees; there's a distant glow from a lamppost, a few yard lights on, but otherwise blackness reigns.

Again comes a spark of light: from across the street, the house of the Willis Whites, the unsociable neighbours who refused Rivie sanctuary when a racist thug pursued her to their gate.

The source of this intermittent light might be matches or a lighter being struck, but it's most likely a small flashlight — yes, a thin beam glints off metal flashing, and is quickly doused.

He fumbles in the dark for the phone, connects quickly with a 911 operator, reports a break and enter in progress, answers questions, listens to instructions. In the front vestibule he paws behind a fire extinguisher, locates an emergency flashlight — heavy enough for use as a weapon. Though the 911 operator warned him to remain inside, he throws on a rain jacket and eases his way out the door.

As best he can make out, a human form is crouched in front of the Whites' door, working noiselessly at some task or other. It doesn't seem he or she is picking a lock. A car rolls by, and in the arc of its lights Arthur makes out what looks like a bear huddled by the threshold. Words have been freshly painted on the door.

The scene suddenly makes sense — in its own bizarre way. It's the long-anticipated return of Donald Stumpit, soldier of the Final Reich. He'd tracked Rivie there on the recent long weekend, and assumed that was her home.

Suddenly another pair of headlights approaches, fast, the wrong way on one-way Beaconsfield. A police cruiser: it must have been patrolling mere blocks away. It screeches to a halt.

Arthur has his light on Stumpit now, as he bolts across flower beds to the sidewalk. He hurls a can of spray paint wildly at the cruiser. A black spume scars its hood and windshield.

Out jumps Constable Louella Baker from the passenger side, her partner from behind the wheel. Mr. and Mrs. Willis White peek from their half-opened door.

"Game over, you sick shit!" Louella shouts as she gains on him, her partner following.

Stumpit crashes over a low picket fence in a last-ditch effort to evade them, and falls on his face. Arthur hears thumps and yells and the rattle of cuffs, sounds drowned under the barking and bawling of dogs and the scream of approaching sirens. By now, the entire neighbourhood has awakened, some residents outside in rain gear, working their phones.

Arthur can't deny his curiosity, and slips across the street. The Whites have retreated inside, behind their big front window, looking confused, apparently unaware of the unfinished, semi-literate message on their front door: "commonist jew hoor lives he—" Followed by a panicky belch of black paint and a squiggly line.

Arthur is startled when Rivie takes his hand. "Let's scram before the TV vans show up." She has a jacket over a men's tall T-shirt but is bare-legged and barefooted. Neither is ready for the media — he's in pyjamas and wet slippers.

Rivie holds back for a second to study the Whites. "What are those two hiding in that house? The mummified bodies of dead babies? Whips and shackles in the bondage room?"

They return to their house. "I'll speak to Louella," she says. "You get your sleep. We can talk in the morning. I need . . . I don't know . . . advice. No problem — it will wait."

Arthur isn't fond of the phrase "No problem." It often masks a problem.

Louella Baker pockets her notebook and thanks Arthur for putting time aside on a Sunday morning. "He's looking at a fistful," she says. "Maybe both hands. Stalking, threatening, malicious damage, resisting arrest."

Rivie, still in shorts and sweaty tunic after her run, joins them in the living room, bringing a pot of coffee, toasted bagels, cream cheese, and jam. She had got up before dawn, when only one sentry guarded the crime scene. A crowd had soon collected and on her return she had to sneak in by the back.

"Both hands?" Rivie asks as she pours coffees.

"Ten years."

"Oh, good, so I'll be getting out around the same time. Hey, maybe he'll get off by claiming he's a victim of a hate crime against a member of the Aryan race."

"Yeah, like I'm the racist," Louella says.

Arthur foresees complications. Stumpit is in custody with a broken nose and he has a lawyer.

"I had to give my boots to forensics to prove his blood ain't on them. My partner saw Stumpit fall face first on the rock. That also accounts for his broken teeth."

Arthur also saw Stumpit fall. He's not sure what happened after, though. There was a fair bit of noise.

He looks outside at the herd of people with nothing to do on a lazy Sunday, most of them massed across the street. Beaconsfield is blocked to all traffic but police vehicles and media vans. A TV crew is interviewing and filming. The mood is sombre. Lots of people with phones, snapping pictures, mailing or posting them.

One of the local attractions is the paint-sloshed cruiser, still in place, Ident officers taking measurements from it. The Whites' flower-trampled yard is cordoned with police tape, and tradespeople with sanders and paintbrushes are waiting to refinish the door. The privacy-obsessed Whites, trapped in their own private hell, occasionally peer from a window, then dart away.

§

After Louella leaves, Arthur asks Rivie what was troubling her last night.

"Oh, God. Abbie Lee-Yeung."

That comes out rapidly, in one breath. Arthur feels a twinge of anxiety that becomes something close to anguish as Rivie blurts out how Ms. Lee-Yeung approached her in Montreal Bagels. "Laid in wait and jumped me. Blocked my exit."

As she pours forth the details, Arthur feels his knees go wobbly, and he slides onto a sofa, enduring a feeling somewhat like being punched in the gut. *After this is over, will there be any chance of seeing you?* That's calamitous. *I will never vote to convict.* That's worse. So much for Plan B.

On painful occasions like this he is often tempted by the need for strong drink; now it assails him. He breathes slowly to let his heart decelerate.

"Arthur, are you all right?"

"I was taken aback, sorry. I'm fine." A deep breath. "Rivie, I don't want to sound pious or pretentiously noble. But let me admit to a view that you may find naive and old-fashioned. It's about the respect I hold for the rule of law. I believe in our jury system — strongly, Rivie, with as much fervour as religious zealots believe in salvation. Trial by one's peers is a bulwark against tyranny. It guarantees that our justice system is, at bottom, democratic, despite its faults."

Arthur pauses, uncomfortable as he hears himself: stuffy and pontifical, rattled by Rivie's growing look of dismay, by the awful plight they face.

"If we allow a jury to be compromised by bias, we then allow rot to set in; if we turn a blind eye to a breach of a juror's oath, we encourage that rot to grow and fester. If our system of fair trials founders we become like Russia or China and all the other autocratic nations with their transparent pretences of allegiance to the independence of the courts." Another deep breath. "Very well, that's my little lecture. Now we need to consider what flows from that."

"I thought everything I tell you is privileged." Her voice is shaky.

"I dare not repeat it unless you waive confidentiality. And we have to talk about that because I cannot ethically and in good conscience serve you as counsel knowing a juror has flat out made up her mind without judging the evidence."

Rivie stares glumly outside, as the police wrap things up and the paint crew erases the "commonist jew" scrawl. The crowd slowly disperses. "Doc warned me not to talk to you. That didn't make sense. At the time."

"Helmut was wrong. Rivie, there are lawyers of ill repute who might abandon ethics over this issue. They might gamble that the truth wouldn't come to light, and risk disbarment. But truth has an oddly insistent way of breaking through. People talk. They share confidences with family, close friends, lovers, clergy, doctors. Who else did you talk to besides Helmut?"

"Um, Lucy, but she . . ."

"Right, despite Doc's warning, and doubtless you passed on a similar warning to Lucy. Which brings to mind a favourite adage: 'If you can't keep a secret don't expect anyone else to keep it for you.' Tongues wag, all the more when loosened by drink and drugs."

"Lucy and I were totally straight, Arthur."

"Not suggesting otherwise. But you can't count on Ms. Lee-Yeung being circumspect, especially if she's as unstable as she seems. A friend with a Twitter account, a leak to the press. Vengeful, disappointed in love, she accuses you of seeking *her* out. It doesn't end there. Security cameras and hidden listening devices are fundamental elements of the new society."

"Okay, but for the record, I didn't see any security cams outside."

"Inside Montreal Bagels?"

"I didn't . . . no, I don't know."

"Who else was in the line to buy bagels at that bakery? Maybe an undercover officer tailing you or Abbie?"

"Then they would know I refused to be compromised."

"They would also know you kept silent about her approach. You would be seen as deceitful for not mentioning that a juror has broken her oath of neutrality. You will have lost all the honour you have gained during this trial."

Rivie sits on the floor, head bowed, trying to hide tears. "Okay, whatever. Tell me what I have to do."

"Release me from the bonds of privilege and silence. A written statement will be necessary. Perhaps an affidavit. I will talk to Nancy, then Azra. Today. No time can be lost."

"And then?"

"Then we meet in closed court with Justice Donahue. Her options are narrow. She can dismiss Ms. Lee-Yeung from the jury and order the trial proceed with the eleven others. Or she could, conceivably, order a mistrial. I will do what I can. I'm sorry."

"Me too. Because we're screwed."

3
Monday, June 3

It is half past nine and they're in a small chambers court on the third floor: the judge, the clerk, the Official Court Reporter, the five lawyers. The room is locked, and Arthur is on his feet.

"Ms. Levitsky refused to speak with her other than to warn her not to communicate further with her. That's in her sworn affidavit. She reported the matter to me. She waived privilege. She did all the right things."

"For a change," says Justice Donahue, who is taking this matter too lightly. Khan and his cohorts seem amused too. Nancy still looks bagged after yesterday's long, loud rant when she learned of the bagel shop encounter.

Arthur insists Rivie's defence is prejudiced if the trial proceeds with eleven jurors. He toils on about the fundamental right to be tried by twelve peers, about the unfairness of Rivie Levitsky being deprived of a sympathetic juror, however misguided.

Donahue gives no indication she's taking this in. She looks up from her *Criminal Code*. "A jury is properly constituted as long as its numbers don't dip under ten. But you're saying, Mr. Beauchamp, that I should override that rule and declare a mistrial."

"Your Ladyship sums up my motion with admirable succinctness."

"Seriously? At this eleventh hour? After all the evidence is in, after three weeks of testimony from a multitude of witnesses. Distinguished experts, many from far abroad, who gave up their time. Also wasted, Mr. Beauchamp, would be the efforts of counsel, and your own skilled advocacy. And were I to succumb to your entreaties, the entire exercise would have to be repeated, clogging court calendars. Let us pity the poor taxpayer."

"Ought justice to be measured in dollars, M'Lady?"

"Motion denied." She makes a sorrowful face. "Now I shall have to explain matters to this young woman." To Miss Pucket: "Please fetch her from the jurors' lounge."

§

On their way up the escalator, Khan offers Arthur solace: "Too bad — that girl may have been your best hope. Tragic for her too, though we're not preferring any charges."

Arthur asks Khan how his mother fares.

"She's comfortable. Alert. She's following our little case, fascinated to know how it will turn out. Curious about you, actually. They say it's a matter of days. But they keep saying that."

"Good luck with your address, Azra. Give it your best."

§

Court resumes in room 6-1 an hour late, to puzzled frowns and mutters from the pews, particularly from the press rows, as they see an empty chair where Juror Twelve used to sit. The judge's explanation that Ms. Lee-Yeung "encountered a personal issue that, regrettably, renders her unable to continue" does little, Arthur suspects, to tamp down speculation. In fact, most people in here, including the jury, probably think that's hogwash. The foreman, the architect, looks troubled. Rumours will soon abound, conspiracy theories will be hatched: Abbie Lee-Yeung committed some great evil. She was clearly pro-defence, so the prosecution found dirt on her. She promised trouble in the jury room, she had to be removed, more proof that the courts are crooked.

So it's not the ideal time to begin an address to the jury, and Azra Khan will have to work hard to grab their attention. He begins with the standard liturgy of advantages granted to the defence: the onus of proof on the Crown, the presumption of innocence, reasonable doubt — precepts he likely won't mention again.

He expends significantly more effort defining conspiracy. "Simply, it's a meeting of the minds to commit an indictable offence enumerated in this book." Holding high a *Criminal Code.* "Such as break-enter and theft — in this case from the Sarnia plant early last September. An offence conceived, engineered, and proudly accomplished by these seven members of the Earth Survival Rebellion." A wide sweep of his right arm in their direction. His left hand holds pages of transcript.

"No one's pretending they didn't do it." He gets close to the jury, amiable, relaxed, confident. "They boldly admitted the crime. Again and again and again."

Khan unfolds a page. "The *New Yorker* profile of Dr. Helmut Knutsen has him outlining the entire scheme while modestly admitting he was its inspiring force. His opinion piece in *The Guardian* just a month ago, titled 'The Necessity of Direct Action,' shows an abysmal lack of repentance. Apparently it was excerpted from a book he's written."

Khan can't resist portraying Knutsen as cold-hearted, reminding the jury he was heard on tape dismissing the late drug-addled Archie Gooch as a "casualty of war."

Another glance at the transcripts. "If Dr. Knutsen was the executive director of the Survival Rebellion, Joe Meekes was the technical director. We have him telling an online cyber journal that the coding system for Chemican's locks and electronics was so elementary he could have trained a chimpanzee to bypass it."

Even Arthur smiles. Khan continues to lightly sketch each accused, employing a cynical wit. He flips a page. "Lucy Wales. Remember this jaunty interview in *Rolling Stone*? 'It was a snap,' said the cheeky self-styled anarchist. 'We waltzed right in and would've waltzed right out again if Rockin' Ray hadn't got blasted on acid and knocked over the equipment rack. They'd have thought it was an inside job.'

"Mr. Wozniak's recall of the events seemed more bizarre with each retelling. As best I can make out he claims that God, having anointed him as the avenger, commanded him to wreak havoc in the Chemican plant. Mr. Beauchamp will urge you to believe he was too intoxicated to know what he was doing, yet he boasted he created a distraction so the others could safely flee. Same article, *Rolling Stone*." He leans confidingly toward the jurors. "So how impaired was he, really?"

Arthur takes this in with admiration and sagging spirits — Khan is charming the jury: getting eye contact, smiles, especially from the women.

"A word about Rivke Levitsky, whose exceptional skill in attracting publicity has generously made out the Crown's case against her beyond all doubt. Sadly, her outspokenness attracted unsavoury interest from a racist thug. Truly, she owes a heartfelt thanks to the Toronto Police Service for resolving that issue with such speed and competence."

He beams a smile at Rivie, who merely cocks an eyebrow, then mocks her for her "cunning seduction of poor, confused Howell Griffin, who obviously still doesn't know what hit him." As to her use of a forged passport, no defence had been raised for the simple reason that no defence exists — unless the necessity defence applies to saving one's skin by fleeing the jurisdiction.

Next up are Ivor Trebiloff and Amy Snider. He doesn't want to lose credibility by overstating the iffy case against these two veteran campaigners, and merely notes they'd housed and hosted Operation Beekeeper and therefore knowingly aided in the objects of the conspiracy.

Having playfully profiled his rogues' gallery, he goes on to question the strategies of their counsel. "In my experience, ladies and gentlemen, when a case seems dead in the water, any good lawyer" — a friendly wave at the defence table — "will grab onto whatever lifesaver comes floating by. And, that, my friends, was a vague, ill-defined concept in law called necessity.

"As Her Ladyship will tell you, this defence is available only in urgent situations of clear and imminent peril when there's no lawful way out. Quite a reach: clear and *imminent* peril when there's no way out. But who can blame my learned friends for trying? When they couldn't come up with a plausible defence, their only option was to try to pull one out of their" — a perfectly timed pause — "hats."

Laughter. At this rate he will soon own the jury. Arthur looks woefully at that empty twelfth chair.

"Almost by definition, the planned, sophisticated burglary of a pesticide plant could not possibly be an urgent reaction to a clear, imminent peril. Let's cut the blarney and see this for what it was. A political act. An act of political protest. More accurately, maybe, a burlesque disguised as an act of protest.

"Ladies and gentlemen, none of us want to live in a society where the rule of law is ignored or trifled with because those of radical views regard it as incorrect and old-fashioned. Because that's where we're going, to a breakdown of law and order, if we allow any alleged do-gooder to violate the law just to get attention — like a wayward child."

This gets a rare smile from Justice Donahue, who has otherwise managed not to betray her enthusiasm for Khan's broadside against the necessity defence.

"Where does it stop? Is the defence also available to everyone who believes in all manner of obscure or worthless causes? Or who merely act on a gripe or a whim? If we allow robbers to get off because they feel morally justified, do we similarly excuse assassins? Is it okay to burn down a tobacco store because too many die of lung cancer? Do we give a free pass to those of firm religious belief who harry or assault an alleged heretic? A gay person? An abortion provider? A sex worker?

"In the words of a renowned British judge, the necessity defence, too liberally interpreted, could, quote, 'very easily become simply a mask for anarchy.' That's right, my friends. Anarchy."

Azra Khan is royally in command of room 6-1. No murmurs of protest sound from the back rows where the Bee-lievers sit. The Sarnia Seven seem just as quelled — rigid in expression, sulky, like errant students scolded by their principal. Arthur is witnessing the Crown Attorney in his finest hour, after weeks of uneven effort, of ducking and dodging blows from his two combatants while burdened by his mother's terrible illness.

He's poised, sure of himself, sure of his message, even as he begins an evisceration of the defence strategies: "'Necessity!' cried my colleagues over there. Their clients had no choice! But of course my friends realized how treacherous was the ground on which they sought to tread. Surely that's why they grasped at a different straw, in nearer reach. It's all Chemican's fault! Blame the victim!

"Remember their devastating cross-examinations of Chemican's senior officer and senior scientist? The bribery, the false tests, the carelessness, the cover-ups, the spills, the scapegoating. A brilliant bit of sleight of hand — it's what the clever magicians do, focus on the devil conjured up, distract attention from the hidden escape hatch."

An unladylike snort of laughter from Khan's lanky young student-at-law is quickly suppressed, disguised as a hoarse cough.

"Ladies and gentlemen, please let me be clear that I share with my learned friends their disgust about Chemican-International's efforts to promote their line of neonicotinoids. We have heard about some slippery and highly questionable efforts in the testing and marketing of their signature product, Vigor-Gro. I hold no sympathy for Chemican. I applaud my learned friends — eminent barristers both — for laying bare its duplicity. But Chemican is not on trial, contrary to what my honourable friends want you to believe."

Arthur has seen this play before: *I am no orator, as Brutus is . . . Brutus is an honourable man.*

"Mr. Beauchamp soon realized that a discerning jury of twelve honest Torontonians was not going to be confused into thinking Chemican was being prosecuted here, so he shifted gears a second time. He embarked on yet another brave and desperate mission — blaming Chemican's director of security. Mr. Howell J. Griffin was the evil genius behind it all.

"Hadn't he hired a junkie drug-pushing hoodlum to guard the factory? The late Archie Gooch, poor fellow, whom Howie Griffin entrusted with the entrance codes to the plant. Somehow Howie Griffin had never got around to installing security cameras in the building. So of course, it's obvious, the whole thing was an insurance scam, and Griffin, needing lots of extra change to support his coke habit, entered into a deep conspiracy with his corporate bosses to use the Earth Survival Rebels as unwitting pawns."

The air in here has become too dense with sarcasm for Arthur's comfort but he fears it's working with most of the jurors.

"And we all know that ploy was quickly deflated when Mr. Griffin took the witness stand. Mr. Beauchamp, to give him credit, then handsomely apologized for insinuating Griffin helped facilitate the Sarnia attack. But my infinitely resourceful friend devised yet another construct: suddenly it wasn't the bees that were in trouble, it was human health.

"Enter Mr. Charlie Dover, a fine young man with a serious disability who may have deserved better than he got from Chemican. Maybe he was severely allergic to Vigor-Gro. Maybe a minute population of this world's inhabitants may be allergic to ziegladoxin. Maybe use of that substance should be suspended worldwide.

"Maybe, maybe, maybe. Ladies and gentlemen, a whole bunch of maybes can never comprise an urgent situation of clear and imminent peril. You cannot conspire to react urgently to an imminent peril! That's the fundamental fallacy in the defence argument."

He moves on to his most telling point:

"Where is the nexus between the direct action undertaken by the defendants, their attack on the neonic plant, and the alleged human health dangers of neonics? When they began their scheming the accused had no clue that Charlie Dover even existed or that trials on humans had ever been undertaken. That point was candidly conceded by Dr. Ariana Van Doorn, the defence's chief witness."

As to the second leg of the test for necessity — no lawful way out — surely the jury could not accept that raiding a factory "is the only way to save the bees and the birds and all of humankind."

Khan reminds the jury that the perils of cigarette smoking were lawfully dealt with by public opposition to Big Tobacco, by political action, by massive suits in damages. Likewise public protest and civil actions led to the downfall of Big Pharma's opiate producers. "Nobody had to scheme and conspire and break the criminal law to save lives from lung cancer and opiate addiction."

Khan has gotten a bit hoarse. He takes a deep breath. This is it, his peroration, he's reaching oratorical climax.

"Ladies and gentlemen, today, tomorrow, and until you render your verdict, you are sitting in judgment of one of the most critical issues of law of our generation: Do we reward those who break the law out of an arrogant sense of rightness — or do we hold the line?

"If you, our jury, don't hold the line, what precedent do you set? That it's okay to burn buildings and blow up bridges because that's somehow going to save the world? Are you prepared to give a green light to acts of terror committed by those who claim to hold the answer to all the world's ills? Or do you stand strong and render a verdict that will deter others who may conspire at truly monstrous evils. I urge you to tell the world: *no* to anarchy, we are not going there, we are standing up for democracy and the rule of law."

4

A single handclap has Judge Donahue searching for the perpetrator as Azra Khan takes his seat in a swirl of black robes. Echoes of his oratory seem to reverberate faintly about the hushed vastness of this courtroom. Arthur feels the suppressed energy back there, spectators fighting the knee-jerk urge to applaud or cry "Bravo."

He's afraid to look at the jury, doesn't want to take in their awed expressions. It's bad enough to behold the glum faces of the Sarnia Seven. Only Nancy Faulk, beside him, seems unperturbed.

Colleen Donahue takes a few moments to let Khan's exhortation sink in before she returns to business. "We have half an hour before the noon break. Would either defence counsel care to begin?"

Nancy rises. "My pleasure, M'Lady. Half an hour is more than ample time to give last rites to the indictment against my clients. There's barely a thimble of evidence against them, so I'll leave it up to Mr. Beauchamp to answer the many misdirected shots Mr. Khan fired at the necessity defence. For the record, Arthur speaks for both of us on that issue."

With a wave toward Amy Snider and Ivor Trebiloff, Nancy presents her clients to the jury as loving, long-time Torontonians who've operated a small antiques business on St. Clair West for twenty years.

She touches on their campaigns for social causes, entertains with an account of their arrests in Mississippi for picketing the church of a racist preacher. Handcuffed together, they fell in love.

That's always a winner. It gets smiles from the jury box.

Her summing-up of the evidence is incisive and succinct: None of the media accounts filed as exhibits point to Amy and Ivor as having played any part in planning the events of September 10. They were portrayed as "close to" or "comrades of" the others, but friendship is no crime. *The Walrus* reported that the store's backroom was "freely available" to the Earth Survival Rebellion, but that spoke only to the couple's generosity, not to an awareness of ill-doing. Anyway, awareness alone does not make one a conspirator.

The van, registered to Ivor Antiques Ltd., was used only for delivery of furniture. On September 10 it disappeared for an evening but was back by the morning. Driving time each way is three hours. Nancy's point: Ivor and Amy likely would not have known it was gone because they regularly closed shop at five and opened at ten.

The couple are so concerned about their carbon footprint they bus to work from their home in York. This detail, along with a few others, isn't in evidence, but Khan seems unbothered. It's as if he expects the jury to cut them loose — presumably as a trade-off for convicting the other five.

Nancy signs off with a reasonable-doubt reminder. In all, it took her twenty minutes.

Her strategy — confidently short and sweet — ought to pay off handsomely, but with juries there's no guarantee. Arthur has too often seen, at trial's end, the stunned faces on counsel who thought they had it in the bag.

"It is twenty minutes after twelve," says the judge. "I'm proposing we adjourn now and return at ten minutes to two."

"I need a fucking drink," Nancy mutters.

§

Arthur commandeers a small table in this gloomy tavern, and as Nancy visits the washroom he re-examines Azra Khan's pitch to the jury. It was brilliant at many levels, folksy and wry with its capsule comments about each accused, then mocking Arthur's shape-shifting strategies. Finally, a vibrant appeal to patriotism and law and order.

Arthur feels his age. He wonders if he has enough left in him to match his opponent.

When he badly needs pepping up he usually seeks a shot of confidence from his wife. Margaret is on Garibaldi this week, or somewhere in her riding at a series of town halls. He gets her recorded voice on the phone. No response on FaceTime. Now he's even glummer.

Too impatient to wait for table service, Nancy brings a tall gin-and-tonic to the table, takes a swallow, and utters a little whoop of relief. Her job is done.

"Can you believe Azra?" she says. "Did he think he was in Stratford? Once more into the breach, dear friends! I mean, what a pile of bombastic shit. Extreme suck-holing to the media. It's all about headlines."

Arthur is shocked at that negative review but he's not revising his own reaction. "Maybe it was a little overblown, but it was damn effective. He did a job on me, likening me to a ball bouncing around a roulette wheel, with no idea where I would land. I was the wily West Coast mouthpiece who thought he could sell hogwash to a Hogtown jury."

Suddenly an omelette appears in front of him. He can't remember ordering it, though obviously he did. His brain has become rusty and shopworn. He's not ready to face the jury.

Nancy picks at a plate of calamari. "Look at it this way — despite all the loaded rhetoric Azra was just wasting words. Donahue is hell-bent on instructing the jury that the necessity defence is bullshit." She mimics, wiggling her nose: "You may not allow this elusive concept to enter into your deliberations."

Arthur has secretly held on to the hope that somehow, like Howie, she might be dazzled by sudden illumination and be persuaded to leave necessity to the jury. He must finally acknowledge that was a wilfully blind hope: she'd proclaimed her intentions well before the trial began.

"Will I also just be wasting words?"

Nancy drains her glass, gestures for the same again, looks hard at him. "You're a great barrister, Arthur, with uncanny powers of persuasion, but you're not going to budge Madam Justice Ayn Rand. Make your pitch. Nothing ventured. Maybe we can still hang the jury. It would help if you offer them a backup defence instead of throwing everything into the necessity basket. Plan C."

Wise counsel. Arthur must dig up one of his red herrings, or maybe create a fresh one, and somehow pump it up with reasonable doubt and hope it will float.

§

He's in the robing room, buttoning his vest with fumbling fingers, still trying to get himself up for his jury address, as his phone rumbles in his pocket. The big furry face occupying the screen confuses him for a moment, and then his heartbeat quickens.

"Bark hello to Arthur." Margaret's voice.

Ulysses stares at small, flat, non-smelling version of old man who deserted dog friend. He backs up a few steps and barks. Arthur barks back, and promises him a huge thigh bone if he can just wait a couple more days. Several barristers are staring at him, so he throws on his robe and finds a private area in the lounge.

Margaret asks, "Have you heard the latest poll results?"

"Poll results? Well, I've been rather out of touch, dear."

"Okay, the election is only two weeks away and already in the bag. Assuming the *Bleat*'s polling procedures can be trusted, approval

546

ratings for Zoller and Shewfelt are running at about ten percent. Our team is hovering in the high seventies."

Our team. Zoë Noggins and the unmentionable Taba Jones. "Well, then, something to celebrate."

There's more good news. Blunder Bay is bursting with spring growth. The chickens are laying and the goats are kidding. No catastrophes, aside from Stoney sneaking off with the Fargo again. The moat around Jeremiah's well is receding and the Garibaldi Historical Society "is panting at the prospect of some kind of unveiling ceremony."

Margaret doesn't ask how the trial is going — Arthur expects she knows the answer. But he confesses it has taken too much out of him. "I swear to all the gods of every known faith throughout the universe that this is my last trial."

"Did I hear you say you'll be here in a couple more days?"

"Maybe even sooner, depending on how fast I can pack."

CHAPTER 25 » RIVIE

1

Monday, June 3

Judge Donahue, who believes everyone has their place — dock, box, stand, or counsel table — keeps a wary eye on my lawyer, who has wandered from his proper station. Right now, Arthur's too close to the jury for her comfort, and I can tell she's dying to order the bad boy to behave.

He's note-less, and gestures with free hands. His voice is so rich and resonant he doesn't need the sound system. Even in the back of the gallery no one cranes to hear.

He pitches pretty hard, now that he's finished his warm-ups. He began with a little paean to Toronto, how well he was received, then explained how our jury system is a bulwark against oppression by the state and powerful private interests, a form of citizens' democracy in which "the people, not the government, not the judges, not the politicians, have the final say."

Then he gave the jury a few congratulatory/sardonic words about Khan's "vigorous" address and a tongue-in-cheek promise to the jury that anarchy won't reign and the skies won't fall if the Sarnia Seven are acquitted.

Azra Khan smiled at that, but his underlings looked sour.

Arthur has a relaxed rhythm going, and is easy to follow, but I wish my eyes would stop drifting to the empty jury chair. It's so forlorn. And symbolic of a situation that is beyond Kafkaesque: ethics demanded that I tattle on an earnest, lovelorn student, thereby ensuring that I get sent up rather than set free. And drag down everyone else.

Arthur's focus is straightforward: heap the shit on Chemican-International, this trial's true evildoer. We are the good guys, we exposed those scumbags. The thrust is that the jury should acquit us on principle, even if they're satisfied we're guilty. Send a message. Help save the world.

He lays it all out, like a good prosecutor, all the evidence against Chemican. The Cook Islands holiday for the EPA boss, the culture of bribery, the falsified tests, the red-winged blackbirds and the hummingbirds, the toxins that stay in the ground and creep into all growing things, into gardens and cultivated fields, into our water, our food, our stomachs, our brains. He warns of the environmental holocaust to come unless something is done.

"Yet Chemican denies harm, rejects honest science, continues on this path of destruction. And I don't trust them, my friends, I don't trust them to tell the truth, and I urge you to find that their witnesses, who are still here, Mr. Wakeling and Dr. Jinks, were untruthful, and because of that, without even considering necessity, there must be reasonable doubt."

This must be the Plan C that Nancy tipsily mentioned to us after she and Arthur returned from lunch.

"Now we know the plant was starting to bleed money and was about to be shuttered. We know a top official wrote confidentially to Mr. Wakeling, 'We'd be better off if it burned down. Big insurance payout.' That's right. A bonanza, a hundred-million-dollar claim, a massive windfall for a creaky old factory with a cash flow problem. And with all that wood framework, it would burn like the *Hindenburg*. I see you nodding, Mr. Foreman, and you should know better than anyone."

Nine out of ten. The mini-mall architect grins sheepishly, pleased that his expertise is recognized. Judge Donahue's face clouds: she doesn't like this overfamiliarity with a juror. Khan seems not to care, as he doodles on his pad, lost in thought.

"Mr. Khan scorned the option I posed, that Chemican's corrupt bosses conspired to use the accused as unwitting pawns to make a big insurance grab. But let me frame that differently: What if these corporate schemers simply gave the accused carte blanche to enter the Sarnia plant, and cause so much damage it would have to be shut down? Whether by arson or explosive device or smashing up sensitive equipment.

"Now we can't say for certain that was the case, but think about it. Ask yourselves if you're satisfied beyond a reasonable doubt that Chemican wasn't complicit in allowing the plant to be targeted by these accused. What we *can* say for certain is that Chemican's trusted agent, Howell Griffin, did consent to an intrusion by my clients."

He reads from a transcript, echoing Howie's earnest tone: "'Anything was possible that night. I didn't care. I was up to here with my job. I was drunk. I was in love. I would have done anything for her.' And he sure did. Howell Griffin gave Rivie Levitsky a blank cheque, gave her the keys to his inner office, gave her his computer's password, gave her the security codes to the Sarnia plant."

That's not quite the way it went down, but no one's objecting.

"Chemican's head of security not only gave consent to an incursion upon that pesticide factory, he practically encouraged it!"

A pause to let that sink in.

I think I'm in love with her more than ever. Lucy still thinks that's a crock of shit. My flush of astonishment and vanity has in fact subsided — punctured by her cutting derision. *I'm surprised he didn't propose marriage while he was on the stand.*

"Griffin boldly admitted he gave Rivie Levitsky full access to his main computer and filing cabinet. Take what you want, he told her. He meant it. So if Mr. Griffin, acting as agent to his employer, encouraged the defendants' direct action, I feel confident in telling you no crime has been committed. If I invite you to walk into my home, Ms. Glockins, and walk off with the silverware — and I'm not assuming you would do that —" (chortles from jurors) "— no one has committed a crime. Well, maybe me, if I was trying to defraud my insurers."

More chortles. Ms. Glockins, Juror Three, social worker, smiles blushingly. Full marks. Arthur has achieved a familiarity with many of these jurors — casual greetings, good-health wishes, exchanges about the weather or the Stanley Cup playoffs, as they chance upon each other in hallways, escalator, elevators.

"Now, you may not be able to find clear, incontrovertible proof that higher-ups at Chemican helped engineer this incursion into their plant. You may find it unlikely they knew Mr. Griffin gave away all the codes and said, 'Have at it, it's all yours, burn it down, tear it down.' But you do know that something stinks. And that aroma alone ought to raise a reasonable doubt about whether Chemican consented to a raid on their plant."

So okay, that's Plan C, I guess, the consent defence. I can read the judge — she thinks Arthur's full of shit — but I can't read the jury. Do they find his concept totally flat-earth far-fetched? Or could it raise a nugget of doubt? Just enough for them to worry over whether Beauchamp was right: What if those kooky idealists *were* used for an insurance scam?

Arthur turns silent, maybe offering a silent prayer, a Hail Mary. Then he's distracted by a tapping sound behind him, and he turns — as do we all — to see Selwyn Loo approaching with his cane. A law student gives her seat to him.

Arthur spends a couple of minutes of special pleading for Rockin' Ray, who was "obviously" too intoxicated by his hallucinogenic drug to know what he was doing while playing his avenger role.

Then he takes a deep breath and gets close to the jury again. "As I leave the consent issue with you, let me turn to the defence of necessity, and try to correct as many of Mr. Khan's misstatements as I can — exhausting all of them would take up too much time."

Okay, we're back to Plan A. Here goes. Can he pull it off? Fingers crossed.

"The necessity defence is historic, recognized from Aristotle's time. Its role in our common law goes back to 1551, thirteen years before Shakespeare's birth, when the scribes of an English court recorded this trenchant comment: some acts 'may break the words of the law, and yet not break the law itself.' And necessity was offered as an example."

Judge Donahue looks restless, maybe annoyed that Arthur is trespassing in her yard: the law.

"And here we are, nearly five centuries later, and that precept still stands, though it's phrased more elaborately: non-compliance with the law — with the *words* of the law — is excused by an emergency or justified by the pursuit of some greater good. Though that principle is not carved on a stone tablet, it has held up."

Donahue's nose begins to twitch. Arthur isn't paying attention to her, has left the counsel table again, is cozying up to the jurors. "The highest court in this land has said: 'the peril must be so pressing that normal human instincts cry out for action —'"

"Stop right there!" As Her Ladyship bawls that, Miss Pucket almost rockets from her chair with fright. "No, sir, you cannot misconstrue Supreme Court citations."

"If it please Your Ladyship, I am in the middle of my final speech to the jury." Arthur looks astonished that she would muscle into his exclusive time with them. "I misconstrued nothing, I quoted verbatim from the Supreme Court."

"Well, you just can't cherry-pick the passages you like. Members of the jury, you will disregard counsel's commentary on the law of necessity. That is entirely the prerogative of the court."

Arthur is unbowed. I think he wanted this small confrontation. "I look forward to Your Ladyship's instructions on how necessity applies to the facts in evidence."

"Or whether it does."

At which point, Khan concludes a doodle which, from what I can make out, is a happy face.

Donahue has an OCD attack: "Mr. Beauchamp, when you address me, would you kindly reposition yourself at your table."

He bows and does so. "My apology, I didn't realize it made you uncomfortable, M'Lady."

Maybe he wants the jury to feel she's one-sided and unreasonable, that's why he digs at her. He boldly continues to talk about necessity, giving a few instances from reported cases. Donahue watches him with eyes hooded.

"A more typical example is this: a mother decides to shoplift from a grocery to feed her starving baby. Would you convict her for that, Ms. Nagler?" Juror Nine, retired botany professor. "No, I should hope, because the offence she committed — that she *planned* to commit — was of infinitesimal effect compared with the harm she sought to avoid."

Donahue's warning voice: "Mr. Beauchamp . . ."

Arthur, piqued, interrupts, before she can get going: "The point I was leading to, M'Lady, is that a planned raid on a factory producing deadly chemicals is insignificant compared to the planetary catastrophe to which these chemicals contribute. Proportionality is a significant factor—"

"That's just one factor. Imminent peril. No way out. How do you meet that? Never mind, just carry on." She shuts up, sensing her heckling has made the jury impatient.

The jurors seem relieved to get Arthur's full attention again, even though they're made uneasy by his evoking of a nearly barren planet.

He asks them to imagine a world without bees, without pollinators, a silent world without the chirping of crickets, without birdsong, a monochrome world of plants that never flower . . . and bleaker yet, a toxic planet, massive crop failures, famine.

With a few brushstrokes, he conjures up a disaster scenario familiar to readers of apocalyptic novels — we're asked to picture our great-great-grandchildren struggling to survive in pockets of civilization as desperate, armed mobs maraud and pillage and rape and murder.

"Mr. Khan railed about anarchy. We are not going there, he exclaimed. But if we can't turn things around, that's exactly where we're going. The breakdown of civilization: that's the anarchy we should fear, that's the anarchy we must resist. And the trigger for that anarchy would be the mass extinction of pollinating insects. That's your urgent, imminent peril, ladies and gentlemen, you can't find anything more imminent than that, it's going on now, and it's accelerating like a runaway train."

His deep voice fills this massive space: "There *is* no way out! Nothing has worked! Despite the pleas of scientists and the promises of politicians, despite school strikes, despite petitions and picketers and marches, the climate crisis accelerates. If all lawful options have been tried and failed, there's no way out, ladies and gentlemen. There is no reasonable, credible, workable way out."

He steps toward us, raises an arm as if to gather us into his embrace. "These men and women should not be prosecuted but applauded. The human testing program that Chemican tried to hide, the neural damage caused to Charlie Dover that they tried to bury — it's out in the open now, thanks to the accused. It's because of them we know that those allergic to Chemican's ziegladoxin are in peril right now, not decades away. The threat is not just imminent, it's *immediate*. And it's nothing less than criminal that Vigor-Gro is still on the market. It's outrageous that Chemican continues to deny the terrible dangers it poses, that they're promoting it with full-page ads instead of issuing a worldwide recall."

Grumbling from the Bee-lievers section has Judge Donahue squinting for culprits. Arthur just carries on, about the human health dangers Vigor-Gro poses. He doesn't risk stepping into the quagmire of stats and actuarial science intended to prove there are other prospective Dovers out there. I don't know if he understands those charts and graphs any better than I do.

But he pulls heartstrings, reminding the jury how the Niagara beekeeper broke down over the loss of her hives. "It wasn't the money, she loved her honeybees, she'd become attached to them. But for Chemican-International, it was only the money, always the money.

"So it has been left to this band of environmental warriors to cut through the smog of greed and denial and inertia, and to shock the world into a stark awareness of the disaster that looms. Theirs was not a crime except by the words of the law. Theirs was a desperate attempt to save human lives. It was an act of courage and salvation."

He might have quit there, on that dramatic flourish; instead his voice lowers, sharing, confiding. "Folks, we live in a time of mass confusion about what is true and what is not. A time when liars abound on the internet and liars dare to shout, 'Fake news!' Try to imagine the celebrations that would take place if my clients were found guilty: corks would pop in Kansas City, and at the head offices of the other pesticide corporations. Their ad agencies and lobbyists would gleefully proclaim that a Canadian jury has ruled in favour of the agrochemical industries and their products. We were right all along, they would say, our pesticides and neonics are harmless, we were victims of fake news."

Arthur turns toward the Chemican group — the veep, the chief scientist, their portly lawyer. All wear scoffing expressions, the lawyer grinning. Not a good look, I think, from the jury's point of view.

"It's not hard to imagine them gloating, is it? In newspaper and TV ads, on Twitter and Facebook. And thus exonerated they will carry on with their false studies, shelling out bribes, hiring scientists to shill for them and perform as talking heads. And they'll continue pumping out their toxic insecticides while forty percent of the million known species of insects face sudden extinction."

He swings back to the jury. "Ask yourselves if in all good conscience you can reward this corrupt and dangerous mega-corporation with even a symbolic victory. You deny them that if you announce to the world that the accused deserve an acquittal."

A big, powerful note, but he doesn't end on it. Once again, Arthur abandons his station, moves in on the jury. His voice lowers, intimate and sharing.

"Remember, it's a serious offence to invade the secrecy of the jury room. Your deliberations are secret. No one may ever tell you what your verdict must be. No one may ever demand to know how you reached your verdict."

He turns back to the Chemican team: "This is a crooked corporation." Back to the jury: "Are you willing to deliver a verdict that exonerates them, a verdict that rewards greed and corruption and heartlessness? What precedent might that set? How would struggling future generations remember that?" Silence as he seeks their commitment. Some engage him solemnly, some nervously, some look away.

"But a decision that makes a powerful statement about the need for a worldwide ban on neonics — that's a precedent that will cause the bells of justice to ring across this entire planet."

A burst of applause from behind me, but Arthur waves the perpetrators to silence before Donahue can spoil the moment by griping at them.

"And should you, my friends, as I pray you will, render not guilty verdicts on every count, reflect on this: history may regard this trial as a turning point. If our planet survives and finds a path to recovery, those future generations — the children of the children of your children — will not only celebrate the outcome of this trial, they will honour those who had the heart and courage and sensibility to do the right thing."

He bows to the jury, bows to the judge, returns to his table, and sits to raucous cheers from the back of the gallery. Miss Pucket bawls for order, but without much effect. The judge seems startled to see the time: it's well past four thirty.

As court is adjourned, reporters barge their way to the door, followed by clamorous Bee-Dazzlers and gabbling Bee-lievers and a miscellany of other Torontonians hooked on this trial. The Chemican team toils along behind with stiff, artificial smiles. Out a side door goes Inspector Jake Maguire, leading the prosecution team.

It takes me a few moments of numbness to realize I'm a little shaken, a little teary, and I'm all alone in the dock. The other six plus Nancy are with Arthur, paying tribute.

He seems weary, so weary, and a little confused as he looks around for someone. When he locates me, his expression is like, how did I do? As if my opinion matters. But I blow him a kiss, and he looks relieved.

But it was Selwyn Loo he was looking for, and he starts on realizing that Selwyn, who has this ghostlike quality, is just behind him. Selwyn smiles broadly as they embrace but tears fall from his sightless eyes.

2

We gather at the Cameron for drinks to celebrate what may be our last evening of freedom. The lawyers were invited, but Arthur plans instead to join Azra Khan and his wife for dinner. Nancy expects to join them but dreads the prospect. Selwyn Loo wants to hang with his old clients, however, and is buying rounds. Tomorrow, he entrains to Ottawa to brief the government on climate crisis strategies.

None of us talk about the trial — it's like a bad-luck superstition — but Doc is unusually gabby, full of himself now that his book's final copyedit is done. Nancy shows a coolness toward him that hints they're disengaging. Clearly, her emotional needs aren't being met. Empathy is not Doc's strong suit.

I finally ask her about the script for tomorrow.

"Bleak," she says. "The judge will veto the necessity defence. Jurors will either bow to her authority or be bludgeoned into submission. That's typically what happens, but sometimes you get a stubborn holdout, someone made of metal. So you get a hung jury, a mistrial, a do-over. Occasionally, when the stars are aligned, you even get a rogue jury. Does this look like a rogue jury?"

Our responses are glum. "Definotly," Ray says.

"Good luck tomorrow," Nancy says. "Pray for that stubborn holdout." She drains her final shooter and takes off.

3
Tuesday, June 4

"It is vital to remember that any sympathy you might feel for the accused must not affect your deliberations. Nor should any repugnance toward their beliefs or lifestyles."

Judge Donahue's smirk doesn't get recorded on the transcript, nor does Nancy's stink-finger under the table.

I confess I had fanciful notions of a twist in the plot: the judge would shock us, would be even-handed in addressing the jury, maybe slightly supportive. The reader would go, "Boy, I sure wasn't expecting that."

But not. She's half an hour into her "charge" to the jury, as they call it, and she's clobbering us. I can hear her thought processes: *Finally, after four weeks of their shit, it's my chance to teach those insufferable, self-glorifying peacocks a lesson.*

I remember my first take on her, back in March: dropping a cold-hearted life sentence on a woman who shot her psychopathic partner. *While I must take into account the jury's recommendation of mercy, I am in no way bound by it . . .*

"Fascist cunt," Nancy had drunkenly hollered at her years ago. There's no way that has helped our case, despite her formal apology. But our counsel have long written off this judge. It's all about the jury now. We don't want their mercy, we just want one stubborn holdout.

Over coffee this morning, Nancy confessed to be profoundly hungover. She overdid it last night at dinner with Arthur and the Khans: a healing of the many puncture wounds from courtroom duels. Her splurge was prompted by her marital war heating up again.

"Likewise, any feelings you may have about Chemican-International Ltd., positive or negative, must not prejudice your views." Positive *or* negative? They have a choice? "The company is not on trial, despite the tireless efforts of defence counsel to persuade you so." Donahue is in one of her rare good moods, finally getting the attention she feels she deserves — the media haven't always been kind to her.

She recites what should be shining principles — onus of proof, reasonable doubt — with the machine-gun speed of a TV ad listing an erection pill's side effects. She then reviews the evidence right up to how Jake Maguire and Gaylene Roberts took us down — "in a most resourceful manner, if you'll forgive a personal aside."

She details the evidence against each of us, saving me for the last — and for the worst, with my conniving ways. She seems to take special pleasure in reminding the jury how I was caught red-handed trying to flee the country with a phony passport. She lays into me for running while my confederates stood their ground, as if nobly facing the challenge. Methinks she really doesn't like me, probably regards me as some kind of prima donna harlot.

Morning headlines have been personally embarrassing. *Griffin Gave Levitsky Blank Cheque for Sex, Lawyer Claims*. Inaccurately, but that was in a shitty tabloid. Other conservative media hailed Khan's speech ("Anarchy, we're not going there") while the allegedly liberal media (i.e., a little less blatantly right-wing) was more impressed by Arthur's call for a verdict leading to the banning of neonics.

Donahue doesn't even go easy on Ivor and Amy, doesn't hint the jury would be justified in letting them off. It might help those two if their lawyer brightens up. Nancy looks grim and depressed. On top of her divorce acting up again — over a nasty text about the depleted wine cellar — the word is out locally, via Doc, apparently, that she had a doubly adulterous one-nighter with Khan years ago. Not smart, Doc.

Mrs. Khan's presence at last night's dinner obviously factored into Nancy tying one on. Lucy and I have trouble conceiving the entity that is Azra Khan's wife. Apparently she's a clinical psychologist and is beautiful. I wonder if she knows Azra fools around. Or cares.

Post-dinner, Arthur joined the Khans on a visit to Azra's mother, who (forgive me) has been dying to meet him. Arthur's gesture was five-out-of-five thoughtful. Ten-out-of-ten.

Having disposed of us seven conspirators Donahue spends some time with Howie, summing up his "rather bizarre" testimony but not otherwise commenting on it. His credibility was for the jury to assess. Then she announces that's it, she has concluded her review "of the admissible evidence."

Here it comes.

"You will be aware that I have not touched on any testimony that relates to the alleged issue of necessity. I am bound to instruct you as to the essential elements of the offences charged and the legitimate defences, but not to defences that lack an air of reality. It is a matter for the court to decide whether such an air of reality exists, and I find it totally lacking. A conspiracy hatched and refined over several months cannot by the farthest stretch of the imagination be seen as an emergency response to an imminent peril."

The jurors' expressions range from impassive to confused to surprised to, in one case, pleased. Tax auditor Mabel Sims has "I told you so" written on her face as she nudges the woman beside her: Juror Eleven, well-to-do Joyce Evans, who has an acreage in Meadowvale and is on the SPCA board.

"You are not to give thought to the necessity issue or anything you heard relating to it, whether from the Crown, the defence, or their expert witnesses. Your verdict, guilty or not guilty, must be based solely on admissible evidence adduced in this room. It must not be affected in any way by feelings of sympathy or antipathy for any person or cause. As an example, any compassion you feel for Mr. Charles Dover is wasted because his evidence is irrelevant."

There's something wrong with this picture. How can Donahue just blatantly order the jury to suppress normal human feelings? How does a judge get to dictate to a jury what they're allowed to consider? Didn't Donahue hear our lawyer proclaim that the jury is a bulwark against oppression? *The people, not the government, not the judges, not the politicians, have the final say.*

"You have sworn to give a true verdict according to the evidence." A quick look at Arthur, her nose twitching, as if it smells the enemy. "You have not sworn an oath to resist anarchy or cause bells to ring across this planet."

Nancy does a gag reflex — I can't be sure if it's faked or real. I scan my fellow future inmates. Nobody seems too distressed, except Okie Joe maybe, who's built a thriving business and has a gaming app that could break out of the pack. Doc looks totally cool with doing time, his quest for martyrdom paying off.

Donahue's next bit is to review counsels' final arguments. She quotes almost verbatim Azra Khan's cartoon sketches of the fumbling schemers in the dock. She rhetorically applauds his sarcastic critique of Arthur's "deep conspiracy to use the Earth Survival Rebels as unwitting pawns."

Arthur's pitch gets a less stellar review. Conveying skepticism with arched eyebrows she lightly touches on his notion of a planned insurance fraud. With a baffled frown, she struggles with the concept that Howie Griffin somehow granted consent to our "attack" on the plant.

Arthur's consent defence was "an unseemly diversion long on speculation and short on proof." She hammered the last nail in with "I daresay you will have little difficulty disposing of it."

There she goes again, telling the jury how to think. No wonder Dickens's exclamation still rings true: the law *is* an ass.

Nancy's jury speech gets even shorter shrift, maybe two minutes. I sit there stunned, wondering if Ivor and Amy are doomed too.

Donahue assumes a weary tone as she starts to wrap up with mantras about reasonable doubt and presumption of innocence. She's like, *Do we really have to go through this charade when everything's so cut and dried?*

Other housekeeping chores include reminding the jury their decision has to be unanimous and that sentencing is the sole prerogative of the court. They can come back to ask questions or have testimony read back to them. They will be put up in a fine Toronto hostelry if they can't agree on a verdict today (which, her hearty tone hints, is as unlikely as little green people rappelling to the courthouse roof from a passing asteroid).

Donahue glances at the clock. Nearly noon. "Before you begin deliberations, please enjoy coffee or tea in the jury room while I ask counsel if I have covered all bases."

The jury is barely out the door when Arthur's on his feet, indignant, demanding the judge recall them and brief them fully on our defences. Donahue's instructions were one-sided and illiberal, her view of necessity repressive. He storms about how it's unheard of for a trial judge to strip the defence naked.

I shiver at that concept. After a month-long trial, this is where we find ourselves, exposed right down to our furry little pubes, denied even a thread of reasonable doubt.

"Thank you, Mr. Beauchamp." Polite, smiling. "Ms. Faulk, do you have anything to add?"

"Yes, M'Lady, with all due respect you failed in your duty to warn the jury it would not merely be risky but ridiculous to convict Ms. Snider and Mr. Trebiloff."

"Thank you. Mr. Khan?"

"The Crown is content."

"Very well. The jury will be advised they can now commence their deliberations. Now, as to the matter of whether bail should be continued while we wait for the jury's return . . ."

Khan jumps in. "The Crown has no objection to a continuance of bail for all accused as long as they remain in the courthouse while the jury is in session."

"Very well. The matter may be moot in any event should they return before dinner."

With the quickie verdicts Her Ladyship has made clear she expects.

§

Four hours later, it is dinnertime and no stirrings have been heard from the jury room. Lawyers, court staff, media, and accused sprawl about in corridors or witness lounges. I'm in one of those, learning pinochle from Ivor Trebiloff, when we get word we are to reassemble.

"The verdict's in," an excited young reporter says as we hurry into 6-1.

That seems not to be the case — the lawyers and court staff scoffed at Donahue's optimism over an early verdict. "They're not going to pass up on a free steak-and-lobster dinner and a night in the Four Seasons," says a court officer.

The jury enter, unruffled, no red faces, projecting a sense they finally feel important, they're playing an active role. The judge bounds to her chair with a jauntiness that I read as put on, and gives them a verbal back rub about the thought and care they're obviously putting into this. She tells them to enjoy their dinner as guests of Her Majesty, and grants them an evening off. We are to return here Wednesday at nine thirty.

4
Thursday, June 6

Here I am, Dear Journal, just tapping away mindlessly after a pizza and a toke with Lucy. Got back here to find Arthur asleep in his club chair with Plutarch's *Morals* open on his lap. I put him to bed. He's been a little harried lately. Me too. I get it, the tension of waiting almost three days for a verdict gets damn gripping.

Local social notes: Sooky-Sue and Richard Dewilliger-James II have asked Lucy and me to an engagement party, according to the engraved cards we got today. If we're still not behind bars a week from Saturday, we might go. After all, he is my bondsman.

I suppose it's too late to try to persuade him she's a narcissistic viper incapable of love. Spooky has closed down her spiritual scam, the church of the Lord Saviour Divine. She's into the big bucks now.

Excuse me, Journal, while I take a moment, the Oriole reliever just walked Grichuk to load the bases . . .

That paid off. Two runs on a wild throw. Hey, Howie, are you at the game? Hope you haven't taped it for later, because spoiler alert: Jays seven, Baltimore five in the eighth.

I get weirded out whenever the screen saver kicks in and "Always Believe" scrolls sideways across it. Are you trying to hypnotize me, Howie? Have you embedded a psychic command into the screen saver that will have me begging for forgiveness for having doubted you? Repeat after me. Always believe. Always believe. You are getting sleepy, your head is heavy . . .

As I wrestle with belief, so does the jury, apparently. They're out for a third night and we haven't heard a whisper.

Nancy thinks they're doing a little rebellion thing, refusing to be pushed around. They're goddamn well going to enjoy a paid holiday before sheepishly returning to court and doing what they're told.

Arthur is less cynical. They're just meticulously performing their duty, reviewing every scrap of admissible evidence, and maybe some that's not, and reading and viewing our media interviews. "They're taking the case seriously, or at least pretending to."

The other possibility is that someone has taken on Abbie Lee-Yeung's promised role and is holding out. It's like a juror has done a Howie, and become a firm Bee-liever. The court officer stationed outside their lounge confided that he'd heard a raised voice or two. Someone being pummelled into submission?

Meanwhile, an irony of this trial is that Charlie Dover's testimony has moved several allergy victims of ziegladoxin, or their families, to reach out to Nancy's office. All with varying degrees of muddled senses of direction. She's thinking about a class-action. Thinking about destroying Chemican. If that happens, I'll happily do my time.

Last out, top of the ninth. The Jays hold on. Always believe.

Back to Arthur. Did I mention he's been acting strangely? In court, he was as advertised, Darrowian, but with the trial over he's become a fuddy-duddy around the house. Leaves lights on. Can't find his slippers. I go down to the kitchen every night to check the burners.

Now that the pressure's off, he's lost his edge? — that should work in reverse. Little slips of paper are haphazardly strewn all over the kitchen and under fridge magnets. *Get suit from cleaners. Pack bags. Pet store, dog treats. Repossess Fargo.* He's homesick, pining for dog and garden and the soft Pacific air.

5
Saturday, June 8

For the fourth straight morning, corridors are taken over by zombies: silent, slow-moving women and men of the press, some pacing, some sitting on the floor, remnants of them outside, smoking. None of them dare wander far, even on this sunny Saturday, because the jury could return at any time.

The press outnumber Bee-lievers and courtroom habitués, whose ranks deplete as the jury is now officially in deadlock. We have no clue who of the eleven is our champion, or how long she or he will be able to resist the others' demands to fall in line. Meanwhile, we're nervous wrecks, waiting, waiting, waiting.

Donahue went at them yesterday, goading them to do their duty: ten minutes of boilerplate about the need to listen to each other, to hear a differing point of view, to not let emotions overrule common sense.

Now it's mid-morning and Donahue has called us into court. She floats in instead of stomping. Makes you wonder if she's on tranks. The beatific expression may, however, just mask irritation that someone is filibustering in the jury room. She doesn't want them fetched yet, wants to discuss "taking the rest of the weekend off out of respect for Mr. Khan's loss."

We all knew his mother's death was imminent, so it wasn't a shock when the end came yesterday. Khan was abruptly called away to her bedside at about midday. His robotic junior, Finley, broke the news to judge and jury. He's now at the helm while his boss attends to funeral arrangements.

She asks for counsels' views. "Mr. Findlay? Shall we take the weekend off?"

The robot rises. "Finley. F-I-N-L-E-Y. If it please the court, I'll need to seek instructions—"

Donahue hates mealy-mouthing. "Never mind. Mr. Beauchamp?"

"Out of a sense of collegiality and my deep fraternal respect for Azra Khan, I would be honoured, as senior counsel, to make a motion to that effect."

"Ah, yes, that would be appropriate," Donahue says, defenceless against Arthur's skill at evoking the traditions of professional protocol.

The old fox has done it again. When the jury comes in — eleven tight, weary faces — they show relief as he urges, out of respect to "our dear friend Mr. Khan and his family," that we all take the weekend off from our labours.

"So ordered," says Donahue, then she expresses the hope that the jury, even though sequestered, will return on Monday "reinvigorated" after relaxing for the weekend. Then she sends the rest of us home.

I decide to cycle the long way to Parkdale. I'm so tense I could snap in half. Paranoia grows. I only recently learned I could get consecutive sentences on my roster of charges, the break-in, the conspiracy, false pretences, passport fraud. The count of uttering, which means using a forged passport, exposes me to fourteen years. All told, I could get up to fifty years. "Highly unlikely," Arthur insisted. "Let me do the worrying."

Easy for him to say.

§

After almost three hours of pedalling haphazardly around town, working the tension out of my system, I vault off my bike, sweaty, bedraggled, hair over my eyes, passers-by staring — hey, isn't she that crazy dame from that eco-terrorist trial?

The door isn't locked, so Arthur is somewhere, but not in the parlour or kitchen, though the kettle is hot and tea makings are on the counter. On the fridge door, a recent scribbled note: *AC Lv 410 Mon. arr YYJ 630*. That translates to an Air Canada reservation to Victoria on late Monday afternoon. Day after tomorrow. Does he know something I don't?

After a glass of milk and a bowl of re-nuked chicken soup, I'm ready to clean up, put on my running shoes, grab some more sunshine, pretend to enjoy one last free weekend. But I'm piqued by that note, Arthur's proposed flight home.

I spy him in his bedroom folding and packing clothes into a suitcase while talking to a hypothetical dog. "Come along, boy. This way. It's a beautiful day."

My lawyer is losing it. I don't want to embarrass him so I return to the kitchen and yell, "Arthur, are you home? You want your tea?"

He wanders in, again giving me his newly trademarked dozy smile. "'And tender love is repaid with scorn, what floweret can endure the storm?'" Though pulled from his unbounded repertoire of verse from long-dead poets, it seems hardly appropriate. Another symptom of a disarranged mind?

He thanks me for pouring his tea, and I ask, "So what are you up to?"

"Just packing a few things."

"You mean, like for your flight on Monday at ten after four?"

"No, for a train trip to Ottawa." Checking his watch. "At two today. Margaret and I made weekend plans, and, ah . . ."

"Oh, God, of course, please enjoy. I'm not prying, but . . . you booked a flight home? On Monday?"

"Oh, well, that can be changed. I just . . . I think we'll have a verdict on Monday. Maybe not. Did you see their faces this morning? When they first came in? The jury?"

"Yeah, they looked pissed."

"One learns to read faces in a court of law."

This is all too enigmatic. He's definitely falling apart. "Read *my* face. If they convict everyone, what happens — will you stick around for the sentencing or will you be in a rush to make your plane?"

He looks shocked. I hate myself.

"Rivie—"

"I'm sorry. That's awful. I'm as jumpy as a cat in a lightning storm. Need to shower, then I'm going out again." I rush him, hug him, nearly cause him to spill his tea, apologize again, then race upstairs belching tears.

It's not him, it's me. *I'm* having a breakdown. It's not just the tension, the waiting. I'm overcome by a sense of longing and loneliness. I'll go to jail with no one to love.

A quick shower, repairs to my reddened eyes, a cap to hide my mangled hair, short shorts and running shoes and daypack, and I'm off, not sure where, I just need to run until my lungs ache, I need the pain of this cruelly sunny day.

My feet take me down to Lake Shore, then east to Harbourfront, up Spadina, where the SkyDome looms. This is my goal, an irresistible force has propelled me here, where there is energy, high spirits, happy thousands pouring into the Dome to watch the Orioles and Jays. I will feel less lonely here, among fellow rooters in the cheap seats.

§

As players warm up on the field I find myself being tugged again, from my bleachers seat, then down, and down, from level to level, toward the diamond, toward the third-base seats. I feel a little jolt on seeing him, in his usual spot, reading a magazine or folded newspaper, sunglasses tucked over a ball cap, clean-shaven, long-haired. The seat next to him is empty. My seat.

I swing my pack off and squeeze past Howie's knees and sit with a "Hi."

He looks at me puzzled, like he vaguely remembers me from somewhere. Then he deadpans, "We have to stop seeing each other like this."

"Seriously, feel free to tell me to fuck off."

"It seems odd, Rivie. Not like stalking, but sort of inappropriate."

"Relax. You won't be seeing me for the next ten years, less time off for good behaviour."

"Good behaviour? Why would they give you points for that?"

So acerbic. I thought he'd forgiven me. Howie applauds, and so do I, as a home run king from eons past is introduced. We applaud again as the Jays take to the field.

"What am I supposed to always believe in?"

"In yourself. In beauty and goodness. In the continuance of life. In love. In the impossible. The idea is to believe something, not sit around jerking off."

"Still doing your Buddhist guru impersonation?"

When he sees I don't buy his bullshit, his face creases into a squinty frown. "Literally and symbolically, I got jerked off by you, Ms. Levitsky. The hand job that shook the world. I am the biggest Toronto laughingstock since Rob Ford."

This is the true Howie Griffin, not the courtroom version. That was protective cover to camouflage his disgrace.

"Why do you still have two reserved seats? How can you afford them? Are you getting back with Maxine?" His ex, who preferred Mozart to baseball, and with whom he recently met over wine.

"Maxine and I are friends. I see the boys regularly. They love baseball."

He pauses to watch the first out, a long, looping fly to left centre. "And I can afford the seats thanks to several dirty Chemican executives."

"Right. You know where the bodies are buried. How much has she jacked them up to? Greta Adelsen, your lawyer."

Now comes his famous lopsided grin. "I couldn't understand why Becky McLean pretended to be shallow. Did her dear old mom warn her that men get turned off by brainy women?"

"Were you blowing shit in there? In court?"

"About being in love with you?"

"Okay, that too. But the whole thing, suddenly being radically green and socialist?"

"I am the converted. I no longer feel like shit. I feel purified."

"And the love bit? Did you mean it? It's okay if you didn't."

A bloop single and a sharp double play end the first half. Howie checks his lineup card against the stats on his sports page. He sighs. He speaks.

"Okay, it was a severe rebound reaction. You played me like an oaf from the backwoods. I lost control of the wheel, went off the road. It was real, it wasn't lust masquerading as love. And then when the whole thing blew up, yeah, I felt totally used and betrayed but I still loved . . . not you so much, the concept of you, who you really were . . ."

We both look up. Standing in the aisle is his redheaded mouth-piece, Greta Adelsen. She holds a big bucket of popcorn. "Sorry, I'm late." Eyes as cold as icicles as she extends the bucket to me. "Would you like to share?"

I'm already up, wiggling into my pack. "No, he's all yours."

6

Monday, June 10

The jury didn't take the weekend off after all — either that or a verdict has been reached with lightning speed. They began working only twenty minutes ago, and a court officer has announced they're ready. There's frenzied excitement in the hallways, loud gabbling.

We all take our proper places and wait while Miss Pucket visits Donahue in her chambers. And we wait. The judge was seen scuttling into the courthouse late, a major aberration for the punctuality freak.

Azra Khan is back, looking wan. He had an exhausting weekend — a service for his mother yesterday at her mosque, then a family event at the Khans' home.

Nancy slouches in her chair and looks grim. Despite the occasional bad mood, she enjoyed this trial, gave it everything — it took her away from her unhappy personal life. That life is now back, her husband seeking an order for an accounting of his wine holdings.

Arthur works on a *Times* crossword. He is calm. He will make his flight. He figured out who the holdout was by studying the jury for the few minutes they were in court on Saturday. *One learns to read faces.* He also predicted the jury would bring in a verdict quickly today.

Arthur got back from Ottawa early this morning, and I haven't had a chance to learn who he deduced was the die-hard. Nor have I had a chance to apologize for my bitchiness on Saturday. *Will you stick around for the sentencing?* You should fall on your knees, bitch, after everything he's done.

Lucy and I spent Sunday doing pharmaceuticals under the moose, laughing hysterically in a deranged celebration of our last day of freedom. She got a kick out of hearing about my farcical episode with Howie. "Told you. His only true love is his dick."

When I came down from our trip I felt like I'd found acceptance. I'm chilled, I'm ready to take what comes my way. I keep repeating that. A mantra.

The judge finally comes sailing in, beaming with relief that she won't face the shame of having presided over a mistrial and thereby wasting taxpayers' dollars. "I understand we have a verdict. Ah, I see Mr. Khan is back. I hope your weekend was, ah . . . not too difficult." She remembers, too late, to jettison her smile. "Are counsel ready? Very well, let's hear from the jury."

And they troop in. This time, I study their faces with more purpose. The foreman, the architect, nervously fidgets over his small but vital role: as the jury's voice, he will read the verdicts. Most of the others are as expressionless as officers of the palace guard, only their eyeballs moving, looking everywhere but at us: they hate themselves for their gutlessness, they can't bear to look upon the plucky band of heroes without feeling shame.

But some seem oddly at peace. Juror Seven, his arms folded in triumph, signalling he'd stubbornly fought and won. Juror Eleven, the SPCA lady, has the smile of a contented cat. Beside her, Mabel Sims, the churchy auditor, looks helplessly skyward, stiff-jawed, chastened, as if she'd just got a going-over from her parish priest. Maybe she heard the angry voice of God. Maybe I'm fantasizing. Something is askew here.

Miss Pucket asks the foreman if he has a verdict. Yes, he has. My mind spins as I continue to focus on Mabel Sims, sitting stiffly in the back row. She has it in for me, was forever glaring at me — I'm Satan's little helper, an arrogant, publicity-seeking infidel.

Miss Pucket wants us to stand as our names are called. Doc rises first, with head held high. Mabel Sims glances at him, then back in the direction of the heavens, as if seeking God's guidance. Or questioning it.

As Miss Pucket reads the first count against Doc, the conspiracy, I pinch myself. I feel pain, so I'm not dreaming. I've just had a revelation. I go to Lucy's ear. "Mabel Sims was the holdout."

"What?"

"Number Ten. The tax lady."

"Say again?"

"We won. We fucking won."

Miss Pucket: "How do you find the accused on count one, guilty or not guilty?"

"Not guilty."

You'd think the courtroom would explode. But an eerie stillness settles in. A mass holding of breath. Her Ladyship's nose vibrates like a rabbit scenting the advancing hounds. Khan sighs and shakes his head, in disbelief or disgust.

Then the second count: break, enter, and theft. Not guilty. Theft. Not guilty. Possession of stolen property. Not guilty.

Judge Donahue seems stunned, unbelieving. Doc is immobile, confused about what just happened, unsure whether to stand, sit, or go. Someone at the back yells, "Yay!"

Donahue hollers, "Remove that person!" The miscreant, a Believer, departs on her own, raising a fist of solidarity. But with that "Yay," with that fist, Donahue must finally feel the full extent of the jury's betrayal.

"Dr. Knutsen, please join us down here." Arthur offers a chair behind counsel table. Absentminded, homesick Arthur Beauchamp is the only composed person in this vast room. Tough cookie Nancy Faulk may be the least composed. She jumps up, does a dance step, hugs Doc, wipes tears.

"Joe Meekes," the clerk calls. Jurors finally look at us, observing our reactions, as Okie Joe gets acquitted on all counts.

I swivel left, right, behind me. There's too much going on right now, too much to take in, everything is just a series of snapshots. Azra Khan stops shaking his head, and bends over his doodling pad.

His minions look like they just came out of electrotherapy. A radio reporter flees to break the news. Another follows. Then another.

An intense vibe comes from the remaining press section as they compose their ledes: *A rogue jury acquitted the Sarnia Seven on all counts today* ... Judge Donahue looks at the media rows with poorly masked dismay — their reviews of her starring role will be disastrous. I can only imagine the state of her panties.

Joe takes a chair beside Doc. Next up are Ivor, then Amy. After they leave the dock, quickly acquitted, Nancy bundles them out to the hallway, where we can hear her whoop.

Lucy rises beside me, squeezes my shoulder, and as she gets cleared she blows kisses toward the jury. Rockin' Ray solemnly bows to them when it's his turn, a gentleman at the end.

I'm up last, accused number seven, the last one busted. And I'm thinking, Right on, I'm free, I'm hauling ass for Golden Valley to celebrate with Mom and Dad. I don't care if it's still black fly season. More power to the bugs!

As we work our way through the several charges against me: not guilty, not guilty, not guilty ... bang! my fantasy dissolves. "Guilty," says the foreman, wincing, clearly uncomfortable. It's the charge of using a fraudulent passport.

Mabel Sims gives me a gotcha stare. I get it — they had to give her something. I was the jury's compromise. I was the lamb sacrificed at the altar of unanimity. And I am now the only person in the prisoners' dock and I'm about to take one for the team, a high hard one between the eyes.

"Defendant will be remanded in custody for sentencing." In Donahue's steeliest voice, her fury at events barely under control.

Arthur is up. "If it please the court—"

Donahue interrupts. "We'll need a pre-sentence report — Mr. Khan, how fast can the probation service deliver?"

"Probably a month, but we will check."

Arthur tries again. "Surely Ms. Levitsky can remain—"

"Mr. Beauchamp, you can argue till the cows come home. Your client is going into custody immediately. Parliament has recognized this as a very serious indictable offence, with a fourteen-year maximum. A custodial sentence seems almost mandatory."

"A higher court, M'Lady, might hear that observation as having come from a mind made up, if not closed."

"Mr. Beauchamp, a higher court might also like to reflect on whether the verdicts that went your way could be sustained. I expect Crown Counsel has already turned his mind to that."

The jury still hasn't been excused, so they must listen to the judge imply they did a shitty job.

"I intend to carefully consider your submissions on sentence, Mr. Beauchamp. In due course. In the meantime, I am ordering a pre-sentence and I am putting this matter over a week, at which time I expect counsel will have agreed on a sentencing date. We are now adjourned."

She marches off without a word of thanks to the jury for their service. The media charge through the door like a herd of spooked buffalo. Court officers usher the rabble out behind them. The jury file out silently, watching as I am cuffed.

My comrades are also required to leave. The prosecution team follows. I am almost alone with Arthur now, except for the guy locking the main door, and two women officers waiting to take me to the cells. But they give us space, a few minutes together.

Arthur goes, "I'm sorry, that seems the price we had to pay."

"A bargain! It's nothing! Everyone else walked! I'll do the time happily, Arthur. It's not going to kill me." I'm almost as enthusiastic as I sound.

"I'll ask the Appeal Court for a continuance of bail. I can get on that right now."

"Don't, Arthur. Please don't rock the boat. We appeal, they appeal — isn't that the way it works? Goddamn it, Arthur, just go, you got a flight at four."

"Rivie—"

"Just go!" I turn myself over to my guards. The cuffs rattle as I blow Arthur a two-handed kiss. "I love you! You were brilliant! When I get out I want to meet Ulysses!"

CHAPTER 26 » ARTHUR

1
Sunday, July 21

"Seen much of Jeremiah's ghost lately?" Margaret can't help taking digs at Arthur's dig — his curious obsession, she calls it. "So when is the official unveiling of whatever the heck is supposed to be down that well?"

Margaret is in Newfoundland and they're on FaceTime. Arthur has to set his phone down to pull on his hiking boots. Ulysses whines impatiently — he resents the intrusion of old human friend's little talking tool.

"The first Monday of August — that's the fifth, I think, British Columbia Day. A confluence of New Agers and senior citizens of the Historical Society have deemed this to be the extravaganza of the century, with both incorporeal and historic significance."

"I'll be there. My Atlantic tour ends Friday, then just a couple of stops in Quebec. I can't wait to see all the disappointed faces when they open the tomb. Can you keep a secret?"

"I made my living doing so."

"I've finally got Environment interested in cliff swallows and res-ident falcons. Keep mum and stay tuned."

Arthur assumes she means the feds may buy out TexAmerica's mining rights and attach the quarry to the existing park. That might be something else to celebrate on BC Day.

"Can you keep another secret?"

"What?"

"I'm retiring from politics. I'm coming home. Full-time."

"What? Why?"

"To keep an eye on you. Blessed is the man that endureth temp-tation, especially when his wife isn't three thousand miles away. Joking. It's time. The party needs rejuvenation and I need a life."

"Well, I am deliriously happy, darling." He can't count the times she has sworn to do this. Never before had he heard such conviction in her voice.

"Good luck on Wednesday, Arthur. Give her a hug from me. Tell her I love her."

And with a loud, anxious sigh she signs off.

§

"Come along," he tells Ulysses, who knows where they're going and bounds ahead toward the north pasture, leaping over six cedar rails with grace and power.

Arthur is in less hurry, and uses the gate, stepping around the poop patties, his emotions at war — he's elated by Margaret's news but dismayed over Rivie, feeling he has failed her. Margaret's big sigh was an expression of her deep concern for the young woman, who in three days will likely be shipped off to a federal penitentiary.

At the hearing last week, Justice Donahue reserved formal sentencing to this Wednesday, having forewarned Rivie she will be condemned to "an appropriate term of imprisonment." Her reasons will be carefully written, the pithy lines widely quoted. Her final stab at gaining honour and respect. Language that will hold up on appeal.

Arthur had argued well, but to predictably deaf ears. Yes, M'Lady, Ms. Levitsky tried to sneak out of Canada with a fraudulent passport. But who suffered injury as a result? Who has been hurt, what property was damaged, what harm has been done to anyone or any thing? Ms. Levitsky earned a sterling pre-sentence report, she's a first offender, deterrence is a negligible factor, surely a suspended sentenced with probation is called for.

It unsettles him that Rivie insists she won't appeal her sentence, however punitive it may be. But there is a rationale: Why encourage counteraction? Though Azra Khan has gone through the motions of filing notices of appeal against the not-guilty verdicts, he has let it be known he has little appetite for fighting a new trial. The public mood is strongly opposed. The Crown has a face-saving conviction. As Rivie put it, why rock the boat? Why risk a new trial with a less sympathetic jury?

Certainly, the chances of being blessed with a similarly brave and defiant jury are slight. The prospects of empanelling another Irish wolfhound lover seem infinitesimal. But that may have been a factor in last month's acquittals because it turns out that juror Joyce Evans, the SPCA board member, keeps a pair of them. Arthur learned that while sharing an elevator with her after the verdict. She'd read about Ulysses's heroic rescue of a toddler in Quarry Park. She showed Arthur a wallet-sized photo of her two, and they shared wolfhound lore until Arthur realized he'd missed his floor.

Ulysses leads him down to a wetland vividly decorated with bracken fronds and the giant, Jurassic leaves of skunk cabbage.

Arthur thought he'd gotten over his obsessive sightings of Jeremiah but there's his scrawny shape moving about in a copse of salal and alder. Ulysses also sees him, because he stiffens. But of course it's a deer, and Ulysses is off faster than a speeding bullet — on what turns out to be another profitless quest, returning to Arthur with his tongue hanging out and a blanket of burrs on his coat.

Up the hill is Stoney's backhoe, consigned to the sidelines while Stoney and Dog do the delicate handwork. Dog, anyway — Arthur can see him from the rim of the well's moat, seven feet down, working with a trowel around the cemented rocks at the base. The laconic little stump of a man waves to him, then continues to plug away.

A pump and generator have been used sporadically to drain runoff from the moat, but the well itself seems dry — though it's no longer a well but a stone column buttressed with timber braces. It has developed a lean that's slightly less angled than the Tower of Pisa.

Dog's boss seems missing in action — then Arthur spots him sleeping with his boots on under a hanging tarp. Pooped out already at noon.

Ulysses slurps him awake, or at least half-awake, mumbling, "I love you, Marylou." A reference to a comely newcomer who offers spiritual bodywork in the Wellness Centre.

Stoney struggles up. "I'm not blaming you, sire, but you interrupted my midday meditation. No offence taken. Let's get to work here."

Rubbing his eyes, he leads Arthur to the moat, talking nonstop. "What we got on our hands here is an enigma. Now, your ordinary well, there has to be a way for water to seep in, but this here's a dry well, sealed right to the bottom. Which means Jeremiah couldn't have drowned, according to your theory."

Arthur follows him down a ladder onto some planks on which Dog squats and scrapes.

"Now normally when you fall down a well, it's because you were hauling up water while trashed on booze or dope. But that ain't the case here, because the element of water is missing. So instead of a fairly comfortable watery death, old Jeremiah lay down here all crippled and screaming for help until he starved to death—"

"Shut up, Stoney. Show me proof this is watertight."

He invites Arthur to stick his arm into a snug tunnel dug under the cemented base of the well.

Arthur declines. "It's not that I don't trust you, Stoney."

2

Monday, August 5

The Day of the Big Dig, a sunny holiday, has attracted a grand turnout for Jeremiah's hoped-for exhumation. The entire Historical Society is here, among many other island dignitaries — including the ever-skeptical Member for Cowichan and the Islands. "Be careful," she hollers down to Stoney, who's chipping away rocks to create an entry point. "He may still be alive."

A tent settlement of overnighting hippies is nearby, including the curious denizens of the Bleak Creek commune, many in loose robes gaily decorated with garlands of flowers and twigs.

The usual barroom habitués are here too, drawn by rumours of liquid refreshments, which, to their disappointment, turn out to be coffee, tea, and lemonade prepared by the Ladies of the Hall. But there are also sandwiches and cookies.

A surprise guest pulled in Saturday: Stefan Petterson, the wild-life-whispering ex-farmhand, whom Solara Lang is putting up for the long weekend. "I couldn't resist," he said. A comment veiled by ambiguity: he may have been referring to the ardent hospitality from his host, who cheerfully strolls about with him and Ulysses.

Margaret aroused Arthur for a sunrise walk this morning and mischievously took him by Solara's house. A sneak peek through an uncurtained bedroom window revealed the pair entwined in presumably exhausted sleep. "I knew it," Margaret whispered. Arthur hadn't; he was nonplussed.

Margaret's buoyant mood — she's been thus since announcing her return to civilian life — is also fuelled by the soon-to-be-announced decision by Parks Canada to annex the quarry to the national park. The discovery of a rare species of bat taking up residence in the caves sealed the deal.

Despite worldwide species loss, despite the climate crisis, despite the wildly ignorant refusals to accept scientific consensus about this warming planet, there have been victories this year, and Arthur proudly counts his own contribution, the defence of the Sarnia Seven and its impact: many governments have been racing to curb the use of neonics; many are accelerating efforts to save pollinators and their habitats.

The one hiccup to the courtroom coup is the vindictive sentence Rivie Levitsky got for her victimless crime: two years in a federal penitentiary. Arthur has no doubt that Colleen Donahue took out her anger at the jury on her, anger stoked by her frustration and her sense of humiliation. Arthur suspects Azra Khan filed notices of appeal against the acquittals merely to placate her.

Rivie's decision not to provoke him by appealing sentence is a strong indicator of forensic craftiness, an essential quality for a winning counsel. When Arthur last visited her, a week ago, he found her studying for her LSAT.

She's taking her sentence well. Could have been worse, she insists: she's in Grand Valley Institution for Women, in Kitchener, Ontario, in minimum security, sharing a cottage not a cell, kept apart from the hardened inmates of the neighbouring cellblock. Arthur now must focus on getting her out on early parole. He will pull no punches. Faulk, Quan, Dubois is working on it.

P. W. Peedles, chair of the Historical Society and pillar of Garibaldi high society, has been watching the hippies with trepidation and distaste, and seems particularly offended by a blatantly exposed breast feeding a baby.

He catches Margaret grinning at him, and pretends he was actually looking at Stefan, a pair of yellow warblers on his outstretched arm. "How does he do that?"

"Inexplicably," Margaret says.

The pump goes on, sucking up the water pooling around Stoney's boots. Dog clambers down to take a turn with pick and shovel. They're close to breaking through, and as the crowd gathers round, the Garibaldi Highlanders pipe band strikes up one of their favourites, something called "The Miners' Lament."

Finally, the opening is wide enough for Stoney to poke his head in and probe with a flashlight.

An exultant call: "Gangbusters!"

A clay jug tumbles out, stoppered with a thick, round wooden peg and sealed with wax. Another jug follows, then more.

§

The well ultimately yields up a dozen such containers, all full. But not Jeremiah's bones. Arthur's pet theory has failed, and Margaret joshes him about that, yet he's glad the old bootlegger didn't die ignominiously in a drunken fall.

The message from his ghost is simple and generous. The jug that is his constant companion on his wanderings was the overlooked clue. "There's more to be found, lads," Jeremiah was saying. "Have a nip on me." This well-aged moonshine is his gift to Garibaldi.

The Historical Society has rescued most of the jugs but Chairman Peedles is persuaded by an enthusiastic show of hands to allow a trio of brave volunteers — Gomer Goulet, Ernie Priposki, and Baldy Johansson — to do a taste test.

About a hundred and ten proof, says Baldy, an expert, twice busted for illegal stills. Gomer remarks on its lingering aftertaste of potatoes and rhubarb. Ernie claims to have tasted heaven. Cud Brown insists on trying. Then Stoney and McCoy and Emily LeMay, and then a couple of jars begin going the rounds.

Some locals leave, some come late, but the party goes on into the long evening. The fumes of these distilled spirits seem to drift about the encampment like low-lying mist, and for the first time in twenty-six years Arthur finds himself a little squiffy.

As property owner and host of this gathering, he felt a duty to stay until all guests depart or take to their tents. But it's dark now, and Margaret, Stefan, Solara, and Ulysses have long gone home, and now it comes to him that he's suddenly alone, and he doesn't have a flashlight.

The sky is clear but moonless and the sole source of light is a bonfire, but it sizzles out as a dark, ghostly form douses it from a pail of water. Jeremiah, a final visitation, putting out the last light . . .

Arthur senses the form advancing on him. Its silence feels menacing. "Hello? Who goes there?" A strained effort at humour: "Friend or foe?"

A husky, familiar voice at his ear. "Friend," Taba says. "Your best friend. Your friend in need."

CHAPTER 27 » RIVIE

1
Monday, October 14

The bad news on this day of Thanksgiving, Dear Journal, is that you are reaching the end, you will be stumbling over the finish line as soon as I type the magic numerals 3 and 0. The good news is I have an agent — she has interest and is batting numbers around. Much editing will have to be done, of course, and much lawyering, because some people may think their reputations were slighted.

I have to thank the Deputy Warden here at GVI for her encouragement of my literary endeavours. I'm supposed to be working in the library, placing books in the stacks, that sort of thing, but they gave me a nook of an office and an old computer with LibreOffice and no internet.

And I'd like to thank my housemate in the next room, Miki Upshaw, for putting up with my constant bitching and scritching and scratching on my notepad. In return I don't complain about her off-key renditions of hillbilly love songs. We along with six others share a cottage, as they call it — it's more like a cheap motel with kitchen facilities. But there's a workshop and a garden and there are courses to take and friends to make. My Indigenous sisters have a firepit and a sweat lodge into which I have been welcomed.

I have got through four months of my two years. Egotistically, it's been tolerable, because I get to enjoy a reputation as a martyr. But to be frank, it's a drag: the uniformity, the routines, the counts, the sense of being constantly watched, the sadness, the crying, the fascism of it all. Nancy Faulk's office has been bombarding the federal parole office about getting me out early. They're collecting affidavits.

And though I'm eager to split from GVI, I needed the downtime — I accomplished a lot by not going out to meetings and demonstrations and not getting shithouse with Lucy. Also, I've been admitted to law school at Queen's, and I've already missed over a month. When it became known around here that I nailed my LSAT, I got enlisted as a jailhouse lawyer. I've helped draft so many complaints and affidavits you'd think this joint would want to get rid of me.

Meanwhile, Dear Journal, let me update your prospective readers as to the various hanging threads. Chemican's SLAPP suit against us has gone moribund, and it looks like the whole damn company is on the rims. Nancy's class-action on behalf of the victims of Dover-Wilson Syndrome proceeds apace — she's hoping for a settlement fast, before they go bankrupt.

Nancy visits often. Her thing with Doc was just that: a thing, a fling. Apparently he caught some kind of virus from her, and that did it. Anyway, he moved back to Montreal. But he's twice been in to see me, and dropped off a copy of his enviro-political book, which is getting attention on reviews pages.

Arthur writes me long, funny letters, and I write him long, funny letters. Margaret Blake writes softer, thoughtful letters. Why is this smart, heroic leader retiring?

Who does not write is Chase D'Amato, so I've been literally written off. But it was never going to work. We're tuned to different vibrations. I crave the city, the human theatre, the games, the struggle and bustle. He craves none of that. He craves the wild. According to Nancy he's no longer at risk: the cops can't make him, all they've got are useless fingerprints. I wonder if he knows . . .

Not a whisper from Howie Griffin, my alternate candidate for male lead. I've decided he's just a bullshit artist.

One day my prince will come.

The gang often visit, separately and in clumps, Lucy most often. Occasionally with Ray, who has finally got off meditation and is back to medication, his normal drugged state.

Mom and Dad have been down twice. They were lovely, and proud of their daughter, but I forbade them from coming more often — it's not sustainable, too many hours to Kitchener, too many miles. I will be in Golden Valley in due course.

Dr. Ariana Van Doorn came to see me when she was in Guelph to give a speech. That was nice. Constable Louella popped in a couple of times when she was here on business, interviewing prisoners, following up leads. She has written a support letter for my early parole.

As to the rest of the supporting cast: Sooky-Sue is now Mrs. Dewilliger-James the Second. She and Dick Two got married over the objections of Dick One, who had checked her out. His wedding gift was a pink slip to his son and a one-way passage for two to the Turks and Caicos to manage his property down there. This is according to Lucy.

Abbie Lee-Yeung apparently had a full-blown breakdown, though according to her parents she has merely taken a holiday out of the country. My heart is with her wherever she is. Obsession can be a terrible thing.

It can also be sick and dangerous. Ask Donald Stumpit, my personal terrorizer. He's doing both hands.

Who else? Those seem all the characters who were important to this memoir. So, okay, that's the way I'm writing it. I'm being called away, so this is a final word from your unreliable narrator. Save. Back up. Close.

"Visitor, Rivie!" the corrections official (i.e., guard) yells from the library doorway. Odd — I wasn't expecting anyone. She takes me not to the regular visiting area but to a private interview room, the kind probation officers use.

Setting down his coffee mug, rising to welcome me, wearing a September tan, about fifteen kilos lighter than when last seen, is my arresting officer, Jake Maguire.

I go, "I'm not saying anything until I see my lawyer."

He looks confused at first, then grunts out a laugh, remembering my mantra from our interview. A little over a year ago. "Happy Thanksgiving."

"Same."

"They treating you okay?"

"Like royalty."

"Seriously. I know the warden real good. Off the record, okay?"

"Sure, totally. They treat me fine. I'm regarded as a high-value inmate. It helps that I'm white and college educated and therefore privileged."

"Right. Nobody can figure out what a nice girl like you is doing in a place like this." He thrusts a coffee mug at me, pours from his Thermos. "Ground the beans myself. Top shelf, but I don't know if they're ethical enough for you."

"How's retirement, Jake? Must be working wonders, you look great."

"Sonia has put me on a low-carb diet. I owe everything to her."

"Including your life." The kiss that returned him from the brink.

He seems to need to contemplate that moment awhile. Then shrugs. "You're supposed to be in law school, aren't you?"

I sip at the coffee. "Tons better than the local dishwater. Yeah, I'm doing what I can by correspondence until I get paroled."

"Let's talk about that. Off the record, Rivie, you got a raw deal. Somebody had to take a dive so the state could save face. You were the diver. Anyway, the game is a little changed now. Azra is going to withdraw his notices of appeal. That'll get you out faster."

I resist hugging this good news bear because that would embarrass him. "Is that what brings you here?"

"Yeah, I'm here to interview you. And then I'm going to testify before the parole board so we can get your ass up to Kingston, to your classes. Though God knows we don't need another smartass lawyer gumming up the system. Anyway, I got friends on the board from when I was on duty. Sharing-drinks-and-laughs friends. They got a temporary absence program, I'll take a shot at that first. Sixty days max, and then we can apply for another sixty, and by then early parole should kick in."

"This is great, Jake." Also puzzling. "Why are you doing it?"

"I'm doing it because the people you got supporting you — I've seen their affidavits — are a bunch of socialists and greenies and liberal hacks. You need me for balance. In the course of this interview you got to tell me Sarnia was a one-off and won't ever happen again. I don't ask you to say you regret it, because that would be too much."

"Okay, I have no intention of committing any future criminal acts."

"Don't grin. Just say it with a straight face. Give me leverage to help you."

I repeat my line with credible emphasis, then ask, "What's the real reason you're doing this, Jake?"

"I told you. You had it rough. It was sickening how the trolls crawled after you like sewer rats. You went through shit with that Stumpit."

"Did you ever start wondering if we were right? About neonics? The insect extinction? *Our* extinction?"

"I think you sold Gaylene. I shifted your way a bit when I learned neonics were nicotine-based. It's a thing I have. But that has nothing to do with why I'm here."

There's something else driving this big gesture. I stare him down. He splays his hands, as if finally allowing himself to open up. "You dames, you and Lucy Wales, you could've made my life a shitstorm in hell. You could've smeared me with the kind of shit that never washes off. You could've broken Sonia's heart. You did an honourable thing." He takes a deep breath. "Never mind, let's talk about how we get you out of here."

"I'm all ears."

But he's hung up on this issue, his good name was stained. "Gaylene and me weren't doing anything, she fell asleep on me."

"Hey, breaking news, your wife knows that. They were laughing about it."

Still, he looks morose. "Azra still thinks we did. You believe me, don't you?"

"Always, Jake. Always believe."

ACKNOWLEDGEMENTS

Dr. Mark Winston, professor of biological science at Simon Fraser University (known to his many admirers as the bee guru), tirelessly vetted the manuscript at various stages before finally giving me a passing grade — after I weeded through hundreds of studies and articles about the pesticides that are ravaging this planet's pollinators. Recommended reading: *Bee Time: Lessons from the Hive*, which won Mark a Governor General's Literary Award for non-fiction.

It has been decades since I practised criminal law, and I cannot find words enough to express thanks to Peter Copeland, a highly regarded Toronto trial lawyer, for updating me on current criminal law and the practice of it in the Ontario courts. Despite my ineffective protests, he regularly sent me limping back to my computer to restructure my courtroom scenes: pretrial issues, trial tactics, questions of law. He also provided many insights into the psyche of Toronto, its history, its places, its people.

My granddaughter, Rachel Woroner, a talented Toronto filmmaker, also helped me with the streets, neighbourhoods, and eccentricities of her city of birth. As well, she picked up some stray sexisms and culturally inappropriate usages which, she counselled, are not in the vocabulary of progressive millennials.

I shared several creative highs with my pal of forty years, Brian Brett — poet, activist, raconteur, bestselling author of *Tuco* and *Trauma Farm*. He was the fomenter of several comedic riffs and twists, and helped sculpt a couple of oddball characters. Rockin' Ray Wozniak is especially grateful for his efforts.

My beloved life companion, Jan Kirkby, professional biologist and dedicated conservationist, blue-pencilled her way through many, various drafts in her role as my editor-in-chief. The very existence of this work is due to her urgings that I compose a novel that takes on the agrochemical giants' wilfully blind efforts to poison our ecosphere.

I am hugely indebted to my longtime friend Jay Clarke, who authors hair-raising thrillers under the *nom de guerre* of Michael Slade, for his steely-eyed focus in copy-editing the final draft. He spotted an embarrassing abundance of typos and time-and-date errata that had escaped less vigilant eyes. My publisher's editorial staff refers to him, with awe, as the Wizard of Flaws.

Peggy Gwillim, recently retired from Toronto's Superior Court Registry, kindly escorted me into Court 6-1, while empty, so I could take photographs as an *aide-mémoire*.

Pender Island's Judy Walker, a dear friend and a talented artist, gave liberally of her time to conceptualize ideas for the cover illustration.